The Bloodstained Shade

The Aven Cycle

Cass Morris

Published by Cass Morris, 2023.

Copyright Page

This is a work of fiction. Similarities to real people, places, or events are entirely coincidental.

Also by Cass Morris

The Aven Cycle
Give Way to Night
From Unseen Fire
The Bloodstained Shade

Watch for more at https://linktr.ee/cassrmorris.

To Heidi,

the best West Highland White terrier in the world,

who was sitting beneath my desk during much of this book's creation.

Miss you, little girl.

DRAMATIS PERSONAE

In Aven

The Vitelliae:

Aulus Vitellius, a Popularist Senator

Vipsania, his wife, a mage of Water, deceased

Aula Vitellia, their oldest daughter, a widow

Vitellia Secunda, called **Latona**, their second daughter, a mage of Spirit and Fire

Vitellia Tertia, called **Alhena**, their third daughter, a mage of Time

Helva, a freedwoman, mage of Time, and Aula's personal attendant

Merula, a Phrygian enslaved woman, Latona's personal attendant

Mus, a Cantabrian enslaved woman, Alhena's personal attendant

Lucia, Aula's daughter

Vibia Sempronia, a mage of Fracture, sister to Sempronius Tarren

Taius **Mella**, her husband

Ama **Rubellia**, High Priestess of Venus, friend to Latona

Fausta, a child, Spirit mage

Marcus Autronius, a Popularist Senator and a mage of Earth

Gnaeus Autronius, his father

Quintus **Terentius**, a Popularist Senator

Quinta Terentia, his daughter, a Vestal Virgin and a mage of Light

Terentilla, called **Tilla**, her sister, a mage of Earth

Vatinius **Obir**, client to Sempronius Tarren, head of the Esquiline Collegium

Ebredus, a member of the Esquiline Collegium

Galerius Orator, consul of Aven

Marcia Tullia, his wife, a mage of Air
Aufidius **Strato**, Galerius's co-consul
Trebius Perus, a merchant
The Crispiniae, the Domitiae, the Papiriae, the Naeviae: other Popularist families

Corinna, Fracture mage and Discordian
    Durmius Argus, her brother, member of the Augian Commission
    Lucretius **Rabirus**, an Optimate Senator
    Glaucanis, his wife
    Arrius **Buteo**, an Optimate Senator
    Decius **Gratianus**, an Optimate Senator
    Memmia, his wife
    Licinius **Cornicen**, an Optimate Senator
    Pinarius **Scaeva**, a Priest of Janus and mage of Fracture
    Salonius Decur, member of the Augian Commission
    Aemilia Fullia, High Priestess of Juno

In Iberia

Vibius **Sempronius** Tarren, Praetor of Cantabria, a Popularist Senator, and a mage of Shadow and Water

Gaius **Vitellius**, a military tribune, son to Aulus Vitellius and brother to Aula, Latona, and Alhena

Autronius **Felix**, a military tribune, brother to Marcus Autronius
Corvinus, a freedman, mage of Water, and Sempronius's steward
Eustix, a mage of Air
Onidius Praectus, commander of a legion
Bartasco, chieftain of the Arevaci, allied to Aven
Hanath, his wife, a Numidian warrior

Ekialde, chieftain of the Lusetani
    Neitin, his wife
    Reilin, **Ditalce**, and **Irrin**, her sisters
    Matigentis, Neitin's and Ekialde's son
    Bailar, a magic-man, Ekialde's uncle
    Otiger, a magic-man, Neitin's uncle
    Sakarbik, a magic-woman of the Cossetans

Content Warning

I trust my readers to know themselves and their limits, and I hope to help them engage with this book on their own terms. To that end, please know this book contains graphic violence, bloodshed, and death in the context of warfare and combat, as well brief violence towards small animals and mentions of ritual sacrifice. There is discussion of past sexual assault, domestic abuse, emotional abuse, and infidelity, as well as the lingering trauma of such events. As this book takes place in, essentially, the late Roman Republic, it also includes depictions of enslavement, class structure, sexism, and patriarchal constructs within the context of the classical world and its mores.

The Story So Far

Before the events of *From Unseen Fire*

Horatius **Ocella** leverages his army as a threat against Aven, forcing the Senate to declare him Dictator for a period of ten years. He proceeds to proscribe his enemies, killing many so he can claim their estates. Many others flee into exile to preserve their lives, including **Sempronius** Tarren, a young Senator from the progressive Popularist faction. His sister **Vibia** and her husband accompany him. Another senator, **Aulus** Vitellius, escapes proscription, but his only son, Gaius **Vitellius**, is held on the border when the commander of his legion refuses to return to the city while Ocella is in power. Aulus arranges the marriage of his middle daughter, **Latona**, to a man he thinks politically-insignificant enough to keep her safe, but she has the misfortune to catch Ocella's attention when she acts to save her older sister, **Aula**, and Aula's young daughter from being executed alongside Aula's proscribed husband. As a mage of Spirit and Fire, Latona suppresses her powers so as not to present a threat to the paranoid Dictator, even as she must use her natural charms to appease his carnal desires.

The events of *From Unseen Fire*:

Ocella's death allows Sempronius to return from exile, along with Ocella's other enemies, setting off a scramble for power as the Republic re-asserts itself in the wake of the Dictatorship. Sempronius, a mage of Shadow and Water who has hidden his talents all his life so that he could pursue a political life, summons a vision that shows him two futures for Aven: one as the beating heart of a thriving network of nations, the other falling into oblivion. Believing the gods have a role for him in creating the better future, Sempronius pits himself against the leaders of the Optimate faction, including the ruthless Lucretius **Rabirus**.

When a riot breaks out after Ocella's funeral, Rabirus takes the opportunity to eliminate Ocella's two sons, to prevent a new faction from forming around them. While Sempronius and his allies work to quell the riot, Latona ventures into the streets, using her magic to protect the vulnerable. Doing so loosens her control over her magic, and it begins erupting in unpredictable ways, which Latona, embarrassed and anxious of the attention it could draw, attempts to tamp back down.

Meanwhile, in the vast expanse of Iberia, a charismatic young leader, **Ekialde**, has been anointed by the Lusetani magic-men and inspired to wage war against the Aventans and other people of the Middle Sea whom he considers to be encroaching on his territory. As he grows bolder, he accepts the help of his uncle **Bailar**, whose use of blood magic deeply unsettles Ekialde's pregnant wife, **Neitin**. When Ekialde's war-bands jeopardize Aventan trade, Gaius Vitellius is sent on detached duty with a portion of his legion. Gaius finds the situation in Iberia is more dire than rumor told, but he befriends **Bartasco**, leader of an allied tribe, and his wife **Hanath**, whose people have suffered from Ekialde's raids.

Gaius's letters home help to convince the Senate to organize a larger campaign in aid of their allies. Sempronius campaigns for praetor, a position which could allow him to lead the campaign—the first step in achieving the future the gods showed him. He begins spending more time with Latona, encouraging her to explore the full power of her magical gifts. Admiration blossoms into attraction and affection, but since Latona is still married, they must tread carefully. To bleed off some of her excess power, Latona weaves protective magic into a neck-scarf which she sends to Gaius to keep him safe in Iberia.

Rabirus, finding Sempronius's growing popularity an unacceptable threat, enlists the help of a dangerous Fracture mage, Pinarius **Scaeva**, to disrupt Sempronius's campaign. He also attempts straightforward assassination. When Sempronius is struck by a poisoned arrow on a hunt, he calls on Latona to use Fire magic to purge the poison and save his life. She succeeds, but this use of her powers frightens her father and annoys her husband.

In Iberia, Gaius finally faces Ekialde in battle directly. Ekialde attempts to use a potion to ensorcel Gaius, but Latona's Fire magic protects him from having his will suborned. Ekialde's forces retreat, and Gaius takes possession of the central town of Toletum, where he digs in for the winter. Ekialde's forces regroup, and his uncle promises greater magic to come.

On the day of the Aventan elections, Latona's youngest sister **Alhena**, a budding prophetess, has a vision of calamity. Her sisters go to observe the vote anyway, but before the procedure is complete, fire breaks out in a nearby district. In defiance of danger and propriety, Latona goes to help, using her magic on a grander scale than she ever has before; she over-spends her efforts, however, leaving her open to attack from Scaeva. Though Rabirus instructs him to leave her alive, Scaeva intends to drain her of her very life force. In the process, he reveals himself as a devotee of Discordia, goddess of strife, and thus a member of a dangerous banished cult—but he is interrupted by Sempronius and Vibia, summoned to Latona's rescue by Alhena. Vibia uses her own Fracture magic to break Scaeva's control, and Sempronius uses Shadow magic to close the void Scaeva ripped in the world. Latona, unconscious during the turmoil, credits Vibia alone with her salvation.

At a Saturnalian revel celebrating the Popularists' electoral victories, Latona quarrels with her husband. Sempronius challenges her to stop holding herself back and to take what she wants from life, and they consummate their illicit relationship. Soon thereafter, Sempronius, victorious in his quest for the praetorship, must depart for Iberia. Latona gives him a gift: a protective scarf, like the one that saved her brother. As Sempronius leaves Aven, Latona vows to stretch her magical power in service of the city she loves, no matter what objections or obstacles others may throw in her way.

The Events of *Give Way to Night*

In winter, Neitin gives birth to a son. She dedicates him to her patron goddess, a gentle lady of water and the home, not to her husband's patron war-god, in an act of defiance. Ekialde surrenders more and more of himself to his uncle's experimental magic.

By spring, Sempronius's legions enter Iberia. He soon encounters Hanath, who informs him that Toletum has been besieged, and that Gaius and Bartasco sent her to find help. Together, they press their way toward the center of the massive peninsula, facing both mundane and magical attacks. Sempronius's rival Rabirus has come as well, taking control of the legions in the south. He hopes to block Sempronius's efforts to win allies and victories in the region, but he is unaware that Vibia placed a curse on him before he left Aven, and his actions more often lead to his own misfortune.

In Aven, Latona seeks greater knowledge and training in her magical arts but is blocked by those who want her to remain in a more traditional womanly sphere—including her husband, **Herennius**. She confesses her liaison with Sempronius to Aula, as well as her ongoing correspondence with him, then is summoned to their family's country villa in Stabiae by Alhena, who has had troubling visions. She soon discovers evidence of Fracture magic, turned to vile use, and she asks Vibia to join her to investigate. Vibia confirms that the magic is Discordian, a sign that Scaeva was not alone in reviving the banished cult. The women spend much of the summer chasing down curse-charms left by an unknown mage who preys on the peasants and enslaved farmers, too poor and powerless to fight back on their own. These charms summon *lemures* in various forms: fiends of the netherworld, torn from their proper place and set to torment the living.

In Toletum, Gaius attempts to hold the city together, under siege not only from soldiers, but by haunting demons called *akdraugi*, summoned by Bailar's magic. The *akdraugi* prevent Sempronius from getting close enough to Toletum to lift the siege; he is saved from their soul-draining powers by the magical scarf Latona gave him. Rabirus's missteps lead him to attack one of Iberia's neutral tribes, driving them into alliance with Ekialde and the Lusetani. This tribe drives north, intending to attack Sempronius's legions before they can lift the siege of Toletum. Running out of time, Sempronius risks using his Shadow magic to scry an answer: the gods reveal only that the answer will come from his ally Hanath.

By the end of summer, the Discordian influence in the countryside vanishes. Aula deduces that the cult may have moved back to Aven to influence that autumn's elections. Latona, Alhena, and Vibia return to Aven and must not only fend off the growing Discordian influence there, but also navigate an increasingly volatile political situation. Latona goes to the Augian Commission, a body of mages sworn to protect the city and investigate magical crimes, for help, but is dismissed as hysterical and turned away. Secretly, the Commission has been suborned by the Discordians. Latona and Vibia work with **Obir,** leader of a neighborhood collegium and a client to Sempronius, to defend his neighborhood from the *lemures*. Along the way, Latona also has to face her own fears and trauma, as to her, the *lemures* take the shape of Dictator Ocella. Good things come in the midst of adversity, however, as romance blossoms between Alhena and **Tilla**, a wild-spirited mage of Earth, and as Vibia and Latona develop true bonds of friendship.

Ekialde uses Bailar's magic and human sacrifice to summon a new horror for Toletum: a plague carried in on a nightly mist. Facing disease as well as starvation, Gaius begins to lose hope. Aghast at what Ekialde and Bailar are doing, Neitin turns to a magic-woman from a conquered tribe, **Sakarbik**, desperate for help in saving her husband from himself.

As Latona uses her magic more and more, its power grows stronger, until one day she does something no mage in centuries has been known to do, calling a live flame into her hand, touching the fire but remaining unburned. She tells no one but her sisters, Vibia, and her friend **Rubellia**, a fellow mage of Fire and a priestess of Venus who had previously helped cover her liaison with Sempronius. Later, a mid-argument slip of the tongue from Herennius reveals that he had profited from her abuse at the hands of Ocella. When Latona rails at him, he hits her; enraged, Latona calls every flame in the room into her hands. She resists the temptation to incinerate her unworthy husband and settles for divorcing him.

During a skirmish, Sempronius finally discovers the meaning of the vision the gods sent him: Hanath and some of the other riders are immune to the Lusetani magic while they are menstruating, as the power of the blood of life negates the power of the blood of death. Despite awkwardness among the Aventan military leadership, Sempronius is unwilling to waste an advantage. Hanath agrees to have as many of her warrior-women induce bleeding as possible, giving them a short window to take out the Lusetani magic-men. Sempronius arranges a trap to provide them the necessary opening; the legions take heavy losses in the ensuing battle, but once Hanath scatters the magic-men, the *akdraugi* vanish, and the legions chase the Lusetani away from Toletum. Bartasco and Hanath are reunited, and

Sempronius honors Gaius with the Crown of the Preserver for what he endured. Meanwhile, Rabirus is approached by a messenger from the Discordians, suggesting he leave off trying to undermine Sempronius in the field and return home to guide political matters there. Rabirus is wary of allying further with the unpredictable Discordians, but, believing he can use them to his own advantage, he agrees. Before departing Iberia, however, he sends assassins north with orders to eliminate Sempronius. They nearly succeed, but Sempronius receives a warning through his Shadow magic.

After Vibia is temporarily possessed by one of the *lemures*, Latona weaves more protective garments for those helping her. The efforts are beginning to exhaust them, however, so when Alhena has a vision leading them to the Discordians' lair, they decide to try to end the matter once and for all—and accidentally walk into a trap. Vibia and the others escape, but Latona is caught by the Discordian mage who has been causing them trouble for months: a fanatical woman, **Corinna**, furious that Latona keeps unraveling her plots to throw Aven into unending chaos. Her attack leaves Latona insensible, tangled in Fracture magic that Vibia cannot break.

Umbra cruenta Remi visa est adsistere lecto,
atque haec exiguo murmure verba loqui:
'en ego dimidium vestri parsque altera voti,
cernite sim qualis, qui modo qualis eram!
Qui modo, si volucres habuissem regna iubentes,
in populo potui maximus esse meo,
nunc sum elapsa rogi flammis et inanis imago:
Haec est ex illo forma relicta Remo.

The bloodstained shade of Remus seemed to stand
By the bed, speaking these words in a faint murmur:
'Behold, I who shared the half, the other part of your tender care,
Behold what I am come to, and know what once I was!
If the birds had signaled the throne was mine,
I might have been highest, ruling over the people,
Now I am an empty wrath, escaped from the flames of the pyre:
That is what remains of Remus' form!
—Ovid, Fasti 5

NOVEMBER
690 ab urbe condita
I

Palatine Hill, City of Aven
   'Helpless.'
   Aula Vitellia did not care for this feeling. Any time life wrested away her control, she flung herself into something she *could* manage. Raising her daughter. Promoting her father's election and her brother's military campaign. Maintaining a commanding presence in their social circle. Never her way, to dwell on fear or sorrow, but to cloak tragedy with cheerful determination.
   When they brought Latona into the domus, still as death, unable to be roused, Aula's carefully constructed defenses proved unequal to the task of regulating her onslaught of emotions. She could only think, *'No, not again, not her, I can't lose her.'*
   The sight of her sister's limp body took her back years, to the day her husband died, murdered by a Dictator's mandate. The day she and her daughter would have been killed, too, if not for Latona's swift and self-sacrificial thinking. *'I'm her big sister. I should've been her protector. But she was mine then, and I can't help her now.'*
   The combined efforts of Rubellia and Vatinius Obir, the head of the Esquiline collegium who had been serving as a bodyguard to the mages on their various escapades, eventually scraped Aula up off the floor. Once her mind settled enough to comprehend that her sister was not dead, only injured, Rubellia gave her more information in hushed whispers. They had told Aulus that she had been hurt in an accident, a stall collapsing in the market, because Aulus permitted Latona these excursions only with grudg-

13

ing allowance. *'If he knew she had been injured magically, he might lock her up and cast the key in the Tiber.'*

Obir returned to his collegium, there being little else he could do for the Vitelliae. Everyone else took it in turns to sit with Latona, in case she should stir. Aulus sent for healers immediately, but none provided extraordinary advice. Keep her still—as though that were in any question. Offer sacrifices to the appropriate gods. Pour water through her insensible lips; broth and honey if she did not wake by morning.

Wracked with guilt, Aula sat down on the edge of her sister's bed, absently smoothing out the azure blankets, as though it mattered, as though Latona would notice. The one person in the world closer to Aula's heart than any other lay in some indefinable, terrible mortal jeopardy, and Aula could do nothing.

She wasn't even entirely certain what had happened. Latona had gone out with three other mages — their younger sister Alhena, blessed by Time; Ama Rubellia, High Priestess of Venus, blessed by Fire; and Vibia Sempronia, blessed by Fracture — to investigate a potential locus of Discordian power. A vision of Alhena's led them to the place, where they hoped to find the villain whose curses they had been chasing down for months.

'She would throw herself into whatever danger, if she thought innocent people were imperiled.' With blessings of Spirit and Fire, Latona worked herself ragged to defend the people of Aven against the wraiths and fiends the Discordians summoned. *'How hard it is, to love and admire your bravery and still wish you had just a little less of it, perhaps.'*

One might have expected her to be cold as death, but instead she burned. Like a fever, but without sweat. Her cheeks held no flush, but a golden sheen.

'All her flames, beneath her skin.'

Vibia Sempronia appeared in the door of Latona's sleeping chamber. "Aula?" Her voice was not soft, precisely; Vibia was not a gentle creature. It held a less biting edge than usual, though, and her angular face was set in lines of worry. "Your father's going to the Temple of Asclepius to offer a sacrifice. I'm going to accompany him before I go home."

Aula started to rise. "I should—"

Vibia held up a hand to halt her. "You're in no state. Rubellia will stay here with you and Alhena until your father returns." Her eyes flicked out to the atrium, grown dim and streaked with eerie shadows as evening fell. "She can give you the rest of the story, if you're up to it. Merula, too." Her right hand twitched, as if prompted by an instinct to reach out. But Vibia was not affectionate by nature, nor anywhere near as close to Aula as she had become to Latona. "I'll return in the morning. Perhaps I'll think of something by then."

A strange comment, but Aula's head was so fogged she did not know if that were due to Vibia's obfuscation or if she lacked some explanatory element.

Vibia's dark eyes went to where Latona's golden curls lay in a tangled mess across her pillow. "I *will* think of something," she said, customary intensity returning to her voice. Aula got the sense Vibia intended the sharpness for no one but herself.

Everyone else was in tears, but Merula was *furious*.

The forces at play went beyond her understanding, but she knew her mistress. Whatever the Discordian had done to her, the domina's magic would be fighting a silent, invisible battle. Neither lack of comprehension nor fear of Fracture magic had stopped Merula trying to beat the cultist woman with a stick, though. *'I should have been crushing her to a pulp for all the evil she is doing.'*

Merula continued to pace the atrium as Vibia Sempronia led a stricken Aulus out of the house. Latona had been back in her father's domus only a few weeks, since divorcing her useless husband. *'Small mercies.'* Bad enough that the domina was vulnerable here, in a home where she was loved and protected. Imagining how her husband would have responded to the situation made Merula want to cross town and stab him, just for good measure.

"Merula." Ama Rubellia, the priestess, touched her shoulder gently. She bore the trials of the evening better than the others—or she covered for it better. Still, she was a far cry from her usual well-put-together, sensual self. Her normally warm brown skin looked ashy and drawn, and her raven hair was loose and frazzled from their ordeal in the Discordian house. "We need to tell Aula and Alhena what happened. The full truth."

In the lararium, little Alhena—not so little anymore, Merula reminded herself, for the girl was almost eighteen and taller than her older sisters—was on her knees, rocking back and forth, whispering endless words to the votive statues of the household gods. *She is blaming herself.*

Alhena's vision had brought them to that charnel house. Prophecy had failed to warn her of the danger to Latona. No doubt she was now asking, or demanding, answers from the silent gods.

"You are thinking they are in a mood to listen?" Merula asked Rubellia.

"Whether they are or not, we must try. They need to know." A breath of a pause. "Honestly, Merula, *I* need to know what happened after I took Alhena outside. If it might help—"

A puff of air sighed out of Merula. "I will tell all I can, but how helpful that may be?" She shrugged. "If the Lady Vibia is not knowing..."

"We've all been shocked," Rubellia said. "Something else may occur to us, as we sift through the information."

Rubellia collected the wretched Alhena off the floor. Tears continued to stream down the girl's face as they crowded into Latona's room. Alhena crumpled next to Aula, resting her head upon her sister's shoulder.

It might have made a pretty painting, fit to adorn some lovely triclinium's walls, in a less dire situation. All the Vitelliae had flame-colored hair, though not the same heat: Latona shone sun-gold, Aula bright copper, and Alhena shocking red, even in the gloomy light of late afternoon.

"Alright." Rubellia stood to the side of Latona's bed. "Let's go over what we know."

Rubellia began the tale: Finding the mountain of bones and other curse material, tall as a man and knotted together. How Discordian magic attacked all of them, heightening their usual proclivities into dangers, Alhena overcome by visions, Rubellia swarmed by emotions of everyone within a thousand paces of that loathsome building.

What Vibia and Latona had felt, no one present could be sure, but they had mastered it better than the others. More experience, Merula assumed; they had been battling the *lemures* for months. Latona set the physical construct of the ritual ablaze, allowing Vibia to dismantle the magical component. "Latona was lifting the flames with her hands," Rubellia said. "It must have taken incredible strength. Magical strength, I mean."

"With her hands," Aula echoed, her voice hollow. "You mean— You mean the way she did the night Lucia knocked over the lamps?"

Touching actual flames was not something Fire mages were supposed to be able to do, not anymore, not in the modern world. That sort of talent belonged to the age of legends, with mages like Circe and Hercules. But Latona had done it, instinctively, when Aula's young daughter rambunctiously crashed into a table full of lamps and nearly set herself and the house ablaze. Disaster was averted only because Latona reached out and called the flames to her palm. Latona had never been able to replicate the feat, until that very afternoon.

"Just so," Rubellia affirmed. "But with intent. She moved them, making sure the pile burned as fast as possible. The *lemures* disappeared when she and Vibia pulled the whole thing apart, and we thought it over. I took Alhena outside. And then—" Her dark eyes prompted Merula.

Merula cleared her throat. "Lady Vibia, she is saying that someone had been there soon before. Because of the torches—Domina had to have something to work with." Another pang of self-annoyance stabbed her for not having noticed. "There were being torches in the walls, recently lit. And then *she* is coming out from hiding." Thinking of her put a boil in Merula's blood. "The Fracture mage. The Discordian. She set it all up. Said Domina and Lady Vibia had been causing trouble." Merula frowned, trying to recall the hateful woman's exact words. "She said they were shutting all the doors."

"Oh." A gasp escaped Alhena, and all eyes turned towards her—all eyes except Latona's, of course, still closed. "That's—that's the sort of thing in all my visions. Doors opening. Bronze doors."

"Bronze for Fracture magic," Rubellia murmured. "And doors to let the *lemures* through. Your visions were on the spot, my dear."

"Not good enough," Alhena said morosely. "I didn't see this happening." A hiccup of sorrow entered her voice, and the tears began to flow anew. Merula vaguely wondered if the girl wasn't in danger of dehydration. "I should have done. I only saw the place, and the magic at work, I didn't—I didn't know the woman would be there, I didn't know she would—"

"Shhhhh..." Aula clasped Alhena tightly, rubbing her back. "It's not your fault, my honey. The gods gave you a few tiles out of the mosaic. You can't be blamed for that." Her eyes were fierce, challenging either Merula or Rubellia to naysay her, as she said, "Continue. Please."

"She said they broke Scaeva's mind," Merula added. "And that they were... were shielding themselves, but only their minds and magic. Not their bodies. Then she touched a column and the whole building is beginning to shake."

"It seemed so from outside, too," Rubellia said. "As though Neptune himself decided to quake only that bit of earth. I don't believe anyone else in the neighborhood noticed."

"That is when Lady Vibia is running outside." Merula could hear bitterness in her own voice, but she did not cast blame. They all should have gotten out. "Lady Latona, she—she is not being able to flee. She trips." Merula tsked and corrected herself; her grasp of Truscan grammar remained imperfect, and she tended to slide back into the habits of her youth. In this, though, precision was important. "No. She *was* tripped. Something in the magic, that is what is tripping her. The Discordian beast, she attacks, and I am hitting her with a stick." Merula blew air out through her nostrils. "I should have been beating her brains in! But I—I am going for my knife instead. I am drawing blood, and then—" Her shoulders drew up tight. "She is doing something, the Discordian. I am feeling as if all my bones are shattering inside my skin. I could not concentrate on killing the—" She chose a colorful phrase in her native Phrygian. Only Rubellia's lips twitched with any indication that she understood the highly uncomplimentary words. "I—I have never known pain like that." Merula looked at the ground, scuffed her toe against the floor. "It is shaming me to admit it. I should have been strong enough."

A sudden warmth startled Merula. Rubellia, she realized, had wrapped her in an embrace. She must have been working some magic, too, because Merula felt the tension bleeding out of her limbs. She wasn't sure whether she liked that or not, being robbed of the tight fury that kept her upright, but Rubellia meant well by it, in any case.

"No," Rubellia said, steady ferocity in her voice. "Do not blame yourself. What this Discordian has been doing is beyond any of us, magical or mundane. It is not a matter of strength, and I will not hear you castigating yourself."

Merula made a noncommittal noise.

"If anyone's to blame, it's me," came Alhena's lugubrious voice. "I should have seen—"

"Not you, either!" Aula said, giving her a shake.

"No one would have been hurt if I hadn't—"

"You don't know that!" from Aula, in the same moment that Rubellia, loosening her grip on Merula, said, "That is absolutely false."

Alhena blinked wide blue eyes up at her. "What?"

"If you had not led us there, someone would most certainly have been hurt," Rubellia said, calm but stern. "We just might not know who, or would not have known until it was too late."

"It wouldn't have been *Latona!*" Alhena wailed. "Or Merula!" Her gaze drifted over to Merula. "I'm so sorry, I truly am, I had no idea—"

Merula shook her head. She was not angry with Alhena for missing some warning, nor even with the gods for their many failures. A girl who had been taken from her home and enslaved in childhood was not inclined to trust the gods overmuch. Her fury was all for the Discordian mage—and a little for herself. *'If I had been more alert, I might have realized—of course there was someone else in the building, of course the mage was still present.'*

Even that, though, was a foolish admonition. There had been so much magic swirling about, so much chaos, which she could feel the effects of but not reach out and touch.

"It matters, whoever was harmed," Rubellia went on, "though we feel it more keenly when it is those close to us. But you did right in telling us, dear one. If nothing else, we now know who to look for."

"Some of us do, anyway," Aula said. "Merula, this Discordian mage—what did she look like?"

The first word that came to Merula's mind was *wrong.* Like a statue come to life and then allowed to go feral. "A young woman," Merula answered. "Between the Lady Aula's and the Lady Latona's age, I would be guessing. Very pale skin. Dark hair. Blue eyes, dark blue eyes, that—" A shiver went down her spine. "Blue like the heart of a fire and the coldest ice at once. Blue like the sky before dawn. Blue such as I am never forgetting." Heat suffused her chest again, but this time of her own making, not Rubellia's inflicted calm. "I will know her if I am seeing her, and if I am seeing her, I am putting my dagger in her *throat*."

After Merula finished her story, the women sat in silence for a while. Not that hovering over Latona would do any good, but Aula couldn't seem to tear herself away. *'She might come through this all on her own. She's the strongest person I know. She won't be taken down by some meddling cultist.'*

A gentle footfall crept near the door, and Aula looked up to see her daughter, Lucia, peering around the doorframe. Aula summoned a brave face; she hadn't had time yet to figure out how she would explain this for a six-year-old's understanding. Lucia had been out with her nursemaid when Vatinius Obir brought Latona in, so she had missed the immediate commotion. "My honey," Aula began, "you should—"

Lucia hurled herself onto Latona's bed. "Aunt Lala?" she asked, shaking her aunt's shoulders. Then, again, in a more panicked tone, "Aunt Lala?"

With no warning, Lucia burst into tears—into a *howl*, fit to rend the heavens. Alhena startled, and Aula had to push her sister away in order to dive for her daughter. "Lucia! What in Juno's good name— My darling, your aunt is hurt, she needs to—"

As Aula grabbed her, trying to drag her off the bed, Lucia fought with all the strength in her wiry little arms. "No!" she shrieked. "No! No no no no no!"

"'No', *what*?" Aula asked, bewildered. "Merula, can you help me—?" Merula nipped forward and, in a deft movement, wrenched Lucia off the bed. The girl's hands were fisted in the bedclothes, though, and she dragged those behind her, jostling Latona. Alhena gasped and tried to stabilize her while Aula disentangled her daughter's fingers from the fabric. "Lucia! You cannot do that, your aunt has to stay still, we can't have you behaving like this!"

The girl paid her no more mind than insensible Latona. As if possessed by some fiend—and considering everything that had happened, Aula did not discount the possibility—Lucia twisted and pushed against Merula, struggling so ferociously that she turned herself upside down in Merula's grip, legs pushing at Merula's shoulders, arms reaching out for Latona. "No!" Lucia screamed. "No, she's *hurt*!"

"Yes!" Aula almost shouted, voice cracking with heartbreak. The truth was somehow all the more horrible, in trying to explain it to a child. Her own tears, held in abeyance this past half-hour, welled up behind her eyes and thickened her voice. "Yes, my darling, she is, and I promise, we're doing all we—"

"No! No, you don't *understand*!" Red in the face, Lucia slapped ineffectually at Merula. "You're not *listening*! Can't you hear her?" Lucia bawled, tears pouring down her cheeks. "She wants *out*! She's screaming for help!"

The pronouncement stunned silence into the assembly. Sensing an opportunity, Lucia wriggled free of an astonished Merula, hurling herself back onto Latona's bed and burrowing in close against her aunt's body. Her howls turned to muffled sobs as Aula cast helpless looks at the others.

Rubellia started toward the girl. "If you'll allow me, I can calm her." Aula nodded. Rubellia eased herself down on the bed next to Lucia, and when the girl did not express objection, she lay a hand on Lucia's back. Slow, smooth strokes, no doubt infused with her empathic magic. Emotional manipulation was a gift of Fire, and though magic-less Aula could not see it in action, she recognized its effects. "There, my dear," Rubellia said, her honeyed voice low. "That's better, isn't it?" A snuffle, and Lucia's flaxen head nodded. "I thought so. Easier to breathe, yes?" Another nod. "Now. What do you mean, you can hear your aunt?"

With another great sniffle, Lucia rolled onto her side to speak to Rubellia. "In my head."

"Is she talking to you?"

A negative shake. "She doesn't know I'm here. She's—she's somewhere else. And they're *hurting* her."

"Who is?" Aula realized both hands were clutched to her chest.

"I don't *know*," Lucia blubbered. "But I can *feel* it." She tucked back in against Latona again, weeping more quietly.

A cold pit settled in Aula's stomach, a new pain added to the agony of Latona's injury, as she fit the pieces of the scene before her into her place. She knew what this was, though iron-cold denial wanted her to reject the very notion. Years ago, she had watched Latona and Alhena come into their powers. She did not want to admit that she had witnessed her daughter's first flowering of a magical blessing.

II

Camp of the Lusetani, Central Iberia

"You must trust the gods."

"Trust *you*, you mean." Ekialde, leader of the Lusetani, their *erregerra*, their god-touched war-king, glared across the fire at his uncle. "I trusted you. I trusted you beyond any man, beyond even my war-band, gave you liberties to explore magics our forefathers abandoned centuries ago. Where has it gotten me?" He made a quick, cutting gesture with one arm, and his sight snagged on the lines inked into his own skin. Another of Bailar's experiments producing mixed results. Oh, Ekialde's arms never tired in battle now, never felt injury or weakness—but how they *itched* anytime his hands were empty of a weapon.

"You won victories," Bailar pointed out. "No leader of the Lusetani has harried the Aventans as you have. You held them in fear and misery for the better part of a year."

"And then they broke your magic, killed most of your fellow magic-men, and drove us back downriver."

Bailar spread his hands in silent not-quite-apology.

Ekialde hissed in irritation and began pacing his tent. Outside, a soft snowfall had begun, though the flakes melted as soon as they touched the ground; it had not been cold enough for very long. Still, a reminder: winter could descend upon the mountains with swift severity.

The Aventans had constructed forts upriver—defensible positions, atop hills, well-secured. Harassing them would be a challenge until spring. *'Unless I can find a way to draw them out.'* The Aventans did not like to campaign in winter; nor did the war-bands of the Lusetani, for that matter. Food was harder to scavenge, shelter harder to establish. *'But we live in un-*

23

usual times. The Aventans would struggle to provision themselves more than us. Perhaps I should consider breaking custom.'

He glanced at his wife, asleep—or feigning sleep—near the brazier. Neitin pointedly refused to acknowledge Bailar's presence, disapproving of his methods and, in truth, of Ekialde's war in general.

'If I asked her, I know what she would say. Toss Bailar to the Aventans in exchange for a truce, then take ourselves back downriver.'

There might be sense in it. At his king-making, the magic-men fed his blood to a tree as part of their divination. The ritual revealed nothing at the time, nor was it meant to. Trees looked farther into the future than other vessels. Neitin had more than once expressed a desire to return home to tend that tree and watch for signs of calamity.

Ekialde did not discount her wishes—but he had more than his wife to consider. So many put their fates in his hands, the hands of the *erregerra* whom the gods blessed. *'A paltry blessing, if defeat is all it led to. I began this venture with dreams of glory. I cannot end it by slinking away under the winter clouds.'*

The men who followed him wanted vengeance on the legions which had broken their siege of Toletum. If Ekialde could not deliver, his position would be weak. Already the Vettoni allies wavered. Some thirsted for that same vengeance against Aven, true, but some wanted to take the fight to more of their local rivals. Others wanted to return west as much as Neitin did.

"The gods chose you," Bailar said. "They saw your strength and your purpose and deemed you fit to—"

"Gods can withdraw their favor," Ekialde snapped. "If they have not forsaken *me*, as you claim, then perhaps they turned their gaze away from *you*, since your magics failed me."

Bailar bowed his head. "Men are fallible. I never claimed otherwise. But the gods *are* with you, sister-son. I read that in your blood long ago. Bandue and Endovelicos will not abandon you."

"What a comfort that will be, when the Aventans plunge one of their spears through my heart," Ekialde shot back. "Or spit me upon those ugly short swords. Or carry me across the ocean in chains."

No; not that. Ekialde would never allow it. He would *make* them kill him, before he submitted to bondage. The Aventans paraded their defeated foes through their city, celebrating their victories by making sport of the conquered. Perhaps it pleased the Aventan gods, but Ekialde would have no part in it.

He glanced at the raven-haired woman sitting in the corner: a Cossetan captive Neitin had claimed, she said, to help her with the baby. Needless, with three sisters always about, but it pleased her, so Ekialde allowed it. So few things pleased her these days.

The Cossetan woman *did* have a way with the baby. Perhaps she had raised her own. She looked to be around forty, old enough for grandchildren, even. Her arms were marked up and down with ink, though the designs were nothing like Ekialde's. She had been a magic-woman among her own people, and that seemed to give Neitin comfort. She rarely spoke, at least in Ekialde's presence, but her face was expressive. She disapproved of Bailar's magic even more than Neitin, shooting him baleful looks whenever their paths crossed.

'Perhaps it was no luck of the Aventans,' Ekialde considered, 'and no disfavor of the gods. What if this woman interfered, somehow, with Bailar's work?'

Ekialde shook his head, dismissing the idea. During the siege, Bailar had remained at the war-camp, closer to Toletum, while Neitin stayed downriver at the civilian camp, with this strange woman at her side. 'And Bailar would know, surely, if someone attempted to curse him or disrupt his work.'

He did not like the suspicion rising within him; it would not do to grow fearful, mistrustful. He must be strong, for the sake of his people.

"I do not know by what power the Aventans broke my magic," Bailar admitted, his voice as close to humble as Ekialde had ever heard. "I intend to find out, if I can. Though our numbers are depleted, there is still much we can do. Let us rest through at least part of this winter, rather than harrying the nearby villages." Ekialde grunted; most of the close-range villages were either their allies or already abandoned. There would be little point in scavenging them now. "I will use the time well, this I promise you."

Ekialde wanted to believe him. He had invested so much in Bailar's promises. Perhaps not all had borne out, but it would be arrogance indeed to presume that any man could direct the will of the gods entirely. 'We are engaged in a dire struggle. Our gods against those protecting Aven. Theirs are *strong, or they would never have stretched their hands so far as our land to begin with. But this is our home. Our gods will protect us, here.'*

Perhaps, Ekialde considered, he had overstretched *himself* in the past year. He envisioned pushing the Aventans all the way to the coast, flushing them out of Iberia entirely—but Iberia was not the Lusetani's alone to command. The Arevaci and Edetani had rolled over for Aven, accepted them. *'And perhaps it was not my place to tell them not to.'*

"Can you protect me?" Ekialde asked, his voice coarse with need. "Can you protect my people? Can your magics call the gods' eyes upon us, lead us to victory against the vile Aventan forces?"

"Yes," Bailar said, and his voice rang with sincerity. "I am sure of it, sister-son. I cannot promise you the particulars of how, but this I vow, with every breath in me: the gods are with you. They will not abandon you. Their eyes are on you. They want this for you, this triumph, this glory. They chose you to defend their lands and their people."

Again, Ekialde's gaze drifted to the far side of the tent. His wife, his son. *'You are what I must protect and defend.'*

The itching under his skin swelled to a burning. He needed to feel the hilt of a blade in his palm, or perhaps the smooth wood of a bow. Yes, that would do: hunting. Fresh meat for the stews, and new furs for his wife and son.

'You need to kill something,' a voice at the back of his head whispered. *'Justify it however you like, but you know that's at the heart of it.'*

Ekialde rose, shaking his head as though that might clear some of the tumult inside it. "I do not know that I can wait as long as will suit you. If the war-band wants action, we will go and find it." He lifted his chin proudly. "We are still capable warriors, even without your charms." Neither shame nor defiance crossed Bailar's face, only steady regard. "Do what you must," he said to his uncle. "Find me... Find me a way to triumph."

Forum, City of Aven

Six days before the Ides of November, all civic and business activity stopped. The day was one of the *nefasti*, cursed days in most Aventans' opinions, and of the *nefasti*, considered among the worst. On this day, the Temple of Janus held a sacred and harrowing ritual, opening its subterranean chambers to priests and a few stalwart worshipers. They opened, too, the *mundus*, the umbilical cord that connected the living world to the beyond. On this day, spirits could walk abroad.

Corinna sniffed in disdain as she crossed a quiet Forum towards the temple. *'Fearful fools.'* The spirits that passed through the *mundus* were the blessed dead. *'Well. Blessed or at least indifferent.'* It took a different sort of power to call forth fiends.

The Gates of Janus stood open, for Aven was at war. That matter in Iberia. Well, it was almost always *something*. The gates had rarely been closed since their construction, but *this* time, they spread wide for the Iberian venture. Corinna had no care for it, except that it unsettled people here at home. A tool she could use, another knife she could twist in the guts of this city.

She bowed her head respectfully as she entered. The priests knew her face, and she wore the black-bordered tunic and mantle of a mage. In the public eye, she was a humble devotee, pledged to Fortuna and Janus. Some few might have heard more of her story, one they would deem sad. A tragedy. A broken bird.

They had no idea.

Corinna had broken herself, not *been* broken. She self-shattered, over and over, taking power from every rip and tear and crack in her soul. The priests of Janus, they liked their orderly divides, their doorways, their gates. Either open or closed, so simple. Either forward or back, so clear. They forgot or else they willfully ignored the *true* potency of Fracture, bestowed in the full-flood-blessings of its strongest and truest patron deity: not Janus or Fortuna, but the Lady Discordia.

No temples to her, not here, and no priests. No worshipers known to the world. Her cult had been banished more than once in Aven's history, most recently by Dictator Ocella. *'She may not be welcome, but there is no keeping her out.'*

Aven sought control, regulation, order, forgetting that its past and its future were written in the jagged lines of chaos.

Like many of those who dared the Temple of Janus on this day, Corinna carried a basket full of offerings, though she kept a cloth tucked over her goods. The priests of Janus would not understand. Fruits of the harvest, they expected, bright and colorful and fresh. The first citrons, the last grapes, soft persimmons and sweet pears, and—most blessed of all—the jewels of pomegranates.

What Corinna offered cost her so much more than any peasant's toil or patrician's coin. Blighted stalks of wheat and blistered fruits, white and powdery and crisping. This, the harvest of her soul, the proof of her efforts on Discordia's behalf. Each one the product of another exquisite fissure in her essence.

The air went from crisp to cold as she descended beneath the temple, surrounded by stones which had not seen the sunlight since they had been laid. Had anyone thought to harness the power when they were cut from whatever mountain quarry gave them birth?

Likely not. Corinna sometimes felt no one but she saw the glorious potential in every day. Everything in the world broke, eventually; everything decayed and went to the realm of Shadow, but first it must dissolve in some fashion: splitting apart or sloughing off or with a grand sudden *snap*. So much power, for those willing to grasp it.

She reached out, shifting the weight of her basket to one hip and trailing her fingers over the stones and mortar. Her skin snagged, so gently, on the bumpy surface. Corinna relished the tug of rough stone against her softness, a reminder. *'You can build from broken things, yes, but they will always still be broken. Temples, mosaics, entire cities. They are made of jagged pieces, and even if you smooth them down, they know what they are, in their depths, and that they will never be the same again. A thing once shattered cannot be made whole.'*

The room at the bottom of the stairs was humble: small and square. The pit at its center was no wider than a man was tall, but a thrill ran through Corinna at its rumbling power. Only mages would feel it as she did, rolling in her blood and bones, a deep thrum, usually muffled by a large glossy stone. Though Corinna could only sense Fracture, a mixture of elements simmered beneath: Shadow, calling from beyond the veil like the howl of Cerberus; Earth at its darkest and coldest, still and sullen; even Water, which slipped between worlds, just as the rivers of the Underworld eased the passage from life into death.

Other worshipers were appeasing the gods, of earth and underworld alike. Perhaps they were praying for lost loved ones. Others implored Ceres for good harvest; she made all things come up from under the ground, after all.

Corinna was making a promise.

The men who shared Corinna's orbit—who *thought* they were using her—they wanted to build things, shiny and solid. They would have to tear their world apart first, and they intended to use Corinna to do it, but then they wanted to remake the world in a frame that suited them better. They had their reasons; her brother and his political friends talked, talked, talked.

Corinna didn't care who won or who lost or why they wanted to fight, but she was happy to turn Aven into a battlefield, while she remained, for now, sheltered and shielded and supported by those oh-so-powerful men. She would take what she needed from them, demure and sweet under blight-white mantles of pressed linen, every pin in place—and she would rend Aven to bits, if her strength withstood the strain.

And that, in part, she would owe to her patroness.

When Corinna's turn to step up to the edge of the pit came, she swayed slightly, cocking her ear as she listened to the music from beyond the worlds. A pair of men in rough spun tunics gave the wide-eyed stare she was accustomed to seeing; one looked on the verge of reaching out, lest she pitch herself over the rim. She offered a beatific smile and in her sweetest voice said, "Beautiful, isn't it? The gods be with you, my friends."

They scurried away.

Corinna flung her whole basket into the pit; it wouldn't do to tip it out and let the priests see what spoils she brought. Then she fell to her knees. She pressed her palms against the joints between the stones and prayed, then raised one hand to her chest, where a bronze medallion hung beneath her tunic and gown; it bore Discordia's forbidden image. If anyone caught her with it, she would simply lean into the madness they whispered about, in all their incomprehension.

But no one would look so close. She had learned her lessons well, practicing her outlawed arts under the very nose of the Dictator. *I will do right by you, Lady. I will give this place to you.*

------ ∽ ------

Camp of Legio X Equestris, Central Iberia

Sempronius Tarren, Praetor of Cantabria and commander of four legions, was buried in letters.

Most were of a political nature. Elections in Aven were approaching,
only a month away, and Sempronius was engaged in a campaign to see his
praetorship extended into the coming year. There was no reason he should
not be offered propraetorial command — but his enemies in the Senate
would object merely because it was *him*. The Optimates, those "good men"
who believed their narrow-minded ways best for Aven, obstructed him on
sheer principle.

So Sempronius wrote often to his allies, the Popularists and those per-
suadable moderates, not only to secure votes in his favor, but to create circumstances favorable to him among the electorate.

Two men in particular received more than their share: Galerius Orator,
one of the two sitting consuls, and Marcus Autronius, a backbencher
among the Senators who was also the older brother of Sempronius's senior
tribune, Felix. Galerius was a man of rare virtue, who truly served his nation
out of duty rather than ambition. He didn't always agree with Sempronius,
but he always heard him out.

Marcus was a tribune of the plebs, an office with veto power and the
ability to put proposals to the Tribal Assembly, and such a valuable conduit
for some of Sempronius's financial motions. At the moment, Sempronius
was attempting to compose a letter that would convince Marcus to stand
for office a second year.

Once, that would have been blasphemy; two generations' past, men
had been executed for the temerity of standing for tribune twice. But the
world changed, and Marcus would now be breaking no ground. He had a
good head on his shoulders and was well-liked in the Assembly. As an Earth
mage, he could never achieve any higher position within the Senate, but as
tribune, he could make a tangible difference in people's lives. *'I just have to
find the words to inspire him to duty.'*

As he finished the letter and pressed his falcon-in-flight seal into the
wax, his door opened. Corvinus, his steward, an ice-blond-haired freedman from Albina, leading another young man, this one scarce out of gangly
boyhood. Both were mages: Corvinus had some talent in Water, and the
boy Eustix was of Air, deft with the handling and direction of birds. "Mes-

sages for you from Aven," Corvinus said, and Eustix thrust out a hand with a packet.

"Excellent!" Sempronius said, rising from his desk. "I've more to send back." Eustix nodded; he had, over the past several months, gained familiarity with Sempronius's habits. Missives in and missives out, a nigh-unending circle. The boy never complained, and certainly he was being paid well for his postal services. "Careful with the top one," he said, handing over a stack of folded papers in exchange for the packet. "The wax hasn't quite dried yet."

"Very good, sir. Ah— So you know, some of those letters appear to have been sent in October. I think a storm that delayed some of them. Three birds arrived all at once."

"No matter. Still faster than getting them by boat and rider." That was why Sempronius had lured the boy away from Nedhena with exorbitant wages; well-worth the expense, especially in autumn and winter, not to rely on the usual channels for information.

"There are two from your sister," Corvinus said. His voice held weight, and Sempronius's eyebrows quirked up. Vibia typically waited for a response before sending another letter. To receive two at once, sent in quick succession, was foreboding.

Sempronius shuffled through the packet, setting aside messages from the Senate until he found the two bearing his sister's seal and neatly pointed hand. "Do you know which came— Ah, yes, she dated them." Careful as ever, Vibia marked the date of composition on an outer corner of each letter. "Thank you, Eustix. Corvinus, sort the ones from the Senators?"

"Of course."

Eustix nodded and departed. Corvinus settled into his chair on the other side of the room, while Sempronius resumed his seat and opened Vibia's first letter, sent in late October.

Brother —

I write to inform you of a circumstance that, I believe, will be of interest to you. I hope you shall receive this information as proof of my full devotion to and love for you, for nothing else would prompt me to pass along what I fear must be termed gossip, particularly when *my own heart is far from decided upon the overall benefit or detraction of the matter as concerns your august self— But in short, here it is: Vitellia Latona divorced her husband. I have been unable to determine, exactly, why. All she will say is that they no longer suited each other, which little explains why she should cast him off <u>now</u>, when that much has been apparent for years.*

'I beg you not to excite yourself too much over this development. Her newly un-husbanded state removes only one of my objections to the idea of you attaching yourself to her. The lady's own character may nearly have removed another, but you are well aware of the nature of my reservations. In any case, there's nothing to be done until you return from Iberia, so do please focus your efforts on that.

'Ever your dutiful sister,

'Vibia'

Sempronius had to laugh; Vibia's tart tongue was apparent even in her pen strokes. He was glad, though, to hear that her assessment of Latona might be softening. Vibia feared for his safety, but just as much for the keeping of his secrets, which any wife might stand in a position to reveal and which would be almost impossible to conceal from a wife such as Latona—intelligent, inquisitive, and endowed with magical gifts.

'You could let her in,' one piece of his soul whispered. *'Trust her.'* The lover's heart would readily submit to that decree, but the rest of him—so long used to hiding his nature, so accustomed to subterfuge, so sure of his course—shuddered to contemplate such a vulnerability. *'Well. It's not as though I can tell her in a letter, so no matter for now. Vibia's right. Settling the situation here and getting home is the first goal.'*

The second letter, posted only a few days earlier, began *'Dearest brother.'* The uncharacteristically effusive salutation concerned him from the start.

'I write now with dire tidings. I have waited as long as I feel prudent. I was hoping the situation would evolve, and I could impart a tale of ultimate victory. But it has been three days with no change. I can only pray circumstances will alter the very moment I set down

my pen—or, failing that, the moment the bird takes off, such that another letter will follow hard upon this first, with better tidings.

'Vitellia Latona has been injured and may be near unto death.'

A cold pit settled in Sempronius's stomach, and his throat grew tight and still. Almost he forgot to breathe as he read the story, set down in thin, sharp lines. She could not put it in such bald terms as to give him all necessary details, not in a letter that might be intercepted by either his Iberian or Aventan foes, but the siblings were long-accustomed to couching their words in circumspection, and from Vibia's description, Sempronius filled in the gaps.

Latona had been attacked. They both had, with Vitellia Alhena, Ama Rubellia, and Merula, by a Discordian mage. A woman, unknown to Vibia. The others got free; Latona did not. Whatever the woman had done to her, it rendered her as insensible as though dead.

Vibia offered no false hopes nor flowery consolations. Rather she promised:

I will write again as soon as there is any change in her condition. I hope you will pass word to her brother, as I am not certain Aulus or Aula are composed enough to have done so yet.

'Keep faith, dear brother. If I have learnt nothing else these past few months, it is the raw force of Vitellian tenacity. Should Pluto desire her company, he may well have to come fetch her himself.

'Vibia'

He rose. "Corvinus."

"Sir?" Corvinus looked up from his sorting, brow pinched in concern. "What news?"

"Ill tidings indeed. Please locate Tribune Vitellius and bring him here. It concerns his family."

Corvinus's pale eyes widened. "His father, the censor, or—?"

Sempronius shook his head. "His sister. The Lady Latona." To his credit, Corvinus's face betrayed nothing, though he was on the short list of those who knew closer to the truth of how much the lady meant to Sempronius. "I'll give you the full story later." He would give Vitellius the same version Vibia said she gave Aulus: the women were determined to keep secret that Latona had been injured magically and while on Juno's business.

Vibia and Latona had both written to him over the past months, telling him all they encountered, first in the countryside around Stabiae and then in Aven itself. Discordian charms and curses, seemingly random but with an increasingly malevolent bent. According to Vibia, Latona flung herself into the challenge with abandon, each encounter stiffening her resolve to get to the bottom of the mystery and find the mages responsible.

Sempronius wished he had been there to witness. He had long sensed untried potential in her, a deep well. Knowing she had finally embraced her power filled him with delight. He had been so sure, not only of her strength but of the gods' intentions that she use it, that he set aside any worries for her safety. Juno and Venus would protect their own. He had been sure.

The possibility that he had misinterpreted the will of the gods was chilling in more than one way.

Another thought passed through Sempronius's mind, even as he hated himself for the pragmatic intrusion: he and Gaius Vitellius both wore focales woven by Latona's hand and imbued with her magic. It was all that kept their heads above water when the Lusetani tried to drown them in blood magic. When mages died, their magic tended to fade; it was why their public works, like aqueducts, had to be carefully maintained by subsequent generations. Latona's death might not only be a personal tragedy; it might place Sempronius and Gaius Vitellius in jeopardy.

He shook his head, momentarily annoyed by the way his mind worked. Usually a benefit, the constant churning. It kept his wits nimble, meant he was ready to respond to the machinations of his rivals, gave him the ability to see possibilities that others missed. He did not care for the moments when it interfered with natural human sympathy.

The door banged open, caught by a sudden gust and torn from Corvinus's hand as he entered, this time with Gaius Vitellius in tow. A tall young man with gingery hair, in whom Sempronius saw echoes of all three of his sisters.

Strange, to think that he had more acquaintance with the ladies of the household, but the two men were far enough apart in age that society had not placed them in much congress until now. Sempronius had been finishing his own tribunate years, on campaign in Numidia, when Vitellius was beginning his, and then followed the years of exile during Ocella's dictatorship. Vitellius spent his early years of military service with the Eighth Legion along the northern border, until his governor dispatched him to Iberia with two cohorts to investigate rumors of unrest. There was alliance between them, both as military commanders and as members of Popularist families, but not friendship. Not yet, at least.

'The poor lad hasn't had time to recover from all he suffered in Toletum.' A siege was a terrible thing to endure in any case; for Vitellius, the agonies compounded. The Lusetani sent first their haunting demons, then a magically-induced plague to ravage the town that they could not take by force of arms, and Vitellius bore the weight of it all upon his shoulders. *'And now I must inform him of another tragedy.'*

Vitellius's eyes retained a half-haunted look, but as Corvinus secured the door behind them, he snapped to attention. "Sir?"

"Tribune," Sempronius said. "You may wish to sit. I'm afraid I have ill news."

III

For once, Alhena had not been left out of the discussion.

Latona had been unconscious for eight days. Eight wretched, unthinkable days. The healers were perplexed; by now, all agreed, she should have wakened or died. They were doing all they could to feed her broth and honey; her body still knew how to swallow, and it still knew how to breathe, confusing the healers further. Out of suggestions, they did their best to keep her clean and shift her weight so that sores would not develop, but no one could wake her. Even the healer-mages that Aulus brought in had been no use.

'But then, they are accustomed to using magic to heal physical ills,' Alhena considered. *'Would a magical wound appear the same? Would they even know to look for it?'*

That was the subject of today's conference between Aula, Alhena, and Vibia Sempronia: deciding if there was anyone capable of seeing the curse at work who might be able to help. They needed someone of an element that could bear witness to the others: Light, Water, Air, or Spirit. Someone with a particular gift for recognizing magical signatures would be even better.

"I know in normal circumstances, we'd look to the Augian Commission," Vibia said, once they settled in the sitting-room. Aula positioned herself so she could still see Latona's doorway, and her gaze anchored there, drifting back whenever she plucked it away. "This Discordian's magic would violate the *tabulae magicae* even if she weren't a member of a banished cult." It was usually the business of the Augian Commission to investigate such matters; the law gave them jurisdiction over crimes involving magic, just as it charged them to ensure that magic did not interfere with state business. "But I think we should consider that a last resort. Latona doesn't trust them."

"No," Aula concurred. "She tried bringing the curse-charms to a Commissioner's attention and was practically laughed out of the room. He implied it was all in her head. If we brought one of them in, they'd probably decide she did it to herself in a fit of feminine hysteria."

All three women seethed for a moment, in communal disgust with the short-sightedness of arrogant men. Then, Alhena offered, "It should be a friend. For them to be of real use, we'll have to tell them what happened. So it must be someone we can trust."

Vibia's nostrils flared slightly. "Trust," she echoed derisively. Alhena took no offense; the disdain was not directed at her, but reflected Vibia's essentially skeptical nature. "Pity that none of us, nor Ama Rubellia, have the necessary skills. Latona should have chosen her friends more strategically before getting herself cursed."

Aula thought a moment, then said, "Davina."

Another scoff from Vibia. "The bath-house mistress? Be serious."

"I am," Aula rejoined. "She's an extremely talented Water mage and she has some skill in the healing arts. She and Latona have always been friendly."

"Friendly is not the same as trustworthy. She'll gossip."

"You'd be surprised how many secrets a bath-house mistress learns to keep."

"You'd be surprised how many they spill. I'd sooner go to Marcia Tullia," Vibia said, naming the wife of consul Galerius Orator. Marcia was an Air mage of considerable talent, and she had used her skill to help pass messages between senators in exile during the Dictatorship.

"She's so severe," Alhena pointed out. "I mean, she's kind, in her way, but... explaining all this to her would be a feat. And I suspect she'd want us to go to the Commission."

"Yes, very law-and-order oriented, our good consul's wife," Aula said. "It's not a bad idea. But it may not be the best one." Her eyes—so much like Latona's that it hurt, when Latona's would not open—flew wide, and she angled herself toward Alhena. "What about Quinta Terentia? We could ask Terentilla to bring her. Tilla's always been so fond of Latona, and you and she have been spending time together lately, haven't you?"

Alhena felt her cheeks go bright red, and she ducked her head so her hair would fall on either side of her face, hopefully obscuring the telltale flush. "Ah—yes, yes, we have. I mean. I haven't seen her since this all happened." She sent notes, though. Not with the full story, but enough of it. Tilla had been there when Alhena had the vision that led to this whole mess. Tilla had witnessed Alhena going into a trance. Tilla had been frantic with worry when she didn't easily shake out of it. Tilla had—

'Tilla kissed me.'

A warm thrill went through Alhena with the memory, an indulgence she treasured, though it felt so utterly wrong to think of pleasure in such circumstances. A shock to them both: Tilla feverishly pressing her lips to Alhena's hair, cheeks, then mouth. *And then I kissed her back.'*

If Alhena hadn't felt such a need to get back home, to tell her sisters what prophecy revealed to her about the Discordian's lair, she might've gone on kissing Tilla forever. It stirred something unknown in her core. Even when she had *been* kissed—and it seemed so long ago now, the betrothal to Tarpeius, a perfectly nice young man who would've made a perfectly nice husband, if he hadn't died returning from his military service—nothing like this eager yearning had swelled within her.

'Did Tilla feel that, too?' There had been no opportunity to ask, and no chance since to sort out what it might all mean. Alhena hadn't left the house since the calamity.

'Tilla has sent a note every day, though.' Nothing in them addressed the topic of kissing, of course, but they were warm and sympathetic and friendly. *'So she's not angry with me, at least. And she's so kind.'*

"Quinta would keep a secret," Vibia allowed, "and if you say Tilla would, I'll believe you." She said it with a slight roll of her eyes, though; prim Vibia disapproved of Terentilla's wild ways. "But a Vestal Virgin turning up at the door would attract quite a lot of attention."

"Attention's going to come sooner or later if she doesn't wake up," Aula said. "I've made excuses on her behalf—told people she's come down with a mild fever—but we can only keep up that pretense for so long."

"What about—" Alhena began, then cleared her throat when Aula's and Vibia's attention snapped toward her. "I mean. I think I've thought of someone. A Spirit mage. Someone who would have good reason to be loyal and keep a secret. And someone who would attract no attention whatsoever coming here."

Vibia lifted a thin brow. "Well?"

"Fausta."

It took Vibia a moment to realize who she meant. "The girl, you mean?" Aula's forehead furrowed in confusion, so Vibia expanded: "She's been Latona's acolyte at the Cantrinalia these past two years. Gawky child, but she looks at Latona like she hung the moon."

"A child, though?" Aula asked, fingers worrying at the neckline of her tunic.

Alhena nodded confirmation. "She still wears the *bulla*. Or she did at the Cantrinalia last month." The protective charm indicated she was not yet menstruating, since that was typically when girls put them aside and began wearing women's clothes, indicating they were—legally, at least—marriageable. Boys waited until their manhood ceremonies at seventeen, a discrepancy Alhena had never thought fair. "I think she's eleven or twelve."

Both Aula and Vibia looked wary. "So young, and largely untrained, I would assume," Aula said.

Alhena knew she was thinking not of Fausta, but of Lucia. The girl had shown no further evidence of magic, after that first night. No more screaming fits, no more claiming she heard Latona crying out in pain.

That was often the way, at her age. The gift came in sudden bursts, unexpected and often uncontrollable, until a child learned how to call down the gods' blessing deliberately—or at least wrangle some awareness of when it would come unbidden. They couldn't even be sure what element it stemmed from, though Spirit seemed a likely guess.

They hadn't told Vibia yet; Aula objected on the grounds that she didn't want her daughter hectored after a traumatic event, and Alhena had to admit that Vibia might not be as delicate as a mother would wish, if she thought Lucia could tell them anything useful.

"But of Latona's own element," Alhena said, feeling more convinced of the rightness of this course as she spoke. "Vibia, you've said you could only get a sense of what the Fracture magic is doing, correct?" A tight nod. "But if Fausta could see more, though she may not know what to do or have the strength to fix it, she could tell you, at least, and you might be able to figure something out."

"She'd certainly come, if we sent for her in Latona's name," Vibia said. "Her family would think it a great honor even without any idea of what's going on."

Aula's face showed less certainty, but she did offer, "Latona has been meaning to take more of an active role in mentoring the girl, there being so few female Spirit mages in the city."

"I think it would do no harm," Alhena said, "and possibly a great deal of good."

"Even if she decided to go carrying tales," Vibia said, "she's a plebeian child of no consequence, so who would listen?"

An ugly truth, but a truth nonetheless. Vibia could be unfeeling in such matters, but at least she never flinched from them.

With the matter decided, Vibia wasted no time in making the arrangements, determined to take action that very evening. They sent word to Ama Rubellia, who offered to accompany the child Fausta across the city.

Aula opted not to be present when they made their attempt. She arranged invitations to a quiet, consoling dinner with Maia Domitia for herself, her daughter, and her father, neatly removing those unpredictable elements from the house.

Rubellia brought the girl an hour before sunset. Fausta was as Vibia remembered, in so much as she *did* remember. In truth, she took small notice of the acolytes during the Cantrinalia. If they were worth remembering, they'd grow into mages of consequence, but so many of them were chosen simply for being the right age, with no particular talent to mark them out.

'So it had been for me.' Vibia had served the role a few times, in her own youth, before it became apparent her powers were not going to flourish into anything to dazzle the nation. Time would tell if Fausta's gift was weak or strong.

The girl was, as Alhena estimated, eleven or twelve, trapped in the age of sudden growth and blemished skin. She wore a simple roughspun tunic, but had clearly made an effort to present herself well: freshly bathed, her light brown hair dressed in three neat plaits which were then bound on top of her head. Her eyes were an indistinct hazel, but keen and alert. She stood close to Rubellia, making Vibia wonder how much calming energy the priestess was radiating. Alhena and Merula kept their distance, determined not to overwhelm the girl; both settled down to pray at the lararium.

"Fausta understands why we've asked her here," Rubellia said, her lovely voice as smooth as ever, "and she knows she is to be circumspect. She also knows to tell us if she feels uncomfortable or frightened, and that we will not force her to do anything that will overwhelm her."

Vibia rolled her shoulders back. "Yes, of course," she said, though she was thinking, *'Little use the girl will be to us if she has a meltdown or flees in terror.'*

"I'm—I'm pretty good at seeing magic," Fausta offered. "It's the first thing I started doing, years ago."

"Excellent," Vibia said. "That's what we need. If you can describe to us what's going on, it may help us determine how to recover Vitellia Latona."

The girl's fingers fidgeted with her belt, twisting the fabric at her waist. "I hope I can help. She's so kind. And everyone knows—well, everyone on the Esquiline, anyway—how much good you've been doing, with all the strangeness." Her hands stilled and her voice dropped to a whisper. "I wish I could be like her."

Vibia and Rubellia exchanged a glance over the girl's head. *'Would you wish that if you knew all she's suffered?'* Vibia wondered.

"Perhaps one day you shall be," Rubellia said, petting Fausta's hair maternally. "And I know Latona would like to help guide you, as much as she is able."

"But we have to wake her up," Fausta said, with a decisive nod. "Alright. I'm ready. I'll—I mean, I'll try."

It took Fausta longer than Latona to summon her magic and settle into its form. Vibia had become accustomed to Latona's particular rhythms and pacing. After so many months working together on the Discordian problem, they had learned to yoke their strengths with instinctive efficiency. The child required a patience that took conscious effort on Vibia's part.

Neither Vibia nor Rubellia could see the power Fausta was invoking, but when it fell into place, the girl drew a sharp breath. "Oh! That's—That's interesting."

Vibia held her tongue, knowing anything she said would come off sharply, and let Rubellia ask, mellifluous and undemanding: "What do you see, dear one?"

"A golden glow, all over her. Like she's wrapped in a shining cloud. That's her own magic. At least, I think." The girl frowned. "But I don't know how that could be, since she's unconscious. I know Shadow has dream-magic sometimes, but I didn't think anyone else could perform while asleep." She squinted, leaning closer to Latona's bed, as though trying to read something far-off. "There's a— there's something mixed in." She shook her head. "No, not mixed, that's not the right—Hmm. It's like when a burr gets stuck in clothing. All those spikes and tendrils, snarled in the weft. It's not hers. Someone else put that there."

"Go on," Vibia prompted. "Tell us about that."

Fausta blinked a few times, then turned her gaze back to Latona. "It's, ah— it feels stuck in her. It's—bronze?" Her brow creased. "Bronze is usually Fracture, isn't it?"

"You *have* been practicing," Rubellia said, giving her shoulder a squeeze.

"Can you get a sense of what the burr is *doing*?" Vibia asked.

"I know it might be hard to tell," Rubellia softened the request. "Putting words to magic can be such a challenge, even for those of us with more experience."

Fausta nodded, biting her lower lip. "It's—You know when you get a splinter? And it doesn't get better until you pull the wood out? Like that. But... magic." A quaver entered her voice. "It's making her magic like a wound that won't heal."

Vibia sucked in a breath, seized Rubellia by the elbow, and dragged her aside. "I think I have it," she said in a low hiss. "That heinous woman—Ohh, she's clever, I must give her that. And creative. We saw that in her experiments, out in the fields and forests. Part of what she was doing was using Fracture to manipulate other elements. We felt it in her little den of horrors, too."

"I remember," Rubellia said.

"I believe that's the nature of what she's done to Latona. She anchored the curse not in some external charm or token, like the ones we've been tearing apart all year, but in Latona's own Spirit magic." Vibia swallowed. "It would explain why she's burning so hot still. Not a fever, just her own magic, roiling inside her." Always astonishing, how hot Latona burned when working magic; in the dead of night, her skin would glow like she was under the noonday summer sun. "As she tries to fight off the curse—"

"The effort fuels it more." Rubellia pressed a hand to her chest. "Blessed Venus. Is that even possible?"

Vibia made a frustrated gesture. "I have no idea! Discordian magic isn't precisely something I was trained to analyze."

Frowning, Rubellia jerked her head toward Fausta, and Vibia realized her voice had risen. Fausta had taken their need for conference in stride, however, and was paying them no mind. She had closed her eyes, holding her hands palms-up at waist level, murmuring prayers.

Lowering her tone again, Vibia continued. "What the girl said, about it being like a burr in cloth. That's easier if the cloth is rough and frayed already than if it's tightly woven, yes?"

Rubellia nodded slowly as she puzzled her way through Vibia's hypothesis. "I think I follow you. Latona's magic was already ragged—"

"She'd put so much of herself out as we dispelled the *lemures,* and I don't think she had much left in the way of defenses."

"So the Discordian was able to sink her claws in."

"But I don't think it was spontaneous. She wasn't merely taking advantage of the moment. She was ready for this—waiting for it. The whole scenario may have been a trap."

Horror came over Rubellia's expression. "She might have had one prepared for you as well. For any of us, I suppose, but—"

"I know," Vibia responded darkly. "Latona and I were the ones undoing her work all over the city. If it was hers alone." Vibia still wasn't sure on that count; the charms they'd encountered had been so different. One mage's experiments? Or the efforts of multiple hands?

In any case, the Discordian mage's ire had been directed at them both; the turn of Fortuna's wheel delivered Latona into her trap and not Vibia instead or as well. *'Glitter-gold and the knife's edge,'* the woman had called them.

"Juno and Venus preserve her," Rubellia said, voice husky with grief and astonishment.

Vibia scowled. "Fine job they've done so far. First that worthless marriage, then what they let Ocella do to her, and now this! If she's meant to be serving them, they might see fit to remove an obstacle or two from her path."

A shadow of a smile cracked through Rubellia's expression. "You're very good, to be so defensive of her, even against the gods themselves."

Vibia huffed lightly, but Rubellia had a point. Not long ago, Vibia had not thought highly of Latona. Affected by the cloud of suspicion, hovering since the reign of the Dictator Ocella, Vibia had doubted her motives and warned her brother off of further association with a woman she judged as ambitious and conniving.

Now she knew: what ambition lived in Latona's heart was only recently-discovered, and its bent was for the public benefit, not her own aggrandizement. Vibia still found Latona's irrepressible altruism a little irritating, but in the same way that her own brother's persistent benevolence wore at her nerves. If it had been a pose, an affectation to impress the masses, Vibia might have disdained them both, but the truly annoying part was how thoroughly they *meant* it.

'All she wanted was to serve you, Juno. She believed you gave her these gifts for a reason.'

Vibia's eyes drifted again to Fausta, another young girl given such gifts. "She could help."

"What?"

"The girl."

Rubellia cocked her head, her usual mild demeanor giving way to a flash of pique. "If you intend on conscripting her into service, you might at least use her name, Vibia."

Vibia flapped a dismissive hand. "She's stronger than I thought."

"Vibia, we cannot ask a *child*—"

"It may not take much!" Vibia said, struggling to remain hushed. "A nudge to disrupt the curse, shake it loose. Latona helped to guide my magic before. If Fausta can do that much, I might be able to sever the connection."

"And then what?" Rubellia demanded. "What if it shatters Latona's mind? Or recoils on Fausta? Do you want to risk that little girl getting snared in the Discordian's trap, too?"

"What other choice do we have?" Vibia hissed. "I'm not saying we *force* her. But we can ask, at least."

"Children are impressionable and often seek to please. They aren't capable of evaluating the danger to themselves."

A muscle twitched in Vibia's cheek. Rubellia wasn't wrong, and she had far more experience with youths than Vibia did, considering how many acolytes she oversaw at her temple. But they had a chance, right here and now, to free Latona, and Vibia could not overlook any tool at her disposal. "She's nearly grown," Vibia said, keeping cool only with straining effort, "and she's going to have to learn how to govern and guard herself soon. If she has even a tenth of Latona's talent, others are going to notice. And in times such as this? With evil cultists running loose in the city?"

"That doesn't mean we have the right to rush her towards—"

"I'm not *saying* we rush her into anything. But look." Vibia jerked her head towards the girl, still radiating piety. "She cares for Latona. She's shown she wants to help. We can at least give her the opportunity to be of further use." Another crease in Rubellia's pretty brow let Vibia know she had not phrased that as delicately as she might have. "And besides," she hurried on, "if we can't wake Latona up, who will there be to teach and protect her?"

That argument cut where the others had not, for Rubellia's shoulders sagged. "We must take every care for her safety. And if she wants out, we release her, immediately."

To Vibia's gratification, as soon as she and Rubellia rejoined the girl, Fausta asked, guileless as a doe, "Is there anything else I can do?"

'*She is young,*' Vibia thought, while Rubellia explained what they wanted, '*and trusting, Juno bless her.*' She hoped the goddess might show this child more tender care than she had Latona.

Fausta's lips parted uncertainly. "I'll—I'll try. But I'm not sure if I have the power, or the control, to be of much help."

"I know you are young in your talents," Vibia said, trying to infuse her voice with Rubellia-like warmth, "but obviously you have no small gift. All you need to do is use your magic to augment Latona's—get it to flare, a bit—and I think that will enable me to sever the connection between the curse and Latona."

"An additional influence may shake things loose, is what we mean," Rubellia supplied. "Like jostling a basket to get to something at the bottom."

Worrying her lower lip again, Fausta glanced at Latona's form, aglow in the lamplight. "A surge of empathy, perhaps? Sort of... threading my magic with hers?"

An encouraging smile lit Rubellia's face. "Let's see, shall we?"

Fausta drew nearer to Latona's body, and this time, reached out and put a hand on Latona's bare shoulder before she began drawing in her magic. Rubellia stood by her, likely pouring calming energy into the girl as a precautionary measure. Again, Vibia waited in trammeled silence for the child to work her nascent magic.

After a moment, Fausta's neutral expression contorted with anguish. She cried out, but did not recoil from Latona's form. Rubellia's hands steadied her, but tears began pouring down the child's cheeks. "I didn't know— There's so much— Ah!"

"Vibia..." Rubellia said, half-warning, half-question.

But Vibia sensed something shaking loose. So frustrating, to know only half of what was happening! She couldn't see what Fausta was doing, couldn't feel the haze of Latona's magic, but she could sense the Discordian curse in sudden revolt, bucking against the imposition. *'Like seeing a lock without a door, or a rider without a horse.'*

"Hold on," she ordered, reaching out to grasp Latona's hands, interlacing their fingers. Still, she expected to find Latona corpse-cold, but her skin remained sunburn-warm, almost painful to touch.

Fausta whimpered, but squared her shoulders, evidently willing to continue. She closed her eyes in concentration, and again the curse shuddered. Pressing her lips together, Vibia reached out for it with her own Fracture magic, probing its ragged edges to find a weak point. *'Janus and Fortuna, show me where to break the hold. And Lady Juno, you might be a bit helpful, too, you know, this is your scion I'm trying to save!'*

The Discordian curse *was* coming loose, but not enough. It was as a fist clenched around a stick: someone else might grab the stick and jiggle it, and the grip might slip, but it would take more force to tug the stick loose entirely. Vibia wasn't sure Fausta had that kind of strength, nor that the half-trained girl would be able to endure much more of whatever was happening to her. *'So I'll have to do what I can about the fist.'*

She worried, though, about the damage that might present to Latona. The Discordian curse was snarled deep into Latona's own powers, and Spirit magic was more closely linked to the soul of the mage than any other element. *'I can't possibly do more harm than the curse is,'* Vibia thought, more hope than conviction.

She wedged her own magic in around the Discordian power. *'Sever. Snap. Break. Break, damn you!'*

Fausta's half-choked whimpers were starting to well into sobs, but she kept her hand resolutely on Latona's shoulder. Rubellia's voice had grown more worried. "Fausta, if you need to stop, we can stop. Vibia, I don't think we—"

"Quiet!" Vibia snapped. "I almost—"

She didn't want to use her magic violently, but she didn't have time to prise every stick of the bur loose from Latona's soul. Breathing in, filling her chest, she wrapped her magic around the curse instead, as best she could with no idea how it was anchored to Latona's own strength. *'Fortuna be with me.'*

Then she *yanked* on the curse, with as much magical force as she could muster. The sensation was horrible: a ripping, tearing feeling, full of splinters and shards, as if she had pulled the wing off a live bird.

Fausta inhaled, gulping, then fainted dead away into Rubellia's arms. "Vibia!" Rubellia shouted. "What did—"

"Recoil," Vibia said, again having to hope she was right. "She'll be— Oh!"

Latona's hands began to shake. The tremors moved up her arms, and then her whole body seized. With a cry, Rubellia eased Fausta onto the floor and rushed to Latona's side. "What did you do?"

"The best I could," Vibia half-whispered. "I promise."

Rubellia was calling for help, and a rush of footsteps soon answered her: Merula, no doubt, and Alhena, and others of the Vitellian household. Vibia stood and looked through the narrow window at the top of Latona's bedroom wall. Since they started, twilight had fallen, the sky purple and thick with clouds. If Vibia concentrated, she could always feel the moment when the blurry line between day and night tipped over, even if she couldn't see the sun on the horizon.

As tumult grew around her, Vibia reached for that slip, that shift. She wasn't sure why the urge to mark the moment had come upon her, swift and insistent, but she drew and slowly released another careful breath.

Latona went limp. Those clustered around her fell silent. The last curve of the sun slipped away in the unseen west, and in the same instant, every flame from every lamp in the house flared-white hot. Those in clay containers burst their vessels, but no one spared attention for the spatter or the flickers of fire that followed them across the tiles.

Latona's green eyes shot open.

IV

Camp of Legio X Equestris, Central Iberia

As he had for three nights, Sempronius dismissed all his servants except Corvinus. He settled down in the center of his tent, all the flaps tied shut, every lamp and brazier doused, with a clay bowl before his knees. Sempronius let his eyes adjust to the darkness: not pitch-black, not quite, not in such an active camp. A faint glow from torches and lanterns bled through the heavy canvas.

The bottom of the bowl was painted black, making the water within as dark as possible. As Sempronius stared down at it, he let the rest of the world fall away: all the sounds of the camp, Corvinus's slow and steady breath in the corner, the slight ache in his shoulders. Nothing could be allowed to exist except him and the shadows—and the scrap of fabric clutched in his left hand. Threaded between his fingers, Sempronius held the focale that Vitellia Latona had woven for him. The gift had, he was certain, saved his life more than once. The focale was a connection to Latona, stronger even than her letters: something not just crafted with her hands, but run through with her magical effort. If anything could help focus his own magic, it would be that.

"I call upon Pluto, Lord of the Underworld," he murmured, his hands resting palm-up on his knees. "I call upon Nox, Lady of Night. I call upon Neptune, Master of the Seas; I call upon Lympha, Reader of Souls." The invocations appealed to his peculiar blend of magic, Shadow and Water together, a method of scrying far apart from the orderly work of the augurs or the spontaneous visions of prophets. Reaching out with his talents, Sempronius sought to peer into the flickers of the uncertain future. "Governors of Shadow and Water, I, Vibius Sempronius Tarren, entreat you. Look here, gods; look here and answer me."

The power rolled to him from every edge of the tent, a flowing tide within the darkness. The surface of the water in his bowl shivered.

"Please," he said in a whisper. "The Lady Vitellia Latona. What— What has happened to her, and what will become?"

The previous nights, he had seen nothing. Only an endless fog on the water, usually a sign that his gods heard him but had nothing to impart. Worrisome, that. Was her fate beyond the knowledge of even the gods? Or did they simply not want to tell *him*, for some unknowable reason?

'Please.' The thought ached from beneath his ribs with every breath, a distraction he could ill afford in the midst of worrying about supply lines, drilling the legions, and maintaining balance between his Iberian allies. Everyone had someone back home to think of and worry about, of course; his concern was selfish, and he knew it.

'None of their dear ones have pitted themselves against a nameless Discordian menace, though. None of them placed their own flesh and soul between the people of Aven and whatever horrors the cultists are conjuring.'

He could imagine her trials, based on what he himself had experienced with the *akdraugi*. Not identical creatures, it seemed, but similar breeds. Men had been haunted to death by them, trapped in a world of nightmares within their own minds, until their bodies gave out. *'It cannot be. She cannot fall to such. So I ask you, gods who look over me, for some answer—or if not my own, then the gods who look over her! She is doing your work with all the fierceness in her heart.'*

A faint noise rippled around Sempronius: a laugh, though not an unkind one. The mild chuckle of a mother, he thought, whose child implored her for a treat. *'Very well,'* it seemed to say. *'If you must.'*

A shimmering golden light came over the surface of the water, like the sun rising over the sea. Sempronius's fingers tightened around the edge of the bowl, and he leaned closer, fixing his mind on the magic swirling within the dark liquid, calling the gods' gifts closer to his heart, that the image might show itself more clearly.

The scintillating light resolved itself into the picture of a glorious bower, teeming with every flower in creation. In the midst stood an enormous peacock, cerulean-and-teal feathers in full display, a thousand eyes wafting behind the curve of his neck.

A figure approached as though from some other other part of the garden: a tall and stately woman, dressed in rose-colored fabric and bedecked with pearls. With her plump curves and auburn tresses, Sempronius might have mistaken her for Aula Vitellia—but no, cheerful Aula did not move with such considered dignity. Nor did Aula wear a purple diadem, bound elegantly about her brow.

Sempronius's breath caught in his throat, half-afraid at what he had been given leave to witness, even in this figurative form, for this could be none but the goddess Juno, Queen of Heaven, greatest of all the divine ladies, and his love's protector.

As she approached, the peacock folded aside his tail feathers, revealing a silk-draped bed behind him. A golden-haired woman lay on it, as still as if it were not a bower but a bier. Her head was turned away from Sempronius's vantage point. Images in Shadow-induced visions were rarely literal. Faces, particularly, tended to blur, but he had no doubt that this was Latona. His heart felt like iron drawn to a lodestone, ready to leap out of his chest and plunge into the water, if that meant reaching her.

The goddess reached a hand toward Latona's brow, smoothing it as gently as a mother with a fretful child. She bent, placed a kiss on the crown of Latona's head, and then vanished. On the bed, Latona's body gave a great shiver, then a gasp, and as she sat up, the surface of the water shattered into golden light again.

Sempronius sat back from the bowl, sighing with his whole body. *'The more fool me,'* he thought, *'not to have asked you first, Lady Juno. I shall make glad sacrifice to you for setting my mind at ease.'*

The soft, indulgent laugh echoed around him again, and then the golden light faded from the surface of the water. Sempronius's magic slid away, back to the shadows of his quarters, its purpose achieved.

Palatine Hill, City of Aven

The first thing Latona saw, upon surfacing from the inchoate void of nightmares, was Vibia Sempronia, frowning at her.

Somehow that was comforting. No fiend drawn from the netherworld could replicate Vibia's unique ability to look exasperated, grateful, inconvenienced, and vaguely amused all at the same time.

Latona sat up, sluggishly. So many other people in the room. Someone hugging her. A great deal of crying all around. Noise, muffled by a head that felt stuffed with damp rags. Everything around her was moving faster than her wits could keep up with, so she chose to focus on Vibia's face, which slowly drained of obvious tension.

"Thank Juno," Vibia said. Her voice was low, barely audible in all the tumult, but the only thing piercing through the fog hazing over Latona's mind. "I should slap you for scaring us all like that."

"Vibia!" a familiar voice exclaimed. Ama Rubellia, sitting beside her. Behind Rubellia, a weeping Alhena. On Latona's other side, Merula, looking equal parts shocked and relieved. Latona ought to say something, reach out for someone, ask what happened—but she couldn't seem to do anything but sit there, blinking in a daze.

Then the matter was taken out of her hands. Merula pulled Latona's legs over the side of the bed, draped one of Latona's arms over her shoulder, and half-helped, half-hauled her to her feet. "Out of the way," she said. "Domina is needing air."

Merula deposited her in a chair in the peristyle garden and moved to stand a little ways off, no doubt to chase away anyone who approached.

Latona looked up, found the pinpricks of a few stars beginning to sparkle in the sky, filled her lungs with fresh air until she thought her ribs might crack, sighed it all out again. "Thank you." The words scratched in her throat. "For bringing me out here, but for what you tried to do with that woman, too."

Merula's arms were folded tight across her chest. "I am trying my best to keep you safe," she said. "I failed with that woman, but—"

"No," Latona cut her off. "No, I will not hear you chastise yourself for that. We were all in over our heads, and I should never have put you in the position of having to face off against a mage of that power."

Merula lifted one shoulder in a shrug, affecting nonchalance. "You were not knowing, before we are going in, how bad it would be."

"I knew it wouldn't be *good*." Latona pushed both hands through her hair. "Merula. How long was I—"

She didn't finish the question, and Merula let it hang for a moment before answering, "Nine days, Domina. Today is the Ides."

"Nine days," she repeated. "Sweet Juno. Fitting, I suppose. One for each of the elements." A bitter laugh trembled in her throat. The breath she drew to steady it was ragged, shallow, and the breath behind it came faster, and the next, and the next. Behind her eyes and at the back of her head and all down her spine and all through her chest, the numbness tore loose, shivered, shuddered. The full force of what had happened, what she had escaped, crashed down on her like a storm-tossed sea.

Nine days in a timeless agony. Nine days of feeling her magic tear at itself like a maddened animal. Nine days that might have turned into forever. Nine days, an eternity, an instant.

"There it is," Merula muttered, as a wracking sob ripped out of Latona. She gulped for air, tears splashing down her cheeks. She wept as she had not done since childhood—wept without inhibition or restraint, for once not caring who saw or heard, not *able* to care, because no room was left inside her for anything but overwhelming terror at the past and profound gratitude for the present.

Too much to feel all at once. The contrary emotions surged into and swirled around each other, shredding away the stupefying haze that had attended her since waking. She cried with such force that her face hurt, cried as though she could make the callous gods hear her and share in her pain and fear and relief.

At length, the storm ebbed, leaving clarity in its wake.

'I'm alive.'

Soft cushions beneath her hands. Tiles beneath her bare feet. Scents of the garden, juniper and cypress and myrtle, mingled with the acrid suggestion of smoke. Cool evening air stirring the hairs on her arms.

'I'm alive. I'm alive, and I'm relatively certain I'm still sane. I am a part of this world, and neither it nor I are in tatters. There is good earth beneath me, not an endless vale of shifting shadows. I have air in my lungs and blood in my veins and life in my soul. That must be enough, for now.'

She let it be, for a moment, before other realities came trickling back to her. Murmured voices beyond the garden. Merula stepping back in, likely having shooed away some rightfully-concerned party.

Latona sniffled, wiped roughly at her face, and attempted to re-establish normalcy. "Who-who was on the floor?" Merula had ushered her along too swiftly for a face to register.

"Fausta. She was helping the ladies to revive you."

"Is she—"

"Well enough. Going home now. I am thinking she has had an educational evening."

'Another debt my soul has incurred,' Latona thought with a sigh. *'I owe that girl better guidance than I have delivered thus far. And now I owe her my freedom as well.'* Fausta's magic must have been what she felt, within her nebulous cage, the surge of crackling energy that shook loose Discordia's hold on her. Then the wrenching pain that followed, magic with a signature she recognized well by now: Vibia, tearing the curse out of her.

Latona stretched out her arms, rotated her wrists, flexed her fingers. *'I am alive. I am whole. Or at least so much as I ever have been.'*

Camp of the Lusetani, Central Iberia

Neitin's eyes were well-washed with tears.

Her sisters had no patience for it. What did she have to weep for? Her husband was as near a god as a mortal could manage. Her son was healthy and thriving. All her worldly needs were tended to. What right had she for sorrow? What cause for discontent?

Small wonder she had withdrawn from them of late, seeking instead the counsel and comfort of the Cossetan magic-woman, Sakarbik.

"When can we go?" she asked in a hush, as they walked around the perimeter of the camp. Neitin wore a heavy cloak, hood pulled up over her tangled chestnut curls. Her son, Matigentis, was cradled close to her chest, beneath her cloak and furs. Sakarbik, by contrast, wore only a light deerskin cape. She seemed impervious to the elements. An aspect of her magic, perhaps, so much a part of the natural world that she could not be harmed by it. "You said the *besteki* would guide us. I do not want—" Her voice snagged around a sob threatening to well up in her throat.

"You do not want to watch your husband fall deeper into Bailar's sway, further into his foul magics," Sakarbik finished for her. "I know it, little mother. I vow to you, I am seeking the path. But—" She sucked air through her teeth. "This is a bad time for it. The world grows ever darker. Perhaps by the solstice, when the light begins to return to the earth—"

Neitin bounced Mati lightly. He had been named at the summer solstice, though born months earlier, in the blasting winds of a winter storm. It might be fitting, to set forth into a new life for him at the winter solstice. "How—" she started, then caught herself. She put such faith in Sakarbik; she did not want to admit doubts or concerns.

But the older woman looked at her without emotion. "What?"

"How will we make our way?" she asked. "In the dark of winter, alone in the wilderness. Will—will the *besteki* provide for us?" She winced at the note of incredulity in her own voice, but she knew so little of these strange spirits whom Sakarbik sought as allies. Bailar had raised the *akdraugi*, fell spirits torn forth from the netherworld by the power of bloodshed. The *akdraugi* had done more damage to the Aventans than the Lusetani soldiers had. Haunting fiends, whose power got into a man's very soul, draining him of the will to live.

The *besteki* were their inverse, good spirits. Sakarbik had worked for long months to summon them. They did not like it here, would not linger near Bailar and his perfidies. But Sakarbik promised the *besteki* could help them escape this place and find home.

'Home.' The thought should have warmed her. Home was a flat blue river and rolling hills, not this rocky terrain and the turbulent water that cut through it in chaotic shocks. Home was a stable village, peaceful and solid and content with itself. Home was safety.

But home, now, meant abandoning her husband.

'He left you long ago, in spirit if not in flesh,' she tried to tell herself. *'He left the path of goodness. He left the place where he could be a father to your children, a leader for your people. What this is, now... this is madness and corruption, and whatever drives Ekialde now, it is not the man you pledged your love and loyalty to.'*

A truth, perhaps, but not a comforting one.

She had every right to leave her husband and return home, whether that meant his village or the one that had given her birth. She had not decided, yet, where to go. Ekialde's village was also home to the tree that had been fed his blood, the night he had been made *erregerra*. Maybe something could yet save Ekialde. Maybe Sakarbik knew some magic that would free him from Bailar's influence, if only she had access to such a powerful token as the enchanted tree.

But Ekialde would seek her there.

"The *besteki* cannot feed us," Sakarbik admitted, "but they may guide us to where healthful things are. But fear not, little mother. I have plans." A wry smile turned her lips. "I've been thinking, since my capture, of how to flee. Some peoples in Iberia yet balk at Bailar's ways and refuse to knuckle under to either Lusetani or Aventan rule. We will not be unaided in our quest to claim our liberty. The *besteki* will help to shelter us from— from whatever Bailar may send after us."

A chill far icier than the autumnal air rolled down Neitin's spine. The *akdraugi* had tormented those who opposed the Lusetani, Aventans and rival Iberians alike. The idea of being herself hounded by those fiends, having them set to harrow her soul...

'He would not do it, surely. Bailar would, but Ekialde would not allow it. He could not.' A feeble hope, which even in silence, Neitin doubted. If he were still the man incapable of such cruelties, Neitin would have no need to flee in the first place. *'And if you take away his son? What parent would not do everything in their power to recover a lost child?'*

Neitin shivered, and Sakarbik turned a rare sympathetic eye on her. "Come on, little mother. Walking is good, to build your strength for what will come, but I feel a change in the air, and we would not want to be caught out if it starts to storm." She placed a hand on Neitin's back and guided her towards their tent.

V

Palatine Hill, City of Aven

On the third morning after she woke, Latona finally felt equal to re-joining the public sphere. Determined to put on a good show, she dressed with care: a sapphire blue undertunic with shining pearl buttons holding the sleeves together, an overgown in Juno's rosy pink, and the light golden mantle she had worn to Saturnalia a year past.

'A garment with happy memories.' That night, she had cast all caution in-to an open flame and thoroughly adultered herself with Sempronius Tar-ren. *'Quite thoroughly,'* she thought, heat filling her. *'Oh gods, please let him come home safely.'* She would need to write him, to tell all that had oc-curred—or as much of it as she could relate in a letter.

Latona added strings of pearls around her neck and had Aula's ornatrix arrange her hair in high fashion, with tendrils curling at her neck and in front of her ears. A touch of carmine on lips and cheeks, a touch of kohl smudged around her eyes, and Latona assessed herself presentable. "It's strange," she commented to Merula, "but I think just putting all this on has made me feel better." Lounging about in loose robes might have been com-fortable and restful, but it did nothing to engender pride in herself. *'I need a bit of that, to get myself going.'*

She joined Aulus and Aula in the atrium before her father opened the door to his clients. Aulus was in the toga of his office of censor, with two thick purple stripes as borders; Aula was resplendent in a green gown that set off her coppery hair to perfection.

Though a late sleeper by nature, Aula rose to greet patrons alongside their father most mornings that he accepted them. She had been mistress of his household in the years between their mother's death and her marriage and re-occupied the role after her husband's assassination. *'No one could ever fault Aula for filial duty.'* Her mind was ever bent towards her father's and brother's careers and what she might do to advance them. Greeting patrons was part of that—even if she was likely as not to succumb to a mid-morning nap once they departed.

Latona squared her shoulders and ventured forth. "Good morning," she announced. "I thought I might put in an appearance, to reassure your clients that I am in good health."

Aula gave a short squeal. "My honey! Should you be up? What do you need? Water? Something to eat?"

"I'm fine, thank you." Part of her yearned for a chair. By tradition, only Aulus would sit to receive patrons, but in light of her recent indisposition, she might be allowed one. *'But that would not show I am returned to strength.'*

Aula continued to flutter. "Are you sure? If you feel the slightest bit—"

"Stop henpecking her, Aula," Aulus said, beaming as he strode to greet Latona. Aulus clasped her head in his hands—though he had lived with three daughters long enough to be mindful not to muss her hair—and kissed her forehead. "My blessings and those of the gods be upon you, daughter. It is good to see you looking so well."

A pang of guilt twinged in her chest. No one had yet told him the truth of what had happened to her, and she suspected no one would. *'How I wish I could trust you enough,'* she thought. He loved her, and in truth, that was part of the problem. When Aulus had most erred in her upbringing, it had been in the name of protection. His worst fear for her was that the strength of her magic would lead her into danger—and so it had.

Only recently had they reached an accord regarding her exercise of her talents in the public sphere. *'If he knew the truth, he would revoke that.'* And since leaving her husband, she was again under her father's control. If he so chose, he could pack her up and send her to a remote country estate, with a guard to ensure she never stirred forth from the property. She didn't think he *would*—and the past few months had also revealed the strength of her own will in opposing him—but she did not want to chance it.

The morning passed in a blur. Aulus had so many clients that he did not require them all to present themselves every day, but there were still a great many to get through, from distant relations and snobbish equestrians down to the freedmen and property-less men of the Head Count.

Some had requests to make of Aulus; others were fulfilling their duty, trading news, and—when they saw Latona—gawping at the Vitellian daughter whose mysterious infirmity had, apparently, been a topic of conversation.

'Thank Juno for Aula.'

She was in top form, smoothly deflecting any impertinent inquiries, with such consummate political skill that none of the querents could take offense. Latona was able to contribute enough to the conversation as to give no cause for concern, and when the last of the clients had been seen to, Aulus departed for the Forum, looking happier than he had in days.

As soon as he was out the door, Latona collapsed onto a couch in the sitting room. "Part of me wants to go to the Forum to hear the speeches," she said, "but I don't think I could make it as far as the next street."

"Poor pet!" Aula exclaimed, sitting beside her and fluffing Latona's hair. "You shouldn't be overexerting yourself."

"I didn't," Latona promised. "I exactly exerted myself." She offered her sister a weak smile. "And now I shall be pleased to sit quietly until lunch. I've invited Rubellia and Vibia over."

"Oh?" Pert curiosity lit up Aula's face.

"Mm-hmm. We need to figure out what to do next. And it's time I explained... well, as much as I can explain. But I think I only have the strength to do it once."

"Well," Aula said, "if you're sure you're up for it. I suppose I can wait."

"You'll survive another two hours' lack of satisfaction, I'm sure," Latona said, leaning against her sister and closing her eyes. "How's Lucia doing this morning?" She had learned, since waking, of her niece's sudden burst of magic and had spent quite a bit of time reassuring Lucia that she was well and safe now.

"She's fine," Aula said, her fingers still moving soothingly through Latona's curls. "Poor mite has had more than her share of nasty shocks by the age of six, but she's resilient."

"We haven't talked about— Well, about how you feel about it."

Aula gave a burbling little laugh, quiet but with a thin thread of hysteria strung through it. "Another mage in the family." Latona chanced stretching out her Spirit magic to brush against her sister's emotions. The effort still ached, but now more like exercising a sore muscle than probing a wound. From Aula, she sensed a discomfiting flurry of anxiety and hope. "I confess,

my darling, it's not what I would have chosen for her. Not with as much opportunity as I've had to see how ungentle the gods can be with those they
choose to bear their blessings."

"We'll keep her safe," Latona said. "I don't know how. But we will."

Aula slipped an arm around her and gave a squeeze, but sadness was
flaking off her. "I know you want to. I know you'll do everything you can.
She's *alive* because of you. We both are. Anyway!" Her tone turned deliberately bright, for she never liked to dwell long on past darkness. "At least if
it is Juno that's blessed her, she won't have to go away for training. She's got
her beloved auntie right here."

"Best be nice to me, then," Latona teased, "or I'll teach her how to put
you in a pleasant mood any time she wants extra sweets."

As the day wore on, Alhena joined them with her cithara, plucking out
gentle tunes, and Latona soon found herself dozing with her head in Aula's
lap as if she were still a small girl. She roused herself only when the steward
announced Vibia Sempronia's arrival. Rubellia had sent a note with her re-
grets; she oversaw a number of acolytes at her temple, and apparently one
of them was having a disaster that couldn't be left unattended.

"I'll go over tomorrow," Alhena offered, "and tell her everything, if
you're not up for saying it all again."

Their meal was small and simple: salted bread, pears, figs, nuts, and
cheese from Liguria. Aula tucked in with customary gusto, but Latona's appetite had yet to fully recover from her ordeal. "Well," she said, tearing her
bread into very small pieces, "where should I start?"

"You can eat first," Vibia said. "I'm in no hurry this afternoon."

Latona's lips curled wryly. "I could," she said, "but frankly, the anticipation I can feel radiating off you and Aula is distracting." The frisson of
it kept provoking her empathic senses—another sign that her magic was
recuperating, when it asked her attention rather than waiting to be summoned. "So I may as well come out with it."

"Between Vibia and Merula, we've heard everything that happened up
to the Discordian attacking you," Aula said. "So that leaves..."

"The magic," Vibia finished. Compassion softened her features a touch.
"I am sorry for it. I can't imagine it's pleasant to revisit, but we must know
what it was, to have any hope of fighting it in the future."

"You're right," Latona said. She closed her eyes, thinking back to the moments before oblivion. "She said she couldn't have me interfering. She put her hands around my head." Latona raised her own hands to illustrate. "And there was... oh, simply incredible pain. Like my skull were cracking open. She told me to say hello to the fiends."

Alhena's breath sucked in, and Vibia's brow furrowed. "And did you? I mean—" She waved a hand. "Not say hello to them, obviously, but did you encounter them?"

"Yes and no..." Latona sighed. "It's hard to explain. It was a bit like a dream, but incohesive. The world around me didn't look like anything at all, just shifting shadows. If the fiends were there, wherever I was, I couldn't distinguish them from anything else. It was like being trapped not in a moment of fear, but in the feeling of it. That—" She clasped a hand to her chest. "That hitch in your breath, the sudden flood in your veins. And, at the same time, not being able to wake from a nightmare. *Knowing* it's only a dream, but not being able to stir yourself awake."

Alhena squeezed her hand. "I know that feeling," she said, low and somber, "but for me, it never lasts more than a few minutes. No matter how wretched the vision is, it always ends swiftly. To have it go on for nine days..."

"I can't say I was really aware of the time passing," Latona said, "but I also can't say it felt swift."

Vibia's face was serious, studious. "What our opponent has been doing all along is tearing open rifts between our world and the world of the spirits, then jamming them open so the fiends could come across," she reasoned. "In this case, it seemed she tried to shove you through the other direction."

"My question is, how much did she succeed?" Latona rubbed her temples. "My physical form didn't go anywhere."

"But was affected," Aula pointed out. "Do we know anything else about this woman?"

Vibia's face darkened considerably. "Not a thing. I'll know her in an instant if I see her again, or hear her voice, but she's unfamiliar to me."

"I know her." Latona passed a hand over her brow. "I've seen her before, I just can't..."

Aula's brow creased, and Latona knew she was searching her mental catalog of patrician families, clients, and associates. "Based on what Vibia told us, she's too old to be newly introduced to society," she said. "Perhaps she was... married to someone and kept in the country until recently?" But her lovely features were screwed up in consternation. "Or a... a cousin brought in from afar?"

"There *are*," Latona noted, "roughly three hundred thousand people in this city not included in our social circles, Aula."

"I suppose." Aula's tone implied she found the estimate too high.

Latona drummed her fingers against her thigh. "I've never seen her at the Cantrinalia. I'm sure of it."

"I *certainly* would've noticed her," Vibia said. "There aren't enough Fracture mages for any of us to get lost in a crowd. But if she's from out of town, that wouldn't be a surprise."

Latona sighed heavily. "I don't get the sense this was some country girl. She knew too well where to strike within the city. Better than she did in Stabiae."

"But if she's from the city, and never attended the Cantrinalia?" Aula shivered theatrically. "I can't imagine that sort of blasphemy."

"Well, she *is* a member of a blasphemous and banished cult," Latona pointed out. "I suspect on the scale of her misdeeds, failing to present herself at the Cantrinalia is on the lesser end."

Vibia rose, abruptly swift. "Aula, I need pen and paper. And to borrow one of your people to run a message."

"Of course." Aula went to Latona's desk at the side of the sitting-room and pulled out paper, stylus, and ink. "Do you—"

"A moment."

Aula's lips twitched at one corner. She still was not entirely comfortable with Vibia's brusque style, but she had learned, at least, not to take it personally. Instead, she went to the doorway and called for Haelix to attend her.

Vibia scratched out a few words, folded the paper twice with sharp creases, and held it out to the waiting Haelix. "Go to the house of Sempronius Tarren. Ask for Djadi, his clerk. Give this message to no one else. Wait and bring Djadi back with you."

Haelix's eyes flicked to Aula for confirmation, but when she nodded, so did he. "It will be done, Domina."

While the errand was run, the ladies took their lunch, mostly in silence. Vibia inquired about some of Alhena's poetry, and Aula seemed only too happy to help turn the conversation aside, allowing Latona some respite. She couldn't be sorry for it, though she was growing frustrated with her own frailty. *And what havoc might the Discordians be wreaking, or at least preparing to wreak, while I'm struggling to recover my strength?* The woman wanted her out of the way, needed to keep her from interfering. But with *what*?

Eventually, Haelix ushered in a young man with bronze skin and riotously curly dark hair. "Domina," Djadi said, inclining his head respectfully towards Vibia. Then he turned to Latona and her sisters. "Honored ladies of the Vitelliae. My greetings on behalf of my master to you all." He straightened, looking warily at Vibia, and withdrew a rolled parchment from the satchel hanging at his waist. "Lady Vibia, you requested these notes."

"Thank you, Djadi," Vibia said, swiftly taking it from him.

"Will there be anything else, Domina?"

"Maybe," Vibia said as she unrolled the parchment. "I don't know yet."

Smiling graciously, Aula gestured him towards the stairs. "Please, take water and anything you'd like to eat in the kitchen."

He hesitated only a moment, intelligent eyes looking curiously at Vibia and the paper, before he inclined his head again and left the room.

"Here." Vibia smoothed the parchment out on the table. The others gathered around her. Inked in what Latona recognized as Corvinus's careful handwriting was a list of a dozen or so names, some with a few notes following them. Vibia's finger ran down the list. "Sempronius made this last year," she said, "before we knew it was Pinarius Scaeva hounding him. It's all the Fracture mages in the city. He was trying to figure out who might—" Her finger tapped on one name. "There. It must be her. Everyone thinks she's a madwoman, and excused from the Cantrinalia and all other rituals on that account."

Latona squinted at the letters. "Anca Corinna?"

Aula gasped, making the others turn their eyes to her. "She's related to—" Aula swallowed. "I mean, I'd need to double-check, but I'm reasonably certain she's related to someone on the Augian Commission." Latona's lips parted in shock, and Vibia blinked rapidly several times. Aula moved to the doorway and bellowed, "Helva!"

A moment later, the Vitellian housekeeper, an Athaecan freedwoman, appeared, all her inky curls concealed beneath an azure blue kerchief. "Domina?"

"Who on the Augian Commission has a sister from the Corinnae? A half-sister, I mean."

Helva's eyes took on the slightly blank look they always did when she was rolling through her flawless memory's vast library, threading her peculiar aspect of Time magic through her mind. "Sextus Durmius Argus," she replied. "A Spirit mage. His mother, a Pallida, married first his father, a Durmius, and after his death, Ancus Corinnus, to whom she bore two daughters, one still living."

Latona sat down heavily as Helva returned to her interrupted work. "Sweet and blessed Juno." She turned wide eyes to Vibia. "I knew they were useless, but this level of corruption..." Her head waggled in disbelief. The Augian Commission held a sacred trust, like that of the Vestals, to preserve the realm of magic from that of government and to ensure that mages did not misuse their powers.

"He's been protecting her," Alhena said. "That's why they haven't done anything about any of it. And probably why she's never been required to go to the Cantrinalia. If he's vouching for her instability..."

Latona's emerald eyes went wide with sudden recognition. "I remember where I know her from." Her voice rang hollow, a lower timbre than usual.

"Where?" Aula asked, sitting up. But at the look on her sister's face, she went ashen. "No. Latona." Her hand reached out for Latona's. "She wasn't—"

"Capraia." Latona nodded tightly. "I didn't remember her name. I— I didn't ask." A thread of shame compressed her voice. "Our time didn't overlap much, I don't think. At least Ocella didn't bring her out into court as often as..."

Aula slid closer, putting an arm around Latona's shoulders. She looked, though, to Vibia. "But why would Ocella have a Discordian mage as a— a pet?" she asked. "He hated the Discordians."

"He may not have known her affiliation," Vibia suggested. "No one in the Temple of Janus suspected Pinarius Scaeva. Or maybe she joined after leaving his court."

"If she's hidden herself for this long—never attending the Cantrinalia, living in seclusion—" Latona shook her head. "It's no surprise she was able to hide even from Ocella."

"Bona Dea," Aula breathed. "How many more of them might there be?"

Vibia's shoulders drew together. "Then we know what we must do," she said. "We expose her, expose the Augian Commission, and expose any other Discordian she's working with."

"It won't be that simple..."

Alhena's voice had gone far-away and her eyes glossy, as they tended to when Time magic stole upon her without fully subsuming her into a vision. The others were used to it enough by now not to interrupt or question her, for any distraction might rip her out of whatever hints Proserpina had decided to bestow.

"Layers," Alhena said at last. "Like fabric upon fabric, some of it sheer and some opaque, the colors blending in confusion..." She blinked twice, shook her head, sighed. "Sorry. Lost it, whatever it was. I get the sense, though, that she is well-protected in more than one regard."

"You'd think the Augian half-brother would be enough to be getting on with," Aula muttered.

Vibia was rubbing her temples. "A few months ago, you turned up at my door with that strange summons from Alhena. I knew what followed wouldn't be simple or ordinary, but I had no idea the scale of disaster we would be in for." She lifted her head. "How do we do this? How do we expose a cult that's supposed to be banished when they're being protected by one of the city's oldest and most venerable institutions?" She made a stiff, irritable gesture in the air. "That's no mere complaint. I'm actually asking."

"It may take more than a moment's consideration to come up with the answer, Vibia," Aula said, heat entering her voice. Latona's still-raw magical senses prickled: tempers were rising. "Dare I say, it may even take us an entire afternoon's worth of—"

"We aren't going to get any closer to a solution by—"

"Latona has only *just* begun to recover from her ordeal, and—"

Latona knew she ought to intervene, say something, cool them down before someone said something spiteful—but an idea had begun to piece itself together in her mind. A bold thought, a course of action no one would predict—and that a great many people might object to. *'But it could work. Not only for now, not only for this crisis, but to help protect against future threats. It could work.'*

Latona rose from the couch and began pacing. The sudden movement interrupted the bickering, and, oddly, Vibia smiled, watching her—a tight, brief smile, but unusual for the rigid woman.

"What we need," Latona began, the warmth growing inside her even as her heart fluttered at her own temerity, "is a collegium."

The other three were quiet a moment, glancing at each other. "You don't mean like—" Aula began.

"I mean one of our *own*," Latona said. Tired though she still was, a now-familiar warmth was building in her chest. "A collegium for female mages. Or—or for any of the mages who never ascend to priesthoods or positions of power, the ones the Senate will never take seriously, but who see what happens everywhere in Aven. The ones doing the quiet work in their neighborhoods. If the Augians and the pontifices won't defend this city, then—" She swallowed. "Then we have to."

Vibia's mouth remained firmly shut. Her expression was scrutinizing, though not necessarily disapproving. Aula, on the other hand, was wide-eyed with skepticism. "It's... it's an idea, my honey, but..."

"We've been saying for weeks that we can't keep this up on our own," Latona said. "The city is too large. We can't be everywhere at the same time. We've already begun building a coalition." She could taste cinnamon on her tongue; this was a *good* idea, a *right* idea, an idea Juno approved of. "Tilla, Davina, Rubellia—They've been eyes and ears, but what if we started training ourselves and others to deal with the Discordians? To—to find out how *each* element might be able to counter their charms or stabilize the effects or whatever else needs doing?"

Alhena's hand shot out, seizing Latona's wrist. "Yes," she said, swift and fierce. Her eyes had gone glazed again. "Not only for this challenge but for those beyond, those in coming years, those which we cannot yet dream—not only for ourselves, but for our daughters, for the forgotten, for the overlooked, for every mage whose path to opportunity has been strewn with caltrops or led them into the wilderness with no guide."

This time when she stopped talking, the other three looked not to her, but to each other.

"Very well, then," Vibia said, lifting her chin. "A mages' collegium it is."

VI

'Every time I think I have a win,' Lucretius Rabirus thought as he stomped his way up the Quirinal Hill, *'someone snatches it away from me.'*

A year before, he had won praetorial office. He had intended to use the office to counter Sempronius Tarren's efforts in Iberia, entrenching his ambitions in mud—but the misfortune had, instead, been his own. *'And not through my fault, but through a curse. A woman's curse, no less!'* When he sought to take vengeance upon Sempronius by other means, his assassins had been foiled. So much for the protestations of ability he had been given before leaving Iberia. And now, when he sought retribution upon the woman who had cursed him, that, too, had failed.

Well. The men who had provided such inept assassins might have been thousands of miles away and out of his reach, but the people responsible for the ongoing vitality of Vitellia Latona were right here in Aven, and he had no compunction about pounding on their door to demand answers.

After cooling his heels in a sitting room longer than he felt appropriate, Rabirus was greeted by Durmius Argus: tall, fair-haired, and seemingly innocuous, if you didn't know he was both a member of the Augian Commission and a devotee of the forbidden cult of Discordia. "Where is she?" Rabirus demanded.

"Alas, honored praetor," Durmius replied, unruffled by Rabirus's aggression, "I do not know if my sister is fit to receive guests today. She is, as you are aware, of a delicate constitution."

Delicate was not the word Rabirus would use to describe someone who regularly engaged in profane rituals, reaching into the gaps between the world of the living and the worlds beyond, dragging forth demons and fiends and gods knew what else. Any fragility Anca Corinna had, she created within herself, dancing on the edge of chaos as her patroness demanded, pushing Fracture magic to its most dangerous limits.

"It was you who forged this alliance," Rabirus said, jabbing a finger at Durmius. "You who brought your sister into it. You wanted my help in covering your efforts, diverting attention from your little cult by calling your actions divine judgment—"

"A mutually beneficial arrangement," Durmius said. "I understand the people of Aven are listening, most attentively, to the stories you and your fellows weave out of our threads. The upcoming elections—"

"Are a month away and yet uncertain. If all is to proceed to our mutual benefit, we cannot have interference, now can we?" These Discordians had been useful, yes, but they were such troublesome allies. Rabirus disliked admitting, even to himself, that he could not control them. The only leverage he had was their adherence to a banished and blasphemous cult—and that leverage was compromised, considering they had infiltrated the very Commission that investigated such matters. Nor did he have hard evidence to use against them in public exposure; they were too careful, never giving him more information than he needed, never putting anything in writing, never allowing him to know the names of their confederates in chaos. "Your sister was supposed to put an end to that interference, and yet—"

"And yet." The interrupting voice was oddly musical. Rabirus's head snapped to the open doorway, where Anca Corinna stood, dressed as she had been every time Rabirus had seen her, in purest white, her hair pinned into a loose coronet.

The siblings did not look much alike, but then, they did have different fathers. Both were tall and slender, but there the resemblance ended: Corinna's hair was raven-dark, and where her brother's eyes were an indifferent brown, hers were an arresting blue. She was not beautiful, in Rabirus's judgment, but one could not easily look away from her. Everything about her appearance jabbed into an onlooker's awareness like a knife, while Durmius Argus had the ability to make himself so innocuous that he nearly disappeared.

'Although in either case, that may be their magic at work, not their physical attributes.' Though Durmius served Discordia, his element was Spirit—an element which could affect others' perceptions. Rabirus suspected that Durmius could make himself authoritative and imposing, if he chose.

Corinna, though, was Fracture all over, and if she had ever been able to blunt the sharp edges it created in her, she had long ago abandoned that effort.

Rabirus wasted no time on preamble. "The hellcat lives, I understand," he accused, crossing to Corinna. "She joined her father, Censor Aulus Vitellius, in greeting his clients this morning, looking fresh and blooming as spring crocus. I thought you were taking care of that."

"I *tried*," Corinna shot back, with a distinctly sulky air. "I *did*. Glitter-gold was unconscious for nine days, no sparkle left, no shine." She paced the room jerkily, stopping and starting, her shoulders twitching in irritation. "But she's stronger than I thought. Not only glitter-gold. Lightning at her core. My curse should have devoured her, should have broken her. I buried it *deep*, her own magic was eating itself, she should have—"

"I don't want to hear what she should have!" Rabirus interrupted. The woman was more lucid today, but she still spoke half in maddening riddles, as though using a code only she understood. "I want to know how you mean to remedy this."

"I can't until I know more about how she broke free." Corinna leveled indigo eyes at him, and Rabirus steeled himself not to shudder. Those eyes were uncanny, cold as ice and no natural shade, dark yet luminous, eyes that hardly belonged to anything human. The Dictator Ocella had had eyes like that. "And when she did, it—it—" Corinna hugged herself, fingernails digging into her own upper arms.

"My sister felt the reverberations in her own magic," Durmius supplied. "It's shaken her. I don't expect you to understand the thaumaturgy, but—"

Rabirus waved a hand, impatient. "I don't need to. When can she try again?"

"We have other tasks as well." Durmius's tone remained mild, but now carried an air of chastisement. "I know you've noticed those. At least, you and your friend Arrius Buteo use them as rhetorical fodder often enough."

Pain in his jaw made Rabirus realize he was grinding his teeth. He took a breath, forcing himself to relax. These people held no power over him—and yet, too much. No lawful authority; Rabirus was no mage to be under the Commission's sway. But, as Rabirus learned before leaving Iberia, the Discordians had taken an interest in him.

"I would suggest," Durmius said, looking between Rabirus and Corinna, "that you both shelve your ire with the Vitellian woman. She is only one mage—"

"Not alone," Corinna trilled. "She is not alone. The knife's edge, they glint together."

"Two mages, then," Durmius said, his eyes lifting briefly toward the ceiling. "We have more. Many more." His hand fell on Corinna's shoulder. "And other plans. Longer plans." Those weighty words held significance beyond Rabirus's comprehension.

Corinna, though, plainly heard their meaning. Her body drooped, losing its frenetic tension. "Yes, yes," she sighed. "Plans." She rolled her eyes then, as though the idea were ridiculous, a mere indulgence she offered her brother. "So many shivers between now and the future."

Durmius returned his attention to Rabirus. "Forget the Vitellian creature, at least for now, and whatever companion in mischief she may have." So Durmius did not know the identify of the one Corinna called "knife's edge," either—or he was feigning ignorance, another tidbit withheld from his supposed ally. "You focus on your work, and we'll do ours. Chaos enough to scare the populace right into your sheltering arms."

I am missing something. Rabirus had been in politics long enough to sense when he wasn't getting the full story. With how jealously Durmius guarded secrets, he was unlikely to gain purchase there—and though Corinna might willingly expose all, Rabirus doubted he'd be able to understand her ravings if she did. *Never mind. Use them as long as they provide mutual benefit, and then drop all association. They are a tool, nothing more. A dangerous one, perhaps, but so was Ocella. Keep your own focus clear, that's what matters.*

For Aven, he had made this bargain with blasphemers. Few men had the strength to do as he did, dirtying their hands in service to the greater good. Rabirus had done so before, steering the Dictator as well as he was able, and learned much from the experience. Now, he would use these Discordians to purge the city of opposition. Out of their chaos, he would create a new order, a restoration of the *mos maiorum* and all it stood for. Sometimes you had to burn a structure down before rebuilding on new, stronger foundations. The Discordians were his fire. *And when they exceed their usefulness, when my power is secure enough that I need not fear their blackmail any longer, I will find some way to extinguish them. I will secure proof and drive them again out of the city.'*

So he pressed a hand to his chest, bowing his head. "Forgive me, Lady Corinna, if I caused any offense," he said. "Your brother is exactly right. I am—I am over-anxious, that is all."

"You *are*," she agreed, in that strange musical voice. "It shivers all over you." A sublime smile lit her face. "I quite like that."

Rabirus schooled himself not to show how much the proclamation unnerved him. "I am honored, Lady." Then he looked to Durmius. "As you said. You to your work, I to mine."

Popularity was, in Marcus Autronius's newly-formed experience, as much a burden as a boon.

Since Quintus Terentius decided to make an ally of him, Marcus had found himself a more noteworthy figure than was his custom. Oh, he was *known*. An Earth mage, a backbencher in the Senate, and, for the past year, a tribune of the plebs. He gained some attention for the measures he put before the Tribunal Assembly—largely directed by Sempronius Tarren from half a world away—but nothing to the whirlwind that surrounded Terentius: a patrician of ancient blood, representative of a family both wealthy and powerful, father to a Vestal Virgin and an Earth mage as well as two promising sons, and the Popularists' chief contender for a consul's chair in the coming election. When he accompanied Terentius in public, they could hardly turn for people wanting to pluck the older man's sleeve, asking him for favors or challenging his latest speech in the Forum.

Even attending Sempronius hadn't been the same: Sempronius tried to keep some public distance between them, so Marcus wouldn't be seen as his lackey. Terentius did not operate with such subtlety. *'He's never needed to,'* Marcus considered. *'No matter what he does, his place in the world is assured.'*

It was why the Terentiae had a reputation for eccentricity: they could afford it, in both literal coin and political capital. Terentius saw no reason not to make Marcus prominent at his side; indeed, he believed it would only help Marcus's own re-election efforts. Suddenly, the people who wanted

Terentius's attention wanted *his* as well. Could he give Senator Terentius this note? Could he ask Senator Terentius about this proposal? Could he ask the senator for a meeting in the forum? Could he possibly wrangle an invitation to dinner?

Another man—like his younger brother, Felix—would have had his head thoroughly turned by the inundation of regard. Marcus thanked the good solid Earth of his nature that he could take it in stride. He listened to all with careful diligence, but only put any further effort into those which he believed had real merit.

Through it all, Marcus was getting an education in political maneuvering. Again, not quite like with Sempronius. Sempronius's mind worked at an unfathomable speed, and at least half the time, he had to be reminded to stop and explain his machinations. He was playing a deeper and longer game, and Marcus had never been sure to what end. Terentius was more practical and in-the-moment, and by observation, Marcus learned a great deal about the finer-grained components of Curia intrigue.

'Though I don't know why he's bothering to bestow such knowledge,' Marcus thought. *'It's not as though my career has any further to go.'*

The *lex cantatia Augiae* prohibited mages from seeking higher office. For centuries, the law had barred mages even from serving in the Senate, but in generations' past, too many families with gifted sons had balked at the restriction. Marcus could be a senator and a tribune, as he was, but could climb no further up the *cursus honorem*. No aedileship for him, no praetorial command, and certainly never any consul's chair. He'd never minded, really, any more than he minded serving as a functionary for more ambitious men.

"I want you to be careful, that's all," his father said, low in his ear as they entered the Curia a few days after the Ides of November. "There've been such strange goings-on in the city."

"I don't think that has anything to do with Senator Terentius's campaign," Marcus said. "Or my own."

"One never knows," Gnaeus Autronius muttered.

Marcus did have to concede him that. The past few years had demonstrated how quickly politics could grow bloody. Last year's election had seen two assassination attempts on Sempronius, only standing for a praetorship. Felix had been caught up in a nasty curse in the Forum, which had provoked the factions into a fistfight.

Then there had been the fires that broke out the day of the election. An accident, so far as anyone could tell—but they had spread so far so fast, done such damage to the Aventine emporiums primarily owned by Popularists, and there had been rumors that they had been set deliberately to disrupt the vote.

Gnaeus sighed as they took their seats—still in the back row, for all Marcus's burgeoning notoriety. "It does make me wonder if I did right," he said, dropping his voice lower so their neighbors would not overhear, "petitioning to get on the senatorial rolls."

Marcus understood why his father might be second-guessing a decision made decades ago. Prominence made them a target. "You did the right thing," he said, equally quiet. "We have the opportunity now to effect change, to make the system less fraught for those who will follow us. And as much as our presence may rankle the Optimates, we are an important symbol for others."

The Autroniae had joined the Senate only after generations of wealth-building. Their ancestors hadn't been among the founding families, those who formed the first Senate hundreds of years ago. Marcus didn't even know who all his ancestors were. They had wandered into Aven in fits and starts over those centuries, and not all voluntarily. His father's grandmother had been a slave taken during the Truscan Wars, and she hadn't been freed by virtue of a magical blessing. Her liberty had been purchased by the man who wanted to marry her. Sometimes Marcus wondered if she had been in love, too, or seizing an available route to freedom when it presented itself.

"We show what is possible," he went on. "A little risk seems worth it."

The room fell quiet as the consuls, Galerius Orator and Aufidius Strato, entered and took their chairs. Autronius, as usual, looked annoyed at having to be present for the day's bickering. The famous general was not, in Marcus's estimation, a man suited for the indoors. He had been elected on the strength of his victories on the northern Albine border and because he had been persecuted by the Dictator Ocella, and he accepted the position because that was simply what men of a certain status did. *I'll bet he can't wait to get back on campaign. I wonder if he'd rather head back to Albina or take over Baelonia as his proconsular command.*

As it happened, the topic was on the docket for discussion. With elections fast approaching, the Centuriate Assembly needed to know how many provinces would be open for the claiming. Some of the current praetors would wish to extend their terms into propraetorial governance—but not all would be allowed to do so.

Sempronius Tarren, of course, intended to see out his Iberian campaign and had written many letters to that effect, to his allies and moderates alike. *'And, because Sempronius wants it, the Optimates intend to stand in his way,'* Marcus thought, as Arrius Buteo, inevitably, rose to speak.

"He is a danger to the Republic, I tell you!" Buteo shouted. "He stole—*stole*—the allegiance of the Fourth Legion from the honorable praetor, Lucretius Rabirus."

Marcus knew the truth of it from Felix, who served as Sempronius's second-in-command, and if he were someone else, he might have risen to shout Buteo down.

That, however, was not his way. Shouting rarely did a consideration any favors. Too, he was conscious of his marginal position within the Senate; a second-generation man from a family that many patricians considered up-jumped, too closely tied to their mercantile origins. As a tribune of the plebs, he also preferred to save his outbursts for when they might truly be needed to interpose his veto on some egregious measure. Staying out of the fray bestowed more gravity upon his words when he did speak.

Others, however, felt perfect security in going on the attack. Quintus Terentius rose to say what Marcus had not. "Your accusation might carry more weight, Buteo, if Lucretius Rabirus were still in his province, not sitting in this very room! From what I understand, Rabirus fled his province in disgrace after a number of tactical missteps which earned him the rightful disdain of the men under his command."

Rabirus rose from his seat, though with none of Buteo's anger or bluster. "I returned to Aven because my presence was no longer necessary in Baelonia," he said. "We dealt with what few raiders had strayed so far south as to trouble our citizens there. Gades is well-garrisoned. I attended to all necessary judicial and financial measures—and returned, I must note, with the tax revenue that the prior governor rather neglected during his own term in office. With the year drawing to a close and the campaign season over, there seemed no call to extend my stay. In truth, I see small need for legions to remain in Baelonia. Sempronius Tarren's foolish war concerns the central plateaus, where few Aventans dwell."

Several men began speaking: some military-minded men challenging Rabirus's analysis, some senators with trading interests eager to remind him that disruption in central Iberia had tangible effects on the coast. After a momentary cacophony, Buteo jabbed a hand into the air. "Lucretius Rabirus has done what is right and proper!" he bellowed, pitching his voice above the din. "He lay down a command where warfare was no longer necessary! A noble and modest course, which our forefathers would smile upon—unlike the self-aggrandizing actions of Praetor Sempronius, so greedy for power that he needlessly prolongs our involvement with the Iberians! We *must* strip him of command and recall him to Aven so he may face—"

"I remind my esteemed colleague," Aufidius Strato snarled from his consul's chair, "that the disposition of provinces and extension of command rightfully belongs to the Centuriate Assembly. Any debate here is mere ostentation."

"We may make *recommendations* to the Assembly, may we not?" Buteo sneered in return. "Surely, in such an important matter as this—"

Aufidius's face reddened, suggesting he was on the verge of an apoplectic response, but Galerius cut in. "I thank you, Arrius Buteo. You remind us of our duty to advise." Before Buteo's expression could turn smug, however, Galerius went on, "Indeed, you have reminded us as much every day we have been in-session for the past month."

A ripple of laughter passed around the Curia, and Buteo's head whipped about to glare at the offenders. No doubt their names were being put on some list for reprimand or retribution.

"I think we can consider the recommendation well and truly made," Aufidius Strato growled. "You want to convince the Centuries? Well, you've got the next damned month to do so."

Judging by their expressions, neither Galerius Orator nor Aufidius Strato would be overly sorry when their terms of office ended. *'But what will the gods give us to replace them?'* Strato had been inoffensive at worst, a man elected on the strength of his military reputation, not any real policy platform. Galerius was that rare breed: a true moderate, a politician who carefully weighed every word and action and who sought always to do right by his nation and his gods. Their influence had steadied Aven in its first year free of Ocella's dictatorship. *'If one can call this past year steady. No telling how much worse it might've been.'*

The next year, Marcus feared, might show them.

Alhena had, of course, offered to go and talk to Terentilla about the mages' collegium.

Before leaving the house, she pulled the pins from her usual tight bun and rearranged them, with her attendant Mus's help, leaving most of the bright red curls loose and flowing down her back. She put on her favorite mantle, a soft dove gray that she thought made her eyes seem more blue, though she blushed at the vanity of her own thoughts.

'You're being silly. It might've been... I don't know. Nothing. An odd moment. A strange impulse. And if Tilla wants to forget all about it... Well, I don't know how I'll ever look her in the eyes again, but I stare at the ground most of the time anyway, so it shouldn't be much of a bar to friendship.'

When she was admitted into the Terentian domus, it was to a great deal of noise. Raised voices rang from the back of the building. Alhena couldn't make out the exact words. They didn't sound angry, precisely, but certainly animated. "If this is a bad time—" she began, but the boy at the door shook his head furiously.

"No, Domina. Lady Terentilla, she has said to let her know at once if you should arrive. I will go!" And he did, scurrying off.

The Terentian home was testament to the family's famous unconventionality, decorated in a mismatch of styles borrowed from across half the Middle Sea. The mosaic in the atrium was Athaecan in design, complex geometrics interlacing with each other; the columns around the impluvium pool seemed to be Abydosian, polished alabaster and gently curved. In each corner stood a statue, though no two hailed from the same culture. Alhena was contemplating one of them, a flat-faced figure with dozens of gold-painted necklaces and an elaborately carved headdress, when Tilla came skittering into the room.

As usual, her dress was haphazard. Her tunic was unevenly pinned, sliding off of one shoulder, and she wore no overgown at all. A loose plait held her brown hair, as many tendrils escaping as captured, riotous curls nestling into the graceful curve of her neck.

Tilla's eyes were bright with merriment and her cheeks flushed as she approached Alhena, and when she reached out for Alhena's hands, their fingers sliding together, a sudden tightness seized Alhena from her throat all the way down to her stomach.

"I'm *so* glad to see you!" Tilla exclaimed. "It's been so—I mean, not to say you shouldn't have been with your family, of course. I was overjoyed to hear that Latona's recovered."

"Y-Yes." Alhena felt dizzy, unbalanced. Was this normal? "I'm sorry I couldn't come sooner, but she—"

"No, not a word of apology," Tilla said. "She needed you. But—" Her voice dropped, eyes darting to the side to see if anyone were listening. "You will tell me everything, now?"

Swallowing hard, Alhena nodded. She didn't know how much information her sisters intended to give to everyone they recruited for this mages' collegium, but Tilla, she would trust with all. "I will. I—" She glanced toward the back of the house. "I would ask if we could sit down, but, um..."

"Oh!" Tilla laughed. "That's nothing. My brother Sextus has a thorny legal case, and Mama and Young Quintus are helping him to argue it out. I was, too, but—" Her eyes sparkled; Alhena felt like she could fall into them. "You're much more interesting. Come on!" She tugged Alhena toward the door. "We'll get no peace here. No—" And for the first time, her self-assured manner faltered, for the briefest of moments. "No privacy." She bit her lip, then grinned. "So I thought a walk. The gardens of Tellus aren't much to see this time of year, but—"

"A walk would be lovely," Alhena managed to say. Tilla could be such a whirlwind, a true force of nature; sometimes Alhena's thoughts struggled to keep up. "You'll be cold, though."

Tilla came to an abrupt halt. "Dis take it, you're right. I wasn't thinking." Quick as anything, she bussed a kiss onto Alhena's cheek, then darted off, saying, "Wait right here! I'll just be a minute!"

VII

When Tilla returned, she had tightened her tunic's pins, especially down the sleeves, added a bright blue overgown, and thrown a pine green mantle over her hair. Concessions to the weather, no more; unlike Alhena's fashion-conscious sisters, Tilla seemed to consider her clothing no more than an animal thought of its pelt: something that needed to be clean, certainly, but only functional, no great matter of ornament.

As the ladies walked, arm-in-arm, toward the Temple of Tellus, Alhena related the full story of what happened at the Discordian den, how they finally brought Latona out of her malady, and what Latona thought needed to be done next.

"A magical collegium?" Tilla echoed. "For women? Well, I must say I like that."

"I thought you might."

"I don't know how much I can teach that's worth knowing, but I'm willing to try. And more than willing to learn." She smiled, broad and open; Tilla was nothing if not candid, a trait she shared with her Vestal sister. "Honestly, just to be able to talk about magic with other women—it never feels quite the thing to bring up at a dinner party, does it? And you're always leaving someone out, if there are others around who don't have the gift. But to have that space for ourselves, yes—" Then she tilted her head, frowning. "A space. Where will we meet?"

Alhena's brow creased. "I hadn't thought of that."

"It can't really be in any of our houses. Too many eyes and ears. And it's not as though we have a tavern to take over, like a proper collegium would."

"I'm sure my sisters will think of something suitable," Alhena said, though she wondered whether it had occurred to them yet.

As they passed from the crowded streets into the temple garden, Tilla carried the weight of the conversation, filling Alhena in on political tidbits she picked up from her family. Things of interest to Aula and Latona, no doubt. Alhena hoped she could keep the information in her dizzied head long enough to pass it along. Everyone was worried about the upcoming elections, looking more and more dire for the Popularist faction, but as important as that was, Alhena at this moment couldn't think of anything except the lanky girl striding at her side.

They settled onto a bench beneath the arch of two pines, a short distance from the meandering path through the garden. The green space wasn't large enough to attract many visitors, but people did pass through now and again. They weren't alone—but they had as much privacy as a city as crowded as Aven was likely to offer to two young women.

Tilla's thoughts trailed off, and oh! how Alhena wished she was clever-tongued like her sisters. Not knowing what to say, now that she had the chance to speak freely, was an agony. Usually she enjoyed silence, and she and Tilla had shared lovely companionable moments before, but now the quiet swelled between them like an oppressive bubble.

Until Tilla, in a casual tone, popped it. "You don't have to be shy, you know." Alhena turned wide eyes to Tilla, who immediately winced. "I didn't mean that. Or I did, but—Dis take it, Mama tells me I never think before I speak, and she's right. You *are* shy, and that's not bad. But you don't have to be shy with *me*, is what I meant."

Alhena ducked her head. One advantage of wearing her hair down was that the curls naturally fell as a curtain, hiding her face—or they did, until Tilla's fingers gently lifted them up, pushing them back behind Alhena's ear. So tender a gesture, and yet Alhena's body tightened in response. "I'm sorry," Alhena said.

"Sorry?" Tilla exclaimed. "What under the great sky do you have to be sorry for?"

"I-I'm not good at this." Her sisters were; she had watched them at it for years, Aula's flirtations and Latona's easy charm. Of course, they worked their wiles on *men*. "I don't even know what this is. I don't have words for it."

Tilla shifted on the bench, angling herself more to face Alhena. "Well. What it *was,* was a kiss." She grinned impishly. "A rather nice one, too, not that I've a broad standard to judge by. As for what it is... What do you want it to be?"

Horrible question, that Alhena had been decidedly avoiding trying to answer. "Tilla, I don't know what—I mean—" She huffed slightly, annoyed with herself. "I'm not completely naive, I mean, I've read poetry."

Poetry that raised a blush on her cheeks every bit as fierce as the one heating her skin now. In her first exploration of the works of Hyacinthe, a project to improve her Athaecan translation skills, she had been so shocked at that lady's ardor that she rolled the parchment back up and hid it at the bottom of a pile of scrolls. She had returned to it the next day—only to read a few more lines, get flustered all over again, and repeat the procedure.

It had taken her the better part of a week to get through the entire scroll, all the while wondering *why* the lyric lines unnerved her so fretfully. Matters of love and even sex, she had encountered before with equanimity, both in her reading and through Aula's imprudent gossip. But Hyacinthe's lines—*sweet Aphrodite, rescue me from despair, for I am drowning, wrecked by my love, overcome with longing for a slender girl*—stirred something that Alhena hadn't known how to look directly at, let alone sort out in her jumbled emotions.

"If it helps—" Tilla said, shifting closer to her on the bench. Their hips were pressed together, and Tilla's fingers interlaced with Alhena's. "—I don't really know how to go about it, either. I've heard stories, though." Her lower lip caught briefly between her teeth, and the glow on her cheeks was almost too lovely for Alhena to bear. "From real people. Living people, I mean. Not that poets aren't real."

"From—Who?"

Tilla laughed, hearty and strong. "Diana's worship isn't exactly like other orders. Well. Minerva, maybe. Maybe Vesta, for all I know, though I confess I've never gotten up the courage to ask Quinta about it." *That* idea was shocking enough that Alhena's face contorted. "I don't get the sense she's of the inclination, though."

"What—" Alhena began, alarmed at herself for daring to venture the question. "What do they say in Diana's temple?"

"I'm almost afraid to tell you," Tilla teased. "I'm worried you may faint." Her fingers brushed at Alhena's hair again, traced the shell of her ear, trailed lightly down the side of her neck. A tingle ran all through Alhena's veins. "Suffice it to say, there's quite a lot to explore, if we're so inclined."

"I—" It was hard to think, with Tilla sitting so close. "I think I'd like to try."

Tilla's eyes were merry as she glanced over Alhena's shoulder. "Your girl's doing an admirable job standing watch on that end. Anyone coming up the path behind me?"

"What? No, but—"

Before she got another word out, Tilla's mouth was pressed to hers. Alhena was mortified to hear a muffled meeping noise of shock escape her — but then, as Tilla's hand slipped around her waist, she relaxed into the kiss, sweet and dazzling at the same time. Alhena always felt so brittle, like fragile Abydosian alabaster that would shatter if anyone tried to grasp it. Tilla had the remarkable power to melt her.

Alhena had no idea what to do, but for once, that didn't matter. Tilla's lips coaxed hers, intimate and instructive. Alhena's fingers shook as she touched Tilla's cheek, and their bodies surged toward each other, like two waves crashing.

Then Tilla pulled back, giggling and gasping at the same time. "I think we might get good at that if we give ourselves the chance."

"But Tilla," Alhena protested, "we—I mean, maybe you could, Diana and all, but you even said—" They had discussed it at a dinner party, how both their fathers would be finding suitable husbands for them soon. Tilla was uninterested but not unwilling, bound by duty and piety if not by desire. "What—What do we do when we must marry?"

"Has your father picked someone for you yet?"

"No."

"Nor mine." Tilla shook dark curls back from her face. "Probably he's dangling me as bait for his political allies, but he hasn't arranged anything yet, and I suspect he's really waiting for the best options to return from Iberia. So, I say we continue doing this, and whatever else we like, for as long as we like doing it and no one stops us."

Tilla's irrepressible grin was infectious; Alhena realized she was smiling, too. A secret was a thrilling thing to have.

The air in the atrium was cold and still. Vibia ordered all the lamps extinguished at moonrise and sent everyone away — servants, slaves, even her husband. He retired amiably, with a kiss to her forehead and no resentment at being sent to his cubicle as though he were a child. Vibia did not interfere with the minutiae of his business, and he did not meddle in hers. It was rare enough that she claimed the privilege, and he trusted she always had good reason to do so.

Their home was far enough from a main thoroughfare that the noise of the city was not too much an intrusion; no distraction from carts rattling by or workmen shouting to each other. A neighbor's dog was barking intermittently, determined to signal his presence to the world, but even that, Vibia could let fade away as she knelt before her altar.

"Lord Janus and Lady Fortuna, look here. I call your power to this place. I call your eyes upon me. You who blessed me, you who laid your hands upon me, open the gate and grant me access to your deepest gifts." She let the invocation hang in the air a moment, reaching out with her magical senses, waiting for the shift. It came with a shiver along her skin, the sign that her perception had slipped into the right place.

Suddenly she was more aware of every gap in the vicinity: every open door, every slit in the window-slats, every chipped mosaic tile. For a moment, the shattering sensation threatened to overwhelm her.

Vibia's chief experience, though, was in control. Instead of panicking at senses that wanted her to believe the whole world was crumbling around her, she drew a steadying breath, leveled her gaze at the taper on her altar, and waited for quietude to settle back over her.

And so it did, all those crevices muting in her awareness. *I am getting stronger,* she realized, *as Latona suggested.* She had always believed herself only weakly gifted, particularly in comparison to her brother's strength in Shadow; perhaps she had simply never pushed herself so far, so often.

Examining that more closely would have to wait. Tonight, Vibia had work to do.

Delicately, she lifted a lead stylus and held its tip above the surface of a small sheet of hammered bronze. "Lady Invidia, Lady Nemesis, I call your eyes to this place. Wrong has been done to me by an impious woman, and I would see the perpetrator punished." With slow, deliberate strokes, Vibia began carving an intricate shape into the bronze. "Her name is Anca Corinna, profaner and blasphemer, abuser of the gods' gifts."

Had Vibia been born to a common plebeian family, a rank where it was not only fitting but necessary for women to turn magical gifts to economic use, she always thought she could have done very well for herself as a purveyor of curses. A Shadow mage might do the work, too, but Fracture had an instinct for finding the perfect words to disrupt an offender's life.

"May her ventures fail. May she expose herself and her many perfidies. May the laws of men and of gods punish her and bring her to justice."

There was a trick to cursing, a narrow line Vibia had learned to walk. Specificity mattered—and not over-reaching. In this case, however, she felt entirely justified asking for a great deal.

"May the strength of her limbs fail her. May her vision dim. May her tongue fall silent. May her womb wither. May her intestines knot. May her spleen and liver grow putrid. May all her health waste away." With each request, Vibia added a flourish to the complex symbol she etched into the bronze tablet. Her hand moved nearly of its own volition, guided by the Fracture magic buzzing through her body.

The parameters set, Vibia reminded the gods again of who she intended these ills for. "Anca Corinna." Vibia carved the letters into the bronze tablet, backwards, for that would strengthen the curse. "Anca Corinna. Anca Corinna. Lady Invidia, Lady Nemesis, if you bring her to torment and destruction, I will offer you joyous sacrifice."

Vibia folded the bronze sheet upon itself, over and over until it was only twice as wide as her thumb. Then she picked up an iron nail and a small mallet. She placed the tip of the nail at the center of the rolled sheet, over Corinna's name, and slammed the mallet down hard.

Pain stabbed into Vibia's head, as though a massive fanged creature had seized her whole head in its maw. Yowling, Vibia dropped the tablet and skittered back on her hands.

"Domina?" someone called from several rooms away. Evidently she had shrieked loud enough to be heard in the kitchen.

"No!" she shouted back, though the agony was so complete that she could not yet open her eyes. "I'm fine! Stay where you are!" Whatever she had unleashed, she did not want to risk any of the household blundering into harm.

Deep breaths, slow and deliberate. With each, Vibia released a strain of the Fracture magic, drawing herself back from the curse tablet. As she let go of that power, the pain began to recede.

Memory rose to take its place. Sempronius had encountered a trap like this a year earlier, when searching out the enemies hounding him within the city. Vibia had recognized the magic as Fracture, but neither of them had known what else to make of it at the time. Now, it seemed this was a trick of the Discordians, a defensive mechanism to protect them from reprisals. A chasm cut into the magical energies of the world, as ditches were cut around a fortress.

Vibia glared at the curse tablet, unwitting vehicle of betrayal. "Oh, you little—"

How, *how* had Corinna done it? A protection only invoked when directly assaulted. It had to be tied to something; such a power couldn't linger in the air, waiting for invocation. *'Not anchored to anything here in my house, either.'* Vibia would have been alerted, if the wretched cultist had infiltrated her own domain.

'So, what has she done?' Vibia wondered where the woman lived, if with her brother Durmius Argus or somewhere else. Surely the dilapidated place where they had found her earlier had not been her home. *'What den does she creep back to?'*

A house could be warded; many artistically-inclined mages made a profitable living painting protective sigils above doorways or cunningly disguised in frescoes or mosaics. *'Possible. She would be protected against curses or scrying so long as she remained within those walls.'* Would the woman risk it?

No, Corinna would not place her safety within walls alone. Oh, her home might well be warded, but Corinna would have something else, something she was never without. She left her sanctuary regularly, planting her fiend-summoning charms all around the city. Her cult was hated, and now she knew that Vibia and Latona were onto her, aware of her schemes, ready and eager to dispel the threat she presented. *'She'll have something on her person. Like a child's bulla.'*

Children wore amulets around their necks, talismans against evil influences and foul sorcery. Vibia had never tried to curse a child, but she imagined if someone did, the result would be much like what she just experienced: a magical impediment thrown in her path, a swift rebuke from the gods who looked after the youth. *'No reason Corinna could not create one with the opposite purpose, so her goddess might shield her wickedness from corrective influence.'*

Brushing her hands off, Vibia stood, taking up the curse tablet as she did. A faint warmth lingered on the metal. *'Useless now.'* She would have to go and toss it in the river in the morning. She disliked touching her tablets after she had worked them and always tried to get them out of the house as swiftly as possible. Knowing this one had gone wrong, its power aborted before coming to fruition, she wanted it gone even more.

'And we'll just have to figure out some other way to stop the Discordian delinquint before her power swells out of control.'

DECEMBER
VIII

Camp of the Lusetani, Central Iberia

A month had passed since Sakarbik showed Neitin the *besteki*.

Five days had passed since Bailar convinced Ekialde to engage in another blood-soaked ritual.

"Necessary, my sweet rabbit," Ekialde insisted, cupping Neitin's cheeks between his callused hands. He used the soothing tone she had once adored. Once, she believed it showed her his true self, the caring young man who wooed and won her, the softness he could not allow anyone else to see. Now the sound of it grated, made her dig her fingernails into the pads of her palm.

'Condescension is not love. I wish I had seen that so long ago.'

But she saw, too, the twitch of fear in the corner of his yellow-hazel eyes. *'No. Fear is the wrong word.'* Concern, perhaps. Or if it was fear, it was the selfish kind: fear of losing face, fear of losing power.

His next words confirmed it. "The Vettoni war-band, they need a show of strength from me," he said. A little hiss escaped him. "Not just the Vettoni. Our *own* people, too. They worry I have lost the gods' favor. The blood will show them they have no cause, and it will give us renewed strength to strike at our foes."

Neitin swallowed around the lump in her throat. "Whose blood?"

"Prisoners the Vettoni took, further north. Some Arevaci who thought their village safe to return to."

Futile though she knew it would be, Neitin had to try to argue, to make him see sense. "Why not use blood freely given?" she asked. "Blood that does not require death? Otiger tells me there is power in that, too." Her uncle had not proved the ally she hoped for against Bailar, but he did have information worth the knowing. "Even Bailar did not always take the blood of death. He used to—"

But Ekialde shook his head, shaggy black hair falling in his eyes. "When he did not know better."

"Strange definition of better," Neitin said. Once, she would have spat the words; now, they were almost a sigh. She was so tired of fighting him, so weary of her voice being heard but never heeded.

His fingers stroked her hair, surprisingly gentle. "I wish I could help you feel it, my love," he said. "Bailar has chained forces no one else thought possible. I was wrong to doubt. Generations of our forefathers could not harness such magic."

'Maybe generations of our forefathers simply had better sense.' Once, she would have said that aloud. *'Once, once...'* Once, she had imagined a very different shape for her life.

She watched because Ekialde asked her to, thinking it might convince her of Bailar's power. *'As though I have not seen it before.'* So much blood, so many slit throats, so many corpses. How was that something to delight in?

Neitin stood as far away as possible. Her uncle Otiger spoke softly to her beforehand, quietly solicitous. "If it does not work, perhaps your husband's confidence in Bailar will be broken once and for all," he said. Neitin was beyond such hopes. If the disaster at Toletum had not won him away, nothing would.

And *almost* it had! *'But Ekialde wants victory too badly. He has wrapped his whole self up in the idea of being erregerra.'*

Beside her, Sakarbik's silent fury had enough force that its heat radiated off her skin. Sakarbik hated Bailar's magic, if possible, more than Neitin did. Sakarbik did not care what happened to the Lusetani, not to the warriors, anyway; her objection was different to Neitin's. She wasn't worried about saving anyone from the perils of a polluted soul. For her, the revulsion was more visceral. "Everything around me stinks of rotten meat," she muttered, nostrils flaring. "Everything Bailar does, may Endovelicos turn his sight away from the wretched man, it is... putrid."

The magic-men took their time beseeching the gods, reading the stars to be sure they had chosen the correct night, preparing their instruments. Then they brought forward their sacrifice.

Three prisoners, all men. One had a sickly look to him, or perhaps merely underfed. The other two were older, with gray flecking their beards. They had all been stripped naked. The eldest had pale bands around his arms. *'He may have been someone of importance in his village,'* Neitin thought, and wondered who had claimed his ornaments, if they would be worn or melted down and reworked.

All her horror remained on the inside as the spectacle unfolded. Not that she had grown inured to the spray of blood; she had run out of tears.

Bailar caught the blood in bowls and did *something* to it; Neitin had never understood the particulars, never sought to, hoped she would never have to. Bailar began marking the foreheads of the warriors in the circle around him. Ekialde first, of course; then his second-in-command, Angeru; then the chief warrior of the Vettoni; then the rest.

Magic or madness, *something* took over each man and woman when the blood streaked their skin. A strange glow behind their eyes, a new vigor in their limbs, a fervor taking over their sensibilities. They began to dance around the fire, howling like wolves, beating their chests, celebrating the new vitality that the death-blood bestowed upon them. Musicians struck up drums and horns.

"Disgusting," Sakarbik snarled, her face contorted with repugnance.

"He will have the Vettoni now, I suppose," Neitin said, her voice cold. "Who would not follow such a man?"

It should have been over. Neitin knew the rhythm of these things, had grown used to the pattern of the rituals.

But Bailar stretched out a blood-dripping arm, pointing across the fire. At first, Neitin wasn't sure why. What did he want? Then, it became apparent: Not what, but *whom*.

Her uncle Otiger.

Two of the dancing warriors obeyed Bailar's whim, seizing Otiger and bringing him forward. They did not need to drag. Otiger went willingly enough, mild as always. "Why is Bailar doing that?" Neitin asked. "Otiger will not take part." That line, her uncle refused to cross, even with as many magic-men as they had lost at Toletum. He offered his other skills, in quiet defiance of Bailar's disdain, but he drew the line at rituals involving human blood.

Sakarbik sucked in a breath, a flash of concern replacing the disgust in her expression. Before Neitin could ask her why, a bronze blade flashed, catching the firelight. It arced through the air, cutting a ragged gash in the dark night. More blood. A guttural, choking noise. A body collapsing, twitching, jerking, as two warriors eased it to the earth with incongruous reverence.

"No." Not a scream, but a half-strangled whisper. Neitin was unaware of having started to move until Sakarbik's fingers tightened on her shoulder.

"You cannot intervene," she hissed. "He is dead already."

And so he was, or near enough as made no matter. Bailar bent with bowl in hand, collecting Otiger's blood, as much as he could gather. Neitin's gut wrenched further when she saw, at Bailar's side, her sister Reilin, heavy with sorrow, but showing no sign of recrimination. No, she was resigned; she would play handmaiden to this tragedy, would tell herself it was ordained, necessary, righteous.

Neitin could not see her husband, did not know if he had witnessed Otiger's death. She did not want to see. Did not want to think that he might have approved this part of the plan. Did not want to witness his capitulation to Bailar's definition of necessity. Blinking, Neitin became aware of wetness on her cheeks, tightness in her throat.

Sakarbik's grip on Neitin tightened, yanking her backward, further away from the fire. "We will mourn him later." Her voice was a growl against Neitin's ear. "I wanted to wait longer, for the solstice, for the sun to return. It would have been easier— But we cannot. We go now."

Still reeling from the shock of seeing her uncle's body fall, Neitin swiveled, turning wide eyes on Sakarbik. "Now?"

"Now. As fast as our legs can carry us."

"B-But we—"

"I made preparations. When I heard Bailar intended a ceremony for tonight..." A hissing noise escaped from between her teeth. "Well. I thought it might be necessary. Clothes, water, food, enough to get us downriver a fair distance."

Neitin swatted Sakarbik's hand away from her shoulder. "Y-You knew this would happen?"

"Not your uncle," Sakarbik said. "I swear to it, little mother. I would have warned him. Would not have let you watch. The sun's colors tonight, they tried to warn me something ill was afoot. For your sake, I wish they had spoken more clearly." She grabbed Neitin's upper arm and gave her a shake. "I know you are shocked. But you must focus. Do not make me slap you."

Neitin swallowed down her fear and horror and nausea and anger. "What must we do?"

"We go fetch your child."

"Irrin is—"

"You will send her here."

Neitin shook her head. "I don't want her to see—"

"Perhaps she should!" Sakarbik snapped. "Perhaps seeing your uncle's body will shock some sense into her, but if it does not—and I doubt it will, given that all your sisters put together do not have half your sense—then she will be drawn into this madness. Everyone knows you want no part of it, and with the blood-haze Bailar is drawing over them all, I think you will not be missed, not for a long time. The *besteki* will cover our retreat."

"Cover our retreat," Neitin echoed. "You sound like a warrior."

"Too much time in this damned camp." She seized Neitin's elbow and steered her away from the campfire. "You get rid of her and gather whatever is necessary for your child. I will fetch our supplies from hiding. And then—we run."

"*Where?*"

But Sakarbik shook her head. "I will not speak our direction aloud, not with fiends in the air. You have trusted me with yourself and your boy till now. Trust me further."

Neitin's heart quavered. Leaving Ekialde, abandoning him to his uncle's madness, that was hard enough. Doing so at the bidding of a woman who, she knew, had no reason to love her or her people—

'*The besteki. You felt the besteki, their power, their—their holiness. They would not attend someone treacherous.*'

That would have to be enough.

Fortress of Legio X Equestris, Central Iberia

Restless by nature, Sempronius had found solid sleep even harder to come by since Rabirus's most recent assassination attempt, and so he was awake, mentally composing his next letter to Marcus Autronius, when the world around him suddenly *tilted*.

No, he realized, grasping at the nearest wall for support. Nothing had happened to the world itself. But his sense of it had been knocked askew, spinning and clattering like a dish nudged off a table. A cold chill crawled over his skin, intangible yet thicker than mere wind, carrying a sense of pervasive *wrongness*.

Just as swiftly, the sensation passed, as though nothing more than a brief wave washing over him.

Restabilized, Sempronius moved from his sleeping chamber to the tablinum-slash-receiving chamber that preceded it within his officer's quarters, intending to splash some water on his face. Because Corvinus slept on a cot in the corner of that room, he tried to keep his footfall soft—only to discover his steward awake, if decidedly more rumpled than usual.

"You felt it, too, didn't you?" Sempronius asked.

"Not as strongly as you, I expect." Corvinus frowned. "Hard to put words to it. Like... oil, but cold, and like no amount of scraping would ever be enough to get it off of me. It woke me up. I thought at first—I don't know." He shook his head. "I was going to say, I thought maybe it was raining and a roof slat had come loose, and I'd gotten drenched in my sleep, but I *didn't* think that. I only wanted to, for whatever sense that makes."

"No, it does. Our minds—particularly in the fog of waking—try to find rational explanations, to reassure our mortal bodies that we are hale and whole."

"But this was not rational."

"Nor, I think, of the mortal realm. But not Aventan magic. Either of us would recognize that. Iberian, then."

Corvinus smoothed out his hair and reached for his cloak and shoes. "Yes. Which means I should go check with the Arevaci magic-men, learn what they experienced."

"The patrol as well. I doubt there's been an incursion, but—"

"Yes. Better to be safe."

Within the hour, Corvinus returned with several answers: yes, the magic-men felt the same thing; no, they did not know what it was, exactly, but none of them thought it good; no, the patrols had not seen or heard anything unusual; yes, the boy Eustix experienced something unsettling as well; no, none of the non-magical populace of the fortress had been disturbed.

Most interesting was the magic-men's assertion that, whatever had happened, it had not happened *here*.

"So this was no attack?" Sempronius asked.

"Not a direct one, anyway. Rather a ripple of some great work elsewhere. They think."

Sempronius had not been idle while Corvinus rounded up information. He stoked the braziers, lit lamps, and begun perusing a sheaf of notes which he kept among Corvinus's documents, not his own: everything they had learned so far about Iberian magic. "I'm inclined to agree. We know they can work at a distance. The plague and the *akdraugi* operated in that way."

"Still a closer range than any Lusetani are right now, though," Corvinus said. "Surely our scouts would have noticed them creeping within a mile of the fortress. We've been quite diligent about maintaining a perimeter around these hills."

"If this was directed at us, they've managed to do so from farther away than we thought possible," Sempronius reasoned, "or else, whatever we felt wasn't meant for us."

"I don't like either option."

"No." Sempronius drummed his fingers on his desk. "Any work creating a ripple like that..." He shuffled the papers before him until he found his notes on correspondence from Vibia and Latona: a catalogue of the Discordian curses they found, the effects, the physical markers, the thaumaturgical theories.

Peering over his shoulder, Corvinus commented, "You think it may be related to what the ladies have encountered?"

"I wouldn't use the word 'related,' no... but I am increasingly struck by the similarities between Aventan magic and Iberian. Resonances, really, far more than traditional thinking would hold." Corvinus's snort indicated his opinion of 'traditional thinking,' and Sempronius whole-heartedly agreed. "Aventan magic borrows so much from the Athaecans—but its roots are in our Truscan origins as much as in what we adopted from Athaecan philosophers, little though modern snobbery likes to admit it. I wonder..." His fingertips traced over some of his notes, particularly those Vibia had shared about the trap that netted Latona. "I wonder if there are answers in those origins. I never noticed such resonance with Abydosian magic, but here... perhaps my Truscan ancestors shared more in the way of thaumaturgy with the Iberians than we've ever realized."

"Or with Tennic peoples," Corvinus added, tilting his head in consideration. "Perhaps that is why so many of us can do your magic, with your gods' blessing."

"Another blow to 'traditional thinking,' if that's the case."

The rationale behind the manumission and citizenship laws favoring those with magical blessings had always been that those were people the gods picked out for "betterment" above their non-Aventan origins. *Would challenging that reasoning lead to greater tolerance of and appreciation for those beyond our borders, and those we bring within them? Or would it jeopardize their enfranchisement?* A hazardous thread to pull on.

Sempronius sat, sighing. The notes before him conveyed so much and yet left so much unspoken, unconsidered. He needed great minds in a room together, able to spin thoughts off of each others' ideas, to find the truth beneath all the layers of observation and guesswork.

One voice, he yearned for more than all the rest, to hear her thoughts, to benefit from her viewpoint.

"Dominus?" Corvinus asked. "What's taken hold of your mind, now?"

Sempronius gave him a rueful smile. "An impossible fancy, that's all. I was just thinking, I wish I could speak to the Lady Latona of these things more openly, as I do to Vibia. My sister provides admirable counsel, but her scope is more... focused." He did not want to discredit her by saying "limited," though it was true. Vibia's nature was decisive and forthright, but not as imaginative or investigative as he sometimes wished. She saw simple solutions, not always the grand array of possibilities.

Corvinus nodded strangely slowly. "Yes... I can imagine the Lady Latona's perspective could be quite an advantage."

"I get what I can through Vibia, of course, but it's not the same as if I could be direct. Especially in letters."

Corvinus shifted his weight, some inner conflict playing itself out upon his face. Then he said, tentatively, "Could you not?"

"Not?"

"Not be more direct with her? I don't mean in letters, necessarily. But when we return to Aven, could you not speak with her as openly as you wish?"

Sempronius blinked a few times. "Not without... without..." The words 'giving myself away' stuck to the inside of his mouth like a thick sauce. Concealing his nature came so naturally; even considering revelation was so alien a concept that his body itself seemed to reject the notion.

Perhaps sensing that, Corvinus continued. "Dominus." His voice was far softer than usual. His conversational tones ranged from no-nonsense to sardonic, but gentleness—well, that was typically something Djadi brought out in him. "This woman, her importance to you... You have not troubled to hide it from me, and I am grateful for that trust. But I think, when you return to Aven, you will not long be able to hide it from all and sundry."

"No," Sempronius admitted. Already, Rabirus had taken notice of his attentions to her, the time they spent together, and Sempronius was convinced only Venus's blessing, delivered through the hand of the sympathetic Ama Rubellia, had kept the secret of their Saturnalian tryst. If they carried on like that after his return to the city, they would be courting scandal. "Nor will I want to." Her divorce opened up possibilities.

"If you mean to bring this woman into your life," Corvinus went on, with the air of someone choosing his words very carefully, "could you not, then, also bring her inside your trust?"

Half of Sempronius wanted to concur, immediately—but the other half hitched, like a wagon caught in a rut. The idea of disclosing his magical abilities tripped some snare inside him, one that sent a panic galloping through his veins and seized around his heart like a fist.

'Why fear it?' In general, that answer was easy: because he had committed a sacrilege for which he could be thrown from the Tarpeian Rock.

But he dared destiny every day of his life, secure that the gods intended far more for him than such an ignoble end. He did not fear being caught out by accident; he was too careful.

Letting someone inside, though—that, he had no familiarity with, had never prepared for. Even someone like Latona. If ever he were to do such a thing, it would require careful handling. Laying the groundwork, far in advance, so she would *understand* why he kept such a secret, why he defied man's laws in favor of divine guidance.

That would be critical. He did not think she would turn him in or expose him, but he wanted her to understand.

Sempronius swallowed, with difficulty. "There would be no one more worthy of that trust, to be sure. But there will be time enough to consider that once we return to Aven." Aware of the haste in his voice, he moved on to proposing theories as to the nature of that night's Iberian magical surge. Corvinus allowed him the evasion without further pressing, but the weight of the suggestion hung like clouds over the moon.

IX

Camp of the Lusetani, Central Iberia

Glorious, glorious night! Ekialde did not sleep till dawn, his blood racing with his uncle's magic, his head dizzied with delights. All the markings on his skin had seemed to dance, and he danced, too, he and all his warriors.

He woke to a chill spreading across his body. The bonfire had burned down to low coals, and with the magic wearing off, Ekialde felt winter's bite. He squinted at the horizon, judging the hour: mid-morning, perhaps. The sky was white and yellow; there would be snow again today. *'So cold, so early in the year.'*

Perhaps it would make life harder for the Aventans and their allies. Already they would be suffering, with the Vettoni raiding their supply lines and so much of the land around Toletum stripped bare. The Lusetani could raid and forage to the south. They could move, would move, as necessity took them, while the Aventans dug in to their hillside, as though walls were all men needed to get them through the winter.

'Wooden walls, only. Not so high or sturdy as at Toletum. They intend no fight before spring. We will surprise them and end this long before then. We will swarm over their pitiful wooden walls, we will catch them without their shining armor, we will be the chaos among them before they can form up in their neat lines. Every advantage of their army, we can defeat. We will!'

Confidence in this plan heated Ekialde's muscles, as though the markings on his skin reached inside of him and stoked the embers of his heart. It was the best he had felt since disaster befell at Toletum. He told Bailar: Find me a way. And Bailar found it. This he swore: new invigoration for the war-band. How could Ekialde doubt, after the bolstering strength of last night? Whatever new charms his uncle had worked, whatever favors he begged of the gods, they sizzled in Ekialde's skin still.

Not enough to chase off the cold entirely, though. Even Bandue's favored *erregerra* needed a warm cloak on a winter morning. *'And my wife. I should like to see my wife.'* It was a fitting morning to make another son to follow in his line. *'Another erregerra, I am sure of it. One to follow after me.'*

The boy Matigentis was a sweet little thing, but Neitin was coddling him. He would be for the magic-men, perhaps, and Ekialde would give him to the gods gladly, for he owed the gods much. *'But with this fire in my blood, certainly now I could put a son in her belly to follow in my footsteps. A war-king greater than myself, one to command the entire Tagus River, drive the Tyrians from our shores as I will the Aventans, tear their corrupt cities to the ground.'* Yes, a pleasant thought, and Ekialde felt himself stiffening in excitement.

As he crossed the camp, he discovered he was not the only one whose blood had been so moved by the night's magic. Here and there, men and women lay sleeping in each others' arms, under the stars. Ekialde wondered that the urge had not come upon him during the ritual, that he had not sought his wife out then—but all his focus had been for the gods. *'As is right and natural.'*

Near his wife's tent, he stepped over one pair of still-slumbering lovers: Neitin's sister Reilin and his own second-in-command, Angeru. *'A good match,'* he thought, smiling. Reilin was becoming a capable spearwoman, and there was no one Ekialde trusted more than Angeru.

Ekialde whipped back the door of his wife's tent, expecting to find Neitin tending their child, or perhaps mending clothing. By this hour of the morning, she would be up and about her usual work.

But the tent was still and quiet and icy-cold. No one within. No babe in his basket. No fire in the brazier. No one had been here in quite some time.

A pit opened up in Ekialde's stomach. *'Perhaps it is nothing. Perhaps it is later in the day than I thought, and they are merely somewhere else in the camp. Perhaps she went to her—'*

The thought snagged. Neitin had few friends in this camp. That Cossetan sorceress she kept as a nursemaid, claiming the woman held the favor of the goddess Nabia, and her uncle Otiger. Otiger, who provided such a noble sacrifice the night before, giving his life, his magical life, so that others might prosper from the power in his blood.

Did Neitin know? Had Neitin seen? She had been... somewhere. The memory was foggy. Once the magical fervor took him, Ekialde's vision had turned dream-like, blurry. In touching the world of the gods and all their power, he lost some sense of what happened in the earthly realm.

If she did know of her uncle's role—well, Ekialde knew that she did not place the same faith in Bailar that he did. She would require convincing. He would show her what wonder had been done, what strength his warriors drew from the ritual. *'And placing that future erregerra in her might have to wait.'* Once he returned victorious, surely, *then* she would see why it mattered so much, the necessity—

But where *was* she?

Ekialde whipped around, back out of the tent. He went to the pair sleeping not far off and nudged Reilin in the shoulder with his foot. "Wake!"

With fluttering eyelashes, she did so, though her expression contorted in confusion at first. Her eyes narrowed at Angeru, wondering, and only belatedly did she perceive the *erregerra* standing above her. "My king!" she exclaimed. As she sat up, her hands pushed on Angeru's chest, waking the warrior as well. "I apolo—"

"Your sister," Ekialde demanded. "Where is she?"

"Neitin?" Blearily, she gestured at the tent. "I assume—"

"No. Up," he commanded. Reilin rose, not troubling to cover her nudity, though she shivered, aware now of the cold winter air. "Find her."

Before long, the whole camp had been roused, and once those who had fallen into a stupor in their nakedness clothed themselves and brought their senses fully back to reality, they searched for the *erregerra's* wife.

"Could she have been taken?" Neitin's youngest sister wondered, casting her wild gaze around the camp. "The—The Arevaci? Or the Aventans?"

Ekialde would happily have blamed either enemy for his wife's disappearance, but inherent honesty forced him to shake his head. "There was no disturbance in her tent," he said. "No sign of struggle, nothing out of place."

"Not nothing." Reilin emerged from the tent, having performed a thorough appraisal. "There are things missing that I think no kidnapper would trouble with. Clothing. Waterskins and blankets. Young Mati's toys." She settled her hands on her hips. "And with the boy and the witch-woman both gone, too?"

"Even under the power of the ritual, no enemy could have slipped into camp." Ekialde's uncle had appeared at his elbow. Whether he had been searching or consulting the gods, Ekialde was not certain. "We did leave sentries untouched by the magic. And in your heightened state, you would have sensed the presence of an outsider, I'm sure of it."

Ekialde rubbed at his brow. "I cannot— I do not think—" The only explanation, that Neitin had disappeared of her own accord, was too impossible to put into words.

Bailar's hand touched his shoulder, cold against his skin. "It is difficult to reckon with," he said in a low voice, "but she has ever been weak in her faith."

Ekialde's nose scrunched up. No, that was not right. She did not share Bailar's fervor, true, but she was a pious woman in her own devotions. That she had little love for Bandue, the war-god—well, that was simply her nature, was it not? She had ever been Nabia's devotee, drawn to the rivers and the growing things. *'I fell in love with her in the spring,'* he remembered, suddenly seeing her as she had been years earlier, when they met during a conclave between their villages. *'Rose-cheeked and wearing flowers, so alive, so happy.'* He had not seen her look happy in a long time. *'Was this my fau—'*

Bailar's words interrupted his thoughts. "Last night's ritual... She would not have understood. She has never seen Bandue's truth. If she mistook our purpose in taking Otiger's power for our glorious cause—"

"But where would she have gone?" Ekialde asked. "And how? She is a sensible woman, uncle, not a fool. To charge off into the wilderness, in the dead of winter—"

"Who knows what influence she may be under?" Bailar's fingers pressed harder into his shoulder. "That Cossetan woman may have said something—*done* something—led her astray, convinced her that there was safety beyond the camp."

Ekialde could not reconcile all these things. Neitin's piety, Neitin's distrust; Neitin's good sense, Neitin's apparent madness. And his son—his son, his *blood*, vanished with her.

"What of the Vettoni?" Reilin asked. "Do they—"

"If they remain in ignorance, let us keep it that way," Ekialde said swiftly. "I think they took small note of her to begin with. If we must explain, we will say that I sent her back downriver for her safety."

"Now?" This, from the other sister. "When you never did before?"

"Then say something else!" Ekialde hissed. "A message from your parents, a spiritual quest, anything! But speak no truth of this to the Vettoni." Their allegiance was newly reaffirmed, after the shaking of their alliance following the loss at Toletum. He could not risk their faith wavering again now. "I must—I must go and find them. Bring them back. My *son*—"

"No. You must go and lead your war-band against the Aventans, as you promised the Vettoni you would do." Bailar still had not released Ekialde's shoulder. "You are *erregerra*; you have your duties."

"But my wife, my son, I must find—"

"Allow me," Bailar said. "Let that be my responsibility, my burden. I have given you what is necessary. You take your warriors and go. Surprise the Aventans in their wooden camp." Bailar's lips arched into an anticipatory smile. "Bathe in their blood, revel in the slaughter, and sing of Bandue's might, my sister-son. Work glorious wonder for the god who loves you. Let me attend to the wayward woman." He lifted his hand from Ekialde's skin at last and flicked his fingers dismissively. "She and her pet sorceress cannot have gotten far. I will find your wife and the boy, and I will keep them safe until you return in triumph."

Ekialde searched his uncle's face, which he had known and trusted all his life. "Their safety is of the greatest importance," he said. "Whatever Neitin has done—for whatever reason—"

"Do not fear, blessed one," Bailar said. "I will not hold her accountable for what that Cossetan harridan may have beguiled her into. She is your queen. She will receive all honors and deference, as is her right."

His wife. He ought to search for his wife himself, and fiends take the Vettoni if they didn't like it. He ought to find Neitin and learn what had driven her out into the wilderness, if it was really the Cossetan woman's prompting, or if something else...

'*You are erregerra. You have your duties. You know what you are best at. What Bandue demands of you.*'

Bandue would not smile on him for haring after a woman in the wilds, even if it were his queen and the mother of his child. Bandue expected glorious victory, and Ekialde had to fulfill his god's expectations. Failure might unravel his whole world—and then what would he offer Neitin, once she was found? What safety could he promise her, if he lost Bandue's favor?

He nodded tightly. "Very well, uncle. Find my wife. Protect her and my son. I—I shall lead our warriors forth this very day."

X

Esquiline Hill, City of Aven

The domus was nothing spectacular, certainly not compared to the grand houses that lined the upper reaches of the Palatine or the Caelian. It didn't even have the flash of being in an up-and-coming neighborhood, but was tucked away on a quiet street, respectable but with no prestige, on the northern spur of the Esquiline. The rooms were small but serviceable; the ceilings a bit low; the walls relatively unadorned.

'Still, it's more house than most Aventans would ever imagine having for themselves,' Latona thought, turning about in the atrium. Months of visiting crowded insulae and apartments above shops to dispel *lemures* gave her a keener appreciation for how the bulk of the population lived. *'And we have so much wealth that Aula has a whole house she'd never even set foot in, standing empty.'* Many would say that was simply the way of things, the gods' blessing upon their family, but it hardly seemed fair.

"We can bring in some simple furniture," Aula said as she swanned appraisingly through the rooms. "I don't suppose we need to kit out all the bedrooms, will we?"

"No," Latona said. "One or two, maybe. It might be nice to have a place for us to stay if we work late. Or for Merula or Hermia to sleep while we work." Vibia's attendant proved dutiful, never breathing a word of her mistress's secrets, but the magic terrified her. If she came along, she'd likely be grateful for a room she could barricade herself within and pretend nothing unusual was happening on the other side of the door. "I'd much prefer to use the space for—for training and experiments." Latona frowned, wondering *what*, exactly, she meant by that. "We'll need the symbols, for all the elements. Raw material to work with. Something like a Cantrinalia altar."

"You know I don't—"

"I know, I'm thinking out loud." Latona rubbed her brow. "And we should set up a study."

Aula cocked her head. "A study? Or a praetorium?" She referred to the command tent of an Aventan legion.

Latona's lips twisted grimly. "Yes. We can bring our maps and things here."

"Alhena's got a proper library under her bed already, I think. I wonder if the priests know how many scrolls she makes off with when their backs are turned."

"Considering how many of them she's borrowed on my behalf, I won't chastise her. Besides, I think she's been copying out her favorites and returning the originals." Latona turned in a circle again, thinking about each room and the use it might be put to. A study, rooms for practicing their gifts, rooms to rest...

"I know it's meant to be private, for now," Aula said, "but are you going to tell Vatinius Obir that you're setting up shop—or something like it—here?"

"I intend to."

"Good. I'll feel much better knowing you can send for his boys if you get yourselves in a fix."

"We might not have to send," Latona mused. "Once he knows we're here, he might set a boy to watching the place." Earlier in the year, Latona discovered that she had protectors in the collegium of the upper Esquiline, set to guard her because Sempronius Tarren had asked his client, Obir, to have a care for her safety.

The arrangement worked out well for them both. Even with Merula always at her side, Latona benefitted from having extra muscle at her back when she traversed the city, and the Esquiline Collegium had called upon Latona when the Discordians began setting curses in their neighborhood.

"Well, I know this house isn't precisely within their domain," Aula said, "but it's close enough as should make no matter. Hopefully they can work out some truce with the local collegium so no one's feathers get ruffled." The city's various collegia were always engaged in competition that ranged from friendly rivalry to outright murderous conflict. Obir's collegium was one of the larger, and thus more respected, and Latona believed he kept good rapport with his neighbors—but territoriality would always be a concern.

"Kitchen's a mess," Merula complained as she came upstairs. "Should be hiring someone to clean it proper."

"It's not as though we'll be hosting dinner parties here," Latona said.

"She's right, though," Aula said. "Just in case. You *might* want to host a dinner of mages sometime. And you can always hire in cooks who wouldn't ask too many questions."

"Let's deal with that if it becomes necessary," Latona said. "If we need food while we're working, there are three thermopoliums on this street."

Aula wandered to one of the walls and ran her finger along a crack in the paint. "Well, it shouldn't take too much to make the place usable, at any rate, and then you can begin inviting your colleagues over."

"Colleagues," Latona echoed, pressing a hand over the slight flutter in her chest. She had never had cause to think of the other mages of Aven in that way before. They came together at the Cantrinalia ritual, certainly, and some other religious rites; they were capable of working together in times of adversity, as they had during the Aventine fires, as she and Vibia had all this year. But it wasn't usual. Latona wanted it to be *usual*, long after they—hopefully—dispelled the Discordian threat once and for all. A proper collegium, an institution that could work toward the city's benefit.

"And if Father wonders why we're spending all our time over here—though I must say, he's been obligingly oblivious to most of your excursions so far—I can always tell him I'm redecorating it in preparation for Gaius's return." Aula grinned. "After all, our dear brother will be in need of a wife once he returns from Iberia, and I imagine they'll want a household of their own rather than staying under our roof."

That thought snagged in Latona's brain. "No," she said. "No, we must... we must tell Father what we're doing. Some version of the truth, anyway."

Aula's eyes went wide. "Truly? You don't mean to keep it a secret?"

"I'm sick of skulking about like it's something to be ashamed of, to be honest with you. I would prefer not to deceive Father any more than we have to. He recognized my gods-given duty, and so I owe him honesty. Or some breed of it, at least." Latona threaded her fingers together, considering the angle she might take. "He knows I intend to be a better mentor to young Fausta. If we told him I intended to do more—to serve as teacher to other children, the way that I would if I were at Juno's temple—"

"Yes," Aula said, picking up the idea. "After all, he couldn't deny you that. It's what you *would* be doing, if not for Aemilia Fullia."

"Yes. I *should* be training any young Spirit mage in need of guidance. That's well within what *pietas* demands of me."

"And it's close enough to the truth not to tempt Apollo's wrath upon your head. No need to mention the *other* half of your mission."

"None at all." Latona sighed, tension dropping from her shoulders. "And think how much simpler it will be, not having to concoct stories and diversions to allay his suspicions."

"I can even bring Lucia here from time to time to make it more convincing. Who knows? Maybe more time around a bunch of mages will bring her gifts more to the forefront."

Though Aula's voice was skipping-light, Latona sensed the tension underneath those words. "Thank you," Latona said, going to Aula's side and pressing her sister's hand. "You really did find us the perfect solution."

Aula tittered. "Not much of an act of generosity, when I'd quite forgotten I had the place. The idea was never for me to live here, of course, just to secure income for me, if it ever became necessary." And it might have, if Aulus and Gaius had shared her husband's ill fortune during Ocella's reign. "So it's fortunate for us that I never got around to renting it back out after the courts decided that, yes, it was my property and untouched by the proscription, though I do wonder what my dear departed husband would have to say about his bridegroom's gift to me being turned to such a use."

"If Lucius were alive," Latona said, "I'd tell him to consider it an act of investment in his daughter's future."

"Yes..." Aula's gaze shifted around as Latona's had, as though she were seeing the possibilities in the space. "I-I won't deny that I will worry for her. I would have anyway, of course, but so much more, with this gift laid on her shoulders. But if she turns out even half as talented as you, my honey..." Aula's jaw set in an unusually hard line, and the merry green of her eyes sparked like flint. "I don't ever want her feeling like you felt. Like she had to hide it and press it down until it was so small she could stow it away in a jewelry box. I want her to be proud of her gifts, and I want her to learn to use them well." Her gaze turned back to her sister, wryly jesting. "Though I wouldn't be sorry if she got into less trouble with them than you have."

Latona pulled Aula into a fierce hug. "If we do this right," she said, "if we get rid of the Discordians and if we establish something like a collegium in truth, maybe Aven will be safer for her and all mages, and she'll never need to."

"Oh, that's the hope of all parents," Aula said, rubbing Latona's back. "A better world for our sprats than the one we grew up in."

"We'll need to lay in extra supplies for the Saturnalia," Vatinius Obir said to Ebredus as they walked down the Esquiline Hill toward the markets. "With the year we've had, we deserve more than a bit of merriment. Some flower garlands, maybe. Plenty of wine, good bread and honeyed buns. Some boar from the countryside."

"May be difficult," Ebredus said. "The dockside boys say the Emporium's been beset with all manner of trouble. Vermin getting into the stores, grain going to mold—"

"Hrm," was all the verbal response Obir made to that. He had accompanied Lady Latona and Lady Vibia to some of those locations, so he knew the likelihood of that trouble being more than ill luck. "All the same, our people deserve some pleasure. I don't mind laying out extra coin if it—"

A cracking noise caught his attention, a few steps behind them. Then scraping, and instinctively, Obir leapt to the middle of the street, giving Ebredus a shove to get him out of the way as well. He had lived in the city long enough to beware falling roof tiles.

The calamity was behind them, however, uphill. Not only one terracotta tile came loose, but a full cascade of them, crashing into the street. A girl shrieked, throwing her hands up over her face to protect herself from the shattering shingles. A woman rushed to snatch a young boy out of the way. The vendors operating out of the first floor of the building rushed to protect their wares, but the tiles crashed into one table, cracking it in two and scattering its display of bronze goods. The clanging of braziers and lamps and household knickknacks raised up further cacophony, even as the roof tiles finally stopped falling.

"Is anyone hurt?" Obir asked, rushing back up the hill. They were not, technically, still within his jurisdiction, since they had crossed below the Temple to Moneta; this was, properly, some other captain's problem. But it was not in Obir's nature to ignore when he might participate.

The gods had been merciful. A few people had been hit with debris, but none had taken the full weight of a roof tile to their heads. Some bruises and scrapes, but nothing worse.

The scare rattled everyone, however. People clustered in small groups, discussing the accident in hushed tones. The usual sort of murmur, Obir thought; well, citizens liked to have something to complain about. Tales would grow in the telling, and any number of witnesses who escaped entirely unscathed would nonetheless be bragging about their brush with death in the taverns and at the thermopoliums tonight.

And, of course, there would be a need to assign blame. The building's landlord would no doubt be a prominent target, but the good folk of the neighborhood might equally well fault a tenant who neglected rituals to the household gods, or perhaps the urban praetor, who had done so little as yet to address infrastructure needs in this part of town. A healthy few days' gossip would pass, and then—

"It's his fault!" cried the woman who had pulled her son out from under the falling tiles, jerking Obir's attention away from his thoughts and the merchant he was helping to gather up fallen braziers. The woman's legs and arms were scratched, flecks of blood dotting her skin as she reached out to point at Ebredus. "Tennic barbarian, I've heard him whistling his curse-music!"

Ebredus's face screwed up in confusion. Obir stepped in between his second and the woman. "He did no such thing, madam," he said. "I know you've had a scare, but your boy is—"

"No!" the woman went on, hysteria straining her pitch. "No, it's just what they've been saying! These troublemakers, they come into the city from gods-know-where, they're jealous of Aven and want to see us suffer—"

"What *who* has been saying?" Obir demanded, settling his hands on his hips. "Who defames this man?"

She blinked a few times, evidently caught wrong-footed. "I've just—I've just heard it around!"

Obir's mouth pressed into a thin line. Many-tongued Rumor, it seemed, had been busy on the lower Esquiline. "I cannot speak for every stranger who passes through Aven's gates," he said, endeavoring to remain calm. "But this man is my second, and I vouch for him. He has no wish to do harm—nor, indeed, any ability to curse roof tiles and bring them crashing upon honest citizens."

"Even if he didn't," the woman said, voice wavering, "he might be bringing the gods' displeasure on us just by being here. That's what—what people are saying."

Another man picked up the thread. "They're saying in the Forum that the gods are angry to see all these foreign travelers taking up residence." He had been retrieving the scattered bronzeware, but he stood now, folding his arms belligerently over his chest. "And listen to you, you're as foreign as he is."

"I am an Aventan citizen, friend," Obir said, striding toward the new challenger, swift and square-shouldered. He did not wish to incite violence, but nor would he duck his head and slink away when his patriotism was challenged. "My tongue has not forgotten that it spoke Maureti first, true, but as you can see, I speak Truscan as well as any man or woman here. I served beneath a legion's banners and am now vowed to the protection of the upper Esquiline. If ever you stroll uphill, you will see that I take my duties seriously. Our crossroads shrine is always well-tended, and our people are looked after so that they may prosper."

"Hmph." The man folded his arms over his chest. "Well, that's as may be."

Sensing an opportunity to diffuse the situation, Obir relaxed his posture, giving the man his best winning smile. He spread his arms wide, with open palms. "Maybe it's time to think about moving uphill, eh? I stay on top of *my* landlords."

The man gave a begrudging chuff. "Been telling ours since the storms last spring that we needed repairs," he admitted, jerking his head at the damaged roof.

"There you have it," Obir said. He raised his voice louder, not to battlefield-command tones, but pointedly, and he pivoted to face the rest of the gathered crowd. "Nothing sinister, no curses. Only rotted pegs and mossy tiles." He locked eyes with the woman who had started the accusations.

"An accident, but fortunately, no true tragedy, yes?" Though uncertainty remained on her face, she eventually nodded. "Good. Pleasant day to you, citizens!"

He turned, as the crowd went back to their work and their conversations. Less tension strangled the air now, but Obir still misliked the feel of the whole thing.

Ebredus waited until they were further downhill before he said anything. "I don't understand. Why did that lady think—?"

"Because of what the damned Optimates are squawking in the Forum," Obir said. He was not, in truth, a highly political man, except for such matters as touched the Upper Esquiline. Being Sempronius Tarren's client meant some things rubbed off, though, as did associating with the ladies of the Vitelliae. "They want everyone unsettled before the elections."

"Hm," Ebredus grunted. "It's working."

"That's not what worries me."

"Eh?" Ebredus arched an eyebrow at his boss. "What, then?"

Obir glanced over his shoulder, back uphill, even though they were far away now. "I told those people it was no curse, and perhaps I was right. Perhaps it *was* only a landlord who should've done repairs over the summer. Perhaps."

He had selected Ebredus for his second because the man was clever, in addition to being tall and solid as an oak. "You think this might be more of the Discordian work?"

Obir shrugged. "I don't know. Only a mage could say for sure. But there have been too many accidents in the streets lately—and too many of them in the districts where people might react like that mother."

He wished his patron wasn't half a world away. Obir knew his world, the world of the upper Esquiline, very well, and he was contented with that—but with the mad blood stirring in the city, he feared that might not be enough. Sempronius would see the connections, would know what hands pulled which strings. He would see the full picture.

Marcus liked sitting in the Forum, though he did wish that the tribunal benches were more comfortable. *'Benches. Why benches, and not a magiste-*

rial chair with a nice supportive backrest to it? The further into my thirties I get, the harder it is to keep a dignified posture all day long.'

The tribunes of the plebs sat in the Forum on all days that were marked for public business—and when they had no other business to attend to. *'And so long as the weather is suitable and our rear ends can endure resting on hard wood!'* Once, in the early days of the Republic, the tribunes had indeed sat out there, all six of them, no matter the weather, to be always available to the public.

The tradition wore thinner over the centuries; rarely did all six tribunes sit at once. *'Another degradation of the mos maiorum for Arrius Buteo to lament. Strange, though, how he never seems to have rhetorical fervor to spare for the institutions which primarily benefited the Head Count and the less-wealthy Classes.'*

He tried to shift forward slightly, stretching out his lower back, disguising the adjustment as a beckoning to the next man in line. "Yes, friend? What's your name and your business?"

"Trebius Perus, Second Class, Tribe of Veturia," the man announced, more loudly than was necessary for Marcus's hearing along. But then, that was part of the point of the tribunal benches: they were public, and as such, so were any grievances aired there. "My business is warehousing and distribution." Trebius Perus was a solidly-built man, pale-skinned but rubicund, fleshy around the middle in a way that suggested he did well in his business. "I own warehouses in the Forum Frumentarium."

A middle-man for grain merchants, then. The Frumentarium was the marketplace for all the grain not directly owned and distributed by the city.

"I need your help in a legal matter involving Licinius Cornicen."

Marcus tried not to wince. Cornicen was an Optimate Senator from a family as old as Aven's hills—which was why Trebius could apply to the tribunes for assistance, as it was their duty to help plebeians in disputes with patricians, to intervene on behalf of those who did not have the wealth, *gravitas*, or legal knowledge to help themselves. The social distinctions mattered less and less with every generation, now that so many plebs had been consuls and thus ennobled their families, but the law retained many vestiges of the days when the difference had been worth spilling blood over.

For all that he was an Optimate, though, Cornicen was one of the sensible ones, and Marcus had little wish to antagonize him. "Speak your concern," he said, "and if there is merit in it, I will take appropriate actions."

Trebius's voice boomed even louder with his next proclamation. "Licinius Cornicen is suing me for negligence, and I want to counter-sue."

'You're not on the stage, fellow,' Marcus wanted to say, but he restrained himself to asking, "And what is the nature of his complaint against you?"

"That I have been careless in my administration of my warehouses, leading to the spoilage of grain and loss of inventory, said loss constituting not only material damages in the matter of pre-contracted sales, but also a potential public menace and threat to the state."

Trebius sounded as if he were quoting the suit against him. *'Did Cornicen write that himself, I wonder?'* Senators weren't supposed to deal in mercantile matters of this kind, but Cornicen always had. Probably he worked through factotums, to keep his hands clean, but the power behind any lawsuit would come from him, not from his lackeys.

Loss of grain *was* a serious matter, though. Adding in the "public menace and threat to the state" charge might be a bit over the top—but with winter coming on, Marcus could not blame Cornicen if true concern motivated him, at least in some part equal with general litigiousness. It took an incredible amount of grain, every day, to feed Aven, to say nothing of the food traded through the fruit, vegetable, and meat markets. *'The city has already been on-edge, and Buteo stirring things up with every speech hasn't helped. If we face a food shortage—'*

"And how do you answer his charge?" Marcus asked Trebius.

"I most vehemently deny it!" Trebius's voice rose to its greatest thunder yet. The man had missed his calling; he could play the largest amphitheater in Athaecum and the audience would hear every word. "I am a cautious steward of all goods under my charge and always have been. I keep clean facilities, regularly patrolled. I keep cats for the vermin, and I hang charms for the same, *and* further charms to ward against rot and pestilence. No man has ever had cause for complaint in my warehouses before!"

Trebius's shouting was at risk of giving Marcus a headache—and furthermore, he did not want all this shouting about spoiled grain to cause a panic in the Forum. Marcus rose from his bench, feeling a stiff creak in his lower back, and extended a hand in the direction of the grain market. "Let us go see, then," he said. "If I can vouch for all that you say, as a sacrosanct tribune, we may be able to convince Licinius Cornicen to drop his suit."

"I still want to counter-sue!" Trebius argued. "For defamation of my character!"

He wouldn't, really, want that; a Second Class man boasted a solid enough income, but he wouldn't be able to out-bribe a senator, so he'd never sway a jury to his favor. "One problem at a time, friend," Marcus said. "Come. Show me your warehouses." As they departed, one of Marcus's fellow tribunes called for the next man in line to state his case.

"So, Trebius," Marcus said, as they walked the length of the Forum. The grain markets weren't far, just on the other side of the Via Nova near the base of the Capitoline Hill. "Tell me: You deny any negligence in your warehouses. But has there been spoilage? Does Cornicen complain rightly about loss of goods?"

Trebius grumbled, but nodded. "There has. I'm damned if I know why, to be honest with you, Tribune." His voice lost some of its theatrical bluster now that they were no longer on display. "I swear to every god—and I'll swear publicly, I'll swear with all the legal rituals—that it's not due to any lack of care or attention from me! I've been in this business twenty years. You think folk would do such business with me if I weren't careful?"

"No, Trebius, I do not." Not senators, at least; the poor might have to make do with disreputable warehousers, but Trebius's clientele spoke to his reputation.

"And it ain't only me," Trebius said, "Every warehouse man is having the same problems, all through the Velabrium."

That caught Marcus's attention. "Every one?"

"Well, every one I've spoken to, at least, and that's a fair few. Not all have had this much disaster, granted. But my friend Crannus, he had a whole shipment of lentils just disintegrate, right into powder. Never heard of nothing like that before in my life. And my neighbor Vesculus, he's mostly in wheat, too, like me, and he's had similar spoilage in three of his warehouses."

"Is it—Hm." Marcus rubbed his forehead. "Something to do with the harvests? Was it a particularly wet year in Sicilia or Alalia?"

Trebius shook his head. "Nah, nothing like that, not as we can tell. The grain comes off the ships fine—and from all over. I get most of mine from Alalia, but Vesculus, his comes in from Numidia."

"Not the harvests, not the ships," Marcus murmured to himself. "I don't suppose anyone could be... tampering with them?"

"We all do patrols regular," Trebius said. "Watchmen and dogs and the like. I suppose someone might slip in here and there, but we mostly worry about theft. Who'd have the ability to spoil a whole warehouse full of wheat?"

"Who indeed?" The back of Marcus's head was tickling, some memory standing up and asking to be recognized, but he couldn't place it.

Trebius sighed heavily as they rounded a corner, moving away from the street and into the warren of warehouses, workshops, and manufactories that crowded the Velabrium. "If its the gods' judgment on us, like them men at the Rostra say, then I don't know why they're judging *me*. I'm a good man, Tribune, I swear it. I honor the gods, I pay my taxes, I do my rituals at home and in the warehouses—"

"I have no doubt of it, friend," Marcus interrupted.

"Ah. Here's one of mine, then."

They went up a ramp into the building — raised, to reduce chances of both dampness and animals finding their way inside. At first glance, all looked to be in order: the warehouse was well-built and dry, with protective talismans painted over the door, as Trebius had said. A man standing by nodded at Trebius, his eyes marking the tribunal stripe on Marcus's toga with apparent interest.

Once they were within, Trebius walked about halfway down an aisle, then tore open a sack. "Look for yourself, Tribune."

Marcus did so. At first glance, the sack didn't look unusual—and then he noticed a black patch of grain on one side. Nothing was wrong with the sack itself; not wet or torn, no fungus or moss attached to it. But in one portion, the grain had turned dark and soft.

He reached into the sack, touching the unspoiled grains first. Hard and smooth, as expected. Then, he reached for the spoiled section.

As soon as Marcus's fingers touched the rotted grains, his skin began to buzz. It was like the time he wandered into stinging nettles as a boy—but no sign of the irritation showed on his skin, no red welts or bumps. The buzzing was not, actually, happening to his body. The reaction was coming from his magical senses. *'Gods above.'*

Someone *had* tampered with the grain—but not in any way that would have been apparent to Trebius.

Marcus withdrew his hand and took a step back. Now that his Earth magic had been awoken, it was in riot, aware of the rot and decay all around him. *Wrongness*, that's what it was, a pervading sense of the world having tilted askew. An itching sensation crept down his arms and up from his ankles; his magic wanted him out of that building, *now*.

But a Tribune could not panic. He had to maintain dignity, and Marcus's nature was not given to impulse in any case. He rubbed his fingers together thoughtfully, though he wished more than anything he could wash them, and gestured down the aisle. One lap around the warehouse; he could manage that, without wanting to crawl out of his skin. He could look as though he were taking proper stock of the entire place. "It's like this everywhere, you say?"

"Yes, Tribune. Not every sack, mind you, but so many of them—all over the warehouse, not just in one corner. And all my fellows say the same."

That made sense, now. A leak would be localized; a curse could strike at random. "I don't know if you know this, Trebius, but I'm an Earth mage."

"I did know," Trebius said. "Part of why I voted for you. Figured, there's a man has the gods' favor. Couldn't hurt to have him on the bench."

Marcus nodded his cursory thanks. "I can feel something wrong with the wheat," he said. "Beyond the obvious, I mean. I can't tell precisely *what*. Earth's gifts don't work like that, and if it weren't, well, grain—if you dealt in fish or something—I wouldn't have any clue at all. But what's wrong here—it's magical. I believe."

All the florid color paled from Trebius's cheeks. "Gods above." He grasped something tied to his belt: a talisman, no doubt, intended to protect against ill luck. "But I—I use charms. Like I said, to keep away the vermin and the rot. I've known the vendor for— He wouldn't cheat me, I'm sure of it."

"I don't think that he did," Marcus said. "But charming against rats and moisture—well, that's different than protecting against other magic."

"But who'd—" Trebius's fleshy jaw worked wordlessly a moment. "I don't understand. I've crossed no mages—I've no enemies—I mean, I have business rivals, sure and don't we all? But no one that would—This is—"

Marcus held both his hands up in a calming gesture. "I cannot make much of a guess, friend Trebius, but if you and all your fellows are experiencing similar troubles, I imagine it has nothing to do with you, yourselves."

The warehouse-keeper's brow creased. "Then—Why? Who would target us? We-we feed the city, we do!" He rolled his shoulders. "Well, we're a part of it."

'Gods, for a swifter mind.' There were pieces here, and they fit together somehow, but he couldn't quite assemble them—not on the spot, not with Trebius in a flutter at his side. "I need more information, Trebius, before I can say anything for sure—and I'm certain you can appreciate that I have no wish to stir up a panic, nor to mislead you in any fashion. For now, yes, I can swear out to Licinius Cornicen that it was not your negligence. But I'd like to bring some other mages in here to assess the damage." A Shadow mage, maybe; they were sometimes talented with rot. Such a rare gift, though, there weren't many of them in the city. 'Perhaps this is a matter for the Augian Commission.'

Like most mages, Marcus preferred to stay beneath the Commission's notice as much as possible. Being around them always felt like sitting under the gaze of his old magister, certain he had erred in his lessons but with no idea what he had done to displease. Some things, though, needed professionals—and there was no one in the city more experienced at recognizing magical signatures and tracking mages than the members of the Commission.

"Trebius, I would thank you to say nothing of this to anyone." Unlikely; as soon as Marcus departed, Trebius was likely to start squawking to his fellow warehouse-keepers. But maybe a bit of pressure could keep the rumors within their circle, at least. "Whoever has targeted you, let them think you ignorant of their schemes. If they suspect you're on to them, well—"

"They may make it worse," Trebius finished, picking up the thought. "Sacred Jupiter."

"May I bring another mage here, to look into it?"

"Yes, yes, of course. I'll tell the guards, if I'm not about, to let you in. Whenever you like."

"Thank you, Trebius. And thank you for bringing this matter to my attention." They were approaching the door out of the chamber now, and only Marcus's inherently steady nature kept him from sprinting for the ramp. *'How did no one else notice this? So much magic, such a powerful curse—and in all these buildings?'* But he had not felt it until he had touched the rotted grain. "I promise you, I will get to the bottom of whatever this is."

And expeditiously he would, too. Aven could ill afford calamity like this at the onset of winter.

XI

Central Iberia

For four days, Neitin had fled through the forest.

She had only a vague idea of where she was. North of the Tagus; mostly headed westward. But Sakarbik changed their direction frequently, cutting jagged lines up and down hills. Throwing off pursuit, Neitin was sure. Every so often, Sakarbik would grab a fistful of pine needles or a clump of dirt, whisper her magical words over it, and then cast it into the air behind them.

For four days, it had worked. Neitin was not optimist enough to assume it would continue to do so.

On the fourth evening, they came to rest in the center of a cluster of trees. Murmuring a low, musical chant, Sakarbik stroked strips of bark, reached out to pinch leaves between her fingers and thumb, bent to inspect exposed roots.

Matigentis watched her in fascination, then pitched himself onto all fours and tried to shuffle in her direction. "Easy, sweet boy," Neitin said, tugging on the back of Mati's tunic to keep him from crawling too far from her. He squawked some nonsense words in response, but his scornful meaning was clear. The past few days had been hard on him. He was too enamored of activity to enjoy being carried all day, whether in Neitin's arms or in a sling. "Come on, aren't you hungry?"

That, too, elicited a scowl. Mati was too old to still be exclusively on the breast. At the camp, they had begun to give him meat drippings, eggs and cheese, supplementing Neitin's milk, but on their flight from camp, Neitin and Sakarbik had agreed that he should take as much from his mother as possible. They had some food left, dried meats and hard biscuits and dried fruits—and Neitin and Sakarbik needed as much as possible.

Still, when Mati gave up on her breast after only a few moments, Neitin gave him a strip of dried goat flesh to suck on and slowly consume.

"We will have better for him soon," Sakarbik promised her, coming back with an armful of branches and tinder. "We are not far from a village that will, I believe, give us some shelter. We can resupply for both us and the boy."

"We should have fled months ago," Neitin sighed, picking up some of the branches and beginning to strip them bare. "When he was lighter, quieter, less mobile. I wish…"

"No sense in that," Sakarbik said, not quite a snap, but not soft, either. "We left when we left. We must make the best of it."

They built a small triangle from the sticks, as soon as they were bare of leaves, and piled the kindling in the middle. As Sakarbik took flint from one of her belt-pouches and began to strike, Neitin tried to get her bearings. The sun set so early, this close to the winter solstice; already it had dropped well beneath the tree line, giving the sky a white-gold glow. "Where are we going?" she asked. "What village will shelter us, I mean?"

Sakarbik's lips twisted slightly. "I do not know," she admitted.

"You don't *know*?" Neitin asked, astonished. "How can we trust—"

"My guidance comes from the gods," Sakarbik shot back. "Do you trust them?"

"Yes, but—"

"My people are far to the south. Yours, far to the west. We will reach neither before we run out of food."

Matigentis popped the strip of meat out of his mouth and fussed noisily, distressed by their sharp tones. "Sa!" he cried, then looked to Neitin. "Ma!"

Sakarbik rolled her eyes, but lowered her voice. "Your son is a natural peacemaker," she commented.

"Good," Neitin murmured, reaching out to stroke his hair.

"My point," Sakarbik went on, as the leaves took flame. They both began tending the growing fire, prodding it with longer sticks. "My point is that we were never going to get all the way to safety in one rush. Not with our supplies limited to what we can carry, and not with what we must do to throw off pursuit. I worry—" A frown creased her face.

"What?"

Sakarbik sighed. "I am trying, very hard, to cover our tracks. But I am only one woman, one magic-worker. Your husband still has several at his disposal, even after so many fell at Toletum. And Bailar..." Her shoulders crept up towards her ears. "I have felt a presence, drawing nearer to us all day. If we can get to a village, enlist the help of another magic-woman—for I believe that is who the *besteki* lead us to—then we may evade them. But I think we have another day or two of walking before we can get there."

"And you're—you're sure this village will be kind?" They were in Luse-tani territory, after all; the villages would be loyal to Ekialde.

"To a pair of women and a young boy fleeing danger? Why should they not be?" Sakarbik cocked her head to one side. Her raven hair was knotted and messy, as Neitin's knew her own must be as well, and it flopped limply over her shoulder. "I do not mean to tell anyone, except perhaps a friendly magic-woman, that you are the *erregerra's* wife, nor this his son. Let them think we are refugees, on our way to rebuild our lives, perhaps in Olissippo. I am sure we will not be the first nor last they encounter."

"There is wisdom in that."

Sakarbik snorted, taking a blanket from her pack and flapping it out alongside the fire. "Of course there is. I said it. Now let me rest my eyes a bit, and try to keep that boy quiet."

Keeping Mati entertained was no large trouble. Though grumpy about his circumstances, he was a sweet-natured child. *'Thanks be to Nabia,'* Neitin thought, as they played at rolling a ball back and forth. It was one of the on-ly toys she had brought with them; any seemed an indulgence, extra weight to carry, but if it kept the child contented, it was worth it.

Neitin maintained the low-burning fire as twilight turned to true dark-ness. A risk, she knew, but these woods were dense; the light would not travel far, and it did not give off much smoke. It was too cold to do without it entirely. In this, as in so much else, she allowed herself to be led by Sakar-bik. Neitin had never before lived rougher than in Ekialde's camp, with at-tendants all around her and a cozy brazier in her tent.

A branch snapped in the woods. A frequent enough sound; there were animals everywhere. Sakarbik assured her that even wolves and bears preferred to keep clear of humans, unless they were truly desperate, and the winter had not yet been so harsh as to drive them to such audacity. Another reason for keeping the fire burning, though.

Neitin had managed to stop flinching at noises from the trees—but this time, Sakarbik sat up, sharp and alert as a hound on the scent. "Get as near the fire as you can stand it." Her tone was so firm, it did not occur to Neitin to question her. She scooted herself and Mati closer to the flames while Sakarbik rummaged in one of her belt-pouches. Mati was sucking on his fingers, looking curious but not yet distressed at the sudden motions from the adults.

Speaking the secret language of the magic-women, Sakarbik moved around them in a circle, sprinkling what looked like sand upon the ground. Then she knelt on the opposite side of the fire from Neitin, pressing her fingers into the earth.

"Whatever happens," Sakarbik said, "do not move. Certainly do not step outside the circle. And hold tight to the boy."

Neitin listened for whatever had set off Sakarbik, but heard only silence. Then she realized—that was the problem. No hooting owls, no buzz of moths or chirp of beetles, no click of bats. No hare or ferret rustling through the underbrush, no lynx padding carefully in a tree. Even the wind had stilled. Despite her heavy cloak and the heat of the fire, Neitin's skin prickled, all her hairs standing on end.

The moan began almost too low to be heard, a vibration Neitin felt in her chest a half-breath before her ears registered it. A hunting horn, she thought at first, but she knew that for vain hope. No man's lungs could sustain so long and even a blast, and who hunted at night?

She thought she knew what would follow: a rising pitch, the moan growing to an awful keen, a pale mist rolling in between the tree trunks. Her heart plummeted to her stomach, waiting for the signs she had seen so often in the war-camp, proof Bailar had set *akdraugi* to track and terrify them.

Yet no mist came. Sakarbik kept muttering in the magic-tongue. Mati nuzzled into his mother's shoulder, lulled by the now-familiar sound of Sakarbik's chanting. Neitin petted his head, trying to take comfort in his downy dark hair, his weight in her arms, his scent. She peered into the gloom beyond their circle of light. Did she see something moving, a blacker patch against the dark forest? Or was it only her imagination?

In the next heartbeat, she had her answer. A shrieking noise, half a whistle and half a howl, split the air, startling Neitin so much that she nearly pitched backward into the fire. Mati began to cry, and she pressed his head into her chest, making futile shushing noises. Sakarbik's chanting grew faster, sharper.

A pounding noise, growing closer in the ever-darker night. A cloud covered the moon, or some eldritch force blotted out its light, and that of all the stars. Closer still the sound, like hoofbeats, charging toward their circle. A shape lunging out of the darkness, hurling itself toward Neitin, and she did not have breath enough to scream, only to give a strangled croak—

A flash of golden light erupted from the ground, everywhere that Sakarbik had scattered her sand. Neitin saw only a hint of a horrible shape, too many legs tipped with cruel claws, before the light hurled it backward into the night.

The light grew into a dome, curling above their heads, and despite her terror, a warmth entered Neitin's chest and flooded her tensed muscles. 'Besteki!' Their protecting spirits, summoned by Sakarbik's magic. When Neitin had seen them before, they always looked like blurry figures, not human, but distinct spirits, bobbing and weaving among each other. Now there was no distinguishing between them, but Neitin could feel their radiant goodness.

Mati's wails subsided to snuffles, even as more of the shadow-beasts flung themselves at the golden dome. Like diseased animals, lacking the sense to know when they were doing themselves harmed, the fiends kept coming. Three or four of them, Neitin thought, though it was hard to tell for sure. They prowled around the outside of the golden dome, scrabbled at its base, tried to leap upon its apex, though every contact repelled them. Were their screeches of pain or merely frustration?

Sakarbik hardly seemed to be taking the time to breathe. Words poured out of her in a near-unbroken stream. Her golden eyes shone wildly in the firelight, as bright and fierce as the *besteki* magic surrounding them. Her fingers clawed into the dry, cold earth. She wasn't blinking. Neitin tore her eyes away from Sakarbik and the dome of light, curling around Mati, her head bent to his. She rocked back and forth, as much for her own comfort as for his.

She had no idea how much time passed before the attacks began to taper off. The yowls that followed their attempts grew less frequent, and the keening noise dimmed. Sakarbik's voice slowed back down, dropping to a whisper. It was longer still before she ceased her chanting. Only then did Neitin raise her head. The golden dome had faded away, but the moon was back out, its lumpen not-quite-fullness much lower in the sky, glowing from behind the treetops. The song of the forest returned, too, the faint cries of hunting birds and the wind stirring the branches.

With an enormous sigh, Sakarbik puddled against the ground, her face ashen. Neitin had never seen her look so tired. "We must go at first light," Sakarbik said.

"You're in no state to—"

"I'll be fine by morning. We must go. Those shadow-beasts will be reporting back to their master, where they found us. My magic can help to cover our tracks, but they have my scent now, and they will follow. We must find that village, resupply, but I fear we will not be safe there long. We must put space between us and that thrice-damned Bailar. Space, and water, if we can manage it."

XII

Esquiline Hill, City of Aven

The house on the Esquiline was not fully outfitted yet, but had already become a base of operations. Vibia and Latona both referred to the study, with its maps of the city and its lattice of helpful texts, as their "praetorium." Aula's joke, at first, but one they increasingly took more seriously.

December advanced, and so did the enemy lines, in the form of spoiled food, unlucky accidents, and the same night-hauntings that had plagued them since the summer. Every day, a new misfortune to add to the map; every day, a new screed from Arrius Buteo and the other Optimates, decrying the moral decay of the nation and the physical manifestations such inattention to the *mos maiorum* caused.

'We push back one fight at a time,' Latona thought as she laced her sandals, the sturdiest—and warmest—she owned. *'Every citizen we defend is a victory. And every day is a chance to find the evidence that will expose the Augians for their treachery.'*

As she prepared for another excursion, Aula fretted. "You've almost been killed by this woman once. I know you want to help—I know you *must*, I know Juno wants it of you, I know, I know—but that doesn't make you responsible for every accident befalling every worker anywhere in the city! What was it last week? A man who fell off a ladder and blamed it on *lemures*?"

"A man whose ladder broke beneath him," Latona said, with exaggerated patience. "And if no more came of it than I was able to give his foreman a good tongue-lashing over the need for new tools if they have any intention of doing proper work, so be it."

Aula rolled her eyes, but Latona could sense the frisson of anxiety running beneath her affected exasperation.

"And," Latona went on, "that was only one street over from that roof collapse two days earlier. People are jumpy and rightly so."

"In the depths of the forest at night," Alhena intoned from her seat at the edge of Latona's bed, "a man might easily mistake a bush for a bear." When her sisters turned to look at her, she blushed, but stuck to her analogy. "I only meant, people who are scared make mistakes. Innocent things seem like monsters. So when we know very well that there have been *lemures* and other wretched spirits in the area—well, we can hardly blame them for attributing accidents or quirks of nature to fiends and spirits."

"Exactly so, pet," Latona said. She reached up, gathering her hair, wrapping it around her hand once, then circling the tail around itself and flipping it over. Merula handed her a pin of polished ebony to jab through it, holding the mass of golden ringlets in a simple knot. "If there *is* Discordian menace at work, we need to know."

"And if there isn't," Aula said, her voice softer, "then you may well be able to dispel some fear by saying so."

"It will do no harm to cool off panicked spleens," Latona said. "Indeed, it may serve our purpose just as well as actually picking apart Discordian curses. They're counting on hysteria taking over the populace. Anything I can do to lower the general state of agitation within Aven's walls..."

Her voice trailed off. If she admitted truth to herself, she knew she could never do enough. The city was too large, and people were too scared. Panic spread ever so much faster than calm could settle. *'They're winning.'* She reached down to adjust her sandal, tightening the strap. *'But I don't have to sit down and let them do so unchallenged.'*

"Are you taking Vibia or Rubellia?" Aula asked.

Latona shook her head. "Vibia's tied up on the Aventine today, and Rubellia—well, she's more suited for training than, ah, combat." Still strange, to think of her life in such terms. Straightening, she smiled over at Alhena. "But I thought you might like to come with me."

Surprise, then fear, then a touch of excitement rippled through Alhena's emotions. "Do you mean it?"

"I do. You said you wanted to be more involved, and this one doesn't sound terribly dangerous. It's in Vatinius Obir's territory, so we'll be well-protected, and since it's not an *umbra* haunting, we can go in daylight."

"Then—then yes. I would quite like to." Alhena stood up, fingers hastily plaiting her loose red curls. "If I can understand the Discordians' work better, I might be able to—I don't know, to recognize its shape in my dreams and visions. Then I might be of more use to you."

Latona wrapped an arm around her little sister and kissed her temple. "I wish you wouldn't worry about being 'of use.' You're perfect as you are."

Alhena's snorting reply was clearly skeptical. "I'm a long way from perfect."

"Yes, well, so is Aula, but she's never let that slow her down."

"Hey!"

It was Obir's second-in-command, the Tennic former warrior Ebredus, who led the ladies to the site of the trouble. The young man who met them there was twenty or so, sun-browned and rope-muscled. He introduced himself as Seppius, and he had a blunt way about him. Not rude, but straightforward. *A natural fit for Obir's domain,* Latona thought.

"Something's wrong, noble ladies," Seppius said. "I don't know how to explain it. But something's wrong."

He led Latona and Alhena to a fountain in a crevice between two buildings. It was typical of this part of Aven: not so ornate as that which you would find on the Palatine or the Caelian Hills or in the public forums. This humble cylinder stood hip-high, with no more ornamentation than a leafy pattern embossed upon its cap, but its purpose was vital. Most of Aven's citizens took their water from fountains like these, part of the vast network springing from the city's aqueducts.

"We've checked—there's nothing wrong with the fountain itself. No cracks or leaks. But the water's got a strange, sour taste to it, and it's been giving folk odd dreams." Alhena perked up a bit; dreams were, after all, more her territory than fiends and demons. "Sometimes people are weak or dizzy after drinking directly from it or washing their faces here. Seems the effects lessen if they take the water home."

Nodding, Latona scrutinized the fountain itself. "You've done a thorough assessment." Not everyone would have thought to have made that connection between proximity to the fountain and the intensity of ill effects. "Let me see what I can determine."

Latona wasted no effort in projecting a soothing energy at Seppius; he seemed well in control of himself, stepping back to give her room to work. She could not see anything uncommon about the structure of the fountain. *'Not that I know anything much about them...'* But it appeared solid and cared-for, not crumbling or mossy. She placed her hands on the capstone, running her palms around the lip.

Alhena was watching her, keen-eyed. She wouldn't be able to see what Latona did, of course, but she wanted to learn, so Latona explained aloud. "I'm going to send my Spirit magic down, to see if I can feel any Discordian influence. Depending on what it is, I might be able to cleanse it myself, or I might need to come back with Vibia."

"Tell me what it feels like, please. The magic, I mean. As you use it."

Whyever she wanted to know, Latona was happy to oblige. She closed her eyes and took a deep breath. "Sending my energy out feels... like a sigh." Her fingers traced the edges of the leafy pattern on the stone. "Spirit senses such differences in things. I didn't know at first, when I'd only ever used it on humans, who are so complex. But then that tree in Stabiae—plants have a different..." Her lips twisted as she tried to frame her words accurately. "It's like different fabrics. There's not only one way it changes. The weight of the cloth, the tightness of the weave, whether it's rough or smooth, whether it might make you warm or leave you cool, how it would drape hung from a body, how it moves—all those things together. Animals feel different, too."

"And demons," Alhena said softly.

"Just so."

"Are the other things, plants and animals, are they easier than humans?"

"You'd think so. The advantage of humans, though, is that with so many thoughts and emotions going on all the time, whatever's most important—or most upsetting or frightening or just most immediate—tends to pop up to the top. Easy to sense what a person is feeling in a given moment; harder to tell what's going on beneath the surface, what they've buried or hidden or forgotten. With things that aren't human, it's like it's *all* beneath the surface."

"What does a tree remember..." Alhena murmured, not exactly a question. "Or a stone... and how long must it take them to do so..."

Leaving her sister to her pondering, Latona rolled her shoulders back. "Very well. Here we go."

With another deep breath, as though she were about to plunge into a pool, Latona pushed her magic *down*.

Sure enough, as she explored, nudging the tendrils of her magic out, she found Discordian putrefaction, slippery and mucous. She felt no anchor, no charm tied anywhere within the fountain, and surely the Esquiline men would have found it, had there been one. Then she realized: the viscous sense her magic was prodding up against wasn't merely magical; it was a substance, the actual vector of the Discordian curse. *'How did it—? Someone must have poured it in.'*

Horrifying thought: In Stabiae and Aven so far, the Discordians tampered with solid matter, trees and stalks of wheat and crates of lentils. A liquid curse was something Latona had never dreamed they could tie to a location. *'Maybe they didn't mean to. Maybe this was meant to infiltrate more of the city's pipes. Or maybe... Gods above, maybe it was a test.'* In Stabiae, the Fracture mage Corinna had experimented with small curses before moving to attempting to cover entire fields, then took what worked and put it into practice in Aven, on a much larger population.

"Latona?" Alhena prompted. "What do you—?"

"Sorry, lamb. There's a lot to consider." She flicked her eyes meaningfully at Seppius, standing nearby with a worried air. Inciting more panic was precisely what she did *not* want to do, and so she would not discuss the possibility of the Discordians tampering with Aven's water supply until they were safely at home or in the praetorium.

Instead, she closed her eyes, sliding back into the flow of magic, and resumed narrating the process of seeking out every crevice where the Discordian curse had lodged and purging it, as she would poison from a body.

As she spoke, Latona realized how much that was once almost terrifyingly unfamiliar had become routine to her over the past months. That, in itself, was alarming. Voicing it to Alhena made her consider the process in a new light, though, and she found herself adjusting her technique even as she described it to her sister.

Then, she halted mid-sentence.

"Latona?"

Latona held up a hand. Unlike Aula, Alhena did not require further instruction regarding quietude.

Amid the expected energies, stone and water and the jagged edges of the Discordian curse, she found something else. Cool and clean, with a gentle flow, swirling around the edges of the fountain. Water magic. Traces of it, weakly formed and without any real structure. Untrained magic, certainly. But *there*, alive and instinctual.

"Seppius," she said softly, "could you come closer, please?" Seppius obliged. Latona opened her eyes slowly, and when she met his gaze, she could feel the truth of it, utterly resonant. "Seppius, has anyone ever suggested to you..."

She bit her lower lip. How to put this? She had no memory of learning she had been gifted with magical talents. No one had ever had to tell her. It had always simply been a part of her, an immutable given circumstance of her life, from her earliest memories. She had only been four when the strength of her gifts was apparent enough that Gaia Claudia took her on as an apprentice. The idea of making it to adulthood with no idea was unfathomable.

In the country, perhaps, it would not be so unusual. A mild talent, manifesting in someone who rarely saw priests or other mages, might go unnoticed for decades, even a lifetime, their gift seen only as a knack for their trade. But here in Aven, in the very heart of the city, where hundreds of mages lived? How could it have happened? *'And if it happened once, gods above, could there be more like him?'*

Seppius was staring at her, confused and curious. "Domina?"

Latona cleared her throat and tried again. "One of the gifts of Spirit is the ability to see the magic of others at work."

He nodded. "Yes, Domina. Everyone says that's why you're so good at rooting out these *lemures*."

"Yes... That's been a boon. But..." Her eyes went to the fountain. "Whoever acted to spoil your waters, theirs is not the only magic at work here."

Seppius blinked a few times. "Domina, I'm not sure I take your meaning."

'Be plain. Talking in circles does neither of you any favors.' Latona reached out again for the cool thread of Water magic, gentle and refreshing and try-

ing its best to fight against the Discordian influence within the fountain. "Seppius, this fountain is well cared-for. I can sense Water magic at work, and unless I miss my guess, it's coming from you."

An uncomprehending stare was all that met this declaration at first. Then Seppius shook his head, laughing. "Domina, you're—begging your pardon, I don't mean to be rude, but you're mistaken. You must be."

"I do not believe I am," she said, carefully, tentatively, "though it may seem incredible."

She frowned, considering. Water could see magical workings, too, sometimes—and certainly ought to be able to see its own, with close attention. *I wonder... if I amplified it enough, would he...?*

She held out a hand, palm up. "Would you allow me to try something?"

He stared at her hand as though he had never seen one before. "Domina, I—"

"Please trust me," she said, fighting the compulsion to use Spirit magic on him to get him to agree. She could, she knew; it would be wrong, she also knew. "This may not even work, but it will do you no harm, in any case, and if it does work, I think you will understand what I mean."

Hesitantly, as though he were trying to pet an unfamiliar dog, Seppius extended a hand and delicately placed his fingertips against hers. It was for Latona to grip more tightly, as though that might augment the channel she sought to create. It did help, in a way; she could feel his pulse.

She couldn't make the Water magic itself stronger. As an inimical element, it would sense the Fire in her and shy away if she were not careful. She focused on the signature alone, that thread of crisp blue lacing around the interior of the fountain. Messy plaits of Water-born energy, an uneven and haphazard latticework. A faint signature, magic worked on instinct rather than with purpose, but also well-worn into the stones where it had lived for so long. An etching, scratching the surface, but indelible nonetheless.

Show yourself, Water magic...' How to convince it? Fire magic, she would have told to burn brightly, to blaze and scorch and flare white-hot. But for Water... *Think of the sun sparkling on the river, the glint and shimmer of a minnow's scales, the roll and tumble over the rocks and pebbles of the riverbed. Show us that shine!*

A sudden rush of cold poured over Latona's arms: the Water magic responding. What Seppius was seeing or feeling, she had no idea; she saw magical signatures as lines of bright color, and her tongue thought she had taken a quenching gulp of freshly-drawn water, but she knew that other elements sensed it differently. Whatever it was, Seppius was looking frantically between the fountain and his own chest.

"No." He shook his head. "No, it can't be—I can't be—" As much fear as wonder lived in his wide eyes. "Someone would've noticed by now, if I was—it's—it's just not possible!"

Latona *did* extend a bit of calming energy towards him then. "This must be quite a shock."

"That ain't the half of it, Domina."

She placed a hand on his shoulder. "I can recommend some people for you to talk to—priests, if you like, but Davina of the bathhouses is both kind and experienced. For now, though, how would you like to cleanse your fountain? As much as you care for it, you might be able to do a great deal of good here."

Man of his word that he was, Marcus Autronius returned to the Velabrium with a member of the Augian Commission in tow. It had taken a few days to get one of them to make space in his schedule.

Too many days, in Marcus's opinion. *'They may barely know me from a hole in the ground, for all that I am a mage and under their purview, but you would think the summons of a tribune of the plebs would be considered with more urgency!'*

Salonius Decur, though, plodded along, his black-bordered toga drawn up over his head to protect his bald pate from the chill, and when Marcus brought him to the afflicted granary owned by Trebius Perus, he sighed with exaggerated patience. "Tell me what you think you see, Tribune."

As Salonius laced his fingers together in front of his stomach, settling back on his heels, Marcus attempted to pinpoint what about the man's tone was bothering him so much. Salonius's demeanor, tolerantly tranquil, reminded him of a magister from his youth, a long-suffering Athaecan man who considered it his earthly travail to suffer the limping arithmetical attempts of his charges.

'*Salonius may have three decades on me,*' Marcus thought, '*but I'm a man grown, a mage born, and a tribune elected. I deserve more respect than an errant schoolboy.*'

He cleared his throat and gestured out to the wheat. "The complainant wished to show me that the rot in his grain was not due to his negligence, but to circumstances beyond his control." This, he had told Salonius before, but the man's vague attention warranted reiteration. "The building is as he says: clean, well-built, magically warded. Yes?"

"Yes, yes, I can see all of that." Salonius sniffed. "The warding work is what I would expect for this district."

Marcus didn't take the time to parse the slight in that comment. "So I came to inspect the grain itself. Nothing's wrong with how it's stored, and the black patches are random, not centralized like you'd expect from a leak or vermin. When I touched the grains, that's when I noticed it—a magical sensation, like stinging nettles." The itch had hit him again as soon as they entered, now that he knew to expect it. "It's some sort of curse, Commissioner. I'm sure of it. But my only element is Earth. I can only feel the damage it's done. I don't know its nature, and I can't trace a signature."

"Hmm." Salonius's calm expression did not communicate an awareness of the severity of the situation.

"I should add, Commissioner, that the good citizen who owns this granary tells me others nearby are similarly afflicted." Marcus had already told Salonius this, too. The more placid Salonius appeared, the more provoked Marcus felt to try and elicit a stronger response from him. "They are concerned—and it is a concern I share—that the city's food supply for the winter may be in jeopardy if this isn't stopped."

Salonius rolled his shoulders back and drew an amulet from underneath his tunic—a bit of rock crystal, symbolic of Light, roughly carved into a shape that Marcus charitably assumed was the god Apollo. "Very well," Salonius said. "Let me see what I can deduce. Step back a bit, would you, lad?"

No doubt for another mage who could see the workings, what Salonius did next would have been fascinating—or, at least, an opportunity to practice their own skills, and perhaps to judge his. Marcus, however, could only watch, grounding his frustration in the depths of patience the gods had given him, as Salonius clutched his amulet and muttered his invocations. A practiced drone, with nothing of inspiration or urgency in it; ritual words, over and over.

When at last the recitation stopped, Salonius unhurriedly wandered down the aisle, then opened a sack of grain. Even from a distance, the rot within made Marcus's skin itch. Salonius touched one of the blackened patches briefly. *'He must feel it. How could he not?'* That Salonius did not recoil, that no revulsion registered on his face—that had to be a mark of his age and training, his dignity and composure.

He came back to Marcus at the same pace, no sign of concern or haste. "Well!" he announced, clapping Marcus on the shoulder. "I'm afraid you're mistaken, my lad."

Marcus resisted the urge to point out that he was thirty-two years old and thus demonstrably no one's "lad" any longer. "Mistaken? Do please explain, Commissioner. What I felt—"

"Oh, there may be a little magic at play—raw stuff, though. How can I put this?" Salonius rocked back on his heels, lacing his fingers together in front of his belly, again adopting the air of an instructing magister. "You're an Earth mage, so you're used to your source of power being all around you, all the time. It's so common that you're, well, dulled to it a bit." Marcus's brow knitted, though he tried to keep any further expression of pique off his face. Salonius picked up on it anyway, perhaps through the truth-revealing insights of Light. "Now, I don't mean that as an insult, lad, no, not at all. More like—It's like going into the hot room at the baths. The weight of the air is tremendous at first, but then, you acclimate. *You* are permanently acclimated to the source of your magic around you—or, as it were, underneath you. So are Air mages, but it's not like that for all the elements. When a lamp is lit or a hearth is kindled, there is then the potential for Fire magic, yes? So too, when something rots, the potential for Shadow and Fracture magic exist. I expect what you've felt here is that potential." He cocked his head to one side. "You're sure you've no Spirit or Water in you?"

"Not that anyone ever noticed," Marcus said, "so I can't imagine how I'd feel Shadow or Fracture at work. What I felt was—was *wrongness*." He wished for a more elegant expression. "My magic told me something was amiss. The grain that should have been solidly of the Earth had been..." He sighed, reaching for a phrase. "Had been disrupted, somehow." Yes, that was the right word for it. With growing confidence, he went on: "As if the essence of the grain—those qualities which make it good and healthful, but also its state of being, its current place between a thing grown and a thing consumed—all that, mangled. Unnaturally mangled. I'm sure—Commissioner, I am *sure* I would not have felt it if it were natural rot. I've seen rotted food before, certainly, and never felt such an offensive abnormality."

"It can be confusing," Salonius said, sidling closer to Marcus. "You're not used to experiencing this kind of magic. But surely this is why you called for me, yes? For my expertise?"

A strange itch started up at the back of Marcus's neck, all the hairs pricking up. Was it only the effect of the cursed grain, or something more? "Commissioner, I am telling you, something is not right here. Something has been—"

"And I am telling *you*—" Salonius's tone changed. A heat had entered it: not an explosion of anger, but persistent, steady, like the hot coals which forged a blade. "There is nothing to be concerned with here. No reason to be anxious. No reason to be curious. You won't forget this all happened. You're too smart for that. But you can stop worrying about it. It doesn't concern you any longer."

Just like that, Marcus believed him. His muscles lost their tension, and his mind cleared. "You're right." His tongue moved strangely, like it had prepared to say different words, but now—now these were the only words that mattered. "Yes, of course."

"I expect you feel a bit foolish."

A tickle in his throat made him laugh. "I do!" he said, surprised to realize it. "I do, I—I can't imagine why I thought this was so dire." He *had*, only moments before, yet now all the concern, all the urgency evaporated like a shallow puddle under bright sun.

"There, no need to chastise yourself," Salonius said, placing a hand on his back and guiding him down the ramp that led out of the building. "It's a burden, serving as tribune of plebs! So many people clamoring for your attention all the time, always tugging on your nerves. Easy to get overwhelmed."

"Yes... yes, there is a lot of work to do."

"And you do your duty well! You have much to be proud of. The gods smile on diligence, lad. Always better too much than too little, eh? But now you know! And you need not concern yourself over this again..."

With each step away from the granary, Marcus's chest felt lighter—though the itch at the back of his neck would not settle, and still he felt sure there had been something else he meant to say.

XIII

Only Merula's utter tyranny over the boy Urco, who watched the door of the Vitellian domus late at night, allowed Latona to slip into the house without repercussions. She and Vibia had been called to two different curse-burdened apartment buildings that evening. The first went easily enough, but the second—the second *hurt*.

The *lemures* had been the vicious kind, jabbing into Latona and Vibia like javelins and trying to wrench control of their own magic away from them. *Pila*, they were calling this variety, named for the legionary weapons, to distinguish them from the haunting *umbrae* or the soul-hungry *devorae*.

The magical signatures were different, too. The first was less practiced in this dubious art. The mage responsible knew the forms of the curse that would crack open the gates between the worlds and let the *lemures* through, but had not anchored it very well. Vibia had been almost disdainful as she unraveled it.

The second, Latona was certain, was the work of Anca Corinna.

"We keep saying we can't continue like this," Vibia grumbled. "We may not be alone any longer, we have our informants, we're setting up a place to work, but there's still no one else who can do *this*."

Latona didn't have an answer. Fracture and Spirit were two of the rarest gifts the gods bestowed upon mages—and most of the Spirit mages in the city with any appreciable power were either on the Augian Commission or closely associated with them. There was little Fausta, but Latona had not yet resigned herself to bringing the girl into danger.

"We'll figure something out," was all she could manage.

"We need to find Anca Corinna and whoever's helping her," Vibia said, "and *end* them."

They had tried to track the Discordian devotee at the center of their troubles, but if she lived at her brother's house, she was well-secluded there, beyond their reach. *'Vibia's right, though. We can't go on like this.'*

The night's effort had drained Latona's vigor. She was learning to moderate her efforts better, not to let too much of her essence bleed out with her magic, but she had to do the work, whatever it required. Dealing with the *pila* was particularly exhausting, since it was in their very nature to steal energy. Latona had had to shield herself *and* Vibia while also guarding against that theft. *'And the damned charm took forever to find...'*

Latona barely managed to slip her sandals off before collapsing into bed, still dressed. When she woke, many hours later, the angle of the sun in the window told her it was past mid-morning. The house was quieter than she expected: no one in the sitting rooms or atrium. "Where is everyone?"

"Your father is already being in the Forum," Merula answered. "Lady Aula went out with him, though I believe her goal is being the market. Helva wanted her to look at a new pork vendor. There is being some problem with our usual? Short supplies, they are claiming?" Merula, never much interested in household management, shrugged indifferently. "Lady Alhena is going to the—the special house. Said she wanted to be working on a translation, and the book is there."

Latona knew what she meant: Aula's house on the Esquiline. *'We really must come up with a better name for it.'* Latona squinted against the light, wondering if she were up for the day or if she wanted to fall back into bed. "Did she go alone?"

"She has Mus with her, of course, and she is with the Lady Terentilla, who dropped by not long after your father's clients left. Lady Tilla is bringing a guard with her, one of her own people." Anyone used to looking after Terentilla's antics was unlikely to be someone prone to gossip, so that was well. "Lady Aula is telling your father that you are having a headache," Merula added, as she herded Latona back into her room and set about the work of putting her in fresh clothes.

"She wasn't lying," Latona said. Her head did ache. *Everything* ached.

"You are needing much food," Merula tsked. "Water, too. And rest. Maybe no running all around the damned city today?"

"I'd be delighted if no calamities required my attention, I assure you." Latona rubbed both hands over her face, massaging life into her cheeks.

"And what of your rest? You were up as late as I was, but you're awfully energetic."

"Yes, but I was fighting no demons, which seems a strenuous use of time."

"Well, you have me there."

Latona spent the rest of the morning, once Merula saw her fed, lying on a couch with a damp cloth over her face, wishing her temples would stop throbbing. *Monstrously unfair to feel the effects of overindulging in wine without having the pleasure of doing so.* Rather than falling back asleep, her mind turned the Discordian problem over and over, retreading old paths without scraping free any new answers.

In the early afternoon, Merula came in and poked her in the toe. "Here is being something to cheer you up, Domina."

"Mmrmm?" was as much of a response as Latona felt up to giving.

"Mail packet. From Iberia."

Latona sat bolt upright, damp cloth dropping into her lap, hand already outstretched despite the dizziness roiling her head. "Give it here, and *do* stop smirking, Merula, your face might stick like that."

"Enh. Worse fates." The smirk turned into a grin, though, as Merula dropped a letter into Latona's hand.

The seal, a falcon-in-flight set into dark wax, set her heart racing: Sempronius Tarren's personal emblem.

Vibia had confessed that she alerted her brother to Latona's condition. Latona wasn't certain how much Vibia knew, and still sensed that she didn't fully approve of whatever she *did* know, but the gesture had been, at the least, a recognition that Latona and Sempronius were important to each other. Latona, too, wrote to him as soon as she recovered.

For many days, they heard nothing back. Longer than expected, thought not yet long enough to worry. Late autumn storms tore through the Middle Sea, and even a magically-guided bird could be lost or taken by a predator.

Latona popped the seal and began to read.

Sempronius wrote, as ever, with awareness that the letter would pass through several hands before it reached her. They had no reason to think any of the carriers would pry—*'Well. Except Aula, who absolutely would.'*—and it wasn't as though she had a husband to take offense any longer, but still, prudence was the best course.

He had chanced one word of errant passion, though, a step further than ever he ventured before. *'Dearest Latona,'* he began, an endearment rendered in sharp strokes and heavy ink.

Latona could almost see him, sitting in the officers' quarters in a snug fortress, perhaps wearing furs over his scarlet tunic and cloak, or sitting near a brazier to fend off the growing winter cold. She pictured him writing the jagged lines of that superlative, *dearest*, in a fit of unrestrained ardor—then mastering himself, remembering himself, to write the rest.

> *'I am more glad than I can possibly express to hear that you are in good health. Since my sister apprised me of your illness, I have implored the gods daily on your behalf. I am sure it is far more credit to your excellent character than to my beseeching that you have recovered, but I give thanks to divinity in any case, and I promised a mighty sacrifice to Asclepius and Juno Cantatia to pay my own part of gratitude.*

> *'I would ask you to take care enough of your precious self that no further maladies befall you—but I know your nature, and I admire you for it. You will, I know, do what is necessary.'*

That mention of Juno Cantatia, the goddess in her aspect as governess of mages, was his only way of acknowledging that he knew her malady had been no mere illness. The following words, *'I admire you for it,'* carried all the more weight. Sempronius had never chastised her for her ambitions, never thought her unnatural for them, never considered her safety a higher priority than her duty to her city and her gods. Warmth spread through her chest, chasing away all the lingering pain and weariness from the night.

Before she could get any further, a commotion in the atrium alerted Latona to her sister's return to the house and, thus, imminent interruption. "What news?" Aula asked, flumphing down onto the couch next to Latona and craning her head to see the letter, utterly without any guile or pretense. "I know it's from *Iberia.*" The teasing sing-song meant she also knew it was from Sempronius and not their brother.

Latona pressed the letter to her chest and gave Aula a none-too-gentle nudge with her foot. "You know perfectly well I'll pass on anything fit for your hearing."

"So? Pass."

"I haven't finished reading it yet!"

"And I should leave you alone to cherish his words in peace?"

"I shouldn't complain if you did."

"I can be quiet." Aula grabbed a pillow and pretended to muffle herself with it. Latona laughed, rolled her eyes, and continued reading.

> *'I hope that, before too much more time passes, you and I shall have the opportunity to compare notes on extraordinary events. The Iberian magic fascinates even as it horrifies—and you are not so delicate, I think, to shy away from the more gruesome aspects of its manifestations. You have endured, I am given to understand, enough to temper your natural qualities into the finest steel.'*

Latona was not so humble as to take no pleasure in that praise. She allowed herself a moment of indulgence, imagining hearing it from his own lips. That and more, whispered against her ear, spoken against her skin by the breath of promises unfulfilled...

She halted the thought before it could progress further, aware that if her cheeks colored, Aula would become insufferable.

> *'May boldness be a watchword for us both, to carry us to good fortune in the coming year. I confess, I'm tempted to daring myself. The legions are well-situated into our camps—proper fortresses with walls and watchtowers, barracks to keep the men warm and healthy, everything necessary to get us through to spring and another campaign season.*

> *'But I am restless. It is difficult to trust in this security with our foes still prowling the countryside. Reports reach us: merchants am-*

bushed, towns raided, supply trains harassed. All our trains travel with protection, but there have been losses, and if they continue, remaining here will become difficult. The region cannot support its own populace and our legions after the past year, with so many crops and orchards burned, others unable to be replanted.

'Yet what should we do? Retreat? That would be disaster, both for the security of the region and—if I may indulge in the fault of self-concern—my reputation as commander. I came here to prove to the Iberians that Aven will stand by them, that we do not abandon those who put their faith in us. How would it look if I pulled back to the coast now, leaving them to the ravening wolves in a harsh winter?

'Too, there have been disturbances of a less predictable nature. No further attacks such as those that plagued Toletum, but oddities unsettling the Arevaci magic-men. They think the Lusetani are trying something new, though they cannot say what that means, only that they have felt waves of power washing over the countryside.

'We disposed of a great many of the Lusetani sorcerers at the Battle of Toletum, but not all. Perhaps they gathered reinforcements from the west; perhaps they merely found some new way to be a menace with fewer men. In any case, I am disinclined to simply wait until they strike at us directly.

'If we cannot retreat, and we cannot remain here, then only one option remains: to take the field. It seems madness, in winter, a contradiction of all military wisdom. Military wisdom, however, has not been sufficient to combat the inventive magic of the Lusetani. I must, perforce, be nimble.'

"What?" Aula asked. "Your face has thoughts on it. What does he say?"

Latona blinked a few times, shaking her head. "He's... he's considering taking the legion, or at least part of it, out of the fortress to pursue the Lusetani."

"In winter?" Aula asked, sitting bolt upright.

"He says they're encountering supply difficulties so far inland, with their foes still harassing the countryside and stalking the major roads."

"Or whatever passes for roads in Iberia," Aula said, shuddering at the consideration.

"And there may be more trouble from the Lusetani magical practitioners that warrants investigating."

"Did I hear you right?" Alhena's head popped around the corner; Mus was still divesting her of her woolen mantle. "The legions are moving out? At this time of year?"

"Not necessarily," Latona replied, "but Sempronius is... considering unorthodox solutions to his problems."

"I thought you were staying at the other house for the afternoon," Aula said.

"I meant to, but Tilla got called back home, and I didn't want to stay by myself." Alhena slipped onto the couch opposite Latona's, her curiosity about the letter more polite than Aula's.

"Your cheeks are red, dear one," Latona said. "Has it gotten very windy out?"

"I— Yes, yes, it must've." Alhena's hands rain over her hair, usually so tightly wound but now falling loose of its pins. "I could scarcely keep my mantle on."

Latona's Spirit magic stirred, but she wasn't sure why. Alhena was fidgety, twisting her fingers into the fabric of her overgown—but then, Alhena was often anxious. Hard not to be, when your head was invaded by confusing messages about the future. "Do you think we might have a storm coming in?"

Alhena nodded. "Not that I've had a vision or anything, but a... a sense of foreboding, more like. I mean, that could be anything."

"But with the winds kicking up, it seems a logical deduction," Aula said. "I'll make sure the household gets shuttered down tight tonight." She wiggled a finger at the paper in Latona's hand. "Anyway, speaking of ill weather—"

Latona likewise returned her attention to the letter. "He says it hasn't been terrible so far. Cold, and some light snows, but nothing to give them real trouble. He counts it a point in favor of making the unusual move to march in winter."

"Still." Aula shivered. "I don't like to think of them wandering the wilds this time of year."

Alhena's fingers shot out and grasped the letter. Latona wasn't prepared for it; her younger sister wasn't the grabby one.

The glaze on Alhena's blue eyes prevented any chastisement, however. Alhena did not even look at the words. She tilted her head, lips pressing thin in consideration. "He will move for advantage. Take a risk in faith. Defy convention because convention no longer serves. Action over stagnation."

Latona and Aula glanced at each other. Flashes of insight came to Alhena unpredictably, but this one felt different. *Is she using the letter as an anchor? A talisman to focus her magic?* Latona wondered. *Could she do that with other objects?*

"Destiny awaits him at the water's edge." Alhena's voice hollowed out. "He is called to it, though whether he knows..." Her eyes tightened, as though trying to see something far-off. "He feels it, even if he doesn't know it. The sudden rush will find him there." Then her eyes shot wide, their bright blue clearing, and she looked at the letter with a perplexed expression. "Uhm." Her voice was back to its usual timbre. "That was odd. I don't..." Ducking her head in embarrassment, she proffered the letter back to Latona, who had to move fast to grab it before Aula swooped in. "I'm not sure what that was."

"Well," Aula said, "Latona's discovered some unusual new talents lately. Perhaps she's not the only one."

"Whatever it was," Latona said, "I thank you for the insight."

Alhena pressed the fingers of both hands to her mouth. A gentle probe with Spirit magic revealed not so much alarm as mystified contemplation. Latona's mind buzzed with questions, but pushing Alhena rarely yielded favorable results, so she decided to leave her sister to her pondering. When Alhena had answers, she would share them.

"If you have the right of it," Aula ventured, "if they choose to fight through the winter and find there's advantage in it..."

"They might be able to win," Latona said, glancing down at the letter again. Her eyes rested again on the first line. *Dearest Latona.* "They might come home soon."

XIV

Three days before the elections, central Truscum saw a storm unlike any in living memory.

The winds came down from the northeast, bringing driving rain and hail with them. A bad enough omen, so soon before voting would begin. Howling winds tore open shutters, ripped tiles from rooftops, and blistered the cheeks of anyone who stepped out-of-doors. Priests of Jupiter begged for intercession; mages of Air and Water tried desperately to mitigate the storm's effects upon their own households. The temples of the Forum and the Capitoline were crowded with people seeking shelter, those who had nowhere else to go or couldn't get home safely.

Everywhere, from the grandest domus to the humblest insula, citizens shivered in fear and prayed their walls would hold. In some parts of the city, the narrow streets flooded, each avenue a rushing river. Worse in the Subura, where so much of that water raced; there, the insulae themselves flooded, water forcing its way over thresholds. Even in finer houses, impluvium pools overflowed, inundated by the downpour.

Overnight, a chill worthy of the Albine Mountains set in, and the rain turned to ice, then snow.

Snow! In Aven, in December! It wasn't even winter yet, in a region which only saw snow once every couple of decades. Children too young to have experienced it before wailed in fright. Fire mages worked themselves to exhaustion, trying to keep braziers and hypocausts blasting as much warmth into the air as possible. The City of Aven, which never slept, always a-bustle with business or holiday, ground to a halt. Citizens huddled with their whole families beneath piles of blankets, out of fear and need, while impluvium pools and fish-stock ponds froze over.

Yet even so wild a storm could not hold sway over Aven for long. The following day, the Ides of December, the sun melted much of the ice and snow from Aven's streets. As citizens swept slush from their doorsteps and pulled their carts out of the mud, the city came back to life—but groggily, tentatively, fearfully.

Marcus Autronius made for the Forum as early as he could, tramping through mucky streets and trying to keep his toga from becoming hopelessly begrimed. The Senate would meet in the afternoon, but Marcus had an instinct—one proved correct when he reached the Rostra and found Arrius Buteo well-advanced in a diatribe. *'Good gods, did the man rise at dawn simply so no opportunity of castigating the masses might be missed?'*

Buteo's face was florid despite the chill lingering in the air—and, to Marcus's dismay, the Optimate orator had already gathered a crowd. People who ought to have been at their shops and administrative offices lingered, listening. Marcus's magic gave him no sense of empathy, no ability to see into others' souls or read their emotions, but he did have a keen sense of solidity. He knew what was firm and what was not; he had never put a foot wrong in his life, for every step landed on even ground.

He had no sense of solidity here. The crowd was uneasy, unsure, ready to crumble. They wanted reassurance—and Arrius Buteo offered them something to cling to.

'Sons of Dis,' Marcus thought, as he drew near enough to hear Buteo's words. He was no grand speaker, would not have dared ascend the Rostra at such a moment. *'But where are the consuls? Where is Quintus Terentius?'* Seeing to their own households and neighborhoods, most likely; dealing with the clients and tenants who needed immediate attention. A noble aim, if that's what they were doing—but an impolitic choice. *'Sempronius Tarren's letters are rubbing off on me. I didn't always think like that.'*

Buteo was in his full stride, voice cutting cleanly through the cold air. "The gods show their disfavor in this!" he shouted, jabbing a finger up at the sky. More than a few people glanced up in fear, as though the bone-white clouds might again open and spit down ice and hail. "For weeks—months!—I have warned you! Have tried to warn you and gone unheeded! For months, as misfortune has befallen the city, from the Colline Gate to the Tiber River, I have warned you. The *gods* warned us, and they warn us still. They are vengeful, but they are benevolent, my fellow citizens! They give us the opportunity to set things right!"

The murmuring that followed this assertion was mixed at best. Some scowling and wagging of heads, but too many of the crowd mumbled in agreement.

"Only by returning to the strictures of the *mos maiorum* can we spare ourselves future pain!" Buteo went on. "We have drifted too far from the precedents set by our ancestors. Our noble forefathers hang their heads in shame!" This he followed with a recitation of Aven's many transgressions: lack of moral discipline, imprudent behavior displayed by wives and youths, the usual litany of vices and indulgences.

Marcus thought he could likely recite the speech from memory by now—but either it was new to some of the crowd, or else it struck their ears with new fervor in the wake of the unexpected and unnatural storm. Too many were nodding along, too many looked on the verge of clapping or cheering their support.

In a way, Marcus could empathize. He did not like haste. He often thought Sempronius's ideas pushed too far, too fast. New ideas were not always healthy enough to take root; they needed careful tending. But that didn't mean he agreed with Buteo's intransigence to any kind of change.

Buteo ended his tirade faster than Marcus expected; he had not had time to shove his way toward the Rostra, and to his horror, Lucretius Rabirus ascended, standing to Buteo's right.

"Remember this, citizens!" Buteo thundered. "When you vote in two days' time—remember that the gods are watching!"

Applause followed his descent from the Rostra, and Marcus's heart sank further into the muddy ground. *'Applause, for that fear-mongering, isolationist old curmudgeon. Gods, these people must be scared.'*

Rabirus was not the rousing orator that Buteo was, and he began by acknowledging that fact. "I ask only a moment of your time, citizens," he said. "And I ask not for myself—Indeed, I ask for *your* good selves, that you hear me and make wise choices when you come to vote. I ask for Decimus Gratianus and Cominius Celer, whom I know to be virtuous men, men whose values align with the *mos maiorum* that has kept Aven safe for so many venerated generations."

The *mos maiorum*, as the Optimates interpreted it, would have kept Aven small. *'If we never grew or changed, we would have been overrun by our neighbors centuries ago. Veii or the Volsci or the Samnites would have swallowed us up. Or the Tyrians would have carved us to pieces.'* Aven became a center of commerce and power because it adapted. Swift change alarmed Marcus, yes, but nothing grew without alteration. That was healthy, whether in a plant or a man or a nation. *'Would they see us living in huts again? A cluster of shepherds, fishermen, and bandits hugging these hillsides?'*

No, of course not. They wanted this wealth and power—but they wanted it in their own hands, not shared with immigrants and freedmen from every nook and cranny of the Middle Sea. *'Nor with men like me. In their estimation, my family should have contentedly remained field hands forever.'*

Rabirus went on: "I know you suffer, and I grieve with you. But I have consulted with priests and augurs, and all are in agreement: These misfortunes are the gods' way of warning us that we have gone astray. Look, and you will see the signs of it everywhere. Foreign-born ruffians and exotic harlots entice our youth to abandon their duties in favor of pleasure. What wonder, that we are visited with harsh weather, to remind us of what it is like to toil? Carpenters, masons, painters prefer ornate, outlandish styles to solid, dignified abodes. What wonder, that our houses crumble and collapse? Bakers would rather make cakes and pastries, fit to adorn the tables of Parthian princelings, than good honest Aventan bread, hearty and nourishing. What wonder, that our food spoils in its granaries and warehouses, befouled and unfit for consumption?"

Marcus cocked his head. The mention of the granaries pulled on a thread at the back of his mind. Not an unusual condemnation. The Optimates decried indulgence in all its forms, and rich foods were a favorite topic of denunciation. But this, in particular... *'I checked the granaries. The spoils were... were nothing. Commissioner Salonius assured me...'*

The counters on the abacus didn't line up. He had been told not to worry. He had *believed* there was no need to worry, even though complaints came to him as a tribune, even though he had verified those complaints himself. He had been so concerned—and then those concerns slipped away, like sand through his fingers. *'Why did I let it go so easily?'* The thought itched, a troubling sting at the base of his skull—but there was no time to contemplate it, for Rabirus's speech continued apace.

"So remember this, friends, as you join your tribes in two days' time to enact that most sacred right and privilege bestowed upon you by the gods who both favor and chasten us—" Rabirus was laying it on thick, but it was effective. "Remember that there *is* a path back to prosperity, if you can be stalwart enough to hold to it. A path back to peace, if you are pious enough to heed the gods' warnings. A path back to the *true* Aven, noble and enduring, if you are diligent enough to honor ancient wisdom."

Marcus's fingers itched. *'A path back. Never a path forward, with these men. Never a path to the future. Only retreading the past, to the benefit of the same few plutocrats, who are so sure that the gods want them to triumph above all other men.'*

Rabirus finished by calling again on the audience to remember the names of Decimus Gratianus and Cominius Celer—Optimates both, though neither had Rabirus's cunning or Buteo's raw fervor. Still, if they won, Rabirus and Buteo would work through them.

Marcus abandoned his notion of taking the Rostra himself. He was no orator, certainly not enough of one to follow those speeches. *'If Sempronius were here... And where in Jupiter's name is Quintus Terentius?'* No doubt he would take the Rostra at some time today, but it would not undo the impact of the Optimates' words, which would be repeated and passed around all the city within hours.

Marcus angled instead for the tribunate bench. *'I can do my own duty, and show myself pious and diligent in that.'*

'Has it been only a year?'

A year and some odd days, Vibia supposed; elections had no fixed date, and last year's had been held earlier in December. This time, the Assemblies chose two days after the Ides. But still—only a year since the last elections, and so much had changed. Only a year since the Aventine fires. *'Only a year since I realized the Discordian blasphemers had a presence in Aven.'*

The snow and ice had melted, but the sky remained an eerie white, as though the gods might yet visit another such hazard upon the city. Vibia usually didn't bother going to the edge of the Campus Martius to await votes, but Latona convinced her, on the rationale that, if Discordian interference should crop up, they would both be there to deal with it.

The lower offices had been filled the day before, by the Tribal Assembly; the ranks of the quaestors and aediles were rarely contentious. Today's votes by the Centuriate Assembly, though, decided the higher offices: consuls, praetors, and the allotment of propraetorships and proconsular appointments. Today they found out who would govern the city in the coming months, who would be given provinces and the legions that went with them, and whether Sempronius would hold on to his command in Cantabria.

Vibia half-hoped he wouldn't. She wanted him back home, to help fend off the threat from the Discordians and Augians. They needed someone inside the Senate, to convey the machinations there, but no one else had both their trust and their capability. Aulus Vitellius's fear for his daughters' safety impaired his usefulness; Galerius Orator could not be approached without more solid proof about the Augian connection; Vibia's husband Taius was a supportive man but blissfully ignorant of magical dealings. Sempronius was the only Senator they could trust with everything.

'Though it would be more useful if he trusted us with everything in return,' Vibia thought, looking sideways at Latona. Sempronius's magic would be valuable to them—but not if he had to keep hiding it. Apart from Vibia's growing discomfort with the deceit of omission, the impracticality would become a hindrance to efficient work. 'No point brooding on it until he's back in Aven, I suppose.' Certainly she could not hector him about it in a letter.

Vibia's wish to bring him home was selfish. He had a purpose in Iberia, part of the gods' greater plan for him, and she understood that, supported it. So despite her private desires, she would hope for electoral victory today.

The women dressed well for the occasion, but it hardly mattered; their mantles were thick wool and wrapped so tightly about them that they might have been giant walking cocoons. An icy wind picked its way through the crowd, finding every gap in the press of humanity to slide between.

"Can't you do something about this?" Aula grumbled at her sister. For once, her mantle was drawn up over her brow, and she was holding it tight beneath her chin. Alhena was fully muffled in hers, almost none of her face showing, just bright blue eyes between layers of silver-gray wool.

"Something?" Latona retorted. "What sort of something did you have in mind?"

"I don't know." Aula's bundled clothing bulged slightly around the middle; she was making a circling gesture underneath her cloak. "Conjure us some warmth or something."

Latona rolled her eyes. "Without a brazier or a hypocaust, Aula, there's really very little I can—"

"Well, you've learned one new trick in the past few months, who knows what else—"

"A trick?" Latona hissed, glancing to see if anyone had heard. "That's not exactly how I would—"

"Oh, you *know* what I mean, and—"

Vibia was about to snap at them to stop bickering, but Alhena beat her to it, jerking her wrap down from around her mouth. "Hush!"

Latona huffed. "You're quite right, my dear. It's unseemly for us to—"

"No," Alhena said. "No, I think they're about to announce results."

Murmurs began to carry word of the election results out of the field and into the crowd. The consuls and proconsular appointments came first. Latona seized Aula's hand through both their wraps as word filtered back, a wave of whispers. Even before it reached them, Alhena was shaking her head, some whisper of Time telling her that not all was as they hoped.

The consuls for the coming year: Decimus Gratianus and Cominius Celer.

Upon hearing the news, Aula groaned, stamping a foot. "Sweet blessed and merciful Juno—"

"She wasn't today," Latona muttered.

"—how on *earth* did Quintus Terentius not prevail? His daughter's a Vestal, for crying out loud!"

"We know how," Vibia intoned. "Lies and swollen presumptions and perfidious advantage-taking."

"Lies and fear," Alhena added. "That last storm may have tipped the scales."

Vibia agreed; *that*, she did not believe Corinna's doing, nor any of her unknown affiliates. Weather was impossibly complex for any mage to command. Merely predicting it strained most Water and Air mages to their utmost; maybe a few in Aven's history could summon a stray cloud to nurture a single garden, but to create a storm large enough to paralyze half of Truscum? No; whatever Corinna's powers were, Vibia felt certain they did not extend so far. *'She and hers can make use of ill luck, though.'*

"I still can't believe it," Aula said. "Are people really that scared? And do they really believe the Optimates will give them security?"

"Evidently," Vibia said.

"Monstrous."

"I don't disagree with you."

Such lovely lies the Optimates told, such sweet falsehoods, and frightened people latched on to such things with fervor. For every neighborhood where men like Vatinius Obir kept the faith, there were three with no commanding presence, where the people could be easily swayed by promises of peace and safety.

'Chin up, Vibia. Maybe they aren't all so credulous. Some might simply have been bribed.'

One light shone amid the wretchedness of the consular results: Aufidius Strato had been awarded proconsular control of Baelonia. "A sop," Aula said, "to those who did not buy Lucretius Rabirus's claims that all is idle in the region." Galerius Orator declined any proconsular command, preferring to remain in the city.

Then, the praetorships: A longer process, a tedious wait. Much needed deciding—which of the current year's praetors would keep their offices, first. Until that fell out, no one knew how many slots would be filled by election, though a few men had declared themselves willing to step down, mostly those whose provinces were either boring or poor.

The key, of course, would be Sempronius and Cantabria.

'Will they split their decision?' Vibia wondered. The Centuriate Assembly consisted of men who had held or were eligible for military service. Unfortunately, with so many legionaries, centurions, and officers in the field, fewer were home to vote. *'But if Aufidius Strato gained his proconsularship, then maybe enough ex-legionaries are left here to understand what Sempronius is doing.'*

It was very nearly the shortest day of the year, and the sun's bleak progression dropped with alacrity toward the horizon. Some of the crowd began to wander away, not intending to remain on the Campus Martius after dark, and their absence only allowed more cold air to buffet those who remained. "It's coming," Alhena said, as the clouds turned pink and yellow.

And sure enough, a few moments later, the word rippled back through the crowd, one whispered name at a time, passed from spectator to spectator.

Sempronius had been given propraetorship of Cantabria. Vibia nodded at the news with tight satisfaction. What an ignoble defeat recall would have been. And Vibia knew her brother: if ordered to return before he considered the job done, he might have defied the Senate and refused to relinquish his command. *'The gods are good in declining to put him into the position of causing such a crisis. But why have they left us a mess in every other regard?'*

XV

Anas River, Central Iberia

Dawn in Iberia had much to recommend it. Nothing, to Sempronius's thinking, would ever rival the first rays of the sun hitting the red rooftops of Aven's hills, but Aurora's rosy fingers looked well as they stretched over Iberian trees and ocher rocks, too.

'And better out in the open than viewed from the wall of a fortress.'

When the Tenth received word of a Vettoni unit repeatedly hassling a town two days' march to the south, a large force left the fortress to squash it. Ten centuries, with Arevaci cavalry—and accompanied by General Sempronius Tarren.

Unusual, for a legion's general to go on such a vexillation, but stagnation did not suit Sempronius. He was tired of trying to assess the lay of the land from verbal reports, hasty sketches carved into wax tablets, and reconstructed memories scribbled on scrap papers—and even more tired of speculating about the strange tide of magic that had swept over the land at the beginning of the month. If a fight could give him answers, then he would take himself to that fight.

Several days after the Ides of December, the vexillation crossed the Anas River and made camp on a high piece of ground. This land belonged to the Tartessi, a tribe ravaged not only by the Vettoni, but by Lucretius Rabirus's forces.

Rabirus's carelessness in mistaking the Tartessi for Vettoni had put the Tartessi on a war footing, before Sempronius's legions had broken the siege of Toletum; only narrowly had Sempronius negotiated an accord, and he welcomed the opportunity, now, to make some kind of amends. While the centuries rested, scouts ventured toward the nearest villages, searching for information about the raiders' present location.

At dawn, Sempronius walked the perimeter of his camp. All night he had tossed and turned, troubled by an itching in his brain as a gentle rain pattered on the roof of his tent. He had not yet received word about the elections, but correspondence made him pessimistic about their outcome. When he settled matters in Iberia, he would be leaving one battlefield for another.

'Well. It was always going to be that. You have your plan, and you have your duty.'

The gods required much of their most devoted servants. Sempronius had been trying to do their will all his life, though the plan crystallized in those first few days after the Dictator Ocella's death, when his magic granted him a vision: three challenges to face, and two futures for Aven. In one, the glory that he dreamed, a city bright and indomitable and filled with the best people from dozens of nations; in the other, the fate he feared, a civilization briefly sputtering to greatness before winking out, its streets abandoned, its temples plundered, its magnificent potential fallen to ash.

The first part of the vision had brought him here, showing him strife in the Iberian countryside and a young man, crowned with stars and smeared with blood. Ekialde, the war-king; the iconography fit perfectly.

Sempronius understood the war-king's goal of driving foreigners from Iberia, as much as he understood the Optimates back home, men whose vision of the world was too limited, who never wanted to grow or change or encounter new ideas. The Lusetani feared Aventan conquest. *'Fair enough. But our presence here need not be obliterating—and there are no few elements of the Iberian way of doing things I'd like to take back to Aven.'*

In a way, Ekialde's war may have brought the integration that the war-king feared sooner, rather than in a quieter swell of time. Tribune Vitellius had made friends of the Arevaci and several other northern tribes, and Sempronius meant to secure those friendships, carving them in marble, not merely sealing them with wax. Not everyone in Aven would like it, no more than everyone in Iberia. *'But this is the future. This is the way to build a stronger world for us all.'*

This was Sempronius's dream, planted in his head by divine inspiration: a federation of nations stretching across the Middle Sea, and maybe beyond, for mutual aid and comfort. People who could trade freely with each other, learn from each other, share their technological advancements and their magics. *'And Aven, right at the center, the beating heart of it all.'* The gods wanted it, and he would do whatever necessary to bring it about.

The second part of the vision had been stranger. For a long time, Sempronius had seen nothing in the waking world to tie to it: a woman standing by a river, dark and terrible and holding a skull whose eyes glowed an unearthly blue. *'The more fool me, to think all the challenges I saw would be my own to face.'* After Vibia's and Latona's letters, he now felt sure that this vision heralded the rise of the Discordians in Aven.

A threat to his plans, a faction that would not just obstruct him, like the Optimates, but would seek to tear down any progress, holding the world in thrall to destruction and strife. *'A menace to all society. The only good thing Ocella ever did was banish them.'* Not the first time their cult had been cast out of a city, but after the dictator's death, they crept back.

In a way, it was heartening. *'They would not need to rip Aven apart if it were not on the verge of becoming all that Discordia abhors. It speaks to our strength—so long as we can withstand the trial.'*

Not that he doubted the capacity of the women dealing with the problem. Vibia was so smart, so stubborn, and Latona had more raw power than anyone he had ever known. Better still, if he read between the carefully-constructed lines of their letters correctly, she finally seemed to be realizing that and harnessing her potential. *'Gods, but I wish I could be there to see it. All the more reason to crush this Ekialde and his blood-fiends as quickly as possible.'*

The third, briefest part of the vision, he did not yet know how to parse. A splash of blood against tiles, fiercely red under bright sunlight. Sempronius told himself not to borrow trouble from the future—but still, staring at rows of tents under the golden glow of an Iberian sunrise, he could not help but wonder: Whose blood? Spilled in a fight or in sacrifice? The blood of life or of death?

"General! General! To arms!"

The panic in Lady Hanath's voice had Sempronius moving almost before he processed her words. They had built the marching camp as they would have for a full legion, only on a smaller scale: tents laid out on a grid, surrounded by a ditch and an earthen wall with spears and spikes driven into it. Sempronius met Hanath as she thundered through the center of camp, still a-horse. Tall, dark-skinned, and strong-muscled, Hanath had proved herself a clever tactician as well as a ruthless warrior over the past few months. Now she looked grim. "What news?"

"Vettoni approaching from the east," she said. "And Lusetani from the west." She pointed first one direction, then the other. "They will cross where the river is shallower, down from the bend, on either side of our camp, and they are almost at the shore." Then, the true reason for Hanath's bleak expression: "General, there are at least five thousand of them, between the two forces. We have been lured into a trap."

"Sound the alarm!" Sempronius bellowed. Immediately horns rang out. "Battle formation, northeast and northwest corners!" Without further word to Hanath, who knew well enough how to muster her cavalry, he turned into his already half-disassembled tent. "Corvinus! Armor!"

His thoughts raced; this was it, the cause of the itching in his mind. *'Damn fool, trying to keep too many things in your head at once, thinking too much of the future, too many steps ahead of yourself, didn't even notice Shadow trying to warn you—'*

The camp was vulnerable. The legionaries would be swift in assembling, but many were not yet dressed. Getting into kit would take time; getting into formation would take time. And then they would have to defend themselves on two fronts simultaneously, outnumbered more than five-to-one.

'Father Mars, look here. Father Mars, bless us now or see us obliterated.'

Corvinus started readying Sempronius's cuirass as soon as he heard the horns, despite the pit in his stomach that always accompanied the onset of battle, and when the general entered the tent, Corvinus began strapping it onto him with brisk efficiency.

"I can do the rest. Send Eustix's bird," Sempronius said. Even without magical direction, it knew how to find its way to its Air mage master back at the fortress. "We'll have to hope the raiders are too busy crossing the river to shoot it down."

Corvinus bent over a trunk lid to scribble the message as Sempronius pulled on his greaves and vambraces. His hand was steady; however much he hated the turmoil of impending battle, panic was not in his nature. *'Dread, yes. Panic, no.'*

"Corvinus," Sempronius said, his voice an urgent hush, "I think I know how to hold off the attack—but I do not have the strength to do it myself."

"Sir?" Corvinus asked, opening the bird cage and securing the note to the creature's leg. The bird was agitated by the sudden noise in the camp, crashing around them as a thousand men prepared for battle. "I don't understand."

"Time is against us," Sempronius said, dressed now except for his helmet. "Did you hear what Lady Hanath—"

"No."

"The Lusetani and Vettoni approach, from east and west. Five thousand of them." Corvinus's breath hitched, his heart going nearly as fast as the pigeon's. "They will be across the river by the time we can get into our lines, and they mean to pinch us between their forces." He held the tent flap so Corvinus could release the bird into the air. "Unless we—you and I, I mean—make it impossible for them to cross."

Corvinus stared as the bird ascended to heaven, hopefully high enough to be out of easy arrow range. Then comprehension dawned in a rapid succession of horrifying corollary thoughts. "Dominus, even the two of us together could not—I only have a touch of the gift."

"And I'm weaker in Water than Shadow, I know, but it will be enough." A wild look had entered his eyes, one Corvinus had seen before, when Sempronius believed he knew the will of the gods. The touch of divinity upon his soul, some people would say; utter staggering arrogance verging on madness, others would assess.

"How we can accomplish this without anyone noticing? If the Lusetani don't murder you on the riverbank, then one of our people may see you working magic," Corvinus went on. "And even if we did manage it, the Prohibition of Mars—"

"I know. I know all of those things. But we don't have the time for niceties. We will be overrun and slaughtered if we don't stop them at the river. We have to do this. We have to do this *now*. We can sort out the consequences later."

Agony twisted Corvinus's gut. Too many things could go wrong with this plan, if it could even be called that. But he had sworn himself to Sempronius's service, for good or ill. Whatever came of it, Corvinus would be at his side. "Let us go then, Dominus." He gestured to the tent flap. "But if I might be so bold to suggest—"

"A little Shadow magic to ease the way?" Sempronius nodded. "Hold still a moment." He placed a hand on the back of Corvinus's neck and began murmuring an invocation to Nox, Lady of the Night, asking her to lend some of her darkness, stretching it beyond the lines of dawn.

The magic shivered over Corvinus's skin as the charm took hold. It would not render them invisible, precisely. Anyone looking specifically for them would still be able to find them; anyone who *knew* where they were would see them plain as day. But no one would be expecting the general to leave camp while his men were preparing for battle, and there was certainly no reason for anyone to look for them along the mud flats.

XVI

They slipped through the gate behind the quaestorium. The vexillation had cleared trees to make room for their camp, but much of the hill was still wooded. Sempronius and Corvinus emerged from the tree line into tall grass at the river's edge. Corvinus saw then that Sempronius had not erred in his assessment of their timing. A few hundred paces downstream, the Vettoni were crossing. Some were already in the water, wading across the shallows, picking their way between the muddy sandbars and helpfully-strewn rocks that dotted the Anas here. The mud might slow them down—but not by much.

Sempronius fell to his knees at the water's edge and stuck his hands in up to his wrists; Corvinus followed his example and did the same. He winced; in the early morning, the river seemed icier than when they crossed in mid-afternoon the day before.

"This river wants to rise," Sempronius said. "Feel it, upstream?"

Corvinus nodded. Immersed in the element, Corvinus's magic flowed with the water itself, and he could sense a swollen mass, many miles away. Rain had fallen in the night; what had been only light showers upon their camp must have been a downpour upriver. Encouraging that water to hurry itself along was perfectly plausible magic. But could they do it fast enough?

"We can do this," Sempronius breathed, as though he heard Corvinus's thoughts—or, more likely, sensed his trepidation through Shadow's discernment. "We can, and we must." His eyelids lowered. "Blessed Lympha, Lady of the Rivers, look here upon your favored children and hear our call. Flood this river. Swell it. Make it rise. Blessed Lympha, Lady of the Rivers, look here upon your favored children—"

Corvinus joined him in the chant, over and over, the same words. No fancy ritual, no poetics, just a simple plea to render aid. He chanced a glimpse upstream, and his breath hitched. The Vettoni were fully massed now, swarming the riverbank. Those first in had reached the near side, though they had sense enough not to charge uphill on their own. Some were going back to help their fellows find a surefooted way across; others were shaking out their tunics, wiping their blades dry.

'How many will they wait for, before beginning their assault?'

Then, as Corvinus's hands were beginning to go numb with cold, he felt it, like a tumbler in a lock sliding into place. The water upstream began to move.

A hard tug within the magic: Sempronius had also noticed the Lusetani on the shore and was giving his power a *yank*, as though the river were a horse and he held the reins. In a dizzying rush, the river responded: a clear, hollow sound rang in Corvinus's head, not unpleasant, and he tasted ice upon his tongue as he added his own power to Sempronius's effort.

Faster, now, faster the river rushed, as though responding to their urgency. Corvinus could almost picture it, careening down hillsides, splashing over rocks, crashing around the trees and shrubs that stood near the banks. He could almost hear it—

No, he *could* hear it, he realized with a jolt of fear. A dull roar in the distance, still far off, but closer with every heartbeat. He pulled his hands out of the water, standing. "I think that's done it," Sempronius said.

"That may have *over*done it."

"We'd best be off."

Sempronius let the cover of Shadow drop from them both as soon as they were back inside the camp. He strode purposefully down the via praetoriana, bellowing instructions and encouragement in equal measure, as though he had been there all along. The centurions had done their duties well; the legions were in a hurry, but well-ordered. Half the men were assembled in lines outside the northeast and northwest corners of the camp. No one had noticed Sempronius's temporary absence.

Corvinus made for the command tent and his duties: organizing healers to receive the wounded, making sure the baggage was packed up in the shameful—and hopefully now unlikely—event of a retreat, and observing the battle so he could later assist Sempronius in composing a report for the Senate.

Sempronius pulled two centurions aside as he went toward the stable. "Once your men are armored and ready, hold them back, you at the porta dextra, you at the sinistra. We'll use you for a flanking maneuver once the foe gets in close." He was swinging himself into the saddle even as the men saluted and shouted their understanding.

Hanath's cavalry waited near the porta dextra. Sempronius pulled alongside her for a moment. "Is all well with your people? Did you have a chance to change horses?"

"Most of us, yes. Not enough for everyone, but those who rode hardest this morning were able to swap out. The rest of our mounts are hale enough."

"Good. What was the ground like coming up the hill? Soft from the rain?" He knew the answer, of course, from his own trek.

Hanath shook her head. "Wet leaves may make things a little slippery, but this area drains well, and the rain was not so hard. We should have adequate footing."

"Unfortunately," Sempronius said, "so will they." With a wry expression, he rode out the porta dextra to give the men in their lines a bolster—but his eyes were on the river. *'Any moment now...'*

And then it hit: A rushing in his head, dizzying and powerful. From below the camp, shouts that turned to screams, a rise of panic in Iberian throats. And the water, crashing and roaring, utterly inexorable.

'Thank you, Lady Lympha. And Father Mars, forgive me.' He had tested the patience of the god of war more than once on this campaign: using the immunity of the Arevaci women to counter the summoning magic of the Lusetani, the sleight of Shadow magic to help him confound the assassins months earlier, and now this. None were *strictly* violations of the Prohibition of Mars. None had been the actions of Aventans after battle had been enjoined. But this, especially, rode right up on that line. *'And the gods are not always known to be generous in interpreting their own laws.'*

Well-disciplined as the legions were, few of them could restrain their shock at seeing the river rise to swallow the very enemies they had been preparing to defend themselves against. Not that they could see much at this angle. The river was only intermittently visible through the naked trees,

so much obscured by their gray trunks and the few brown leaves still clinging to branches. It was enough, though, to tell a compelling story for the
onlookers.

"Hold steady!" Sempronius shouted. As the river continued to crash
and roar, Sempronius rode from one corner of the camp to the other, peering to get a better look at what was happening. His magic filled in what his
eyes could not see: a river engorged, tearing through its banks, ripping up
grass and rocks, churning an angry white as it rushed downstream. What
men were midriver when the surge hit were surely dead; many on the banks
might be, too.

He risked opening his magic further, to give him an advantage, and immediately wished he hadn't. Death was ever the realm of Shadow, and Water was a conduit. He *knew* that, and yet he had not expected the inundation of agony.

It gave him no joy, this slaughter. *'What a waste.'* War in general typically was. An opportunity, yes, he knew that well enough. He needed this
war to set up a stronger coalition for Aven in the future. But each man who
died choking, just as each man who fell to a blade, was a life that might have
been turned to a different, fruitful purpose.

*'I do the best with the world I have, but sometimes, mighty Jupiter, I do
wonder why you let us devolve from the golden era into this turmoil and strife.'*
If such an era had ever existed, outside tales and legends.

So many died out of Sempronius's sight. And yet, some lived. Some
were already on shore, scrambling high enough above the surge not to be
dragged back under; some, improbably, clawed their way out of the churning roil and found their way to land.

'Father Mars, we owe you an honest battle yet.' He looked to the nearest
centurion. "Sound a march." A short whistle signal set the legionaries to
motion, with careful tread, in perfect unison. They did not move swiftly,
not a charge down the uncertain slope of the hill. Measured and disci-
plined, every step. That was the strength of the legions; each man knew his
place, guarded his neighbor, sought not personal glory but collective triumph. They came through the trees and locked shields, pressing through
the tall grass to meet their foes.

After that, it was a simple matter of cutting down the would-be as-
sailants who had not drowned. Or, it ought to have been simple. Trapped

between the advancing cohorts and the swollen river, the fighting men had nowhere to go, no recourse. Sensible men would throw down arms and hope for mercy.

The Lusetani, it seemed, were insensible. Every one of them who emerged from the water, drenched and half-choked, flung himself into battle as though all the odds were on his side and victory assured. *'Do they love their war-king so much?'* Sempronius wondered, watching the battle from the back of the lines. Most days, he would not have held himself so much aloof, but his magical exertion had left him weaker than he cared to admit. *'Are they so eager to join their honored dead?'*

But no—this was more than mere devotion, more than zeal for a glorious death and riches in the afterlife. These warriors fought like men possessed, wild-eyed with fury, hardly seeming to notice when a gladius penetrated their guts. They fought with full strength—until they died.

From his position amid a square of defenders, with the crimson legionary standard snapping above him, Sempronius watched one Lusetani warrior hurl himself against the shield wall over and over again. Each time, he took a hit; each time, he flung himself again into the fray, not seeming to mind the blood and viscera flowing out of his person. He was an ox of a man, broad-shouldered and dark-haired. Every bit of skin that showed outside his leather armor and fur wraps was dotted or hatched with markings. Snarling defiance, he hacked away with his curved blade, looking for a joint between the shields—until he fell down dead, all at once, like a puppet whose strings had been cut.

The hairs on the back of Sempronius's neck stood on end. *'There is magic in this... This may have been the work performed at the Kalends, a profanity with force enough that we felt it at a distance.'*

Despite the horror, his legions performed exactly as they were meant to, striking each foe until they stayed down, no matter how much gore and grit that required.

When the fighting was over, Hanath joined Sempronius at the shore. Her men and women had done their job, skirting the wings of the camp to track down any of the foe who attempted to flee—or who made mad charges up the hill on either side. "We have captives," she reported, sidling her horse alongside Sempronius's. "A number of the Vettoni, seeing the river take their fellows, chose surrender over death."

"Not a one of the Lusetani did so," Sempronius said. "They died to a man. Eventually."

One of Hanath's eyebrows cocked. "Eventually?"

Sempronius gestured at one of the nearby corpses — hacked into three pieces. "They were... insistent."

A hiss passed through Hanath's teeth. "More magic, you think?"

"I cannot think what else. A man whose guts are out or whose arm is off usually falls. These went on until there was quite literally nothing left in them."

"Pity," Hanath said. "I'd have liked the chance to interrogate one of the Lusetani. But perhaps the Vettoni are sensible enough of their ally's plans that they will yield some useful intelligence."

"We can hope." As they walked the sodden battlefield, Sempronius's eyes stayed alert, looking for the leopard-skin cloak that the Lusetani king was known to wear. *It would be too much to hope that we might find a fallen god among these bloated heroes.*

Hanath's eyes, too, scanned the breadth of the wrecked riverbank. "This is most unusual," she said. Saplings and small boulders had been torn loose, cast upon the shore; so had a great many bodies.

"I've seen the Iteru flood like this," Sempronius said, allowing a note of puzzled speculation into his voice, "in Abydosia."

"As have I," Hanath said, "and some others in my homeland, but not here."

Sempronius rubbed his forehead with the back of one hand, squinting at the curve of the river around another hill to the east. "Perhaps it rained much heavier upriver than it did here?"

"Perhaps." Hanath was plainly unconvinced.

He sighed, as though equally at a loss to explain the rescuing flood. "Or perhaps the gods blessed us. Maybe Lympha saw our peril. Or the Iberian gods—who rules the rivers, here?"

"Nabia. Though she is not typically vengeful."

"Well, someone else, maybe, who objected to the perfidies of the Lusetani blood-mages." Hanath's head bobbed slightly, allowing the possibility.

"Whatever the cause, I shall give thanks for our timely salvation. We were caught short of our full preparation, and it might well have been our corpses littering this hill instead."

"It would have been a stiffer battle, to be sure," Hanath said, "and in unfamiliar territory, with no easy bolt-hole to retreat to."

"I don't like that we were so easily lured here." That, at least, was unvarnished truth. Sempronius should have considered that the Lusetani were canny enough to arrange such an ambush. "But now that we are here, we might as well press south and make sure no more Vettoni are lurking in the area. It will be some days before we can cross back across the Anas, I think."

A soft snort from Hanath. "Indeed. This river will be some days in calming itself." Her teeth showed in a slowly-growing grin. "And yes, I think it right and well that we make our presence here felt."

XVII

City of Aven

That year's Saturnalian revels were subdued. Too much of the city was still gripped with fear; others could not afford the expense, or did not want to be seen flaunting wealth when others economized. And the Popularists were, plainly, depressed. The turn of the year would see their opponents installed into nearly every major office in Aven, which did not feel much cause for celebration.

But the gods required their due, and so there were still feasts, still rituals, still gambling and gift-giving among both the high-stationed and the low. Dominus Aulus, Merula thought, actually seemed determined to make the slaves' feast even jollier than usual, bringing in musicians and dancers. The door-boy Urso was made Lord of Misrule and tromped about in the dominus's purple-striped toga, giving ludicrous orders which Aulus and his daughters scrambled to carry out. Merula had thought the custom strange ever since arriving in Aven and generally declined to participate in the foolery—but she did enjoy the food.

The following morning, Merula rose with the dawn so she could exercise and train before beginning her morning duties. The cook let her use the herb garden, so long as she didn't trample any plants. It was a good place to practice precision work and close-quarters moves.

When she came back upstairs, she was surprised to find Domina Latona already up, dressed, and wrapped in a warm woolen mantle. She held out a hand, urging Merula, "Come with me."

At first, Merula thought the domina had some reason to head to the house on the Esquiline—but if that were so, she would have simply said it. They went up and over the crest of the Palatine, coming down into the Forum near the Temple of the Vestals, but instead of continuing north toward the Esquiline, Latona banked eastward, leading Merula to one of the large basilicas where the magistrates did their work in dozens of alcoves and small chambers. Today, they were open and busy after being closed for the long Saturnalian holiday.

Women like Latona did little business for themselves. Widowed Aula had more rights and property of her own, but divorced Latona fell back entirely under her father's authority. *'So what could she be needing with the magistrates?'* No legal rights, no ability to make contracts, no property—

Merula's stride hitched. *'Her property.'*

She realized, now, which magistrate Latona had them queuing for. The one responsible for overseeing the manumission of slaves. "Domina?" Merula asked. "You—You mean to—"

Latona turned toward Merula. She had that fierceness in her face, like a provoked lioness, which Merula recognized as a sign that she would not be shaken from her intended path.

"I mean to make sure that if something happens to me," Latona said, "you will not be left in an awkward position. Not that I think my father or Aula would—" She sucked in a shaky breath. "You would have been freed in my will, in any case, but that might not be enough, depending on the circumstances. My father's agreed to this. I'd have done it sooner, but he took a little convincing. I've been thinking of it ever since the... the Corinna incident." She withdrew some papers from the folds of her mantle; Merula had gotten so used to her carting thaumaturgical treatises around that she hadn't even noticed them. "Everything's in order, but I wanted to be the one to... Suffice it to say, Merula, I am ever more acutely aware of how fragile all our lives are. There's no guarantee that my family would be able to protect you, if the worst occurred. So I must put you in a position where you can protect yourself."

A strange gift, to have rendered back that liberty which had been hers at birth. A complex gratitude and not-gratitude, to receive it.

"It doesn't mean—" Latona rushed to add. "That is, you'll be free to leave my family's service, if you wish. But you can also stay, with the wages due a freedwoman. No one's going to turn you out into the street. Not ever."

Merula contemplated that for a long moment. Some of the enslaved women in Numerius Herennius's household had asked her, once, what she would do if she were freed. She had not answered them, silly chickens that they were, with no right to know her hopes or dreams. She had ideas, though—not quite plans, nothing so well-formed.

It had always seemed too distant; a likelihood in the far future, but certainly not before she turned thirty. Merula imagined something like a gladiatorial *ludus*, a place of training and fitness, but for women like herself to learn the skills necessary to be, as she was, a bodyguard. There would be money in it, she thought; other women, like Lady Latona, would realize the benefit of having such protection. A male bodyguard got noticed; a female one, ignored. Some of the city's collegia might pay to have their women trained, too, the better to defend their neighborhoods.

She could not strike out on the endeavor immediately. Never mind not having enough money—she also had no idea how to run such an establishment. *'I will be having much study ahead of me.'* Gods, was she going to have to learn to do *accounts*? Helva would teach her, no doubt—but what a humiliation, having to sit patiently and take lessons from that cold and judgmental creature. *'Perhaps there is someone else.'* She had friends all across the city, after all. It would take time and dedication, but she could learn.

In the meantime, however...

"I will stay," Merula decided. "For now. For a while, most likely."

Latona smiled broadly, but her shoulders sagged with relief. "Thank Juno. I don't know where I'd find anyone I could trust quite as I trust you."

Awkward with such emotions, Merula rolled a shoulder, casting Latona a sidelong gaze. "Anyway. If I am leaving and you are getting yourself dead, as surely you would within a week, how am I to be getting on with that on my conscience? To say nothing of my reputation."

Latona laughed. "I'm not sure I care for that assessment of my self-preservation instincts—"

"Is being accurate."

"—but I'm grateful for your tender regard for my person."

They came before the magistrate after only a few more moments. The domina had worn her *tunica magicae*, with its prominent black borders. Its magic today seemed to be in shortening the line, although the magistrate himself did not give it a second glance. "State your name and purpose," he said, glancing up from the wax tablets and papers strewn about his table.

"Aula Vitellia Secunda," Latona said, giving her legal name, "here to support the petition of manumission of Merula." A light touch at the base of her back propelled Merula forward.

The magistrate looked up from between bushy dark eyebrows. "Your own property?" he asked, naturally skeptical. So few women owned anything in their own right.

"My father's," Latona said, producing the necessary paperwork. "But my responsibility."

The man took a moment to peruse the paper, and Merula's chest tightened. Would he find some reason to deny the petition? Some cause to yank away the jewel of freedom dangling before Merula's eyes?

But he cleared his throat, setting the paper atop one of his stacks. "Alright, then." He pushed up from the table and came around the side toward them, picking up a slender wooden rod, evidently some sign of his office.

Merula glanced hesitantly at Latona. "I am not knowing what—"

"Here." Gently, Latona maneuvered her so she stood in front of the rod-bearing magistrate. Latona's hands rested lightly on her shoulders, and Merula tried not flinch as the magistrate rested the rod on top of her head.

"Out of the laws of the Quirites and the divine twins Romulus and Remus, as sanctioned by the Twelve Tables and by my authority as a civil magistrate," the man rattled off, in the practiced tone of one who said these words often, "I do recognize the claim to independence of one Merula, previously the enslaved attendant of one Aulus Vitellius Caranus, his interests here represented by his daughter, Aula Vitellia Secunda, acting under his direction, permission, and instruction. Aula Vitellia Secunda, what is your will?"

"It is my will that this be a free woman," Latona said, "with all the rights and privileges of a citizen of Aven."

"Let it be so, in the sight of gods and men," said the magistrate, in the same vaguely bored monotone. He lifted the rod from Merula's head and tucked it under his arm. Latona guided Merula to turn around, facing away from her, and then she lifted her hands from Merula's shoulders.

'Is that it?' Merula wondered. 'A few words and a little gesture, and I am freed?'

That, it seemed, was it, for when she turned back around, Latona's hands were clasped to her chest. "Libertas smile upon you, this day and always, my dear."

Merula wasn't sure what to say. Words of thanks were not quick to rise to her lips. So she stuck with a less complex truth. "I will be glad for her favor, Domina." Still a technically appropriate word, which many freed men and women used for their employers, but a habit she might try to break.

"Nice day for it," the magistrate added, more conversationally, as he moved back to his seat. "Moved by the Saturnalian spirit, eh, Domina?"

"Something like that."

He looked directly into Merula's eyes for the first time. "Well, getting you into the census should be a small enough matter. Tribe Palatina, I suppose?"

"Indeed," Latona affirmed. The urban tribes were defined by what quadrant of the city they lived in—and almost all freedmen and freedwomen ended up in the urban tribes. It weakened the strength of an individual citizen's vote in the Assemblies, since each tribe voted as a whole—but since, as a woman, Merula wouldn't be able to vote, that hardly mattered to her.

Getting into the census, though, that *did* matter. Little enough now; she would only be among the Head Count, the property-less mass of citizens at the bottom of the social heap. *'But not forever. Someday, I am having property. Libertas be good to me, for I will make this so.'*

The magistrate shuffled through the items on his desk, locating one particular wax tablet—evidently the day's tally of manumissions. "And what name will you be going by, freedwoman?"

Some slaves went back to the names of their youth, or Truscanized versions of them, but Merula did not remember hers. The first thing she remembered being called was "girl," by the foreman at the farm she had first been sold to. "Trouble," too, as soon as she had grown old enough to be willful. A trader had given her the name Merula, hoping an Aventan name might fetch a higher price.

However ill-bestowed by a stranger, she supposed it was as good a name as any. *'And I will not be needing to learn to respond to a new one.'* So she lifted her chin and replied, "Merula will do just fine. Vitelliana Merula."

Rarely did Discordia's devotees risk congregating, but on the last day of the year, a passel of them slipped into Durmius Argus's secluded home.

His residence was more private than that of most patricians. Many men, particularly those of political ambitions, left their front doors standing open in the daytime, a signal to any passers-by that they had nothing to hide. Even in supposedly private chambers, there were always servants and slaves, coming and going and standing and waiting. From the cradle to the crematorium, Aventans born to wealth were rarely alone a moment in their lives.

Not so here. Durmius's doors remained shut most days; no jeopardy to his reputation, of course, since he could not climb the *cursus honorem* and had achieved the utmost in his own field when he was appointed to the Augian Commission. That same appointment rendered him unimpeachable and untouchable, nearly as much as a Vestal; his closed doors were no cause for suspicion.

And he *did* admit visitors, guests, and clients. If it was not so often as other men of his class, well, he had pious business to be about, didn't he? Much better conducted in a tranquil environment.

"The time is ripe," her brother said to the figures, some hooded, some bareheaded, who filled the small dining room. "We must change our focus now. The city is frightened. Their fear gives us opportunity."

Her brother was a planner. Corinna was not. Plans fell apart so readily, at the slightest diversion. She rather liked them, for that reason, or at least she enjoyed watching her rivals' plans disintegrate. Her brother's made her nervous. *'We should not be laying our goals out like this, step by step. Act, then see what happens, then act again. That's the right way of it.'*

Durmius continued: "It will no longer accrue to our benefit to continue our campaign of minor aggravations. But we can now claim a certain degree of protection for our larger efforts, our greater goals."

"You speak of your ally," said one of her fellows from deep within his hood. "The political creature."

Did that man know Lucretius Rabirus's identity? Perhaps; some of their number did. A useful tool, Durmius insisted. Corinna doubted. They worked at cross-purposes, for all Durmius endeavored to persuade Rabirus otherwise. *'Even my brother does not fully comprehend, though.'*

How could he? Discordia had not touched his heart, not truly, not as she did those she blessed with her talents. Durmius still thought in terms of cycles, of purging and growth, of a little necessary disruption to earn greater gain in the future. Fortuna, more than Discordia. He did not embrace that disruption was the *point*, the goal all by itself.

Corinna did not blame him for this. He did his best. Perhaps someday, Discordia would open his eyes further.

"He is better positioned now," Durmius said, "to deflect the apparatus of the Aventan state from taking interest in us. To a point. A continued campaign of city-wide disruptions would jeopardize his ability to provide cover. All to the better. Petty mayhem is well enough, small succor to our lady, but we can now think in larger terms. Conserve our strength and make one grand push, something monumental enough to crack this city at its core and allow strife a proper reign."

He was doing that *thing*, Corinna noticed. Spirit magic's trick of making himself seem taller, stronger, more important. He wore authority like a cloak, easily swung on or discarded. Typically he kept it off, but he chose well the moments to don it. Even Corinna found herself susceptible to his persuasion then, a compulsion tugging within her ribs.

Then his demeanor shifted, blue sky after a cloud. He spread his hands open, smiling. "So. Let us plan."

They did, though Corinna hardly listened. What it was necessary for her to do, Durmius would let her know—and she would do it, or not. No few of the other Discordians were men like her brother, either untouched by the goddess's gifts or only lightly given her blessing, and their concerns expanded outside of the immediate. They wanted to weave the goddess's works into politics and economics, into the rise and fall of nations.

'Foolish. Every nation falls, sooner or later. What glory it may be to witness, and if I can, I shall—but these plans, these plans they make! What do they expect? That all the world will lie down neatly for them?'

Corinna knew it was not so. If it were, all her lovely gates would have stayed open. If it were, glitter-gold would never have emerged from the nightmare realm where Corinna had trapped her. *'It should have worked. It should have broken her in so many beautiful ways! The fiends should have eat-*

en their fill, and then if she returned, she could have been one of us, one of Discordia's blessed, maybe then she would have seen the magnificent shattering—'

A pity, though the idea of having an implacable enemy was somewhat satisfying. Lady Discordia was detested even among the gods, after all.

Durmius went on, explaining what he intended their fractious group do in the coming months. Corinna examined the cracks in the mosaic on the floor, each sharp angle and rough edge. She already knew her brother's calculations, and she largely approved, at least on a thaumaturgical level. His political machinations bore little relevance. She was eager to test her magic further, and this plot would give her an avenue for doing so. It *would* require more assistance, to be sure. More hands, a safer space than this bolt-hole, and perhaps the magic of others to supplement her own. No one else in the group had her strength, but some caught on to her methods more swiftly than others. They might be useful.

Once his compatriots departed, Durmius turned his attention back to his sister. "I will join you again tomorrow evening," he said.

"Just you? Or all this company?"

"Neither. I'll be bringing one other. Someone I'd like you to meet, for I think you will have much in common." His lips turned up in a smirk, as though at some private joke. "We'll call him my New Year's present to you."

JANUARIUS
691 ab urbe condita
XVIII

City of Aven

Most temples saw heavier traffic on the Kalends of Januarius than on other days of the year. The New Year wasn't only a lucky day; it was a day when the gods' ears were assured to be open and available to mortals below. Olympus felt closer, and Aven liked to make the most of it.

Latona began her New Year's Day at the temple of Juno Cantatia. Many Aventans considered it good practice to petition Janus first among the gods at the turn of the year, since he was the gatekeeper of Olympus. Pleasing him might make it easier to reach the ears of the other deities. But Latona offered her reverence first to the goddess who most blessed her and whose will she was trying, so hard, to perform in the city. After that, she dropped a New Year's gift off at the Esquiline Collegium: a basket of baked goods to share amongst themselves, with a freshly-embroidered enchanted token for Vatinius Obir, as thanks for all his efforts in looking after her.

From there, she intended to visit the Temple of Venus to give that lady her honors and perhaps have a bit of a chat if Ama Rubellia weren't overwhelmed. Then, Janus and Bellona. A full day of walking for her and Merula; Alhena had her own devotions to attend to, and Aula was paying social calls with their father. They were all to meet in the Forum at midday, then walk together to ask Bellona to protect Gaius and bring him home.

The Temple of Venus was such a crush that Latona struggled to keep her empathic abilities under control. Her grasp on them had grown much more refined, but concentrated intensity could still overwhelm her. Just as well that Rubellia was too busy for more than a kiss on the cheek and a quick blessing, with a promise to catch up later; by the time Latona exited the temple, she was badly in need of air.

Fortunately, the gardens of the nearby Temple of Tellus provided shelter. "Gods above and below," Merula grumbled as they slipped into the comparatively secluded lane. A cluster huddled around the shrine at the entryway, but past that, few people dallied. "One would think the temples were not being open any other day. You ought to draw lots."

Latona laughed at the idea. "Low draw has to rise early, best draws may dawdle in after midday?"

"Something like that."

Even in winter, many of the trees here were green—some by nature, some encouraged by the efforts of Earth mages, for Latona found tiny, verdant tendrils of light around their bases if she looked hard enough. Stone pines created a canopy, insulating this strip of land from the busy city around it. Spiky cypresses and junipers were arranged along the path, with benches placed between them. Ivy grew over brick walls and snaked its way around the trunks of larger trees.

Latona loved Aven, all its noise and color and productive pandemonium, but today, she was glad to choose a secluded bench between two junipers and take a moment to clear her head.

She and Merula had not been there long when another walker approached. The hairs on the back of Latona's neck stood on end as soon as she glanced up, though the newcomer's face was obscured by her close-held snow-white mantle. Latona and Merula both rose, sensing danger.

"I thought you might be here." The voice had a strangely lyrical quality, piping up and down with an odd cadence, and unnervingly blue eyes gazed at her as the woman drew back her mantle. Anca Corinna, bold as anything, standing only a few paces away and smiling.

Merula snarled, reaching for the dagger she always kept strapped to her thigh—but Latona put a hand on her arm to stop her.

"Indeed, little wildcat," Corinna purred, "murders in furtive circumstances are one thing, but in broad daylight with so many witnesses close at hand? Rather another, I think."

"What in Juno's name do you want?" Latona demanded, trying not to think of the agonizing void this woman had tried to consign her to.

Corinna cocked her head to one side, contemplative. "To see you," she said. "To speak with you, glitter-gold. Surely a great many people want to bask in that shine. Why should I not be one of them?"

The malice radiating off of Merula was a palpable distraction, but Latona did not want to block out her magical senses. She would need every one of her wits about her, physical and metaphysical. "I cannot think what we have to say to one another. You are a criminal and a blasphemer and you tried to murder me."

A peal of laughter, high and unrestrained, rippled from Corinna. "You're right, you know!" she said, utterly delighted. Then the mirth vanished, leaving cold iron in its wake. "And you can't prove a thing, nor do you have any authority to haul me in front of."

"All the more reason to be slitting your foul throat and dumping you in the river," Merula growled.

"Yes," Corinna agreed. "Most likely. But you've had that chance once, wildcat, and missed the mark. I don't mean to give you another." Her gaze slid back over to Latona. "Anyway, it's you I wanted. Our prior conversation was so abrupt."

Latona's heart thundered against her ribs. Fear, in part. Body and soul recognized this woman as a threat. Beneath that, though, a more complicated emotion: almost excitement, almost *eagerness*, blended with the trepidation. Here was a chance to know her enemy.

"Very well, Anca Corinna," she said, pronouncing the name carefully to make sure the women *knew* she had been identified. "Let us chat." She gestured off the path, suspecting the conversation would not benefit from being overheard.

Latona and Corinna remained several paces apart, even as they withdrew beneath the many-forked branches of a myrtle. 'Myrtles are Venus's tree,' Latona thought. 'My territory. Oh, blessed lady, cast your eye upon me and keep me from danger.'

She had no Fire to draw on here, no torch or brazier or glowing embers. If Corinna attacked, she would have only the strength of her own heart and blood to rely on—only Spirit magic, set against its inimical element. Merula stayed at Latona's elbow, no doubt ready to carry through on her homicidal promise should an excuse present itself.

Corinna gave no sign of imminent threat, however. She was stroking the tree's branches, all the places where animals or weather had stripped away the bark. "I imagine," she said in that odd, lilting tone, "that you are as curious about me as I am about you."

"Only in that it is wise to educate oneself about threats," Latona said, but the words tasted of dishonesty. She *was* curious about Corinna. Another female mage in the city with so much power, dedicated to her cause—but why *this* cause? Why something so perverse and harmful?

"I confess," Corinna said, "when I saw you on Capraia, I never imagined you would prove so formidable an opponent."

Ice shot down Latona's spine, and her chest and throat tightened. All memories of Capraia were locked at the very back of her memory, things she could not manage to discard but never wanted to take out and air. Her time there, captivity in all but name, hostage to Ocella's whims for the sake of her family's safety, had been a prolonged nightmare. She lived for months with her heart in her throat, every moment a cautious dance: be pleasing, but avoid notice; be valuable, but not useful; smile and smile and never let the Dictator see her shudder at his touch.

In months past, she had confronted this dark period again and again. The *umbrae*, when they appeared to her, took Ocella's form as he had been on Capraia, predatory and prowling. The thickness in her throat, the buzzing warmth that snaked down her forearms and itched in her palms, the fear that seized her jaw and pricked at the back of her eyes—all this, she learned to work through. As hard as she might try to slam a door between herself and those memories, she could not deny them entry entirely, particularly not when a fiend assumed her tormentor's shape.

And now Corinna spoke of it, so casually, as though they had merely been on holiday together on that gods-forsaken island. *'She says it to unsettle you. Do not award her the victory. She wants you to fight—she wants discord, of course.'*

With great effort, Latona relaxed her hands. "I must confess," she said, as mildly as she was able, "neither did I."

"Yes, you were a mouse of a thing then." Corinna's limbs were loose, her shoulders low, her hips swaying. "Just another pretty Fire mage, and everyone knew what use Ocella found in those. Venus's girls, all shine and no steel. Ornaments and toys."

The old fear thudded in Latona's core. No matter that the man was dead; the thought of him sparked defensive instincts in her and always would. "I made a bargain," was all she would say.

"Oh, don't think I count that against you." Corinna laughed, an unsettling tintinnabulation. "No, no. We must all use whatever tools come to hand…" Her attention drifted, her neck craning over her shoulder, gazing off at the surrounding hills.

Under her breath, Merula muttered, "Leave this madwoman, Domina. What value is there in speaking with a cursed beast?"

Latona knew she ought to walk away, for the sake of her nerves if nothing else. Yet the fascination persevered. *'This woman is my dark mirror. Inimical elements, inverted values, utter opposites in so many ways, and yet…'* Little though she cared to admit it, she could see likenesses, too: in endurance, in ferocity, in devotion.

She risked probing Corinna with her empathetic magic, a tentative brush. She did not want to extend much of herself; Fracture could seize and warp her magic, but she wanted to know what this woman *felt* like. Expecting a torrent of conflicting emotions, a wild disarray of the soul, what she touched instead was like a cloud of unspun wool, hazy and indistinct. She could get no easy read.

Not without provocation, at least.

"Is that what set you on this path?" Latona asked. "Ocella left his mark on so many. I know what Capraia did to me. What did it do to you?" Corinna's eyes fixed on her, fast as a striking snake, but she gave no verbal response. Latona felt a frizzle of energy, though, hot and defiant lacing through the murk of Corinna's soul. "Did it give you this thirst for destruction, this desire to annihilate? Did it push you into the arms of Discordia?"

All the languidity snapped out of Corinna's body. Now she resembled far more the fiend-summoning adversary Latona had faced down, intent and furious. The unearthly blue of her eyes struck like an arrow, like Ocella's. "Do not do that," Corinna warned. "Do not. Ocella may have altered *you*, but he made nothing of me that I was not already." She lifted her chin, implacable pride in every angle of her face. "I see what you're trying."

"Do you?"

"A way to explain me, to rationalize me, to *lessen* me through some reason." Corinna tsked loudly. "You should know better, glitter-gold. Never try to reduce another woman down to something smaller than she is."

"What *are* you, then?" Impatience and temper both were rising past her ability to bank them. "A zealot? That much is clear. But what—"

"No!" Corinna's fingers curled, and Latona kept her own Spirit magic ready to provide defense, should she lash out. "I will not let a story be made of me that is not of my own devising. I will not be dismissed as a madwoman or a tragedy. I have not been broken." Her lips curled in distaste. "That's what you think, isn't it? What you want to hear? That something broke me, something snapped my poor fragile wits and left me a blasphemer?" No musicality in her voice now; rather the shriek of a kestrel in the dive. "I have not been broken. I have broken *myself*, in glorious service to Lady Discordia, and I have never sorrowed for it."

Revulsion warred with a warped sort of respect in Latona's heart. Still she could not sense Corinna's emotions, not exactly, but a hundred jagged edges pressed back against her magic. "You claim you were born like this, then? Born with a shattered soul, fit only for destruction?

"I don't know," Corinna half-sang, her head lolling to one side. "I don't recall it. But from the moment Discordia set her hand upon me, I was marked, every bit as Juno and Venus marked you. Who would you be, without their influence? Can you separate yourself from the gifts they gave you, from the way those gifts shaped you?" Latona had no ready answer, and Corinna sniffed in disdain. "Of course not. No more can I. So I will be utterly damned rather than award Horatius Ocella credit for *my* making. But you!" She laughed, too loud, too unrestrained. "You created yourself from his ashes, I think. Born like the phoenix of the east, able to rise only through destruction. What you are is a reaction to the damage he did. Can you deny it?"

She wanted to; passionately, she wanted to. But Latona's power had only flared after Ocella's life ended. The threat of him hemmed her in for so long. Even after his death, the black mark he had put upon her reputation continued to haunt her. In trying to escape that legacy, she was nonetheless responding to it. And how could she deny his ongoing influence on her life when every mention of him stifled her lungs, put a weight in her stomach and a tremor in her fingers? When the damned *umbrae* took his form to spook her?

So she did not deny it. Instead, she said something true, forcing the words past the tightness that stretched from beneath her ears down into her chest. "I am made of many things, many experiences."

"No doubt, no doubt." The lyric quality returned to Corinna's voice. "And it *is* impressive, don't think I don't see that, how you spun pain into strength. But to what end? You still place bounds upon yourself." Corinna's feet began to amble. Merula tensed, though Corinna had not angled in their direction. "Lovely glitter-gold, so eager for others to see her sparkle. But oh, if you let go of that, if you took all those fences away, how you could *blaze*! What fine chaos you could create, what beautiful tangles, what a gorgeous storm."

"If this is a recruitment speech," Latona growled, "you may spare yourself the breath."

"You want change, though," Corinna challenged. "I can feel it in you, practically screaming."

"I want change," Latona admitted, "but I will not burn the world down to get it."

"It's what my brother wants, too," Corinna said. Her tone was casual, but Latona leaned forward slightly. *This* might be useful, might make this whole awful conversation worth it. "And all his friends. They talk so, talking and talking, I grow quite weary. They want the world torn apart so they can make it anew. A *different* new than yours, I expect." Corinna smiled, too prettily. "You could try to beat them at their own game, if you think you're strong enough. Brave enough. Try to tear it down faster, build it back stronger."

At last, Latona felt something in Corinna's emotions that she could get a grip on, a revelation of the true woman, underneath the disorienting haze. "But whoever wants it," she said slowly, tentatively testing her understanding, "will have to beat you, too. Does your brother know that?"

Corinna's eyes widened; for the first time in the conversation, Latona had scored a proper point. Mention of Durmius Argus provoked an odd loop of emotion from Corinna, but nestled at the core was *anger*.

"Does he know," Latona went on, "that your goals are not aligned with his?" A guess, but each pulse of Corinna's increasingly frantic emotions told her she was close to striking true. "You're not in it for the rebuilding. You want to do your lady honor. A new order wouldn't do that. You want to tear everything apart and just keep tearing. Does your brother know, and he thinks he can control you? Keep you from doing as you please? Or have you played him false? Your own blood, who shelters and protects you, have you misled him in such a fundamental thing?"

Dangerous territory; Fracture's energy sizzled in Corinna now. She could draw strength nearly anywhere. The snap of a twig, the crumble of a stone, any break, any border. *'Her strength is everywhere.'*

But a more encouraging thought followed hard upon: *'So is mine. Mine exists wherever I am, for it is in my own heart and blood.'*

She flexed her fingers, concentrated until she could feel her pulse, ready to draw from its strength if Corinna took action, and went on, pleased to have wrested control of the conversation. "If you and your brother want to tear Aven apart, it's not just me who will stand in your way. There is far greater strength in unity than in your breaking, and I mean to build upon that strength. Senseless ravening or studied corruption, it doesn't matter. Our coalition will be far stronger than your kin-devouring collection of blasphemers. And we will not let Discordia take this city."

Sharp cinnamon on her tongue, tingling in her fingertips, a slight golden haze over her vision—something about this was drawing Spirit magic, unintentional.

Corinna seemed to sense it, recoiling from her—but she smiled, too. "Ohh, you will try, glitter-gold. *Please* try. Such pleasure there will be in shredding what you assemble."

Then she darted away, faster than Latona or even Merula could react. She had chosen her moment well: as she dashed down the path, a magister herding a group of small children came wandering through. Latona and Merula could not pursue her without raising a scene.

Neither magister nor children stopped Merula from wrenching free her dagger at last, then turning and, in a swift snap of her arm, sinking it into the trunk of the nearest pine, grunting in frustration as she did so. "I hate that woman, Domina. I *hate* her."

"You are not alone in that, Merula." Beyond what she had done to Latona herself, Corinna had committed any number of crimes, many unforgivable. The woman was well worth hating. "But I think I may understand her a little better now."

Latona could not continue on to Janus, not after that, but the walk home was far from pacifying.

"Find me something I can set on fire," Latona told Merula as soon as they were back in the house. "A nice, controlled little fire. I'll do it right by the pool in the garden."

"Is being on your own head if you set the furniture ablaze," Merula said as she headed for the kitchens.

At the same time, Aula popped her head out from the sitting room. "Why are we setting things on fire? And what are you doing back? I thought we were meeting you in the Forum in another hour or so."

Latona pressed her lips thin, not wanting to air her news where many others might hear it. "Get Alhena and meet me in the garden."

The garden of the Vitellian domus was set around a rectangular pool, both longer and shallower than that in the atrium. They decorated with trellises more than trees, overgrown with ivy, though a few junipers did stand near the columns. Alhena kept songbirds, twittering in their elaborate cages.

Latona settled down cross-legged at the far end, hoping she looked enough like One About To Do Magic to keep the household staff at a distance. Merula brought her a large clay dish with an assortment of kindling and odd ends tossed in it: strips of wood and bark, rags ready for discarding, husks from shelled peas and a few other greens. Then she plunked a bronze lamp down next to the dish and stood several feet back, arms folded over her chest.

Latona's blood leapt to have fire so near, even if it was only the gentle flicker of an oil lamp. It called out to her, heated her skin, sizzled in her blood.

Grasping the flames still did not always come readily, as much as she had practiced, but her emotions were riding high enough that today, they hopped into her palm as obediently as a trained sparrow. Latona rolled the fire up and down her fingers like an acrobat with a ball, feeling its painless warmth on her skin. She concentrated on the heart of the flame, white-hot and exuberant, eager to play.

After a few moments, her sisters sat down on either side of her, Alhena folded up neatly on the tiled floor, Aula throwing a pillow down first. "So," Aula said, eyeing the flames warily, "what in Juno's name happened to put you in such a mood?"

Latona related her encounter, attempting to keep her tone as cool and steady as possible, channeling all of her heat and ire into the flames in her palms. They became an extension of her *anima*, bleeding the sharp edges off painful memories and taking the burden of her troubled heart. It gave her someplace to steady the emotions she perceived from the others too: Aula's mounting anger and indignation, Alhena's quiet fear and deep-nested defiance, Merula's continued impotent rage and regret. Steadily, the white core of the fire grew, edging out the red and orange.

"So," she said when she had told the tale, "not the morning I intended to have—but I do think I learned something of worth. And..." She sighed, then let the flames roll off her fingers at last, tipping them into the kindling in the clay dish. Hungrily, they seized upon the driest bits first, snapping and hissing like voracious little lizards. "And she may have a point."

Aula made a half-choked noise. "Diana's tits, she certainly does not!"

The unquestioning rancor towards their foe made Latona smile. Whatever Aula's faults, disloyalty could never be counted among them. "She did, though. At least in the matter of... of Ocella." In the dish, the flames popped and flared. "It's something I can even admire in her. She gives him no credit for her making."

"Well, neither have you!" Aula sputtered.

Nearly the same words Latona had shot back at Corinna, but she saw the weakness in them. "Not credit, precisely but..." Latona settled her shoulders back. "I wonder if I haven't granted him too much power. What he did— Well, it's been over a long time. Years. He's been dead for years, too." She twirled a finger over the bowl of flames, twisting their shape into a ragged spiral. "Perhaps I should be... should be over it, by now."

Aula regarded Latona with her usual protective fury, but when she spoke, her voice was ice cold. "You don't ever have to be 'over it.' That is no obligation upon you. What he did to you, that violation, that isn't—that isn't something you must simply get over or dismiss or forget." Aula drew a deep breath, and it shook when she let it out. "I don't think I'll ever be *over* seeing Lucius's blood on the floor."

Latona reached over and squeezed her sister's hand. Aula so infrequently spoke of her own pains, always burying them beneath layers of duty and aggressively determined cheerfulness. Alhena held her tongue, as she so often did, but scooted closer to both of them, lending her silent, unjudging support.

"Being affected by that violence," Aula continued, "it doesn't mean I've let it or Ocella define me. They haven't *made* me. Even if it never goes away. Even if it's always a little part of me." Her pretty lips turned up in a knowing smile. "A part I put in a box and stuff to the bottom of the trunk of my mind. That it exists does not define me. That I still feel its weight does not mean I am made by it. And it does not mean I've granted the man responsible for that pain any ongoing power in my life."

"You are no less for your scars," Alhena half-whispered. "I mean. I never thought so, anyway. You weren't brave *because* of him, even though he forced you into a certain way of showing it."

"Yes," Aula said. "That was all you, my dear, and always has been, even when, well!" She gestured at the flames. "When your light hasn't been given enough air and space to burn as brightly as it should. *That's* the core of you. In spite of Ocella—and Father, and your useless husband, and Aemilia Fullia, and anyone else. Not because of them." She chucked Latona under the chin. "Juno and Venus must be proud."

"You two are the very best of sisters, you know," Latona said. She thought of Corinna, secretly at odds with her brother; of the Crispiniae, always sniping at each other and competing for attention; of Maia Domitia, whose only sisters had died in childhood. "How lucky we are to have each other."

They sat in companionable silence, watching the flames as Latona allowed them to burn themselves down, her turbulent emotions purged, at least in part, at least for now. Alhena rested her head on Latona's shoulder; Lucia wandered in with her kitten and sat in her mother's lap.

"Gods above," a soft voice said. Aulus, returning from his work, was standing at the edge of the garden, smiling. "I should have you all painted."

Aula moved Lucia out of her lap and rose, brushing her hands on her skirts. "I'd be happy to be immortalized in art," she declared, grinning broadly. "I think we'd make a very fine fresco, so whenever you want to hire someone, we'll arrange ourselves accordingly. Are you ready to go to Bellona?"

"Yes, at last. So much to attend to at the start of the year—but we should get going so we're back in time to ready ourselves for dinner. And!" Aulus added cheerfully, crooking a finger at his granddaughter. "I have good news for you, Lucia. It's a small family affair, so they've said you may come and take your supper with Neria and Nerilla, if you like."

Lucia gasped in delight, squeezing her kitten to her chest. "Truly?"

"*If,*" Aula clarified, "you have your bath now, while we're at the temple, and let Gera do something with your hair."

"Can she make it look like Aunt Lala's?"

"She can try, my love," Aula said, steering her daughter towards the edge of the garden.

Latona stood, lifting the clay dish in her hands. As her family gathered up cloaks and shoes, she walked down the length of the house and set the dish before the altar. The fire could safely burn itself out there; that felt more honorable than dousing it. "These flames sought to provide me solace," she said in a hushed voice. "And so, blessed Venus, I dedicate them to your glory."

Anca Corinna returned home in a flurry of clouded emotions. She thought the texture of Vitellia Latona's magic familiar by now, burning so bright, but there in the garden, something *else* had flowed through it. Something *more.* '*Something not her own, I think.*' Something drawn *through* her, more like.

Corinna did not know what it was, nor where it came from, and that pinched at her confidence.

To assuage herself, she spent the afternoon unraveling a bedsheet, tearing it thread by thread, so when her brother came in the evening—as she had forgotten he promised to do—he found her sitting in a heap of tangled fibers, much more contented than hours earlier.

Durmius gave the scene no more than a considering blink before ushering forward his companion, a reed-thin man swathed in charcoal-gray.

Corinna leapt to her feet, drawn by the power shivering off of him, beautifully chaotic, splinters and snarls. "Who are you?" she breathed giddily.

"His name, I think you will recognize," Durmius said. "Scaeva, I have told you before of my sister, Anca Corinna. Corinna, this is Pinarius Scaeva."

A pioneer, truly, a visionary. Oh, how Corinna wished she had seen it, his work during the Aventine fires, tearing open a maw that would devour whatever tried to fight it.

"You were broken."

"I was, lady." His voice rasped; his eyes did not quite focus on her.

"We have reclaimed his mind," Durmius explained. "Salonius and I took great pains—"

"Pity."

Corinna did have to admit, though, that he was of more use when in control of his faculties than as a drooling, raving mess. A little less Discordia's, perhaps, but a better tool for her cause. *Once we've won, we can return him to her bosom.* Breaking his mind a second time would be simpler than putting it back together.

She strode to him, clasped his head between her hands. "You are *blessed.* Discordia has smiled upon you as she has few others." She pressed a kiss to his brow. "What a glorious creature you are."

Scaeva swayed; his smile was a touch vacant, but he nodded. "I do, I do feel closer to her than once I was."

Durmius gently touched his sister's shoulder, drawing her a step back from Scaeva. "We are grateful for your restitution," he said. "At this time, as we gather our powers for a show of true devotion to our lady, your participation will be most welcome."

Still Scaeva swayed, his thin frame shifting from one foot to the other. "I will do my best, of course..." he began, vaguely, but then intensity seized him. "Yes, yes, we have opportunity now. A nation on the brink, so many people with so many wants, such desire, such greed and anger and beautiful *strife*, boiling just below the surface."

As his rant picked up speed, Scaeva changed languages every few words, from Truscan to Athaecan and back. *'He cannot even keep his mind fixed in one tongue,'* Corinna thought, delighted, envious.

"Strife, glorious strife, we could unlock so much of it. The gates, they beckon, they rattle, they clang. Bronze gates, such beautiful music. Openings, here and there, here and here, here and—" His wobbling head snapped toward Corinna, and he lifted a shaking finger. "It was you, wasn't it? You found the way."

False humility always grated on her. "I did," she announced with full-throated pride. "I learned to unlock the barriers, to wedge the gate open, and I showed the others how." And open they stayed, unless someone meddled.

Scaeva giggled. Incongruous, in a man of his age and appearance, and Corinna thrilled at the dissonance. "But the biggest gate of all, the true breach, that would take much more, I think? Yes?"

"Yes," Corinna said. "To throw it open so wide that no one, no glitter-gold or any of her associates, could close it again—that would be a worthy endeavor."

Scaeva's pale eyes were almost entirely consumed by the black of his pupil. "Trouble, though. Opponents."

Corinna's heart swelled with fury, swift and fierce, the utter indignity of it all. "You understand, don't you? She stopped you, too, they both did. Glitter-gold and the knife's edge."

A sneer curled Scaeva's lip. His next words were more grounded, closer to the world-dwelling man he had once been. "The golden one must have grown stronger. I'd have finished her off easily. She'd poured out so much of herself—"

"She still does that. I almost had her, too." Oh, what a thing it was to speak to someone who understood! "She *is* growing stronger. Her gods stand with her, and she learns fast. Her and—"

"Yes, the other," Scaeva nodded. "The other, so keen, so sharp, so fine, and the—the—" A queer look crumpled his face, tight and peering. Then he shook his whole body, like a wet dog. "There was something else, but it's too hard to see. A shadow on a dark night."

Corinna frowned. What had reached her of those events was less than rumor. Magic itself had written part of the story. One of her brother's colleagues in the Augian Commission, an Air mage, had visited the scene to read what signatures remained. Scaeva's, of course, and glitter-gold's effusive Spirit energy splashed all over, and another Fracture mage's—Vibia

Sempronia's, the knife's edge. He had mentioned traces of another power, but they had faded. Corinna had assumed it was glitter-gold's sister, the little prophetess, but something about Scaeva's words now made her wonder.

"We will find the missing pieces," Durmius assured him. "We will give you what you need—both of you—to prepare the way for our lady's glory."

"Yes," Corinna said, grasping Scaeva's hands. Let glitter-gold say what she liked about unity and strength; with another *true* disciple at her side, Corinna could break any bond.

XIX

Fortress of Legio X Equestris, Central Iberia

Soon after the turning of the year, Sempronius Tarren received a packet of letters with some good fortune mixed among the ill tidings. Of the wretched turn of the elections, he had heard already. Vibia reported the installation of the Optimates into their offices with tart efficiency, then shared two bits of advantageous news: that a quaestor was headed for Tarraco, to take over administrative duties there while Sempronius remained in the field, and that Aufidius Strato, given proconsular command of Baelonia and its legions, had set off for Ostia the very afternoon he'd been sworn into the office.

This, Sempronius shared with Felix and the Arevaci chieftain Bartasco, both of whom had been taking dinner in his quarters when the packet of letters arrived. "General Strato intends to set off immediately!" he announced. "A year and a half in Aven was too much domestication for him, it seems. He is eager to rejoin a legion and take the field."

"Dangerous to travel now, is it not?" Bartasco asked, frowning.

"Hazardous, certainly," Sempronius agreed. The open seas were stormy and uncertain this time of year, but a boat that hugged the coast would be safer. "He has only to find passage for himself, though, which makes things easier. If Fortuna blesses him, he could be in Gades by early Februarius." The idea thrilled Sempronius. "If he brings the Second up from the south, we could crush the Vettoni between us, then push the Lusetani westward."

"In winter?" Felix asked, surprised. "Leave the fortress, before the campaign season starts?"

"Why not?" Sempronius asked—though there were several good reasons, all of which he had answers for. "The Lusetani and Vettoni clearly intend to. Why should we sit here and allow them to plunder the country-

189

side? Our vexillations won't be enough to quell them entirely." Though, following the incident at the Anas River, his had made short work of the remaining bandits in that area. "We leave a garrison here—" A garrison could begin training new recruits, drawn from the local populations of both Iberian and Aventan towns. "—but if we can press an advantage, we ought to do so."

Bartasco and Felix eyed each other. "The weather could prove risky," Bartasco said, "but we would be moving down out of the heights, where the winter is milder."

"And many of our men were already hardened on the Vendelician border," Sempronius said. "Damp and chill won't trouble them. The newer recruits—well, they'll bundle up. Your magic-men, how are they with weather?"

Bartasco stroked his bushy red beard—in need of a trim, as was Sempronius's hair, though he kept himself well-shaved, to present the image of a controlled and dignified Aventan leader. "They can often tell when a major storm will come," he said. "The sky-readers look for certain signs."

"Well, tell them to keep their eyes wide open. We'll mark out some places to retreat to if ice and snow are bearing down on us. Otherwise, we press toward the coast. We take every inch of ground from the Lusetani that we can. Supplies will be a challenge, but I've talked to the quartermaster, and he has some clever ideas."

Felix looked more excited by the moment. Bartasco remained contemplative—not an ill thing. If Sempronius's notion had holes he hadn't thought of yet, he wanted them pointed out before he broached the idea with Onidius Praectus, who led the Fourteenth Legion from its fortress on the opposite hill. Before they could discuss further, however, Corvinus entered with a scrap of paper in his hand.

"Excuse me for intruding," he said, "but I've received an odd note from Tribune Vitellius, brought by an advance rider." Vitellius led the latest vexillation, a short patrol only a few miles downriver and back. "They're not far away, and he has a... a gift for you."

Sempronius lifted an eyebrow. "And here I thought Saturnalia had passed."

There were not *no* secrets in a fortress this size; Sempronius managed to keep his magical abilities sheltered, despite the close quarters. But there were certainly *few* secrets, and so even though Vitellius arrived after nightfall, all of the Tenth Legion seemed to have turned out to witness his arrival, once word spread from the sentries upon the wall.

Sempronius decided to meet Vitellius openly; the whole legion had interest in this, whatever it was, so they may as well see it. *'And it serves me well if my reputation is for candor in my dealings, not subterfuge.'*

Gaius Vitellius came down the via praetoriana at the head of a narrow column. Some of his men dispersed to the stables or the quaestorium to stow gear. Sempronius could not see what marched behind the legion's banners, but it was setting up a stir among the men as it passed. Felix squinted and twisted his neck this way and that, trying to get a better view; Sempronius stood perfectly still. It would come to him. No need for impatience.

Vitellius drew to a halt before him, saluting. "General, well-met."

"We hear you've brought us something," Felix said, still peering down the camp's central lane. "Feeling cryptic, were you?"

"To be honest, I wasn't certain how to put it in words." He rotated, gesturing others forward. "Saying that I have an Iberian captive doesn't do justice to the spectacle."

Vitellius's specialists brought forward a man strapped to a pole—dangling from it, in fact, lashed by his wrists and ankles. A leather strap was between his teeth, cutting bloody blisters into the edges of his mouth. The pale yellow of his wool tunic was brown and maroon with blood beneath his ribs. His hands and forearms, his neck and jaw, all were inked in the manner of many Iberians—but not with the bluish-black markings Sempronius had come to expect from the Arevaci and Edetani. The swirling lines and carefully arranged dots all over his pale skin were crimson.

'Well. That's probably not auspicious.'

Watching the procession, Bartasco lifted a bushy eyebrow. "Is it the Aventan custom to string up their prisoners like pigs for a banquet?"

"There was no other way," Vitellius said. "Even once we took him down, he still fought. It was this or a cage, and cages are too much trouble to transport."

"Took him down?" Sempronius asked. "In battle, I presume? How long ago?"

"Yesterday. Gladius strike to the gut," Vitellius confirmed. "Lift his tunic, you'll see. It's like the others. He shouldn't be alive, and yet—" Vitellius gestured broadly with one hand.

"Lusetani?" Bartasco said. "Not Vettoni?"

"As near as I could tell, yes, Lusetani."

"As Hanath said at the Anas River," Bartasco said. "Friend Sempronius, I would like for my magic-men to examine this captive."

"Just what I was thinking."

"I'm curious myself," Felix said. "Winning this war will be a lot simpler if men who are stabbed fall as they ought to."

They took the prisoner to the quaestorium, a long building that stretched toward the wall behind Sempronius's command quarters. The quaestorium was mostly the quartermaster's domain, a place for holding supplies and plunder, but it was also generally the place in a legionary camp best equipped to hold onto captives. They stretched the Lusetani warrior out on a table, binding his wrists and ankles to each wooden leg. Still he writhed and bucked, grunting and moaning beneath his gag.

Two of the Arevaci magic-men flanked him, with Bartasco and Sempronius standing a few steps away; Felix and Vitellius farther back still, near a few of the highest-ranked centurions that—for transparency's sake—Sempronius had invited to observe whatever was about to occur. On the outside, Vitellius looked every bit the stalwart Aventan soldier, but his anxieties were pulsing so forcefully that Sempronius was tempted to send him away to rid himself of the distraction.

'No,' he amended, upon closer inspection with a brush of his own Shadow magic. *'Not anxiety, not fear. More... distaste.'* Vitellius did not want to be there, witnessing this event.

Strange, and not strange. The young tribune was not above ordering torture when circumstances dictated; it was how he had garnered valuable information, long before Sempronius arrived in Iberia. Ordering it and bearing witness to it weren't the same, of course, but Sempronius did not think mere queasiness was behind Vitellius's reticence now. *'He's seen too much of this. The blood magic, the fiends, the unnatural creations. I should send him home. Give his soul respite.'*

Soft chanting from the magic-men around the table drew Sempronius's attention back. Though he had picked up some of the Arevaci dialect in the past several months, that was not what the magic-men spoke. The cadence was all wrong, the consonants snapped in different places. The magic-men of Iberia had a language all their own.

Sempronius's own Water magic could not see the workings of such different gifts, not in the wispy colors he was accustomed to. Its energy buzzed around him, though, setting all the hairs on his arms on end. His fingertips itched, and his chest ached with the yearning to understand these strange enchantments. Seeing magic without knowing its secrets was like sitting down to a feast yet being told not to eat a bite.

The warrior on the table continued to struggle, bucking against the ropes that bound him. His wrists were chafed raw, blood seeped from the corners of his mouth, and the wound in his belly would never improve, yet he gave no sign that he felt pain or indeed had any idea that he was injured. That battle fervor could take over a man was commonly known; in the heat of the moment, a warrior might not feel a wound. But to remain insensible of it a full day later?

'This is more unnatural sorcery.' And until he knew it better, Sempronius would not risk underestimating its peril.

The Arevaci magic-men ran their splayed-open hands up and down the warrior's form, hovering just above his skin. Each part of him went still in turn, paralyzed by their mystical efforts. The warrior's eyes alone retained their untrammeled fury, silently raging against his captors.

"This is like no magic I have ever seen," pronounced the elder of the two magic-men—or so Sempronius had judged him, by the length and hoar of his beard.

"And those are words I have heard all too often," Bartasco grumbled. Sempronius was glad for Bartasco's interjection; he didn't feel it was his place to chastise the Arevaci magic-men, but he too had grown weary of their inability to explain their opponent's maneuvers. "You've had some effect on him, at least. Tell us what you *do* know."

"He's alive," said the younger of the magic-men.

"Still alive, yes," the older said. "Because of these." From inside his furs, he withdrew a bone needle; with that, he prodded the red markings that whorled over the warrior's body. As soon as the point touched skin, the man began to seize, an agonized howl ripping from his throat.

Sempronius fixed the elder magic-man with a hard gaze. "Explain. As best you are able."

"The markings, they are... a conduit."

"For what? Be specific."

The magic-man's shoulders moved in diffidence. "I cannot be specific, because this is beyond our powers. I can make guesses."

Sempronius's jaw ached, and he had to consciously cease grinding his teeth. "Make them. Now and in detail."

The magic-man huffed slightly, but he made a conceding gesture. "It is as though they are inviting the *akdraugi*—or something like them—within their very skin. It may be not exactly those spirits, but... some other force, drawn from worlds beyond. It may be the invocation of Bandue the war-god himself."

"None of those are encouraging prospects," Felix muttered from behind Sempronius.

"No. They are not." Sempronius glanced down at the groaning warrior. "I take it some spirit—never mind its nature, philosophy can wait—enters their body and, what? Keeps them alive when they ought to be dead?"

"Keeps them moving, at least, until the very last moment."

"A man who loses an arm," offered the younger magic-man, "loses blood swiftly. He will fight like a god until his blood is spent, and then, no more. A wound like this, though—"

"A wound like this can take much longer to kill a man," Sempronius said. "Yes, I know." He had seen enough gut wounds in his life, and he thought of his friend Vatinius Nisso, whose passing he had eased. "Is he feeling pain?"

"I should not think so," the elder magic-man said. "The spirits inhabiting him do not let him, for if he did, he would know himself for dead, and perhaps cease to fight."

"I would almost say," ventured the younger magic-man again, "that the spirits *eat* the pain."

"Curious. Do you think—"

In that instant, the warrior gave a great lunge, bursting all the bonds upon him, leaping up from the table. He grabbed the elder magic-man's head between his hands and smashed his forehead into the man's face, then whirled, seizing the table and hurling it at the younger magic-man. Next he dove straight for Sempronius—but Autronius Felix was there first, too fast for him, jamming his short sword between the man's neck and collarbone, driving down hard toward his chest. Even that did not suffice to slay him, though his blood sprayed in every direction.

Bartasco came from behind, kicking hard at the back of the warrior's knees. He staggered, still growling. Bartasco seized him by the hair, stepping on the back of his legs to pin him in place, and Felix, moving fluidly, yanked his sword free and swung again at the warrior's neck. The gladius was a stabbing implement, not built for slicing, and it took several blows to hack the man's head free from his body. Bartasco cast it to the earth as soon as it was severed. Felix took a step back but kept his sword ready, watching as the body toppled to the ground.

Still, the man's eyes were wild with hatred, and his lips continued to form curses, several breaths longer than should have been possible. His fist pounded the earth three times—and then all motion ceased.

A long silence followed. The younger magic-man was tending to his elder, and Vitellius went to call for a medic. Felix swore and pushed blood-damp hair out of his eyes with the edge of his hand. "If we have to kill each of the bastards a few different times before it takes," he said, "it's going to be a long winter."

"No," Sempronius said darkly, never minding the blood splashed over his own limbs and garments. "We must make it a short one. As brief as possible."

Western Iberia

In the deadest part of the winter, the sunlight was weak, hardly more than a limpid white glow from behind the clouds. This river was not the Tagus, far too deep and wide to cross without a raft or boat, but one of its tributaries. And it was *frigid*. "I don't know if I can do this," Neitin whimpered, backing away. Sticking one foot in had been too terrible, and she was already so cold. Sakarbik had insisted they strip naked and put their clothing in their satchels, which Sakarbik would balance atop her head. Neitin's arms were full of Matigentis. "And he's so small. The shock of the cold..."

"We have no choice," Sakarbik said. Her voice had no heat to it, no anger, but was hard as granite, utterly unyielding. "Crossing will make it more difficult for both worldly and magical hounds to follow us. And if you want to keep pressing south and east, we must cross at some point."

Neitin regarded the water with trepidation. She loved rivers, most of the time. She had grown up on the banks of the Tagus closer to the ocean, where it was a broad azure ribbon cutting through green countryside. Months earlier, Neitin had waded into the Tagus to bless her child and ask favor of the gods. Beneath the full strength of the summer sun, she had stood in the shallows, cool and refreshing water lapping at her legs. But with dead leaves around her feet and bare branches above her head, this stream looked dark and unforgiving.

Sakarbik was in up to her knees. "You won't get any warmer standing there!" she called over her shoulder. "And I have your clothes!"

A regrettable truth.

Squeezing her eyes shut and whispering a prayer to Nabia, Neitin stepped in again. One foot, then the other, sliding against the smooth stones of the river bottom.

"Downriver first," Sakarbik instructed. "Then we will cross."

Neitin understood the principle; she had spent enough of her life around hunters and trackers. If they came out directly across from where they went in, it would not be difficult to pick up their scent again.

Her feet tingled with the cold. *What will happen when we do have to cross wider and deeper rivers?* Perhaps they could find another friendly village, on the shore this time, someone with a fishing boat or a raft... Sakarbik's contacts thus far had been very kind, and Neitin would have liked to have stayed with them longer, but that was impossible with *akdraugi* on their heels.

The river stones were slick with algae. Neitin was almost glad. The more she had to concentrate on keeping her balance, the less attention she had for how cold she was. The wind had kicked up to torment her, she was sure, more frigid where it cut across the water than it was over land. She didn't even have her hair as a protective cloak; Sakarbik had made her bind it up on the crown of her head. Again, sensible; she would not like trying to dry it in this chill.

After a time, Sakarbik determined that they had gone far enough downstream. She whistled to Neitin, turned, and began wading her way to the far bank.

'Surely it cannot be but so deep,' Neitin thought, shivering as she reoriented herself. *'It's not that large. It can't be too deep.'*

Turning aside exposed Mati to the wind, which his mother's back had previously shielded him from. He began to fuss, squirming in her arms. "No!" he shouted, tiny hands curling into fists. "No, no!"

"I quite agree, my love," she murmured, pressing a kiss into his hair. "But we have to. Not much longer, I promise."

The current grew stronger as she stepped further from the shore, and the water was now up to her hips. It brushed Mati's feet, which made him squall and kick. "No! No, bad!" the boy howled. Neitin had to squeeze him tighter, trying to keep his flailing limbs under control.

Step by agonizing, careful step, she progressed across the stream. The water pushed at her, so eager to coax her under. For the briefest of moments, Neitin wondered what it would be like—to let go, to let the current have her, to become a woman all of ice and cold. *'Nabia rules the waters. Falling into her embrace... there are worse things...'*

But Mati's increasingly aggrieved shouts brought her back to herself. She thought instead of the warmth of his skin against hers, the scent of his hair, the pains she had taken to bring him into this world and to protect his every breath. *'I have dedicated us both to Nabia, but that does not mean she may claim our mortal flesh just yet!'*

Sakarbik had nearly made it to the other side now, and she hadn't gone more than waist deep. That was reassuring. Neitin tried to follow in her path, though in the moving water, it was hard to tell where she had stepped. The riverbed seemed to be sloping back up toward the shore. "Not much further," she said, as much to reassure herself as Matigentis.

Her foot slipped.

Her right leg slid out from under her, and for a heart-seizing moment, she thought she would go under, unable to wheel her arms for balance—but one of Mati's lurches reeled her weight back in the other direction. She nearly over-corrected, and Mati wailed as the cold water splashed up his legs and back, but she found solid footing again.

She stood still a moment, chest aching with labored breath, before she could convince herself to continue on. Slower now, more cautious, testing every rock with her toes before shifting her full weight to it. Her hands around Mati were an unforgiving clamp, but she forced herself to be unmoved by his outrage.

Only when they were safely ashore and she set him on solid earth did her fingers loosen. She smoothed his hair, rubbed his cheeks, tried to pat warmth back into his legs. "I'm sorry, little love, I'm sorry. I know, I know, shh-sh-sh. You're all right, see?"

Sakarbik already had the boy's tunic and wrappings out from their baggage. Once he was fully dressed, ensconced in a blanket, and mollified with a strip of dried goat meat to gnaw on, the women retrieved their own clothing.

"D-Do you think that will have worked?" Neitin's teeth chattered and her legs were wobbly. As soon as she had her tunics and leg wraps on, she started to sit—but Sakarbik grabbed her by the elbow.

"We'll get further into the tree line before we rest. And I don't know. I'm not sure the *akdraugi* can cross water on their own—but I'm not sure they can't."

"Can-Can the *besteki*?"

"The *besteki* are where we are, little mother, have no fear of that."

"I never want to do that again."

"But you will if you must." It was not a question.

"I will," Neitin said, looking at her son's tear-streaked face. "If I must."

XX

City of Aven

Marcus felt like a hound that had been pursuing the same hare, day after day. *'There's a fable about that, I think. And the hound doesn't come out looking well.'*

He had lost his tribunate during the December elections. It stung a little, though in such a year, with so many Popularists losing office, the edge was blunted. Even Quintus Terentius had lost his bid for the consulship, and so he bore no ill will toward Marcus for failing in his admittedly unusual attempt at a second tribunate. What did trouble Marcus was that, at first, he had not known why the people had deemed him unworthy.

Three times, he had examined granaries and warehouses. Three times, he had called in a member of the Augian Commission to verify his findings. And three times, he had left that meeting with the Commissioner with the sense that he had over-reacted.

It had taken his wife, the good Poppaena, asking him why on Tellus's green earth he kept having the same conversations over and over again for him to realize something was dreadfully amiss.

Since the turn of the year, he had taken to walking the streets of afflicted areas, hoping that—He hardly knew what. That some magic would call out to him, some wounded bit of Earth begging for attention, giving him a clue, a thread to follow.

Mostly all it got him was well-exercised legs. He had not caught a hint of new cursework springing up. *'Good. That's a good thing,'* he told himself.

And yet it was *odd*. Why should the affliction come to such a sudden halt? And why did Marcus feel this pressure at the base of his skull, vague but insistent, driving him to return to the scenes?

The sun was falling beneath the rise of the buildings, which meant it was time to go home. His father expected him and his wife for dinner that evening, when no doubt Gnaeus would have another mild lecture about problems beyond his purview. He had solved Trebius Perus's immediate problem, gotten Licinius Cornicen to drop his suit; he had remedied similar issues for other afflicted tradesmen and merchants. That was all his tribuneship had required, even when he held the office, and it was far more than anyone should expect of a citizen who was neither patron nor business partner.

'I expect better of me, is the problem. I may not be as bold as my brother or as clever as Sempronius Tarren. Certainly not as self-assured as Quintus Terentius or as nimble-tongued as Galerius Orator. But I... I must do something. I lost face with the citizens because I put too much faith in the Commission. For whatever reason, they didn't want me looking into this—but the people saw that I did look into it, and then did not fix it. They were right to judge me harshly for it. I judge myself.'

He could not simply close his eyes to this problem. Whether he unraveled the mystery of the Augian Commission's impotence or not, it was still his moral duty to find out what afflicted the people of Aven and to remedy it, if that were within his power.

Marcus was about to turn out of the Velabrium when a figure stepped out of a doorway and seized him by the elbow. "Hey!" Marcus shouted, rearing back. Hard to fight in a toga, but loud noise and the impression that he was willing to scrap might throw an attacker off their intent—

But Marcus's assailant had a thin face with frightened eyes. *Terrified* eyes, in fact, and then Marcus realized why: the person who had grabbed him was a woman, slender and flaxen-haired and wearing a slave's collar. *'For her to lay hands on a citizen—What's going on here?'*

Lowering his voice, Marcus stepped to the side of the road. "Easy now, no harm done. What's the matter?"

She dropped her eyes, knitting her fingers together in front of her. "Those men have lied to you," she whispered. Her voice had an accent Marcus couldn't place, thick around certain consonants and short on the vowels. Albine, maybe, or further north. "The black-bordered toga men." The Augians, she meant, but perhaps did not know the right word. "I saw you before. When the black rots came. It happened for months, in many places. But everyone who tried to bring it to those men, they were dismissed."

"How do you know?" Marcus asked. Surely the woman had no magic herself; she would have been manumitted if any had manifested.

"My master is one who had a similar trouble, before the Saturnalia," the woman said. "Having no luck with those men, he sought different help. Mages who broke the curse."

Marcus felt a patter in his chest, faster, harder. Other mages knew of this? Well, that made some degree of sense, he supposed. He was not such an egotist to think no one but he noticed a problem. But who were they? Why had they not brought the matter to public attention? *Perhaps they are poor. Or if not poor, then... well, lower-status.* Magic opened avenues to great income, but not everyone could make best advantage of that, particularly the weakly-gifted. *Someone weakly-gifted could not have broken this curse, though.*

The woman's eyes shifted up and down the street; she seemed a rabbit ready to bolt. Marcus made his voice as soothing as possible—and with his fingers, formed a subtle sign of grounding, which he cast down into the earth beneath their feet. He could not manipulate emotions like a Fire or Spirit mage, but he had some small ability to make a person feel more stable, more certain.

Failing that, he could keep her from running, using his gift to pin her feet to the ground where she stood—though he misliked using his power in such a way and sought to avoid it. "Who are these mages?" he asked. "Did they help others, beside your master?"

The woman nodded, gnawing on her lower lip. "Many others, I think. Here and across the city."

She had not, he noted, answered the question of identity. "How do I find them?"

"There is a place you can go," she said. "A house on the northern spur of the Esquiline Hill. A red door, with a sigil painted above it. It looks like this." The woman turned to the wall and traced a figure in the dirt that clung to it: a nine-pointed star, three triangles on top of each other. Nine points, for the nine magical elements. "If no one answers, you must try again another day. They are not there always. Or so I understand. But if you reach them, they will come. They will help. They always help."

So many questions, but Marcus thought this woman would have few answers—and fewer she would be willing to relinquish to him. She hugged her own arms, more jittery with each breath. "I thank you for your assistance," he said. "Rest assured, I bear no ill will for your having grabbed me. I shall forget it the moment I turn away from here. But I do wonder—Why risk yourself to help me?" If anyone had seen her grab him, after all, retribution might have fallen on her head whether he wished it or not.

"When food runs short, magistrate," the woman said, hardness overtaking the fear in her eyes for the first time, "I know whose mouths they take it from first. When there is trouble in the city, I know whose blood will pay for it."

Anca Corinna's chambers in her brother's house were set apart, behind the back garden, rooms that might otherwise have been used for storage. A single maid was allowed in to tidy, and now and then a physician came to look in on the young woman, known by all to be out of her wits. *'Such a convenient explanation,'* Corinna thought, running her fingers along the cracking plaster of the wall. *'Everyone nods sadly and sympathizes with my brother, and then they ask no more questions. Too awkward, too uncomfortable. Simpler to forget I exist.'*

Many people did, and Corinna thrived in their disregard. The implication that she must be shut away, left alone, not disturbed gave her so much freedom, and her brother saw to her comforts: chambers of her own, not only for the physical necessities, but a place to *work*, a room where no one would venture, with no proper windows, only small vents to let out the smoke from lamps and braziers.

For so long, Corinna had enjoyed its liberty in isolation, but one guest, she now admitted: Pinarius Scaeva, whose soul rang in the same brazen tones as her own.

A scandal, to entertain him in seclusion, if anyone knew of it, but no one would. The door behind the gardens was not worth anyone's observation. Corinna came and went from it as she pleased, without ever having aroused interest from either her brother's household or the neighbors. And now Scaeva entered with similar lack of attention.

He, alone among the other Discordians, both *truly* understood their purpose and had power enough to do something about it. The others were like her brother: men who considered Discordia as the means, not the end. *'Shameful impiety, gross insult to a goddess older than Olympus itself.'* Yet she could not fault them for it. Their short-sightedness and self-interest were human frailties, and she did love frailties.

Still, that meant it fell to her to work divine will in the world—to her, and to Scaeva, whose boldness and experimentation had already achieved so much. "Tell me more," she insisted as they sat about the low-burning brazier. Both were wrapped in wools; the winter continued cold, and the hypocaust did not run under this part of the house. "When you nearly broke through, at the Aventine fires. I want to know how it worked."

"Not nearly, little one. I *did* break through, opened the gate, let it in."

"What? You must give it words, I insist."

Scaeva's smile was slow and wistful, like a man remembering a long-deceased lover. An odd look on him, a decidedly unromantic figure, for all that Corinna admired him. His scraped-back gray hair, thin face, and vulpine features did not inspire ardor—but his passion for his patroness, *that* transformed him, made him beautiful in ways both strange and sublime. "The maw," he said at last, lips and jaw shaping the word with careful reverence. "Another child of dark Night, kin to Discordia, brought forth from Chaos's realm."

Corinna leant forward, fingernails pressing into her knees. She had never reached such a place; when she split the worlds, she had always reached into Pluto's realm, calling forth the *lemures* from that dread domain. To reach through and touch the void, the gaping space between the earth and the heavens, oh, that she scarce dreamed of! "Tell me," she demanded. "Tell me what it is like, and teach me how to get there."

He dipped his head, demurring. "What it is like, I can hardly say. I dared not venture my own *animus* in; I but opened the door and made invitation." A faint smile touched his lips. "I would be madder than I am, had I ventured through in any real sense."

Corinna laughed and clapped her hands appreciatively. Yes, they *were* both thought mad, when the truth was that they saw the world through more open eyes than most others. Scaeva could be inscrutable sometimes, even to her, but that was no failure of his, no madness, only another way of expression. Today was one of his more lucid days, though his speech still snapped between Truscan and Athaecan with no warning, with the occasional word of Tyrian thrown in.

Following required nimbleness, but even when Corinna lacked verbal understanding, she understood Scaeva's *meaning*, his *intent*. They were so alike, compatriots of their blessings, speaking the same language of the soul no matter what tongue framed their thoughts.

"It is," he went on, "the realm where all the elements were born, and where they exist still intermingled. The womb of all creation. All gods, all forces, all magic, it all comes from there. I but opened the way, a little, and what came out was..." He sighed, his head falling back a little. "*Magnificent.*"

Corinna had no doubt. "More. Tell me more. You know now what I have done. How is this different?"

"Mmmm." Scaeva tented his fingers, consider. "It *hungers*, like your fiends. The maw is drawn to magic above all things. The gift of our blessings, we feel it as an ability, yes? Something we *do*. But the maw, the maw, it perceives magic entirely differently."

"As food?"

"Food, yes, and a fountain of wine, and a river to immerse in, and the breeze that wraps around hot skin. Something to be consumed, enjoyed, lived within. Insatiable and inexorable. It hungers, it hungers, it yearns, it devours." He shivered slightly, but smiled still.

"Could you do it again? Reach into the void and coax forth the maw again?"

Vaguely, he nodded. "Oh yes, yes. I'm sure. With the right inducement..."

But what would that be? Corinna's fingers tore at the already-frayed edge of her mantle, pulling threads loose from the neat weft and warp. *'There must be another path we can follow. If he did it once, we could do it again. Both of us, stronger and better. A maw to unravel Aven at its bones, drown it in Discordia's gorgeous strife...'*

For such a large work, she would need the right opportunity. After all, when Discordia set strife among the gods, she did not stride to Olympus on an ordinary afternoon. She chose a time when her actions would have the greatest effect. A time both favorable in the stars and weighted by others' emotions. The wedding of Thetis, attended by all the gods. Discordia's most famous story, when a golden apple set off the war that destroyed ancient Ilion and ravaged most of Athaeca as well. The proudest moment in history for her devotees, when one sly action made the earth rattle and quake.

'And then, then, we can shatter them. Break their control. Break everything they have to give. Overwhelming force, a tear in the world too massive for them to grasp. A gateway to let chaos in, too fierce and terrible for them to close. I will need the right tools. And the right time.'

Until she could find—or engineer—that precious moment, though, other work needed doing. "Another question, friend Scaeva. To break an assembly, to cause enmity to rise between friends, to—to cast the golden apple."

"Our lady's work indeed." He nodded thoughtfully. "I have done this. You want to invoke *furillae*, cousins to the goddesses of vengeance. The divine Furies punish the wicked, but the *furillae* make no distinction. They will take whomever they find. I used curse-dirt to give them a path, once." He told her of a brawl in the Forum, instigated between strangers. "It faded quickly, though. The trouble with curse-dirt. A little water clears the deed."

Corinna drummed the fingers of both hands against her cheeks. "But if we found a way to anchor it... and a way to *direct* that fury, not at random but against a single target..."

There would be a way. There *had* to be a way. The *furillae* would be her instruments of vengeance, against glitter-gold and the knife's edge and all their fellowship. *'No. More than vengeance, I owe Discordia more than that. They want to stop her. They think their union will defeat her. So that union I must break.'*

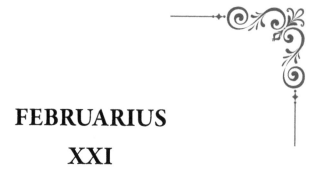

FEBRUARIUS
XXI

Camp of Legio X Equestris, Western Iberia

The horn that blew the alert had hesitance in it, a slight note of confusion, and when Sempronius came to look out between the stakes driven into the earthworks surrounding the camp, the sight did not illuminate his understanding.

Since late Januarius, the Tenth and the Fourth Legions had been on the march. The Tenth pressed downriver, while the Fourth moved south to rejoin Aufidius Strato's Second Legion. The Fourteenth remained at the winter fortress erected near Toletum, under the command of Onidius Praectus, to safeguard that region and its supply chains. The Tenth and the Fourth had won victories, but with difficulty; not all of the Lusetani were marked with the magical designs, keeping them alive past nature's intentions, but enough to cause trouble.

A sizeable group was approaching the camp. Mostly men, all afoot and moving at a pace that communicated no hurry. Iberians, but they were not near enough for Sempronius to guess what tribe. They bore no insignia, no trophies. The man at the lead held only a single long pole, with no blade attached.

"What do you suppose they want?" Felix asked.

"I won't know till I know who they are." Sempronius turned to the nearest guard. "If they show no more threat than this, let them in the gate."

Most of the group stopped out of arrow-range, but the pole-bearer and two others continued on to the gate.

They called up in their own dialect, and one of the Arevaci answered them in his own, near enough to each other for comprehension. Sempronius understood most of what the man said, though he waited patiently, wearing a blank expression, until the Arevaci translated for him. "They are of the Vettoni," he was informed, "and they wish to negotiate."

"Does he speak for all of his people?" Sempronius asked. "Or only for a few?"

He waited through another exchange. "All," the Arevaci guard said. "He comes bearing the good will and fresh hopes of Tarbantu, their chieftain." After a moment, the guardsman added his own observation. "The naked pole is a symbol of their intent. They bear no weapons and no malice."

Sempronius arched an eyebrow. No weapons, he could believe; no malice, after years of fighting, was more of a stretch. "Tell them to wait," he said, then turned to one of the Aventans beside him. "Find Lord Bartasco or Lady Hanath," he instructed, "and one of the Arevaci magic-men. I want to see if there are any signs of magic upon them."

The Vettoni waited with apparent patience while Bartasco and one of his magic-men consulted. Only when they agreed that there was no indication of either physical or magical threat did the Aventans open the gates and allow the Vettoni delegation into the camp.

Once they were inside, Sempronius took their measure. The man holding the pole was hardly more than a boy. He had a beard started, but his sandy hair was so fine that one had to look closely to find it. To his left stood a gruff figure, an older warrior with knotty black hair and a missing eye. On his right, a woman, slight but muscular, paler-skinned than the two men, dressed in the same kind of short tunic that Hanath preferred. Her left arm bore a large scar above the elbow, as though she had at some point in battle attempted to defend herself with a shield but caught the blow above its protection.

Under the scrutinizing eyes of the legion, the delegation walked up the center of the lane, straight to Sempronius Tarren. Sempronius felt Felix tensing at his side, ready to leap into action should the youth decide to do anything clever with that pole, supposed symbol of their good intentions or not. He could see now that it was a young tree, stripped of branches but not bark.

When they were yet a few paces away, the youth turned the pole sideways and dropped it to the ground, where it clattered and bounced a few times before settling. All three of the visitors sank to their knees, placed their hands in a triangle shape before them, and bowed their foreheads down to their hands. "Get up," Sempronius said, embarrassed. "We don't do such things in Aven."

Once someone translated for them, they all rocked back on their heels, but only the youth stood. "We are representatives of the Vettoni." He spoke in labored Tyrian and in a voice deeper than Sempronius would have expected. "We have the blessing of Tarbantu, lord of our people, beloved of Endovelicos. We have come to sue for peace."

"You are welcome to this camp, if peace is your true intent," Sempronius answered, also in Tyrian. There were echoes behind him in both Arevaci and Truscan: Hanath translating for those of the Iberians who did not speak Tyrian, and Vitellius doing so for the Aventan soldiers, fewer of whom probably spoke it than the Iberians, for whom it was a language of trade. "You will forgive my suspicions, however, considering how much blood lies between us. For what reason should we trust you?"

The youth lifted his chin. "I am Tarbantu's son," he said. "Our noble lord places my life in your hands."

That might mean much or little, depending on how well Tarbantu liked this particular son, but Sempronius chose not to comment. "The goal of Aven has always been peace and stability in Iberia," he said. The Vettoni woman's cheek twitched; she likely had her own opinions about how Aven pursued its peace and enforced its stability. "We had peace," he added, "until the Lusetani broke it and the Vettoni joined them. So tell me, what has renewed your devotion to good order?"

The youth rolled his shoulders back. "We can no longer stand beside the Lusetani. They have... have crossed a line."

Unimpressed, Sempronius raised an eyebrow. "You were happy enough to benefit from their sorcery for the past two years."

"For so long, it seemed a worthy innovation. Elsewise we would not have submitted ourselves." He lifted his eyes, and Sempronius saw a bit of a challenge in them. Not entirely displeasing; it was good to know these people still had spirit left. "We are the largest tribe in the region. Our territory stretches from Segontia to the first bend of the Baetis River. We joined with the Lusetani not because they were mightier warriors than we, but because their magic-men were attempting feats out of legend. Who would not seize upon such a power, to give them advantage?"

"So," Sempronius asked, "what changed?"

"Your own victories of late, particularly at the river, which show the gods' favor upon you. We do not wish to lose more of our own by pitching ourselves against such a powerful foe." The youth's face altered, losing its defiance. "Too, we are... We are troubled by the Lusetani's latest magical endeavors."

Sempronius folded his arms over his chest. "Their latest only? Do they so far outstrip the prior horrors? Be clear in your meaning."

The youth glanced over his shoulder at the older man, who grumbled something—evidently of assent, for the youth drew a deep breath, then said, "We have reason to believe their magic-men are befouling the bodies of the dead, ripping them from their rest. Trying—"

He wanted to appear strong and certain, yet fear clung to him, a deep smoke that Sempronius saw through Shadow's intuition.

The young man wet his lips and began again. "They are trying to wake the dead. Not only use their blood. Not only call forth spirits from the netherworld. Not only keep mens' spirits trapped to their bodies even after those bodies should fall. They want to set dead men to fighting." He paused, then repeated, harder, "Actual dead men. Fodder for your swords to chop through, for your arms to grow tired trying to defeat."

Three waves of murmurs broke out, as those words filtered through the assembly in each of three languages. Sempronius raised his right hand without turning to look at any of the whisperers. He had strong enough command of his legions; they quieted.

If the youth spoke true, then the Vettoni brought them not only a truce with one opponent, but intelligence on the other. Opportunity glistened. "It is a comfort to know," Sempronius drawled, "that Tarbantu and the Vettoni draw the line at necromancy."

Most peoples of the Middle Sea did. Even the death-and-afterlife-obsessed Abydosians had given up the attempt to re-animate bodies centuries ago. It should not have been possible—but after the past year, Sempronius would discount nothing.

"Are you prepared to discuss terms?" he asked.

The youth's throat worked over a swallow, but he nodded. "I am authorized to negotiate on behalf of my father. We offer—"

"No." Sempronius's voice was hard and swift as a javelin strike. "That is not how this works. We will tell you what we demand, and you will decide if you can accept that, or if peace must be delayed further." He allowed his demeanor to soften. "Naturally, we must discuss this. I offer you the hospitality of our camp. You will be given food and water. Wine, if you like it. A place to rest." He gestured with two fingers, and two men came forward, one Arevaci and one Aventan, both of whom spoke some of the Vettoni dialect. "My people will see to your comfort."

The youth nodded again, tightly, but behind him, the older man and the woman exchanged skeptical glances. *'Hard to fault them for mistrust.'* They had no way of knowing that when Sempronius Tarren promised hospitality, he would die before transgressing against it. The guest-right had sheltered him on his desperate flight out of Aven, when Ocella proscribed him; he owed the gods eternal recompense for that. The Arevaci and Aventan men would eat with them, to show that no tricks were intended.

"Good," Sempronius said. "We will speak later, then."

Vitellius's skin was dewed with fear. The idea of Lusetani magic raising corpses—it was too terrible to think about, and yet all his mind could do now was conjure images of horror. The mist which had crept over the walls at Toletum, stealing in around the camp, only now instead of living warriors, dead men swarmed over the palisades. Dead Iberians, some of them, men they had killed once only to have to attack again—but dead Aventans, too. Dead Mennenius, his friend, as he had been in his last moments: his face deformed by purple blotches, his hair drenched with sweat, his form shrunk and withered.

Yet in Vitellius's imagining, the resurrected corpse did not lose strength as the living man had. Keening like the *akdraugi*, the dead Mennenius came at him, sword in hand, demanding *why*? Why had Vitellius not done more to save him? Why had he asked Mennenius to come to this gods-forsaken place to begin with? Why should not Vitellius be dead, too?

Vitellius shook his head hard as he entered the praetorium. *'It cannot be so. It will not be so.'* Even if the Lusetani *had* gained such nefarious power, surely they at least needed the body to work with. Mennenius received all his funeral rites, as had every man who died of the mist-borne plague, and had been properly cremated.

No matter how he told his imagination to settle down, however, his heart thundered with unspoken fears. He took his usual place around Sempronius's table, hoping no one else would notice how unsettled he was.

"Lord Bartasco," Sempronius said, "I rely on you and your magic-men in this regard. Is it possible? Could the Lusetani do this?"

The pallor in Bartasco's usually ruddy face was answer enough. "It should be impossible," he said, "and yet so should all else that they have done. I can see where this would build on the bloody arts they have been practicing upon their warriors of late. Knowing what they have been capable of, and knowing their leader to be a man of no conscience, I must say yes. Yes, it may be possible."

"He did not say they have yet succeeded," Hanath pointed out. "He said they were trying."

"We must not give them time enough to succeed," Sempronius said. "We must take this peace with the Vettoni and then move against the Lusetani with all swiftness. General Strato has arrived in Gades and is making his way north and west. If we add the Vettoni's powers to ours, we can drive the Lusetani like hinds before the hounds, leave them nowhere else to flee, and end this war."

"I agree," Bartasco said.

"And I," Hanath agreed, "and yet we must not be so eager for their aid that we forget their transgressions." Her expression was cloudy and fierce, the same Vitellius had seen whenever they encountered a pillaged Arevaci town. "There must be some recompense from the Vettoni. If we wink at their offenses now, we shall be fighting them again next year."

"A hard thing," Sempronius said, "to punish them with one hand while extending the olive branch with the other."

"I concur with Lady Hanath." Vitellius was not aware of having opened his mouth until he heard his voice. His arms were folded tight across his chest. "General, the Vettoni were responsible for at least as much chaos and destruction as the Lusetani. More, perhaps, to our own people and to merchants attempting to reach the coast. We need peace, but it must have a price."

"I know that." Sempronius's voice was cold but steady. "But we must be precise in how we thread this needle."

He sighed, and Vitellius inspected him carefully. *For all that my sisters report the Optimates rail against you as a power-mad warmonger,'* he thought, *'you don't actually much like conquest, do you?'*

A vanquished tribe typically pleaded only to avoid total annihilation. When Rufilius Albinicus pacified Albina, he sent tens of thousands of Tennic tribesmen to the yoke. Some went straight to the grain fields in Alalia and Sicilia, others to the mines of Pannonia, and some all the way to Aven, to enter service in households. The way of things, the spoils of war. The fighting men expected their share of the profits from such ventures; so did the state, for that matter, which bore the cost of the conflict, and so too would their Iberian allies.

"The Vettoni will be expecting to pay a penalty," Vitellius said. "I do not think they are so foolish as to think they will win peace without giving up something in return."

"Then we must determine how much to demand," Sempronius said. "We have legions to pay, after all." He lifted his eyes to Bartasco and Hanath. "And you must ask what is fair for your own people."

It was Hanath who stepped forward, snatching the wax tablet from Sempronius's desk and beginning to carve figures into it. "Let us find out, then, what price we set upon putting an end to this."

"They are a populous people," Bartasco said, "and their range is far. Many villages, and they are not so itinerant as the Lusetani. They have farms, even mines. Whatever penalty we impose upon them must be enough that they do not think of making war against us again in this generation."

"I want to make it so they have neither need nor desire to make war upon you ever again," Sempronius said. "But that is a different matter of diplomacy." He looked sad, Vitellius thought, not victorious. His shoulders drooped as he joined Hanath in hunching over the tablet. "Corvinus, I require your brain. Help us run some figures."

It was as good a deal as the Vettoni had any right to expect, Sempronius knew. Had Aven and the Arevaci been the suppliants, the Vettoni would have enacted their own retribution upon the defeated. And Hanath was right; peace did have to have a price, or it would not be valued.

Still, Sempronius misliked how much the Shadow in his nature exalted in dispensing penalties upon those who could, perhaps, be made into solid allies. That same part of himself resonated when it heard the *akdraugi* howl, and had looked into a void and wanted to put it on a leash. The ugly part, the part that wanted to conquer and control so no one could doubt his strength or his purpose, the part that yearned to remake the world in the image of his choosing and damn the cost.

'My soul is no nastier than any other man's,' he reminded himself. *'The gods have just given me the power to see and know frailties, in myself as in others. I will use what I can to improve our world, as the rest of the night is necessary for the productivity of the day. But I must be ever wary, ever cautious, and never give full vent to Shadow's temptations.'*

Thinking so, he missed his sister. Vibia walked a line even finer than his and held herself to excruciatingly precise standards of behavior to be sure that she would never tip over to the wrong side of it.

'This is a good deal, and I can improve upon it. If we win this war, if we defeat the true enemy, I can improve upon the rest. We can make further treaties, and all the peoples of Iberia will prosper, such that it will no longer be worthwhile to make war upon their neighbors, nor upon Aven.'

This time, when the Vettoni approached, Sempronius seated himself in the manner of a magistrate. He had not gone so far as to don a toga, but he eased back in his chair, one foot sliding forward, the traditional pose of a patron greeting his clients. Whether the Vettoni would read the statement of power in this or not, he had no idea—but the Aventans assembled would, and they needed to see their general, their governor in a position of authority at this crucial moment.

The young man's body twitched forward slightly, as though he were about to go into the elaborate bow he had earlier, but he remembered himself and held his spine straight. "Have you reached a decision?" he asked, voice strong and carrying, despite the thickly accented Tyrian consonants.

"We have." Sempronius gestured to Lord Bartasco and Lady Hanath, standing on his right side. "This agreement involves not only the powers of

Aven, but the peoples of the Arevaci and the Edetani." The Vettoni had ravaged other tribes as well; their tragedies would have to be ameliorated in
some other way at another time. Sempronius could only focus on the allies
who fought alongside the legions. "We expect and will take action to ensure that you honor your agreements with them as well as with us."

"We hear and understand this," the youth said. "As I have said, my father desires that the Vettoni return to peaceful life. We wish to honor our
neighbors and will abide by the terms of the agreement that involve them."

Words. Easy words, or weighty, depending on the man who spoke
them. Sempronius did not have time enough to take this young man's measure, so he would have to live in hope. "Good." Sempronius put out a hand,
into which Corvinus deposited the wax tablet, now neatly imprinted with
what the leaders had agreed. Formal papers would be drawn up in all relevant languages, assuming Tarbantu was amenable. Not all Iberians kept
careful records, the way the Aventans did, but they had enough trade with
merchants to understand the concept of a contract, at least.

Pitching his voice to carry over the crowd, Sempronius read their list of
demands: the money to be remitted to Aven, the Arevaci, and the Edetani,
either in coin or in equivalent goods; the trade agreements, details to be
negotiated further; the captured territory returned to the Arevaci and Edetani; the cessation of violence against merchant caravans passing through
Iberia; the concession of a few border villages to the Arevaci.

The older Vettoni man sucked on his teeth when he heard the amount
demanded, and the woman's scowl deepened the lines of her face at the
mention of the villages. The youth, however, dipped his chin once. "All this,
I can agree to on behalf of our chieftain."

"A fine start," Sempronius said, and the youth winced, but did not argue. "Of those men who took up arms, you will submit one-half to the
yoke, to be sold in the markets of Gades. In addition, five hundred civilians
with useful trades."

The youth paled. "One-half of our— We cannot—"

"Unless," Sempronius went on, as though the young man had not interjected, "the Vettoni are willing to aid us in our efforts against the Lusetani. We wish to make an end of this unpleasant affair, that all of Iberia
may again know peace—and live free of any blasphemous horrors haunting
their days and nights."

He allowed that reminder to settle over the Vettoni a moment. Even the fierce woman dropped her eyes, shame replacing the bitterness on her face. Through his magic, Sempronius could see the fear snaking through all of them. The Vettoni were proud, yes, but whatever the Lusetani were up to, it had truly unsettled them. A cruel advantage to press—but press Sempronius would.

"If you fight beside us," he continued, "then in recognition of such friendship, we reduce our demand. One-quarter of those who took up arms and three hundred civilians."

This was the course they had chosen, he and Bartasco and Hanath: to make the penalty look like an abatement by setting first a higher price. If it worked, Aven and the Arevaci would both come away with most of what they wanted, and the Vettoni would, with luck, not feel themselves too badly-used.

Hanath thought the offer too generous, particularly with regard to the civilians, but Bartasco's argument won out. It was more important to blunt the Vettoni's military power; a quarter of the Vettoni's five or six thousand fighting men would be a significant reminder, but not a crippling one.

"That is still a high demand," the youth ventured. "Our people—"

"Perhaps you would prefer it to be all of you," Sempronius said, hardening his voice to steel again. "Do not think that when Aven chooses to be generous, that we are naive as well. You made war upon your neighbors. You murdered non-combatants. You disrupted trade. You slaughtered unarmed merchants. You ruined fields and orchards and vines. Your actions have had financial consequences, not only for the Arevaci and Edetani, but across the Middle Sea. And you gave aid and comfort to the Lusetani, whose blasphemous horrors you say you now abhor. You assisted them as they unleashed fiends and demons upon the earth." The youth's cheek twitched. The woman scratched awkwardly at the scar on her arm. "For all this, you must pay."

No more would he say. Over-explaining would only weaken his position. He watched, his expression impassive, as the Vettoni ambassadors turned to each others, murmuring. Then the young man looked back. "I-I must go to my father," he said. "I was authorized to negotiate a peace, not a second war with a new foe."

"Then go," Sempronius said, "and return quickly. This offer expires at midday tomorrow."

XXII

City of Aven

The Lupercalian rites took place before the Wolf's Cave, at the southwest foot of the Palatine Hill. Not a long walk from the Vitellian domus on most days, but the festival was always well-attended, and the crush of people in the streets made it difficult for the family to push their way through, even with Aulus in his censorial toga, Latona and Alhena in their mages' tunics and mantles, and Haelix and Pacco looking large and imposing.

"I don't see why it's so important we get right to the front," Alhena grumbled, once her father had moved away to speak with one of his clients. "We're not married, so there's truly no reason for us to be looking for help with fertility this year."

"We might be married soon!" Aula protested.

Latona jostled Aula with her shoulder. "You just want a better view of the runners."

Aula grinned. "Guilty, I suppose. It's a shame Publius Rufilius isn't back in town, but I hear the young man they selected from the Caecilian clan is *quite* the handsome fellow." She poked Latona in the arm. "Anyway, it behooves me to peruse the specimens. There's always a chance Father might decide to make me marry one of them."

"I seriously doubt either of this year's officiants are within his consideration." With Optimates in charge, the young men of their houses had been appointed to the Lupercalian rites.

"Who's the other?" Alhena asked.

"Gratianus's nephew," Aula said with an eyeroll. "Both as fine-looking and quick-witted as the rest of the family, from what I understand."

Alhena shifted uncomfortably, pulling the edges of her mantle around like a bird drawing in her wings. Latona and Aula could stand at the front

217

if they wanted; Alhena was increasingly uncomfortable with all the talk of husband-hunting and fertility-boosting. Longingly, she thought of Terentilla. *'As long as we like and no one stops us.'*

Someone would, sooner or later; girls of their status had to marry. If Aven's political situation hadn't been so unsettled the past few years, Alhena would have been wed and breeding long ago.

'If I must, then I must. But I don't have to like it or go looking for it before it's ordained for me.'

As Aula and Latona talked, Alhena let her mind wander. She was composing in her head—not one of her magical treatises, today, but a lyric poem in Tilla's honor. Whether or not she would ever have the temerity to let Tilla read it was as yet undetermined. *'It'll be too derivative of Hyacinthe, whatever I do.'* Orderly words of thaumaturgical reasoning came easily to her; the free-flowing forms of poetic verse were, ironically, a matter of greater labor.

A cry went up down the road, and Aula wriggled in anticipation. "That'll be the start!" she declared, flinging her mantle off her arms. It was too cold a day to wear a short-sleeved tunic, but Aula, no doubt, wanted to show off a shapely wrist, in case anyone desirable should take note. Latona, shaking her head, folded back the edge of one of her sleeves with an air of resignation. Alhena stayed firmly bundled behind them.

The cheering from the crowd swelled as the runners drew near: two young men, designated priests of the Lupercal, stark naked but for the strips of goatskin tied around their waists. Their faces were smeared with blood and milk, and they laughed as they ran, lashing out with their whips, freshly-fashioned from the morning's sacrifice.

As they drew near, Aula squealed in delight and thrust her arm into the street, lurching forward enough that, as the runners passed by, Alhena lost the barrier between her and mayhem. A splash of blood, just a fleck or two, spattered Alhena's cheek. She blinked, and the world around her vanished.

No, not vanished. *Emptied.* Not only of people, either. All the familiar buildings had disappeared from the surrounding hillsides. No Capitoline triad to the northeast; no insulae at the base of the Aventine to the south; no homes and temples on the Palatine; no Circus Maximus across the street.

No street, in fact, but a marshy track at the bottom of the Palatine Hill, muddier than the hillsides and overgrown with weedy tangles, and beyond that, a few men in rough, dark tunics. *Shabby* tunics, really. *'Did they weave those themselves? Surely no woman could be proud of such work.'* Overtop the disreputable garments were draped sheepskins and tanned hides, ragged at the edges. *'Who in the gods' names—?'*

She was too far away to see their faces clearly, but she could tell that they were fully bearded, their hair worn much longer than most Aventan men's. They stood in front of a cluster of ramshackle huts at the base of the Aventine Hill, built of straw and daub, hardly high enough for a man to stand up in. Sheep and goats grazed all around, and one man carried a fishing-trap in the direction of the Tiber.

Then a horn blasted from over the Capitoline Hill, and a handful of men began charging down the slope. They outnumbered the men in the hollow between the hills, but not by much. One man darted inside a hut and re-emerged with a spear in one hand and a knife in the other. Fearless, he raced to engage the attackers, and others followed him, some with bladed weapons, others with only their shepherding crooks or other tools.

One man hung back, though Alhena did not think out of fear. He raised a hand to the sky. Where he pointed, a dark cloud gathered, and within the cloud, flashes of white light began to draw together—

The vision faded, and the true world crashed back in around Alhena, impossibly loud and filled with so many people. "Sorry, dear, I know you weren't looking to get struck." Aula was rubbing the blood off Alhena's cheek with a corner of her own mantle. *She* had gotten a thorough splatter, decorating her right arm like a set of bracelets. "I almost fell right in the street!" Aula laughed. "Did you see?"

"Everyone saw, you shameless flirt," Latona said. A modest streak of red marked the back of her hand, though whether a direct strike or a splash off of Aula, Alhena wasn't sure. "I don't know why everyone always made a fuss about *my* decorum when you're as subtle as a stick in the eye."

"Widow's privilege," Aula trilled. "Every comedic playwright knows it. We're *supposed* to be brazen and outrageous."

"You're something, all right."

"It was well worth it. That Young Caecilius might not have the wit to vote the right way if the Senate were debating whether to stand in the rain or take shelter, but did you *see* his—"

"Hard to miss it."

"And the way his ass-cheeks—"

"Yes, those too."

By that point, Aulus was coming back from tending to his clients, so the lascivious commentary came to an abrupt halt. He looked pleased at the blood smears on his elder daughters. "It's good fortune one way or another, my dears. Maybe not the, ah, usual way, but good fortune nonetheless, I'm sure."

As they turned back for home, with Aula humming merrily and Latona quietly informing their father that she'd be spending the afternoon training young Fausta, Alhena stayed quiet—not that anyone found that unusual—and contemplated her vision. *'That was a window into the past.'* The vacant hills, the straw huts, the *beards*. Aven, yes, but Aven many centuries ago, before the refinements of Truscan government or Athaecan architecture.

'But why? What did Proserpina mean for me to witness?' A raid on a bunch of shepherds did not seem a noteworthy occasion, and Alhena could not imagine what relevance it had for the modern day.

She gnawed on her lip. *'That was so much more direct than my usual visions, too.'* A scene had played out before her, not a tangle of symbolic signifiers. She didn't experience the emotional tug that so often attended her visions, the impending doom or hectic need, the nerve-fraying concern or looming despair. *'You would think that would make it easier to comprehend.'* All she had, though, were questions.

Alhena blew out her cheeks in frustration, thinking, not for the first time, that if the gods wanted mortals to do their will, they might be less obtuse about making their intentions known.

Domus Magicae, Esquiline Hill

The girl moved slowly down the path, examining each plant. Juniper, myrtle, ivy. Not much else was green yet, but she even hesitated over the dormant plants, scrutinizing them carefully. Then she paused at a skinny juniper tree, one of several in a line at the very back of the garden, against a wall painted pale yellow. "This one," she announced, touching its bluish-green foliage. "It's... it's had a nick in the bark healed."

"Good!" Latona applauded. "Very good, Fausta!"

They were together with Terentilla in the small peristyle garden of the Domus Magicae, a name that no one recalled bestowing upon Aula's house on the Esquiline, but which everyone in their as-yet-small cohort had begun using. Out in the sitting room, Merula sat at a desk, scowling at a pair of wax tablets, one of which she periodically attacked with a stylus. Even learning book-keeping, it seemed, was a violent task for the Phrygian freedwoman. Alhena was with her, head bent over a pile of Athaecan poetry.

Terentilla leaned against a column, arms folded over her chest. "She's eight for eight!" They were practicing Fausta's ability in seeing magical signatures. They would send Fausta out to sit with Alhena for a few minutes while Tilla worked Earth magic on something in the garden, then bring Fausta back in to determine what had been altered.

"Thank you for helping," Fausta said shyly, hardly daring to look at Tilla.

"Happy to be of use!" Tilla said brightly. "Though I'm better with animals than plants, Latona, I told you—"

"Yes, I know, but consider the impracticalities of bringing a menagerie into the garden."

"Fair, I suppose."

"Fausta," Latona said, redirecting her charge's attention, "can you tell me what Tilla's magic feels like? How would you describe it?"

She asked as much for her own curiosity as to test the girl. All mages who could read magical signatures did so a little differently; for Latona, magic had shining colors and, when running particularly strong, a taste.

Fausta's brow wrinkled in concentration, and the fingers of her left hand rubbed together. "There's a greenish haze. It gets clearer, sharper if I focus—but that starts to hurt my head."

"It will get easier with time," Latona promised.

"And it feels—it feels—" Fausta bit her lip. "Like new growth. Bouncy, like... You know how you can snap a dry twig, but not a fresh one, still on a tree? Like that."

Tilla's boisterous laugh filled the air. "I suppose being able to bend rather than break is fortunate."

Fausta's cheeks pinked. "I'm sorry, I didn't mean any—"

"Oh, no, don't mind me!" Tilla said. "It's almost impossible to give me offense." She bent at the knees, getting onto Fausta's level. "And believe me, my brothers try nearly every day."

"You have brothers?" Fausta asked.

"Two of them! Do you?"

Fausta nodded. "Two as well. And a sister."

"The same as me!" Tilla said. "So we shall have to be great friends."

Latona mouthed "thank you" over Fausta's head. The girl's potential swelled like a cloud before a storm—but a cloud in danger of being blown to pieces by the wind. Confidence, that was what Fausta needed. *'Confidence, and the company of other mages, which we can provide.'*

A knock sounded at the door, turning Latona's attention. Perhaps it was Rubellia with her acolytes, or Aula to check in, or Vibia with some news, or some poor wretch from the nearby neighborhood, coming for aid. There had been fewer and fewer of those since the start of the year, though Latona was at a loss to explain why, with Corinna's threats looming over her.

But no—neither pupil nor petitioner had turned up on the doorstep. Instead, she found herself looking into the startled brown eyes of Marcus Autronius.

"Senator! I—"

"Lady Latona!" He gave his head a little shake. "I did not expect—" Then his shoulders slumped. "Actually, I don't know what I expected."

Latona opened the door wider. "Senator, why don't you come in? I think that, whatever brought you here, it would be better discussed inside."

He obliged, if with a touch of hesitation. *'Well,'* Latona considered, *'a married man, a recently divorced woman, a supposedly private house.'* Under other circumstances, scandal-fodder indeed.

The sight of the other women drew the tension from Marcus's spine. "If... if I had thought about it properly, I suppose I ought to have guessed. Ladies, I mean, if not you in particular. You have the means, and more... not anonymity, but... A man of similar means, I might've crossed paths, might've heard something in the Curia, but... Gods, what ignorance, not to even think..."

Fausta had crept out from the garden, staring wide-eyed at Marcus. She was only now becoming less shy and awkward around her mentor; being faced with a senator, a former Tribune of the Plebs, appeared to have overwhelmed her. "Merula," Latona called. "Are you by any chance ready for a break from your studies?" A whuff of air let Latona know she had guessed aright. "I thought so. Would you mind walking Fausta home? It's almost sundown, and I don't like to think of her on the streets alone."

"Yes, Domina," Merula said, popping up from her desk with alacrity. Strangely, fierce as Merula was—and as many men in the city were thoroughly intimidated by her—little Fausta liked her. "Come on, gosling," she said, taking Fausta's hand. "We will be stopping at the thermopolium on the corner, yes? They put nice flavor on their honey mushrooms..."

"Leave the door open, Merula." No one passing by would be able to overhear them, if they sat beyond the atrium, but to leave one's door open was to proclaim that one had nothing to hide. *And we'll have to get used to that, if we're to be a proper collegium.* For now, it might at least give Marcus some peace of mind.

Once they had gone, Latona gestured for Marcus to join her, Alhena, and Terentilla in the sitting room on the far side of the atrium. Tilla positioned herself with an eye on the door, while Alhena curled up on a couch next to her.

"Senator," Latona said, "perhaps you had best back up and explain how you came to be at the door of our little establishment."

So he did, telling in blunt terms a tale that Latona found all too familiar. Cursed warehouses and unnatural rot were perfectly of a piece with the battle she had waged all autumn. *Yet word did not reach us of all those locations. How much damage did the Discordians do outside my notice? How could we not have seen it?* But it was a big city, and they had only their own lattice of friendly informants to rely upon. That would not catch everything.

Still, it troubled Latona deeply. *That they were capable of this much wreckage... We knew there must have been others working with Corinna, but how many?*

When Marcus finished his story, his head sagged. "I don't know how I kept losing the thread of it," he confessed. "These people came to me for help, and I-I did what I thought best. I tried. I went to the mages who should have been able to do more."

"Do not blame yourself, Marcus," Latona insisted. "You have been played upon most cruelly." Then it was Latona's turn to tell *her* tale—all of it, sparing nothing, from the first discovery in Stabiae to the true nature of the mysterious illness that had felled her back in November.

As she spoke, Marcus's face grew paler and paler. "Oh, Latona," Marcus sighed when she had finished. "Why did you not come to someone else with this?"

"To the Augian Commission, as you did?" she asked, with a mirthless laugh. "I did, actually. I begged Salonius Decur for help, and he dismissed me as hysterical. Told me all this was the result of peasants neglecting their piety."

Marcus hung his head, back bent, his hands folded between his splayed knees. "I wish I could say you should have come to me," he said, "but we—Forgive me, Latona, I have always thought well of you, but we—we—"

"Our families are political allies," Latona supplied. "And, I hope, friends. But we have not, till now, been yoked by intimacies such as those which the practice of magic can elicit."

He lifted his head a touch, with a faint smile. "Yes, that's... that's a good way of putting it."

Their eyes met, and Latona knew a bond had been forged in that instant, fixed in iron. Their friendship now would not be a matter of overlapping social circles and political allegiance; they had both experienced something wretched and transformative, both been marked by it, both attempted to fight against it. They were comrades-in-arms.

"I expect if Salonius could have worked upon me as he did you," Latona added, "he would have done so. But he knows me for a Spirit mage. He could not risk my discovering his treachery. As it was, I found him merely useless, until we uncovered the link between Anca Corinna and the Augians."

"The attempt— He—" Marcus's eyes widened in understanding. "He used magic on me. That's why I kept forgetting what was so important, why it just fell out of my head. He must have..." His brow creased. "Salonius Decur is Light and Air. Truth and the mind... but if he warped those intentions, if he wanted to *obscure* the truth..."

"Light can dazzle," Alhena offered. "Illusion is one of that element's talents. And Air has dominion over the mind. Together, they could certainly tamper with your natural sensibilities." She blushed. "Or... or so I've read."

Marcus's head wagged. "What a fool I've been. I—You must understand, ladies, my tutelage was rudimentary. My talents are modest at best, so it was never worth investing in highbrow tutors. I had not imagined— I did not know such things were possible."

"I knew it was possible," Latona said, "though I cannot recall any practice in living memory."

"Manipulation of that kind is forbidden," Alhena confirmed. "Outlawed by the *leges tabulae magicae*. It's considered a violation of a free man's will, and thus an affront to liberty."

Latona's teeth ground together in barely-suppressed fury. "Another crime to add to the Augians' tally, it would seem." Her fingers dragged through her hair, loosening pins. "Tilla, if Marcus brought this matter to your father, what do you estimate his reaction would be?"

Tilla thought a moment. "He would want to believe it. But he would need proof before he could do anything about it."

"And Marcus's patron, alas, would no doubt want to help us, but is a few thousand miles too far away to be of use in the present moment." Sempronius's absence stung acutely now, when they could benefit from his keen mind, his political acumen, his ability to see many moving pieces of a greater problem. *'Well. It falls to me, then, I suppose.'*

She settled her shoulders back. "We have—as you've discovered through your own informant—people around the city who alert us when something magical has gone awry. We are trying to build a stronger coalition—a collegium of magic." She let those words land. Marcus showed no shock or disapproval, so she continued. "I can tell you more about that, what we'd like to do, but you, Marcus Autronius, you can go places we cannot, talk to people we cannot."

His shoulders sagged again. "I've been of small use so far."

"Well, I mean to make you of use now." A bold way to speak to an unrelated man, a senator and a former tribune, but Latona's instinct guided her rightly: Marcus was a dependable follower, not a leader. He heard a strong voice calling him to service, and he sat up straighter. "You have access not only to the Senate but also, I think, many merchants of the city, yes?"

His cheeks colored slightly. Senators were not, technically, supposed to have mercantile interests. His family had made their fortune in that way, however, and though they employed a factotum to give them legal coverage, the Autroniae still governed many of their own affairs. "Yes. My father and I both— We have contacts."

"Then you can keep ears and eyes open in those parts of the city, as well as within the Senate."

"The Senate?" Marcus asked. "There's no magic in the Senate, the... the Augians..." The thought caught up to him as he said it. "Gods. I hadn't followed that through."

"Shocked us, too," Tilla said.

"What we don't know yet," Latona said, "is *why* the Augians would be mixed up in this. Durmius's sister, yes, but what effect would that have on the others?"

"Even for love of a sister, it beggars belief. The Augians are..."

"Sacred," Alhena finished, hugging her arms around her knees. "But what would you not risk for your brother?"

He frowned, brows knitting. Latona sensed the conflict in him, weighing piety and duty to the state against fraternal bonds. "Felix may be a handful, but he'd never put me in a position like *that*," he determined. "But if I had some other man as a brother, someone traitorous, someone I could not reach or sway from his dark course... I hope I would be stalwart enough to find some other way of balancing my loyalties." He shook his head, as though to dismiss the contemplation. "But I can't imagine that my familial devotion would be sufficient to sway my peers. When I stood as tribune, for example—no, I can't imagine it. Good men... good men would not join in such a conspiracy."

Latona almost envied him his faith, shattered though it now was. "Not everyone is as stalwart as you, I fear. Many men are only good until the right temptation presents itself."

Marcus cleared his throat, rolling his shoulders awkwardly. "The other thing I can't figure out, though, is why they seem to have... stopped? At least they did in the Velabrium. I don't know if—"

"Here, too," Tilla confirmed. "Latona and Vibia have dispelled a few curses since the new year, but far fewer than during the autumn."

"Most of those we've found this winter looked to be older," Latona said. "Placed months ago, likely, and only now taking enough of an effect to be noticed." Weaker charms, too, she thought; either Corinna's early efforts or else from the hand of an as-yet unknown comrade. "But Corinna made it clear she had further intentions. She may be only waiting for the right moment to strike. This is just a—a storm gathering strength before it breaks."

Marcus sighed. "I'm sorry. I've done nothing but drop new troubles on your door."

"No!" Latona said swiftly. "No, not at all, Marcus. You have given us new information, which is always useful."

"If you've time," Alhena said, "I'd like you to look at the map I've been keeping. Of-of all the Discordian curses we've found. We should add those from the Velabrium to it."

"And I meant what I said," Latona added. "You are privy to the goings-on in the Senate."

"Your father doesn't—?"

Marcus already knew their secret; it seemed worth trusting him with further details. "My father," Latona said evenly, "rightfully worries for the safety and security of his daughters. He knows we've formed something of a society for magical education, but the extent of our activities remains beyond his awareness. If he knew, he would want to stop us. But, Marcus, you must understand, for so long we were the *only* ones rendering aid—"

"No," he interrupted. "No, I do understand. I do. The—the people of this city need protectors, and the men who ought to fulfill that role abdicated their duties." He swallowed, hard. "I will do what I can to help. It may be little enough, but... I will do it."

"And we will be glad and proud to have another ally." She put out a hand, and after a confused moment, Marcus shook it. "Welcome, Marcus Autronius, to the collegium of the Domus Magicae."

XXIII

Lusetania, Western Iberia

Two and a half months of journeying finally brought Neitin back to familiar territory. Her heart leapt the first time she recognized the bend of the river, flatter and wider now, sluicing its way through flatter terrain.

They had to leave its shores, though. Her mother's people had a village further downstream, but Ekialde's home was up a steep rise—the last of the western *mendi,* the mountains that the Lusetani held sacred. *'He always liked the thought of that,'* Neitin thought, bouncing Matigentis in her arms. *'As though being from the mountains made him tougher, stronger than us river-folk.'*

At Neitin's insistence, they turned aside. Sakarbik scowled and muttered—but then she consulted the skies and, for reasons of her own, agreed. "The path leads to that village," she declared. "I cannot say why. Endovelicos does not see fit to tell me. I expect he knows we will find out soon enough." Her brow was pinched with irritation, though; even a god's directive was not beyond Sakarbik's scrutiny. "I do worry, though. A place so well-known to your husband and his uncle. It may call their hounds back to our scent."

Neitin worried about that, too. Since crossing the river, they had been lucky, not so much as a hint of an *akdraugo* on the air. Perhaps they traveled too far for Bailar's magic to hold. He, surely, would stick close to Ekialde. *'And why waste so much power on a woman he doesn't want to find?'*

Ekialde might miss his wife. At least, Neitin hoped he would, hoped there was enough of her husband left in that fiend-ridden flesh to do so. But Bailar? Bailar likely thought himself well-rid of a nag.

228

Matigentis pulled on her hair, and as Neitin unwound her curls from her son's fingers, she realized: *'He is worth more than I am. Bailar may hunt my son, Ekialde's blood, even if he would not care for me.'*

She no longer knew what safety looked like. Perhaps they would flee to undreamt-of lands, across the sea to the northern isles, where her mother's people sometimes traded for tin and hunting dogs. Or south, to the deserts and mountain ranges that lay across a narrow strip of water. *'Anywhere. I would go anywhere to keep my boy safe.'*

First, though, she owed her husband one last thing. She had left him, not yet abandoned him in her heart. *'And if there is any hope he can be saved, if he can be brought back from the brink, I will find it here.'*

Fitting, somehow, that they would return to this village so near to the anniversary of Mati's birth. *'Forget that first year, my dear one. Let it form no part of you, leave no mark on you. I will raise you in Nabia's loving arms, out of Bandue's bloody sight. Somehow. Somewhere.'*

As they drew near the village, Neitin's pace slowed, her eyes on the sky-line. "There's no smoke," she said. "No fires. With as cold as it's been..."

"There is no one in the village," Sakarbik said.

"How are you sure?"

"Seeing through the *besteki*'s eyes. It is abandoned."

What had happened? Many of the village folk had gone along with Ekialde in the war camp, but certainly not all. Many women and children remained behind, along with those too old or infirm to tramp about in the wilderness. *'Did they leave to find shelter elsewhere?'* Though harshly cold, the winter had not been overly snowy. Perhaps it had been worse here, though; the *mendi* could be prone to strange winds and sudden storms.

'Or were the people taken?' In gathering his forces, Ekialde left few men to guard the towns he left behind.

"No danger to us, at least," Sakarbik said, continuing to trudge toward the village. "No people means no one to sell you out to Bailar. And no fires doesn't mean we can't make one. Come on. We'll be better for sleeping un-der a roof tonight."

Everything was as Neitin remembered it: a cluster of round huts in the midst of a clearing, with a fence of wooden stakes. How small it looked now, after spending months gazing at the walls of Toletum across a dis-tance. Neitin had seen large cities before, had been to Olissippo in her youth and looked upon the sea-without-end, but nothing else had made this home seem a trifle.

"He could have brought riches back here," she said, more to herself than Sakarbik. Mati crooned and babbled at the sound of her voice, making noises of agreement. "We could have made this a proper town. Real walls. Better houses. A center of trade. He had taken enough in spoils to satisfy our people for years, to make sure none of us went hungry or cold. He had the opportunity. And instead—what?" Tears stung the backs of her eyes. "Instead he chased some vision of blood and glory."

"Blood and glory are like strong wine," Sakarbik said. "Sweet and intoxicating, yes. Drinking much of them makes you want more and more. And then, they poison."

The wind moved tree branches and leaves, but there was no other sound but their own footsteps. Normal, in the woods; terrible, in a place that should have rung with the voices of families, the clang of smiths at work, the sizzle of stews cooking over hearthfires. Under her many wraps and the furred cloak, the hairs on Neitin's arms stood on end. She whispered a prayer to Nabia beneath her breath as they approached the center of town.

When they came to the far side of what had been Ekialde's hut, though, a strangled cry ripped from her throat.

In this place, the magic-men of the Lusetani had named Ekialde *er-regerra*. In this place, they had cut his arms and caught his blood in bowls and read it for signs from the gods. In this place, they had fed that god-touched blood to a sapling, binding two lives together, so that the health of one would reflect the fortune of the other.

What had been a strong, straight tree now bent nearly in half. Its bark flaked away from the trunk; its leaves were desiccated husks. The branches were gnarled, twisting themselves into knots. The exposed heartwood was a horrible color, like congealed blood.

Neitin set Mati down and dropped to her knees, reaching out towards the mangled flora as if in supplication. "Oh no," she breathed. "Oh, my beloved husband..."

Less sentimental, Sakarbik snorted, "What did you expect? You told me he tied his soul, his power, his lifesblood to this tree? Well. Now you see what comes of that."

If Neitin looked closely, the ragged shapes left by the disintegrating bark mirrored the ink designs Bailar put into Ekialde's skin. *'To make him strong,'* she thought bitterly. *'To bring the gods' power into him. So sure he knew best, Bailar, so certain he heard the gods in ways no one else could. So sure that he has led many men to their deaths, has ordered those deaths, has organized the death of the man he thinks he is raising up to greatness.'*

She began to weep and could find no shame in it, not when her chest felt like a spear had been rammed through it, not when everything inside her felt so unbearably heavy. *'I tried, husband. I begged you! I tried.'*

Had there ever been a real chance, to alter the course of his life? Or had the gods truly destined him for this dark and blood-soaked path all along?

Matigentis stood beside his mother, head tilted. The tree captured his attention, but he kept glancing at Neitin, distressed by her tears. "Ma?" he questioned. "Ma? Wha?"

Swiping at her cheeks with the back of her hand, Neitin turned toward Sakarbik, without getting off the ground. The older woman was also staring at the tree, her upper lip curled, her shoulders drawn up toward her ears.

"C-Could this be fixed?" Neitin asked. "The *besteki*. Their powers. They've protected us. Can they heal?"

"Heal? Yes. Heal *this*?" Sakarbik blew air out through her nostrils. "I do not know what could heal this."

"But can we try?"

"Why should we?" Sakarbik snapped. "He has chosen his fate, plain enough."

"If it can be reversed, though," Neitin pleaded, "if the *besteki* can drive out Bailar's influence, if he can be restored—think what suffering will be spared! If he gives up this quest and returns here. No more killing. No more foul rites, no more perversion of magic."

Sakarbik's weight shifted, and her lips twisted. She was considering it.

Neitin pressed on. "You said yourself, the path led here. Endovelicos wanted this. Why? Only to break my heart? Maybe—Maybe there is yet good to be done. Maybe the *besteki* have more of a purpose than only shielding us. I don't know. Of course I don't know. I have nothing of magic in me." Sakarbik quirked an eyebrow; Neitin did not know how to interpret her expression. "So please. Can we try?" Neitin's throat worked around a lump; her voice warbled. "Please?"

"Very well, little mother," Sakarbik conceded. "We can try."

Tagus River, Western Iberia

The Vettoni agreed to Aven's demands. As a show of good faith, their chief told his son to remain with the Tenth Legion, half-guest, half-hostage.

Word came from the south, too: the Vettoni cut their deal just in time to avoid conflict on both their borders. General Strato was pressing north with the Second Legion, all a-fire to meet the foe in combat, never mind that it was the middle of Februarius, at least a month before sane people thought of campaigning.

'What about this entire venture has been sane?' Vitellius thought, staring into a campfire outside the tribunes' tent. The Vendelician border had occasionally been harrowing, but at least there he knew what to expect. Since he had set foot in Iberia, nearly two years earlier, unpredictability reigned and the uncanny ruled his life.

"Excellent news about Strato, eh?" Autronius Felix, back from whatever duty he'd been placed on for the evening, thunked himself down beside the fire. "I knew the old man couldn't keep away from a fight. Once he heard Sempronius was on the march, no way was he going to sit behind the walls of Gades and wait for spring."

Vitellius glanced up at the sky, more hazy-gray than properly black. Low clouds obscured the stars entirely and blurred the light of the half-moon into nothing more than a silver blotch. "I only hope it won't get us into trouble we can't get out of," he said. "Larger armies than ours have been felled by a single bad storm."

"Ah, don't be gloomy." As he warmed up, Felix began stripping off the extra wrappings around his hands and legs. "Don't you know? Sempronius has Fortuna's favor." He tugged on a tight bit of fabric with his teeth, unsnagging it from his greaves. "Mars's too, probably. 'S'why they keep handing him improbable victories. Anyway—" He spat a bit of thread that had come loose, then began coiling the wrappings. "We're almost out of the heights, the scouts say. The weather further downriver is more like a Truscan winter, or so I hear. Might get damp, but we won't freeze to death.

And if all goes well, we'll be home by summer!" Felix furrowed his brow. "You're not married, are you? No wife waiting back home?"

Vitellius shook his head. "Not yet, though I'm sure that's on my father's list of intentions for me once I return." His eyes went briefly heavenwards. "And if not his, my sister Aula has mentioned it in no few of her letters."

Felix laughed, scooting himself closer to the fire. "You are a man well-blessed with sisters, Vitellius. Even that little one is quite charming, but Aula's the life of every party, and no mistake."

Strange, as ever, to think that other men knew his family better than he did. Alhena had still been a child when he left Aven. Latona had been sixteen, growing into the beauty he understood was now somewhat famous, and not yet married to the husband she'd since divorced. And Aula had been just swelling into pregnancy, growing the niece Vitellius had never met.

He knew all that had occurred in his absence, of course. His family were frequent correspondents, particularly while he was still at the secure posting on the Albine-Vendelician border. It wasn't the same as *being* present, though.

"Well, I know how it is, having family on you about that," Felix went on. "My mother writes me all the time about how nice Marcus's wife is. No children yet, but it took my parents some time, too, before they managed to produce us, so she's not worried. But not so *un*worried she doesn't want me to forge an advantageous alliance for the family."

"I think my sister might want me for her friend Maia Domitia," Vitellius confided.

"Really?" Felix said, with interest. "Were you acquainted with her before leaving town?"

Vitellius shook his head. "Our fathers were friends. I knew she existed, but no more than that."

"She's lovely," Felix assured him. "A true beauty in a classic mold, I promise you. And good-natured."

"I'm not sure my father would choose a widow for me, but she does have experience running a household. And proven fertility. Two daughters, Aula tells me." He sighed. "I think that's why she wants me for her friend. The lady is having difficulty finding a husband who wouldn't want to separate her from her daughters, and Aula knows I'd never... I mean, of course

I wouldn't..." Aula, too, had a daughter and reason to eye remarriage warily on her behalf. "Always seemed foolish to me, the men who try to pry their wives away from the children of their first marriage. Not likely to make a very happy household."

"No," Felix agreed. "Personally I see no sense in ever making a lady unhappy, if you can manage to avoid it."

Vitellius shrugged. "Can't say I've had much opportunity one way or the other."

"No?" Felix's brow rose in disbelief. "Not on the Vendelician border? I heard the Albine girls were sportive enough."

How to explain to Felix, who joyously took pleasure wherever it was offered, that Vitellius had always thought it unbefitting to meddle with the local girls? At the border fort, he'd been a senior legate, a position of authority among the local community. Taking up with an Albine girl always seemed both unwise and unfair.

To redirect, he said, "I thought your tastes ran toward the Iberian. Who's that girl you've been, ah, keeping company with?"

"Sterra!" Felix declared, laughing. "Hoo! Talk about not wanting to make a lady unhappy. If I displease her, she'll run me through from one side while Lady Hanath gets me from the other." He was grinning, more pleased than alarmed by the prospect of getting mauled for his romantic entanglements. "Truth be told, I'm getting fond of the minx. I've half a mind to take her home to Mother and see what the family makes of *that* marital arrangement." He stretched his arms above his head, as though working out a kink in his shoulders. "But that wouldn't be fair to either of us, really. She's not a citizen, so it wouldn't be properly legal. Anyway, she's not cut out to be an Aventan matron, and it'd be a real pity to leave a beauty like her home alone while I go back out on campaign."

"Is that what you intend?" Vitellius asked. "Back out as soon as possible?"

"Oh, yes. What about you? Think you've got another campaign in you?"

In truth, Vitellius could hardly wait to put cuirass aside and don the toga. "As soon as I'm back in Aven, I'm sure my father intends to point me toward the law courts and prepare me for the Senate. I'll be eligible soon enough."

"Ahh, more's the pity!" Felix said, clapping him on the back. "My father's already got his senator in my brother. Oh, I might go in some day, I suppose, but there's no rush, so if I want to sign up for another campaign, well, we'll find someone to put me on staff again, I'm sure. They won't be as clever as Sempronius—but maybe that means their campaigns will take longer!" Felix laughed, as though the prospect were appealing, not horrifying.

'He hasn't been out here as long,' Vitellius remembered. They weren't far apart in age, but their careers had been very different. *'He did a short campaign in Numidia, then time in the city, then here. He didn't spend all of Ocella's dictatorship patrolling the Vendelician front and trying to keep moss from growing on everything in sight. He wasn't—He wasn't in Toletum, he didn't see—'*

An unfair thought. The men in the field had faced *akdraugi* as well. *'What did they make of you, and you of them?'* Felix was so boisterous, so lively. The *akdraugi* might have found him a delicious treat—or, he might have been too much for them to chew.

"You really do like it, don't you?" Vitellius asked, with genuine wonder. "This life, I mean. The marching and the fighting and all."

"Of course I do! Makes me feel alive." But then something serious crossed Felix's face, and he scratched his forehead. "To tell you true, Vitellius, out here, I feel like I know what I'm about. Y'know? Like I can follow the plan, do what I'm good at, and not cause anyone embarrassment. Too easy to find myself at loose ends in the city." As swiftly as it had fallen, the somber aspect fled, with another of Felix's incorrigible grins. "For instance, you should've seen the Saturnalia party the Papirae threw last year. There was this dancing girl, name of Pyra—well, so she claimed, anyway, I'm sure that's never what her mother called her—a Fire mage, and you wouldn't believe the flexibility—"

A horn from the perimeter of the camp interrupted what no doubt would have been a colorful tale. Vitellius and Felix were both on their feet in an instant, reaching for their discarded helmets and greaves, moving to find their centurions and prepare for another battle.

XXIV

Domus Magicae, Esquiline Hill

"Months, I've been trying to get my hands on texts like these," Latona complained, standing with her hands on her hips as Marcus unloaded a sackful of scrolls onto the work table.

"We're going to need another storage lattice," Vibia commented from where she stood nearby, arms folded tight. Though disgruntled at Latona's unilateral decision to bring Marcus Autronius into their fold, she grudgingly admitted his potential utility.

"*Months*!" Latona went on. "And you can walk into any temple and take what you like, without obstruction."

She sighed with envy. So many doors were barred to the women of the Domus Magicae on account of their sex—though Latona also had an extra hurdle in the shape of Aemilia Fullia's enmity, as the High Priestess of Juno had requested that many temples deny Latona, specifically, access to their libraries.

"Wait till Alhena sees these," Vibia said. "She may faint with delight." Some of the black-bordered scrolls, indicating thaumaturgical texts, looked like no one had unrolled them in generations.

"I just grabbed anything that seemed like it might be vaguely related to your—to *our*—work. Much of it might be useless," Marcus said, with a note of apology. "And these—" Rummaging deep, he extracted the last few. Fresh scrolls, newly inked and rolled. "—I asked a bookseller for. Copies of the *leges tabulae magicae* and the *lex cantatiae Augiae*." A rueful smile. "If we're going to nail the Augians to the wall, I figured it would behoove us to build a solid legal case."

"Quite right," Vibia said. "Let us crucify the wretches upon every point of their transgression."

A savage sentiment, but Marcus nodded grimly. "For what they've done, they well deserve whatever retribution the law demands. I also wondered if—" Marcus cleared his throat, wincing. "I'm sorry. I don't want to sound like I'm, ah... being prescriptive. Or—or trying to take over here. This collegium, it's *yours*, not... Hm."

Discomfort shimmered off of Marcus in small ripples, worsening when Vibia fixed him with a cold stare. Latona got the impression he wasn't *opposed* to working in such ways with women, just unused to it and confused about the etiquette.

'As though there were etiquette for what we're doing.' It made her miss Sempronius all the more, for he never displayed a moment's awkwardness or unease at the idea of yoking their strengths together.

Taking pity on Marcus's hawing, Latona said, "Marcus, we value your advice and promise not to take offense." She flicked a warning glance at Vibia. "Please, what are you trying to say?"

His cheeks colored, but his shoulders lost some tension. "I only wondered if you had any thoughts about, well, what comes *next*? If we manage to expose the Augian Commission, and if it's as hopelessly corrupted as we fear... What next?"

"What and who replaces the blasphemers, you mean." Latona ran her finger along the edge of the desk. "I *have* considered it, and strong though the temptation is to say 'nothing and no one'..." She tapped at the edge of one of the legal texts. "The *lex cantatia Augiae* was written for a reason."

Not one, she realized, she was very familiar with, despite its impact on her life. It arose from a time in the early Republic that saw both a rash of magical crime and a single mage's disastrous transgression. Dolosus, his name had been, the last mage to climb the cursus honorem above the entry ranks. It was his fault that Marcus would never be more than a Senator and Tribune.

"Non-magical citizens *do* need protection from unlawful magical interference in their lives," she went on, "and obviously someone needs to adjudicate that protection. But within what structure? With what checks upon power, so it cannot again be abused as the Augians have done?" She spread her hands wide. "I have no answers, yet."

"Nor I." Marcus was quiet a moment, contemplative as he helped Latona sort the pile of scrolls into neater stacks. "I think there are many who prefer it, that the Augians are so far removed from other systems of power," he said. "It removes magic from our politics. Or seems to, and that in turn seems comforting. But it also insulates the Commission from precisely the checks upon power that you mean. If they were thoroughly integrated with other structures, rather than off to the side, the corruption within them might never have gained hold."

Vibia's posture relaxed, shifting to curiosity. "A keen appraisal, Marcus."

"I-It's not unlike the Tribunes, in some ways," Marcus said, thrown only a little by the mildly insulting note of surprise in Vibia's voice. "Both part of the Senate and not. Beholden to law and to a certain portion of the Aventan citizenship. But the Commission hasn't been renegotiated over time the way the Tribunate has."

"No one's ever had the nerve," Vibia said. "Even Senators not under their governance know they could have a magically-gifted child someday. No one wants to incur their wrath."

Latona frowned, trying to untangle the thorns in her mind. "It's a prestigious position, but it doesn't pay, does it?" Marcus shook his head. "Thereby closing itself off from anyone who doesn't already come from a wealthy family."

"I think you're right."

"She is," Vibia affirmed. "Mostly patricians, a few plebeians of noble family. All senatorial class, *maybe* one or two equestrians."

"That keeps the Commission small. No one of the lower Classes can afford to take the post."

"I hadn't thought of that," Marcus said, "but it is monstrously unfair, now you mention it. The Senate has Tribunes to balance it out, and to look out for the interests of the lower Classes. Why has the Commission no similar counterpart?"

Latona settled her shoulders back. "Perhaps because no one has ever demanded it."

A warm surge hit her blood, faint cinnamon hit her tongue: Spirit magic rising unbidden again. Not uncontrolled, as had happened shortly after the Dictator's death—but not by conscious summoning. *'Why? Where is that coming from?'*

Before she could chase it down, Marcus continued. "Well, perhaps some of these texts will shed light on the decisions of the past."

"And help us make better ones for the future," Latona added.

The paint was the color of blood mixed with bronze, and Corinna thought that fitting. She dipped two fingers in the gritty mixture, then smeared it on the wall in a long, curving stroke.

Carefully, so carefully, Corinna had crafted this curse, using all she had learned: Scaeva's example of the curse dirt, her own experiments with snarling her magic into someone's *anima*, and a hefty dose of—she was not too proud to admit it—her brother's prudence. He'd approved of her scheme, or what she told him of it. He'd helped her acquire ingredients and refine the mixture, and even now stood watch at the end of the alley so she would not be interrupted.

She might have drawn anything. Half the walls in Aven had graffiti on them: political slogans, tavern recommendations, phallic images, men boasting about their sexual partners, trivial messages between neighbors, some lout proclaiming "I was here" as though anyone would care. For Corinna, the magic was not in the image or message; she drew no sigil or word square, which Durmius warned her might attract attention as a work of magic. *Always so worried about drawing notice, my dear brother, always fretting...*

No, the magic was in the paint itself, similar to the techniques some artists used when crafting illusory murals or protective charms. So Corinna wrote poetry—none of her verses praising Discordia, of course, she could not be so pointed. Instead, she penned a few oblique verses about the fall of Ilion, another city doomed by Discordia, but a common enough subject of art that no passerby would think it strange.

She dared not try the pigment yet on the house of another mage, who might sense the work. She began strategically, with those already inclined to do what she needed and who had no magic of their own. *A little nudge is all it will take, and they will do the rest. Splendid strife, Discordia's purest work, to stoke the fires of enmity in mortal souls.*

The effect would not be so strong as Scaeva's curse-dirt, but Durmius said that was better. The effects would be subtle, seem natural, raise no alarm. *Fret, fret, fret...*

Still, she decided to agree with him. If her marks drew no notice, they might survive longer. Oh, they might wash off in the rain, or be scrubbed off, or painted over, but until then, they would call *furillae* to this place.

Anchoring the intention, that had been the hardest part, but for the right price, most households had a disgruntled slave willing to sell a few fingernail clippings or strands of hair pulled from a mistress's brush. That ensured the *furillae* would not be drawn to just *anyone* passing by.

Nor would their targets turn their strife blindly upon the world; Corinna had no bodily token from those she most wished harm, but she knew the shape of their magic, and she taught that to her curse. Once the *furillae* took up residence, focused antipathy would grow within their hosts.

'*I have no golden apple to cast,*' she thought, putting some finishing touches on her lines, '*but let this deed bring Discordia joy, done in her honor.*'

XXV

Tagus River, Western Iberia

The battles were growing bloodier.

After his long slog south, after Toletum, Vitellius would hardly have believed it possible. But the Lusetani-blood warriors grew in number, no matter how many the legions cut down. Again and again, they faced fighters who refused to lay down and die.

Vitellius signaled to the centurion to blow his whistle, cycling the front line of soldiers through. The manuever was precise, drilled into every legionary from his earliest enlistment: how to fall back without losing ground, turning and sliding at the exact moment the man behind you brought his shield forward. An efficient maneuver, part of what made the legions a formidable machine. Ideally, each man fought at the front line for only a few moments before falling back.

They held to that, but it had less benefit when the battle went on for so long. When the enemy kept coming, long after they should have been defeated, it wearied limbs and souls alike.

It made the battle a gruesome business, too. Dismembered limbs and severed entrails were a part of warfare—but not usually so prominent a part, in the Aventan experience. The gladius was a fairly tidy weapon, as such things went. Pierce the stomach or lungs; wait for death to follow. It *could* be used as a slashing weapon, but in the normal course of Aventan battle, that was incidental: an advantageous strike at a kneecap, a defensive blow to an incoming arm. It wasn't the weapon's intended purpose. With these Lusetani blood-warriors, however, sometimes the only way to stop them fighting you was to hack them apart, joint from joint like a slaughtered cow.

'And even then...' Vitellius watched, gorge rising in his throat, as the legions had to step over and, ultimately, *on* a Lusetani man, his skin marked from throat to wrist with the cursed crimson patterns. His arms weren't hacked off, but had been so badly damaged that he could not lift a sword any longer. As the legions pressed on toward his fellows, he continued to bellow his war cries, as though he were a man whole and ready to triumph, not nearly a corpse and about to be trampled into the mud.

'At least he is only nearly a corpse.' Vitellius kept a sharp eye open, lest any of those dead bodies rise and try to fight. So far as they knew, the Lusetani magic-men had not unlocked that particular gate.

Yet.

Again, Vitellius signalled; again, the men at the front of the line fell back to make way for those behind them. He had no idea how long this battle had gone on, but the sun had not crested the treetops when they began. Now it was at least a handspan above. *'Longer than a battle should go. Where does he get the men from?'* To be sure, not every one of them was a deranged blood-warrior. Most of the fighters withdrew, sensibly, when injured. But with each battle they fought, a higher number were those who would not, perhaps could not, yield.

Vitellius was about to give another signal when a horn blasted off to his left. He had been entrusted with the right flank; Felix was somewhere off to the far left, with the General in the middle and cavalry behind each of the wings, ready to dash out and harass at need.

Vitellius listened: an echo. This call came from Felix's wing, relayed through the center. When he recognized the sennet, his blood hitched in his veins.

'Akdraugi,' that call indicated, though for Vitellius, it meant, *'Run. Run and hide, but you will never be safe, never secure, never live free of haunting.'*

His own men echoed the call. To their credit, the legionaries held their lines, kept pressing forward as if nothing had changed—though the men in the rows farther back from the front were glancing around nervously for the tell-tale mist.

Vitellius wrapped his horse's reins more tightly around his hand. Slow, deliberate. A physical action to relieve some of his internal turmoil, but nothing would quiet the horror screaming at the back of his mind. Sweat beaded on his temples and the back of his neck.

'*You are still protected,*' he reminded himself, for he still wore at his throat the focale woven by his sister. So much power, in a simple red scarf. '*They cannot touch you while you wear it. Not in the same way, at least. They cannot invade your mind. You will not be ensorcelled by them.*'

He would not—but what of his men? Vitellius's own safety came at the price of guilt. Leadership was always a heavy burden, but since the death of his friend Mennenius, Vitellius questioned, more and more, if the honors were worth their weight.

The mist came, but patchily. Not the overwhelming fog as at Toletum; here the *akdraugi* appeared as unpredictable smudges around the perimeter of the Aventan ranks, not a unified and persistent surge.

"Strike drums!" Vitellius bellowed. They had, after all, much practice at this: music helped to keep the mind clear, the wits grounded. Cheerful tunes were best, and so the animated rhythm that the drums struck up, augmented by jubilant horns, jarred terribly with the grotesque combat still going on at the front.

Vitellius's lines held, and they rebuffed the *akdraugi*. '*Thanks be to you, Father Mars.*' He took it for a sign that the Lusetani had not been able to replenish the numbers of their magic-men. Enough to work foul deeds, clearly, but not so many as had given them the upper hand for so long at Toletum.

As he scanned toward the south, however, the situation did not look so rosy. The lines had grown jagged; men were faltering. The *akdraugi* were thicker there, perhaps, or the blood-warriors more numerous, less easily dispatched. '*Or perhaps there's some new horror to confront.*'

Vitellius could do nothing from his position; not directly, anyhow. But he could give the Lusetani something else to think about. "Cavalry!" he shouted, reeling his own horse around.

He had a number of the Arevaci and Edetani with him, though not Lady Hanath herself. Felix's little minx Sterra was there, though; Hanath and Sempronius had not intervened in their affair, but nonetheless placed them on opposite ends of the battlefield when possible.

"On me!" Unsheathing his sword, Vitellius began a charge around the far right flank. Any pressure he relieved from the center would be a boon to the men fighting there. '*Father Mars, go with me. Father Mars, look after me. Father Mars, bless me.*'

Generals were, in the usual course of events, not meant to return to their camps covered in blood.

Sempronius was no coward, but he knew the sense behind the strategem. High-ranked officers led from the back, or at least within a thick cordon of guards. The man with the plan, the man with the authority, he needed that protection. His death could set chaos among an entire legion, lead them to break ranks and fall to disorder.

Sometimes, though, there was no choice.

When Sempronius's center lines faltered, he raised his standard and brought his small cavalry unit between the block of infantry in front of him and Felix's wing. It helped; the cavalry appearing in their midst caught the Lusetani by surprise. Or, at least, it did those who were still capable of surprise. Sempronius wasn't certain their blood-warriors would even notice if they took a hoof to the chest or head. It bolstered the legionaries, too, seeing their general take the field, watching the scarlet banners and bronze standards in their midst.

The Lusetani brought their bloody warriors in full force and managed to raise *akdraugi* in greater numbers than the legions had faced since To-letum. They had aimed well, too, splitting the ethereal forces at the point between Sempronius's center and Felix's wing. Felix had reacted swiftly, as had Sempronius—but it did not save every Aventan or Arevaci life.

That night, as he sluiced the blood off his arms and legs, Sempronius sighed. "We are gaining the upper hand," Sempronius said, more to himself than to Corvinus, "but at cost."

Corvinus was, at that moment, the only other occupant of the tent, and so they could speak freely. He was setting out fresh clothing and readying Sempronius's armor for cleaning, which some low-ranking tribune would be given the honor of seeing to. "May I ask, sir," Corvinus ventured, "what did you expect?"

He had thought—foolishly, arrogantly—that his press downriver would be an easier victory, with the Vettoni pacified and General Strato swooping up from Gades. "I confess, I had not expected the Lusetani magic to continue giving us such trouble."

"Pity Lady Hanath didn't manage to spit *all* of their sorcerers on that spear of hers."

"Indeed." Sempronius rubbed his forehead, dripping water on his face. "We must find a way to neutralize their magic without *using* magic."

"Without using magic in battle," Corvinus pointed out. "Without using it offensively. The Prohibition of Mars draws a distinct line. The legions have always used defensive magic in their shields and armor. And our efforts at the Anas River demonstrate that the god is not affronted by the use of magic before battle is enjoined."

The thought of what they had done that day made the spot between Sempronius's shoulders itch. "We pressed our luck at the Anas—no, *I* pressed our luck, I can pass none of the blame for that onto you."

"Thank you."

"Ha. At any rate.... That Father Mars withheld his disfavor then does not mean he will show similar lenience a second time. I should like not to tread upon his patience any further, if we can avoid it." Sempronius returned his hand to the basin of water, scrubbing a stubborn bit of dirt or blood lodged underneath a thumbnail. "And if we must test the boundaries of his good will, then it must be I alone who takes that risk. But better that we find a way to best them without violating his Prohibition any further."

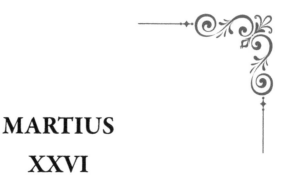

MARTIUS
XXVI

Just when Vitellius thought the monotony of battle might break him—one day so like the next, facing down blood-warriors and fiendish *akdraugi* in fits and spurts, battles that churned on and on, grinding up men and dirt in their wake—he found himself summoned, alone, to Sempronius Tarren's command tent early one morning.

When he arrived, the scout Dorsus was there, along with a man he did not recognize, but could identify as Vettoni by the manner of his golden jewelry. "Tribune Vitellius," Sempronius said, warm but businesslike. "I have a task for you, if you are willing to give up the life of camp and battle for a few days."

There was no obvious irony in Sempronius's voice, but Vitellius felt the edge of sarcasm anyway. "Yes, sir," he replied. "Always willing to serve, in whatever capacity Aven requires."

Sempronius's dark eyes rested on him a moment. "Yes. I know." The weight of the general's regard lifted, and he gestured to Dorsus and the Vettoni man. "Our scouts have something interesting to report. It's a distance downriver, and you'll have to take a circuitous route to get there without running afoul of the Lusetani forces, but I'm intrigued by what they suggest."

"And what is that, sir?" Vitellius asked. "If I may?"

Sempronius glanced first to Dorsus, then to the Vettoni man. "They think they've found Ekialde's home village," he said. "That may mean much or little. He's been in the field so long, it's hard to imagine there's anything of value there. But I would rather know than guess—and, if we can capture

246

his home, that may bear some psychic weight upon his men. Any of them left that still have their own senses, rather than fiend-riddled brains, at least."

Vitellius nodded. "I will go at once, and return with anything of value."

"The Lady Hanath will go with you." Sempronius must have seen the confusion on Vitellius's face, for he prompted, "Does that trouble you?"

"No, sir," Vitellius said. "I will be most grateful for her company. I just... I would have thought she had greater value here."

Sempronius gave him a wry smile. "The gods know that the Lady Hanath is a boon to any company she keeps. But the gods know, too, that it would be impossible to keep such a woman from doing as she pleases—and having heard the report from our Vettoni ally, it would please her to see this village. We'll manage without her, somehow. Her lieutenants are good women and men, capable of directing the cavalry in her absence, and she may well be of use to you in..." Sempronius's easy flow of speech hitched briefly. "In identifying whatever you find in this village."

It took several days to reach the village, with the Vettoni scout leading the way, and Vitellius, Dorsus, and Hanath keeping a wary eye on him, lest this be some trap. The Vettoni were allies, true, but not yet fully trusted. How could they be, after so many long months of raids and bloodshed? All very well for the general and the chieftain to come to an accord; men of the lower ranks needed proof before they would trust their erstwhile foes.

But all seemed legitimate. After cutting north, through high plateaus where the brown grass frosted overnight, they crossed a tributary of the Tagus, ascended another hill, and found themselves outside a village walled only by outward-facing spikes.

They tied their horses at the front gate and went in armed, not knowing what they might find, some garrison or group of bandits or even a knot of blood-warriors lurking, ready to rush out and slit all their throats.

No need. The village was quiet as the shore of the River Lethe.

It set Vitellius's hair on end. He mistrusted quiet. Quiet generally meant something horrifying lay in wait somewhere.

Not just quiet, but still. No motion, no sign of life anywhere, except for the smoke of the single fire that had led them this direction. That persisted, beyond the first cluster of huts. Every house looked long abandoned. The gardens planted alongside some of the huts were either dry and barren, or else overrun with weeds and ivy. Here and there, roofs sagged with neglect and the weight of storms. Dorsus even pushed open doors as they passed; no one came forth, no domicile bore signs of life.

Then, in the center of the town—or what passed for its center, though some Aventan homes boasted atriums larger than this space—stood a dying tree. Bent and gnarled, its bark flaking off and exposing blood-red sapwood.

Ice ran down Vitellius's spine, the chill of plunging into a frigidarium pool, a chill that woke his soul instead of inviting it to sleep. That tree felt *wrong*. Looking at it made him think of the *akdraugi* and all those long months in Toletum, waiting each day and night for the haunting spirits to rise and try to drown the hearts and minds of ever poor soul living within the walls.

Perhaps because the wretched memories swarmed him, it took him a moment to notice the small figure curled around the base of the tree.

Hanath had noticed her, certainly; the Numidian woman had gone still as a hunting leopard. Dorsus and the Vettoni scout, too, had reacted quicker than Vitellius. Both had hands on their weapons, though neither had drawn.

A woman alone, or so it seemed. Hard to tell her age while she was prostrate, but she had sun-brown skin and thick, dark hair. What purpose could she have here? What threat might she pose?

None, Vitellius wanted to think, but he knew that for naiveté. A great deal, he knew to suspect, but wanted to believe that an overreaction, born from years' worth of tribulations.

If she heard their approach, she gave no sign of it. Another set of footsteps broke the silence, however, coming out of the hut closest to the tree: a second woman, this one older, with silver streaks in her dark hair. She held a young boy by the hand. A year old, perhaps a little more, walking unsteadily with her assistance. When she halted, he fell back on his rump, evidently finding that the soundest course of action.

This second woman spoke in an Iberian dialect, dissimilar enough to Arevaci that Vitellius only caught about half the words. Hanath, though, had better fluency in various Iberian tongues, on top of her Tyrian, Truscan, and Athaecan; life as a trader's daughter had given her a gift for language. She exchanged a few brief sentences with this dark-haired woman.

"She means us no harm," Hanath said at last. "She is Cossetan. She is not the boy's mother. The mother is there, weeping." She jerked her head toward the tree.

The Cossetan woman said something else, which made Hanath widen her eyes. She repeated the words, seeking clarification. The Cossetan affirmed her statement, nodding resolutely.

"The boy's mother," Hanath said, turning her astonished gaze to the woman at the tree, "is the queen of the Lusetani. Ekialde's wife."

Vitellius blinked a few times. "Well," he said, looking between the supposed queen and the young boy. "That, I suppose, would count as something of value."

The sound of voices slowly penetrated Neitin's fog of grief. She had heard so few other than her own and Sakarbik's since leaving the Lusetani camp; the magic-women in the villages where they sought brief refuge, that was all. But now she heard—was it possible?—men.

When that possibility finally made it past the layers of sorrow and confusion, she sat up, twisting to see them.

A strange party. One man of the Vettoni, by the look of his garments and jewelry, ruddy-skinned and bearded. Beside him, a tall, dark-skinned woman with hair worn in dozens of small, bulbous knots. Behind, two men in scarlet tunics and leather cuirasses, one pale-skinned and ginger-haired, the other much browner. The ginger-haired man held a helmet beneath his arm. A crested helmet. Scarlet clothes, and a crested helmet.

The details came together in Neitin's grief-addled mind, and she shot to her feet. These were Aventans. Aventans! Somehow, so deep in Lusetani territory. Somehow *here*, in Ekialde's own village, two Aventans—who had discovered his queen, alongside Sakarbik and her son. "Don't harm them!"

Neitin cried out. Her voice creaked; she had used it for little but weeping in the past two days, since Sakarbik's last effort at healing the tree failed.

The Aventan man frowned. Had he understood? His eyes went sideways, to the dark-skinned woman beside him. Some words passed between them, then the woman spoke: "I am Hanath. This, Vitellius." She indicated the man with the crested helmet. "He speaks some of the Arevaci dialect." Her own voice was thick with mixed accents; Arevaci, yes, but also something else, vaguely familiar but too far off for Neitin, in her panic, to identify. "But not Lusetani. I translate, yes?"

An opening, at least. They were armed, all of them; the Aventans had those ugly short swords, the Vettoni a curved blade, and the woman a long spear strapped to her back—but no one had a weapon in hand. Neitin swallowed. "I have a little Tyrian," she said, then repeated the words in that language. She learned it in youth, when traders from Olissippo frequented her home village.

"I have some Tyrian as well," the ginger-haired man said, with careful enunciation. "Between the three of us, we may make some conversation?"

It would have to do. Neitin gestured to Sakarbik. As she spoke, she slipped between Tyrian and Lusetani as she had the words. "Please don't harm them. The boy is—is innocent. This woman was my slave. She is Cossetan. They are, I think, allies of the Aventans."

The dark-skinned woman murmured clarification when necessary, in the strange, halting cadence of the Aventans, hard and soft sounds mixed together, vowels high and long. Some conversation passed between them; Neitin heard the word for the Cossetans a few times. The Aventan gestured for Sakarbik to come forward. He looked her up and down in a perfunctory way, though his eyes rested longer on her forearms, marked with ink, and on her golden eyes. He spoke two short words, which Hanath translated. "Is this true?"

"True," Sakarbik said. The Cossetan and Lusetani dialects were close enough that they had never had trouble understanding each other. "I have served her for a year."

"If this is as you say, you are free to go."

Sakarbik snorted. "Go? Go where? My village was annihilated by the Lusetani raiders. Those who lived were taken to Gades or Olissippo to be sold."

Hanath arched an eyebrow and relayed that information to the Aven-tan. "You wish to stay with the queen?"

Sakarbik's shoulders tightened. "We made a bargain, she and I. I would see her and her child safe. What do you intend?"

"We intend nothing," Vitellius said, in Tyrian, once Hanath translated Sakarbik's words for him. Already the tangle of languages was dizzying. "Our general will decide what is to be done with her."

Sakarbik had sharp eyes, and they darted between the enemy group. "Only four of you? I did not hear more horses."

"Four of us here," Hanath said, cold warning entering her voice. "More are close. And *two* of you, with a small child, and neither of you warriors." She lifted a thin eyebrow. "I see your markings, magic-woman. You could try something against us, no doubt. But others will come. If you flee, others will find you."

"Sakarbik," Neitin said, weary to her bones, "do not fight them. At least do not do so on my account, and as you say, your people have no quarrel with them."

Vitellius took a tentative step forward, looking directly at Neitin now, and speaking in Tyrian more fluid than Neitin's own. "Our general is a com-passionate man," he said. "Particularly where women and children are con-cerned. I cannot say what he will intend for you, but you will come to no harm, nor your child. I think you will be safer with us, than staying alone here. If raiders found you, or slavers coming up from the coast, they would not care whose queen you were."

'*Queen.*' The very word made Neitin flinch. She had never felt a queen, in truth. She had never held authority. Nor had she ever had any chance to govern alongside her king. All her queenship had been life on the hunt, pursuing Ekialde's and Bailar's mad dreams of conquest and slaughter.

"We do care," Vitellius went on. "It makes you valuable, and Aven pre-serves what it values."

Neitin turned her attention to Hanath. What could a man's promise of a woman's safety mean, after all? But from another woman— Not that their sex were without cruelty, but it might be easier to trust her. "Tell me," she said in her own tongue. "Is what he says true?"

Immediately, the woman nodded. "You have little reason to trust me, I know," she said. "I am wife to an Arevaci chieftain. But you will see here a

Vettoni man at our side. We made peace with them. The Aventan general desires peace. I think he desires it above all things, because he thinks peace can be more prosperous than war."

'If he truly does so, then we have that much in common,' Neitin thought.

Hanath continued: "He has treated fairly with the Vettoni." Her eyes cut sideways at their companion. "More fairly than would please some whom the Vettoni harmed," she added, her tone sharpening. The Vettoni man did not react. With a sigh, she returned her focus to Neitin. "He will treat fairly with you. I would stake my honor on it." She nodded to Vitellius. "This man, I have known for nearly two years. We have shared many trials—including the horrors that your husband raised up against us."

Neitin dropped her eyes. She was not responsible for Ekialde's bloodshed or Bailar's perfidies; why did she feel ashamed of them nonetheless?

"He is a good man," Hanath vowed. "A warrior, as I am, with all that implies. But a good man. He kept many alive in Toletum when they might have starved, fallen to disease, or gone mad. He will not harm noncombatants. If you, your son, and your companion present no threat to us—and vow to try no magical tricks—then we will escort you safely to our camp. There, the general will treat you as an honored guest."

Neitin wished she and Sakarbik had some language to speak in that neither Hanath nor the Vettoni would understand. *'Well, if they take me for a queen, I should play the part, and a queen would not shy away from unpleasantries, I think.'*

She put out a hand for Matigentis, who rushed to her side, though his wide eyes were on the newcomers. "Do you think she is trustworthy?" Neitin asked Sakarbik. "I value your counsel. What would you advise?"

Sakarbik scrutinized Hanath and Vitellius. Then she cast her gaze up to the sky: gloomy and grey this day, threatened with clouds but not yet raining. Whatever she saw with her golden eyes, beyond Neitin's perception, it led her to nod. "Yes. The woman has honor. She is a killer, but not a liar." For her part, Hanath did not look displeased with the assessment. "The man... darkness hangs heavy on him. He has suffered. He grieves. But in this, I believe he speaks true: he will not harm you or Mati."

As much reassurance as Neitin could hope for. The stranger had a point: they were lucky not to have been taken by raiders or slavers already. Another tribe might push in from the east or north; the Tyrians might move up-river and take a fancy to plundering the abandoned mountain villages.

Neitin looked back at the tree, her heart aching. Several times, Sakarbik had tried to heal it—and perhaps, through it, Ekialde. Nothing had worked. Once, she got leaves to sprout, but they immediately turned black and crumbled to dust. Other times the tree began to shake and quiver, sloughing off more bark and bleeding more crimson sap. "You said the path led here," Neitin said. "To this village. You said Endovelicos wanted us here."

"I said it led here," Sakarbik agreed. "I did not say it ended here."

"I thought..." Neitin sighed.

"I know you did," Sakarbik said. "It was not a foolish thought. Certainly, in a devoted wife, an understandable one. But now I think this was not our purpose here."

Strange path, to take them so far to the west only to deliver them into the hands of their foes. *I begged Nabia for aid, and she did keep me and my boy safe. Sakarbik asked Endovelicos for wisdom, and now she advises me to go with these scarlet strangers.*

Neitin lifted her son in her arms, settled her shoulders back, lifted her chin, and tried to sound like a queen. "I will go with you," she said in Tyrian, as though she truly had any choice. "I trust in your honor, and that of your general. The gods will bring down a thousand curses upon you if you play me false."

Solemnly, Vitellius inclined his head. "It may mean little to you, my lady, but I will swear by the gods I hold dearest, Jupiter and Mars, and by the ancestors of my family: we will not harm you, and we will do all we can to prevent anyone else from harming you."

Neitin knew little of Jupiter and Mars, but swearing by one's family carried significance. She turned, then, to Sakarbik. "You owe me nothing," Neitin said. "You made sure my child would be free of Bailar's blood magic. It is enough. Go. Go home and find whatever peace you can."

"I will travel with you a while longer," Sakarbik declared, her countenace far more regal than Neitin's. "These Aventans have a goal in mind, I do not doubt. Perhaps at the end of their path, I will find a new life for myself. And it may be..." She glanced at the sky again, as though looking to it for direction, then stepped closer to Hanath. "What if I could help you?"

"Help us?" Hanath's face communicated skepticism.

"My people are friends to the Aventans, is it so?"

"Those of them who are left, yes," Hanath said, without pity.

Sakarbik nodded. "Then it is, in fact, my duty to give aid where I can." Her voice hardened to a growl. "And even if it were not, I have personal reasons to want to see Bailar of the Lusetani laid as low as low can be."

Hanath hesitated, then spoke with Vitellius in his own language for a moment. "Bailar," Hanath asked. "He is—not your king, but—?"

"He is the king's keeper," Sakarbik said, and though it stung, Neitin could not deny it. "He is the magic-man at the heart of all your troubles, the foul genius behind all the fiends and fetid magic. He is an affront to the good use of magic in this land, and he must be stopped."

"In this, we agree," Hanath said. "But the Arevaci magic-men have been unable to summon sufficient defenses."

Sakarbik smiled secretively. "We left Ekialde's camp long ago, before the winter solstice, but I had long months to observe Bailar before that, and it is possible I may know things your Arevaci magic-men do not. I will need to speak with this general of yours."

"Let us begin our escort," Vitellius said, once this too was translated. "General Sempronius Tarren will, I believe, take great interest in you both."

XXVII

Esquiline Hill, City of Aven

As Februarius wore into Martius, the Domus Magicae grew busier. Many days, Rubellia attended with her acolytes, letting them practice their talents with a little more seclusion and less room for embarrassment than the temple afforded. Fausta came every afternoon that her family could spare her. The Water mage Davina stopped by occasionally; she was not well-lettered, though exquisitely numbered in the running of her business, and she and Merula sat together, teaching each other. Vibia even invited Rufilia Mulagonis, a talented Fracture mage against whom she had long harbored a degree of envy. Rufilia's visit was brief, but warmer than Latona anticipated, and she had high hopes that Vibia would decide to trust Rufilia enough to bring her in on future curse-breaking efforts.

'*We are building something here,*' Latona thought, warmth coiling inside her. '*Slowly, perhaps. But we are building.*'

What the women of the Domus Magicae learned, Alhena wrote down. Her corner of the tablinum was stacked high with wax tablets, slates, and papyrus, notes and notes scribbled down whenever something interesting happened. She had confessed to Latona her intention to compile the notes into treatises, and then to create a system for them—a structure for teaching and investigating.

Latona was thrilled about Alhena's work; they would need solid plans to convince a wider audience of the merits of their collegium. Every building, after all, had to have solid foundations before it could reach for the heavens.

On the afternoon of the Nones of Martius, Latona and Alhena were alone in the study, poring over the texts from Marcus Autronius. Nestled within a legal commentary on one of the earliest cases that the Augian

Commission had prosecuted, Latona discovered a reference to the reason for the Commission's founding: the tale of Dolosus, the notorious mage-consul whose ill-fated rule had convinced the city not to trust mages with such power.

Dolosus took the consulship at a time when Tennic tribes were streaming over the Albine Mountains and into Truscum. Latona had never before studied the details, but now she learned that Dolosus sent a series of increasingly offensive ambassadors to the Tennic chieftains, the last of whom turned murderous. The Tennic tribes, with good cause, swore revenge and came south to get it.

Then followed a sequence of political and military missteps, as Dolosus failed to take the threat seriously. When the Tennic warriors breached Aven's gates, Dolosus panicked—and in his panic, called upon Water magic with sufficient force that the Tiber overflowed its banks and flooded half the city. A concatenation of disasters followed, piling magical mishap upon magical mishap.

"The common version of the story says that the gods punished Dolosus for his hubris," Latona told her sister. "But from what I'm reading here, it seems like Dolosus was simply an utter fool! His consulship was full of blunders from the start. It wasn't the gods' wrath that brought doom on Aven; it was Dolosus's arrogance and stupidity. What if—" She huffed; the presumption that magic and power could not, *must* not mix was so deeply ingrained that she struggled to frame her thoughts around it. "What if generations of Aventan men have been barred the cursus honorem based on his ineptitude, not on divine judgment?"

Alhena made no response; her nose was buried in a scroll. At first Latona thought Alhena's focus might have stopped her ears, but then she said, "If it were so inherently improper... if it were truly blasphemous... it does seem odd that the Republic made it two hundred years before the gods took offense. To say nothing of the kings who founded the city in the first place."

Straightening, Alhena proffered her scroll to Latona—one of the older texts, left furled for so long that the paper stayed curved even when unrolled, cracking along lines of fiber rather than smoothing out.

"There's something very odd about that one," Alhena said. "It talks about the Divine Twins, and their division of responsibilities in founding the city."

Latona nodded. To Romulus, the army and construction; to Remus, the law and religion.

"It starts to talk about Remus's magic, with more specificity than any text I've ever seen, but using such different language. Whoever wrote this—well, wrote it first, at least, I'm sure this is a copy—did so before Tyrian and Athaecan influences on the way we practice magic grew so strong."

Latona frowned. "What do you mean?"

With a sad sigh, Alhena reached for one of her wax tablets. "The worst part is, I don't *know*, entirely. So little survives from the age of the kings, and almost no one in the early Republic thought it worth writing about. But Truscan magic was less formalized and philosophized than that of the Athaecans. They didn't think about the elements in the same ways we do. I'm not certain they made division between them at all."

Instinctively, Latona boggled at the notion. Of course there were nine elements; every schoolchild knew that.

But once she began to pull at the thread, more unraveling followed. There were more than nine gods; more than nine ways gifts expressed themselves. An Earth mage devoted to Diana was not, as Terentilla continually proved, the same as one devoted to Ceres, nor to Pomona or Flora.

Too, talents crossed over between elements. Empathy belonged to both Fire and Spirit, even Water in some cases. The ability to see magical signatures cropped up in mages of several elements.

Latona sat forward, elbows thunking on the table, chin propped on one hand. "If what we've been taught isn't the only form our magic can take..."

"Yes," Alhena said wryly, "it rather dizzied me when I first chased the idea down, too. But anyway, that text—it doesn't use elemental language when it talks about Remus's magic. It hints at what he was capable of—and then it just breaks off, and starts talking about the codification of certain rituals at the Temple of Saturn."

"You said it seemed like it had been copied."

"Oh, I'm sure of it. That papyrus isn't as old as the words are."

"If it's been copied, it may have been altered."

Alhena nodded. "I think it has. But by whom? And why? What—what information would they be hiding?"

Latona pushed to her feet and started pacing. "Information about Remus. Remus, who was both statesman and mage. A Spirit mage—or so we think. So we've been told." She tapped her thumb against her lips. "Told by whom? Tradition, our teachers... but who told *them*? Who was the first person to attach that term to him, if as you say, the earliest Aventans wouldn't have? Why was it important to them to narrow future generations' perception of him?"

"To narrow..." Alhena echoed, considering. "Remus is held up as an example to Aventan mages. But if the example no longer fits the laws of the times—"

"—if his reach expanded beyond what later generations found permissible—"

"—then people like the Augians, both now and in the past, would benefit from erasing that knowledge. From... from making sure no one *could* use him as an example to step outside the bounds the Augians set."

Latona gave a woeful little cry. "Oh, what a despairing thought! If they've destroyed it all, if that history is lost to us—"

"It might not be."

"Hm?"

Alhena shifted on her bench, tucking her legs beneath her. "I. Um. I had a strange vision a little while ago. At the Lupercalia."

As Alhena told her story, Latona tried to piece it together with the revelations in their documents. The tale invoked ancient days indeed: bare hills, shepherds' huts, marshwater in the Forum.

Too, it was a stranger kind of Time magic than either of them were familiar with. When Alhena finished, Latona asked, "Why didn't you say anything when it happened?"

"Well, you and Aula were rather distracted by Young Caecilius's, um, merits," Alhena replied, with a hint of tart reproach. "And I wasn't sure what to make of it, at the time. It *was* rather disorienting. But the two men—"

"A warrior and a mage. The Divine Twins?"

"I-I don't know." Alhena's shoulders drooped. "I wish I could say for sure. I was too far away to see if they looked alike. And the beards didn't help, and it ended so fast—"

"But why else would Proserpina show you that particular moment in time? She rarely troubles you without a pointed purpose." Golden warmth blossomed in Latona's chest. "I'm right about this. I'm sure of it."

Alhena's agreement was wary. "Well. It's why I mentioned it. If-if I managed that again, to reach back there... maybe we could learn more about the truth of him. Remus. I mean. Only I haven't the slighest idea how to go about it. The Lupercalia created special conditions."

"Then we'll have to create our own, somehow," Latona said, unperturbed, then gestured at the scrolls. "And in the meantime, now we've got something to ask our friends to look for. Any text about the time of the Twins that they can find, any rumor they've heard, any fragment of poetry or scrap of song, even!" Latona's excitement grew as the possibilities spun out before her. Cinnamon, the taste of cinnamon, *yes*, this was *right*! "If the truth has been expunged from official records, it may yet live on in some bit of nonsense doggerel."

This was it, the hare they needed to chase. Grounds to challenge the supremacy of the Augian Commission with, and that not even the Optimates could argue against, since it would draw from the most revered of Aven's forefathers. *'And, within that, inspiration for what we can build anew. A system both fair and just, offering protection and opportunity to all Aventans. A chance to let us write our own rules—and our own destinies with them.'*

A few days later, Alhena explained her sister's theory to Terentilla as they strolled through the markets northeast of the Forum. Ostensibly, Tilla was on the hunt for a birthday present for her brother, and she poked through the stalls as she listened. "Funny thing it would be," she said, "if your sister managed to beat the Optimates at their own game, invoking ancient rites to force a change in the law." Tilla's fingers fumbled the bronze pin she'd been toying with, and it thunked heavily back to the merchant's display. "Sacred groves, that really is what she's doing, isn't it?"

"It's what she wants, anyway."

Tilla gave a little laugh. "Strange. We wouldn't think that odd in your brother, or mine. Yet here we are, always held to laws we have no part in making."

"She'll have to work through them, and people like Marcus Autronius, of course."

"At least if it's your brother, it'll still have her name on it, in a way." Tilla grinned, shouldering Alhena gently before picking up the pin for renewed examination. "The *lex cantatia Vitelliae*. Nice ring to it, eh?"

"I think your cart's rolled quite a way ahead of its horse." Alhena hadn't yet seen the shape of the future of these endeavors, and she feared to tempt the Fates.

Tilla decided on a garnet pendant for her brother, and the women continued their stroll around the base of the Capitoline Hill. Alhena hadn't received any specific visions about her brother in Iberia lately, but a twinge in the back of her mind suggested *something* was happening there, and she wanted to drop by the Temple of Bellona to offer her hopes that it was something *good,* something that would bring Gaius home.

Before they reached the Field of Mars, however, a high voice called out Alhena's name. She turned, but it took her a moment to place the figure approaching, as they were not well-acquainted.

Aemilia Fullia, High Priestess of Juno, was a slight, dark-haired woman who moved with practiced grace. Conscious of her status, she performed accordingly. She must have been on her way uphill to the Temple, for she was dressed in full regalia, with two subdued acolytes in rose-colored robes trailing in her wake.

Too confused to render a proper greeting, Alhena could do no more than blink in wonder. Tilla, affected neither by bewilderment nor protocol, scrunched up her face, saying, "Aemilia? What do you want with us?" She looked at the ground behind them. "Did we drop something?"

A scowl briefly appeared on Aemilia's face before she recomposed her expression to one of benevolent concern. "No, not at all. I'm only glad to have caught you. For days now, I've been thinking, *hoping* to have some way of extending the necessary influence, and now here you are." She clasped her hands. "Juno's hands must be at work."

Earnestness rang in her voice like the clap of a dented bell. "Um," Alhena said. "Good?"

"I very much hope it will be." Aemilia drew closer; she wore a cloying rosewater perfume, and Tilla's nose wrinkled. "It concerns your sister."

"Yes," Alhena said, cautious. "I was rather afraid it might."

"Word reached me that she is, once again, seeking to overstep her bounds." Another step, too close now. "That's she's convening some society, an assembly of disgruntled mages." For all her slightness, Aemilia had an imposing presence, and Alhena would have shied back if not for Tilla beside her. "And that she wants it to be a collegium, of all the absurdities!"

Passers-by were pausing to overhear; Aemilia's religious garb made her worth noticing, and the people of Aven generally considered public conversations to be free entertainment.

Alhena resisted the urge to pull her mantle up to obscure her face, and she tried to keep her chin steady, as her sisters did when facing a rival. "It is a civil enterprise, as any citizen of Aven might attempt, and no concern of yours." She swallowed, feeling like a rock had lodged in her throat. "And if you think I would be your messenger of dissuasion—"

Aemilia waved an impatient hand. "I've given up on trying to rescue Vitellia Secunda from her own foolishness. Clearly that is a lost cause. No, my dear, I hoped I might be able to persuade *you* not to take part in her vulgar pretense."

Anger sparked inside Alhena, a bright and sudden heat that she hardly knew how to manage. How *dare* this woman? "She is my sister," Alhena said, sharpening the syllables of each word. "She will always have my support."

"You're still young," Aemilia argued, "and for all your father's tardiness in getting you married—"

"Her intended husband did *die*, you know," Tilla interjected.

Aemilia ignored her. "—I should hope your future has much more in store than trailing at your sisters' hems."

It might have been a clever ploy, on someone else; Aemilia did not know that Alhena had no desire to strike out on her own and would happily rest in her sisters' shadows all her life, if so permitted. "I think we have nothing more to say to one another," she said, trying to imitate their dignity. "Tilla, let's—"

"And Quintilla Terentilla!" Aemilia said, before they could move. "You should heed this warning as well. Your family may have a reputation for eccentricity." Her cool eyes roved over Tilla's haphazardly draped tunic and gown. "But you are of an ancient line, and you should be conscious of that dignity."

Tilla snorted in a pointedly undignified manner. "My ancient line doesn't get to determine how I live my own life."

"Your sister is a *Vestal*," Aemilia pleaded. "Surely that means something."

"It means she sees through to the truth of things," Tilla countered, shifting herself in front of Alhena. Her posture grew broader, slightly aggressive. "She can tell pure hearts from those of mean, jealous cats." She tilted her head, dark curls swaying, and took in the small crowd of onlookers. "What must she see when she looks at you, I wonder? Shall I ask her? Perhaps in a public place, where all might hear the answer?"

A murmuring stirred up around them, and Aemilia stepped back, smoothing out her garments. "I am sure your sister would express nothing but regard for a fellow devotee of our divine protectors," she said primly.

"All the same." Tilla's smile put Alhena in mind of a wildcat baring fangs. "I'd love to find out."

Aemilia lifted her nose and turned away. "Think on my warning," she said. "It was kindly meant."

Snorting again, Tilla looped her arm through Alhena's and tugged her away, towards the Temple of Bellona. Those who had gathered to watch the spat went back to their business, but Alhena only released her tight-held tension once they walked a fair distance. "Thank you for the rescue," she said, clutching at Tilla. "I was running out of bravery."

Tilla brushed a quick kiss to her temple—a kiss that would look like friendship, to any observer, but that made Alhena want to melt into her nonetheless. "Don't be absurd. You've deep wells within you. But that woman was itching for a set-down, and I don't care a brass obol for her lofty position."

"It's odd, though... She's passed along her supposedly-well-meaning concerns to Father before. But to try to prise me away from my sister? And then bring you into it?"

"Not her usual style, hm? People like her deal in whispers and backchannels, not public haranguings."

"Latona gets under her skin. She knows Latona should hold her position, and that frightens her."

"Don't make excuses for that little shrew," Tilla chided playfully. "You've no obligation to play fair when someone wishes harm on your sister. *I* certainly wouldn't."

"No, I know. Still... it's odd. And it..." Alhena worried her lower lip. "It makes me wonder who else she might be so bold with."

XXVIII

Camp of the Lusetani, Western Iberia

Every day, it slipped from his fingers a little more, that dream of glory, that *promise* the gods had given him.

Two years ago, Ekialde had been the fiercest warrior in three generations of Lusetani, blessed by Bandue, an unchallenged *erregerra*. On his own, he had been those things, fierce and strong. His own heart, the might of his arm, the quickness of his mind, those had made him a leader of men.

Sometimes, he felt that still. When the power moved through him, when the lines on his arms and spine buzzed with glorious vitality, so heady and intoxicating that he felt it in every part of him, down to the bones—*then* he remembered what that was, what it meant to have the blessing of the gods, to work their will in the world and know that it was good.

The strength faded swifter and swifter each time.

Now, when he had been too long without a satisfying fight, his arms and legs trembled. His body could scarce function except in combat—or when supported by his uncle Bailar's tinctures and potions, supplements to the magic that lived in his skin.

Shivering so hard that his teeth chattered, even in mild weather, he pointed an accusing finger at his uncle. "More," he demanded. "You said this would work. You promised many things. Ensorcelled Aventans, devastating plagues, easy victories. My *wife* back, my *son* back."

"I have done everything in my power," Bailar said. "No one knows so well as you how hard I worked. The gods may hold plans beyond my understanding."

It was what men said when they had erred, terribly, and did not wish to own that mistake.

Well. They were of a piece in that. Ekialde *could* not own his, not with so many people still depending on him. Not with what he encouraged in so many of his warriors, how he praised them for following in his footsteps and giving themselves over to Bailar's magic. "Give me what I require," Ekialde growled. He did not have the patience for any further philosophical wranglings—nor, if he did not get the tonic soon, the strength to stay upright.

In this, at least, Bailar remained reliable. His potions had ever been effective, the best of his work, apart from the *akdraugi*. He promised greater discoveries—that business with the corpses, his ongoing experiments—but the promise was, as-yet, unpaid.

What was in the potion, Ekialde did not ask. Blood, he knew that much. Some of his own, some from his enemies. The rest was secret, prerogative of the magic-man. Bailar warmed it over the fire, poured it into a clay cup, and passed it to Ekialde.

It smelled of damp earth and rusted weapons. The taste was worse, but Ekialde was well-used to it by now. He chugged the concoction, throwing back his head and pouring it down his throat, guzzling it in his aching need.

Strength returned. Heart returned. Without looking at his uncle, he cast the clay cup to the ground and stalked away.

'One final victory,' Ekialde promised himself. 'That's all I need. One last, grand push against the Aventans. Kill their commanders. Scatter their forces. Then, perhaps... then I claim triumph. Return home. Rest. Heal. Find Neitin. Find my boy. My sweet rabbits both...'

Camp of Legio X Equestris, Western Iberia

"They were alone," Gaius Vitellius reported. "The queen and the child, with the Cossetan woman. She claims—the Cossetan, I mean—she claims to be one of their magic-women."

Sempronius gazed at the two women, the spoils of Ekialde's home village. If Ekialde styled himself a king, then the wretched creature clutching her squalling child hardly looked the part of a queen. She was well-formed, her bistre hair shot through with reddish tones. A fine enough specimen of Lusetani womanhood, if one who had been living rough for some time.

Shadow's intuition revealed a heavy cloud of sorrow on her, much like the one weighing on Gaius Vitellius. "And you found her—where?"

"Curled around the base of a dying tree."

Pressure at the back of Sempronius's head told him to heed those words: Shadow, alerting him to oncoming darkness, but Water, too, recognizing the touch of magic in the world. *'Curious.'*

He took one step toward the women. The Cossetan did not flinch, but the supposed queen drew her shoulders up toward her ears, turning away slightly, as though to shield her child. "Does she speak...?" Sempronius prompted.

"Tyrian," Vitellius answered. "The queen, I mean, does. The Cossetan has Iberian dialects only."

"Ask Hanath to join us, please," Sempronius directed, his eyes taking in all they could assess about both of these strangers. "Your Iberian has come a long way, Vitellius, don't think I disparage your fluency, but I want to be sure there are no—"

"I understand," Vitellius said, nodding as he departed.

Sempronius did not step forward this time, but fixed his eyes on the queen. "You speak Tyrian?" he asked, in that tongue, before changing over to Iberian that was halting at best, even in the Arevaci dialect: "I could try your tongue, but I may run out of words."

The queen blinked a few times, then collected herself enough to reply, in Tyrian, "Let us try what we have in better common."

Sempronius gestured to the chairs in his tent and took his own. The Cossetan sat readily enough, even though her face wore wary puzzlement, the look of one who did not understand the dialogue but did not intend to miss out on meaning nonetheless. The queen lowered herself, slow and cautious, murmuring soft words to the child still clutched to her.

"Your name, honored lady?"

"Neitin," she said, and gave herself no titles, no regal styling. "The child is Matigentis. My companion, Sakarbik." Sakarbik blinked at the sound of her own name, but otherwise held her face impassive.

"I am Praetor Sempronius Tarren," he said, "sent here to eliminate the threat your husband presented to Aven's interests in Iberia."

Distrust and suspicion emanated from the Lusetani queen. Sempronius respected her for that; a credulous woman would have been a disappointment. "I do not care what reasons you came here for," she said. "It is no business of mine." She drew a deep breath, setting her shoulders back. "I cannot tell you anything worth knowing. No secrets to unfold, no hidden knowledge to help you prevail."

Perhaps it was true; Shadow gave him no indication that she was lying. "Honored lady," Sempronius said, "I cannot expect your trust. But I will say, nonetheless, that I mean you no harm. Nor the child." She froze like a doe caught out by a hunter, terrified for her life but unsure whether to flee or fight. "I am not in the habit of murdering defenseless women and children, nor torturing them for information. Furthermore, I am... intrigued." The word prompted a question on her face; evidently it strained the extent of her Tyrian. "I am curious," he amended. "If you are the *erregerra*'s wife, why then were you alone and unguarded?"

Her eyes went to the floor. "I had my reasons."

"No doubt." Leagues from her husband's army, without any guard. Had she been left there, abandoned? Or had she parted company from them?

The tent flap stirred; Hanath entered, looking curious, but she did not interrupt, only crept along the perimeter of the tent, eyeing both the Lusetani queen and the Cossetan stranger.

"I-If you speak true," Neitin ventured, "if you mean us no harm? Then I—I promise to give you no trouble." Her child said something; it sounded like words, but Sempronius did not know if they were proper Lusetani phrases or simply the babbling of an infant. Neitin patted his hair, shushing him a moment, before she continued. "All I ask is safety, for me and my boy. I know he is—he is your enemy's son, but—"

"I have said," Sempronius cut in, "I am no danger to children. Even the children of my enemies."

Images came unbidden to his mind: the Dictator Ocella's young sons, butchered in their own home. Innocent children, despised for their sire's sake. Sempronius had tried to save them; he had failed.

Gazing at the black-haired child—the Iberian princeling—in his mother's arms, Sempronius made a solemn vow: not again. Whatever this boy would grow to be, whatever the Fates intended for him, he would have the opportunity. Sempronius would assure that, so far as he was able.

"You must be tired, Lady Neitin," he said. "If you will allow my people to escort you—or one of the Lady Hanath's maids, if that would be better?"

The young queen nodded vigorously, and Sempronius cut his eyes to Hanath. "Sterra, perhaps?" Felix's paramour was friendly and reliable, and Hanath nodded her assent. "Yes. My lady, if you are willing, one of the Arevaci girls will take you to a tent where you can have some privacy and comfort. A bath, a soft bed, whatever you and your son require. Let the girl know, and it shall be done. We can speak further when you have rested."

After the queen departed, Sempronius looked to the Cossetan woman. "My sincere apologies for anything you suffered while captive to the Lusetani," he said. Hanath translated, for Sempronius's Iberian, while improving, was not up to a full—and likely to be nuanced—conversation.

"It was not you who took me," the woman replied, also through Hanath's aid. "I might blame Aven for negligence, I suppose, but your duties in this region have always been... uncertain."

"I mean to rectify that vagueness," Sempronius assured her. "Tribune Vitellius tells me you claim to have a power that can help us defeat the Lusetani for good and all."

"Help, perhaps," the woman clarified. "I can make no promises on behalf of your troops. But I can, I think, give you a way to nullify their foul magic."

"Truly?"

"If you have magic-men with any sense at all—"

Here the Cossetan and Hanath broke off, squabbling for a moment among themselves, Sempronius assumed over the slight to the thaumaturgical capacities of the Arevaci. As much as he valued his allies, he was inclined to side with the Cossetan in this respect; the Arevaci magic-men had not, after all, unraveled the conundrum. At every turn, in fact, the superior magic of the Lusetani stymied them.

After a few sharp-toned exchanges, Hanath sighed and resumed translating. "If you have magic-men with sense," she reiterated, "I can show them what to do. It will require many of us, to work on a scale sufficient enough to counteract Ekialde and his uncle's forces." This was the first Sempronius had heard of an uncle; he slotted the information away for further perusal. "It stretched my talents to protect the queen and her little son. To summon enough strength to render the whole of his army bereft of their blood-born vigor — that will take much more than I may manage alone."

"And what is it you have that may help us?"

Sakarbik lifted her chin, dignified as any queen. "You have lived long in fear of their *akdraugi,* I think," she said. "Let me introduce you to spirits of another sort."

To prove her good will and the power of her magic, Sakarbik arranged a demonstration.

Not wanting to rile the soldiers, Sempronius allowed her to do so in his tent, with his two most capable tribunes, Felix and Vitellius, and Lord Bartasco of the Arevaci observing. He wondered about including Vitellius, so soon after a journey and ill at ease with Iberian magic—but the young man gave no indication of displeasure at the task.

Sakarbik pulled back the rugs in Sempronius's tent, exposing the earth below. She took a pouch from her side and scattered a mixture upon the ground: herbs, but other materials, too, flecks of stone that caught the lamplight. Then she stood in the midst of the circle she made, her hands held palm-up almost at the level of her shoulders. Similar to an Aventan supplication, but not so humble. This woman looked as though what the heavens did not readily yield her, she would *grab.* Sempronius smiled. '*Perhaps we have something in common.*'

As soon as Sakarbik began to sing, Sempronius's Water magic leapt to attention. Her voice was not exactly beautiful, but low and rolling through words of a chant he could not understand, and its power was evident as soon as she began. He forced his face to remain impassive, but inside, his magical sensibilities wanted to dance with excitement. Whatever she summoned would have real force; his Shadow magic remained quiet, dormant, and so he did not fear that force.

As the song went on, Sempronius glanced sideways to Bartasco. The Iberian chieftain shook his head in answer to the mute question: no, he could not translate. Sempronus had suspected as much. The Iberian magic-men had a language all their own, separate from the everyday dialects.

Sakarbik thrust both hands into the air—and one of them held a dagger. Wherever that had been hiding, she produced it so swiftly that Sempronius hardly saw the motion. Felix took a step forward in front of Sempronius, ready to defend, but Sempronius put a hand on his shoulder, easing him back. The worst that would happen, at his guess, was that the woman would cut herself.

This, she did not do. Sempronius was grateful; the use of human blood in magic was not inherently evil, but with all they had suffered under the effects of such power turned to foul purposes, placing his hopes of salvation on something similar would have caused significant unease.

Instead, Sakarbik flung the dagger down at the earth with such force that it embedded itself into the ground. "Endovelicos of many faces, Endovelicos who blesses my sight, here!" she cried, words close enough to the Arevaci for Sempronius to understand them.

Then she stepped back, waiting.

Outside the tent, an owl shrieked. A wind fluttered the flaps of the tent and flickered the lights from the lamps. A mist began to form in the middle of the tent, rising up from the dagger Sakarbik had flung into the earth. Vitellius drew a sharp breath, and Felix looked no less ready to draw his sword, but Sempronius remained passive. "There has been no blood," he reminded them. "Whatever this may be, we know what it is *not*."

The mist took slow form, a few rounded figures bobbing in mid-air. None of them had distinct shapes; they seemed to merge and flow through each other. After a moment, they began to sparkle gold. They emanated warmth and power, *such* power that Sempronius's thaumaturgical sensibilities were in near riot. Had he been a Fire mage, every flame in the tent would have blazed out of control.

Gazing at the shapes offered no comfort. They were not spirits of consolation and relief. No, he felt *summoned*. In their glimmer shone the reminder of all he intended to do, all he had not yet done. The weight of ages pressed at his back, urging him to shape the future.

"*Besteki*," Bartasco breathed in awe. He was gaping, and Sempronius did not blame him. He had to tear his own eyes away to check the reactions of his tribunes. Felix's face registered shock, but heightened energy, too; he looked invigorated. And Vitellius...

Vitellius wept. Silently, motionlessly, tears flowed down his pale, freckled cheeks.

A curiosity to examine later. Sempronius turned his gaze to Sakarbik. "Honored lady," he said, addressing her as he would any mage of Aven, "can you explain?"

With Bartasco's translation help, she could. "These are *besteki*. Good spirits. Protectors. They guarded me and the little mother on our journey."

Still, they pulsed in mid-air, their ethereality incongruous in the military surroundings of Sempronius's command tent. They took no human-like shape, as the *akdraugi* sometimes did. No faces, no limbs, just nebulous energy given a semi-tangible form. *'But what good will they be to us in defeating the Lusetani?'*

As though reading his mind, Sakarbik said, "They can do more than float. Much more, when there is need. When we fled from the camp—for if the little mother will not tell you, I have no reason not to—"

Sempronius quirked an eyebrow. *'So the queen left of her own volition. Fled, her companion says.'* It would be worth knowing more, but that story could wait.

"—Bailar sent his wraiths after us. *Akdraugi* to track us. To what end, I cannot say. Ekialde, I am sure, wanted his wife and son returned safely. I can attribute no such altruistic motive to Bailar." Her face contorted in revulsion. "Well. The *besteki* shielded us from the *akdraugi*."

"Shielded?" Felix echoed. "Could—I mean, could you get enough to shield an entire army?"

"I am not certain," Sakarbik admitted. "But they... they communicate with me, in a way. Hard to explain. Not words, exactly. They are not human, never were, so there is no human language for them to express. But they still give me senses—where to go, what to fear, and now, what they want."

Sempronius lifted an eyebrow. "And what is it they want?"

"To purge the *akdraugi* from this earth." The ferocity in her voice was stirring. "They could not do it before. They were not strong enough—nor I as a magic-woman powerful enough to call them in more than fistfuls. But I have grown stronger, this past winter. I understand them better. And with more magic-men and magic-women, I think we could defeat the *akdraugi* and their master." Her yellow eyes flashed in the dim tent. "Once and for all."

A tempting prospect. Sempronius knew better than to be drawn in by optimistic promises, however. "Forgive my sluggish Aventan mind," he said. "We are assured by specifics. These *besteki*, if you summon enough of them—What is it, precisely, that they could do? Shield us from the *akdraugi*? Shield us from physical harm?"

"Praetor Sempronius Tarren," Sakarbik said—in Truscan cadence, he noted, either a quick study or more familiar with their language than she let on, "enough of these *besteki* could, I believe, cleanse the Lusetani of the *akdraugi* influence." A slow, ravenous smile spread across her face. "They could then summon no fiends, and I think their maniac warriors would find that their unholy strength deserted them. The *besteki* would chase the hellish spirits from their bodies, leave them only as they were before: men."

Sempronius stood for a moment, watching the *besteki* circling in the air. *'Men, we can defeat.'*

It was worth trying. They would be fighting in any case. And Iberians raising Iberian magic against other Iberians—that would not offend Mars. Such things happened in other nations all the time. The Prohibition applied only to Aventans and other peoples who honored Mars. Mars had never told them—at least not in Sempronius's hearing—not to take advantage of the thaumaturgical maneuvers of their allies.

"What do you need?" he asked Sakarbik.

"I can make a list," she said. "We may have to get creative. The herbs, this time of year..." She clucked her tongue. "Difficult. And other elements... If you have anything of the Lusetani that can be broken apart—armor, talismans, even bodies."

"There are always bodies." With each battle, more of them, hacked ingloriously to pieces and trampled underneath hob-nailed boots until their strength at last gave out. "We can supply you, if it will help."

Her nose crinkled. "I do not like it," she said, "but evidence of the perfidy does call the attention of the gods. Ashes, perhaps, would be best. Let us keep the blood of death out of our dealings, if at all possible."

"I quite agree, honored lady."

Sempronius sent Sakarbik off to rest with the Lady Neitin, then he turned to Bartasco. "Do you think this a worthwhile plan? I will countermand it, if you do not."

The Arevaci chieftain kept glancing back at where the *besteki* had been, till Sakarbik dismissed them. They all did. The spirits left an intangible residue. Sempronius wondered how long it would take to fade, and if he, not much given to dreaming, might find his sleep affected this night. "I do, General," Bartasco said. "I... I had thought the *besteki* something out of legend only. But I had thought the same of the *akdraugi*, until I saw their power ripped from between the worlds." His broad shoulders moved in an uneven shrug. "There is much beyond my understanding, but those spirits.... Those felt *good*, yes? Wholesome. Everything the *akdraugi* are not."

"I'm curious," Sempronius probed, for *wholesome* was not the word he would have reached for, "what did you feel, when you looked at them?"

Bartasco blew air out through his mouth, rustling his whiskers. "How to put it in words... I remembered what it was to be welcomed home, at the end of a long journey. To put down a load and rest in one's own bed."

"A comfort I hope you may enjoy again soon, my friend," Sempronius said.

"Yes, we have all been long from our proper homes, but it... it didn't make me homesick or weary. It was just... a reminder. A steadiness, embedding itself deep beneath my ribs. A promise, even, that I would know that warmth once again."

"And you?" Sempronius asked of Felix. "What did the *besteki* make you feel?"

"Invigorated," Felix answered without hesitation. "Full of life. Like the very best of fighting and fu—pardon me, Lord Bartasco," he amended partway through, coughing. "I only mean—the very best of all sorts of *action*. Chariot races and victorious battles and raucous parties." He touched his own chest, beneath his heart. "Lord Bartasco is right, it felt like it came up through my ribs, filling all my blood with energy." With a laughing sigh, Felix shook his head. "I wouldn't mind seeing them again, General, I will tell you that."

Sempronius elected not to include Vitellius in his survey. The young man was still a half-step behind Felix, holding close to the tent wall. He was no longer weeping outright, but his cheeks bore the tracks of tears yet. "Felix, go and find Eustix," Sempronius commanded. "I want to communicate with Strato and Onidius, let them know we may at last have advantage enough to secure victory. Lord Bartasco, I believe the Lady Sakarbik will have need of your magic-men."

"Indeed!" Bartasco said, with relish. "We've dragged them along this far, and little enough help they've been. If that Cossetan woman can put them to use, then thanks be to Endovelicos, Jupiter, or whatever other gods are listening."

Once Bartasco and Felix had gone, Sempronius gestured to Gaius Vitellius to come forth from the shadows. "Is all well, tribune?"

Vitellius nodded thickly, clearing his throat in the gruff way so many men did when they wanted to cover an uncomfortable emotion. "Yes, sir. Very sorry, sir. I didn't mean to..." His gaze moved back to the center of the room as if dragged. "I'm not sure what I expected of her magic, but it was not that."

What had he felt? What sensation had lodged beneath his ribs, tugging on the innermost corners of his soul? To Sempronius, the *besteki* pulled upon his ambitions, his lifelong quest to reshape the world, but to Bartasco they echoed the comfort of homecoming, and to Felix, the joyous tumult of physical achievement.

No simple spirits, these, and gods, how Sempronius wanted to study them more, to learn their nature and their possibilities.

To Gaius Vitellius, he gave an understanding nod. "Indeed," Sempronius concurred. "I only hope she can bring the Arevaci magic-men up to the mark. This is well beyond anything they've managed so far."

"I didn't—I mean, yes, sir, we'll need that, but I meant more than the scale of the power." His head swayed helplessly. "I had not thought, after all I've seen here, that Iberian magic could produce something so beautiful."

XXIX

Tagus River, Western Iberia

It took several days to prepare the magic. From the Nones to the Ides of Martius, Sakarbik worked with the Arevaci magic-men, and even with Eustix, the Air mage messenger.

Sempronius wanted to watch it, every incantation, every maneuver, every invocation. His curiosity thirsted for answers to so many questions, everything he had wondered about Iberian magic since arriving in this land. No matter if some parts were peculiar to these people and their gods; he still wanted to know, wanted to use Water's insight to see where the different forces came into play.

He could not, of course. Those same days that Sakarbik and the magic-men needed to prepare their charms, Sempronius needed to prepare his strategy.

Dorsus and the other scouts rode throughout the nearby terrain, finding a suitable location. Large enough to serve as a battlefield, wide and flat, but with ground soft enough to receive the Cossetan woman's charms.

"How do we lure them there?" Hanath asked, looking over the flat scrape of land on the north side of the Tagus River. They were much closer now to where it turned sharply south, towards Olissippo. The winter campaign had brought them farther from Toletum than Sempronius would have expected.

"We let them know we have something they want."

Hanath's dark eyes widened. "You mean to use the woman and child as bait?"

"I mean for Ekialde and this fiend-summoner of his to know we have them, yes," Sempronius said. "I have no intention of bringing them anywhere near the field of battle, but Lady Sakarbik thinks we can lay a trail, draw the enemy forces in—draw Ekialde, *specifically*, not one of his subordinate war-bands. He will be looking for his son."

"What man would not?"

A cruel token to play, perhaps, but Sempronius weighed the scruples of it and found himself satisfied with the balance. Ekialde and his forces had caused enough death, mayhem, and destruction, even *before* they began to alter the natural order of life and death. If he had to play upon a father's love to bring this ugly business to an end, that was a bargain well worth the making. "Then, once we have his attention, we use traditional measures to drive them onto the field where we want them. Your cavalry will be important there."

"Fear not, Sempronius Tarren," Hanath assured him, "we are as eager as you are to put an end to their wretched reign."

On the Ides of Martius, they were ready.

Sakarbik seeded the field with her charms, assisted by every magic-man they could find from the Arevaci, the Vettoni, and the local villages. Sakarbik spread, too, traces of the Lady Neitin and her son—clippings of hair and nails, which she said would draw the attention of Bailar and his *akdraugi*. How she had gotten them, if the lady knew she was being used in such a fashion, Sempronius opted not to inquire.

That morning, with dew clinging to the grass and an entirely natural mist rising over the water of the Tagus, the Tenth Legion and its auxiliaries waited on the outskirts of the chosen field. Vitellius and Bartasco had command in the lowland, overseeing the centurions and the Arevaci forces. Sempronius placed himself and Felix on high ground nearby, at least at the start; from horseback there, he could see the Lusetani camp in the distance. Smaller now than at Toletum. Already some of the Lusetani had marched forth, following the Sakarbik's trail.

'Where is the mage Bailar in that throng? Following the scent of his prey? Or directing from a safe location?' He witnessed, too, the ride of Hanath and her cavalry, curling wide to the north, then coming up from behind the Lusetani, intending to drive them toward the plain.

The movement of so many people all at once looked strange from such a distance, almost unreal, like something playing out in his mind, not in reality. Yet here they were. The sun had barely risen, but battle was imminent. Men would die this day, and perhaps a war would end.

"They're moving," Sempronius said. "Signal to Vitellius to be ready."

Visual signals only, for now. They did not want to alert the Lusetani to the extent of the trap awaiting them. They knew they were heading into combat, no doubt; likely they embraced it. But if any of them still had the sense to spot unfavorable odds, Sempronius did not want to give them the opportunity. Sempronius's standard-bearer dipped and lifted the banner of the Tenth Legion, with its barking dog emblazoned on a scarlet field, three times. A moment later, a standard-bearer on the plain did the same.

Still and quiet, Sempronius watched. The fog was burning off the river as the sun rose higher. Like flocks of birds, the Arevaci cavalry and Lusetani horde moved. The cavalry was not riding at full pace, and they had to spread out to pursue the full Lusetani force, which had fanned out when rushing out of their camp.

Too far, Sempronius realized. "They're breaking off to the north side." He swore beneath his breath. "The cavalry caught them too far from the battlefield."

Felix peered where Sempronius was looking; his vision was not quite so acute as Sempronius's, but he could hardly miss the mass of Lusetani as they moved like starlings, a dark flutter across the pale yellow plain, cutting too far too the north to reach the prepared ground.

"Someone has to drive them back," Felix said. He squared his shoulders, tightening the strap on his helmet. "I told you that you could count on me, Praetor. Now is the time I pay that promise." Before Sempronius could react, Felix slapped his horse's reins and urged the beast onward. "Cavalry!" he cried out, lifting a fist in the air. "On me!"

Sempronius did not countermand the order. Felix was right. Something had to be done, or the entire venture was lost.

But there were not enough of them. Most of the cavalry had gone with Hanath, attempting to pinch the Lusetani in and drive them toward the intended battleground. Only a rump remained—and, though Sempronius hated to admit it, the Aventan cavalry lacked the caliber of the Iberian locals. The blood-marked warriors might not be stopped even by horses, once they were in a charge. His hope was that Ekialde had enough sanity remaining, and enough control over the men driven by magic, that he would pull them back, and thus stumble onto the prepared ground.

Heart racing beneath a stoic demeanor, Sempronius watched as Felix's cavalry thundered down the hill and around the northern side of a copse of trees. The foliage, just starting to bud, obscured his view as the riders encountered the advancing Lusetani. Long minutes passed while he could not know who prevailed.

Then, at last, the tide of Lusetani warriors turned. They began moving south again, back toward the river—and toward the battlefield Sakarbik and the magic-men had prepared as a trap.

Without knowing if brave Felix had survived his charge, Sempronius gave the order for his remaining guard to move off the hill and rejoin their compatriots.

Ekialde's blood buzzed in every vein, thrilling to the danger, the imminence of a fight. He had hoped to find some small cohort, perhaps scouts, holding hostage his wife and child. Instead, from the trees at the far end of a field of dry yellow grass, an entire legion emerged, all scarlet cloth and clanking armor. Their footsteps thumped like his heartbeat, a call to battle, a call to glory.

Whatever game their cavalry had been playing, he no longer cared. His arms itched, and hunger ached inside his core. The need to kill surged through his muscles, crowding out other concerns. The spirits within him needed blood, *Aventan* blood, and Ekialde meant to let them feast.

His warriors obeyed his call, even those whose skin bore Bandue's blessing as his own did. They were not insensible, not uncontrollable. Still men, not beasts. They knew where a better fight would be, more worthy of their honor and Bandue's approval.

Across the field they charged. The Aventans halted their advance, bracing in their neat lines, from the copse of trees to the north almost down to the river's edge.

Two shields parted, dead in the middle, and someone stepped out. Hard to see, even as Ekialde raced closer. A woman, he thought. An *Iberian* woman.

He could not slow down; his muscles would not let him, arms and legs pumping on toward the battle, despite a sudden misgiving in his mind. Keen though his eyes were, he could not be certain, but he suspected it was the Cossetan his wife had taken as a slave. *'What would she be—?'*

Other holes had opened up in the Aventan line, admitting other figures. None in armor; all in robes. *'Magic-men,'* he realized. Now he urged his legs to move faster. *'We must kill them before they can finish, as they slaughtered our summoners.'*

He was still a long distance from them, though, when the woman flung something down into the earth. All the men followed suit, then the shield wall opened again and the legions moved forward, swallowing the mages.

Across the broad plain, the air turned hazy, as though a dust storm had kicked up. But this was no dust: the ground was solid beneath them, even damp close to the riverbank, and what rose in the air was no ocher dirt, but a golden, glimmering vapor.

Ekialde had never seen anything so beautiful.

Here and there, it coalesced into small clouds, hovering mid-air, flowing around and sometimes through the Lusetani warriors. They emanated serenity, soft and lulling. For a moment, Ekialde wondered if he had died and stumbled through to the world beyond, eternally caught in a gilded, glowing dawn.

All around him, the other Lusetani warriors slowed, even the blood-marked, looking around as though in a daze. Some had tears on their faces. Others were breathing heavily, almost gulping for air, clutching their chests, enraptured.

The radiance seized Ekialde's heart, tugging out his softest memories: his mother's voice, his wife's laugh, his son's tiny fingers and toes. A sound like a song rose all around him, rolling along with the mist, clear and mellifluous. Music that the gods might play for one another, this, dulcet and decorous and ringing with unadulterated beauty.

Then, the beauty turned to horror. The honeyed song lost its gentle airs and clanged, harsh and loud. The golden glow no longer soothed, but scalded; not tranquil clouds, but steam from boiling water, shockingly hot. Ekialde tried to back away, but the brazen gleam was everywhere, inescapable.

All the battle-fervor had gone out of him. His blood did not surge with eagerness for the fight; it sizzled within his veins, frantic and desperate. Like stinging nettle within his skin, like the heat of a thousand hearth-fires, a pain more profound than any he had known. The skin of his arms grew red and itchy, as though afflicted by horrible sunburn, and the agony inside felt as though it would shatter his bones.

His blood-marked warriors doubled over in agony, clawing at their own arms, legs, backs, anywhere they had been marked with Bailar's sanguine ink. Ekialde's own markings, too, felt as though they were trying to tear their way loose of the rest of his skin.

It came to him, then, what the golden mist was. *'Besteki.'* The natural enemies of the *akdraugi* and all such fiends. They saw in the blood-marks a threat, a foe, and they would root it out with the thorough efficiency of bees who had caught a hornet within their hive. Only myths and legends, he had thought, but so had the *akdraugi* been, before Bailar raised them.

'Bailar.' He should have known better. Should have anticipated this countermove. Should have sensed the trap. *'I put all my faith in him. All my strength. My life, in his hands. Every time he failed me, I made excuses. I said he was interpreting the unknowable gods. I thought... I thought...'*

Deep down, he did not want to admit what he had thought: that any setback could be overcome, that any horror was worth it, for the sake of his glory.

The Aventans began to march, but Ekialde did what he loathed, turning his back on the battle. His uncle was somewhere in the rearguard. The intent had been for him to summon *akdraugi* again, but there would be no point, not here in a flood of *besteki*.

Bailar needed to answer for his failures.

XXX

As victories went, this one was not glorious.

Sempronius could take a degree of pride in it, for the strategy involved: the lure, the magical nullification, the symmetry of fighting the *akdraugi* with their inimical spirits. But the fight itself? No; that was not a matter of pride, only grim satisfaction.

The battlefield was bloodier than usual, for the magically-enhanced Lusetani warriors were coming apart at the seams. Blood gushed from their markings long before any Aventan blade touched them, seeping from the whorling designs as though their flesh was trying to separate from itself.

The non-magical warriors were a mix. Some were dazed by the *besteki*, utterly stupified. Some recognized the futility of the moment and lay down their arms, surrendering themselves to captivity. And some chose to fight on, against the odds, even with their brethren howling and practically disintegrating around them.

No pride in this, no glory. Only a brutal end to the conflict. By midday, Sempronius judged, the entire Lusetani army would be dead or captured.

'But where are the two who matter most? Their war-king and his pet sorcerer?' If they lived and escaped, they could prove a threat to Aven and the peace of Iberia again—maybe not soon, but on some future day. Sempronius desired peace, true and lasting, prosperous and productive. *'So I must find them.'*

He rode along the left flank of his army, the legions moving with ruthless precision. Sakarbik and the Arevaci mages were in a knot at the very back on this side, far from the fighting. If things took a sudden disastrous turn, they could be protected, or else melt into the marshes at the riverbank and hope to avoid further notice.

To the guards riding along behind him, he said, "Stay here. Watch over the Lady Sakarbik and the Arevaci magic-men."

"Sir—" one of the guards started, but Sempronius held up a hand.

"I will be fine. We need our allies safe." They had done their part; gods willing, they would not be needed again.

Sempronius's own magic, though, might yet have a role to play.

He rode along a narrow strip of yellow grass between the fighting men and the thicket of trees and weeds that grew by the riverbank. *'Gods who favor me, look here,'* he thought. *'Surely there is blood enough to count as a sacrifice. I call upon Pluto, Lord of the Underworld. I call upon Nox, Lady of Night. Governors of Shadow, I, Vibius Sempronius Tarren, entreat you. Look here and guide me.'*

With delicacy, he reached out with his Shadow magic—and reeled in his saddle. Darkness was everywhere, clouding out the rising sun and the golden glow of the *besteki* alike. Everywhere one of the Lusetani blood-marked warriors lay dying, the shadowy vapors filled the air. Sempronius had to withdraw his magical senses or be overwhelmed. *'Pluto and Nox, I ask you—help me find one thread of this Iberian magic. The leader of them all, their parent and original. Guide me to that man, and I will do you great honors.'*

Ekialde was bleeding, though not from any wound inflicted by an Aventan blade or an Arevaci spear-thrust. He had not clashed swords this day, and he made it to the rear of his lines without encountering a single foe.

'Bandue would be ashamed.' But Bandue had thrust him into Bailar's willing embrace, into all his schemes and plans.

Covered in blood, but without a fight. It seeped through his skin, through every pore. The lines inked into his arms and chest and back wept. With each drop, he grew weaker. *'I am sorry, my darling rabbit,'* he thought, wondering where his wife was, if she sorrowed for him. *'Perhaps I should have listened.'*

The cavalry caught up with the back of the lines, and more crashed in from the north. Now Ekialde saw how thoroughly they had been netted, driven like deer to the killing-place. He evaded the horsemen and horsewomen, ducking and weaving through a chaos of men, half retreating, half trying to press onward into battle still, as though they might somehow relieve the forces rendered useless by the *besteki*.

Bailar, though, would be somewhere near. The man knew how to hide. As the battlefield turned back into forest, at the base of the hill, Ekialde knew to search for him. Someplace the cavalry would overlook as they harried the Lusetani forces, someplace tucked away. Beneath a fallen log, perhaps, or cringing in a hollow between two boulders, or up a tree.

Ekialde found his uncle not up a tree, but beneath one. The winter rains had swept the soil away from the roots of a massive holm oak, leaving a hollow on one side big enough to fit a man in.

"Come out," Ekialde growled. "Come and see what you have done."

Like a tortoise sticking his head out from his shell, Bailar came forth from his arboreal hideaway. His eyes widened when he saw Ekialde's skin, bubbling blood from the pores. "Endovelicos preserve us," he said, clutching at the talisman around his neck.

"He has not," Ekialde panted in reply. "He has turned against us. Do you know what they have out there? What the Aventans have fighting on their side now?"

Bailar shook his head, but even as he did, understanding dawned. "No... No, they could not. The Aventans could not raise *besteki*, there is no chance."

"So you did know it was possible!" Ekialde accused. "You knew a way existed to counter your magic? The magic you promised would be stronger than any other?"

Bailar's head shook. "No. I did not *know*. I have never seen *besteki*. Never summoned them. Never known anyone who had. I did not think—it did not occur to me that anyone would be able to call them forth. They are gentler spirits than the *akdraugi*."

"They are gently shredding my army to pieces, then. Gently flaying the souls of all my blood-warriors."

"It may be that—"

"I have had enough of your lies!" Ekialde bellowed. "Enough of your begging, enough of your promises!" His chest cracked with the pain of admittance. "I might have been a strong chieftain, if not for you! I might have lived to see old age, lived to watch my sons and their sons thrive! But you—You convinced me the gods had some magnificent path in store for me! So I followed."

"You wanted to be convinced," Bailar responded, cold as winter. "You wanted to be told you were the gods' own vessel. You charted that path in your own stars. Do not blame me."

"I did not ask for—"

"No?" Bailar took a step forward, challenging, never mind the curved blade levelled in his direction. "You did not tell me to find you ways to win? To do whatever was necessary to secure victory?"

"And have we won?" Ekialde flung a hand back in the direction of the battlefield. "My men are dying by the score with each step the Aventan legion takes! My blood-warriors are like this!" He shook his gory arms at Bailar, spattering him with crimson. "Worse than this! Falling to pieces! And my wife and child—my wife and child—"

That pain was too terrible; he could not frame his tongue to it. *'I am sorry, Neitin, I am sorry. Gods grant I may have the chance to tell you so.'*

Bailar spread his arms wide, still trying to conciliate. "I did warn you, sister-son," he said, "that no man can accurately predict the will of the gods."

"Yet you claimed to know *my* fate, that Bandue intended me for victory and conquest."

"I thought he did. I did not lie to you, Ekialde. This I swear."

Ekialde's sword, drawn for battle what seemed half a lifetime ago, was still in his hand. He advanced on his uncle. Bailar tried to back up, but found himself tripping over the roots he had so recently hidden beneath. "You vowed to protect me," Ekialde said. "You promised I would be invincible. You never wanted to admit a weakness in your plans, never warned me about their flaws, not until doom was upon us. Why, Bailar? Why did you push me down *this* way of interpreting the gods' signs?"

Bailar's tongue was still a long moment, his dark eyes unfathomable. At last he said, "You are not the only one who thought you had a great destiny, sister-son. I believed it was my purpose to explore magic no man ever had. And this seemed the best way to get to do it."

For that, so many had died. For that, Ekialde had surrendered his soul.

There was no joy in the kill when his blade drove between Bailar's ribs, only the squelch of viscera and a last croaking gasp from the man who had been mentor, instigator, and kin.

It purged nothing, when the corpse lay at his feet. Ekialde's skin continued to seethe blood, and his heart still felt shattered.

A noise behind him. Hoofbeats, approaching in no hurry.

"Ah. I see you have spared me the effort of killing him," a strange voice said, in thickly accented Arevaci. Ekialde turned to see a lone man on horseback. Aventan, wearing a more impressive helmet and cuirass than any he had seen before. Not the young leader he had nearly ensorcelled before Toletum. No, this had to be that man's superior officer, the one who had brought reinforcements, broken the siege, broken all of Ekialde's good fortune.

'Fight!' Ekialde ordered his body. *'Fight him, damn you!'* His hand shook; his fingers could barely grip his sword. Still he tried to hoist his arm in the air, lurching at the stranger.

"Stop that," the man said, still in his borrowed tongue. "Fool-man, there is no need—"

That was all Ekialde heard. The last of his strength left him, and the world turned black before he hit the ground.

An ignoble end to the fight, for a warrior who had caused strife across so much of Iberia, who had won so many battles and skirmishes.

Sempronius dismounted and drew cautiously near the young man, in case it was a feint. But no, the youth was out cold. Not dead yet. The blood spilling from his skin was horrible to see, but not enough to threaten his life.

"We will make a better story of it," Sempronius promised the unconscious *erregerra*. "For both our sakes. A proper fight, man-to-man. A bit antiquated for my people's tastes, but better than this." An Aventan victory was only as impressive as their opponent was strong, after all. "Perhaps that mage betrayed you in the middle of it, and that's how I managed to vanquish you."

He took the sword from his side and daubed it in the free-flowing blood, then jammed it into the earth beside him. Both of his elements were screaming now: Water felt magic pouring out everywhere, untrammeled by the magic-man's death, and Shadow felt the darkness drowning the young king's soul.

With effort, Sempronius pushed that awareness to the side. Now was a time for the tangible world, not thaumaturgy.

He straightened and blew a whistle, summoning nearby riders. He needed witnesses to Ekialde's fall and the blood-mage's death—and he would need help tying the young man up and bearing him back to camp.

One of his junior tribunes was among the riders who answered his call, but not Gaius Vitellius or Autronius Felix. Worry pinched the back of his neck. Had Felix survived his wild charge, turning back the Lusetani force? Had Vitellius, in the thick of the battle, held his ground? He would have been better defended than Felix—but like Felix, like Bartasco, like Sempronius himself, he would not have shied from action if he thought the strength of his arm or the influence of his presence would make a difference. *'I will find them. One way or another, I will find them.'*

As ever, temptation lurked at the periphery of his consciousness. Shadow knew Pluto's realm better than any other element; if he reached out, he could likely learn if either of their shades were in transit. Using magic that deep on a battlefield would be madness, though. Death was too much a presence here. *'The River Styx will be crowded today.'* Sempronius wouldn't say he would *never* be able to distinguish one soul's passage from the rest, but he could not manage it and still perform his duties as commander. *'I'm not certain I could manage it and retain my sanity.'*

With the help of the tribunes and the other riders, Sempronius got Ekialde trussed up and slung over the back of his horse. A further indignity, but less so than being dragged behind the horse. That fate, Sempronius relegated to the sorcerer—a truer author of all their ills, he suspected, than the young man whose people had placed their faith in him.

By the time they emerged from the copse of trees, the battle was all but done. The *besteki* were fading to golden wisps. *'Spent, or sated?'* He had not seen enough to know if they were purely defenders or predators, feeding upon their foes.

With nowhere to retreat, the opposing forces had fallen or surrendered, and there was nothing left but the mopping up. Most of his legion had already fallen to spoil; the Lusetani warriors wore gold enough to make any soldier feel the effort worthwhile, and blood would wash off bracelets and rings easily enough.

Sempronius did not race across the field, eager though he was to regroup with his lieutenants. A solemn procession better suited the state of affairs. Slowly, he crossed the field back toward the hill where he had begun the day.

The legionaries took notice as he passed. Most stopped their looting to salute, either of their own volition or chivvied by their centurions. As Sempronius made steady progress, the soldiers saw the man draped over the back end of his horse. Perhaps they recognized his face, or his leopard-skin cloak, or noticed the band of gold around his brow. One way or another, they saw him for the king he had been. Sempronius sensed it in the murmurs, rippling across the battlefield as the last glow of the *besteki* ebbed away.

"*Imperator!*" a legionary cried, raising his sword in the air. "Sempronius Victor! Imperator!"

And others picked up the call, echoing across the field. "Imperator! Imperator! Imperator!"

It was the word used for a true victor. The word necessary for a man to claim his right to a triumphal parade. A title that only the legions could bestow. An acclamation, prized above all other honors in the Aventan Republic. An honor that had sometimes been purchased, yes, but that meant so much more when bestowed unbidden.

Had Sempronius expected it? No; not with such a battle as they engaged in. Had he hoped for it? Of course; every Aventan commander did, to say nothing of every ambitious politician.

Could he accept it?

It had not been a glorious battle, but the legions needed it to be. After so many months—years, for some of them—fighting fiends and shadows, they needed to feel they had vanquished the foe properly, not that the foe vanquished himself through his hubris, like a figure in Athaecan tragedy.

'Let them cheer, then. Let them write the story in their minds now and tell it to their sons in years to come.'

He gave little outward sign of their acclaim. He would not appear self-satisfied; would give no sign of pride. He only raised a hand, acknowledging with a stone face perhaps the greatest advantage the legion could have granted him.

XXXI

Autronius Felix was badly wounded. He went into a thick cluster of the blood-mad warriors, strayed too far from the rest of his unit. First, a pellet fired from a slingshot caught him in the helmet. Not a direct skull-cracking hit, but enough to unbalance him and send him tumbling off his horse.

He regained his seat eventually, but only after fighting for his life. An Iberian curved blade caught his left forearm above the greave, tearing it open to the bone.

Vitellius found him half-swooning in his saddle when the battle was over. Felix's arm hung limp at his side. An entire chunk of flesh was missing, and what remained was a bloody ruin.

"Gods," Vitellius gasped, grabbing the reins of Felix's horse and shouting for one of the Arevaci cavalry to help. Vitellius wrenched off his focale—his sister's gift, still imbued with her magic—and tied it tight above Felix's elbow, hoping to staunch the flow of blood and maybe, if they were lucky, impart a little healing magic into Felix's body.

They rushed him back to camp, but it was clear there was no putting the shredded pieces of his arm back together. "It must come off," the healer said, pitiless. "At the elbow. We can do it quick, cauterize the wound, leave you with most of your arm."

Felix's eyes met Vitellius's, searching for some answer, some reassurance. They both knew what a grim prospect he was facing. A man maimed in honorable military action was due honors, but he would also be pitied. And he would have no further career. All Felix's hopes of another campaign, all his bluster and joy in the fight, that would be over.

"I would not wait," was all Vitellius could think to say. "If infection spreads..."

Tightening his jaw, Felix nodded. "By all the gods, then, Vitellius, find me the best wine we have. No, not the best—the strongest. I couldn't give one of Bacchus's swollen balls what it tastes like, so long as it renders me insensible."

"You know what this is?" Felix said, when Vitellius returned with a full jug of unwatered wine. Local stuff, an Iberian red, unrefined but potent.

"I—What?"

"It's because I'm just too handsome," Felix said, putting out his right hand for the jug. "Not fair to the rest of you louts, really. Gods had to—to even the scales somehow." The pain was evident on Felix's face. He was drenched in sweat, and his eyes rolled, unfocused. He did, with help from Vitellius, manage to lift the jug and drink deeply.

"Here," the medic said, scooping a tiny portion of powdered seeds from a glass jar in his kit. "Datura," he explained, dumping the minuscule treatment into the wine. "You'll be delirious for a day or so, but trust me, it's better than feeling what I'm about to do to you."

"Haven't got a bigger spoon?" Felix joked.

The medic was not one for grim humor. "Any more would drive you mad permanently or possibly kill you. I'm trying *not* to do that." He turned his glare to Vitellius. "You're in the way. Go. I'm sure you have other business." He did, but leaving Felix seemed unbearably cruel. "He'll be unconscious in a moment," the medic sighed. "My assistants and I need room to work. It's a delicate business, amputating a limb from a living man. I can't just go at him with a cleaver."

"Go on." Already Felix's words were slurring. "'Spect this fellow's goin' wan' strap me down."

"Too right," the medic mumbled. His assistant had leather cords in hand.

Swaying, Felix fell back against the cot, head lolling. "Tell th' Gen'ral... Tell 'im... did m'best..."

"You did brilliantly, Felix," Vitellius assured him. "Saved the day." He pointed a finger at the medic. "So *you* save *him*."

The war-king of the Lusetani could be held in no common prisoner's quarters. In any case, the quaestorium was full-to-brimming with other captives, the men without blood marks who had seen sense above glory and thrown down their arms in the midst of the *besteki*-guided battle.

Ekialde was placed, instead, in a tent of his own, with guards stationed on all four corners, and fettered, hand and foot, one chain secured around a tentpole. Though the young man no longer looked capable of lifting a child's practice sword, let alone one of his own formidable weapons, Sempronius did not want to take chances. Whatever sorceries had invigorated the *erregerra* might yet resurrect themselves.

The fallen king's needs were tended to: food, wine, a bath, a fresh tunic. The blood had stopped pouring out of the markings that decorated half his body when he had been taken off the magically-seeded battlefield, but they still wept now and then. He had been offered the services of a healer, Arevaci or Aventan, but declined. The sole request he made: to see his wife and his son, if it were true that the Aventans held them captive.

Sempronius had every intention of granting his request, but he was in no haste to do so. If the man had information about the magic that so enhanced his power, Sempronius wanted that intelligence.

While the Lady Neitin spoke passable Tyrian, Ekialde did not, so Sempronius brought one of the Arevaci translators with him. Hanath and Bartasco were busy in the auxiliary camp, tending to their own people, but they assured him this man was familiar enough with the Lusetani dialect to serve his purpose. He brought, too, a canvas folding-stool; Aventans sat to communicate that they felt no threat in their surroundings.

The sight of Ekialde, sagging on a low cot, shoulders slumped, hands dangling between his splayed knees, did not fill Sempronius with joy or satisfaction. Ekialde's actions had made both the war and his defeat necessary, non-negotiable, but as Sempronius gazed on the young man, all he could do was mourn the *waste*. The waste of a promising young man's future, the waste of so many lives both on the battlefield and in the pillaged towns, the waste of a year's crops and yields.

'At least I brought peace in time for this year's planting. Central Iberia may begin to recover.'

Ambition mourned those losses, but Shadow, pressing at the edge of his awareness, reminded him that even rot and decay had their purpose, however destructive. Sempronius could admire the Lusetani for their drive to press the limits of what was known, what was assumed to be possible, what was thought to be lost. Ekialde's failures were born of an ambition of their own, and of a willingness to experiment.

Those things, properly harnessed, could be a benefit. *'Have been already. If Ekialde and his pet mage had never raised the akdraugi, would Lady Sakarbik ever have needed to discover a way to raise the besteki?'*

Ekialde looked up when Sempronius entered. There were small red spots upon his tunic, where his markings had wept since he had been given fresh clothing, but not many of them. "So," Ekialde said, through the translator, "you are the man who has conquered my country."

"So," Sempronius replied, "you are the man who tried to conquer all of Iberia."

"Not conquer," Ekialde insisted, "only to purge it of malicious foreign influences."

"Not conquer, either," Sempronius rejoined, "only protect our friends, allies, and traders from malicious assaults."

They regarded each other a long moment, two men assured of the rightness of their goals. Beneath Ekialde's weariness, lingering pain, and the cloak of Shadow hanging about him, Sempronius could see remnants of the man who inspired so many to follow him. His yellow-hazel eyes pierced like lightning; if he used them to good effect, that alone would make enough of an impression to sway many hearts. He was handsome, too, or had been before the effects of bloody sorcery took their toll on his body. A strong jaw, fine dark hair, broad shoulders.

Yes, he must have been the very image of a king when he was in full health, wearing the golden circlet and leopard-skin cape which Sempronius had in safe-keeping.

"I understand you wish to see your wife," Sempronius said after a moment. He took the moment of translation to pop open the folding stool and seat himself. Easier to appraise this young king from eye level than looking down upon him.

"If it is true you have her," Ekialde replied. "I have seen no evidence but the trickery left by that Cossetan sorceress."

Sempronius shrugged. "We have a woman who claims to be your wife, and the Lady Sakarbik affirms it," he said. "Whether she is or not, I cannot say, never having made your queen's acquaintance before my people found her in your home village, curled around the base of a dying tree." Ekialde's flinch was small, but Sempronius caught it, there in his left cheek and eye. "A pretty woman, I think. Short, round face, dark brown hair and eyes. She had a child with her, about a year old. Hair as black as yours. Didn't catch the boy's eye color."

Ekialde nodded slowly. "That... that would seem to match her, yes. What have you done with her?"

"Treated her kindly and as befits her station as a captive queen. She is in good health, and your son, though her spirit suffers."

Ekialde's jaw trembled. "Any spirit would, to be held in bondage."

"Mm. Yes. But I think this agony pre-dates our acquaintance." He lifted an eyebrow speakingly. "Or do I have it wrong? Did she part company with you under pleasant circumstances?"

The king turned his head away, as though the tent walls were more interesting than Sempronius. "Tell us what you plan for us. Or shall I guess? I have heard what you Aventans do to your captive foes. You march them through the city, that your people may jeer and hiss and mock the vanquished."

The pause while the translator relayed words back and forth might have frustrated a different man, but Sempronius enjoyed the opportunity it gave him for reflection and observation. Too, it gave him the chance to improve his own understanding; the Lusetani dialect was not so far removed from the Arevaci, but in the words he recognized, he could hear differences in the way they pronounced certain consonants, a little softer on the S, a little harder on the C and G.

"It is our custom," Sempronius replied mildly. "The gods have their demands, and so does the populace. It may be imperfect, but I find it a better way of treating the vanquished than draining their blood and using it for foul magic."

The war-king gave no visible response, but asked, "And then what? Execution?"

Sempronius lifted one shoulder, unconcerned. "It is the usual way. You might have avoided that fate, had you treated with us as the Vettoni did."

Ekialde snorted, proud even in his fetters. "What life would it be, to see my people broken to the will of foreign masters? We, who were so strong, who prevailed over the Bastetani and the Cossetans, who nearly threw you Aventans out of our lands once and for all?"

"You fought with bravery," Sempronius acknowledged, "though that would mean more had your successes not been wrought as much by your uncle's bloody hands as by your own merits." *Now* the young man winced, casting his gaze to the ground. "I confess curiosity," Sempronius continued. "We Aventans, as I think you've gathered, do not use our magic in warfare. So the uses you contrived for it are new to me, and I am one who is intrigued by new things."

When this was translated, Ekialde's yellow eyes slid back to Sempronius. "You were happy enough to use Arevaci magic, if not your own."

Sempronius spread his hands. "You may not know this about Aventans, but we are a legally quarrelsome people. We are experienced at finding..." He suspected the word "loophole" might not translate, so he went with, "alternative methods, to evade that which is forbidden." He sat forward, mirroring Ekialde's posture, with his elbows on his knees and his hands clasped before him. "And it is our strength and our pride to combine our own strength with the strength of our allies."

Ekialde's lip curled. "Your vassals. Your instruments. Or would you have me think you treat them as equals, the foreign nations you lash to your interests?"

At that, Sempronius hesitated before replying, weighing whether to respond on his nation's behalf or his own. Aven had not always treated its client kingdoms with favorable terms, nor did it treat them all equally. The wealthy states were both cosseted and plundered; the impecunious, dismissed and ravaged.

But this was not the future Sempronius Tarren wanted for his nation. This was not the vision of a thriving Aven the gods had granted him.

In the end, he settled for saying, "You would need to apply to Lord Bartasco and Lady Hanath for their opinions on the merits of friendship with Aven. I do not believe they have found us lacking." Before the translator finished, Sempronius went on, so Ekialde would have no opportunity to interject. "The Arevaci, too, reviled your methods. The Edetani, the Cossetans, even the Vettoni, in the end. Educate me, *erregerra*." Ekialde's eyelids flickered when he heard the Lusetani word on an Aventan tongue. "What were you doing that was so abhorrent, even to people closely related to yours? The man you killed, the mage—what did he do, to frighten them all off?"

Ekialde's gaze dropped to the floor again. "He said it was necessary. That it would work the gods' will, through me."

'Yes,' Sempronius thought. 'We all believe that, those of us who seek to shape nations. I certainly do. And each of us hopes that we are right and everyone else who believes it is wrong.'

Ekialde stretched out his arms, examining the crimson-brown markings etched up and down them. "I trusted him," he said, softly. "I let him... I didn't even know what this all meant. That concern was for the magicmen, with their secret language and their communion with the stars. My uncle knew about those things, not me. Not my place or purpose. I was supposed to be the warrior, Bandue's favored son. I thought. I..." He sighed. "I thought it for the best." The softness hardened, as though he remembered, then, his audience. "So if my story is sung, by my people or anyone else's, let that be its heart: I did what I believed necessary, to protect and exalt my nation."

A sentiment Sempronius Tarren could appreciate. 'You fell for that which I guard against, every day.'

The temptations of ambition, the urge to seize more power than he ought, the promises made by unearthly powers. Sempronius had heard that siren call more than once. So far, he had always been strong enough to turn aside.

'Yet someday, ambition may catch up to me, and I may end no better than this poor wretch.'

But Ekialde had also revealed his ignorance of the methods behind Lusetani magic, which meant Sempronius's task was complete. He rose, taking up his folding stool. "Tell the guards if you require anything—more food or water, fresh clothes, fresh bedding. We do not mean to keep you in squalor." He waited for no reply, but turned and left the tent.

'Just a boy, really,' Sempronius thought. 'An extraordinary one, perhaps, or he might have been. Bold and resolute. If not for his uncle-mage, what might he have become?'

Pointless to wonder now, however the shadows of impotent futures danced at the edges of Sempronius's awareness. Those were seeds which would never grow to fruit.

"Let his wife in to see him," he instructed the centurion at the front of the tent. "She can bring his child, if she likes. Have one of the Arevaci translators listen to their conversation."

And now, Sempronius had other concerns—other seeds to plant and nurture. He had given the Lusetani blood sorcerer's body to Sakarbik and the Arevaci magic-men; he needed to learn if they had discovered anything noteworthy. He needed to check on Felix in the infirmary, to ensure that the amputation had been successful and, if possible, assure the young man that his career was not over, though potentially redirected. He needed to meet with Bartasco and Hanath to discuss future treaties: the division of spoils from the Lusetani, the release of Vettoni hostages, a more permanent state of relations between Aven and the Arevaci.

And he needed to plan how to get his legions home.

'Olissippo, I think, rather than Gades.' A shorter distance, continuing down the Tagus with no need to cross other rivers or venture back into the mountains. Not, strictly speaking, Aventan territory, but Olissippo was a merchants' city, another colony from Old Tyre, like Massilia in Maritima. There would be boats enough there to carry the Tenth Legion home to Aven. *'And there, the next phase begins.'* He filled his lungs with a deep breath. *'Each step carries me closer to the fulfillment of my vision. One pace at a time.'*

To the esteemed and venerable fathers of the Senate —

I write with joyful tidings and news of victory. The cunning and discipline of the Aventan legions, together with the resourcefulness and bravery of our Iberian allies, have overcome the fearsome sorcery of our opponents. The leader of their corrupt magic-men is dead. I have their war-king in my custody, along with his queen and prince.

Most importantly, we have broken the bloody hold the Lusetani had on this land. With the Lusetani defeated and peace restored among the other tribes, Iberian trade can resume without fear.

Our merchants and those of other nations will find these hills and rivers once again safe for transit.

I will not, reverend fathers, bore you with details of this victory: not of the long winter spent defying the weather, nor of the bold actions of General Aufidius Strato as he pressed up from Gades; not of the clever ruse devised by a friend among our allies, which lured the Lusetani into a trap, nor of the precision executed by our honorable centurions. Such stories are prized by soldiers, to be spun and respun over the fires of their age, once the vigor of youth has faded. They will be told and retold in years to come, when these good men have retired in wealth and comfort and seek to impress their sons with tales of their youthful deeds. I need not waste the Curia's time on them.

No, what the Curia wants to hear, I am sure, is of diplomacy: I attach copies of treaties negotiated with the Arevaci, the Vettoni, the Cossetans, the Edetani, the Tartessi, and what rump remains of the Lusetani. I encourage the Senate to ratify these treaties without amendment. Aven has made promises; Aven must hold to them.

If you are unconvinced, reverend fathers, of the need to forge such bonds with our Iberian allies, then I look forward to debating the matter with you in the hallowed hall of the Curia. I shall see you soon.

I intend to return to Aven, bringing home the Tenth Legion, as soon as passage can be arranged from Olissippo. The Eighth Legion remains with Onidius Praectus near Toletum; the Fourth and Second are General Strato's business, but I believe he intends that the Second return with him to Gades while the Fourth posts near Detania, to ensure harmony among our coastal allies.

I look forward, as well, to discussing the future of Aventan cooperation with our Iberian allies. There is much we can offer each other. A system of roads in this land would be a boon to all, for example—but such details will take both time and investment. What a thing it is, honored friends of the Senate, to have the opportunity to build strong bonds with strong people! What a blessed state, the gift of the gods, when virtue and advantage dwell together in so mutually-fortunate a circumstance! I am certain you understand, as what honorable man would not?

I remain, faithfully executing Aven's interests in the eyes of gods and men, with piety and humble duty,

Praetor V. Sempronius Tarren

To my friend, Marcus Autronius —

I hope this letter finds its way to your hand before Galerius Orator reads his out in the Curia, though of a necessity I must send them in the same packet. I present you and your family a mixed blessing.

For the good news: We have won the war against the Lusetani. Your brother Felix acquitted himself with exceptional valor, leading a charge against the Lusetani blood-warriors, without which we would not have been able to execute the strategem that won not only the day but the entire conflict.

Mars himself must have guided Felix in that hour—but Felix did pay a price for his heroism. Not a mortal one, fear not that. He has lost his left arm below the elbow.

The wound was grievous indeed, or such a remedy would not have been necessary. His prospects of recovery are excellent. The flesh begins to knit, and the medics say it shows no further sign of infection or contamination. He smiles through the pain and has made any number of self-deprecating jokes about his condition, but rest assured, I have a keen eye out for damage done to his spirit.

This will alter the path of his life; perhaps not so much as he fears. I have tried to remind him of the General Petronius Aegidius, who lost a hand in the Tyrian Wars, had a metal one fashioned in its place, and thereafter went into battle with equal fervor, successfully capturing twelve enemy camps—but I think it may be too soon for history's example to be of any comfort to him.

I will bring him home, and he will reshape his future from there. Please render my sorrow to your excellent mother and father.

Yours in good faith,

Vibius Sempronius Tarren

Dearest Latona,

How weak a thing it is, to write a letter where so much must be pressed between the lines. We both have stories to share in more detail than ink can render, I know. Perhaps it is best not to force these scratchings to bear more weight than they must, for if the gods are good and the winds fair, I may be able to greet you in Aven before summer.

We draw near to Olissippo as I write this — a city I have long wished to look upon, here at the edge of the world, grand outpost of the Tyrians who first ventured beyond the Gates of Hercules — and while I hope to sample its splendor, my intent will be on returning myself and my legion home. The stories reaching me from Aven prompt a swift return.

There will be other years, other chances to visit. What I have set in motion in Iberia will, no doubt, require much careful diplomatic attention in the years to come, and I should not be sorry if Aven sees fit to send me back someday.

Forgive my imaginings. For too long, my attention has been fixed on the immediate next step necessary to win this war. Relieved of that burden, my mind is taking liberties. It creates all sorts of tantalizing possibilities for the future.

I am pleased to report that your brother is in good health and, while no man can know the shape of fate, likely to remain so until I can return him to Aven. He has served our nation with the highest honors, and I intend that such service be acknowledged and appropriately recognized. Without his stalwart defense of Toletum, indeed, without his early approach into Iberia, matters might now be a world different.

War may always have strange effects on a man's psyche; a war like this, all the more so. Our soldiers will return to Aven with scarce-believable tales: much to boast of, true, and no doubt many will find that their stories are ample currency in a variety of transactions. But those tales do not reveal all. Well — You have experience enough with terrors. I need not detail my speculations. Only know that your brother has been a hero, with all the good and ill that may entail.

I look forward to delivering him to the bosom of his family soon. I look forward, as well, to greeting your lovely sisters and to speaking with your estimable father. He and I have many significant matters to discuss. All this pales, however, to the chance to enjoy proper conversation with you again, my dear friend, for the sound of your voice carries far more splendor in it than dry paper can convey.

I remain yours, with a full heart,

S.

XXXII

Carinae Hill, City of Aven

Aula far preferred attending parties where only Popularist families were in attendance, but with the political waters churning, she could not afford to be snobbish when it came to events of mixed allegiance. She had to know whose power ebbed and whose flowed, where the swirling threat of Charybdis might lurk, and where she might find unexpected halcyon lulls.

So, when she attended dinner parties like that thrown by the Crispiniae in late Martius, Aula did her best to keep her ears open and her tongue a little more guarded than was its natural wont.

By the time the fruits were served and the guests were milling about to admire paintings and dancers, liberated from the confinement of their couches, Aula was buoyed by a few successes.

She'd gossiped with garishly-dressed Papiria Dola and discovered that her youngest sister was engaged to marry one of that year's aediles.

She'd chatted with Collo Nedius, the honored historian, and convinced him not to dedicate his next book to the current consuls.

She'd had a quiet word with one of the attendants trailing behind Licinius Cornicen and discovered that, should a few sestertii find their way into his path, he might be willing to furnish a list of the most prominent frequent visitors to his master's house.

She'd flirted with Young Caecilius and quite discombobulated him, and though he was a fool scarcely capable of stringing a sentence together, he let slip that his father was planning to introduce a new tariff on Iberian grain, hoping both to weaken support for the war there and to shift trade relations back in favor of the Menaphon in Abydosia. Aula knew several

Popularist Senators who would make use of that tip and perhaps head Old Caecilius off before he got started.

'*All in all,*' Aula considered as she made her way down a colonnade with bright frescoes on its walls, '*a fine evening's work. And the Crispiniae always do set a nice table.*'

While Aula enjoyed using guile and charm to coax information out of unsuspecting conversational partners, she was also not above eavesdropping—and for all her bright copper hair and usual vivacity, she had a talent for it. The hairs on the back of her neck went up, before she turned a corner into a sitting room, as she heard her sister's name spoken by someone inside.

"—always said Vitellia Latona was a grasping little schemer, and this shows he was always right."

The voice belonged to Glaucanis, wife to Lucretius Rabirus. Aula's nostrils flared in irritation, but as she was debating how to take the vicious weasel down a peg, new voices threw her off-guard, for unlike Glaucanis, they did not belong to women whom Aula thought of as enemies.

"It's madness, is what it is." That was Crispinilla, younger daughter of the evening's host. "What makes her think she can set herself up as—as what? A teacher?" Crispinilla giggled, high and smug. "An unofficial priestess? Madness."

"She's not mad." This, Aula recognized as the elder daughter of the house, Appia Crispinia. "But she is, what, twenty-three? And no children? I suppose she does need *something* to occupy her time."

The implication infuriated Aula as much as its unexpected source. '*Just because you've been more or less constantly pregnant for the past six years, Appia, doesn't mean that is the only function of a woman's life.*' Aula knew it distressed Latona to have no children, though Aula believed the blame lay squarely with her worthless ex-husband, but even so—Aula had one, and while she loved Lucia more than life, the little girl wasn't *all* there was to her life. '*Politics, fashion, friends—Diana's tits, I don't begin and end at my womb!*'

"Well, I think it's left her unbalanced, and Aemilia Fullia agrees with me," Glaucanis said, prim and self-satisfied. "As though she's trying to emulate Jupiter, not Juno, of all the absurdities."

"*Dux femina,*" a fourth voice tittered—Memmia Gratianae, Aula thought, wife of the consul. A cutting remark: a term used for some mythological heroines, perhaps, but in real life, it meant a too-masculine woman, one who did not know her place and attempted a military authority. "Woman general," it meant, as risible and ridiculous a creature as a sow with ambitions to fly like an eagle, a figure of utmost contempt.

"No wonder her husband put her off," Crispinilla sniffed. "Who would want to be wed to that?"

"No sane man, that's certain," Glaucanis said, sounding gleeful.

"I don't understand the purpose," Appia said, with a tone of true befuddlement. "What does she mean to achieve?"

"Nothing," Memmia answered. "Nothing at all. It's another way of making a spectacle of herself. She's gluttonous for attention."

But Glaucanis countered, "I don't know about that. *Dux femina,* like you said, that's more than pretentious preening. That's arrogance beyond reckoning. She has political ambitions."

All four women laughed at the ludicrous idea, and Aula could not remain silent. With a burst of energy, she swept into the sitting room, yearning to give each of them the tongue-lashing they so richly deserved.

Yet the words did not come. Of all the things she could think to say, none were powerful enough, none would *hurt* these women enough.

So she drew a mantle of dignity down upon herself and simply glared at each in turn. Memmia's jaw dropped and her eyes went wide. Glaucanis and Crispinilla were surprised, but unrepentant. Only Appia Crispinia was sufficiently abashed to lower her gaze.

Lifting her pointy chin, Glaucanis challenged Aula. "Well? If you've come to defend your *dux femina* of a sister, go on."

"I will not bother bandying wits with you, Glaucanis," Aula said, her voice iron-cold, bereft of its habitual merry bounce. "What a waste of breath that would be for both of us. You know yourself for an envious liar, and it will rot your soul." She turned sharply to the Crispiniae sisters. "You two, though, should be ashamed. Our families have long stood friends to each other, and it grieves me that you would speak such poison. Latona has never wished you anything but good fortune."

"She—" Crispinilla began, but Aula wasn't minded to hear her parry.

"May many-tongued Rumor repay you in kind for this." Aula whipped back around and, plastering an amiable smile on her face for the sake of whomever else she might encounter, went to summon her litter and guards. She would not remain in this house a moment longer than necessary.

Domus Magicae, Esquiline Hill

Terentilla was a daily revelation.

Over the past months, she and Alhena had shared explorations, unhurried but joyous. They took what time they could, away from their families and other responsibilities, meeting in gardens or in the Domus Magicae when no one else was about.

Terentilla was absurdly beautiful in the afternoon sunlight that streamed through a high window in one of the cubicles. Even when other people were about, Alhena adored gazing at Tilla when the sun put a glow on her brown skin and got lost in her dark, riotous curls. And when they were alone in the house, there was a comfortable couch to take advantage of.

Alhena knew she had no great experience with kissing, but she thought Tilla must be the sweetest kisser in the world. She always tasted of excitement and fresh air. *'This is what kissing a nymph must be like,'* Alhena thought as they lay side-by-side, arms tangled about each other. *'No wonder gods are so fond of it.'*

Tilla rolled Alhena onto her back and started plucking at the shoulder-pins holding her gown together. She was not slow or gentle, but Alhena didn't mind, eager for what would come next.

That had been one of the early glorious revelations. Alhena had never given her breasts much thought. They were just *there*, something to tie a sash under. But the first time Tilla's fingers cupped one of them, the first time she drew Alhena's gown and tunic down, the first time her blessed lips closed around Alhena's nipple—then Alhena gained new appreciation for her own assets.

She reached for Tilla's gown, too, slipping loose the knots that held it up, tugging her tunic until it fell down. Tilla's breasts were shallower than hers and higher-set. Alhena adored them. Diana surely looked thus, strid-

ing bare-breasted through the forest on her hunts. Alhena's hands enfold-
ed around Tilla's ribs and slid up, until her thumbs brushed over the small
buds. Tilla shivered and growled at the same time, then dove down on Alhena with such eager ferocity that Alhena laughed. The giggle turned into
a gasp when Tilla nipped at her neck, then drifted over her curves.

Tilla had less patience than Alhena, which, she reflected, was probably
a good thing, or else they'd never get anywhere. Tilla kissed and licked
everything within access, and then she went hunting for more. Her left
hand reached as far down as she could manage without taking her lips from
Alhena's chest and tugged Alhena's skirts up to get beneath them.

Alhena's whole body pulsed with glorious tension, each breath catching
inside her ribs. Tilla's fingers slid up her leg, no light touch, but strong
and purposeful. They found the heat between Alhena's legs, stroked at the
crease of her thigh, then pressed ever-so-intently onward.

A month ago, Alhena had no idea such bliss could exist; now, there
were times when she could think of nothing else but its magnificent pursuit. She! The shy girl, the one in the corner, the bashful little thing who
would rather be home with a book, struck by Cupid's bolt. She breathed in
the scent of Tilla's hair, pressed kisses to her crown, arched up into Tilla's
persuasive touch.

When Alhena was not quite upon the precipice of euphoria but had it
in sight, Tilla paused. "Oh, don't tease me, Tilla, please," Alhena begged,
turning her head to find Tilla's mouth.

"You know I wouldn't," Tilla said, half-mumbled through another kiss.
"It's only, I thought I—" Suddenly, Tilla sat up straight, head cocked. She
swore and yanked her gown back up, pulling the shoulder-ties back together. "Someone's at the door!"

Alhena's eyes went wide. "I thought we bolted it!" she hissed.

"I suppose we didn't," Tilla grumbled, re-wrapping her belt. "So there's
a lesson for us. See? We have furthered our education here today, precisely
as our families believe we're doing."

"Not *precisely* like, I don't think," Alhena said, repinning her own gown.
"Who is it?"

Tilla pulled the last pins from her hair and shook it loose, brown curls
spilling everywhere. She could get away with that; everyone knew her hair

was improperly coiffed most of the time anyway. "I'll go see while you repair yourself," she said. "Your pin is, um... somewhere."

"I'll find it. Go! Or whoever it is will get suspicious."

Alhena pulled her hair loose, too, combing it with her fingers. *Fortunately, I'm no notable follower of fashion, either.* A simple low knot should arouse no suspicions, as long as it was reasonably neat. After Alhena tidied herself, she untidied the room, moving papers and wax tablets to give the illusion that work had been in-progress.

"Look, Alhena!" Tilla said, too bright, as she came back. "Rubellia's here!"

And so she was. Ama Rubellia, preternaturally beautiful as ever and so composed in her garnet-colored gown with its perfect falls, glided into the room. "Your sister's on her way, too," she announced. "With your niece, I think. Apparently little Lucia is evincing more empathic abilities, so Latona wants my advice on helping the girl to shield herself until she's better able to control the flow." She clasped her hands in front of her. "We want to record it, properly—all the things our mentors taught us but that no one ever bothered to transcribe. Would you have time to help? I know you've been working on turning the more advanced work into treatises, but I think a basic curriculum could have quite a lot of value."

Now Alhena blushed for multiple reasons. She wondered if they came in different shades or blended until her face resembled a pomegranate. "I'd be pleased to be whatever help I can be, of course."

"And I, ah, I should go!" Tilla said. "My mother's probably wondering what's become of me by now. I think we've got some dinner or other to attend tonight. So I'll—I'll go." Her eyes shot all sorts of meaning in Alhena's direction, but with Rubellia's gaze on her, Alhena could do little to reciprocate.

After Tilla left, Alhena sat down at the little chair behind her desk. "Um. So. Rubellia. I'm happy to transcribe while you and Latona work with Lucia. And we can, um, polish it up later?"

"I think that would be lovely," Rubellia said, folding herself onto another chair—and, blessedly, not onto the recently-vacated couch, where Alhena draped a distracting, no-one-has-been-here-in-a-while blanket. "No doubt you could lyricize it far better than we can. You're such a devoted student of poetry."

Mirth brightened Rubellia's voice. It often did, so Alhena wasn't sure why it struck her as odd. "I, um, yes? I do love... love to translate." At the moment, the only lines popping into her head were once more from Hyacinthe. *'Come, immortal Aphrodite, in your chariot of gold, and release me from grueling anxiety.'* She cleared her throat, moving a few papers from one pile to another, with no idea what was written on them. "I don't know how much I could manage on my own, though. I mean, from my own... my own pen, as it were."

"You know, Alhena," Rubellia said, her tone airy and unconcerned, "if you had wanted a little more time, I'd have been happy to have kept your sister chatting outside for a while."

Alhena blinked several times. "A little—Time for—Um. What?"

Rubellia's gentle smile would have shamed the most inveterate liar in the world. "You and Tilla, my dear. I'm terribly embarrassed to have brought you up short. It's practically sacrilege, by my reckoning."

Alhena's blood didn't know whether to plummet to her feet or boil out her ears. Her mouth opened and closed wordlessly, and she knew she must look like an eel that had flopped its way out of the water.

"I've known for a while, I'm afraid," Rubellia continued, as though Alhena were not in danger of having an apoplexy right in front of her. She inclined her head with a pointed expression. "It's hard to keep things like that from a Priestess of Venus, let alone one who is also a Fire mage. The air between the two of you is scorching most of the time, and right now, you are ablaze with frustrated desire." Her lips quirked up at one corner. "I've half a mind to dunk you in the impluvium to cool your ardor. It's really quite distracting."

Mortified, Alhena turned her back on Rubellia, both hands covering her face. "I cannot—I simply cannot—"

Rubellia laughed, but it was a warm sound, not mocking. She rose and stepped closer, putting a hand on Alhena's shoulder. "Of all the people you should not be embarrassed in front of, my dear, I believe I should take first rank. If any amorous act yet remains on this earth that can shock me, I confess I rather look forward to discovering it."

Alhena peeked over her shoulder. She'd lived with Latona long enough to suspect when someone was using empathic projection on her, but the effect took hold nonetheless. Her heart rate slowed; the knot in her stomach uncoiled. It *was* impossible to hold onto shame in Ama Rubellia's presence. She radiated acceptance and understanding. *'The warmth of Venus.'* Not a touch Alhena had ever particularly thought to need.

"You won't—" Alhena gulped. "You won't tell my sisters, will you?"

Rubellia cocked her head to one side. "I certainly won't if you don't want me to. I'm good at keeping secrets, Alhena. It comes with the territory. I believe you could trust them, though."

"It's not that I don't trust them," Alhena rushed to clarify. "It's just that I—I—I'm not ready for them to know. For the conversations." For it *would* mean conversations. Her sisters were talkers.

Rubellia rubbed Alhena's back in soothing circles. "They'll figure it out eventually," she said. "They've had their heads so deep in this Discordian business, and now assembling the collegium, that it's kept them distracted, but Latona has gifts similar to my own, and Aula—well, Aula has a nose for scandal nigh-unrivaled in the city."

"I know." And she did. It was a miracle she and Tilla hadn't been caught already. "I... I guess I should start preparing for that, maybe. What to say. How to explain. I know it's... it's abnormal."

Rubellia's head bobbed in consideration. "Not much talked-of, perhaps. Not as much enacted as other types of desire. But more frequently felt and yearned for, I expect, than many women can freely acknowledge."

"I never would have, if not for Tilla," Alhena admitted, as Rubellia stroked her hair. "I didn't even *know*. Not—not at the top of my mind."

"That's often the way. We know what we're expected to want, and the tower of that expectation can cast all else into shadow. But Venus blesses more than one type of intimacy."

"Maybe I *should* let you tell my sisters," Alhena muttered, rubbing at her face. "You'd explain it much better than I will."

Another light laugh, like the ringing of bells. "In the general, perhaps. I could never speak the particulars for you."

"The particulars?"

"Why Tilla?"

Alhena thought on that a moment, and Rubellia let her. The attraction had approached Alhena sidelong, so stealthy that she hardly knew how to describe it. She had felt warmth for Tilla, swelling long before they first kissed, but what built it into something more?

"I feel... safe when I'm with her." She frowned. "Which is odd, because it also feels like being caught in the middle of a thunderstorm, with wind and lightning crackling all around me. But I... I enjoy it."

Rubellia bent over and kissed the top of Alhena's bright red curls. "Hold onto that feeling, my dear," she advised. "It can carry you through many challenges."

When Aula told Latona what she had overheard at the Crispiniae's party, terror and defiance each tried to seize Latona's heart. "I... would've thought better of Appia and Crispinilla," she said slowly, sinking onto her bed. "Appia in particular. We've never had a cross word between us. And Crispinilla can be a jealous little piece, but still..."

She bit into her lower lip, wondering at the reason for such surprising enmity. Crispinilla had flirted with Sempronius Tarren, true, back before he'd left for Iberia, but Crispinilla was eager to remarry, and he had not been her only target. Even if word had gotten out about his correspondence with Latona and people were whispering about the implications of their friendship, she didn't think Crispinilla would have taken it personally.

'What other reason could there be? Does Old Crispinia share their assessment?' She hoped not; the elderly woman was someone whose esteem was valuable, both in social capital and personal pride.

"I'm telling you, Latona, something was odd about it," Aula insisted. "I've been thinking about it since last night, and I..." Her lips scrunched up in perturbation. "I don't know. It wasn't just that it was Appia and Crispinia. This wasn't typical gossip. I mean, *dux femina*?" Latona winced at the insult. "That's more than snide gossip. More than factional rivalry, even. They were being peculiarly vicious, and it worries me. If that grows, it could become dangerous for you."

Latona rolled her shoulders back, trying to slough off the hurt feeling. "Glaucanis and her set have always hated me. They've always gossiped. It's never damaged me irreparably."

Aula's voice dropped low. "Hasn't it?"

Latona's jaw trembled. Such gossip had been half the reason she had spent so much of her life trying to avoid notice, not wanting to be thought a flirt, or a slut, or ambitious. *Juno's mercy, it's the reason you stayed married to Herennius for so long, for the thin shield he provided against it.'* And it was part of why, for so long, she never allowed herself to realize how much power lived inside her, how far she could take her magic.

"It's not fair," Latona whispered. "I finally start... start *living*, in the way I'm sure Juno wants... and so swiftly, they want to slap me down. It isn't fair."

"Of course it isn't." Aula sat down beside Latona, taking her hands. "Have you never noticed the difference, my honey, between the kinds of hate that women of our world are prone to? Often as not, it's boredom. We feud and gossip because those are the forms of power permitted to us, and they pass the time. But when real malice gets beneath it—that's when you've done something to make them *angry*."

"But what?" Latona sighed.

"Your collegium, of course. That was the focal point of their mockery. You transgress, my dear, and so they must punish you, because if they do not, if no one does, if you succeed in pursuing your grand desires, and build something enviable, something that gives you security and honor and a sense of purpose—something that, were you a man, would give you *auctoritas*—then what does it mean for them, who have failed to do the same?" Aula smiled sadly. "A bird may be content in a cage, so long as no one forces it to notice the bars."

Heaviness settled in Latona's chest, or tried to. The half of her that had been terrified, hearing Aula's report of the conversation, now ached in resignation.

The other half, though, screamed its resistance. She had too much to do, to give up now. Maybe it was hubris, maybe ambition, but there were Discordians to expose and a Commission to cleanse and she did not think it could happen without her. She didn't *want* it to happen without her.

Old terrors had sharp claws, however, and their tug prompted her to ask, "Should I—?" She didn't even want to say it. "Should I stop? Go back to trying to work in... in the small ways, without attracting notice?"

"No," Aula said. "No, I would never want you to go back to making yourself small. I could not bear to watch you cage yourself again."

Latona flung her arms around her sister's neck. "Thank you. You're the best, most supportive—"

With a mirthless laugh, Aula gave her a squeeze. "Yes, I know. But it's true. It would break my heart. We may have to... to rethink our strategies, is all."

Releasing her, Latona sat up. "Our strategies for the collegium? Or for... You're thinking of Father's career, and Gaius's."

"I'm thinking of it all," Aula said. A hint of an impish grin flickered across her face. "I can't do magic, after all, so my brain's all I've got to contribute."

"That's worth a great deal."

"I should think so!"

Latona rubbed at her forehead. "Father should know what people are saying," she said. "He should hear it from me, rather than letting rumor reach him."

"No," Aula said. "He'll hear it from me. I'm the one who told Glaucanis to go rot, for one thing!" Laughing, she reached out to tug affectionately at one of Latona's curls. "And you've had to defend yourself to him enough times. It's my turn to do so on your behalf—and I'll work on him until he's ready to officially propose your mages' collegium as part of the Popularist legislative platform!" Aula squared her shoulders. "It won't be easy. But we can turn this to advantage."

"If anyone can, it's certainly you."

APRILIS
XXXIII

Olissippo, Iberia

Like a bright bead on the end of a chain, the city of Olissippo gleamed at the mouth of the Tagus River. It came into sight gradually, with no ridges to cross nor dramatic promontories to round. Olissippo began as a smudge of white at the horizon and steadily insinuated its presence into the awareness of travelers heading toward it.

Though friendly to Aven, Olissippo was a free city, of no particular allegiance, long unmoored from the nations of its founders and their descendants. Its land-facing side had high walls, to protect from raiders; the seafacing side, plenty of watchtowers to warn of the approach of pirates.

Considering it impolitic to bring his army beneath the city walls, at least before he negotiated transportation for them, Sempronius had the legions make camp a few non-threatening miles north. He sent a messenger to the city's ruler, called the Navarch, and soon received an answer, inviting him to meet and proposing to do so, most unusually, on the ocean's shore.

While the legions dug trenches and built palisades as they had all the way across Iberia, Sempronius and his officers rode the short distance to the edge of the world. There they stood on soft golden sand, staring at water without end.

"Bona Dea," Felix breathed, and Sempronius was glad to hear it. He had insisted Felix attend him, even though he was not yet fully comfortable ahorse without his left hand. The ride was easy, however, and Sempronius wanted to give Felix something to inspire him, something to stir his spirits.

He had not counted on how deeply the view would affect *him*, too. Awe vibrated within his chest, filling him up, as he contemplated the truth of the Endless Ocean.

The Navarch of Olissippo had erected a pavilion on the sand, much like patricians would at the seaside resort of Baiae on Crater Bay. The season was early for it, with a chill wind off the water whipping the sides of the tent, but Sempronius suspected the Navarch was showing off. The tent's fabric looked to be costly linen, dyed a deep indigo. As he drew nearer, he saw embellishments in Tyrian purple, a reminder of the city's origins and its lasting wealth.

The Navarch's attendants scurried about, taking charge of the horses as Sempronius and the others dismounted. The first figure to emerge from the tent was, surprisingly, familiar to Sempronius, with curly hair of a deep brown, a neatly-trimmed beard, and a long striped tunic of blue and green, secured with knotted cords about his chest.

"Shafer!" Sempronius proclaimed, throwing his arms wide in greeting. "I thought you were in Gades." He spoke in Athaecan, the only language the two men had enough in common for easy conversation.

Sempronius first met Shafer ben Nassim, an Asherite, in Tamiat, during his exile. Like Hanath, Shafer belonged to a trading family. They operated in many of the old Tyrian ports, ferrying goods between them and ancient Abydosia. For a man who desired to know as much of the world as Sempronius did, a friend like Shafer was invaluable; his work took him all over, and he was a dedicated correspondent. For years, the two men had written messages to each other twice over, so that Shafer could practice his Truscan and Sempronius his Petraean.

"Ah, I move back and forth between these fine cities," Shafer said. "I was meant to return to Gades a few days ago, but I heard you were on your way here, so I determined to stay to greet you. Our honored host is a friend and was good enough to invite me along today. Come in! Let us make all the necessary introductions."

To Sempronius and Bartasco fell the duty of a long discussion with the Navarch. Sempronius was gratified that the Navarch gave Bartasco the courtesies due to a ruler of equal authority, for all that Bartasco's home village of Segontia would fit inside Olissippo twenty times over, with room to spare.

The Navarch's advisors showed a variety of heritages in both their bodies and their clothing, testament to the mix of Tyrian, Athaecan, and Iberian influences that mingled in the ancient city. While Felix, Hanath, Vitellius, and the rest strolled on the beach, chatting with the lower-ranked Olissippan dignitaries, Sempronius and Bartasco went within the tent to sort out business matters: how many officers would be welcomed to stay within the city, with whom the legions could arrange transport back to Aven at fair rates, what tariff Olissippo would impose for any slave-trading conducted at its ports, what personal gift the Navarch would accept in thanks for his indulgences.

"We are grateful to you for ridding the land of that war-fevered boy," the Navarch finished. "We have some Lusetani here, you know, but it's more Oestrimni. City folk for long generations now, not people of river villages and mountain huts." He shook his head. "We were fortunate the Lusetani did not turn our way this time, as they have done when raiding in the past, but still, the whole business was bad for trade."

"War generally is, in the short term," Sempronius said, "but I mean to make prosperity out of it in the long view."

"Good. Good!" The Navarch waved a hand. "I weary of business-talk. Please, you and your officers must dine with me tomorrow evening, when we have time to prepare a proper feast."

"We would be most honored, Your Eminence."

The Navarch rode back to his city with his advisors, leaving the functionaries behind to pack up the tent. Sempronius found Shafer strolling near the water's edge with Hanath, who seemed to be enjoying herself tremendously. "Blessed gods of the sea and sky," she was laughing when Sempronius approached. "And what happened when the camelopards got loose?"

"As you might imagine, mayhem reined. The dancing girls went running in every direction, tables knocked over, grapes and figs flying everywhere—and one lone flautist kept playing the same tune, resolute as though divinely instructed to finish out the verse."

Hanath wiped tears of mirth from her eyes. "Sempronius! You are missing a good story."

"Camelopards in the court of Chrysos?" Sempronius verified, clapping Shafer on the back. "That's always one of the first tales he tells a new acquaintance. It's how he establishes himself as such an affable fellow."

Despite his joy in seeing his friend, Sempronius's gaze drifted out once more over the waters of the Endless Ocean. Shafer smiled with satisfaction, hands on his hips. "Quite a sight, is it not?"

"A mighty thing," Sempronius agreed.

"It never leaves me, this feeling of wonder," Hanath said. "However much may change on land, whatever we frail humans do to shape our destinies, *this* is eternal. The waves crash upon this shore as they have always done and always will do."

"Beautifully put!" Shafer cried in delight. "Are you a poet, lady?"

Hanath snorted. "Certainly not. But if you are, I give you leave to steal my words for your own use."

The sheer expanse of the ocean, its staggering *possibilities*, tugged at something deep inside Sempronius. The Athaecans had once used the curvature of the earth to calculate how wide it must be, to go all the way around and come out again on the other side. No ship could ever make such a journey, of course. Even if suppositions about sea monsters, churning storms, and devouring whirlpools were untrue, no vessel could hold supplies for so long a voyage.

But how far might a ship travel, before it had to turn back? If not straight out to the west, how far north or south? What might be out there, besides roiling water? With as vast as the world had to be, Sempronius had to wonder: other nations, other peoples, other magics?

"Shafer, tell me," Sempronius said, "for I am unable to contain my curiosity—"

"A surprise to no one, I think," Shafer interjected, with a wink at Hanath.

"—Your northern trade routes, what are they like? Are your connections with the coastal Tennic tribes?"

"Some, but so many of the Armoricans and Vendelicians don't stay still long enough to establish relationships. They may be there one season, gone the next. If you keep going, though?" He bent, sketching in the sand with one finger, approximating the shape of the coastline north of Iberia. Then, a second shape, north and west of the mainland. "The peoples of those islands, they do not move about. They settle. They farm. They *mine*." His smile was close-lipped but wide with pleasure. "Good tin comes from those lands, and they trade with us regular."

"Tin, you say?"

"Tin and copper."

Hanath offered, in a teasingly conspiratorial tone, "I hear they have ice in their veins, the gray-skinned and white-haired people of the north, and that they have made a compact with the gods to protect their isles from invasion with ship-breaking storms and monstrous beasts."

Shafer laughed, standing back up. "If so, they keep that to themselves."

"Are the routes reliable?"

"Depends on the time of year, much like the Middle Sea. There *are* bad storms as you approach the islands. They are less seafaring than we, reluctant to sail away from their isle, but in the calmer months, it is possible to reach their southern shore. They expect us by now and are always eager to trade."

Possibilities clacked through Sempronius's mind. Those islands were little more than rumor to most Aventans. The Armoricans and Vendelicians guarded their overland trade routes fiercely, never allowing traders from the Middle Sea to meet their northern neighbors. But an approach from this western promontory... *'What would it be,'* Sempronius thought, *'to be the first Aventan man upon those shores?'*

"Wine and citrons and incense for them," Shafer continued, "and metal and hunting dogs for us. It suits everyone. In the winter months, we look south."

"To Mauretania?"

"Indeed, indeed. And, sometimes, when traders are bold enough, to the peoples across the desert."

Sempronius startled. The popular belief in Aven was that the Endless Desert was, well Endless—or at least in the same sense as the Endless Ocean, large enough to be impassable. There were civilizations south of Abydosia, in the east, but beyond the desert in the west? Aven knew less of that than of the Serean Empire. "Tell me."

"To be honest with you, friend, it is so risky that we do not dare the venture often. Oh, they have marvelous commodities, to be sure! Ivory, nuts, leather. Fine crafters as well, working in wood and bone and beads.

But the journey is too long and arduous. Too many men die." He crouched again, adding the coast of Mauretania and the land beyond it to his sand-map. "The Bulging Cape, here, is a place to put in, but the sea is challenging. Many ships founder. We can't support a permanent trading post, and over-land, you would still be moving through desert." He spread his hands. "Alas for the loss, but until the gods change the winds south of Mauretania or gift us with unbreakable vessels, trade routes are unfeasible." He grinned at Sempronius, too-knowing. "Come, friend. Is your world not big enough already?"

Sempronius smiled back. "Never, friend. While there is knowledge for the gaining, never."

Shafer returned to the city, with promises to see them all at dinner the next night. Upon their return to camp, Sempronius and Hanath were still discussing the beauty of the Endless Ocean, up to the door of Sempronius's tent, where Corvinus met them. "If you have a moment, I have a request for your presence."

"From whom?" Sempronius asked.

"The Lady Neitin."

Sempronius and Hanath exchanged expressions of intrigue. "Far be it from me to refuse royalty," Sempronius said. "By all means, send her in."

Hanath rolled her shoulders. "I shall leave you to the forlorn princess." She rolled her eyes; she too, of course, was the wife of a prominent Iberian chieftain, but neither she nor Bartasco had ever given themselves majestic airs.

"No, stay. If you care to, I mean, I won't keep you from other business, but whatever it is she wants, your perspective would be beneficial."

Hanath's head wagged in consideration. "As you like it, General."

A moment later, the guardsman returned, this time leading the fallen queen of the Lusetani. She was a curiosity. For all the honors bestowed upon her, she did not seem accustomed to royalty, certainly not in the assumptive nature of the Abydosian or Parthian royal families, born to the purple and bred in its arrogance. Proud, but not haughty. Resilient, not unyielding.

She remained hard to look at for long. Though her body had recovered from her mysterious ordeals, her spirit had not. The clouds of tragedy veiled her still, and Sempronius had to drive his magical sensibilities into recession in order to meet her eyes. If Gaius Vitellius had been draped in Shadow following the siege of Toletum, then Neitin of the Lusetani was drowning in it.

"Lady Neitin," he said, cool and even. "I understand you wished to see me."

They spoke, again, in Tyrian. "I did. I have a request." She offered him no honorifics, even as a supplicant. Sempronius could respect that. He held no authority over her, after all, except that which he had seized. "Before arrangements are made for leaving Iberia, I wish to beg mercy for my husband."

Sempronius leveled his gaze at her. She was not, by his guess, a silly or simple woman. "He is an enemy of my nation. An enemy of much of Iberia, too. All by his own making. An enemy to anyone who wants the line between our world and the netherworld firmly drawn."

"I know. I know. But... His soul is in agony," Neitin pleaded. "You have much cause to hate him. But I think—" She swallowed. "I think you are a man of honor. Sakarbik tells me the *besteki* favored you, took your part in the battle. Her magic could only do so much. The *besteki* will not grow where foulness reigns. She says. And as I trust her, I think you must be a decent man, for all that you have been our enemy. I understand it is the custom of your people to parade your conquered foes. But I ask you to look at my husband and—and see—" Tears were slipping down her cheeks now, but she held her chin strong, as dignified as any other queen Sempronius had met or could imagine. "See that he will not live to be such a prize. The fiends he bargained with are devouring him from within. I plead for mercy."

Her assessment was not unfounded. Ekialde had not weathered the journey to Olissippo well, growing ever thinner, his dark hair rapidly graying, his skin sallow and shriveled.

Sempronius rubbed his chin with his thumb. "You wish for him to have a quick death, here in Iberia, rather than in Aven?" He glanced to Hanath, who shrugged. Dead was dead, her expression indicated.

"I wish him reclaimed," Neitin said, "from the demons that gnaw on his soul. My companion, Sakarbik—She believes she can do it by—by invoking the *besteki*. The good spirits, who are—" She frowned. "I am not certain of the word. Like 'opposite,' but... harmfully so."

Sempronius did not know the Tyrian word for it, either, but he knew what she meant. "Inimical," he provided, in Truscan, then switched back to Tyrian to explain. "Like Water and Fire, Earth and Air, Light and Shadow."

She might not have realized he meant the magical elements, but she nodded. "Yes. The *besteki* will drive the bad spirits out from his body. They began to, during the battle, she says. But they were not full enough." She frowned. "Not... not enough of them together." She was struggling for the word again; Sempronius thought she meant something like *concentrated*, but he gestured for her to go on. "Sakarbik says he... He will not survive this." Her eyes lowered, only a brief moment, before she straightened in dignity again. "It will likely be painful, if that would give your troops some sport to witness. But I would see it done. I would prefer he die as himself, the honest man I once loved, than as this curse-hounded monster he became."

Sempronius looked past her to Hanath. In Truscan, she said, "Lady Sakarbik has thus far played us fair. I do not know what reason she would have to do anything to this war-king's benefit—except, perhaps, the mercy of death, for the sake of his wife, whom she seems fond of."

He gestured to Neitin. "What do you make of her?"

Hanath paced around the Lusetani queen-that-was, looking her up and down. "Have you ever seen a mongoose?" He shook his head. "They are small animals. Like a weasel, but with a sweeter face. Soft-furred, and they can be tamed. Some in Cirte keep them as pets." She stepped in close to Neitin, an obvious ploy to unsettle the woman. Only the smallest flinch betrayed her; she kept her eyes on Sempronius. "But show them a snake, and they are the fiercest fighters in the world. This woman, I think, is a mongoose."

"And are they honest creatures? Or do they play false, like foxes?"

"I do not know them for tricksters," Hanath said. "And this one—I think she has honest intent. I think she has suffered and seeks a way out of that suffering, as any of us might. But if you allow this, I would have swords at the ready, in case she shows her teeth."

Sempronius contemplated. Aventan custom *did* want to parade its prisoners, true. Defeated kings were the highest prize of all, the greatest treasure on display during a triumphal parade. But they were not necessary. So many of them chose death over capture. The people of Aven would not question it, if Sempronius had only some of the war-king's lieutenants to march along the triumphal route—and, of course, a captive queen.

Too, transporting a man like Ekialde might be more trouble than it was worth. Even if he did survive the journey, he would be a poor prize. *Any general could defeat a decaying wreck like Ekialde was now.* It proved no prowess of any kind, and might in fact damage his reputation. *'I cannot afford that, not with Lucretius Rabirus always ready to seize upon the barest cause for criticism.'*

He could not ignore, either, the tug of curiosity. Another chance to view the *besteki*, to see them summoned, to analyze the magic used to call them. So many questions remained. What *were* they? Were they spirits he might recognize by another name, or something else, peculiar to Iberia? How did the magic-woman summon them? Charms and chanting, yes, but that did not reveal the true thaumaturgy beneath the ritual. *'I have here the chance to learn more about Iberian magic than any Aventan before me. How could I pass that up?'*

Weighing these considerations, Sempronius came to a decision. Whatever Ekialde had become, he had been a king anointed and revered by his people. His methods may have been repugnant, even blasphemous, but they had been *bold*. For that, perhaps he did deserve a more noble death.

"Very well," he told Neitin. Her shoulders dropped in relief. He lifted a finger. "But we shall have guards of my choosing, and Arevaci magic-men observing. If this is acceptable to you, I am willing to grant your request."

XXXIV

She would have wished more privacy.

The Aventan general had not decided to display her husband to all his troops, though he might have done so. Nor had he granted total seclusion. A number of his highest-ranked companions would be present, the men who in Iberian terms might have been his war-band, the men who wore red-crested helmets. The chieftain of the Arevaci attended, and his Numidian wife, with many of their magic-men.

'Not that their efforts will be needed.' Sakarbik had prepared this ritual and eschewed all assistance. She chose the place, too, close to the water's churning edge, declaring the ocean to be a powerful conduit.

"Why?" Neitin asked her, as they walked down the sand. "You hate my husband. You owe me nothing. Why grant him this peace?"

Sakarbik glanced down at Matigentis, held on Neitin's hip. "For the boy," she said. "I think your son has a fine destiny ahead of him. The stars concur. But his father is a shadow in his path. If I can clear that shadow, the gods will think well of me for it."

Salty wind whipped at Neitin's hair and garments as her husband was led forth, his legs unfettered but his arms still in chains, surrounded by a cordon of stoic-faced legionaries. Ekialde wore a fresh tunic of purest white. *'Like a sacrifice.'* He offered no resistance. Had they told him the purpose of this excursion?

Matigentis did not know his father well enough to reach out to him or react to his presence. His attention was all for the golden bangles Sakarbik had given him to play with.

The legionaries drove a stake into the sand, methodically, just another chore. If they had any notion of participating in a sacred ritual—or a fearsome tragedy—no sign of it showed in their bodies or faces. '*Who are these Aventans, that extraordinary circumstances can be so unremarkable to them?*'

Ekialde's chains were hitched to this post. He stood, a shell of his former self, head dragging, shoulders loose. Yet they placed his crown back upon his head anyway, an act of either honor or mockery. No one jeered or hissed, so perhaps it was only an acknowledgment. This man had been a king, and his queen asked that he die as one. '*As though a band of beaten gold made any difference at all.*'

Already, tears dampened Neitin's cheeks and a suffocating pain ached in her chest. '*This is not how it should have ended. How we should have ended. It should never have come to this.*'

Sakarbik left her side once Ekialde's chains were secure. She had her pouch of herbs and other magical elements at her waist, a dagger strapped to her hip. Neitin had witnessed this ritual, or some form of it, many times, but never inquired as to its particulars. It worked; that was all she had needed to know when the *besteki* shielded her from Bailar's hounds. She had no right to demand deeper knowledge now.

Sakarbik walked in a circle around Ekialde, sprinkling her magical concoction upon the sand and speaking words in her sacred language. As soon as the circle was completed, Ekialde's body *changed*, tightening in odd places, his head lolling about feverishly.

'*She warned you,*' Neitin reminded herself. '*She said it would be painful. Horrible, even.*' And this was only the beginning. '*It will be worth it, for him to die his own man, not Bailar's creature.*'

As Ekialde twitched and shuddered, Sakarbik came to stand directly in front of him. Too close, Neitin thought. If Ekialde lunged, she was within the range that his fetters would allow. Yet Sakarbik stood, fearless, and spoke the words that might save the soul of a man she despised. Her sonorous chant rode the wind to Neitin's ears, familiar in its queer cadence.

Sakarbik took out the same dagger she used upon the battlefield. It had begun its life as a simple tool, but war and purpose consecrated it. She gripped it firmly in her hand and *struck*, a swiping blow at Ekialde's chest. No killing gesture, but a slash that drew a spray of blood. "Endovelicos of many faces, Endovelicos who blesses my sight, here!" she shouted, then fell to her knees and thrust the dagger into the sand up to the hilt.

Crablike, she scuttled back, as though she could not waste the time it would take to stand and turn. Her invocation was so strong that nearly immediately, the golden glow of the *besteki* coalesced.

Not now the gently bobbing forms that had first showed themselves to Neitin, nor the gathering mist of the battlefield. These *besteki* swept into the air and formed a dazzling whirlwind around Ekialde's form. It caught Mati's attention. He cooed, reaching out a chubby arm toward the bizarre spectacle. Neitin pressed both hands over her heart, hardly breathing,

All at once, the strange storm *tightened*, diving through Ekialde. The golden light poured into him through every line upon his skin, filling him until he glowed. Beautiful—and terrible, for he howled agony fit for the gods to hear.

Matigentis recoiled, wrapping himself around his mother's leg, when Ekialde began to scream. Neitin gathered her child up, cradling his head to her bosom, shushing him half-heartedly as she watched her husband writhe in agony.

Whorling lines of blood appeared on his tunic, excreting from the markings inked onto his chest. Crimson liquid dripped down his arms, too. Crimson at first, at least; after a moment, it turned purplish, then black. Rivulets of the foul liquid crept down his legs, seeping into the soil beneath him. He looked ready to crumble, crash to his knees, but the eerie force of the *besteki* held him upright even as they ravaged his body.

It was too much. Neitin started to turn away, but a hand dropped onto her shoulder; the Arevaci chieftain's wife, Hanath, had come up behind her so stealthily that Neitin had not noticed. "You asked for this," the woman reminded her. "You requested it. Turn not aside from your own doing."

So, jaw trembling, Neitin forced her gaze back to the man who had once been her husband, chained to a stake and tormented by cleansing spirits. Sakarbik had not moved since the *besteki* appeared. She was still supine, propped up on her hands, watching Ekialde's ordeal with the fixed intensity of a hunting cat. Neitin could not be sure she had so much as blinked.

With each buffet of the golden spirits, Ekialde's body shook and shuddered. First he would jerk forward, as though shoved in the back, then fold in upon himself, chin tucked to his chest, his whole body hollowing around his core. His toes dug in the blood-slickened earth, twisting with each contortion of his body. His hands were like claws, each finger strained and taut.

A high, clear whistle sliced through the wind and Ekialde's howls alike. A piercing sound, but not unpleasant. For a moment, Ekialde's entire body glowed as brilliant as the horizon at dawn, a white-gold of fearsome intensity, aching with promise and unfulfilled power. Then, the *besteki* vanished, diving back into whatever crevice between the worlds they had come from to begin with.

Ekialde' body fell, limp but not unconscious, to the ground. Only the susurration of the waves broke the silence.

Neitin's heart lurched beneath her ribs. *'It is him again. This is my husband.'* She set Matigentis down and darted forward, too fast now for Hanath's grasp to find her again, and from the corner of her eye, she saw Sempronius Tarren lift a hand to stay any other intervention, though he himself stepped closer.

She gathered Ekialde up in her arms. He was coated in his own blood, already drying, flaking off his skin. Plenty of it still smeared on her, though. She didn't care. She could see her husband's eyes again, a hazel that was faintly yellow, clearer and softer than they had been in years. He was weak, his breath rickety, his pulse thin and thready.

"Ekialde. Ekialde, I—" What to say? That he was dying? Surely he knew. That she had helped to orchestrate this end? A burden for her own soul, not his to bear into the afterlife. That she loved him? So long since she had framed those words.

"I am sorry, my rabbit." His voice was a whisper, a dry leaf disintegrating to powder at a touch. "I am sorry."

"I know, my dear one," she whispered, smoothing back his hair. "I know."

His eyes found the sky, a vivid blue with occasional white clouds streaking across it. He drew a long, deep breath. "I am sorry I went so far away from you," he sighed, and Neitin was not sure whether he spoke to her or to the god of all gods, Endovelicos, whose many faces saw all things in his creation. He dropped his head, gasping for air. Then he found her eyes again, managed to lift a hand to cup her cheek. "I think I will not see you again for a long time, little rabbit."

"You will see me, though." Her tears splashed upon her cheeks. "The lands beyond are eternal. A-A few years between your passage and mine will make no difference." Not to him, at least; the time would pass as nothing. It was for her, left on this living earth, to toil out weary days until they could be reunited.

Ekialde's chest heaved, rasping. "Mati—Our boy—"

Neitin did not want to turn away, did not want to take her eyes off her husband, in case that was the moment his spirit fled him at last. Yet she felt another presence at her side. Hanath led the boy by the hand, then faded back.

Mati's lower lip quivered, though he looked almost too afraid to cry. Ekialde reached out a hand, but did not touch him. "By Nabia's will, you may not even remember this, my son," he said, "but if any of it lingers, remember I bid you this: Listen to your mother." Mati burrowed himself into Neitin's side, hiding his eyes from the gruesome form of his father. Ekialde's lips twitched, almost a smile. "Sensible lad. Turn away from these things. I wish... I wish..." Fresh blood bloomed on his lips now, the last of his life flecking away. "I wanted to give you everything. Both of you."

'All I wanted was you, you stupid ass,' Neitin thought. Ill words for a man to carry with him to the world beyond, though. Aloud, she said, "I had your love," though what she meant was, *'I had it for a time, too short a time, but so sweet while it was mine.'*

Another weak smile was all Ekialde could manage before, with one last rattling breath, life left him.

The world stood silent a moment. Even the wind stilled, pausing to bear witness to the passing of this one man. Then Neitin's head fell back, and she howled out all the pent-up agony of the past two years.

XXXV

They let her sob upon the shore a very long time.

They took away the ravaged form that had once been Ekialde. They took her son, handing him to Hanath, and Neitin allowed it. Most of the Aventans faded away, back to their camp. A small guard remained, and Sakarbik, and they let Neitin weep until she had no more strength for tears.

They waited, too, until she rose on her own. Night had fallen, and the ocean wind dropped to a mere whisper. Sakarbik came to her side, and together they began the long walk back to camp, with guards trailing behind them.

"I will be leaving you now, little wife," Sakarbik said, when they were back within their allocated tent. "The Aventans will be arranging transport to go back to their home, and you will go along with them. But I vowed I would not leave these shores, and I do not mean to."

Neitin would not have thought anything could hollow her out further, but Sakarbik's words did. She had come to depend on Sakarbik, and not only for her magic. The older woman's brusque manner and utter fearlessness kept her steady through their long winter's flight. For Sakarbik to leave her *now* felt a cruelty.

'No,' Neitin chided herself. '*She owed you no duty. She performed this last service out of kindness. You have no right to ask more.*'

Mati would miss her, too; she had become more of an aunt to him than Neitin's own sisters. Nor would he know those women, who should have been the trees supporting his growth. Reilin was dead on the battlefield, and of Ditalce and Irrin, Neitin had been able to learn nothing. They were not known to be among either the captives or the dead.

Neitin liked to think that they had escaped with some of the other women and elders who had accompanied Ekialde's campaign. Perhaps they were even now finding their way back to their home village, further up the broad river. Neitin hoped they were safe and would live to see babes of their own, but it seemed impossible that she would ever be free to find them.

Neitin steadied herself with forced grace. "Of course you must go. Thank you for... for all you have done."

Sakarbik acknowledged the gratitude with a sniff. "The Aventans will not misuse you, I think. I spoke truly earlier: the *besteki* seem to like this Sempronius Tarren. Whatever he may be, he is not a cruel man. He did not allow his soldiers to rape when they overtook Lusetani villages, and even plunder was kept reasonable. I think he will protect you."

"Protect me so I can walk in his parade." Neitin lacked the vitality to be angry about it, but that made it no less horrific a prospect. "Guard me as he would some valuable jewel or exotic animal."

"Better than no protection at all."

"And what then? A life as a prisoner in their city?" She had heard that Aven was fifteen times as large as Olissippo, but that had to be exaggeration. Her imagination could not encompass it. "What becomes of me and my son once we have lost our novelty?"

"I cannot say. I will tell you this, though: The road of your stars is longer than you think."

Impossible to believe that, with the weight of despair crushing her down.

"Before I go, there is something you should have. It may be of use to you in that foreign city." Sakarbik settled her shoulders back. "I grant you this gift, for your own self and for the sake of your boy. I told you: the stars believe he has a grand future."

"The stars told Ekialde the same thing," Neitin said. "I would accept a humble but happy one, for Matigentis."

Unconcerned, Sakarbik shrugged. "Maybe that is what they mean by 'grand,' in his case. Who can say? The point is this, little mother—" She grasped Neitin's chin, forcing her to meet Sakarbik's intense gaze, hot like a lightning strike. "I want to pass something on to you. A gift. *My* gift, insofar as I can bestow it. I never had a daughter."

"You—What?"

"I never had a daughter, and all my sons are beneath the dirt. I have no one else to give this gift to."

"I don't understand." And then, suddenly, she did. "No. No, Sakarbik, this thing is not possible."

"It is, I assure you."

"The gods choose, and they did not choose me!" Impossible, utterly impossible.

"Do you think the gods choose only at birth?" Sakarbik shook her head. "Sometimes, it is so. Sometimes, it is the result of great study, years of dedication and practice and sweat. And sometimes, it is a gift. I do not have time to give you all. Perhaps I should have started long ago, but.... Ah. Well. Perhaps you do not deserve all that I would give to a Cossetan daughter or daughter-in-law. But this much, I can give, freely and with a good heart and, I think, with Nabia's blessing." She spoke a few words in the magic language. "Now. Repeat them back."

Neitin complied, though they weighed strangely on her tongue. She imitated Sakarbik's exact cadence, more of a gallop than everyday Lusetani.

"Good. Now this."

It took several tries, but eventually Neitin had it all, several lines of Lusetani magic, embedded in her memory. "But Sakarbik, I cannot—I do not—"

"Those words," Sakarbik insisted, "spoken with a full heart and with certain offerings, they will give protection. The offerings—you need alder wood and crushed angelica, at the least. Other things will help." These, Sakarbik listed. "Then, a connection between earth and sky."

"The daggers you thrust in the ground," Neitin said. "The amulet of mine that you smashed."

"Yes and yes." Sakarbik nodded decisively. "Bring these things together, in all your fierceness and devotion, and the *besteki* will find you."

A thin, hysterical laugh wheezed out of Neitin's throat. "I am about to be taken from this land. Stolen away to a place I can scarcely imagine. Different rocks, different hills, different people. Our gods are not there. Our—"

Sakarbik slapped her cheek. Not hard, but a quick pop, like a mother reprimanding a wayward child. "Our gods are wherever we are, foolish thing," she chided. "And there have been Iberians in Aven long before now. If you have no faith, they may ignore you, true. But if you hold yourself steady, *here*." She pressed hard at Neitin's chest, above her heart. "If you do not forget this land, if you do not forsake the gods of our people, they will still hear you." She let her fingers fall away from Neitin. "And I think you will see this ground again, someday. Your son's stars... Hm. Perhaps best not to know too much."

"You would leave me with such ominous words?"

Sakarbik tilted her head. "It does not mean his fate will be a tragic one. It means you should not try to interfere with it. You gave him a mother's blessing; you asked the gods of your heart to look after him, and the war-god to look away. Let that be enough. Meddle in his fate too much, and you may bring about the end you fear."

Part of Sempronius would have liked to linger in Olissippo, indulging his fascination in the ancient city and the seashore's possibilities. After a few days, though, the larger portion of Sempronius's soul itched to get home.

'You've done your work here. You've fulfilled this component of the vision you received. And Vibia and Latona have at least begun fulfilling the second.'

Remarkable as their efforts had been, Sempronius knew the conflict was not over. While any of Discordia's devotees remained in Aven, the threat remained. And there were still the Augian Commission and Lucretius Rabirus to contend with. *'The social and political wars may be as terrible as the magical one, in the end.'*

On the Nones of Aprilis, the port of Olissippo was a-bustle with soldiers embarking and with many leave-takings. "I shall be sorry to see you go," Bartasco said, clasping hands with Sempronius. "Though I will not be sad to return to Segontia. It has been too long." His mouth smirked beneath the beard. "I confess to you, as age creeps upon me, I find I prefer the life of the townsman to that of the soldier."

Sempronius laughed; Bartasco could not have been any older than he himself. "And I the statesman to the general, friend."

"Keep those nimble wits about you, eh?" Bartasco said. "And keep my wife safe in your monster of a city." For Hanath would accompany a contingent of the Arevaci to Aven, ambassadors and celebrants, proof that Aven and Iberia could work together as friends and forge strong new bonds.

"Keep *her* safe?" Sempronius countered. "The day Lady Hanath needs a politician like me to keep her safe is the day the Endless Sea dries up to a desert." They both laughed, but Sempronius made a more sober promise: "I will look after all your people to the best of my ability, Lord Bartasco, and see them safely returned to you when their sojourn is done."

"May it be the start of many fruitful exchanges," Bartasco replied.

"Indeed. So I intend. And if you need anything here, send to Onidius Praectus at the fort near Toletum."

"I shall do that. And you must write!" Bartasco said. "I have learned some of your Truscan letters by now, but I will need to continue to practice."

"As I must continue to school myself in the Arevaci tongue."

A whistle blew in the distance and was echoed several times, as though a flock of birds uttered the same piercing cry: the ships' crews, calling stragglers to come aboard before the tides changed. "Farewell and not-farewell, Sempronius Tarren," Bartasco said. "If never our eyes meet again, still our words and hearts shall reach across the sea."

Sempronius left Bartasco to say his goodbyes to his wife. It was more of a pang than expected, walking away from his friend and ally. *'I wonder why,'* he contemplated as he strolled along the docks, listening to the crash of the waves and the shouting of sailors. *'I have departed before from places I never expected to return to, have left behind those dear to me.'*

Then, he had not owned so keen an awareness of the ongoing challenges entwined with leavetaking. He and Bartasco would be the pillars supporting a web between Aven and Iberia, but such things were fragile. Whatever he did to mold his dreams into reality, a federation of proud nations drawing strength from one another, for the betterment of all, it could easily be undone, by spite or opposition or mere bad luck. What one generation built, another might destroy. If he or Bartasco were to die before the knots between their nations were firm, who would step up to resecure them?

'So much rests on chance.' The domain of Fracture, his sister's element, awkward for him to engage with. *'I shall have to weave this net as strongly as I can. Strong and flexible, like a spider's web indeed, able to bear the buffets of the winds of chance. And I shall have to make sure I do not die before the work is finished.'*

Sempronius checked in on each of the ships before boarding his own. He had split the tribunes and other ranking officers among the vessels, and he would rotate among them any time they put into port, even if only long enough to take on water. Less than a month's journey, if Neptune were kind—and Sempronius had sacrificed profusely to encourage him to be so. They would hug the coast, to lessen the risk of being caught in storms, and Sempronius could take a few days in Tarraco to settle provincial matters there.

"Very well," he said, and a profound satisfaction settled in his chest, warm and full. "Let us go home."

XXXVI

Domus Magicae, Esquiline Hill

"It's strange no one's spoken to me." Vibia paced behind Latona, whose forehead was flat on her work-table. Her casual tone showed rather more curiosity and rather less consideration for Latona's misery.

That afternoon, Latona had intended to work with young Fausta. At the appointed hour, the girl did not arrive at the Domus Magicae. Her mother did.

Whether from fear or shame, the woman had not been able to meet Latona's eyes. She stammered apologies, yet remained firm in her determination: Fausta could not continue her studies with Latona. The family's patron had raised an objection.

This patron was an equestrian Latona had never heard of, but a little pressing revealed that *his* patron, in turn, was Rufilius Albinicus, the former consul and esteemed general. The orders had apparently been passed down the chain of clientele.

As with the Crispiniae, Latona knew of no direct insult or offense given to the Rufiliae family, so this was a personal intervention into her affairs, but for no personal reason. It escalated matters past gossip and scheming; for a man of Albinicus's stature to involve himself, even obliquely, added considerable weight to the arguments against the Domus Magicae's existence.

She would have to tell her father, or play the coward and let Aula do so, despite the risk that if things kept up in this fashion, he might exercise the paternal authority she had convinced him to slacken.

"I mean, really," Vibia went on. "No one's said a word to me. Or *against* me, not that I or any of my people have heard. But I'm as openly connected to this as you are."

"Are you annoyed," Latona asked, tilting her head to one side without raising it from the table, "not to be snubbed?"

"No. Not as such. But it does make me wonder *why*."

Latona dragged her body upright only to slump in her chair. "You're not as... overt as Aula and I, maybe? She sticks her nose in everyone's business, and I—"

"Draw notice even when you don't mean to," Vibia finished. "Maybe. But when you think how fiercely the Optimates hate Sempronius, it's strange no one's tried to sully him by smearing me, when they're going to such trouble to tarnish you."

"It's not even coming from the Optimates. It's from our own people. Our allies."

Vibia gave Latona what was probably supposed to be a comforting pat on the back. In recognition of her deficits in that arena, however, she said, "I'm going to go find Ama Rubellia and tell her you're more in need of her than any of her chirping little acolytes right now."

"That's very kind of you."

"It's not. You're useless when you're moping, so I'm working to my own benefit."

After Vibia left, Latona attempted to retrain her mind on her research. Marcus Autronius continued to supply them with papers, bought or borrowed or purloined, and among the latest set had been a commentary on the *lex cantatia Augiae* that was only a decade removed from the law's institution. The author, a senator from the then-recently-conquered city of Sentinum, objected to the law's prohibitions in language that Latona suspected would be useful, if she could focus on it.

Vibia was right, though; she *was* useless while moping. So she abandoned intellectual efforts and went to lay on a couch in the garden with a brazier in front of her, playing idly with the flames until emotional reinforcements arrived.

They came in triplicate: not just Rubellia, but Alhena and Tilla. All had the compassion not to speak of Fausta's involuntary withdrawal from their circle. Alhena played music, Tilla told tales of what mischief her brothers had gotten into during the recent games, and Rubellia sat at Latona's side, embroidering with quiet grace and suffusing Latona with a steady supply of calming emotion.

The peace was not to last.

Late in the afternoon, a visitor came to the door. Merula, who had been studying her numbers all afternoon, stirred herself to greet the newcomer and bring her into the garden with the others.

Marcia Tullia was a woman of forty years or so, her dark hair touched with a few dignified shots of silver. Her eyes were a paler blue than Alhena's, like a winter sky, and everything about her dress was perfectly correct and precise.

"Marcia!" Latona's emotions tangled. Marcia Tullia was one of the foremost mages in Aven and wife to Galerius Orator. A friend, in a distant way. Latona intended to approach her about the collegium when they had a more impressive plan—but the recent bespeckling of Latona's reputation had stalled that intention. "Would you care for water or wine, Marcia?"

"Water, thank you."

Tilla passed the jug and cups to Latona, her face showing keen interest in what might be about to unfold. None of the others showed any sign of leaving the room, nor would Latona ask them to. *They have as much stake as I in whatever Marcia has to say.*

After sipping her water and pronouncing it lovely, Marcia set the cup down and adopted an orderly pose on her couch. "Latona, I think you know I am not one to waste time, so I'll get right to it. I've heard a little about your endeavor here, and it concerns me. I should like to determine if those concerns are founded or not."

A hot flush spread to Latona's cheeks even as a cold rock settled in her stomach. "I cannot confirm or allay suspicions without knowing what you've heard."

Marcia's lips twitched slightly, a sign that she knew what Latona was doing: trying to get information before yielding any of her own. "Word has spread that you intend to form some sort of society of mages—of female mages, no less—and that you further intend to set yourselves up as a type of collegium, providing magical services and training to the... to the less prominent of the city's mages."

"You make it sound very formal," Latona said, summoning a light laugh. "I guarantee you we're not charging tuition fees." The attempt at levity died in her throat with the unamused stare Marcia leveled at her. *Can*

I risk telling her more? The Discordians, the Augians... She would be every bit as horrified as Vibia. But she would want proof.'

Proof they did not yet have.

Before Latona could decide what to risk, Marcia lifted her chin. "Latona, I want you to know I speak out of no malice. I have always appraised your skills highly. It is why you stand for Spirit during the Cantrinalia."

Latona's cheek twitched. *'I stand for Spirit because no one else in this city has power enough to earn that right,'* she thought, but she swallowed the flare of pride.

"Yet I am deeply concerned," Marcia said, "that you are stepping out of your appropriate sphere with..." She gestured about the space. "...this endeavor."

"I wonder," Ama Rubellia said, serene as ever, "if you might enlighten us." She gave her sunlit smile, so gentle, so ease-putting. "What is it you *do* think an appropriate sphere would be? For you and I are both, I think, examples of different manners in which a mage may seek to do the gods' will."

"You are, of course, an exemplar of Venus's service," Marcia answered. "But Latona is not you. She is not dedicated to a temple's service."

"Only because that vicious cat at Juno Maxima wouldn't let her," Tilla murmured. Alhena seized her hand and squeezed it in warning.

"And she is recently divorced," Marcia continued, as though Tilla had not spoken. "The boundaries of her life are different, and she ought to heed them." Her cool eyes fell on Latona again. "A mages' collegium, Latona? Truly?"

Latona swallowed around a growing lump in her throat. "It seemed the best way to spread education to those who need and desire it," she said. "So many in this city receive less magical instruction than is their due, and increasingly I think some of those we consider weakly-gifted have instead been only weakly-trained." She had not forgotten Seppius, his talent a secret even to himself, any more than she had forgotten the looming threat of Scaeva and Corinna and the Augians. "I owe service to this city, in Juno's name, and this is a way I can serve."

"Is it a proper way, though?" Marcia countered. "Is it the *best* way you can serve?"

"It's needed," Tilla challenged, despite Alhena's increasingly desperate grip on her fingers. "Diana's ti—tenderness, Marcia, you know how it is for women like us, and *we* all had the benefit of indulgent fathers and considerable resources."

Marcia's attention diverted slowly, as though surprised to find Tilla and Alhena still there. She regarded them with a creased brow. "And when those indulgent fathers find husbands for you? Will they approve of your spending your days here with your heads in books, rather than tending to your own households?"

A tense ripple of emotion fluttered out of both Alhena and Tilla: swift, sudden intensity prodding Latona's Spirit magic. In each, a tight, heart-skipping beat, though Alhena's was more fearful, Tilla's laced with anger. *'What on earth...?'*

"I like to think," Tilla said, her voice harder than its usual joviality, "my father will choose a husband who understands my needs."

Rubellia's cheeks were pink; Latona suspected she was directing calming magic in Tilla's direction, now, too. Yet her voice remained even as she said, "Marcia, you must see the benefit in making sure that every Aventan blessed by the gods has access to the training and education to make the most of themselves."

"The training and education fit to their station in life, certainly," Marcia replied. "The *mos maiorum*. Aven's traditions exist for a reason. They keep things in balance, for the common good."

Something wasn't making senes. Marcia Tullia was not Aemilia Fullia; she was known to be rational, reasonable, willing to consider alternate points of view. Yet she seemed to have made herself stone, not Air. She and Galerius were moderates, not committed to the Popularist faction, true, but Latona had never known her to be intractable.

"What you are proposing," Marcia went on, "will unsettle people. Some might see it as an attempt to extend the powers of mages beyond what the *leges tabulae magicae* allow." She nodded in the direction of the rolls and rolls of books occupying the tables, desks, and lattices all over the Domus Magicae. "You've read a great deal of history, I think. What happens in a society when people fear mages more than they respect them? What happens when people feel that mages have an unfair advantage over other citizens?"

Latona's fingers flexed and curled against her thigh. Fear of unfair advantage was much of why the Augian Commission had been established centuries ago. *And now it is corrupted. Should people not fear that? Blind faith in these institutions has not served us well.'*

Her next words were dangerous, and though she knew it, she spoke them anyway. "Perhaps the *leges tabulae magicae* need re-assessment, to fit the needs of the modern age."

"The city is much larger now than once it was," Rubellia swooped in, sparing Latona from further perilous statements at least for the moment. "People with magical potential do sometimes slip through the cracks—"

"Small adjustments, then," Marcia allowed, "and properly done, through appropriate channels like the Augian Commission."

Latona managed not to twitch; Tilla did not manage not to snort. "The Augians," Latona said, trying to choose her words with care, "have had centuries to adapt with the city's growth and with changing times. They have not done so."

"Your renegade behavior is not the answer. A collegium? People will see it as a threat, Latona. A collegium has *power*, if not on its own, then as a weapon in the hands of a patron. What would yours be?"

No honest answer would suffice, because the truth was that she *did* want her collegium to gain power—power enough to challenge the Augians and change the restrictions on magical education and exercise. But nor could she lie; Air mages could smell falsehoods.

"A school," Alhena said quietly. "There's precedent. From the Truscans, that is, before the Ilionians and Athaecans came—"

Marcia gave no indication she heard Alhena, her exasperation reserved for Latona alone. "Honestly! Even if all you say is true, even if this were all necessary and right with the gods—and I do not mean to suggest that I cede those points—what would make you think that *you* are the correct person to shoulder the responsibility?"

"Juno has given me gifts," Latona said, echoing words spoken to her father a few months earlier, "and I intend to use them. To do otherwise would be to dishonor her."

"Juno's gifts..." Marcia shook her head in dismay. "I appreciate that your husband was not a political man, and that your father does not rely on you as he does Aula, who had the dual benefit of your mother's instruction and a politically-minded husband." Latona flinched, stung by the unexpected assault on her upbringing. "So perhaps you do not have a real sense of what it is, to bear burdens on behalf of the people of Aven. Starting a collegium, a true one, would be a massive effort. This isn't something you can just *play* at."

Vitellian temper, Venus's fire, Juno's pride, some combination of them all ignited within Latona, trampling her myriad insecurities and the warnings against making an enemy of Marcia Tullia. "You think I am playing at this?" she asked in a low growl. "You think this is the action of some bored, pampered brat, at loose ends without husband or child to occupy her time? That I *dabble*?"

"I think you have not consid—"

"You can't have it both ways," Latona said. Marcia's jaw snapped shut in surprise; not many people dared interrupt her. "I can't be a silly little girl playing at importance *and* a dangerous threat to the established order. And if I must choose one or the other..." She stood, propelled to her feet by fury. "Gods, I have *suffered* for this city and its people. You have no idea what we've been facing, because most of Aven's mages turn their gaze aside—"

Rubellia's fingers touched her wrist. "Latona..."

But she was beyond the reach of any calming influence now. "No, Rubellia. Marcia has gifted us with her unvarnished honesty. Well and good. I should do her the same courtesy." She flung an arm out, pointing to the door. "We have been the *only ones*, Marcia. Me and Vibia and—" She held back Marcus Autronius's name, not wanting to implicate him if Marcia did not already know his involvement. "And the other women here. We have been fighting a terror for nearly a year, and because of the way magic works in this city, because we could not *trust* the system designed to govern it, we did it alone! So yes, I sought to do more. I sought to build a better system. And I will march straight into Tartarus before I let someone tell me I have not considered what it means, to bear a burden for this city."

Marcia looked no less composed than usual, but her poise sharpened. She stood, hands folded neatly in front of her. "I am glad I came to speak with you," she said, each word a carefully-threaded needle. "I am glad to have gained clarity on your efforts here. I will have to consider what to do with the information."

"Merula!" Latona called. "Please see the Lady Marcia out. I believe we have said all that is necessary."

Marcia took her leave without another word to Tilla, Alhena, or Rubellia, almost as though she had forgotten they were there. Latona hardly breathed as she departed, sandals padding in quick steps against the tile. Only when the door closed and Merula slid the bolt shut did she let herself draw a harsh gasp of air.

"Well," Tilla said, "that's thrown a stick at a hornet's nest, for sure."

Hot tears, *angry* tears splashed down Latona's cheeks. That Marcia could think so little of her, could challenge not just the merits of her plan but her capability to enact it, even her devotion to the city—it was infuriating.

But when the cold reality of her own words crashed down, terror took anger's place.

If Marcia chose to make life difficult for Latona, she could do much more damage than Aemilia Fullia. She could bar Latona access not only to materials but to *people.* That, in turn, would hurt Latona's family. Her father's and brother's careers would be damaged if they were seen as having an imprudent woman in the household. Marriage prospects for Aula and Alhena would evaporate, even for little Lucia, years off yet from any betrothal. *'All those years I spent trying to avoid social ruin, and now look what I've done.'*

Moaning, Latona half-collapsed at the waist, hands on her knees. "Ohhh, gods, what did I do? What did I do, what did I do, what did I do?"

"You, um," Alhena began, "you told off one of the highest-status mages in Truscum."

"Thank you, Alhena, I believe her question was rhetorical," Rubellia said softly, moving to rub Latona's back.

"And what do I do *now*?"

Soothing warmth spread from Rubellia's hand into Latona's muscles. "My dear, you now have the advantage of having committed yourself wholly to a path. Never mind the wisdom of it. The only way out is through."

"Through?"

"Through the course you've chosen. You may never make friends of women like Aemilia and Glaucanis—"

"And who would want to?" Tilla put in.

"—but the Crispiniae and Rufiliae and others like them can be persuaded by action. When they see what you do and how it will benefit the city, not tear it down, they will relent. And Marcia..." Rubellia frowned, an unusual expression on her placid face. "She'll come around, I'm sure. I couldn't get a hold on it, but there was something odd in her emotions today." She shook off the thought. "So, that is what you must do. Hold to your course, however the storms buffet you. Learn all you can. Expose the Augians."

"And reinvent magical governance." Latona straightened, wiping at her face with the back of her hand. Summoning confidence felt, in that moment, like trying to draw water from a bottomless pit. "Simple as that."

MAIUS

XXXVII

In the days that followed, Latona kept her head down and her mind on her work, letting Vibia and Aula field their remaining alliances. For some reason, they were not attracting the same measure of disdain. Latona sequestered herself in the Domus Magicae, attempting to teach herself law without the benefit of a magister, drafting and re-drafting arguments for re-legislation of the *lex cantatia*.

Alhena did her best to help, compiling notes and evidence, rooting much of it in ancient traditions, which might find common cause with some of their usual political opponents. Alongside that work, she also began transforming those notes into treatises, not just on history and law, but on thaumaturgical practice.

"You could publish these," Tilla said, looking over a scroll on which Alhena compared the Athaecan and Truscan theories of magic.

"Don't be absurd," Alhena said, frowning at the tablet in front of her.

"I'm not." Tilla set the scroll back in its cubbyhole carefully. As wild and reckless as she could be, Tilla was always precise when it came to handling Alhena's work. She slipped up behind Alhena, brushed her hair aside, and pressed a kiss to the back of her neck—a risky move, with Latona muttering to herself in the next cubicle and Merula exercising in the garden. "Those treatises are *good*. I mean, you write well."

"You're very kind in your assessment, I'm sure."

"I'm not that, either," Tilla laughed. "Do you know how long it took *me* to learn to read? Couldn't be bothered. Nothing interested me. But your works are... captivating."

Alhena set down her stylus and tilted her head up at Tilla. "Would you think that if you weren't in love with me?" Her voice wobbled a bit on the words, still strange to say.

Tilla, ever the opportunist, snatched a kiss before replying. "I would. I love my sister, too, if in rather a different fashion, and everything she writes bores me to sleep."

Shaking her head, Alhena returned to her tablet. "Well, however captivating the prose, it wouldn't matter. No one would read thaumaturgical treatises written by a woman."

Tilla gave her horselike huff, meandering around to the other side of the table. Alhena suspected she wanted to argue, but Latona's current travails made a counterpoint difficult.

"Thank you," Alhena whispered, "for not abandoning us."

"What?" Tilla squawked. "Alhena—"

"I wouldn't blame you, I mean. I'm grateful, but I'd understand. If it reflected poorly on your family—"

"You ridiculous goose, look at me."

Alhena did, and despite her turbulent emotions, it was still a pleasure. Tilla's brown skin glowed with warmth all the more now that the weather had turned fine and she could spend more time outside. She wore little jewelry, a few copper bands about her arms and fingers. Her belt was loose and her tunic, as ever, hung off one shoulder; her long-since-discarded overgown lay over the back of a chair.

All this, Tilla gestured at. "I am aware," she said, with less bounce in her voice than usual, "that I am a figure of ridicule in certain circles. Even those who purport cordial relationships with my family. But my parents and brothers and even holy Quinta have always loved me and stood by me." An impish smile curled her lips. "We Terentiae are not creatures of fashion. If the rest of society casts you out, we may cleave to you all the more just to be different."

That coaxed a small giggle from Alhena. "I should have more faith in you," she admitted quietly.

"You should!" Tilla said, with only faint reproach. "The advantage in having a Vestal for a sister and a famous eccentric for a grandfather, is that they both provide a fair bit of coverage for one's own oddities, in different ways. But even if they didn't, my sweet, it would be a poor showing if I abandoned you at the first trial."

A flurry of activity at the front door—which Latona insisted on keeping open, a statement of her honesty and virtue—drew Alhena's attention. "News!" Aula cried. "Where are you all?"

Tilla and Alhena met her in the atrium. Aula was pink-cheeked and dewy with exertion, looking in better spirits than any of the Vitelliae had felt in many days.

Latona appeared in the door of her study, looking, by contrast, as wretched as ever, with dark circles under her eyes. "Heavens, Aula, where did you run from?"

"The Forum, at a good clip, and you'll understand why." Smile beaming, emerald eyes twinkling, she announced, "The Tenth Legion has landed at Ostia. Our menfolk have returned home."

Via Ostiensis, Truscum

The closer they drew to Aven, the more a heavy weight lifted from Gaius Vitellius's chest. Each of his horse's strides brought him nearer to the moment when he could lay down the burden of military office.

Not immediately, of course. He would not be discharged until after Sempronius's triumph. The tribunes, like their commander, were considered still under arms, though their war was ended. They could not enter the city bounds until they were discharged.

'Soon, though. Soon.' Vitellius had grown weary of being responsible for other men's lives, at least in so direct a fashion as the job of a tribune entailed. *'If the gods are good, Aven will ask me to serve in a different capacity.'* He would go to the law courts and into the Senate gladly, but if he never donned his cuirass and crested helmet again after the triumphal parade, he would count himself Fortuna's favored child.

The march from Ostia to Aven took half a day. How pleasant to be back on a proper road! After years in Albina and Iberia, trudging through mud and stamping against hard rocks and tripping over pebbles, Vitellius had nearly forgotten what it was like. The legion moved faster than they had in all those months toiling across the plateaus and riverbanks.

The sprawling villas they passed were strange to Vitellius's eyes now, so much larger than any farmhouse in Iberia or Albina. The enslaved men and tenant farmers worked in larger groups, too. *'You will have to get used to that again. There are more people in Aven alone than in all of Baelonia.'* The largest cities he had seen in years were Nedhena and Olissippo, and he'd spent far more time in towns the size of Toletum or smaller villages. Aven dwarfed them all.

Closer to the city, the farmlands became obscured by the mausoleums and funerary monuments lining the road on both sides, some simple rectangles, others enormous and ornate. The Vitellian monuments were on another road; he would pass no ancestors today. He saw many soldiers' markers, though, each one inscribed with the name, rank, and unit of the deceased, along with how many years he had served and any honors he had won. Men from the same legion or cohort were often clustered together, even included on the same monument, their memories tended to by their burial clubs.

'Gods, how many thousands more will there be now? How many stones will grieving families and burial clubs erect with the words 'died in Toletum,' 'died at Libora,' 'died by the Tagus River' marked upon them?'

He wondered what road Titus Mennenius's monument would be on. He would like to contribute toward it, if Mennenius's family would not consider it a presumption. *'If not for me, he would have been safe home more than a year ago.'*

Caught up in maudlin thoughts, Vitellius almost did not notice when Autronius Felix sidled up next to him. Even with his missing hand, he was still an able horseman, adjusting for the weight imbalance and managing his reins. "That man," Autronius Felix said, "never rests. Not for a moment! Not in his mind, at least."

"Hm?" Vitellius asked, eloquently.

"Sempronius!" Felix replied. "He's back there right now, riding alongside one of the wagons, making poor Corvinus try to write on a wax tablet while bumping along, working out plans to improve the port at Ostia. Expanding the harbor and such, to 'remove impediments standing between the grain deliveries and the people of Aven.'" These last words, Felix delivered in a passable impression of Sempronius's cadence and tone. Then he laughed. "I swear by Apollo's golden prick, if that man weren't so damn capable, he'd be extremely annoying."

"His capacity for realizing his goals does beggar belief," Vitellius agreed. What amused Felix caused Vitellius mild alarm, though he could not quite explain why, even to himself. Perhaps it was that Sempronius wore so easily the burdens that Vitellius was eager to set down. Not lightly; Sempronius was never cavalier with the lives under his command. To the contrary, Vitellius had seen the man mourn—and seen him take desperate actions that mourning might be prevented.

But it never seemed to cost Sempronius any measure of *functioning*. Vitellius had seen Sempronius frustrated, had seen him angry, had seen him frightened, even, but in all these months, he had never seen Sempronius seem unsure. Always, another plan to implement, a new angle to approach a problem from. Impressive, certainly! But uncanny, too, and it left Vitellius ill at ease around his commanding officer.

'Perhaps I judge him unfairly. Perhaps he conceals his inner turmoil, hiding it in the back of his soul so that the troops will not lose faith.'

Perhaps—but he did not think so.

'Well. If he is guilty of hubris, that is for the gods to both determine and punish.'

As soon as the walls of Aven came into sight, Vitellius's heart swelled within his chest, a palpable ache that dizzied him. He swayed in the saddle briefly before grabbing his pommel to steady himself.

Felix grinned sideways at him. "Forget what it looked like?"

"A bit," Vitellius admitted, though the truth was more that he had forgotten just how dear a place could be. The walls, the riot of red rooftops, the crests of the temples poking up from the seven hills and reaching toward the sky—all those things were, as it turned out, imprinted on his heart, indelible.

Palatine Hill, City of Aven

"No, no, no, no, *no*." Aula plucked the pins at Latona's shoulders and yanked her gown right off her. "You are *not* wearing that color."

"I look good in blue," Latona objected.

"You look *fine* in blue," Aula said, throwing open a trunk. She cast the garments into utter disarray in a heartbeat, hurling wool and linen hither and thither in her sartorial quest. "But you look dazzling in emerald, radiant in fuchsia, and scintillating in scarlet." She straightened, a fist of finely-woven wool in her hand. "Yes. Scarlet."

"Ohhh, Aula." Latona drew an unsteady breath. "Don't you think it's a bit obvious?"

"Think of it this way, my honey." She whirled the length of cloth around her sister's head and flapped a hand for assistance. A visibly amused Merula stepped forward to hand her pins. "No, the gold with the lion's head, I think, Merula. And find earrings to match. Latona, the man hasn't seen you in nearly a year and a half. Do you want to greet him looking like a docile little mouse? No. No, you do not."

Latona had not expected a chance to respond, so it did not surprise her when Aula nattered on without so much as a pause for breath.

"You need to look like a goddess. Anyway, it's *thematic*. It's the military color! You're honoring the legions." She frowned, rubbing the bright red fabric between her fingers. "What do we think for a mantle? One of your *special* ones?" She meant one of the Fire-enchanted mantles, woven for protection from the *lemures*. "Or the pale gold?"

"Gold," Alhena said from her perch at the edge of Latona's bed. "The reds aren't a perfect match."

"Ah, well. Gold, then. Though I do worry that takes away from the shine of your hair."

"My hair," Latona said, snatching up her earrings in an attempt not to be treated *entirely* like a doll, "makes statement enough on its own, thank you. And may I point out, *you're* not wearing legionary red."

"With this hair? Of course not! It clashes." Aula's hands were quick, draping and tucking and pinning until the gown hung to best effect, its soft folds accentuating Latona's rolling curves. "Same reason Alhena can't wear it. You're the only one who can manage it. Well, Father, I suppose, but of course he'll be in his censorial toga." Aula was resplendent in a grass-green gown with a saffron border, which did set off her coppery hair nicely. She had amber cuffs and a necklace to match, with jangling golden earrings. "And Alhena is charming in lavender, though I do worry you'll look washed out next to the two of us, dear."

"I don't mind," Alhena said. "I just want to look nice and… well, grown-up. Gaius hasn't seen me since I was a gangly little girl, after all." She did look lovely. Her bright red hair had been not twisted back in its usual severe knot, but combed to a sheen and half-braided into a coronet over her brow. The lavender gown was paired with a cerulean tunic, rose-colored earbobs, and a lilac beaded necklace, all of which warmed her pale skin and set off the vibrant beauty of her hair.

"I still think this is too showy for me," Latona said. "There's no need for me to make a spectacle of myself." She was thinking of all the accusations leveled against her in recent days: ambitious, presumptuous, scheming, arrogant. "I don't want to be tarted up like a common she-wolf."

"Tsk! No common she-wolf, darling, I'm sure you'd fetch a very high price."

"Aula," Alhena said in a warning tone.

Abruptly, Aula sobered. "Yes. I know what you're worried about, my dear. That was a poor joke, at such a time." She hooked a finger into the hair behind Latona's right ear. With a deft motion, she teased a curl out to bob invitingly against Latona's cheek. "But think of it this way, my honey: if the conquering heroes, fresh off their victories, are seen to stand by you, it will only help matters. Maybe it won't win everyone over, but it may well stop the public snubbing. No one—well, no one except the Optimates, and we don't give a fig for their opinion—will want to be on the wrong side of the triumphing imperator."

"Or I'll drag him down with me."

"Don't be morose." Aula lifted her chin. "We are the *Vitelliae*. We are going to the camp of the Tenth Legion upon the Field of Mars to greet our brother and, yes, the victorious general who masterminded the Iberian campaign and who is likely to be elected consul later this year. Eyes will be upon us, and so we *will* look our best on this august occasion, and vicious busybodies can chuck their opinions on your appearance in the river, and throw themselves in right after."

Latona rolled her eyes, then yelped as Aula pinched color into her cheeks. "Are you *ever* going to stop doing that?"

"Not likely." She flicked Latona's mantle once on each side, arranging it over her shoulders, as though it would stay there while they trekked halfway across the city, then grabbed Latona's hand. "Come on!"

XXXVIII

Eight years since he had seen his family, and yet Vitellius was not sure he was ready to see them so *soon*.

The Tenth Legion made camp upon the Field of Mars, traditional for an army awaiting approval of a triumphal parade. Odd, how a legion *there* was perfectly appropriate, but one at the same distance anywhere else around the city would be perceived as a threat, as when Horatius Ocella used military might to force the Senate to declare him Dictator. Until discharged, this was the only proper place for military men in a civic setting: the domain of Mars, his patch amid the enormous cluster of influences that was Aven, a short walk from the Forum and yet a world apart from it.

'Perhaps it's better, that they come here to greet you.' His father's house would have more gawkers. Aulus Vitellius Caranus was a censor of Aven and a patrician of ancient blood besides; the homecoming of his son would be an event for the whole neighborhood to behold, never mind all of his clients and hangers-on.

That time would come, no doubt, but on the Field of Mars, Gaius Vitellius could forestall it. The soldiers might quirk a curious brow at the presence of a togate official and highborn ladies in their midst, but it would not be anything worth stopping their work for.

Gaius made sure that his armor was shining, his tunic spotless, his crest well-brushed. He tied on the focale his sister had given him, noticing only then how the color had begun to fade, and some of the embroidery was pulling loose. He had worn it and washed it so often, trusting in her magic to keep him safe, even redeemed it and somehow gotten it clean after using it to staunch Felix's blood.

Gratitude mixed with guilt. *'Here I stand, ready to be welcomed home by my loving family. But Mennenius's ashes lie in Toletum. His family has no one to enfold back to their bosom. And Felix comes back maimed, his future prospects uncertain. Why should the gods have smiled on me and not on them? Is it only because I'm lucky enough to have such a sister?'*

Gaius met his family near the border of the Field of Mars, not wanting to put them through the challenge of navigating the forest of tents. It made perfect sense to anyone used to a legionary camp, and perhaps his father would still have remembered how to find his way to a tribune's quarters, but better that they need not wander through the camp without him.

Trepidation fluttered in Gaius's chest when he saw them: his father, wearing the regalia of his office, his sandy hair gone much grayer than Gaius had imagined; his sisters, a tiny flock with vibrant plumage; the household attendants, a cordon around them, some men that Gaius recognized, if vaguely, others that were new faces. *'This is home, now. Or will be, as soon as you're discharged. These are your people, as they always have been. They love you. They will love you, even if they learn of your failures in Iberia. They love you, and life will go on.'*

Aulus strode forward with his arms wide. "Gaius," he said, clasping his son's head in his hands and kissing his forehead. "My blessing and that of the gods be upon you."

"Thank you, Father," Gaius said, and was surprised at how much he *meant* it. His father's words might have been part of an ordained ritual, but still Gaius had not reckoned on how much he needed to hear them, how powerful they would be after so long a separation.

Aulus's eyes went heavenward, his hands still cupping Gaius's face. "Let it be known that I will make sacrifice to Jupiter, Mars, and Bellona in thanks for your valorous conduct and your safe return."

"Only so valorous as I had to be," Gaius replied, embarrassed. He should have known they would want to fete him, to show off the son who returned home with laurels, who was being awarded the Crown of the Preserver, however little he felt he deserved the honor. He would have to steel himself to hearing words of praise.

Aula, never one to stand on formality, particularly when it came to matters of family, rushed forward next. "Gaius, darling!"

As she flung her arms around his neck, Gaius cracked a smile. "Good to see you, too, sis." Only a year apart in age, they had been close growing up, until their educations split in different directions, the martial and the marital.

Of all his sisters, he knew Aula best. Alhena was so much younger, and Latona spent more of her childhood in Juno's care than in her family's. But Aula had been his playfellow, his rival for their parents' attention, his stalwart supporter as he began his career. Her letters always sounded like her, too, effusive and energetic, so that everything about her now remained familiar.

Everything except the flaxen-haired girl trailing behind her. She hung back, evidently considering herself too old to hide behind her nursemaid's skirts, but not bold enough to approach this stranger-uncle unbidden.

Gaius knelt, setting his helmet down beside him. "Hello," he said, in a soft voice. "What have we here?" He tilted his head to one side, then the other. "A water nymph? Or some dryad? However did my father tempt one to the city? And why have you come to this strange place?"

The girl blinked owlishly at him a moment, then burst into giggles. "No!" she insisted. "I'm not a nymph or a dryad. I'm a girl!"

"A girl?" Gaius said, affecting incredulity. "Are you sure you're not an oceanid? Or one of the Hesperides?"

"No!" Lucia howled in laughter. "I'm a girl, and I'm your niece Lucia, and I am six and three-quarters years old!"

Gaius allowed himself to fall backwards on his rump, clapping a hand to his forehead. "It can't be! My niece Lucia?" She nodded heartily. "But I expected to find her a baby still!"

Lucia put her hands on her hips, chiding him, "I haven't been a baby for a *very* long time!"

"Lucia," Aula said in an instructive tone, "why don't you tell Uncle Gaius what you rehearsed for him?"

Gaius righted himself back to his knees, and Lucia clasped her hands in front of her. "'Just as when Jove the wretched earth afflicts with pouring rain and vicious hail, so this sudden storm with no less rage strikes the distracted Tyrians. Cold terror freezes their blood; their eyes rove wild; shouts and cries lift to the heavens and shake the stars. This, the strength of Aven, triumphant against dire odds, bright in dark hours, bold in the face of fear.'"

The lines were familiar. "That's well-spoken, Lucia," he said. "Truscanulus, I think?"

"She has quite a memory," Aula said with pride. "Can rattle off reams of the stuff already."

"I wanted to recite it for you because it's about great heroes," Lucia said. "And Mama told me you were very brave in Iberia."

Gaius reached out to stroke her hair, and she was comfortable enough now not to shy away from him. "I did my best, little one," he said. "As we all must."

Aula put out a hand for her daughter. "Come, Lucia, let him say hello to your aunts."

Obediently, she skittered to her mother's side as Gaius stood, but she cast over her shoulder, "When you come home, you can meet my kitten! Though she's not really a kitten anymore, she's gotten quite big."

"I shall look forward to it."

Latona came next. She looked different than he remembered. Older, of course, though she had been nearly a woman grown when he departed. Still, something in her had not just aged but deepened, though he could not immediately decide what made him think that. "Sweet sister," he said, embracing her. "You saved my life in Iberia, truly. Without your magic, I'd be..."

The thought caught in his throat, unexpectedly grim. *I'd be dead, several times over. I'd have been ensorcelled by Ekialde. Or I'd have gone mad when his demons swarmed Toletum. Or I'd have caught his plague.'* Sorrow for Mennenius, never far from his heart, throbbed beneath his breastbone.

Latona's expression softened, and she clasped a hand to his cheek. "We can speak of it later, if you wish." He had forgotten the sound of her voice, low and lilting, or perhaps it had not held so rich a timbre eight years ago. She spoke quietly, too, words not for the ears of any passers-by. "Or never, if you do not. But I love you, and I am only sorry I could not do more."

"What you did was wonder enough." He kissed her cheek, hugging her again, this time with more true feeling, not merely the custom of greeting. "Thank you."

She held him fiercely, and after a moment, the ache in his chest lifted, and the pinch at the back of his skull eased. Not gone, but lessened. He could straighten, coughing to dispel the awkwardness. Had there been magic in that? Well, he would not fault her for helping his emotions to smoother roads.

Then, Alhena, who was shuffling from one foot to another. "Alhena," he said, tentative, unsure how to approach this sister, nearly a stranger, someone he might not have recognized had she not been standing with the rest of his family.

But no—he could see their mother in her eyes, the same blue as his own. She was taller even than Aula now, but when he held out his arms to her, Alhena hesitated—then crumpled into them, burying her head in his shoulder.

"I missed you," she said. "Oh, Gaius, you don't know how worried I was, all the things I saw—"

"Saw?" he echoed. "Your goddess gave you warnings about me?"

She nodded, straightening. "But it was so hard to know what they meant."

"If it's any consolation, I was *there* and I didn't know what was going on half the time." A truth, and Alhena's lips quirked at it. "Come on," Gaius said to his whole family. "Let me show you all off to the general. He's shown me great favor."

"I am pleased to speak with any man who has good things to say about my son," Aulus said, beaming. "I confess, I am eager to hear what he intends to do next. Sempronius Tarren always does have so many plans."

"Yes," Gaius said, with a kernel of unease. "I've learned that over the past year."

As soon as Gaius turned down the corridor of tents, walking and talking alongside their father, Aula reached out and pressed Latona's hand, grinning wickedly. Her fingers went toward Latona's face as though to pinch color into them again, and Latona slapped her away, caught in a twist of conflicting emotions.

Something was wrong with Gaius, a deep trouble he dared not show on the outside. She felt it gnawing deep within him. Spirit knew a wounded soul, and Gaius's throbbed with unhealed hurt.

'Sempronius did warn me. Perhaps I can get Gaius to speak more of it later, once he's properly home.' She would not prod at such tenderness here, in the midst of tents and horses and the tumult of an army camp.

Despite this new-born concern for her brother, Latona could not lie to herself about the warm anticipation coiling in her chest, tighter and tenser with each step that took her closer to Sempronius. Heat below her sternum, deeper and heavier than a fluttering heart. *'It was near here that I saw him last,'* she remembered, *'not knowing if he would return.'*

Aula, as was her wont, kept up a merry chatter as their little parade crossed the Campus Martius, full of effusive praise for Gaius's efforts, assuring him of what a reputation he had won for himself and how certain his election into the Senate would be, asking questions about the camp and its business. Latona gave silent thanks, for the loquaciousness spared her from trying to concentrate through the buzzing haze of expectancy.

Her heart leapt, a hot jump almost like fear, when Gaius called out, "General Sempronius!" And indeed, there he was, speaking with two other men outside his command tent.

It took all Latona's effort not to fling herself at him. So long, her eyes had thirsted for this sight, and now she could drink her fill. He looked much as he had when he left. A deeper tan on his skin, a little sun-lightening in his sable hair, but still strong and hale. What caught her near-breathless were his dark eyes, lively with all the intensity of his nature, and the broad, genuine smile as he turned to greet them.

"General," Gaius said, stepping to the side, "I know you've seen them more recently than I, but I must beg a brother's privilege to formally present my father, the Censor Aulus Vitellius, and my sisters: Aula Prima, Vitellia Latona, and Vitellia Alhena." The formality was ostentatious—a show not only for the general, but for any onlookers, more of whom gathered here, near the commander, than had taken interest at the border of the camp.

"You may indeed!" Sempronius stepped forward to clasp arms with Aulus Vitellius. "Honored Censor, I have been more grateful than I can say for the assistance you have rendered me within the Senate."

"And I have been glad to do so," Aulus replied. "You were, it would seem, entirely correct in your assessment of the Iberian problem."

"Perhaps," Sempronius said. "It's a complex place. Our future relations there will require nuanced calculation."

"Mm." Aulus's face conveyed a great deal. "Ever the specialty of the Senate."

"Determined minds will find the answer, Censor, I'm sure of it." Sempronius turned, then, to the ladies. Quite correctly, he greeted Aula first, taking her hands and kissing the fingers of each. "My dear Lady Aula, what a pleasure to see you again, even lovelier than when I left."

"And you as silver-tongued as when you departed," she teased, grinning. "I'm glad that the sparkling society of Tarraco and Olissippo didn't lure you away from home permanently."

"No society could be said to sparkle, lacking your wit and delightful company."

"Sweet Juno, I'd forgotten how delightfully he flatters!" Aula crowed, even as she artfully put an arm around Alhena and swept her little sister forward. "Go on, General, see if you can turn Alhena's pretty little head."

But with Alhena, Sempronius adopted a more reserved air, bending over her hand but not actually touching his lips to her fingers. "Lady Alhena, if I may make so bold to comment, you're looking more elegant and grown-up than ever. How do your studies progress?"

"Yes," Alhena blurted. "I mean, they're—they're going well." Her cheeks were pink, as they still so often were under direct attention, but she managed a wobbling smile. "That book you gave me was quite interesting," she continued. "I've been writing my own commentaries on it. And on some other works. Um. All thaumaturgical texts, but they're... they're intriguing." Her blue eyes darted down. "We've been thinking a lot about how magic is taught and transmitted. Your sister may've told you. So I've written some thoughts down. I don't know how many people would find interest in them, though."

"I assure you I would," Sempronius said, solemn. "Your devotions do you credit, and a keen and agile mind ought always to be appreciated."

"Thank you, General," Alhena said. "I hope always to do my best in serving my gods and my family."

Aula squeezed her shoulder in encouragement—then neatly used the gesture to usher Alhena out of the way. "Latona's turn!" she chirped, and as she steered Alhena back into Gaius, she also redirected their father's attention. "Oh! That reminds me. Father, tell Gaius about that conversation you had with the Naeviae brothers at, oh, which dinner party was it? When you were discussing—"

At last, Latona found herself the object of Sempronius's attention. How wily Aula was, how deft a puppeteer, turning their menfolk's attention aside and leaving Latona for last, which granted her both a measure of privacy, as much as possible in the midst of camp, and a little more time.

A curve at the edge of Sempronius's mouth suggested that he had not missed the significance of Aula's maneuvers, either. Even the chaotic noise of the camp dulled when their eyes met, and a radiating heat spiraled out of Latona's heart, as though trying to envelop the two of them in a private world, if only for a moment.

"Vitellia Latona." The words were husky, and a flood of emotion poured off of him as he took her hands.

His lips burned hot against her skin, and she thought of the last time they had touched. His kiss had seared then, too, and her heart had been a-tremor with fear—of discovery, of her own boldness, of the possibility that he might not return from Iberia. Now she was alight with joy—but a joy that she had to keep trammeled, at least for the time being.

'Gods, why did I not divorce Herennius sooner? But in four months—in four months, I am free.' That thought gave her strength enough to stamp down, hard, on the impulse to curl a hand around his neck and kiss him with all her pent-up passion.

Instead, she inclined her head in a gesture of respect, trying to look as though he had not surreptitiously stroked the sensitive skin in the center of her palm. "Imperator." It came out much breathier than she intended. *'Oh sweet Venus, to have been able to greet him alone!'*

"I cannot thank you enough for your many kindnesses during the campaign," Sempronius said. He flicked his eyes down, nodding at his own neck—where he still wore the focale woven by her own hands. "With your faithful correspondence, I feel as though I hardly left the city. Duty may have called me away, but my heart—" His eyes were like embers, and Venus's Fire sang through Latona's blood, filling her with impossible longing. "—I assure you, always remained here."

A few steps away, Aula gave a fluttering laugh—too loud, Latona realized, a warning bell. Flushing hotly, she pulled her hand from Sempronius's grasp, though with reluctance, and his skin kept contact with hers as long as possible. *'He is as loath to let go of me as I of him,'* she realized with bubbling jubilation. "You were good to indulge me," she said, aware of how entirely she was failing to give her voice a matron's proper modulation. "I've been most privileged to enjoy a correspondence with our famous hero."

"Yes!" Aula said, whirling back to them and looping her arm through Latona's. She was grateful for Aula's steady presence at her side, if she could not wrap herself around Sempronius. "We've been fortunate to get such detailed information, since our brother is a poor correspondent," Aula added, crinkling her nose in Gaius's direction.

"I was under siege, Aula," Gaius said, though his aggrieved expression was colored with fondness. He knew he was being teased, and knew how to respond to Aula.

Latona was glad for it; it was more normal—or at least she presumed it was, for she had to admit, she had no idea what might be normal for a brother she hadn't seen in years. The sense of throbbing pain from within his animus ebbed a bit, though.

'Well. The gods and I both know what a balm Aula's relentless chatter can be.'

The moment Sempronius set eyes on Latona, approaching with her brother and sisters, the rest of the world dimmed, leaving only her, burning bright in her scarlet gown. Sixteen months in the field had not diminished his ardor in the slightest. Fortunately, many years of legal training allowed him to carry on a sensible conversation without giving away how consumed his mind had become with the prospect of slipping those golden brooches from her shoulders and enjoying once more the unobscured glory of her person.

'And she divorced her feckless pigeon of a husband,' he thought, with glee that was marred by the following thought: 'In October. She is not free again, properly, until Sextilis.'

Aventan custom required divorced women to remain unwed for ten months—long enough for any tardy pregnancies to reveal themselves. Any fool could observe Latona now and know that Herennius's seed performed no better in the last months of their marriage than at any time before, but nonetheless, Sempronius would have to be patient.

'No reason not to speak to her father in advance, however,' and indeed he intended to do so, once he could enter the city and make the request with all due solemnity. *'A little time, my bright-burning star,'* he thought in Latona's direction, *'and we may hope that no one would begrudge an affianced couple some measure of privacy.'*

Aloud, he announced, "Come, Censor! Allow me, if you will, to pass along the introductions. I think you may find it most edifying to meet the representatives of our new Iberian allies."

Lady Hanath made for a charming ambassador. *'What good fortune we have in her,'* Sempronius thought, watching as she made Aulus Vitellius laugh. *'Easy in any company, quick-witted and observant.'* Her Numidian birth, too, made her less a barbarian than the Iberians in Aventan eyes. She was cosmopolitan, had grown up in a thriving trading center, spoke half a dozen languages as though they were her mother-tongue. She would *impress.*

'And we need that. If we are to forge these bonds, ratify these treaties, build a strong coalition, then we must convince the Senate and the people alike that Iberia is not merely a backwater to be plundered, but a worthwhile investment of resources and a potential wellspring of new talent.'

Hanath had chosen well in the coterie that attended her across the water, too: young men and women of good sense, not easily overawed. They would not gawk at the massive city of Aven, but cast a contemplative eye upon it, dignified and stately.

As Gaius and Aulus chatted with Hanath, Sempronius allowed himself to fall back a bit, enough to re-engage Latona in conversation. Aula saw the maneuver and grinned, which encouraged Sempronius to believe he could count on her to provide as much of a curtain as was possible in their surroundings. "So much to say, and so little opportunity to say it." He kept his voice low, not a whisper, which would attract more attention than a rumble of conversation.

Latona kept her eyes ahead, watching her family, but her cheeks colored. "You'll be back in the city soon, once your triumph is approved. Then we can anticipate, I hope, many opportunities, conversational and otherwise."

Gods, this woman! *'The Fates must truly fear what we might be able to accomplish together, for every time we knock a barrier down, another arises be-*

tween us.' Simple enough to defeat, this one, the vagary of time, but no less a frustration.

Not wanting to jeopardize his composure, he allowed himself only political conversation. "I understand you've had an... eventful few months."

"We haven't been able to put the half of it in writing," Latona said. "Has Vibia—?"

"She came this morning and told me everything she couldn't put in letters." Sempronius's eyes drifted to the city wall, rising beyond the edges of the camp, separating the Field of Mars from the Capitoline Hill. "I'm itching to get back in there and help. Now that the army's back, and so many of our faction with it, we may mount a political defense to bolster your magical one." He rolled one shoulder, with a faint crack. "Among the many things I should like to detail to you are my *precise* feelings about the Augian Commission and its subversion."

Latona released a tight sigh. "Yes. I have many words of my own on that subject, though I fear the vocabulary required is unladylike in the extreme."

"Ladylike behavior," Sempronius said, unable to stop himself, "is often overrated."

Her eyes cut toward him, emerald darts piercing straight to his core. "How fortunate, then, that I have determined to behave as pleases me, rather than as propriety would command."

Her boldness delighted him; for so long, he had hoped she would reach for her full potential with both hands. How sorry he was to have missed the intermediate steps of this transformation, but how exultant he felt to have the chance to witness its full flourishing.

Then she gave another sigh, softer, more regretful. "Although, Vibia may have told you, that determination has had... social repercussions."

"She did," Sempronius said, "and I intend to mount a defense just as vigorously in that regard."

"I look forward to any and all demonstrations of vigor," she almost-whispered, and again Sempronius called upon long-practiced techniques to keep his face composed.

Hanath looked to be wrapping things up with Gaius and Aulus. Sempronius exhaled, irritated. "Not enough room or time for a proper conversation here."

"Or anything else," Latona murmured.

"Indeed." He bent as close as he dared. "I have to see you," he breathed, hardly more than a whisper. "As soon as I'm allowed within the city. I'll send a message."

Latona nodded tightly, though she twisted away from him, restoring the bounds of propriety in case her father or brother should turn around. "Do," she said. "Oh, please do."

XXXIX

"Fortuna pisses on us!"

Arrius Buteo was in full fervor, if not the most nuanced expression of his rhetorical capabilities, as he stormed around Lucretius Rabirus's office.

"Why couldn't the damn man have had the decency to *die* in Iberia?" Buteo squawked, waving a hand in the air. "Plenty of people did! Instead, we must suffer his arrogance, his self-satisfaction. He arrives home bedecked in glory, having vanquished a sorcerous opponent, with a princess in tow! What are the people to make of that?"

Rabirus knew full well what they would make of it: a consul, in seven months' time.

"And now he sits outside the gates, holding court on the Field of Mars!" Buteo continued. "Do you know who's been to see him?"

"Any number of tiresome Popularists, I imagine."

Buteo snorted. "Oh, the usual suspects. Quintus Terentius, no doubt angling for a consul's chair alongside this upstart's. The Domitiae and the Crispiniae. I understand Aulus Vitellius even dragged his whole coterie of daughters along!" That thought snagged Rabirus's attention. The middle Vitellian daughter deserved blame for so many of his own misfortunes—and she and Sempronius Tarren shared a connection beyond mere familial alliance, Rabirus was sure of it. That might be useful. "But not only them! Oh, no. Rufilius Albinicus has gone, and Strato's brothers, and Galerius Orator—"

"Galerius Orator has long been a friend of his, for all that he presents himself to be a moderate," Rabirus said. "His presence there is none so surprising."

"Is Licinius Cornicen's?" Buteo snarled. "That jackal, I've half a mind to cast him out of our company—"

"Don't be so hasty. He may well have been gathering useful information for us."

"*Four* ex-consuls from the decade before Ocella's reign have been to see him. *Three* former censors. He's hardly had time to pitch his tent, and he's hosted half the notables of the city!"

"We can still use this," Rabirus interjected. He'd had plenty of time to contemplate it. Sempronius Tarren's damned birds had winged their way home with news of his victory, and of the legions proclaiming him imperator, with annoying celerity. "Everything he does—every action he takes, every person he speaks with, every word out of his wretched mouth—we must cast in the light of a man seeking power beyond that which the laws of Aven provide."

"A Dictator?" Buteo asked. "We position him as a man seeking to do as Ocella did?" He wagged his head in consideration. "Perhaps. I could make something of that. Seeking to grasp the power that once expelled him from the city, yearning to visit the indignities he suffered upon his rivals... Yes, there's something to that."

"For a start. But I think we can build from there."

Buteo arched a bushy eyebrow. "Worse than a Dictator?"

"You've heard the proposals he's making, or thinking of making. Land redistribution, grain dole revisions, settling his veterans in strategic locations. The last man who made proposals on the scale that Sempronius Tarren desires—"

"Was Antonius Archus," Buteo finished. "Yes, I know my history." It had been a hundred years since Archus's time, but his story served as a warning to would-be demagogues.

"And how was Archus defeated?"

"They said he wanted to be king. Slandered him with the title of *rex*."

Buteo interlaced his fingers in front of his stomach and twirled his thumbs around each other: a sign that he was considering the matter with more than his usual reactionary fervor. "It's a dangerous accusation on both ends," he said. "It might snap back upon our own hands. However much we consider his actions—his damn near entire *being*—in defiance of the *mos maiorum*, he has yet to transgress in any legal capacity. He stoked that damned war in Iberia, yes, but it was legally declared."1

"He didn't take hold of the Fourth Legion legally," Rabirus retorted. "He was governor of Cantabria, and the Fourth was assigned to Baelonia."

"And we can only lean but so heavily on that argument without exposing *your* weak flank. Unless you can prove he bribed them to defect to his leadership—?"

A hopeful question, but Rabrius had to shake his head in denial. Nothing had lured the Fourth away except the promise of fortune and glory. Dull things to hope for, but legionaries were, as a rule, dull men, fit for their role as swordsmen and little else. They had seen, in Sempronius, a man offering to let them fight instead of staying safe behind city walls. Of course the meat-headed fools had leapt for the opportunity.

"My point is only this, Rabirus: If we accuse him of wanting to be a king, we had best be damned certain it looks like he really does."

An idea sprouted in Rabirus's mind. "We may yet have a way to block him from his goals, or at least to delay them. And perhaps... perhaps to lure him into such a blunder, one that would allow us to make that accusation with solid proof beneath our feet." How he responded would dictate what they could do from there. If he bent his head and obeyed the directions of the Senate, well, they would not have to deal with him for months yet, not in any official capacity. *'But if he refused to accept such a decision... if he balked, if he took any action to try to circumvent the will of the Senate... then we could indeed pin monarchist aspirations to him, and the people would believe them.'*

Buteo's brow furrowed. "What block? How do you mean?"

"We would need the strength of all our allies. No defections, no objectors."

Buteo flapped a hand. "We have control enough over our faction. If we say a vote is imperative, they will follow us. But what do you mean to do?"

A slow grin spread over Rabirus's face. "Stop the demagogue's ambitions dead in their halters."

"We have a problem."

Marcus Autronius had come to the Campus Martius. Not for the first time; he had visited his brother before the tents were even up. What had passed between them, Vitellius could not say, but Felix seemed cheered afterward, more his usual self than beset by the moodiness that had, not without cause, shadowed him of late.

Marcus had come to the Field every day since the legions arrived, in fact, though not only for his brother's sake. As one of Sempronius Tarren's most trusted go-betweens, he ferried messages in and out of the city that remained, for now, off-limits to the imperator.

Corvinus, too, was permitted access, since he was no military conscript; Vitellius understood that he had been sent not only to set Sempronius's own household back in order, but to arrange accommodations for Lady Hanath, the other Arevaci, and the captive Lusetani queen.

Today, Sempronius and his tribunes were more at ease than had ever been the case in Iberia, sitting in chairs around a low-burning fire that chased off a late-spring chill. Not that Sempronius could be said to be truly at leisure. He shuffled through letters while Vitellius and Felix played at dice.

When Marcus approached, however, he set the papers aside, plunked a stone on top of them so they wouldn't blow away, and rose to greet his friend.

"A problem?" Sempronius tilted his head. "Please don't think I'll blame the messenger, Marcus. What's amiss?"

Despite Sempronius's assurances, Marcus still winced, clearly uncomfortable with bearing bad news. "The Optimates are blocking approval of your triumph in the Curiate Assembly. They've got their pet tribune vetoing any discussion of it, any time anyone so much as mentions it. They'll keep you out here until after the elections before they'll approve it."

At least Marcus was not politician enough to obfuscate his meaning or dance around a tender issue. "They—What?" Felix spluttered. "How can they deny— He was declared imperator on the field of battle! If that doesn't warrant a triumph, I don't know what—"

Sempronius held up a hand to forestall further vociferous defense from Felix. "I presume their purpose is to prevent me from standing for consul, unless I give up the triumph."

"Exactly so."

Sempronius swore and kicked at the dirt. "Seven months, they would keep me waiting. I can't keep legions sitting on the city's doorstep for seven months. It begins to look like a threat."

"I believe it would utterly content Rabirus and Buteo if the people thought you meant it as such."

"Half the reason to force the impasse, I suspect." Felix's expression was a storm in full fury; Sempronius's was somehow more dangerous, clouds that had gathered, pregnant with potential, but not yet spitting their lightning.

"Much easier to denounce you as a power-mad would-be dictator when they can point out their windows to your army—"

"The *people's* army," Sempronius corrected.

"Unfortunately," Marcus ventured, "you already have a mark against you in that regard, at least in the eyes of some."

"Because of the Fourth."

"Great swinging balls of great Father Mars, he didn't *ask* them to defect!" Felix shouted.

"And he handed them right back over to Aufidius Strato when he showed up," Vitellius added. "Rabirus has no one but himself to blame for that."

"*I* know that," Marcus said, "and you all know that, and even many of the people of Aven agree with it, whether they have real knowledge or not. But it's the sort of thing the Optimates are using to establish a pattern of un-republican behavior."

"And I can't even be present to refute the accusations." Sempronius's hands clenched. "Then, of course, never mind my ego, there are the practical concerns. If I triumph, then afterwards we can place the legions on leave until the new praetors take charge of them and take them back to Vendelicia or set them to building roads through Iberia. If they sit here, they're owed wages. The people will consider it an extravagance, a pointless waste of treasury funds. The legions, meantime, will think themselves ill-used for not getting their bonus paid out. Cranky legionaries are dangerous legionaries."

As ever, Vitellius stood in awe and alarm at the speed with which Sempronius's mind worked. Rabirus and Buteo had come up with a way to nettle Sempronius no matter what he did, jeopardizing his standing with the very groups of people whose support he most counted on: the plebs and the army.

"This is why I came straight from the Curia to warn you," Marcus said.

Sempronius paused his pacing, giving Marcus a solemn look. "You're a good friend. Better than I deserve, I'm sure, and I haven't done enough to repay your many kindnesses."

"You brought that stupid ass back alive," Marcus said, nodding at his brother.

"If not in one piece." Felix waved his partial limb. "But that's on my own conscience and nothing to Sempronius's detriment, I assure you."

"And perhaps a little wiser than when he left," Marcus went on, a peculiar hardness in his voice, one that made Vitellius wonder what had passed between the brothers on other occasions. "That counts for quite a lot."

"All the same." Sempronius's fingers tore through his hair, and a gutteral growl escaped him before he mastered himself. "Fine." The first time he said it, it was almost too low to hear. Then he straightened his spine, lifted his chin, and repeated, "Fine. Then I will waive my right to a triumph."

All of the onlookers stared, mute with shock, for a moment. Vitellius was only sure he'd heard right because the others were mirroring his astonishment. A triumph was the goal of every Aventan leader, the pinnacle of military success. A chance to be not just honored, but a *god* for a day, cast in Jupiter's own likeness, treated to every ceremony that the city could offer. It fixed a man's deeds in the minds of every citizen, emblazoned for future generations to remember. To have the opportunity and give it up was unthinkable.

"You—" Felix's head shook in bewilderment. "You would abandon the chance to triumph? You would hand the Optimates that victory over you?"

"A small enough victory, to secure a far greater one for myself. I was still proclaimed imperator, and I can use the prestige of that," Sempronius pointed out. "The Senate can't take away what they did not bestow. I'm still entitled to certain honors. And I'd rather be a consul than a triumphator. I must be able to campaign, and I cannot allow the Optimates to cast me as a villain lurking on the doorstep. If they are determined to block me in this fashion, then, fine. My ego, I daresay, can take the blow."

"What about—" Vitellius cleared his throat. "Forgive me, sir. I don't mean to—"

"No, speak," Sempronius said.

"The troops may feel themselves jilted of honor." A triumphal parade was a chance for the legionaries to show off, too. "And you said you wanted to honor the Iberians, as well."

"I can fix that," Sempronius said. "One of this year's aediles owes me a favor. I'll take over responsibility for one of the days of the Ludi Tyrenni at the end of the month."

"Fitting," Felix said. The Ludi Tyrenni had first been instituted after another military victory, when the Tyrians had attempted to invade Truscum.

"We'll have the legionaries march in a procession, whichever ones are on leave in the city, anyway. They'll have to go unarmed, but we can still make a good enough show with banners and the spoils of war. It's a bit long to wait, but the Iberians intended to stay in the city until late summer, and I doubt anyone will be marching the legions back to Liguria immediately."

"We can always delay the question of what to do with them," Marcus offered. "Back to Iberia to build roads, or back to Vendelicia to patrol the borders. In either case, there's no immediate need to serve." Marcus waved his hands as though weighing matters on a scale. "All to one place? Or the other? Or split them? One legion to each frontier? But which new praetors should govern them?"

Sempronius made a short gesture of approval with a closed fist. "Yes, that's excellent. Keep the Senate from settling on a recommendation for the Centuriate Assembly for a few weeks, so they can get their glory before they head back out. I'll ask Lady Hanath what she thinks would be right for her people—I'd love to show off their cavalry skills in some way. Perhaps as part of the *venatio*, or else in compliment to the races."

"A triumph without a triumph," Felix said, grinning. "I like it."

"I... worry," Vitellius said. "The Optimates will—"

"Not be pleased, but when are they ever?" Sempronius waved a hand. "I can also make a valid argument that I owe the people this from my own prematurely terminated aedileship." It took Vitellius a moment to remember; Sempronius had barely started his own year as aedile when the Dictator Ocella had driven him from the city. A debt long-forgotten by most citizens, no doubt, but an arguable pretense. "This victory was not mine alone. The legions deserve their accolades—especially those of you who spent so long mewed up in Toletum. And I do want Aven to see our Iberian allies and cheer them, to begin thinking of them as friends, not barbarians."

"The dead, too," Vitellius said, before he could catch the words. "There—there should be something to honor the dead."

Those dark eyes landed on Vitellius, quietly assessing, and Sempronius's mounting energy stilled like a waterfall caught in a sudden freeze. "You may be sure of it. These men faced what no legion before them ever has. They deserve as much honor as the living." Then, just as swiftly, the freeze snapped, and Sempronius was back in the flow of his plans. "There will be a monument at my Temple to Victoria, but that's not enough. Something in the midst of the Circus Maximus, something large enough to command attention—Well, I'll figure that out. Marcus, today, you will return within the city and announce my intention to forfeit my triumph. Make it formal tomorrow when the Senate meets. Today, I will give discharge notices to the higher officers and instructions to the centurions. Tonight, I will re-enter the city, without pomp. Tomorrow, I will speak from the Rostra." He fixed each of them in turn with a hard look. "Not a word of my other plans, about the Ludi, agreed?"

An order, not a question, though Sempronius would have no authority over them once he stepped back within the walls of Aven. *'Well, the Autroniae are his clients, I suppose.'* Over Vitellius, he would have no official power—but Vitellius nodded his agreement anyway. However nervous the man's ambitions and machinations made him, Sempronius was still one of the most prominent Popularists.

For Vitellius, the decision was a welcome one: the sooner Sempronius released his officers, the sooner Vitellius could lay off his armor once and for all.

The following day, Aulus Vitellius led his family and a bevy of clients down the Palatine Hill to the Forum, that they might all hear the speech.

It was a pointed statement of support and solidarity among the Popularists. The censorial toga always gathered a bit of attention, but Aulus rarely trooped forth with so many of his clients in tow. Where their gaggle went, others followed, if only to see what the fuss was about.

Evidently Gaius had not been alone in disseminating the information. The Forum was even more crowded than usual, and most of that crowd was milling about the Rostra.

Aula craned her neck about, glad that Aulus had decided this outing did *not* require her daughter's presence. Observing the crowd was much harder with a six-year-old in tow.

Yes, there were the Terentiae: Quintus and his sons, at least, no sign of Terentilla. There, Gnaeus and Marcus Autronius, with their wives. And there, the Domitiae, no doubt eager to welcome their own sons back home. Rufilius Albinicus, too, with General Strato's brothers.

'A strong show of military support for Sempronius.' Aula wondered how much of this had been Sempronius's own arrangement, how many missives he might have been distributing across the city in recent days. 'If he's done this properly, as soon as he's done speaking, each and every one of these allies will turn to their own portion of the crowd and start whipping up support.'

Aula became aware of her mantle fluttering, bapping against her arm as though buffeted by the breeze—but the air in the Forum was still. The culprit was not Boreus or Zephyr or any other god of the winds, but Latona. Unlike Aula, her attention was fixed firmly on the Rostra. Her left leg was bouncing, though, and her fingers drummed endlessly against her thigh.

"You are vibrating like a plucked lute-string, Latona," Aula said, poking her sister in the arm. "Do stand further off. It's distracting."

Latona barely seemed to hear her, but with a heaving sigh, Alhena nudged her aside to switch places. "She's been like this all morning, didn't you notice?" Alhena's voice was low enough not to attract the attention of their father, who was standing on Aula's other side, speaking with one of his clients. "Ever since the note from Gaius came. She's been in a tizzy."

Aula snorted. "Hadn't expected to find *him* back within the walls so soon, I expect." Before Aula could opine further, the tenor of the crowd changed off to their left. She went up on her tiptoes, but Alhena's hand came down on her shoulder.

"I'm taller," Alhena said. "If you *don't* peer up, I can see over you."

"Well!" Aula said. "Tell me what's—"

"He's arriving, of course. Gods, everyone's trying to shake his hand. It'll take him ages to get to the podium at this rate."

It did take quite some time, but it afforded Aula the opportunity to judge the crowd. Eager, curious, almost ravenous for their new-minted hero. An imperator was always a popular figure; whatever truth lay behind the exaggerated stories that reached Aven's ears, that distinction bolstered the legend. Technically, in forfeiting his right to a triumph, he had also yielded the title and its attendant rights—but the people called it out to him nonetheless.

When finally Sempronius Tarren ascended the Rostra and became visible to the whole assembly, a roar of cheers echoed across the Forum. He bore it mildly, raising a hand in recognition, but impassive in his expression. *'Dignified. He does not want to give the impression that he enjoys the acclaim.'*

He wore his senatorial toga, nothing more elaborate. Aula had wondered if he meant to display himself in the toga candida, signifying his intent to stand for consul—but no, it would have been tacky to do so this early in the year. Sempronius was bold, even impertinent, but never inept.

When he adopted the traditional pose of oratory, the crowd hushed. They had come, after all, to hear what he would say. Sempronius let the quiet hang in the air a moment longer than necessary, forcing them all to feel the weight of it, before he spoke.

"Good people of Aven! I return with joyful news from our provinces in Iberia." What followed then was an accounting of the legions' victories. Much of this was already known, thanks to his diligent correspondence, but Sempronius told it with particular vigor, and the audience seemed to lean forward as one, drinking in his words.

Aula's own family was not excluded from that captivation. *'Gods,'* Aula thought, looking at Latona's parted lips and dramatically heaving bosom, *'the good General had best intend to make an honest woman out of her with all haste. This is almost embarrassing to behold.'*

Sweet, though. And if any woman deserved to be foolishly captivated by love for a man, and to have that copious devotion returned in equal measure, it was Latona, after the farce of a marriage she'd endured.

Aula suspected that, given liberty and security enough, she herself could manage quite well finding pleasure outside consecrated nuptial bonds. A degree of independence and license suited her. Latona, though, would best thrive with a partner. *'She's as much Juno's as Venus's.'*

When the recitation of the legions' deeds in Iberia—always the legions' deeds, never his own, all credit to the fighting men and their allies—was completed, Sempronius paused and changed the rotation of his hand, his palm looking inward now, a gesture of humility. "Good citizens, I know many of you may be wondering—why, with these victories, with these honors, do I not march in triumph? Why do I appear before you in the toga virilis of a senator, not the toga picta of a triumphator? Why are these brave legionaries not displaying themselves before you, with the spoils of their victories?

"This, I answer: It meant more to me to return among you, to be with the people of Aven, for whom I have labored, than it did to ride in a chariot, paint my face, and play at the role of Jupiter Optimus Maximus for a day. Nor did I wish to sit on the Field of Mars in leisure for months, awaiting the Senate's pleasure, when I could be back inside the Curia, working for your gain. Why should I sit idle, when there is so much to be done? Why should I rest on my laurels, when so many cannot rest their toils at all? Why should I enjoy honors, when it is the people of Aven who deserve recognition for their deeds and their devotions?"

"The Optimates will brand it false humility," Aulus said sideways to Aula, "and I daresay his intent is not to be humble in the slightest—but he really would prefer to work than to rest idle."

"And the role of triumphator," Aula concluded, "means far less to him than that of consul." Aulus hmmed his agreement as the speech continued.

"And so, I have declined the honors that might have been pressed upon me, in order that I could walk among you again, that I could hear your concerns and seek to remedy them. But think not, good people of Aven, that I mean to cheat the legions of their due accolades!" Sempronius went on, turning his palm outward again. "I introduce my good friend, Ulpius Turro, to explain all."

Ulpius Turro was not the orator Sempronius was, nor so fine to look upon, and a murmur in the crowd attended his words. Aula was close enough to the Rostra, though, not to lose the thread: Ulpius, one of the aediles in charge of the upcoming Ludi Tyrenni, had been so impressed by Sempronius's piety and sense of obligation to the city that he had been moved—divinely inspired, perhaps, although Ulpius's rhetoric was unfirm on that point, which Aula considered a missed opportunity—to implore

Sempronius Tarren to take responsibility for the first day of the games. Sempronius had agreed, and the Tenth Legion would receive its due honors as part of the festivities.

"What bribe did that take, I wonder?" Aula murmured to her father.

"Cheaper than a triumph," Aulus replied, "and neatly arranged." He huffed slightly. "Serves Buteo and Rabirus right for blocking the vote on the triumph. He may not get the official honors, but he'll reap the rewards of the populace's attention, for certain." Aulus sighed, shaking his head with a touch of dismay. "Wait till the Optimates catch wind of this, though. They'll howl like Cerberus, claiming he's once again circumventing the *mos maiorum*. Too clever for his own good, that man."

Aula glanced aside, past Alhena's curiously furrowed brow to where Latona stood, hand pressed to her chest, with eyes for nothing but her still-distant paramour, and wondered what other repercussions Sempronius's temerity might have.

Neitin was not sure what she had expected.

The camp outside the city limits had been much like every other camp along the way, except that its outskirts were surrounded by buildings. If she did not look too high, she could ignore those and see only the familiar red and brown canvas tents, the bronze standards and flapping flags. Just as they had been in Iberia, and not so different from the Lusetani war camps in which she had spent the past few years, though cast in different colors and a still-foreign tongue.

Beyond, though...

Beyond the limits of the camp stood the City of Aven, almost grotesque in its enormity. Its walls stretched for miles and yet could not encompass it. Buildings spilled forth from its sides like entrails from the stomach of a slaughtered deer, splattering themselves around the countryside.

Neitin had known the city would be large, larger than anything she had seen, but her imagination had not been capable of envisioning the sheer magnitude. Aven dwarfed Olissippo, heretofore the largest city of her acquaintance. Olissippo could have fit on *one* of Aven's famous hills, which rose above the barrier of the walls, all their gleaming roofs and rickety constructs competing for dominance on the skyline.

Thus far, Neitin had not been taken within those walls, not even after the camp broke up, at least in part. She did not understand the particulars. Some of the men were placed on leave and allowed in the city; others were being sent away; some few would remain on the field. But she and her son, it seemed, were destined for another place.

They traveled in the company of the Numidian woman and her Arevaci entourage, across the river and southward. "It is called the Janiculum Hill," Hanath explained to her, a gesture of some small kindness. "Foreigners are not permitted to dwell within the city limits. Not officially, at least. We may be guests, we may travel within during the day, but our abodes must be outside the walls."

"What a barbarous custom."

Neitin bounced Matigentis, stroking his hair. He, at least, was untroubled, no matter how often they moved. He had even taken the sea voyage in stride, and with far less illness than his mother. Here, every sight captivated him: so many colors, so many people, so many noises.

"Enh," Hanath said, shrugging her shoulders. "It is part idiocy and part sense, I think. You will see how crowded that city is soon enough. They have little room as it is. But it is also pigheadedness, a rule set by men who fear everything beyond the ends of their own noses." She huffed. "Well. Much may change, under the right guidance." Hanath flapped a hand. "Never you mind, queen-that-was. You will be more comfortable on the Janiculum, I am sure. The houses are bigger here, and the air fresher."

Where Hanath and the Arevaci were staying, Neitin had no idea; nearby, she presumed, but she and her son were handed into the custody of a togate man and his plump-cheeked wife, neither of whom spoke a word of Tyrian, let alone any Iberian tongue. They seemed welcoming and gentle, but Neitin remained wary. They were, however bright their smiles, her jailers. This, she understood.

The house *was* large—more than twice the size of even her father's mud-bricked home on the Tagus River had been, let alone the huts of Ekialde's village. Neitin was given two rooms of her own, with plush beds and sumptuous wall-hangings. There were even windows, though they were high up and—if escape had been a notion—far too thin for a woman with her hips and bosom to squeeze through.

But escape was not a notion. Neitin had put herself into Aven's hands and would have to bear the consequences.

Two men stood outside her rooms at all times. They looked innocuous enough, and when she opened the door, they did not threaten, but spoke to her in what she took for a questioning tone. If she patted her stomach, they brought more food. If she made a motion like bringing a cup to her lips, they brought more water or wine. Once a day, they brought a deep basin of water in which she could wash herself and Matigentis.

Fresh linens for the bed, clean tunics sewn in the Aventan style, combs for her hair, even perfumes and toys for her child—anything she could think to want was presented her. But never was the door left unattended, and never was she permitted beyond it without escort, even to walk in the walled garden.

"Is this how we live, now?" she asked her son, who was supremely occupied in the possible movements of a little toy soldier he had been given. An *Aventan* soldier, Neitin noted. The wooden doll had fully articulated joints and could be positioned in any number of ways, but his body was painted legionary red, and upon his carved head sat a little horsehair crest. "For how long do we go on like this? Will they forget us? Or sell us? Or make some other use of us?"

Mati, busily stomping his soldier through the landscape of a potted plant, made no reply.

XL

The day after Sempronius's bold return to the city, while much of Aven still reeled from his declination of a triumph, Latona went to the Domus Magicae in mid-afternoon.

All had been arranged, mostly by Aula and Merula. The lovers agreed to arrive separately, so no one on the street would be likely to see them both, and this day, the door would remain closed and unanswered. Latona arrived first, by design. With Sempronius besieged with clients and allies, it made sense for Latona to be the one who spent more of the day in seclusion.

Latona combed her hair until it shone like sunlight, then spent more time than she would have cared to admit having Merula arrange and re-arrange the ringlets. Finally, Merula's patience wore out. "Is only going to be coming down as soon as the general arrives, I think?" she snapped. "What point is there in putting all the pins in to begin with?"

A valid point.

Then, cosmetics, perfume, changing from the gown she'd worn in the street into something more alluring, putting on jewelry, and fussing over all the adornments a second and third time. As the appointed hour drew near, Merula took herself to the kitchen to oversee the light meal that Aula's rented girl was preparing for later in the evening. *'Much later, with any luck.'* Relief at being dismissed was plain on Merula's guileless face.

Latona spent the next half hour moving from couch to couch, trying to arrange herself with artful elegance, twitching her skirts into different draping patterns, wondering if her figure showed to better advantage seated or reclining, or perhaps lounging over a rolled pillow...

'Idiot,' she chastised herself, falling back into a heap of cushions in a decidedly inelegant posture. *'You're acting like a girl with greensickness. He*

knows what you look like. He's intimately acquainted with the particulars. And he comes here a-purpose. It isn't as though you need to stage an elaborate seduction like some Parthian princess in a bad play.'

Sempronius did not knock. He arrived close to sunset, slipped through the bright red door, and latched it behind him. Only when it was secure did he pull the hood of his cloak down and turn to find Latona in the atrium.

For a heartbeat, he could have sworn that Venus herself had descended Olympus. Lamps and bright-burning braziers glowed all around Latona, who reclined on a plush couch, bathing her in golden light. So often in the wilds of Iberia, he had envisioned her, but the sight of her now, absolutely radiant and draped in a fuchsia linen so fine it hugged her every curve, put his imagination utterly to shame.

The tableau lasted only a moment. As soon as their eyes met, she came to her feet, clasping her hands in front of her. "Dearest—" she began, but before she said another word, he crossed to her, and they crashed together like a wave upon the shore. Sempronius took her face in his hands and kissed her with the pent-up passion of so many long months; Latona melted into him, twining her arms about his neck. She smelled of cinnamon and myrrh, heady and entrancing, and he breathed her in like nothing else could assure him of life and vitality.

One of his hands fell to her hip while the other clasped the back of her head, pressing her to him. As often as he thought of her, he had not realized the overwhelming power of this *need* to feel her close, to assure himself that she was real and truly here, in his arms, no dream and no vision, but the only woman with a claim on his heart and very soul.

At length, Latona broke away from him, drawing in a panting breath. "What a beast I am," Latona purred, "pouncing on you in the vestibule before you've gotten your cloak off."

His hand curled under her chin. "I like it when you pounce," he said, remembering the first time she had kissed him, soot-covered and standing an alley not far from the scene of the Aventine fires.

A low, lustful noise escaped her, and her fingers clenched at the fabric of his tunic. "Then come into the lioness's lair," she teased, stepping back to lead him farther into the house.

Only then did Sempronius take notice of his surroundings. A small domus, as Latona had told him, as compared to the Vitellian home on the Palatine. The atrium was small, with a pair of sleeping chambers on either side—and most of those, it seemed, had been given over as practical spaces for magical study, filled with various tools of thaumaturgical craft. Beyond, Sempronius glimpsed a small garden, a modest triclinium, and a tablinum with ample proof of all the work of the ladies' collegium: a rack of scrolls, a pile of slates, and a number of votives representing the elements.

Pride surged through him, only enhancing the lust that had him in its grip. Latona and Vibia and the others had *started* something here, something with real potential to shape Aven's future. He wanted to know everything, every detail of their work, every plan for the future, how he could help.

At the present moment, however, curiosity did not prevail over decidedly less cerebral concerns. His whole body ached with wanting her, a sensation as welcome as it was unusual. "So... No one else at home?"

"Merula's downstairs with the girl that Aula rented to fix some supper for us." Her eyes flicked up provocatively. "Assuming you intend to stay that long?"

With a growl, Sempronius caught her tightly about the waist. "I have no intention of going anywhere for the next twelve hours, at least."

He scooped her up and made for the nearest sleeping chamber that actually had a bed, rather than an assortment of magical paraphernalia. Latona laughed, hearty and free, a sound that shot joy through Sempronius's blood and tightened the need coiling at his core.

This would be different from the last time. No quick union and hasty parting, with the fear of discovery looming over them. They had privacy and an entire night to spend together—to spend *on* each other. And Sempronius intended to make the most of every moment.

Much later, Latona called down to the kitchen for dinner, which Merula brought up with a decidedly insouciant expression. She looked at the excited flush on Latona's cheeks and rolled her eyes. "Oh, do hush," Latona said as she took the platter from Merula's hands.

"Am not saying anything, Domina."

"Your face is eloquent."

Merula snorted. "Is not my place to be judging. Better this than you mooning after him from a thousand miles away." Her expression softened slightly—only slightly, approaching though not reaching a smile. "And he is being a better man than your husband, at least."

That being as fine an assessment as she was likely to get, Latona kissed Merula's cheek and went back to her lover in the triclinium.

The food was succulent, but Latona found she had little appetite. Food had such *weight*, and she wanted nothing to bring her back down to earth. So they talked, more than they ate, tucked up into each other on the couch.

Sempronius told her of the beauty of Olissippo and the Endless Ocean; Latona shared nugatory tidbits of gossip, those things not been worth setting to paper during his campaign.

She knew he would still want to know more of the Discordians and the *lemures,* just as she was ravenously curious about the *akdraugi,* but those themes were too dark to be allowed to puncture their glimmering bliss. Nor did they speak of political concerns: of the Optimates' maneuvers and Sempronius's countermeasure, of his plans for alliance with Iberia, of the settling of his veterans, land bills, or citizenship extensions. Time enough for all of that later.

A ripple in his emotions unsettled the placid relaxation. Anticipation, even apprehension, a touch of nerves. Strange sensations, from a man who was always so sure, so bold.

"May I venture a curiosity?" he asked.

"Hm?"

He was looking down at his wine cup, swirling the liquid about the bottom of the cut-glass bowl. He lifted his eyes before asking, however; Sempronius Tarren was not a man to shy away from his interrogatives. "Why did you leave your husband?"

Latona blinked a few times. That was not a question she had expected, and it took her a moment to find her tongue.

"I'm very glad for the decision," Sempronius added. A wry smile touched his face. "And not only for selfish reasons. I am glad for *you*. It was an indignity, that your glory should be dimmed by an unworthy partner. But you knew that long ago. You admitted as much before I left for Iberia. So what final peppercorn broke the mule's back?"

She had told no one except her father and sisters. Too humiliating, too great a vulnerability. In this moment, though, she realized that if she trusted anyone else in the world, anyone beyond her own blood, it was Sempronius Tarren.

Her only concern was how he might react. He had such fierceness in him, such protective instincts—and his clients included men like Vatinius Obir and his collegium, who, fine gentlemen though they were, did not scruple from applying irrevocable solutions to problems.

'Then again, if Herennius's body turned up in the Tiber River one day… well, I can't say with honesty that I'd much mourn.'

Sempronius's eyes were still on her, prompting. With a shaky breath, she answered, "He struck me."

The change in him was imperceptible on the surface, but the chill rushed over Latona's magical senses like a flash flood. "He dared?"

"He dared. Not out of nowhere. We were having the worst row of our marriage." Her lips quirked up a bit. "It started with my refusal to share my correspondence." Sempronius lifted an eyebrow speakingly, but did not otherwise leaven his countenance, cold and still. "I think he startled himself, in doing it," Latona went on. "And I did very nearly set him on fire in response."

Sempronius's expression still did not lighten. "Incineration," he said, with slow deliberation, "would have been too kind."

"Yes, well, I didn't fancy having to explain that to the Augian Commission, even before we found out about their corruption. And I'm not sure how my father would have felt about having a murderess for a daughter."

Sempronius rotated a shoulder, adjusting his lay on the couch, and in doing so shook off the iciness he felt. A sense of Shadow still hung over Latona, though, the weight of words yet unsaid, secrets unspilled. He pressed a kiss to her temple, leaving room for her to continue.

"I should have divorced him ages ago, but I was afraid. Afraid of what people would say. And now..." She laughed mirthlessly. "Now I have cast myself into the flames of public shame anyway."

"Not shame, I think. Not from what Vibia's said." He touched her jaw-line softly. "But tell me."

So she did. A long tale, sketching the beginnings of their collegium, the unexpected cessation of Discordian activity, Alhena's vision at the Luper-calia and the path of inquiry it set them on, then the responses to that in-quiry: Aemilia, expected; the Crispiniae, Rufilius Albinicus, Marcia, and others, surprising.

"That doesn't sound like Marcia at all," Sempronius said, concerned. "She does not always approve of me, I know, but in the past, her words of warning came from a sensible place. Something else must be going on..."

"What plagues me most, Sempronius," Latona said, voice weak, "is fearing they are right. Not about everything. Something has to be done about the Discordians and the Augians, obviously. But the fear that... that I am not, in truth, the one to do it. That it's far too large a problem for me to tackle, too much risk, too little hope of achieving the reforms I desire. That it is only arrogance and hubris making me claim the duty."

"No, beloved." His thumb stroked her cheek. "The gods have made a demand of you. and supplied you with the means to do their will. There is no hubris in that."

So he told himself, again and again. So he believed.

"I have tried to hold onto what I feel when I'm doing something *right*, something for Aven," she said. "It's... it feels like summoning my Spirit mag-ic, but instead of swelling when I call, it comes of its own volition." Her face lightened with the memory. "I taste cinnamon, and I see as through a gold-en veil, and I know Juno is with me."

"No doubt she is." His hand grazed her shoulder, lifting a lock of gold-en hair and stroking it between thumb and finger. "And I do not think she will abandon you. This trial will end, and you will shine."

Latona curled against him, her head tucking against his chest. "I hope you are right."

Would it help her, to know his own story? To know how, all his life, he had defied the customs of man in favor of the mandate of the gods?

Perhaps. But he did not think it would help in this moment. She needed bolstering now, not to have his burdens added to her own. There would be time—so much time, if the gods were good—in which to unravel his secrets and place them safely in her keeping.

So he held her, warm and close, and pressed a kiss to her hair. "I think I may drop by your father's tomorrow. In the afternoon, once he's finished with his clients. Or perhaps I'll try to catch him in the Forum."

Latona blinked, twisting to look up at him. "Tomorrow?"

"I know we can't wed until ten months have passed since your divorce, but I want all Aven to know that you and I stand together. What you have done, setting yourself against forces that seek to tear this city apart—I admire you for it, so fiercely. We could be a force like Aven has rarely seen, in all its long history, and form such a union as would set this city to quaking. I defy the Optimates, the Discordians, or Olympus itself to stop us."

She did stop him, then, with a kiss. "Blasphemy," she chided when they parted. "Don't tempt the Fates."

His hand sank into her hair. "I would for you," he said. "For you—and for Aven."

She laughed, even as he rolled her to her back and began exploring her throat with his lips.

XLI

The following afternoon, when Aulus returned from the Forum, he wasted no time in summoning his middle daughter to his office. His expression was not exactly grim, but tired and serious, like a slab of weathered granite. *'Why is it,'* Latona thought, *'every time I'm in this office, I feel like my only choice is to chip some piece of him away?'*

Aulus drew a deep breath and released it as a sigh. "Well, my girl," he said, "I had an interesting conversation in the Forum today. One that surprised me, I must confess, though I have been given reason to believe it may not come as a shock to you."

Latona did her best to affect a demure expression. "If you mean to say you've had an offer for me, then no. It would not be a shock." Aulus stared at her for so long that she felt compelled to offer some further explanation. "We've been good friends for some time. We corresponded while he was in Iberia, and—"

"I do not wonder at how it came about. I could see an affinity between you before he left. It's only..." Aulus rubbed at his forehead and looked up at the ceiling. "Three daughters at home. People ask why, and I always have an answer. Waiting for the right offers. For the war to be over. For a time when I'm less busy with censorial work. But the truth is, Latona, I am trying not to repeat my error." Weariness wrote itself in the lines of his face. "With Herennius, I... I did as I thought right, in the beginning. I will always maintain that. At first, it seemed suitable."

"At first," Latona said, offering what mitigation she could, "it was."

"But you became unhappy. That much was clear. Even before you divorced him, I was questioning my judgment. It's why I held off finding new matches for your sisters. I don't want any of you girls in that position again." His eyes had tears in them, and Latona's magic shivered with the weight of emotion sloughing free. "I love you all, more dearly than I can express. I want you safe *and* happy, and I have not known how to arrange both."

Latona could not hold herself aloof. She left her seat and knelt next to her father's chair, reaching up for his hands. "We are none of us safe, Father. The gods throw stones in our paths all the time. But I would be happy with him, because I am assured of his admiration and respect."

"I do want to see you with a man who respects you," Aulus said. "And I admit, he may well be an answer to the social difficulties you've been encountering." He shook his head, and for a moment Latona worried that his old dismay at her goals was going to rear up again—but Aula had done her work on him well. "I don't know why some of our friends are behaving so foolishly about it. Magical education *ought* to be a matter of public concern, and I see no danger in saying so." He waved a hand. "But I digress. The point is, with Sempronius returned from Iberia as Aven's rising star, a beloved imperator... his reputation may shield yours, and his voice could lend weight to a Popularist call for attention to the matter."

"I agree," she said, annoying though it was that her reputation required a masculine shield once again. "And he will be glad to stand with us. Vibia and I have kept him apprised of our work."

"But, my dear, while he might offer protection, he is also dangerous." He held up a hand to forestall argument. "I don't mean that he's vicious or malevolent. I do not believe he would ever intend any harm towards you. But harm follows him." He reached out and touched her hair lightly. "He is a man with noble intentions; I do not doubt that. He has accomplished a great deal, and his goals for the city are altruistic—if rather showy. But he is also a man who attracts contention and strife."

"Should I spurn him because his rivals in the Senate resent his success? Because those noble goals of his are threatening to the men who hoard their power like jealous magpies?" She attempted a smile. "If women declined to marry men whose political ambitions might attract trouble, I think Aven would quite soon face a declining population."

"He courts the Optimates' disfavor, Latona. This trick he's pulling with the games, taking the triumph they wouldn't grant, that's only the start. You've never seen him in the Senate—he's the crow tweaking the wolf's tail, daring sharp jaws to snap around him." He flexed his right hand, then curled it around the armrest of his chair. "The Optimates don't just hate him, Latona. They want him dead."

"I do remember."

They had both been there, after all, when an envenomed arrow found its way into Sempronius's shoulder and Latona purged the poison with Fire magic. Aulus would not want to hear that Latona would prefer to be there when Sempronius faced such threats, there to assist him, protect him, save him if need be. So she took another angle.

"He has such vision." Her voice rang with earnestness, with the strength of her belief in the man she intended to marry. "Such brilliance. Such *hope*. He's kept that, through all the darkness of the past years. He still believes his dreams for Aven are achievable—and he makes me believe it, too. He's going to do great things, Father, and I want to be with him as he does."

Aulus leaned forward, cupping her cheek with his hand. "This is what I have feared. What I tried to avoid. You will be a target, my dear. Men who want to influence Sempronius, for good or ill, will go through you. Not all of them will be polite, and some may become violent."

Those words might have scared concession into her, once. She had spent so many years ducking her head, trying not to draw notice.

'No longer.'

Latona rose, taking a step back from her father. She cupped her hands in front of her, and with a thought, drew a flame from the nearest lamp into her palm.

Though she summoned it gently, Aulus still flinched—not so much in fear of the flame, she was sure, as in response to powers he had not yet figured out how to reconcile with his mental construction of his daughter. She kept the flame small, burning low and orange, but she nudged its shape with her magic, curling and twisting it until it appeared as a rose blossom.

"I do have some ability to protect myself," she pointed out. With a mental nudge, the fire-rose flared white-hot, before she drew it back down to a lambent glow. "And I have no doubt that Sempronius will devote his resources to protecting me." She closed her fingers around the flame, extinguishing it. "I will be as safe in his house as I am in this one."

Aulus held her gaze a long moment, and Latona let him sit with the consideration. "I will give my blessing to this union." Latona's heart leapt in her chest, despite the resignation coloring her father's voice. "If nothing else, I feel I owe you that much, considering the mess Herennius turned out to be. In many ways, it is an exemplary match. Yet I cannot pretend I will not worry. I will always be your father, my darling girl. Your safety will always be more important to me than anything."

Perhaps that was a father's prerogative, but in seeking to keep her safe, Aulus had denied what she was and what she had the potential to become. And so, for many years, she had denied it to herself. *'No longer,'* she thought again.

"I give my consent," Aulus said. "And I must hope I will not come to regret it." He rose, and Latona moved to embrace him, kissing his cheek.

"Thank you, Father."

He smiled weakly. "Go on, tell Aula she may begin making plans. She's only got three months, after all." His eyes rolled ceiling-ward. "Gods know how much of my money she'll be able to find a way to spend!"

When the note arrived, Corvinus, Sempronius, and Djadi were together in the dominus's tablinum, tallying figures, simultaneously settling matters from Iberia and preparing for Sempronius's contributions to the upcoming games. *'And after that, the small matter of a campaign for the consul's chair,'* Corvinus thought, trying not to despair over the columns that Djadi scribbled into a wax tablet.

The plunder from Iberia had not been tremendous to begin with, and Sempronius was dispersing most of it to the legions and the Iberian allies. For himself, he accepted *gifts*: it was an acceptable means of bribery among the senators, who were not, strictly speaking, meant to engage in trade. But to serve as a conduit for introductions, to facilitate trade agreements among others, that was within the bounds of legality—and if those parties felt moved to proffer a contribution to the man who made their new partnerships possible, well, who would be so churlish as to refuse?

The trip to Olissippo had been their saving grace, in truth, and the stops made along the way home, establishing new contacts between Aventan and Tyrian traders and the Iberian miners and the craftspeople in the interior of the peninsula.

Those gifts had to be turned into real money, though. Many of Sempronius's new associates bestowed him with goods, not coin. Corvinus had kept a watchful eye, making sure everything loaded onto a wagon came back off again and went to its appointed place.

The work of selling the merchandise began as soon as they reached Ostia, but it all took time, and while Sempronius's creditors were inclined towards patience, they still wanted to know on what schedule their investment might be returned to them. That assurance might, in turn, depend upon the elections, still months off.

Political victories never came cheaply.

So deep in the documents, Corvinus hardly noticed when the door boy scurried in with a paper, which he handed directly to Sempronius. As he read, Sempronius's lips curved up slightly. He went to his desk and scribbled a return message on the other side of the paper.

As the boy ran back out to relay the response, Sempronius settled his shoulders back, clasping his hands behind him. "Corvinus, Djadi, I am pleased to inform you that I shall be marrying the Lady Vitellia Latona in Sextilis."

Djadi's eyes lit up. "Felicitations, Dominus!" he cried, then smiled over at Corvinus. "It will be a fine thing to have a lady of the house, will it not?"

Corvinus nodded; if nothing else, it would free him of many of the household management tasks that had fallen under his stewardship ever since Tita Aebutia died, several years earlier. Vitellia Latona had been married before, so she knew how to run a home. There would be none of the halting awkwardness of a new bride testing out her powers of command. A period of transition, to be sure, as the lady would bring some of her own staff with her—but Corvinus did not think her violent little maidservant was interested in domestic governance, and so he did not anticipate any serious power struggle among the ranks of the servants and slaves.

Corvinus glanced down at the papers in front of him, then up at Sempronius. "Dominus, it may be indelicate to ask, but..."

"Gods above and below!" Djadi blurted out, less afflicted by tact than his partner. "The lady will have a dowry, yes?"

"A considerable one, so I understand," Sempronius said in a demurring tone. "Her father and I will be working out the details over the coming months, no doubt." He lifted an eyebrow eloquently. "Don't get too excited, Djadi. I mean to make sure plenty is set aside for her comfort and protection."

"Still..." Djadi's fingers traipsed over his columns again, and Corvinus had no doubt he was already factoring in the flexibility their budget might have with an infusion of Vitellian funds.

'Fortunate that we have a few months to plan.' Tita Aebutia's old chamber had been used as guest quarters for years; it would need to be aired out and cleared of any lingering personal touches, so the new mistress could decorate as she pleased. Corvinus would need to prepare for an accounting of the household finances; some wives liked to stay on top of such things, while others cared little, but Corvinus did not mean to be caught out unprepared for an audit.

The staff had to be apprised of the imminent change, reassured that their positions were not in jeopardy and that no one would be laid off or sold away, but accustomed to the idea that some roles might be re-envisioned, depending on what staff the new matron introduced.

A worthwhile thing to learn in advance. Corvinus reached for a spare wax tablet, intending to pen a note to Latona's attendant, since he *thought* she could read. Sempronius had stylus in hand as well, though Corvinus could not discern the nature of his message before he heard a familiar voice cut above the household bustle.

"Oh, get out of my way!" came a sharp voice from the atrium. "He's in his study, I presume?"

"Yes, Domina, but—"

"But nothing!" A moment later, Vibia Sempronia appeared in the doorway to the tablinum, dark eyes fixed on her brother. "*Out*," she commanded generally. Then, without breaking her gaze on Sempronius, lifted a finger straight at Corvinus. "Not you. You stay."

XLII

"Marrying." Vibia let the word drop like an iron weight once the door to the tablinum was firmly shut. "You intend to marry. You intend to marry Vitellia Latona."

Sempronius blinked once before making any reply. "*How* did you find out already?"

"Oh, it's across half the Palatine by now, brother, and it'll hit the Esquiline before dinner," she snapped. "You know how slaves and servants gossip—and *this*? This is prime grist for the mill." Another woman would have flung an arm wide in gesticulation; Vibia made a tight gesture, flicking at the small window at the top of the wall to indicate the city beyond. "I hear you brokered the deal in the Forum, for Juno's sake, and yet you wonder how word spread? And you allowed it to do so before you told me!"

Sempronius lifted one of the wax tablets sitting before him. "I was, even this moment, writing to you—"

"A letter?" Vibia's nostrils flared. "You were going to tell me in a letter, when we live not—"

"I was inviting you to *dinner*," Sempronius said, "so we could discuss the arrangements like civilized people."

"You should have discussed it with me *before* making such a momentous decision!" Vibia cried. "Since when do you commit yourself to something of this magnitude without at least having a conversation with me first?"

Sempronius set the tablet down and folded his arms over his chest. They stared at each other a long moment, unspoken words sizzling in the air. No one, after all, could exasperate like a sibling.

Sempronius and Vibia had ever been closely bonded, children born to aging parents, too far in years from any of their cousins to form other strong familial relationships. Both had been imbued with a sturdy sense of responsibility; both kept each others' secrets. Vibia watched Sempronius's early ascent—and his early fall, when Ocella grew jealous of a young man's growing popularity and potential. She and her husband went with him into exile. She loved him. She was devoted to him. She would do anything to help him toward his goals.

And she could say to him what no one else in this world, perhaps, could. As he grew more powerful, as his legend began to overshadow the truth of him, he would *need* someone to say those things. Who else's duty was that, if not his sister's?

'Well.' Resignation settled between her ribs. *'Perhaps a wife's.'*

Sempronius rolled a shoulder, cracking the joint. "What's this really about?"

"It's about your utter lack of forethought and—"

"No. It isn't."

"Oh, it most certainly is," Vibia hissed.

"No, you wouldn't have rushed over here in such a state merely to chastise me. That could've waited till dinner. You're not only mad I didn't tell you. You're mad about the marriage itself."

Vibia's eyes narrowed. "I have my reservations," she said. "You know I have had my reserv—"

"You know you won't be able to bully her like you did Tita Aebutia," Sempronius commented.

"I didn't *bully* poor Aebutia. She needed guidance." It wasn't Vibia's fault that Sempronius's first wife had been a timid creature. Sweet and obliging, to be sure, and no simpleton—but fragile. In some ways, it was a blessing she died before Ocella's reign began; trying to endure turmoil, proscription, and exile would have crushed her, a fluttering moth caught in an unforgiving fist. "Latona will not require shepherding—at least not in matters of running a household. She's done it before; she knows what she's about." She settled her shoulders back. "And honestly, Sempronius? I'm happy for *her*. After that vile crustacean she was shackled to for so long, she deserves a husband she actually likes." Her jaw set tightly. "She deserves a husband who will be a true *partner* to her."

"I intend to—"

"Sempronius!" Vibia's teeth were on edge. Had he really not thought this through? Did he not see—?

"You have to tell her, Dominus." Corvinus's gentle voice from the side of the room. Vibia glanced sideways at him. Half of her resented his intrusion—but then, she had wanted him present for exactly this reason. "Your choice of bride poses some unique challenges to life as you have currently structured it. The Lady Latona is a mage of considerable talent and natural power. Unless I miss my guess, it's one of the things you would most celebrate her for."

"And this is cause for concern because—?"

Vibia wanted to spit. Either he was so besotted that he had lost sight of reason, or he was playing the dullard for some fool reason of his own.

Corvinus took a more tactful approach. "I do not imagine that yours will be a marriage of genteel detachment, husband and wife living in different spheres even when in the same home. You have, I have seen, opened your heart to this woman, and while she may be well worth the effort, there is a danger in having someone so capable near you. The lady is too clever. Too perceptive. And a mage of Spirit besides, one who can see magical signatures. She will see yours, probably sooner than later. She will figure it out, what you have hidden for so long."

"And gods help us all in such an event," Vibia added tartly. "You haven't been here, Sempronius. You've heard the stories, but you haven't seen her in action. You haven't seen what she can do, and you haven't seen what fuels her. I have. I have seen her protective. I have seen her frightened. And I have seen her *angry*." Vibia's fingers clenched tight. "Please do believe me when I say you don't want to invite that down upon your head."

Sempronius's gaze dropped to his desk. Rare, to catch him without a ready witticism to throw back in her face. It called pity to her heart—but not mercy.

"Furthermore," she said, "in the event that you think I am exaggerating, or if you think her love for you would preclude the full force of Vitellian temper from exploding in your direction—Perhaps you are correct. Even still, you owe it to her to tell her. What an insult it would be, to let her enter into marriage with you, all-unknowing."

"You did not always think so highly of her," Sempronius said, without raising either his eyes or his voice.

"No," Vibia admitted. "I did not. But the past year has given me opportunity to know her, Sempronius. You must unburden yourself of this secret where she is concerned. Anything else would be unworthy of you and an insult to her."

Sempronius glanced aside to Corvinus. "And you agree?"

"I do, Dominus," Corvinus said. "If you cannot trust her with the secret—then you should not be marrying her."

Truth lived in their assertions. Sempronius could acknowledge that. *Did* acknowledge it, but still he hesitated to agree with them. Too many things were yet unsettled, too many dice still in the air.

"It's not for lack of trusting her. I'd already determined to tell her, in fact. But I must... I must choose the right moment."

"I might suggest," Vibia said acidly, "that the ideal moment was *before* brokering the union with her father."

"You know what she's been going through. The rumors, the—"

"I do," Vibia said. "Better than you do, since I've *been* here."

"So can you not understand my hesitation in adding to her present trials? I want to free her from burdens, not add to them. At least for a while. She's spent too much of her life being forced to tiptoe. Why give her one more thing she has to calculate and conceal?"

Vibia did not look impressed by this argument. "You might let her decide for herself what burdens she's willing to shoulder."

"And furthermore—it will put her in more danger."

"It is a risk, Dominus, that we have accepted," Corvinus said. "It is an undercurrent of our lives, to guard this confidence—but we have chosen it."

"A wife is higher profile than a sister or a steward," Sempronius said. "Men who oppose me will target her. Even if she never intentionally let the secret slip, they may have other methods. Gods only know what—but you told me how they played with Marcus's mind, so I am not willing to rule anything out of the realm of possibility. She cannot reveal what she does not know."

"But if she *does* know, she can be prepared for whatever form the attacks may take." Vibia's cheeks were flushed with her continued irritation. "She won't be in less danger for being ignorant."

Again, true, and he knew it.

Underneath the nobler reasons for holding his secret close—reasons which Vibia and Corvinus had neutralized with customary precision and merciless candor—Sempronius was forced to admit the other, darker excuse.

He was afraid.

An uncustomary and unwelcome emotion, but now it crowded in on him from multiple sides. He feared for Latona—a cold horror filled him at the thought of anyone harming her to get to him—but he feared for himself, too. The instinct for hiding his magical nature went bone-deep. His own parents hadn't known.

Sempronius thought, then, of the *erregerra* Ekialde, and of his little queen, sheltered now in a villa on the Janiculum Hill. *'Ekialde did not trust his wife, did not let her share in his decisions or his secrets. Had he been wiser and let her in, he might not have come to such an end.'*

Because Neitin might have talked her husband out of his ambitions.

And there, another fear: what if this changed Latona's view of him? She shared his vision for Aven, expressed the desire to chase it down alongside him—but what if this changed her view of those goals? What if she could not see past his transgressions? What if she didn't understand, as Vibia did, that the gods had called him to obey their imperative above all mortal laws?

He hoped she would understand. She felt Juno's call in her own heart—but she was, as she had told him, on guard for hubris within herself as well. *'What if she considers my secret an offense against both gods and man? A blasphemy, to presume I know divine will, as well as a crime?'*

She might try to stop him. Or...

"She might rescind her acceptance." Startling, to hear the quaver in his own words. Not this the voice of the demagogue, the orator, the battlefield commander.

"She might," Vibia agreed. "She might be furious with you for not telling her before you proposed. She might be horrified at your impious presumptions. She might be afraid of what will unfold." Vibia pursed her lips thin, nostrils flaring. Then she seemed to arrive at some decision, and her voice softened, though not so much that anyone who knew her less well would hear it. "But truly? No, I do not think she will refuse you." Her eyes rolled slightly. "Latona is aggravatingly loyal, in addition to being obnoxiously good-hearted. She will be confused, alarmed, and, yes, perhaps angry. But that heart of hers will go out to you." She reached up, brushing at his hair. "I think she'll see you as someone else in need of her protection. And the woman does love to serve that role."

"Aven could ask for no finer shield," Sempronius said, quiet, tapping his fingers on his desk.

Vibia touched his chin, forcing him to meet her eyes, sable to sable. "Tell her. Trust her. You may find a better ally than you ever hoped for."

The following afternoon, following clients' hours and Curia matters, Sempronius Tarren went to the Vitellian domus on the Palatine. Lady Aula received him, as Aulus had gone forth. "Spreading the news to his clients and cousins, I believe," Aula said. "And deciding who might be important enough to invite to a celebratory dinner in a few days' time."

"I have come," Sempronius said, "to see if I might steal a bit of time with my bride."

"Oh!" Aula twittered delightedly. "Of course you may! Where will you be spiriting her away to?" A twinkle in Aula's eyes reminded him that the little house on the Esquiline Hill was, after all, hers, and thus she had likely been the architect of their tryst.

Would that they could spend the afternoon in such an indulgence. Tempting—but no. Vibia and Corvinus were right. This had to be done. He owed it to Latona not to delay any further, and putting it off would not make the task any easier. "It's turned out to be such a fine day that I thought we might take a walk up the Aventine. The temple I've been constructing there is nearly done."

"What timing!" Aula exclaimed. "A temple to Victoria, just at the moment you're celebrating your own victory."

"One might think I planned it that way."

"One might!" she laughed. "Gods, you don't know how good it is that Latona's marrying a man with some political sense this time around. Let me go find—Oh! Here she is!"

For Latona had come from the back of the house. She was dressed simply, a deep green gown over a cinnamon-colored tunic, with her hair wound in a single coronet braid. Still she took his breath away. *'I shall have this privilege, to see her thus, every day. I will see her full of glamour, but I will see her unadorned as well.'*

Assuming, of course, that she did not throw him over after his confession.

He cleared his throat, unaccustomed to the awkward jitter buzzing in his chest. "I thought we might take a stroll over to the Aventine temples."

"To see Victoria?"

"Just so."

Aula practically shoved her sister at Sempronius. "Go on!" she said. "All to the good that you're seen in public together as word of the betrothal is spreading. But be home for dinner; I'm not sitting with whoever wheedles an invitation out of Father without your company!"

As they walked the short distance from the Palatine to the Aventine, Sempronius delighted in being able to walk arm-in-arm with her. Merula, as always, trailed behind her mistress, a magnificently unconcerned chaperone. They talked of small concerns and light matters: gossip from friends and family, the dinner party her sister was planning, the trouble his cousins were giving him, how happy Djadi was to have Corvinus back in town.

They came, then, to the rise of the Aventine Hill that had once been just another rocky outcropping below the Aqua Appia. Now, a massive edifice of wood and stone towered over the scenery. The porticos had columns of Abydosian granite, gleaming in contrast to the darker podium and the terracotta rooftop. The courtyard in front of the temple had a beautiful fountain in a large basin, burbling away with waters fed by the nearby aqueduct.

"Not done yet," Sempronius acknowledged as they ascended the stairs. "There's still painting to do, and not all of the murals are in. I wanted to oversee some of them myself, anyway. And of course, the goddess's statue will go in last, once her home is complete."

"Oh, Sempronius," Latona said, holding a hand to her chest. "It's spectacular. More than I'd imagined." She turned to him, shining in the spring sunlight. Her smile poured warmth right through him. "Do you know," she said, stepping closer with a coquettish sway in her hips, "the first time you brought me here, to show me the site—I wanted so desperately for you to kiss me that day."

One of his hands settled on her hip; the other brushed through the curls at the side of her face. "I assure you, I was thinking of it."

She tilted her head, eyes sparkling. "Well, then?"

He obliged, thoroughly.

When they parted, Sempronius glanced over his shoulder. "Merula, could I impose upon you to grant me a few moments' privacy with my betrothed?"

Merula snorted. "Not as if you'll be debauching her in the open air, I suppose," she said, shrugging one shoulder.

"What faith you have in us," Latona drawled. "Go on. Take a stroll."

"I will not be going too far, Domina," Merula said. "If you are needing assistance—"

"If Discordian demons or Optimate thugs descend upon us, you mean?" Latona was teasing, but they *had* been cornered by Lucretius Rabirus the last time they walked this path together. "Then I shall scream quiet pointedly, I promise you."

Merula wandered off, evidently interested in examining the half-finished murals depicting Aven's earliest military victories, and Sempronius brushed another kiss onto Latona's hair. "I have something for you." From his pinky finger, he drew a small ring and held it out to her.

"A betrothal ring," Latona said, smiling as she took it. It was a fine piece: not too showy or grand, but with delicate goldwork, a design of vines and grapes around the band, set with a garnet carved into the shape of a blossoming rose. "My, you *have* had an industrious day."

"Wait." His hand covered hers. "Before you put it on, there's—there's something we should discuss."

Latona's face dropped, and she sighed—far too heavily for one who had not yet been given weighty information. "Yes," she said. "It's been on my mind, too, and you've been so kind not to mention it before now."

Sempronius's brow creased. "I don't—"

But Latona, having evidently steeled herself to this conversation, barreled on. "It's possible," she said, "that I may not be able to provide you with heirs."

Sempronius blinked, thrown by the unexpected turn of the conversation. Was *that* what had her so concerned?

"I don't know for certain," she went on. "There were times, more than a few of them, that I thought I had conceived—but nothing ever came of it. And I am nearly twenty-four. If—If I were going to, I mean—"

"Latona." Sempronius had to cut in, unable to bear listening to her castigate herself. Not when his purpose was his own confession—and not when she was so far from deserving any blame. "Far be it from me to cast aspersions on another man's virility, but I do feel obliged to point out that the problem might not have been *you*, my dove."

Her lips twitched slightly. "I confess the thought *had* occurred to me." Sempronius was unable to suppress a smirk, but if anyone had earned a touch of mockery, it was Latona's wretch of an ex-husband. "But there's no guarantee!" she went on. "If Juno—Well, perhaps she has other plans for me than motherhood, and if that's the case—"

"Then we'll adopt," Sempronius said. "Simple enough. Vibia's considering it, you know."

"Truly?"

"Truly. They're in discussions with Ulpius Turro."

"Mercy. His wife breeds like a rabbit. What are they up to now, six?"

"And a seventh is suspected." He twirled a lock of golden hair around his finger and tugged on it playfully. "Maybe we'll get number eight." He kissed her again; he couldn't help it. *'Gods above, I cannot wait to be married to this woman.'*

That thought knocked him back down to reality.

"Latona," he said, drawing back from her. "That wasn't what I wanted to discuss at all."

"It wasn't?"

"Not even remotely."

"What, then?"

It took him too long to respond. Aula would have peppered him with more questions, trying to draw out whatever thoughts tangled on his tongue. Latona waited patiently—although not *so* patiently that she didn't reach out with a tiny tendril of Spirit magic.

What reached back shocked her. Given his serious mien, a little anxiety was to be expected, even if she did not normally associate that emotion with Sempronius. But what her magic touched, at a light probe, was sheer, shaking, ice-cold terror. *'What in the name of all the gods at once...?'*

She took him by the elbow and drew him over to the temple steps. "Come on, sit down," she said. They did, and she reached for him with the hand not still clasping the ring. "Whatever it is, it can't be as terrible as all that."

His laugh sounded bitter. "Oh, Latona. I—" He looked down at their joined hands, his thumb rubbing over her knuckles. "I have not, I fear, been entirely honest in representing myself to you."

Latona's mind spun. What could he mean? If his finances were not as impressive as he tried to make the populace believe, well, that would not differentiate him from half the ambitious senators in the Curia. Such an impediment could be overcome. She had dowry enough—since her father had wrested it back from Herennius's control—to cover a great deal of ground.

What if it were not that? What else *could* it be? Some... some mistress, perhaps? Unlikely, but... A secret child? Was that why he did not fret so over heirs?

"Sempronius," she said. "Please do just tell me. My imagination is fertile enough to invent far worse than whatever it is you hesitate to say."

"You think that," he said, quite softly. "Well. Perhaps it's easier if I..." He closed his eyes, and though his lips moved, there was no sound.

Then, the world around Latona shifted. Her magical sensibilities thrummed like a plucked lute-string, awakened to another signature, to magic in use. *'But that's... No, that isn't... that isn't possible...'*

She cast about to see if anyone had approached, unnoticed. No, they were still alone—and when she turned back to Sempronius, with Spirit's sight fully engaged, the spectacle harrowed her to the bones.

A deep pulse of mingled violet and indigo shimmered around Sempronius's form, undulating toward the clear-running water and reaching out for the shadows cast by the many columns. Water magic, and Shadow, and the only source—the only possible mage responsible—

No. Latona did not want to believe it. Could not believe it. Could not explain to herself.

Latona stood up and skittered back from him. She wasn't consciously aware of having dropped the ring—but it fell on the stone between them with a hollow *thunk*. "Gods protect us."

XLIII

Sempronius got to his feet, and as he lost concentration, the magic seeped away, receding back into the ground and the bubbling fountain.

"You fool."

Not what he had expected by way of a reaction.

"Oh, you utter fool." She pressed a hand to her chest, half-collapsing forward as though she had been struck in the gut. "What have you done?"

"Latona, I—"

But he could find no other words. He didn't know what else to say.

"You hid this? For how—" She stopped herself, no doubt guessing how long, at least in estimate. Few mages manifested powers after childhood. "You've kept this a secret."

"No one could know," Sempronius said. "No one. I had—I had so much to do. I knew that of myself long before I knew—"

"Sempronius, this—this is not only illegal. This is—" Her hand tapped against her chest, as though trying to re-establish some rhythm there. "You—You—"

"It is illegal, I confess that," he said, "but I believe, I have always believed, that it is right. The gods gave me their blessings. They intend me to use them. And I assure you, I have never yet been smote."

"That better not have been a joke." Latona's voice had dropped to a timbre suitable for a funeral.

"No. No, Latona, I only meant—" He dove forward, reaching for her hands, but she snatched away from him. The ache in his chest when she did was shockingly painful. "The gods want this of me." The certainty of it rose in his throat. He had never before had to justify to anyone the choice that so dominated and drove his life. "They have guided me and protected me every day of my life. They gave me these gifts, and they gave me the strength and wit to use them."

"You think that will matter?" Latona hissed, fear sparking sharp anger in her voice. "You think that will keep your fellow senators from throwing you off the Tarpeian Rock when they find out?"

"I have kept this secret my entire life, Latona."

"It does not follow that you will do so for the rest of it," she countered. "There will be a reckoning, someday. Maybe not soon, but—" She shook her head, mouth slightly agape. "This cannot remain a secret forever. It is not the way of the world."

"I have had decades of practice."

"Decades when you were not so great a man as you are now." Tears sprang to her eyes, glistening in the bright sun. Sempronius was the cause, and he hated himself for it. "Decades when you were not under such scrutiny. An imperator, about to run for consul—To bring yourself to these heights, bearing this great a burden—" Half a sob choked out of her. "Oh, my dearest. The gods love to set men up, to be sure, but they also love to watch them fall. You have tempted the Fates too far."

"There were always going to be challenges," Sempronius said. He darted forward, this time swift enough to catch Latona by the upper arms. "You knew that in wedding me, there would be—"

"This goes beyond 'challenges,' Sempronius!" Latona gasped. "This is not some quarrel in the Senate! You—You are not consecrated! You've never been through the rites, you do not attend the Cantrinalia, you—"

"It has all been in service to Aven," he pleaded. "I would never have risked it, Latona, if I did not believe it was what the gods required of me, please believe—"

She sagged in his arms, laughing mirthlessly, hysterically. "Oh sweet Juno! I knew your ego was considerable, beloved, I did, I even found it charming, but this is hubris beyond anything the poets have written!" She pulled away from him, pacing the tiles. "I don't understand. I don't understand *how*. How do you decide to do this? And how do you—do you *keep* making that choice? The choice to deceive and mislead, with so much at stake..."

"I have been at this for so long," he said. "Since I was a small child. So small, I don't even remember how it started. I don't remember *deciding* not to tell anyone. I just know I never did, never felt I should. Later on, I attributed it to the Shadow in my nature—"

"Your *nature*?" Latona rounded on him with the tense muscles and ferocious expression of a caged lion, and Sempronius remembered Vibia warning him about her anger. "As if this were a fable about a frog and a scorpion?" She shook her head tightly. "You're a man, Sempronius. Not a scorpion. You can make choices about your nature, how you express the gifts you're given—" A pained expression twisted her face. "When I think about the years I wasted, making myself and my power so small... And you! With all the doors of Aven already open to you, you feel the need to—to break down this wall as well?"

Tears stood in her eyes now. Sempronius wanted to go to her, to hold her, but knew she would only wrench away again.

"I have agonized," she said, "over every step, worrying that it went too far, that I was pressing my luck with gods and men alike. You *know* that. You saw me struggle with it."

"I *encouraged* you," he said, hoping that would be some defense. "I never wanted it to be a struggle for you. You deserved, you have always deserved, to use your power without apology or hesitation. The gods have plans for you, too, and I longed to see you embrace them, and you *have*, and it's so beau—"

"You said," she interrupted, "just before you proposed, you told me... you told me there was no hubris in what I did. That the gods made a demand, and I had to..." Her hands came up to cover her face, her nails digging into her hair. "But you didn't *tell* me!" The words were a cry, stabbing Sempronius's heart. "You didn't tell me you believe that because you've been *living* it for—for how many years?"

"I'm sorry, Latona," he rasped. "Not for what I am, nor what use I've made of it. In that, I have only ever done as the gods required." She made a strangled noise, half-laugh, half-sob; her breathing had become erratic, panicked. "But I am sorry, I am so sorry, for not telling you sooner, for—for treating you as though you were anyone else—" His voice cracked, and his feet moved toward her of their own accord. "Because you are *not* like anyone else, Latona, gods, you're unlike anyone I've ever known. I should have told you. I should have trusted you, much earlier."

He didn't know what else to say. Everything about this conversation was foreign territory. Sempronius did not know how to plead; he had no practice at it.

At length, Latona dropped her hands and straightened her spine. She shook out her hair, lifted her chin, and met his eyes. "I need to think."

"Does that mean—?"

"It means," Latona said, stooping to pick up the ring she had let fall. She did not put it on. She did not hand it back. She clasped it tight within her fist. "It means I need to think. You have pitched an astonishing weight on my head. I could not have imagined..." She shook her head, then raised her voice. "Merula!" she called. "Merula, we're going home!"

The girl's dark head popped out from around a nearby column. She might have heard most of the conversation.

Latona looked back to Sempronius. "I will... I will have something to say to you soon, no doubt. I—"

But words failed her. She turned her back on him and strode swiftly towards Merula.

Alhena was feeding pine nuts to her birds in the atrium when Latona returned home, much earlier than expected. She saw the glint of tears on her sister's cheeks as she passed. *'Oh, no.'*

Aula noticed, too, and sprang up from her couch. "Latona? You're back early. Father's only—"

"I'm sorry, Aula," Latona said, heading straight for her room. "I cannot possibly come to dinner. I don't care how dull Father's guest is. Tell him I'm overwrought." Her hand came up, pinching hard at the bridge of her nose.

Aula rounded on Merula. "What's wrong with her? What happened?"

For once, Merula's shrug appeared genuinely confused, not merely insolent. "She is having some disagreement with the senator. I was not close enough to be hearing clear."

"Disagreement? What in Jupiter's name could he have done in the space of an afternoon?"

"Enh. Men." Merula rolled her eyes eloquently.

"No, but—"

"Something about hubris?"

"Well, the man's certainly—"

"*Please* go away, the both of you!" Latona shouted, flopping onto her bed. "I need space, for Juno's sake."

Aula looked ready to push in anyway, but Merula reached past her and wrenched the door shut with a forbidding expression. Aula shuffled from foot to foot for a moment, then turned away, grumbling, back to preparing herself for dinner.

Alhena waited, long after Merula went down to the kitchens. Latona wasn't really taking a nap, Alhena was sure; she was in far too excitable a state. But she needed time. Alhena, understanding that more than most, lingered outside her bedroom for a long while, until the sounds of muffled weeping within fell away. Then, gently, she pushed the door open, slipped inside, and closed it behind her.

Latona was sitting at the edge of her bed, elbows on her knees, both hands tangled in her loosened hair. Pins were strewn about the floor, and her sandals had been kicked to the corner. She was shaking, as though the effort of holding herself together were almost too much to bear.

Alhena eased herself down beside her sister, waiting to see if she would also be ordered to leave. When no imperative came, she folded her hands in her lap. "I'm sorry."

"For what, dear one?" Latona wiped her eyes, a dashing gesture as she attempted to compose herself.

'*She doesn't have to do that,*' Alhena thought. By now, she ought to understand. After all they had been through, Alhena didn't need her sisters to put on a brave face for her.

Alhena shuffled her feet against the floor, dropping her gaze to her toes. She need not say anything. No one would ever know. But that thinking had caused Latona's current pain, and Alhena could no longer endure the guilt, which had grown from a mild tingle at the back of her mind, only an occasional reminder of the burden, to a weighty and gnawing beast.

Still, steeling herself to the task was no simple matter. "It... It wasn't my secret to tell, is the thing."

"What wasn—" The word died on Latona's lips; she was no fool. "Sweet Juno," she breathed, swaying backward. "You knew."

"I did. I'm sorry."

Latona's mouth worked silently for a moment. "For how long?"

"Since— Well. I wasn't sure until after the Aventine fires. Before, I knew he was important. That he had to be there. I didn't know why—but I guessed. And then, with all that happened..."

Eyes widening in understanding, Latona raised shaky fingers to her lips. "Bona Dea. The Aventine fires. It wasn't Vibia who—"

"Vibia certainly helped," Alhena said, "but no, it was not all her doing. You'd—You'd have to ask him, to find out exactly what happened." Her voice trembled, as she realized it was no certain thing that Latona and Sempronius were still on speaking terms. "Anyway—since then, I've had some visions that indicated—I saw him in Iberia."

"Using magic?" Latona's hand fluttered down to her throat, as though she might choke herself and stifle any further revelations. "On campaign, among the legions! He—"

"I don't think he ever violated the Prohibition of Mars!" Alhena rushed to clarify. Admittedly, she wasn't *sure* he hadn't, but that illumination would not help Latona right now. "There was something about a river. I'm not sure of the details. The visions come in odd bits and pieces."

Latona released a low, hissing breath. "I was so shocked when he told me... I keep thinking of new implications. All the laws he's broken..."

"We've been thinking ourselves that some of them might need breaking," Alhena ventured. "Or, at least, reforming."

Latona's face was still with consideration. Then she said, voice low, "The wretched thing is, I don't even know that I think he's wrong. He has such vision... but our laws would never have let him pursue it. But I'm so... I'm so *angry*, Alhena, that he never told me. If not before he went to Iberia, then... That he could *propose* without telling me, and knowing how much I've wrestled with how to use my own powers... I'm angry, and I'm a little insulted, and I'm so *afraid* for him."

"I think that's all... I mean, I think you've a right to all those feelings."

Latona hardly seemed to hear her. "Someone's going to find out. Secrets don't stay secret in this city. It's an astonishment he's managed to get this far, but sooner or later, he will slip up. Or someone will be cleverer than him. Juno's mercy, as though renegade Discordians and corrupt Augians weren't enough to be worried about, and now—" Dawning thoughts slackened her face, and she turned wild eyes to Alhena. "Do you know? If someone will find him out, or when or how or—"

Alhena looked down at her hands, picking at one thumbnail with the other. "I was really hoping you wouldn't ask that."

A strangled noise eked out of Latona's throat. "Then that's my answer."

"I don't know for sure," Alhena said. "It could be—it could be anything. Mere symbolism. Or so far off in the future that the world will change and shift by then and what I've seen will be irrelevant." Alhena bit her lower lip. "I don't—I don't want to cause you unnecessary distress."

Moaning, Latona bent forward, ramming the heels of her hands into her eyes. "This is unbearable. I don't... I don't know what..." Her breath caught in a gasp, and this time when she dropped her hands, tears flowed freely down her cheeks. "Of all the things that might have happened, I hadn't imagined, I could never have imagined... Oh, Alhena, what do I do?"

Alhena looped an arm around her sister's shoulders. Being in the position of comforter, not comforted, was unusual. "I'm the last person to give advice on anything involving matrimony," Alhena said softly. "But think about this: If that happens. When that happens. Whichever it ends up being. When a day comes that Sempronius has to face such a trial... Do you want to let him face it alone?"

XLIV

Everywhere Corinna looked, she saw broken things.

The warp in the wool, the crack in the stone, the lightning that split the sky. Each knot, each tear, each fissure called out to her.

Where people would break, too. The things that would fracture a soul. A little digging, and she could name any man's terrors—and any woman's, too. Perhaps that was why the *lemures* responded when she called. *'An affinity between us.'*

So when her brother, eight days before the Ides of Maius, indicated that the time to act had finally arrived—that she need hold herself back no longer, that the straining of her heart could thunder free—Corinna knew what she wanted to do.

Her brother chose his time for political reasons. The return of the legions had unsettled the city. Mostly by way of eager excitement, but even that, Corinna could use. Routine had been disrupted.

What happened in the Curia interested her only so far as it caused further disquiet. Times of political upheaval provided fertile soil for Discordia's strife to flourish, like so many weeds shooting up to strangle weaker flowers and erode the roots of trees. *'Such a shame Dictator Ocella threw the Discordians out of Aven in his time, because oh, what lovely havoc we might have wreaked on his behalf!'*

These Optimates did nearly as well, though, with their implacable hatred of their opponents. Pinarius Scaeva had confided to Corinna that he had been drawn to Lucretius Rabirus and taken his commission because of how many splinters the man's soul had. A creature of strife, even if he did not wrap himself in Discordia's patronage, even if he thought he was reaching for order. "Everything he touches becomes a shard," Scaeva had said. "He could provoke enmity between a cloud and its rain."

Useful, that.

As her brother wrapped up his explanation of how he would use the chaos she created, Corinna wrenched her attention away from contemplations of pretty destruction. "So?" Durmius asked. "You have your license now, you and your fellows. Do what you can, and our friends will both cover for us and make puissant use of it. Are you ready?"

"We have been ready for months," she replied, growing a little more tart. "We would never have paused at all, had you not insisted. But we were diligent. No idle winter for us, no slack spring." Tormenting glitter-gold had been a fine diversion, and a necessary one, since she threatened all Discordia's glory, but that work was nowhere near as satisfying as what Corinna had planned. "We have prepared. We are ready."

"When can you begin?"

She lifted one shoulder and let it drop. "Tomorrow seems a fine day."

Latona spent a listless night in her room, staring at the walls, the ceiling, her own feet, anything at all. She made excuses to her father, then listened to the muffled dinner conversation floating from the triclinium. She discarded her day clothes for a sleeping tunic and lay awake as the dinner noises faded, as Aulus's guest departed, as the domus wound down its daily activities and set itself to slumber.

The moon briefly clipped the long rectangle of her window. Outside, the muted bustle of the city went on, as it ever did, carts and wagons rolling in while fewer people were on the streets.

She must have slept, at some point, for she could not account for every hour of the night, but it was a fitful and unsatisfying business. When dawn illuminated her chamber, she rose and went to the garden instead, for a change of view. In an hour or so, when her father's clients began to arrive, she would still be out of sight, so no matter that she was still in her sleeping tunic, her hair loose about her shoulders.

'Blessed Juno,' she thought, looking up at the sky as it shifted from rosy-gold to pale blue to cheerful azure, *'what am I supposed to do?'*

As the household woke, Latona, her magical sensibilities raw from insomnia and distress, *felt* each soul moving through the house: servants and enslaved attendants cleaning and cooking, her sisters rising, her niece quarreling with the nursemaid, her brother shuffling around in search of a task, her father making ready for his clients. Then, when the clients came, an onslaught of *need*, everyone *wanting* something.

Latona draped her arm over her eyes and tried to block them all out, listening instead to her own heartbeat. *'Steady, steady... Whatever the answer is, you won't find it if your head's addled... Find steadiness...'*

She found, at least, a little more sleep, dozing on the garden couch until a presence intruded further upon her than anyone else that morning had dared. Aula, she knew without opening her eyes, strained beyond her ability to contain her curiosity.

"Alhena says I shouldn't pry," Aula said, settling down on the couch next to Latona's. "And I won't. I promise. I—Well, of course I *want* to, but Alhena insisted, and you know how she gets." Latona let her arm drop her from her eyes and fixed her sister with a sideways glare. "Oh, don't look at me like that. Naturally I'm curious. And I'm worried. But I... I won't ask questions. I promised Alhena I wouldn't. I wanted you to know that... that I'm here. If you want to talk."

Latona *did*, and she didn't. She hardly knew how to put words to the tangle.

"Or—Or I could talk, if you want," Aula went on, never able to long endure a silence. "I could tell you about dinner last night. You'll never guess who Father's guest was."

And as Aula set off onto a monologue about the backbencher from the Curia who had somehow conned their father into a dinner invitation, Latona tried to let her tightly-wound soul loosen a little. Aula's anxiety pricked her conscience and reminded her that drowning in self-pity was no sort of option. She'd given herself one day to mope; tomorrow, she would have to resume forward action.

"The only cheerful note to it all," Aula said as she wrapped up her tale, "is that Father let me pick our next guests. So I'm going to invite Maia Domitia and her brothers."

In an attempt to take part in the conversation, Latona said, "You're flinging her at Gaius, I take it?"

"Maia's capable of doing her own flinging, if she likes. You can't deny it'd be a good match, though."

It was; their families were aligned politically, and like the Terentiae, they had taken Latona's part in the broiling gossip-war. Gaius could bond over common military experiences with Maia's brothers, Maius and Septimus. He would never try to part Maia from her daughters, and Lucia's favorite playmates would become her cousins.

"It would be helpful," Aula said cautiously, "if you were up to your sparkling self when they come over. Or something like it. Help me sell both Father and Gaius on the idea."

"I've already talked him into one betrothal this month," Latona said, more sourly than she'd intended to. "My charm may not extend to a second." She pushed herself to a sitting position and heaved a sigh. "You're right in one thing, though. I ought to clean myself up. I'm not doing anyone any good like this."

Before she could rise from the couch, however, Alhena came into the garden, her bright hair loose about her ears. "Something's going to happen," she blurted. "I can't get a fix on where. I mean. *Here*, in the city, but—"

"Easy, my honey," Aula said. She took Alhena by the hand and drew her down onto the couch. "Take a breath, then take us along with you."

Alhena did, though the gulping inhalation was unlikely to actually calm her. "I had another vision. Like the ones last year—bronze gates opening, all the clanging noise. But here, in Aven, on every hill, in every hollow, from the Tiber River to the farthest walls. The stones of the streets split apart, and the channels between them ran with blood, and the blood turned to liquid bronze." Another hiccuping gulp of air. "It's the Discordians, Latona. I'm sure of it. And tonight—tonight is—"

"Gods," Latona breathed, realization landing like a stone in her gut. "The Lemuria. I hadn't even thought of it. How absolutely stupid of me."

"It wasn't stupid," Aula said kindly. "They've been quiet for months. You had no reason to think—"

"But I did!" Latona wanted to slap herself. She had been so distracted, first by the social upheavals, then the dizziness of reuniting with Sempronius and becoming betrothed to him, followed by the shock of his revelation, that she had given no thought to the calendar. "I guessed they were storing their efforts up for something big, and this is a perfect opportunity."

The Lemuria took place over three days and nights: the seventh, fifth, and third days before the Ides of Maius—unlucky days, *nefasti*, when sensible citizens kept themselves indoors and did not tempt the Fates. Like those days when the *mundus* was uncovered, the gates between the worlds of the living and the dead stood open, but while the *mundus* invited the beloved dead to return and take a peek at the world they left behind, the Lemuria was a time to appease the souls of uneasy and vengeful spirits. A time to guard against the *lemures* and all their ilk, who would take advantage of any opportunity to cross the threshold and make trouble.

Days ideally suited for the Discordians' purpose.

"So what do we do?"

The plaintive note in Alhena's voice hit Latona at the core. *'Blessed Juno, I took on this responsibility, but I have no answers.'* Again, the fear, that she'd taken on more than she could shoulder, that hubris had led her to this pass.

She rose and began pacing. "Without knowing more—without knowing where they may strike, or in what fashion—the best we can do is be alert." Latona's fingers twined around a lock of her hair. "Tonight is only the first night of the Lemuria. If their previous pattern holds—testing themselves first, before escalating to greater horrors—then we may pray that whatever they have planned for this first night will not be irredeemably horrible."

A weak, frail hope. Pathetic, really. *'I consign this city to a night of potential terrors, all because I cannot see a better solution. Great and blessed Juno, if you want me to protect your city, show me how to do so!'* But the goddess, as ever, was silent.

So Latona went forward with what *was* in her control. "I'm going to send notes to all of our friends. The ones we have left, anyway. Vibia, Rubellia, Terentilla, Marcus... If nothing happens, I'll look like a fool, but we should all be alert."

"You won't look a fool," Alhena said in somber tones. "I'm sure of it. Unfortunately."

"You should tell Vatinius Obir, too," Aula suggested. "He knows what to be alert for within his own territory." Latona nodded, tugging on the hair now tangled around her fingers. "And I expect Vibia will tell..." But she cut herself off, wary of the mystery of whatever was amiss between Latona and Sempronius.

The thought was another itch in Latona's mind. Previously, yes, she would have told Sempronius along with the others. He was so keenly concerned with the city's welfare, and he had resources.

Now, half of her wanted to tell him more than before, to bring his magical talents into her fight, another weight on her side of the scales against the Discordians—but the other half trembled to do so. Apart from the fact that communication between them was currently fraught, getting him involved risked his exposure.

No time to think of that now. Aula was right. If Vibia thought he should be involved, either as a magical or purely civil force, she would tell him. It did not, yet, have to be Latona's problem.

Latona cleared her throat and straightened her spine. "Very well. It's not much of a plan, but it's what we've got. Maybe if we put all our heads together, we'll come up with something more proactive, but until then, the least we can do is all be vigilant."

Aula shifted on the couch. "Latona. You... You don't have to play the general for us, you know."

"I—What?"

Aula stood, moved to her side, and gently removed Latona's hand from where it was abusing her hair. "We are your sisters. I can understand how for Vibia, for Fausta, even for Rubellia, for everyone outside these walls, you feel the need to look strong and sure. But you need not play that role for us."

Latona's jaw trembled. "I don't know what to do, Aula," she said, hardly above a whisper. "I am so tired of always feeling three steps behind Corinna and her cohort of horrors."

"Me too," Alhena intoned. "Do you think I haven't asked Proserpina why she doesn't give me a little more notice, or more specific guidance?"

"You are both," Aula said, "still mortal. And the gods are, I am given to understand, both fickle and inscrutable."

Latona pinched Aula's arm, though more out of habit than anything else. "Don't blaspheme."

"Oh, they've heard worse from me. My point is, you're doing the best you can with what they've given you. *Both* of you." Aula's eyes cut meaningfully over to Alhena. "So. Let's send those messages. Tell everyone to be alert tonight. And then we take the next step when we know what ground our feet will land on."

XLV

It had been a long time since Gaius Vitellius observed the rites of the Lemuria. Many domestic rituals went unmarked on campaign. Vitellius was not impious, but a man at war paid the dues necessary to keep him alive and to bring him victory, trusting in the citizens back at home to tend to the other gods and their requirements.

Once home, though, he found himself yearning for the simple familiarity of such customs. He rose in the middle of the night to join his father for the ritual. In older times, entire households participated, banging pots and pans to chase malicious spirits away. Hardly anyone did that anymore. *'Rural folks, maybe,'* Vitellius guessed. But if every household in the city observed that particular rite, the din would be enough to wake any gods sleeping on Olympus.

Aulus hadn't emerged from his chamber yet, but Gaius was surprised to find Latona sitting in the atrium, wearing a loose sleeping tunic, gazing at the altar. Her hair was unbound, but, strangely, she had draped a crimson mantle over her curls. A beam of moonlight shot through the hole in the ceiling, casting her in an ethereal glow. Her gaze was faraway, and something about it made Gaius sad, until she noticed his approach and turned to him, smiling. She patted the bench beside her. "Father's still preparing," she said, keeping her voice low, "but I expect he'll be out soon."

"Couldn't sleep?" Gaius asked, settling next to her.

"Didn't want to."

The way she said it plucked at Gaius's instincts. The night-fog on his brain cleared enough that he wondered why *this* sister would be the one sitting up, far more alert than he felt.

Then the significance of her mantle struck him. Crimson. The same crimson as the focale she had woven for him.

"You think something's going to happen tonight. Something magical." A tight nod. "Why?"

She hesitated, drew a long breath, sighed it out. "There's... a lot I haven't had the chance to tell you," she said, "about what's gone on here the past year."

"Father mentioned something. Some trouble with curses?"

She nodded. "For several months last year. Lady Vibia and I lent our blessings to help dispel them, particularly in neighborhoods where there was no one with enough skill or training to do so."

"Yes, Father said you'd been involved in, um, unusual charity work."

A flicker of pique crossed his sister's face before she tilted her head up, looking at the stars through the hole in the atrium ceiling. "I suppose you might put it that way, yes."

A few years earlier, Vitellius might have left it at that. When he departed Aven, his sister had been a teenager whose magical talents were restricted to minor empathic readings and keeping the hypocaust heating properly: domestic gifts, tidy and small. What Aventans expected from female mages.

But since then, he had witnessed for himself what power a woman working magic could wield. He had *felt* it, been saved by it. For all that weaving was a feminine task, the focale she made for him held more power than any Fire-forged armor Vitellius had ever seen.

He had watched, too, as Sakarbik's magic, so much stranger to his eyes, ensorcelled an entire battlefield. A woman's magic had triumphed over a man's when Sakarbik's golden clouds drove the nightmarish powers of the blood warriors to their defeat. And Latona herself, though he had not yet had much opportunity to observe her, seemed different, more sure of herself now. A force to be reckoned with, in truth.

Driven by that awareness, he asked, "How would *you* put it?"

She leveled an assessing gaze at him. "I would say, not without cause, that I have been a shield standing between the people of this city and more monstrous terrors than they have faced in recent memory."

The statement had been a test, Gaius sensed, to see if he would laugh or naysay her.

When he did neither, she went on: "Not the only shield, to be sure. But one of too few. The instigators have been quiet for months now, but we think tonight..."

"The curses," Gaius interjected. "What was their nature?"

Her fingers touched the edge of her mantle. She opened her mouth—then closed it, looking anxious. "I don't want to say, right now," she said. "The world is too fragile on a night like this. My words might attract undue attention from the very things I'm hoping to avoid."

That was answer enough. The purpose of the Lemuria was to settle the spirits of the unquiet dead. For Latona to be concerned on this of all nights spoke much of the nature of the potential danger. A cold knot twisted in Gaius's stomach at the thought. *'The curses she fought... if it was like the akdraugi...'*

Latona frowned at him. "What's wrong?" When he did not answer, she pressed, "Gaius, my Spirit magic is primed fit to burst right now, and your emotions just popped like oil thrown on a hot pan. Don't pretend. Tell me what's wrong."

He swallowed around the sudden lump in his throat. "I just... I thought about this ritual, what it really means. I've... I've a lot more dead spirits on my conscience than I used to. I'd very much like for them to stay quiet. That's all." His sister took his hand, and despite the cool spring air, a warmth spread over his skin, as though he'd been basking in summer sunlight. "Are you—?"

"A little calming energy," she said. "I'll stop, if you'd rather I didn't."

"No. No, it's fine. It's very kind of you, really. I just wasn't expecting it."

Latona smiled. "I wasn't expecting you to notice."

"I got... more self-aware, I guess you'd have to say. When the—" Gaius didn't want to say the word *akdraugi* right now, in the dark night, any more than Latona had wanted to name her own demons. "The Lusetani magic had a number of peculiar effects," he offered instead. "I learned to be alert for them."

She nodded her understanding. "Tell me more later. I'd be interested. And Alhena, too. We've been making a study of our thaumaturgical understanding of what happened here. A comparative perspective from foreign magic would be well-worth the examination."

His lips quirked. "You sound quite the scholar."

"More Alhena than me, but thank you. We have been trying."

At that moment, a door opened at the far end of the house, and their father came forward into the atrium, with his steward right behind him. Aulus didn't look surprised to see them, though Gaius thought he might have lifted an eyebrow at Latona's mantle. "What pious children I have," he commented. "Or what insomniacs."

"Something in-between the two," Latona quipped.

They sat quietly as Aulus performed his invocation before the altar. He washed his hands three times, his steward changing out the basin with each lavation, to replace it with fresh water. Then he took up a dish of black beans and began his perambulation of the house. After every five or six steps, he stopped and tossed a handful of the beans behind him, saying, "These I cast; with these I redeem me and mine."

Gaius became aware that Latona had gone still, like a lioness in the stalk, her eyes focused on the altar across the room. Slowly, she began flexing and curling her fingers. "Latona?" he asked in a whisper. "Is it—?"

"I don't know yet," she replied, just as hushed. "There might... there might be something..."

Their father continued his progress toward the back of the house, resolute in his duty. How many times had he performed this ritual with nothing unusual occurring? Surely for most Aventan citizens, that was the way of it. *'You do what is necessary to appease the gods, and you go about your life. You don't expect the unnatural to actually break through and intrude upon your peace, not in the modern age.'*

Vitellius had seen horrors enough not to trust in ritual alone. And when Latona shot up from her seat, wild gaze darting about the atrium, it was enough to harrow him, to send his thoughts reeling back to those horrible nights in Toletum, besieged by demons, with no safe place of retreat.

"I can feel it..." Latona hissed. "But I can't... I can't feel *where*."

Vitellius stood as well, his eyes searching the atrium, useless though he knew it to be.

The night, till then, had been cool, but in an expected way. The natural shift from a spring day to a spring night, which would dew all greenery upon the morning. All of a sudden, though, the air around Vitellius turned to ice. No fog rolled in, but Vitellius had the same sinking sensation in his gut as when the *akdraugi* cascaded upon Toletum's walls. Profound unease, a soul-deep awareness that something was wrong in the universe, and he had no power to set it right.

Then he saw it: a shadow, coalescing out of the atrium pool. "No..." he groaned, even before it took form, anticipating what would come. "No, no...."

It was what he had dreaded, all those months in Iberia, what he most feared when he heard that the Lusetani were attempting to raise the dead. The smoky figure rising out of the water pulsed and thickened, steadily becoming less of a formless shadow and more the image of a man. One man, in particular: his friend Mennenius, dead these long months, dead because Vitellius had not been able to protect him from Lusetani magic.

His cheeks were wet. "I'm sorry," he gasped. "I didn't... I didn't know how to..." But the shade of Mennenius only shook his head, denying him any absolution. An ache radiated out from Vitellius's stomach and seemed to consume his whole body. The world at the periphery of his vision dimmed, turned grey, all his awareness narrowing to the specter hovering in front of him, to his dead friend's face, reproachful and judging.

Pressure on his shoulders. Latona, he realized, gripping him. He couldn't see her, though. Only the spirit. "It's not real, do you hear me?" Barely. Her voice echoed, like something far away. "Gaius. Gaius! That isn't whoever you're seeing. It means *nothing*. Their spirit is, I'm sure, safe in Pluto's kingdom, but— Oh, sweet blessed Juno, Gaius, I am sorry, but I have to do something about this." The weight on his shoulders lifted. "It's not here," he heard Latona say. "Damn. Of course it isn't. How would they have gotten something in—"

A noise near the front door. Vitellius felt, vaguely, that he ought to do something, but the agony clouding his brain dragged his attention back to the specter of Mennenius hovering before him.

Latona grabbed the light from one of the lamps hanging by the door. Not the lamp itself. Only the flames, curling around her fingers, providing illumination in the dark street.

Even without the fire, Latona knew she would look mad if anyone saw her, dashing out into the street in the middle of the night, barefoot in a sleeping tunic, but this was too important for her to care. Gaius was netted in some fiend's spell, and since her father hadn't re-emerged from the back of the house, she assumed another spirit transfixed him. No good dispatching each of the *lemures* in turn; she had to find the source of this summoning and put an end to it.

'Where's Vibia when I need her?' On the other side of the hill, of course—and possibly dealing with demons of her own. Latona's intuition, or perhaps some aspect of her Spirit magic, told her that there were little tears in the fabric of the world all over the city tonight. *'You cannot fix them all, not now. Find this one and put an end to it.'*

Harder, without Vibia. Latona realized how much she'd grown accustomed to working in tandem. But she had experience, much more than when first stumbling over these curses in Stabiae. She could wrap her hands around the thread of *wrongness* infiltrating the world and follow it to its source—nearby, an ugly pulse somewhere on this block.

Foosteps behind her—but a familiar presence. Merula, roused by the commotion in the house. "Domina," she growled as she came up behind Latona. "Is being very foolish of you to come out here alone."

"Sorry," Latona murmured. Merula was right, of course; Latona had acted on instinct and on the assumption that this would be like the curses they had dispelled the previous year, anchored to a charm. But it could as easily be Corinna herself, or one of her associates, lying in wait. *'And you could've walked right into another trap.'*

"Well. I am being here now." Merula had donned one of the protective crimson headscarves. She had, also, seized a lamp, and her wicked knife was gripped tight in the other hand. "Do what you need."

Latona let the flames curled around her fingers jump back to the lamp. Her fingers missed the comfort of their warmth, but this would be easier if she didn't have to spare attention to make sure she didn't set her clothes or anything else in the vicinity ablaze. Merula held the lamp high, her head turning left and right, swiveling to stay alert for dangers, while Latona crept down the street.

They did not have to go far. Latona followed the thread of the Discordian magic past other houses. Inside each, she heard weeping and muffled shouts. *'Oh, I am going to make Corinna pay for this, somehow.'*

She started to turn into an alley between another domus and a four-story insula, but Merula caught her arm. "Me first. Just in case."

Latona stayed close behind as they investigated the alley, negotiating their way past the fullers' barrels, stacks of amphorae, and assorted baskets. "There!" Latona said, pointing past Merula at one of the amphorae. "I think it's in that."

Sure enough, when Merula tipped the amphora over and kicked off its lid, a bundle of bones and viscera, wrapped in black cloth and jabbed through with bronze pins, tumbled out. It was a larger parcel than most of those they'd found the prior year, and foul magic emanated from it with such strength that Latona staggered, falling against the wall.

"Domina?"

"I'm all right," Latona said, gathering her wits. "It's a powerful charm."

"Can you—?" Merula's face pinched. She didn't want to imply that Latona couldn't handle it any more than Latona wanted to admit she wasn't certain.

"No choice but to try," Latona said, kneeling. "Keep a lookout behind me. And—" She raised a hand, calling a lick of flame back to her fingers. "Thank you for that."

She let the flames do as much of the work as she could. At her urging, they leapt to the charm, eager to devour it—but they popped angrily and changed color to a pale, milky green. They would not be enough. Latona used Fire to channel Spirit, closing her eyes and focusing all her effort on driving out the thorny Fracture magic which struggled to survive within the charm.

Inimical elements were vulnerable to each other, and the Discordian magic fought back against her with the ruthless instincts of a cornered weasel. Sweat broke out on Latona's brow; her blood buzzed within her veins. She could sense, too, *lemures* approaching. *'No. I'm not having any of that.'*

She pushed harder, using every scrap of her fury to chase down the Fracture magic and leave it nowhere to turn. It spiked and jabbed back at her, a thousand needles trying to stab through her emotional defenses. Latona had become practiced, though, in forging shields. *'Venus, make my heart strong. Vulcan, give my soul armor. Fire protects, so protect me now, that I can protect this neighborhood, this city, these people.'*

Vibia could unravel these charms at their core; Latona had no choice but to flood them with her own power until there was no room for anything else. Her forehead and the base of her spine grew sweat-damp with the exertion.

Finally, she felt the Fracture magic dissipate. When she opened her eyes, the flames had gone out, and the paving stone beneath the crumpled heap of bones was scorched and cracked.

"We'll deal with that in the morning," Latona said, rising with a wince. "Gods. I feel like I ran to the Capitoline and back."

"Inside, Domina." Merula's voice brooked no argument.

More of the wretched curses were out there, she was sure, but, aggravatingly, Latona knew she didn't have the strength to do anything about them. Not right now.

This one, she was certain, had been deliberately placed. Close enough to the Vitellian domus to afflict them, far enough away to be planted without arousing immediate suspicion. *'Planted how long ago? And how many might there be?'* A dormant charm could be nearly impossible to detect until invoked. *'The whole city could be seeded, and we might not know until it's too late.'*

No sooner were they back inside the house than Lucia launched herself at Latona, flinging her arms around her aunt's waist. The girl was hiccuping through her tears, unable to speak. Latona stroked her hair, murmuring soft words of comfort, then looked up to where Aula stood a few feet away.

"Lucius," Aula croaked by way of explanation. "For both of us." She dropped her voice, stepping closer. "Father... I'm not sure. He won't say. Mother, or his brother, maybe. I tried to keep the household in their rooms once we realized... I think they're mostly all right." A weak smile. "Alhena didn't see anything. Had the sense to stay in her room with her eyes closed and block it all out."

Aulus and Gaius were both in front of the altar, now ablaze with lamps, their hands held up in offering. Latona lifted her niece into her arms, then crossed the atrium to them with Lucia's face buried in her neck. Aulus did not turn to her immediately, but his arms drooped and his head sagged. Then, like a man burdened with a great weight, he pushed himself up from the floor.

"Did you—?" Aulus made a vague gesture. "Did you stop—that?"

Latona nodded. "I did." Pride bid her add, "That's what we were doing last year, Father. Vibia and I. That's what we were fighting. That, all over the city."

Perhaps it was not the time for that assertion, but Latona wanted him to *know*. She would never have hoped for this misery to befall her own family, but perhaps now Aulus would understand the importance of her work and the power she could wield.

At the moment, however, he was too thunderstruck to do more than nod. "I may have questions for you in the morning," Aulus said, his voice papery and weak. "I cannot frame them now." Without another word, he went to his chamber, his steps lethargic and shuffling.

Latona kissed Lucia's head. "It'll be all right, dear one," she whispered, though she did not know how. "Go back to bed." Exhausted by the ordeal and her tears, Lucia allowed herself to be passed off to her mother. "Merula, give me a moment. I promise I'll come to bed shortly."

"I will be fetching some vervain for you," Merula said. "I think you are needing what rest you can get before a busy morning."

"Too likely."

Then Latona and Gaius were alone in the atrium again. He dropped his hands and settled back on his heels. Latona sat down next to him. "I've been worried about you," she said softly. "Since you got back. And now this... The *lemures*, they take shapes they know will unsettle you. Someone who died that you... you feel you have unfinished business with. And I imagine, in Iberia..." She didn't know a tactful way to finish that sentence.

Gaius did it for her. "In Iberia, I saw many men made corpses. I expected that. There were dead men in Vendelicia, too. You get used to it. Sort of. But the way of it..." He drew a shuddering breath. "The Lusetani were attempting necromancy, in the end. Did you know that? And now this..."

Tears spilled freely down his cheeks. Latona reached out to rub his back, leaving him the space to decide if he wanted to speak more or not. Eventually he swiped at his face, dashing the tears away.

"I had a friend," he said. "Titus Mennenius. Junior tribune. He was... he was only in Iberia because of me. I suggested it, when we were back in Vendelicia. Thought it'd be good experience for him, and I... I wanted the company."

"He knew the risks, same as you," Latona said. She would've sent more calming energy his way if she had any to spare.

"None of us knew the risks of Iberia, though. Not when we went in. He—he took ill when the Lusetani sent their damned mist-borne plague into Toletum. And I..." He choked back another sob. "Your gift saved me there, too, you know. But I just keep thinking, I might've saved him. Even after he fell sick, if I'd given the focale to him. It might've burned him clean of the pestilence. But I... I made a choice. A selfish choice." The words spilled faster now, a confession tumbling like a waterfall. "I made a choice. I looked at the situation, and I decided my life was more important than his. I was the commander. I had to... to stay fit... I couldn't risk losing that protection."

"You *did*. You absolutely did, Gaius." She edged closer to him, hugging both her arms around his shoulders. "More lives than his depended on you."

"But how do I live with myself now? Knowing I made that calculation. Knowing I-I have it in me to be so cold, so heartless?"

"If you were so heartless," Latona insisted, "you would not now be weeping for his memory."

He sniffed, trying to bring himself back under control. They sat in silence a long while, lamp lights flickering all around them. There would be no swift fix to the shadow on Gaius's soul, Latona understood. No easy remedy. Some wounds, time alone could mend, but company had the power to bleed tension from a dark night.

XLVI

Domus Magicae, Esquiline Hill

Vibia only needed to look at Latona to see the night's travails written on her face. "You too, I see." She sighed. "Too much to hope that the incident was isolated."

She had left her house not long after dawn, and still had not been the first to arrive at the red door on the Esquiline Hill. She found Latona in the study, bent over a desk piled high with papers and wax tablets. Her hair was loosely braided, and weary lines on her face made her appear much older. Vibia's sense of Fracture picked up frayed edges and spiky points. *'Small wonder. All we've been through, all we've tried, and now it feels like we made no progress, for all those months.'*

Latona was, as ever, in ceaseless motion, pacing from one end of the desk to another, pausing to rearrange papers or scribble something down on a tablet. "No, it was quite widespread, it seems. Father's clients were queuing outside the house when I left, and many were murmuring of horrors in the night."

"What are we going to do?"

Latona's fingers tightened against her desk. "I don't know." The aggravation grinding in her voice, Vibia knew, was directed at herself, not at Vibia. "Our piecemeal method of responding to their assaults never worked, not as thoroughly as we needed it to. And now!" She shook her head. "Well. We wondered why they'd been quiet for so long. Evidently in preparation for *this*, an attack that's such a hydra we can't hope to strike off all its heads."

"Time, then," Vibia said, "to go for the heart."

Latona's fingernails drummed her agitation on the wood. "You mean Corinna herself."

"And any of her associates we can nail to the wall." Vibia kept her frustration more contained than Latona, but her fury was no less, thunder rumbling beneath her skin. She wanted the Discordians to pay, wanted them to *hurt*, in recompense for all their treachery.

"I agree. I just can't see how. With luck, more heads will help us find a way through. I sent to everyone we can trust. Short though that list is these days. But Rubellia's on her way, Alhena's off fetching Terentilla, and Aula's gone to Maia Domitia to begin rallying non-magical support. I also sent to Marcus Autronius, because I knew he'd want to know, though he'll be expected in the Curia today. I just wish..."

She pursed her lips, and neither of them finished the sentence. It did no good to wish that they had more allies, that Marcia Tullia hadn't taken against them and warned off half the mages in the city.

Latona brushed through a variety of papers, though Vibia didn't think she was taking in any of them. "Anyway. We'll enlist Obir and his collegium, too."

Vibia nodded. "I'll ask Sempronius about other resources."

"No doubt," Latona said, her voice suddenly icy, "he has many."

There it was, the full throat of what had been, till then, only a whisper of unease. Vibia met Latona's eyes, always so expressive, and saw an open field of hurt and anger. "He's told you." A tight nod. Vibia blew out a puff of air. "Gods above, when the man decides to do something, he doesn't waste time."

"You knew." It was not a question.

"Since he was a child."

Latona's mouth pressed thin again, and her cheeks were pink. "I don't... I don't want you to think I blame you or hold any ill feeling. Of course you couldn't tell me. Of course you protect your brother's secrets."

"Of course." Vibia wasn't about to argue that point. Her loyalty to Latona was yet in its infancy, for all the intensity of its creation. Her loyalty to Sempronius was, despite the corrections he might sometimes require, a thing fixed in steel, unyielding and never-tarnished.

Latona's throat worked before she could go on. "It's still difficult, though. Knowing that you... that you've known, and you must cover, that you..." Latona pushed her hair back from her face, straightening her spine and drawing down her mask of courtesy. "No. Forgive me. Now is not the time for—"

An odd pain nicked at Vibia, seeing Latona affect conscious propriety with her. Once, she would have welcomed the coolness of distant civility as an excuse not to have to explain any further. Now it seemed awkward, unnatural between them. "You want to know if I approve of his course of action." Vibia folded her hands. "I worry about the secret getting out. I've imagined the consequences a thousand times." She gave Latona a pointed look. "Rarely so often as when he took up with you. But whether it's *wrong*? It simply doesn't figure into my considerations. He is my brother. I will support and protect him. That is all there is to it."

Latona was quiet a long moment, chewing on Vibia's words. She wanted to be angry. Her instinct was to be angry, but that was unfair. *'Is there anything you wouldn't do for your sisters? For Gaius? For Lucia? Is there any crime any of them could commit that would turn you against them?'*

No. Of course not.

It would be unjust in the extreme, then, to blame Vibia for similar familial defense. *'If blame is even the right word. For her or for him.'*

She kept shuffling papers pointlessly. "I don't know if I think it's wrong, either," she said, without looking at Vibia. "With all we've learned about the Augians, and with all we're starting to suspect about who made these rules in the first place, what they were hiding, what misconceptions or outright lies led to their creation..." She sighed. "I certainly don't think Sempronius is a new Dolosus. But I am troubled by his deception and the dangers that attend it."

"For what it's worth," Vibia said, "I think he should have told you long ago. I think he *would* have, if he hadn't been halfway across the continent for over a year. But proposing before doing so was... unjust."

"On that, we agree."

Untangling her feelings about Sempronius's mendacity would take more than she had in her, if she were to keep her wits clear enough to take on Anca Corinna and her associates. *'I must put it away. All of it. That will be a problem for if we make it through this. If I pitch myself against Corinna with my mind and soul shaken, then that nightmare of a woman will shatter me.'*

Closing her eyes briefly, Latona summoned every scrap of the fortitude she had employed to steer herself through other ordeals. Then she opened them and returned her attention to her desk, trying to locate one of Alhena's notes about a possible connection between *lemures* and elemental conduits between the worlds.

She affected a lightness she did not truly feel, knowing it would not fool Vibia for an instant. "Well, as I said, I've no ill feeling towards you over it." A pause. "Complex feelings, perhaps."

"That, I think," Vibia allowed, "is fair."

Latona shook her head and shoulders, sloughing off the awkward conversation and her rattled emotions with it. "We really must focus."

The thunderous chaos in the Curia was not of Rabirus's precise design, but he gloried in it nonetheless.

The fiends had visited his neighborhood, too. A nuisance, that, and one he intended to direct Durmius Argus to remedy—for he had no doubt whose hand had directed this well-timed calamity. After so long losing faith in all his allies and subordinates, it was pleasant to realize that one of them was capable of formulating and executing a worthy plan. *'Even if I would've appreciated some warning.'*

Rabirus had been in the midst of his household's midnight ritual, barefoot and casting beans, when the shade appeared: Horatius Ocella, as he had been in his final days. Pallid and emaciated, his ocean-dark eyes hollowed out and ringed in black, his lips chapped and bleeding. No words, no speech from the specter, but fields of accusation written on his face.

'Wretched presumption of the fiends to take such a shape.' Rabirus had served Ocella in order to serve the nation, and he had taken advantage of Ocella's decline and death for the same reason. *'What guilt should I feel for those actions? Why should a shade appear to reproach me?'*

His wife had not been awake; what his son had seen, Rabirus had not asked, only told the boy to master himself. Rabirus did not know precisely how the Discordians summoned the *lemures* or what power controlled them, but he knew they could do no physical harm. No harm at all, in fact, if a man's mind and soul were strong enough. The *lemures* held no power over a man who did not fear.

Judging by the reverberant voices bouncing off the Curia's walls, Aven had few fearless men in it.

"It is an ill omen!" Arrius Buteo hollered. "Never before—*never*, not in living memory nor in the annals of our history—has the Lemuria been so disturbed!"

"It must have been at *some* point," Licinius Cornicen drawled unhelpfully, "or the ritual would not have needed to exist in the first place."

Arrius leveled a glare at Cornicen. "Never since the *mos maiorum* was determined by our forefathers. For hundreds of years, the actions of every paterfamilias in his home served to protect the city from exactly this sort of—of ruinous upheaval! The good people of Aven, disturbed from their beds! Their homes invaded by malicious spirits! Honored fathers, this can only happen when we fail in our pious duties, in our devotion to the proper way of things, and the gods withdraw their protection from us!"

Another round of shouting and counter-shouting broke out: Quintus Terentius shaking a fist, the Naeviae hollering from the back bench, Old Crispinius croaking his opinion through angry wheezes.

Neither of the consuls seemed up to the task of managing the mayhem and forcing the senators to speak in turns and by hierarchical precedence. Decimus Gratianus's spine was straight, but whenever he opened his mouth to speak, it flopped like a fish's, wordless and helpless. His eyes darted about the room, always a beat or two behind the whirlwind pace of the conversation.

Cominius Celer was even worse, slumped in his chair, the dark circles under his eyes testament to his exhaustion. He had a large family, Rabirus recalled, and lived in a crowded neighborhood; no doubt the *lemures* had taken a heavy toll on him.

With the consuls impotent to instill order, volume and presence were the only things making one man heard above the others: dignity, gravity, and sheer lung-power. So much the better; Rabirus could make use of that.

He stood, adopting oratory pose; the visual signal was enough to prompt instinctive quiet in some of the assembly. "Can we wonder at the cause, august fathers?" Rabirus asked. "What could have displeased the gods so?" Now was no time to play coy with rhetorical questions, however; he pointed an open hand straight at Sempronius Tarren. He was near Galerius Orator, the Autroniae, and a few others who had not yet joined the shouting, but bent in whispered consultation with each other. "The cause sits among us, my friends. A man who has brought turmoil back to this city. Who has invited Iberian barbarians to walk our streets and avail themselves of our hard-earned prosperity. Who used, we hear, tainted foreign magics to win his battles! And who is indulging his ego, trying to hold a triumph in all but name by attaching himself to the Ludi Tyrenni? *This* is who has offended the gods!"

"Yes, yes!" Arrius Buteo cried, picking up the thread. "These sacred days have been disrupted by so many transgressions of the *mos maiorum.*" He, too, jabbed an accusatory finger at Sempronius. "Let him answer to that, if he can!"

Weary Cominius Celer rubbed his forehead. "Very well. How do you answer this, Sempronius Tarren?"

Aggravatingly unruffled, Sempronius rose and spoke in a measured voice. "I deny the allegations, and I trust my fellow senators and the people of Aven are canny enough to recognize them for what they are: the vitriol of a general who returned home in disgrace rather than in triumph."

Outwardly, Rabirus did not dignify that with any reaction, but inwardly, he fumed. *'Because of you, and those women you rely upon in most unmanly fashion. Women's magic cursed me and haunted me, all on your behalf, all so you would succeed where I failed. My actions were correct in every particular; you and those women hobbled me.'*

Sempronius continued: "To answer each accusation in its particular, first I say that the idea that a few dozen new foreigners in this city suddenly tipped the balance into chaos is absurd. Aven is home to people from many nations, and long has been. Some are citizens; some are not. Some are here to trade; others to learn. Many of the august fathers sitting in this room owe their blood to men and women who were once strangers here—as were not Romulus and Remus themselves, in the beginning, fleeing the persecution of a northern king?"

Some murmuring attended this, though Rabirus considered it a gross exaggeration, considering the Divine Twins originally hailed from a town twelve miles away. Hardly the same as welcoming barbarians from distant nations.

"Further," Sempronius went on, "the Arevaci are not living within the bounds of the city walls. They are staying on the Janiculum and the Campus Martius, as is right and proper by the dictates of the *mos maiorum*. I can see no cause for the gods to take offense at the actions of those who have been allies to us. That alliance allows me to refute Rabirus's second point: that of foreign magic on the battlefield." He spread one hand in a gesture of allowance. "The Arevaci and other Iberian allies used their own magic to combat that of the Lusetani. Their gods do not take offense at it. But no Aventan soldier had any part in it except good honest sword-work, as Father Mars intends for us. No Aventan magic touched the soil of any battlefield, nor afflicted any man engaged in combat. So it has been for ages, when we fight alongside peoples whose battle-customs differ from our own. This, too, is part of the *mos maiorum*. Father Mars and blessed Bellona never voiced objection before; why would they begin now? Why bless us with victory in the first place, if they did not like the manner of our winning it?"

Arrius Buteo began to voice a counterpoint, but Cominius Celer snapped at him from the consul's chair. "You wanted him to respond to the charges, so let him finish!"

Another aggravation. Cominius was of their faction, always voted the right way, was willing enough to take instruction when it came to proposing or blocking legislation, but he was a man easily bored by the nuance of politics. '*No doubt he wants this done with as fast as possible so he can get home for lunch and a nap.*'

Sempronius shifted his stance slightly. "As to the final accusation, when this body decided I had not earned the honor of a triumphator, I yielded the title without argument or complaint. I welcome the input of this august body on my intention to assist with the upcoming games. I have long felt that, as unjust exile interrupted my term as aedile, I owe the city a debt. I am now in a position to pay it. I wish, too, to see our legionaries and our allies honored, and in the games, I have found that opportunity. Far better than a triumph, in fact, for it will place the focus and honors where they rightfully belong: with our fighting men! What need have I to ride in a chariot, my face painted and wearing golden laurels?" He actually laughed.

"I have no desire to play at being Jupiter, my friends. But to see our legions rewarded for their bravery? Bravery which they demonstrated despite harrowing conditions? And to honor the dead, who gave their lives to secure Aven's interests at home and abroad? Yes, I shall confess to that aspiration. If there is illegality in it, I welcome correction."

With that, he sat down. Rabirus seethed as the Popularists and even some of the moderates clapped their approval of the speech. It was, Rabirus had to admit, neatly done; he could not continue to press his points without looking like he was against honoring the legions.

"Yes, yes, well," Gratianus said, waving a hand for quiet. Sempronius's speech had allowed his mind to catch up with the conversation. "If we're quite done with petty bickering, we still have a problem to deal with."

"What is there to be done before tomorrow night?" Buteo snapped. "If we are not to take reasonable action—expelling all those responsible for this calamity from the city—then we can do nothing but rely upon the piety of our citizens and *hope* it is enough to dispel the threat."

XLVII

Before the second night of the Lemuria, Gaius Vitellius spent as much time out-of-doors as he could manage, as though soaking in the spring sun would shield him against the dark spirits of the night.

Foolish, but better than sitting around all day waiting for doom to fall.

He walked the streets, observing the thousands of lives moving through them. Aven was anxious. Not so bad as Toletum during the siege, but the wire of tension ratcheted tighter with each hour. People still went about their duties: merchants hawking wares, magisters teaching children, butchers chopping up chickens and pigs, cooks toiling in thermopoliums, artisans of all trades working their crafts. But they did so with a wariness, ginger and suspicious, glancing over their shoulders and scrutinizing their neighbors.

It was a joy to go unrecognized. Divested of his tribune's crimson but not yet ready to take up a senatorial toga, Gaius moved through the city in a plain blue tunic and plainer brown cloak. The quality of the fabric, as well as his few rings and bracelets and the fine leather of his shoes, betrayed him as a man of means, but not as a patrician of one of Aven's most important families. Just a man, red-haired and freckled, who looked strong enough not to be worth crossing, and thus could walk unmolested.

When he returned home, the door was closed. Unusual, before sunset. Once Gaius opened the door, he heard sharp voices echoing from the back of the house, and realized why it had been shut. His father and Latona were in the middle of a row.

"I cannot negotiate this, Father," Latona was saying when Gaius crept towards the garden. "You said you would allow me to do my work, Juno's work—"

"Latona, do you know how dangerous it is?" Aulus countered. "Never mind these fiends and spirits—and yes, I *do* credit that this situation has gotten out of hand, and I do not discredit your talent nor your sacred duty, but Latona! The city at night, there are drunkards and robbers and—"

"On such a night as this? Even the most impious of men must have been rattled by the hauntings on the first night of the Lemuria."

"You credit their sense of self preservation too much," Aulus said dryly. "Many men would see only opportunity in this disorder, an opening created for them by the fears of others." He made a cutting gesture with one hand. "No. I cannot permit it."

"You *said*—"

"And you said you would be careful! And discreet!"

"I have every intention of being both of those things."

"Your actions would negate certainly one if not the other."

Gaius cleared his throat loudly. Two sets of emerald eyes snapped to him, sharp enough to spark flint. "Um," he said, "if it would ease your mind, Father, I'll go with her."

He wondered if Latona would object. Instead, she strode to his side, clutching his arm. "Are you sure?" she asked. "You don't even know what I mean to do."

"You mean to fight these fiends, somehow, somewhere." Cold slithered down his throat and into his gut at the thought, but he would be no safer tucked up in bed than anywhere else. At least if he went with Latona, he might feel as though he was of some use.

"I do," she confirmed. "And so I ask again: Are you sure you want to be there?"

He managed a nod. "I do. I..." He turned to their father. He had felt the power of the *lemures*, too; surely he understood the importance of Latona's work.

'In fact, I'd wager that's exactly why he's presenting an obstacle. He has been shaken, and so he wants to protect us all.'

Gaius could sympathize with that reaction, but he could also see what it overlooked. "I can safeguard her physically, while she attempts to safeguard all of us in the magical realm." He had no idea if it worked like that at all, but then, neither would their father. "I would be proud to do so, whatever the danger."

Aulus pressed his lips thin. "Still..." he said, "just the two of you, if you were set upon..."

"And Vibia, and Merula," Latona rushed to add. "Two mages, neither of us without defensive talents, and two others to watch our backs."

"Hrm," Aulus said. "Merula *is* quite as fierce as any gladiatrix." He sighed. "Very well. If your brother accompanies you... then do as you must. As... as Juno demands, and may her grace go with you."

After the sun set, Gaius tied his focale around his neck, strapped a dagger to his belt, and joined his sister. Strange, to wear the focale without his armor. Now wearing only tunic and cloak made him feel exposed, not free. *'And yet my sister has been waging war against demons in her gowns.'*

Once they were out in the street, out of their father's hearing, Gaius asked, "So where are we off to?" Latona had draped her crimson mantle over her head, and Merula wore a headscarf in the same color knotted over her curls. Gaius wondered how much magical weaving his sister had done in the past two years.

"Downhill to pick up Vibia Sempronia first, then the Esquiline," she answered, heading off with a brisk stride. "We have friends there, and they've been targeted before." She worried her lower lip. "But we need more information, and while we search for it, Aven suffers." Her shoulders drooped as though under a heavy weight. "We've been playing cat-and-mouse with our opponents for so long, Gaius. I'm tired of chasing them. I want to strike true, true enough to free Aven from their predations once and for all."

"You're thinking like a general," Vitellius said.

"Don't mock me, please, I'm far too tired to keep up."

"I'm not. I wouldn't. Not... not about something like that." He knew too well what it meant, to take responsibility for other men's souls. A few cohorts had strained his endurance, and here Latona was shouldering the burden of the largest city in Truscum. "Latona, I... I know I haven't been home long. I've no right to... well, any sort of an opinion on your life or what you do with it, really. But I've... I've seen things beyond..." He struggled for suitable words. "You're part of a world I've brushed up against but cannot have any control over," he attempted. "I don't understand it. It terrifies me. But I trust you with it."

She was quiet a moment, then said, "That differentiates you from our father, then. He can't control it; it terrifies him; but he endures my part in it out of necessity, not trust. He doesn't know what to do with me." She spoke with a sad, resigned weight. "He never did. He and Mother handed me over to Gaia Claudia, this strange, too-powerful girl-child they had somehow created. When I returned, I was Mother's problem, briefly, then Aula's, then my husband's. My whole life, he's tried to keep me safe." Her brow knitted in frustration. "But he's also always hoped someone else would know what to do with me."

They had both been brought up, as all Aventan children were, to revere their father as the infallible head of their family. Now their worlds had expanded past what Aulus Vitellius could get his hands around. "He wants me to settle back down," Gaius said. "Marry. Serve in the law courts, then join the Senate. Just as if... as if nothing else ever happened. He knows exactly what to do with me, but I don't think I can follow that path anymore."

She looked sideways at him as they walked. "What would you do instead?"

He laughed helplessly. "Gods only know. Not... not 'instead,' perhaps. But 'also.' I'd like to do something more than just wander my way up the *cursus honorem* because that's what's expected."

"Well," she said, with forced levity, "I'll contemplate. If anything tremendous comes to mind, I shall be sure to inform you and any other relevant authorities."

"Much appreciated, dear sister." He'd always known Aula was witty, but Latona's slyness was taking him by pleasant surprise. "But you, though! Whatever your disagreements with Father, they won't matter much longer. I can't imagine that the general—I mean, that Sempronius will seek to hinder you in your magical endeavors. He has great respect for magic; I saw that in Iberia."

A strange expression flitted over her face, one Gaius did not know how to interpret. Too complex to be the joy of a bride. Pained, almost. But it vanished almost as soon as he noticed it, covered as Latona assumed what he was coming to recognize as a customary countenance of composure.

"Sempronius does not have the same attitude on magic as Father, you're right."

"Is he—I mean to say, has his sister involved him in this effort at all?"

"He's been working on other mundane support for us," she replied, smooth as alabaster. Before Gaius could say anything else, Latona lifted a hand and flexed her fingers. Some of the flame from Merula's torch leapt to them. "Dark, isn't it?" she said casually. "So many houses are shuttered. Not that I blame them. I only wish it would do any good."

An unsubtle way of ending the conversation, but Gaius let her have it.

It would never cease to be strange, watching his little sister wielding such power, and yet it sat well on her. As a girl, she had never looked comfortable with her gifts; now she wore them as easily as a favorite gown. There was a rightness to it, like seeing the Curia full of togate men, a ship coming into port, or the sun rising over the hills in the east.

Some key component of her story eluded him. He felt the gap of it with an intuition he did not think he would have had, before Iberia.

He wasn't like Aula. He didn't want to pry. Latona had left him space in which to tell his story; he afforded her the same courtesy, should she decide to do so. *'But a general does not take time before battle to unburden himself of private troubles.'* And she was, as he said, now a general in her own way.

The Esquiline Hill at night had grown to be familiar terrain over the past year, but Vibia twitched at every unexpected noise nonetheless. A year of slipping about the shadows with Latona had not yet broken her of the instinct to flinch.

The intrusions were few enough, though; the city was still and quiet, unnaturally so. Even in a good year, few men chose to move their goods on the nights of the Lemuria, wary of attracting the attention of malicious spirits. After what had happened already this year, almost no one seemed to be risking it.

It was too cold for mid-Maius. Vibia had a cloak tucked about her shoulders, as well as the protective red mantle of Latona's weaving, but still the air nipped at her. Only the weather, or some foreboding of the evening's duties? *'It isn't right. I shouldn't be out here, shouldn't have to do this.'*

She allowed herself only a brief space to indulge in such whining, even within the confines of her own mind. What matter that she shouldn't have to? What difference, that the institutions that ought to have protected the city had instead betrayed it? She was here; she had power; she had to act. *Should* didn't enter into it.

'But I would dearly love to stick a knife in Anca Corinna's eye, if it mean I could spend the rest of my nights at peace and in bed, instead of wandering around chasing down her damned shadows.'

Gaius Vitellius stood sentinel to one side of them, Merula to the other, alert for any physical dangers. Vibia couldn't decide if Vitellius's presence pleased her or not. Helpful to have another set of eyes and hands, yes, and a man who could fight—though of course he could carry no sword inside the city limits, only a dagger little different from Merula's.

Vibia sensed broken pieces in him, worse than Latona's. What they suffered in Iberia had affected Vitellius's *animus* in a profound way. *'If danger comes, will he crack entirely, or find a way to weld those shattered edges together again, stronger than before?'*

A cold gust of air raced down the street—an unnatural gust, prickling the hairs on Vibia's arms and her magical sensibilities. She whipped around, grasping for the channel that Fracture's power was cutting through the world. "Vibia?" Latona asked. "Is it—"

"Coming from uphill." Vibia started walking, following the direction of the magic. Latona, Vitellius, and Merula fell into step behind her.

The trail led them to a serrated cliffside, a jagged face of stone forcing a break in the line of houses that curled around the hill. *'Edges will ever give strength to Fracture magic.'* Vibia's own senses tingled with the shearing power of the rock.

Several channels of Fracture magic now sang out to Vibia's veins, slicing through the city and converging—where? Vibia planted herself at a crossroads and took out her consecrated bronze knife. "Lord Janus and Lady Fortuna, look here. I call your powers to this place. Show me the way. Show me—"

Another icy blast of wind hit them, and Vibia realized, too late, what she had done. The magic didn't care who summoned it or what god they prayed to; its force, cast out from Vibia, eagerly joined the rest of the power pouring through the city—and Vibia herself was caught in the undertow.

XLVIII

Such lovely work, such magnificence. The Discordians had built their charms, and now invoked them with concentrated purpose, snapping animal bones and bird wings and the necks of little rodents. Each break was a locus of Fracture magic, and when blended with the power of death, held in their hands, the conduit to the netherworld widened. Corinna's breath came quicker as the edges of the world peeled away, letting the fiends in. Her skin flushed, her fingers flexed, the core of her tightened in eager anticipation. *'Yes, yes... Sweet lady, yes!'*

Drawing on the strength of those around her, Corinna reached into the split in the world and called forth the *lemures* in various forms: haunting *umbrae*, so easy to call now, so eager to come and drive men to madness; *devorae*, soul-hungry, spirits that ached for life and would feast on whatever they found of it; and last, the *furillae*, her little furies, summoned now in greater strength and numbers than her painted curses had drawn.

Dangerous spirits, all. Hard to hold balance, not to give over entirely to them. Sometimes, Corinna ached to do so, to let them have her. *'But then who would work Discordia's glory? Who would open the way for more of them? Durmius is right. I must hold myself firm of purpose.'*

The *devorae* had jagged forms, darker and more opaque, like they were made all of shadowy teeth. Corinna had never seen their beauty so distinct before. When she first raised them, in Stabiae, they were less substantial. And the *furillae* burned like tiny fires cast loose from any source of fuel, brilliant red and orange against the dark of the night. Gorgeous, and their intensity shivered inside Corinna's veins. *'This is the power of our forces combined. This is the sign of our strength and our lady's favor.'*

With this, they could shred an entire city.

It would take, as her brother had insisted, the right moment, an ideal confluence of occasion and opportunity. Tonight, the Discordians only practiced, delivering the city a fright that would prime it for the final night of the Lemuria, when they would summon all their strength and set the ritual over all Aven, every altar a conduit, every household a gateway. These beautiful creatures would be given their liberty.

What would happen after that, Corinna could not be sure, but her toes curled to imagine it.

The wind changed direction, as it would before a storm, and dragged magic in its wake. It raised the hairs on Latona's arms and stung at the back of her neck. Her crimson mantle scorched wherever it touched her skin; an illusion, Latona knew, but a painful one nonetheless. Fracture magic, assaulting her shields and boundaries. *'How far will it reach, tonight? How many souls will be affected?'* It was everywhere, sluicing through the streets like water in a torrential storm. Latona had to dull her own sensitivity to seeing magic at work, or the entire world would have been awash in a bronze tinge.

"Vibia, what are they doing now?" No response. "Vibia?"

Vibia rotated strangely, like a statue placed on a cart. Fear like a cold stone dropped into Latona's stomach. *'No. No, no, no...'*

With a grimace of disdain, Vibia raised her hands—slowly, as though she weren't used to operating her limbs—and pulled the crimson mantle out of her hair, tossing it aside. Her eyes took on a strange glow, orange-red where they should have been white.

'What is this? Not what we've seen before, what got into her?' Some spirit had taken advantage of Vibia opening herself up to magical influence. The rivers of bronze energy diverted eddies to course through her, wrapping themselves around her heart.

"Domina?" Merula queried.

"Be ready to grab her," Latona said, deliberately calm. "Both of you. Disarm her if you can. Try not to hurt her."

"Her eyes," Vitellius said, voice quaking. "Latona, her eyes."

"I see them."

"What—?"

"I don't know."

Vibia's head tilted at an awkward angle. "Ready to play hero?" Her voice was her own, not taken over as it had been the year before, in the wheat field near Stabiae. Yet it had an unusual quality, hollow and oddly musical, like the ring of a far-off bell clung to each syllable. "So *good*, Vitellia Latona, so nice, so sweet, so responsible. Playing the savior now to make up for having stood mutely beside so many of Ocella's horrors."

Latona flinched. She had; no denying that. She had believed, then, that there was no other choice. Whether she would believe the same now, make the same choice, was pointless to speculate. But it was a well-aimed barb, a carefully honed bit of nastiness. *'Whatever is inside her wants to hurt me. Why? How does it benefit from that?'*

Merula and Vitellius moved to flank Vibia, each with cautious steps, trying not to excite her attention. *'Keep her focus on you, Latona. If they can restrain her, you can work on driving the fiend out.'* So she swallowed around the lump in her throat and said, not to Vibia but to the thing occupying her, "What is it you want? You've been summoned here for some purpose. Do you even know what it is?"

The vermilion in Vibia's eyes flared. "Do you have any idea what it's like, watching my brother fawn over you?" Vibia's lips, suddenly dry and chapped, curled in a sneer. "What a humiliation for the family. The celebrated imperator, the hero of Iberia and conqueror of the Lusetani, panting at the heels of a power-hungry slut."

An old fear, that accusation, one Latona had been fending off for years, since the day Dictator Ocella first cast his eyes on her and commanded her compliance. It might have been easier to shrug off if not for the recent resurgence of those whispers, kindling doubt.

Vibia went on: "And one who makes such a spectacle of herself. Runs in the family, I suppose. Fire in the blood, they always said that of the Vitelliae, and Jupiter knows your elder sister is vulgar and presumptuous, parading herself in the Forum. But you!" Vibia laughed, thin and cruel. "Your ostentatious goodness, always flinging yourself into some danger, such noble self-sacrifice, and for what? So that someone will pat your head and say, 'Good girl, well done,' at last?"

Latona's chin trembled, but she held back any other show that those words struck closer to her core. "I will always choose innocent lives over my own dignity, this I confess." She stayed stock-still, watching Vibia, waiting for Merula and Vitellius to act.

"A spectacle," Vibia repeated. "Self-aggrandizing puffery. You think you have what it takes to make a difference? You think you can usher in reform, install new order? You're a disgrace, and you'll never win, not when this city is perfectly poised to fall into chaos."

Merula and Vitellius made no sound as they struck; they must have given each other some visual signal behind Vibia's back. Both dove for her in an instant—but before either reached her, Vibia thrust out both arms, without taking her eyes from Latona. As soon as her fingers touched Merula and Vitellius, they shuddered, their motion arrested, howling in agony. *'Not again, not again! How did the fiend give her that power, how did Corinna—?'*

There was no time to sort out the magic involved, how Vibia had manifested this power to invoke pain or why the mantle and focale were insufficient protection. Latona summoned her own power as a shield, spinning Fire and Spirit together in a golden glow. *'If I can envelop them inside it... If I can reach Vibia with it, maybe it will drive out the spirit...'*

Vitellius fell to his knees; Merula's arms wheeled in futile panic. Before they could recover, Vibia dashed forward toward Latona.

Latona reeled back, but not fast enough; Vibia's fingers closed around her throat. Though thin, they were surprisingly strong; Latona coughed and sputtered, clawing at Vibia's hands with her own. The bones pressed hard against her windpipe and curled around, squeezing off the flow of blood.

Fracture magic crackled against her Fire-spun shielding; the golden glow held for now, Latona did not feel the soul-wracking pain that seized Merula and Vitellius, but she did not know how long she could keep it up—and it did nothing against the physical assault.

Latona's vision started to blur. *'If I pass out, I'm dead.'* The thing controlling Vibia would throttle her. Or worse, trap her back inside the nightmare that Corinna had sent her to months earlier. Rising panic threatened to shatter Latona's grip on her magic. *'No, no, no, I will not allow it, I will not go back there, I will not, I will not!'*

In desperation, Latona wrapped her magic around her own fear, remembering how she had once defeated a pair of rapists during the riots that followed Ocella's death. She scooped up her terror and thrust it into Vibia's psyche, blasting her with a concentrated dose of Spirit magic. Vibia's grip slackened, but Latona was growing weaker. If she couldn't concentrate, she couldn't work her magic or keep up a shield—and if she couldn't breathe, she couldn't concentrate. She lifted a knee, trying to kick at Vibia, but to no avail.

Then Vibia screamed, reeling back, and a hot splash of blood spattered Latona's face as the pressure on her throat disappeared. A furious blur with short chestnut curls had impacted Vibia from the side, and Latona saw the flash of Merula's little knife. Vibia's arm was bleeding openly, rivulets, near-black in the dark of night, coursing down towards her elbow.

Latona wasted no time; she pushed another wave of fear into Vibia, a current of Spirit magic to shake loose the fiend inside her. She felt something give, a flutter of the demonic hold. She wanted to make another push, but she could scarcely draw breath.

Vibia hurled herself at Latona again, but Merula intervened, showing no sign if she feared a repeat of the curse-pain upon making contact. She stepped between the two mages, bracing her legs wide to absorb the impact. Merula's long hours in the gymnasium, sparring with gladiatrices, paid off; she moved with terrifying speed, slamming an elbow into Vibia's stomach, then bringing clenched hands down between her shoulderblades when the woman doubled over. Latona thought that would be the end of it, but Vibia leapt up again, the fiends within her spurring her on.

This time it was Vitellius who intervened. He used her own momentum against her. As Vibia lunged forward, Vitellius bent and rolled Vibia over his shoulders. If the scene hadn't been so horrifying, it might have been funny, with all the rose-colored linen whirling in the air. Vibia landed hard on her back, the air huffing out of her lungs.

Before she could recover again, Merula was upon her, straddling her chest, knees pressing down Vibia's arms just above the elbow. Then the knife was back out, held to Vibia's pale throat. Whatever lurked in her had a sense of self-preservation for the body it occupied, it seemed, and was unwilling to attack again while so threatened.

Vitellius knelt, capturing Vibia's arms, binding them with his focale, and pinning them to the ground above her head. Vibia screamed, so loud it would surely attract attention from the locals. *'Unless they're all dealing with similar troubles,'* Latona thought, scrambling over to Vibia's side.

She placed her hand on the knotted focale. "Get out of her," Latona snarled, fixating all her remaining power on the charmed fabric. Spirit and Fire, gold and red swirling together against the bronze whirls of Fracture dragging Vibia away from herself. "*Out.* Blessed Juno, restore her to herself, bring her back."

Vibia's body seized violently, elbows and feet rattling against the stones of the street. None of the other three showed mercy; Merula and Vitellius held her pinned, and Latona continued to push, her magic shuddering against the Discordian power.

Finally, Vibia fainted dead away.

At first, no one moved. "Could be shamming," Merula said.

Latona touched Vibia's face, then peeled up one of her eyelids. The vermilion light had left them. "I don't think so." Her voice rasped, and she became aware of how much her throat hurt. "It feels... it feels like the Discordian power eased." She lifted her head. "We should go, though. We need to get away from here."

They made slow progress toward Obir's collegium, Vitellius carrying Vibia, Latona leaning on Merula. Every stride hurt; Latona stumbled frequently, her legs wobbly, her lungs burning as though she had run to Ostia and back. When they were about halfway there, Vitellius paused, setting Vibia down on a platform, the kind usually home to some magister and his class. "I need to readjust. Unless, Latona, you think—"

Vibia stirred. Merula's hand went toward her dagger, but when Vibia's eyes opened, they stayed white. She pushed herself unsteadily to a sitting position, rubbing her temples. "Gods above, my head..." she muttered, then looked up at the others. "It's me. Just me, rather. No one and nothing else in residence."

"How can we be sure?" Vitellius asked.

The withering look she bestowed upon him was answer enough; purely human and unmistakably Vibia.

———— ⁂ ————

"So you were aware?" The rasp in Latona's voice twisted another pang of guilt in Vibia's chest. "You knew what was happening?"

"Every moment," Vibia said, as Vitellius unwound the binding focale from around her wrists. "Latona, I—" She shook her head. "I'm sorry. For what that *thing* made me say. I didn't mean any of it."

Latona pressed her lips together, then she said, with careful measure, "You did, though. Part of you did. Some of it, at least."

It did not sound like an accusation, but the weight of judgment came down on Vibia's head anyway, because the terrible thing was, Latona was right. The words had not sprung up out of nowhere. Whatever fiend had inhabited Vibia, it did not have the power to invent, nor even to interpret. It dredged up what was already within a person, the darkest, ugliest scraps. All those words had been inside her, even if she never would have spoken them aloud of her own volition. Even if she didn't really believe them. She had thought them, if only ever for the blink of an eye, an involuntary contribution from the recesses of her soul. An animal's instinct, to defend her own and savage anyone else who came too close.

Latona scrutinized Vibia a long moment, while Vitellius stood by awkwardly and Merula glared. Vibia was sure the Spirit mage was reading her emotions, and she didn't care for it, having this shame exposed.

Then, Latona sat down and flung her arms around Vibia. "It's alright." She squeezed tight, clasping Vibia's thin body to hers. "It's alright. We are not our worst thoughts."

Relief swept over Vibia, surprising in its intensity, too much to be merely gratitude that the incident would not complicate her relationship with an ally. "Gods, you really are annoying," she said, returning the embrace. "And I do mean that. You're supposed to be furious with me or terrified of me or something."

"Seems like a waste of energy," Latona said, pulling back to give her a smile. "And gods know what words might've come out if that thing had slipped inside *me*."

"Hm," Vibia said. "A thought to chew on." She pressed her hands to her temples again. There wasn't enough vervain and willow in the world to abate the throbbing inside her skull. She wanted to sleep for a week, but with that option decidedly unavailable, she pressed on, grimly determined. "The night isn't a total loss. I know what they're trying to do. I could sense it, through that fiend. What they're preparing for. Tonight was just a test—an experiment."

"They like to do that," Latona said.

"Yes, which is troubling. It speaks to a level of control I wouldn't ascribe to Discordians. Externally imposed, perhaps, by Corinna's brother or the Optimates. But you can already feel it, can't you? The flow of power is ebbing."

Latona frowned, glancing around them. "You're right. The magical density is much less. So what are they preparing *for*? What's their goal?"

Vibia sucked in air, hardly wanting to put it into words. "They're trying to crack open every lararium in the city. I expect they'll do it at midnight on the third day of the Lemuria."

"When every paterfamilias is performing the final ritual to appease the dead," Vitellius said.

"Indeed. They will instead be inviting the *lemures* to stroll right through into our world." Vibia's hands moved in slow circles against her temples. "Every foul spirit the Discordians can tempt along for the fun—the *umbrae*, the *devorae*, whatever in Janus's good name took hold of me tonight. And not just, I think, from the underworld. I think they want to punch through to... to whatever is beyond it, or between..." Vibia frowned, trying to frame what she had sensed. Difficult, to put words to something so inhuman. "To the space between the worlds, to the void where creation began."

Yes, that felt horrifyingly right. The Discordians would reach for more than mere hauntings. Spirits from Pluto's realm would not be sufficient to truly drive the city into destruction. They needed a power more primal and instinctive to achieve their true goal: strife.

The absolute essence of Discordia. The thing she wanted the most.

They would need to reach into the realm of Chaos itself and draw forth its raw, sundering essence.

One look at Latona's stricken face indicated she had reached the same conclusion. "They will crack this city open like a rotten cask," Latona said. "Every soul within the walls at the mercy of their worst instincts. Every petty dispute. Every jealousy. Every fit of temper. Every nasty thought given voice and, perhaps, strength of arm."

"Everything that separates us from the beasts, stripped away."

"Worse. Beasts kill for need, not fun or revenge or envy."

"Can they really do that?" Vitellius asked. "To overpower the rituals of so many households?"

Vitellius sounded horrified and curious, not skeptical, so Vibia gave him a fair answer. "Yes. They are fanatics, not merely going through the motions of ritual. They can clearly summon a great deal of power. They've prepared well, finding places rife with Fracture energy. And on the third night of the Lemuria, when the boundary between our world and those beyond is so thin? Yes. If they cry out to the void with every scrap of their rotten souls, the void will answer resoundingly."

Latona grasped Vibia's wrists, and her voice was hollow with horror. "Vibia. Could they affect the Field of Mars?"

Vibia thought the pit in her stomach could have sunk no lower, but Latona proved her wrong. "Oh gods. The soldiers."

A legion of men, awaiting their chance to march during the Ludi Tyrenni. A legion already haunted, already burdened with terrible shadows on their souls. A legion who had seen horrors and chaos and then come home, thinking themselves safe. A legion still under arms, who would pay no heed to the laws prohibiting weapons of war within the city if they were curse-maddened and demon-ridden.

Crestfallen, Vitellius sat down, his rump thudding onto the stones of the street. "I don't... I don't..." Stricken, he looked to his sister. "They will break, Latona. I don't like to say it, not of my men, but after what they suffered in Iberia, a force as powerful as we just witnessed... they will break under its strain. And the streets will run with blood."

They sat in silence, contemplating the coming horror.

Finally, Latona passed both hands over her face, scrunched her fingers into her hair, and stood up. "Very well, then. Tomorrow, we tell the others, and we figure out a plan of attack. It's as simple as that."

"As simple as—?" Vibia scoffed. "Latona, did you hear me? Those Discordians are ready to bring half the city down around their ears. They have assembled their full force, and they are well-prepared. We've had trouble taking them on one at a time."

"So let us fix ourselves to the purpose. We have a day and a half to organize ourselves. You tasted their power and their intentions. Can you trace it to its source?"

Denial was on her tongue, but Vibia checked it. She had felt the channels that Discordian magic had carved into Aven, the power sizzling along those lines. "I think... I think I could. Not now."

"No," Vitellius agreed. "The four of us together don't have the strength to fight off a weasel at the moment, let alone deranged cultists."

"But now that I know what to look for, I should be able to find the traces."

"Then tomorrow," Latona said, "we find those traces. We hunt them down. And we figure out how to put an end to their threat before it can rend this city apart."

Janiculum Hill

Something was wrong, desperately wrong, across the river.

Two nights earlier, Matigentis had been troubled with restless sleep—not an unusual occurrence since leaving Iberia. The lady of the house poked her head in, and Neitin felt the urge to apologize, then resentment at the urge, since it wasn't by her choice that her son was here to disturb anyone's sleep.

Despite their lack of a common language, though, Neitin understood well enough when the woman clucked sympathetically. She wanted, it seemed, to help, so they took it in turns to sit with Mati. Every time he started to drop off, he would shake himself bolt upright again, wailing incoherently. Only near dawn had he settled down.

On this night, he again woke crying, wide-eyed and reaching out for his mother. Instead of allowing himself to be mollified, however, he pointed up at the windows. "Bad!" he screamed. "Bad, bad, bad!"

Neitin could see little; the Aventans cut the windows in their city homes high and long, allowing light in and heat out, but minimizing how much of the foul air from the street entered a house. Wise, if frustrating.

Yet his was not the only commotion. Neitin's Aventan custodians were also awake and evidently in some distress, judging by their brisk words and wild gestures. After some time, the man sent a messenger out, and not long after, the front door banged open. Long-legged Hanath entered, with two women and two men attending her.

"What's going on?" Neitin asked. The Numidian woman had visited her twice since their arrival in the city, but not in the middle of the night.

Hanath gestured for one of her men to go talk to the Aventans while she took Neitin and Mati aside. "I do not know," she said, voice somber, "but the city is in an uproar. We heard it on the Campus Martius, too, but whatever the trouble is, it stays within the walls, for now." She nodded her head at the Aventan couple. "Gregorius sent word. He thought you might benefit from a little extra company tonight."

Neitin heard a hesitation in Hanath's words. "Company?" she asked. "Or a little extra guard?"

"Both. A precaution, only."

Neitin sniffed, shifting Mati's weight to her other hip. He was still snuffling and red-eyed, but Hanath's presence was a distraction from his distress. "It's not as though I'm going to take the opportunity to bolt."

"That isn't what he's—" Hanath caught the sentence between her teeth, but not before Neitin realized her meaning.

"Not more guard *on* me," she said. "More guard *for* me."

"I think you're safer here than in the camp," Hanath said, "or else I'd take you back with me. But yes. There's been an odd trouble in the city. I mean to speak with Sempronius Tarren about it tomorrow, because all I can get out of anyone in camp is that it's something religious, some ritual gone awry." She flicked her fingers. "Not enough information. But whatever it is, some in the city seek to blame outsiders. And a foreign queen may be a target, if any of them figure out where we've stashed you."

Outside, the winds howled, rattling shutters and stall canopies, and Mati started crying again to match it. With an air of distraction, Hanath removed one of her beaded bracelets and gave it to the boy to play with, but he dashed it aside, pointing now at the front door. "Bad!" he sobbed. "Bad! Bad, papa!"

Hanath's eyes snapped toward him. "What did he—?"

"Bad, papa!" Mati repeated. "Papa-bad!"

"I-I don't know," Neitin said, shaking her head. She hadn't been sure that Mati would remember his father. What would make him use the word now, though, she could not imagine. *'Unless...'*

Hanath was staring at the child. "What do you know?" she asked him. "What is it you see?"

"Bad!" he insisted. "Bad, bad, papa-bad!"

"Do you think—" Neitin swallowed; she did not want to follow her own thoughts down this road. "The religious trouble you mentioned. These storms. Whatever they are, do you think they might be similar to... in some way reminding him of... the *akdraugi*?" Just speaking the word made her shiver, and a well-timed gust of wind shrieking outside did not help. "And, thus, of his father?"

Hanath frowned. "I am not well-acquainted with Aventan spirits," she said, "but the soldiers in Toletum, they spoke of similarities between the fiends there and those of their homeland. It is possible."

Clutching Mati close, despite his wet sobs and wriggling, Neitin edged back a step, as though retreating further into the house would be any help. "I thought we left it all behind," she said. "I thought it was over. I..."

Then she remembered Sakarbik's last words and parting gift to her. Still, she struggled to imagine that she could summon protection as Sakarbik had. *'But if those fiends cross the river, if this evil spreads out of that city... I must try. I must protect Mati.'*

Hanath's people had taken up stations at the door and within the atrium. Hanath was staring up through the hole in the ceiling, as though the sky might provide some answers. Not even Sakarbik could have learned anything from it tonight; the stars' milky glow was hidden by charcoal-gray clouds, whipping across the night sky.

"Hanath?" The woman's attention turned back to Neitin. "Tomorrow, will you bring me—or have someone bring me—a few items?"

Hanath arched an eyebrow. "Strange time to be thinking of a market trip."

Neitin's jaw trembled; how foolish she would feel, asking for these things if it did not work.

Yet Hanath had seen Sakarbik's work. Hanath had been part of the army taking advantage of her sorcery to win a battle. Surely, she would not mock the effort.

"I know a charm," she said. "Sakarbik said... she said it might protect me, like the *besteki*... if anything happened here. It may not work, but..." She tried to turn the knot in her stomach into a source of strength, standing up straighter. "But if there is a chance to protect my boy, I want to try. She said it would work, if I had faith. That Nabia would find me, even here."

"Sakarbik was wise," Hanath said, slower and softer than her usual tones. "I have visited many lands, and my gods have always been with me, no matter how far I travel." She settled her shoulders back. "Very well, queen-that-was. Tell me what you need, and I shall play market-girl for you. It will do no harm to try."

XLIX

Dark clouds loomed over Aven the next morning, an oppressive blanket pressing down on the city, attended by a damp chill more appropriate for November than Maius.

Vibia and Latona retraced their steps from the night before, attended by Merula and two boys on loan from Vatinius Obir. At a crossroads, Vibia paused to close her eyes and summon the memory of the previous night, harrowing though it was. She could not read magical signatures, as Latona did, but she recognized the imprints that Fracture magic left on the world, making her work today more like tracking animal prints. The spirit that assaulted her left traces behind, as did the magic used to summon it. "This way," she said after a moment, drawing them south and west.

As they walked, Vibia paused to note oddities: markings on street corners, knots of cord looped around bushes, bits of bone and gristle scattered in alleys. So many things that could be mistaken for ordinary rubbish, but Vibia felt the taint of Discordian magic upon them.

"Gods," Latona breathed, the fifth time Vibia stopped to examine a charm. "If they've done this to the whole city..."

"That's why we must find the source," Vibia said, "and stop the heart of them. We'll never find them all, and even if we did, we'd never have time to unravel them." She broke and scattered each charm she found, but otherwise expended no energy in destroying them, choosing to conserve her strength. She rolled a fractured chicken bone between her fingers, considering. "What I felt last night, the magic in the air... that's how she's invoking so many charms at once, over such a large area. But it must take a phenomenal amount of power..."

"Or a phenomenal number of mages," Latona said. "We never have worked out how many Discordians there may be."

Vibia shook her head. "I don't think it's the number. Not all of the Discordians will have her strength. Certainly not in Fracture magic, though we know some of their allies bear other gifts. But Salonius Decur's Light and Air wouldn't help with this, and there simply aren't enough other Fracture mages with the talent. No, she's relying on the Lemuria, on the weakness between the worlds..."

And something else. Something Vibia was missing, but aggravatingly could not grasp.

She sighed, dropped the bone, kicked it, and resumed walking.

They followed the trail to the Forum. "It all convenes here," Vibia said as they emerged from behind the long basilica on the Forum's north-eastern edge. "I can feel similar channels cutting down from the Palatine, the Caelian, the Capitoline, out of the Subura and the Velabrium... they're all knotting up in the Forum."

"That makes sense," Latona said, brow furrowed, "and it doesn't. The Forum is the heart of the city. An ideal place to strike, perhaps, but a hard place to hide evildoing."

Even with half the city scared into hiding by the past nights' events, the Forum remained busy. Togate men hurried about, their arms full of tablets and scrolls. Magisters chivvied their students along. Priests emerged from temples to conduct rituals and read auguries.

'Priests.'

On a sudden instinct, Vibia turned toward the Temple of Janus. Latona, trotting to keep up, whispered, "I thought you said they wouldn't use the *mundus*, because it's consecrated to the beloved dead, not the restless."

"It's still a locus of power, and a breach from this world to another. They may have found a way to pervert its sacred purpose, or to use it in some other fashion. I hope I'm wrong."

The closer she drew to the Temple of Janus, however, the worse her suspicions became. A fraying sensation jarred her nerves. *Something* was near... not the nexus of power, perhaps, but close...

Leaden-cold horror slunk down her spine when she found the source. "Latona." She grabbed for the other woman with a heavy hand. "Latona, look. Look at the priests."

The priests of Janus were arrayed before the temple, conducting a rite, no doubt meant to ease the final night of the Lemuria as best as they were able. In their midst stood a man with pointed features, waxy skin, and thin gray hair scraped back from his forehead: Pinarius Scaeva.

Latona's face went ashen, her voice hollow. "What in Juno's name is he doing there?" The last anyone had heard, the man had been a gibbering wreck, kept in seclusion out of pity and charity.

His wits had not returned in full: his rolling, unfocused eyes confirmed that. *'But the High Priest would never take the risk that he might cause a disruption.'* Religious rites were notoriously strict; any error meant starting over again from the beginning, so as not to offend the gods. *'So he must be in control of his faculties. And if he is, if he's rejoined the Discordians and yoked his strength to Corinna's...'*

Latona pulled on her elbow. "We have to get out of here," she said. "Before he takes notice of us. If he has his wits at all, if he remembers... I don't want him realizing we're aware of him."

For some reason, Vibia could not tear her gaze away. "We should have killed him," she said, "but we didn't like the idea of angering Janus by murdering one of his priests. I thought we'd done a thorough enough job that he would never be a problem again. But we should have killed him."

"Still can," opined Merula from behind them. "Always better to be killing men who want you dead when you have the chance."

"But not *now*," Latona said. "Come on. Let's get somewhere we can think about what this means."

Hardly had they turned toward the Palatine Hill, however, than a voice called out to them. "Ladies? Lady Vibia, Lady Latona?"

Vibia swallowed exasperation. *'Gods above and below, who is it and what could they possibly want?'*

Latona mastered herself better and more rapidly. As she swiveled, Vibia saw her demeanor change, a practiced smile dropping over her face, a relaxed posture taking over the tension and fear. "Senator!" she said, voice smooth as honey—for approaching them was Galerius Orator, in the formal garb of his office. No clients attended him, though—odd, for a man of his station on business in the Forum. "What a pleasure."

His smile was wary. "I'm glad to hear you say so. I know you and my wife, ah... well, I know you've quarreled lately." He rubbed at his hair, which had more silver streaking the blond now than before his consulship. "I hope you know I hold no ill will, though I confess that I... I share my wife's hesitation, about your doings, but... perhaps we should speak on it more some other time. I know law, not magic, and where the two meet, there's always tension." He made a short gesture with one hand. "I digress. I'm sorry. I'm... I'm a little rattled."

"I can tell," Latona said. So could Vibia; his anxiety jabbed at her like thorns, but even without her magical gifts, his discomposure was evident. Galerius Orator had a gift for speaking, yet now his words tumbled and halted like a boy's at his first rhetoric lesson. "Forgive me for saying, Senator, but though much of the city was disturbed these past few nights, I think you suffer a more... specific tension."

Galerius nodded. "It is why I'm glad to have run into the two of you. Whatever the merits of your, ah, your educational endeavors... Marcia gave me the impression that you've dealt with oddities of this type before. I thought you might... that maybe you could help."

Latona flicked her eyes at Vibia; Vibia nodded. Despite their disagreements with Marcia, doing a favor to Galerius could only help them. *'And we might well need his assistance in turn, if our way of solving the Discordian problem provokes legal trouble.'*

Latona put on one of her warming smiles. "If it is in our power to do so, we would be honored to offer assistance."

"Thank you," he almost sighed. "I—Would you walk with me?" Galerius explained his troubles as they approached the base of the Caelian Hill, Merula and the collegium boys still trailing behind. "It's my wife. Last night, she... she lost composure, when those *things* rose up during the Lemurian rites."

Vibia quirked an eyebrow, wondering how much of an understatement "lost composure" was.

"I have seen many people deeply affected by them," Latona said. "There is no shame in it. The spirits are, by their nature, meant to harrow mortal souls."

"This was worse than fear, Lady," Galerius said. "The first night, yes, that's all it was, but this... it was as though some fiend got *inside* her."

Vibia only half-listened to the rest of his tale, for she already knew its shape. Marcia had suffered something very like her own trial, inhabited by a Discordian demon that dredged up the worst pieces of her, the most vicious instincts and unpleasant shades of personality. *'Blessed Fortuna, how many of those things were loose in the city? How many more of them might be unleashed tomorrow night?'*

By the time he finished the story, Galerius was nearly in tears, though he kept his voice steady. "If you know anything that might help, ladies, I... as I said, I know you quarreled, but—"

"That doesn't matter," Latona said, faster than Vibia would have. "These fiends are a threat to all, and I assure you, I have no desire to see Marcia suffer."

Galerius lowered his eyes. "I care for her a great deal," he said. "I cannot bear to see her so tormented. If those things come again..."

"We're trying to prevent that," Vibia said. They were nearing the Galerian house now, and with each step, the sense of wrongness that Discordian magic provoked grew stronger. Corinna and her fellow had evidently reserved an extra-potent curse-charm for this stretch of the Caelian.

"So you recognize this?" Galerius asked, with pathetic hope. "You can fix it?"

"We will try," Latona assured him. "Although I should warn you..." She hesitated, and Vibia suspected she was deciding how much to tell him, knowing that his willingness to hear might have been affected by Marcia's opinion. "There is one night left of the Lemuria. We have reason to believe worse will come. Our hope is to safeguard the whole city."

"Not one woman alone," Galerius said, understanding her meaning. "I should not take you from—"

"To the contrary," Latona said. "You may be providing us with valuable information. I simply don't want to promise more than we can perform, with storm clouds still on the horizon."

They continued to talk, but Vibia stopped listening as they drew near the Galeriae's green door. She felt a deep-pricking thorn here, a bramble of Fracture magic, like so many of the charms they had untangled. "Where are you?" she muttered.

"Lady Vibia?" Galerius asked.

"There's something here. Not in the house. Too hard to plant them inside a private domus. But somewhere..."

She found it under an eave of the domus's south-facing wall, a place well-protected from wind and rain, since another building loomed above it and quite close by. Unlike the scrupulously clean front of the domus, this wall had a smattering of graffiti, like most alleyways in Aven.

Vibia stared at the offending script with utter loathing. A few lines of mediocre poetry, written in a crimson-black paint, undistinguishable from the other words and pictures marring the wall, except that these radiated malevolent energy.

"Look!" she demanded of Latona, gesturing, and heard a gasp indicating Latona understood.

Vibia wanted to spit, but she settled for uttering an unladylike word that raised Galerius's brows. "This is what did it. This is what turned her against you!" She gestured at the space between Latona and the painting. Now that Latona drew close, Vibia could *feel* it; the curse was tied to Latona's essence.

'Corinna knows the feel of her magic, maybe of her very anima. Of course she would. The attack last year gave her what she needed. Gods, I've never heard of a curse being able to do that, but there's no reason it shouldn't. You can tie a curse to a name or a lock of hair or a fingernail. Why not a magical signature?'

Galerius cleared his throat. "Ladies, please... What am I looking at?"

"A curse, Senator," Latona said. "A Discordian curse."

"Discordian?" Galerius shook his head in disbelief. "No... That cult was banished, there aren't any left in the city."

"I assure you," Latona said, gentle but firm, "there are."

"And Marcia, she's... Would her own magic not have sensed such a thing?"

Frowning, Latona squinted at the painting—though Vibia noted she kept her distance from it. "Not unless she was looking for it. It's... it's cloaked, somehow. A hidden weave in the... No. Shadow and Fracture together? Hm."

As Latona murmured to herself, her attention diverted from Galerius to the thaumaturgical conundrum, Vibia fixed Galerius with a hard look. "Get water. Consecrated water, if you can, but *anything* to wash this clean. Leave no trace of it. Scrape the rock if you must. And we need to see Marcia."

"She's been like this since the dawn," Galerius said, when he showed them to his wife's chamber. Merula had insisted on coming with them, in case the fiends provoked violence, but the collegium boys had been set to helping clear the curse-painting from the outer wall.

Marcia lay, ashen-skinned and disheveled, much as Latona had after Corinna's attack, except that her eyes were open. Open, but not alert. She gazed unseeing at the wall, not seeming to notice their company.

Small wonder, since barbs of Fracture magic were strewn throughout her anima. A hundred irritants, embedded and infectious.

Latona held a hand to her mouth, shaking her head in mute horror. "Gods," she murmured. "There's so much. Little bronze needles, everywhere. Each one small, but..." To her eyes, Marcia must have been radiating bronze.

"But together, they have a large effect."

Probably that was how the curse went unnoticed for so long. One needle alone could have slipped by anyone's awareness. *But bit by bit, jab by jab, they poisoned her.* Enough to erupt into enmity against Latona. *Why didn't Latona see them when Marcia confronted her? Were they too slight then?* Perhaps if Latona had known to search for them, but if they stayed small, stayed subtle, even cloaked... *Until the Lemuria. Until all that Fracture magic flooding the city inflamed them.*

Grudging respect for Corinna's talent rumbled beneath Vibia's revulsion for her blasphemy. The woman was skillful, no denying that, and dangerously clever.

"Fortunately, Senator, we have experience with this," Vibia said. "Latona will purge with Spirit, and I'll draw out the Fracture."

The words might have meant much or little to him, but he nodded, stepping back. Latona took one of Marcia's limp hands; Vibia seized the other.

It took much longer than unworking a curse-charm. Each barb had to be teased free individually as Latona's relentless Spirit magic shook it loose. Vibia was reminded of a time when, as a small child, she put a hand into some nettle, and how patiently her nursemaid had pulled loose every stinging fiber.

Patience had never been one of Vibia's prize virtues, but stubbornness was, and she called on that now, grinding her teeth and refusing to relax until Marcia's anima was thoroughly cleansed. Color returned to her cheeks, and finally, the spark of life returned to her eyes.

When Marcia roused, Latona dropped her hand, stepping back quickly. Galerius rushed into take her place. "Marcia? Are you well? Are you—are you—?"

"I... think so?" She sat up a little, looking confused. "I'm very tired, husband. And— Latona?" Marcia blinked a few times, as though barely recognizing her. "What are you—?" She turned half away, rubbing her temples. "No, I... Something's not right..."

Latona looked crestfallen, moving beside Vibia. "That should have worked."

"It did. But the demons have been gnawing on her a long time," Vibia growled. Her anger was mostly directed at Corinna, but she kept some for herself and what she had missed. "Whatever grabbed her last night was an intense manifestation, but the little fiends have been poisoning her for... I don't know. However long that painting's been on the wall. Remember how you felt, when you woke up? The effects may take some time to clear."

Latona nodded her understanding, but still looked disappointed. No doubt she'd been hoping for a more dramatic recovery.

'Some gratitude and an apology wouldn't go amiss, either, but we may have to wait for those. If they come at all.' For Marcia's harsh words, though exacerbated by the Discordian fiend, would have had some basis in her true feelings, just as Vibia's had, to her shame.

"We should go," Latona said. "Let's... let's leave them be."

Vibia returned to her home, needing to rest and to think, but Latona went back to the Esquiline, first to return the boys to Obir's collegium, then to the Domus Magicae. She, too, needed to think, but she wanted to do it surrounded by books and notes, ensconced in her magical haven.

Her thoughts roiled like a stormy sea. *'Corinna's using magic in ways I'd never dreamed possible... I should have, though. Should have guessed, at least, after those early experiments... Scaeva, what he did was strange and new, too. They're working together, they must be. He's her way in to... the temple? The mundus? A breach between worlds...'*

Unraveling thaumaturgical mysteries was only half her problem. She still had to figure out how to stop the Discordians, without fully knowing their plan. *'If only we could get to them before tomorrow night...'* But Corinna and Scaeva lurked in the respective protections of family and temple, and even if they had been within reach, others of their cult might remain in the city to continue their work.

To end the threat once and for all, they would have to find the Discordians after they gathered, but before they started wreaking havoc. *'Vibia felt the Fracture magic centered on the Forum. That may mean—I hope it means—they will all be gathered in one place, not scattered all over the city.'* Many mages working together could create more powerful results, though Latona doubted Corinna would appreciate the irony in relying upon collective effort to create a sundering effect. *'Where will they meet? At the Temple of Janus, most likely, or near it.'*

Latona took up a wax tablet and began scribbling other places that might prove a locus for Fracture magic: the sheer cliff face of the Tarpeian Rock, the Curia, the river's edge. As she formed a list, her mind kept churning. *'We find them, and then what?'*

She knew, but did not want to admit it to herself.

'Corinna would have killed you. Her actions might kill many more. You must put an end to it. But gods, when did I become the sort of person who contemplates murder?'

Little though she liked it, the moral quandary was easier to settle than the practical. *'We'll have to overwhelm them. Obir's collegium... maybe some of my brother's men, if he can trust them. If you manage to stop her, the magical signatures will remain. There are others in the city besides the Augians who can read them. It will be clear that intervention was necessary.'* Legal trouble might still follow, but that would be a problem for her future self. *'If we do not prevail, there will be no law for it to matter.'*

But if she did prevail, there would still be the Augians to contend with. Latona could only hope that proof of Discordian action, organized and empowered, would sway opinions in her favor.

She had history on her side, too. Months of research had shown her the threat the Discordians presented to civilization. They had been a thorn in Aven's side for centuries, if one infrequently trodden upon, and related groups had plagued the city-states of Athaeca and Ionia even longer. Some blamed them for the fractious nature of the Menaphon dynasty, ruling Abydosia over each others' dead bodies. Most famously, Discordia herself had been responsible for the Ilionic War, when a great nation fell and took so many semi-divine heroes down with it.

Ever the Discordians struck at a state's stability, overthrowing kings, outraging oligarchs, agitating rebels. Aven, half-chaos by its nature, had a sort of innate resilience, able to bend with upheavals rather than break under their force—but it had been many generations since Aven reckoned with this kind of magical power leveled against the populace.

'Vibia and I might be dismissed as hysterical women, but we will have witnesses.' Gaius would swear any oaths necessary on her behalf. Vatinius Obir was a respected businessman, known for running his collegium well; his word would carry weight. Marcus Autronius had been a Tribune of the Plebs, and though he was no longer sacrosanct, he was still admired. *'And then, of course, there's...'*

Merula's voice broke into her thoughts. "What are you doing here?"

Latona had left the door closed on this ill-omened day, but she had been too deep in thought to hear it open. She knew who it was before he spoke.

'Too many things have happened today,' Latona thought. Curse-hunting, and Scaeva, and Marcia, and Latona hadn't had time to process any of it yet. *'I'm really not sure I have the strength for this.'*

But some things needed saying, and there might not be another opportunity.

Merula blocked Sempronius's path, arms folded and eyes glaring. Her grudging approval of him had evidently been withdrawn until such time as her mistress rendered permanent judgment. "My lady is desiring no company at the moment," she was saying. "And just because you—"

"It's alright, Merula," Latona called out, appearing in the atrium. "I will speak with him."

Merula looked over her shoulder. "You are being sure, Domina?"

"I am." Her voice was cold and blank, like uncarved marble. "We will need him tomorrow night, in some capacity. And so we must speak."

With a disdainful sniff, Merula closed the front door behind Sempronius, then retreated to the garden.

For a moment, all he could do was drink in the sight of her. Weary and disheveled though she was, hair in a tangled coronet, dark circles beneath her eyes, still her glory shone through.

Fierce love for her, her bravery and her compassion and her capability, roared in Sempronius's heart. "I came to apologize," he said. "Again. More. And to see if... if I might be of service to you."

Latona hugged her arms around herself. She looked desperately unhappy, and Sempronius hated to be the cause of her sorrow. "What I want to know, what I need to hear, is this: Why did you not tell me?" He heard her heartbreak in her voice, and the pit in his chest deepened. "I trusted you with everything, Sempronius. If we'd been caught, that night at the Saturnalia, I could've been—" Her breath faltered, and she finished, "ruined."

He knew she was thinking *killed*. It wasn't fashionable to murder a wife taken in adultery these days, but it remained legal.

She continued: "I've let you in on my secrets, and I have put myself utterly in your hands. All the moreso if I marry you. Why, with all the intimacies we have shared, did you not tell me before you proposed?"

"I should have. I should have trusted you. All I can say is that I am not in the habit of divulging this to anyone."

Her fingers were pressing hard into her upper arms. "Well. I've thought about whether your excuses for general concealment have merit, and that's... that's a longer conversation. A conversation for *if* we get past the next two days."

Despite the qualification, hope blossomed within Sempronius. She made the allowance, at least, was not condemning him outright. She was not discounting the possibility of a future, and one together.

A wall existed between them and that future. "I regret that my timing was... less than ideal."

Her tired eyes lit with sudden heat, and Sempronius realized his blunder. "Less than ideal? Because it coincided with the Discordians threatening to bring the city down around our ears? Or because it didn't occur to you to unburden your soul until *after* you'd secured the betrothal contract?"

"It wasn't that it didn't occur—" he began, then bit down on the thought. She did not want to hear further justifications.

"What hurts the most is the lack of faith in me," she said. "Beneath the shock and terror—and I am frightened, Sempronius, so very much, about what will happen when someone unfriendly discovers your secret. The Augians are not only corrupt, but allied to your enemies, to men who have already tried to murder you on several occasions. To hand them such a weapon as this..."

She was right, of course; Vibia had expressed similar concerns to him often. He understood their fears, but the threat of discovery was why he had perfected hiding his talents. Beyond those precautions, dwelling overmuch on the possibility seemed to show a lack of faith in the gods who set him on this path.

Latona shook herself, as though sloughing off the political implications. "And I'm terrified, too, of the consequences of your hubris. To be so sure you know the gods' designs... I cannot imagine it."

Sempronius did not know how else to be. He could not remember a time without that certitude. He tried to guard against conceit, but his confidence in the gods' plans for him was unquestioned. He simply *knew*.

It grieved him that Latona did not feel it for herself. Her magnificence, her power, they should have given her utter security in the rightness of her goals and plans—

"But beneath all of that," she went on, "I'm hurt."

A sharp pang of contrition hit him in the core. She had been hurt so often, by so many unworthy individuals. He did not want to be among their number. He wanted to celebrate her, encourage her, help her to shine, not hurt her. "I am more sorry for that than I can say."

"I don't need you to be sorry," she said, irritation spiking in her voice. "I need to know that it will not happen again, not because you are sorry, but because you truly have the faith in me you always claimed to." Her green eyes bored into him, rightfully merciless in their accusation. "I thought you saw me as a partner. That I could work alongside you, yoking our strengths together."

"That is what I want," he assured her.

"How can I believe that, when you hid something of this magnitude from me? Both a strength and a vulnerability, something that puts me in danger but also something I could have *helped* you—!" Her jaw clamped shut, and she shook her head. "Your confidence in me, it seems, had limits."

"Please believe," he said, with slow precision, "that my faith in you is ever undimmed. The failure was mine, my weakness and fear, and no reflection on you."

"So you say." She drew a shaky breath. "If you trust me, if you mean to treat me as a true partner, then prove it."

Sempronius was not fool enough to ask how, to make her set out a task like a magister testing a student. He just nodded with grim determination, accepting that he would have to figure it out for himself. "I vow that I will."

Latona's shoulders rolled back, and her expression shifted, smoothed, losing its raw honesty. Through Shadow, Sempronius *felt* her drawing down a mask, and it anguished him. He wanted to be the person with whom she needed no guise nor guile, no well-practiced placidity, no hardened gloss.

A privilege he had lost, and would have to earn back.

Her voice was clear and clipped now. "As I said, none of this will matter if we don't make it past tomorrow night. So, if you would like to be of use, accompany me to Vatinius Obir's, and put your military minds together on a plan of attack."

L

The ominous weather did not abate on the morning before the final night of the Lemuria. Augurs across the city muttered in concern; their birds would not fly, huddling in their cotes. A sacrifice at the Capitoline revealed a goose without a liver, and on the Palatine, an owl sat upon the Hut of the Twins and would not be moved, even as the sun rose high.

Ill portents, all.

Vibia sent members of her household outdoors nonetheless. "You go to Vatinius Obir, on the Esquiline, and you tell him I require assistance. Then you go to these households," she instructed, giving them a list: the Crispini-ae, the Rufiliae, Aemilia Fullia, the Gratianae, everyone who had stirred up rumor and doubt against Latona in the past months. "If there is any graffiti on the walls of their houses, wash it off. If it will not wash, scrape the paint clean."

Vibia did not have time to check every house herself. She was not cer-tain this would work, since they could not purge the afflicted individuals themselves, but perhaps it would at least stop whatever the Discordians had planned for tonight from making things worse.

"If someone asks what we're doing, Domina?"

"Tell them it's a public cleaning on orders from the urban aedile," she said. A lie, but by the time anyone verified it, the work should be done. "You must be finished by dusk. Now go."

At the Domus Magicae, Alhena sat in the small garden, cross-legged upon the ground, cutting into pomegranate after pomegranate and casting the seeds into dishes that were scattered all around her. The air was thick with incense, and she was begging for aid.

'There are not enough of us,' she thought. 'If all those clanging gates break open, we will be able to do no more than protect a few patches of the city, where our friends are. And how long will that last?'

She remembered the words that had haunted her dreams for so long now, the fragments of poetry written upon the bronze doors she first witnessed in Stabiae, and blazing beyond the rest, the horrible promise: All worlds shatter.

'Not ours, not now. Oh please, gods who love us, not ours, not now.'

And so she prayed for insight. 'Any advantage I can give them, Lady Proserpina, any advantage at all. Please help me. Help us.'

The message that eventually came was not what she had expected.

"Eat." Merula shoved a bowl of fruit and a dish of bread under Latona's nose.

Latona huffed, pushing the bowl aside. "I'm busy, Merula."

The fruit and bread reappeared beneath her face. "You are being up since dawn and eating nothing but almonds. This is not sensible. This is weakness. You want to be weak?"

Latona grumbled wordlessly but snatched at the bread, then followed it up with a few apricots and strawberries. "Happy?"

"No. Keep eating. Unless you *want* to fall over and be no good to anyone at all?"

"Merciless tyrant."

"Stubborn pig."

Latona ate another apricot. "Thank you."

She had been weaving all day. The Fire-charged crimson fabric tumbling off her loom was loose and snarled with errors, but no matter; it was only going to be torn into strips anyway, that every one of Obir's fighters would have protection. As she wove, her mind churned through all she had read in the past months, searching for answers.

"I think I've figured out what type of fiend it is that possessed Vibia, and Marcia, and maybe the others," she said, swallowing. "It's called a *furilla*—"

"I'm happy for you. Eat more; explain less."

Before Latona could clear the plate, however, her younger sister rushed into the room. "Come here," Alhena demanded, holding out a hand. Latona gave it unthinking. "It's *you* he wants."

Latona blinked. "What?"

"Remus. He—I don't know how to explain it. Just... Just do this. Link your power to mine. You've done it before. I mean. Not to me. But you've—you've threaded Fire with Spirit. Your own elements. And you boosted that Water, with the young man and the fountain. So you can affect other elements, even those inimical to yours. And Time isn't, it isn't inimical to anything, it couldn't be—"

"Alhena, slow down. I don't know what you want me to do."

"Thread your magic with mine," Alhena said. "I think—if I've understood him, I *think* this should work. Draw my magic along with Spirit's power. I'll see to the rest."

Alhena's eyes were wide, too-blue, and Latona knew better than to put her off in such a mood. She took Alhena's other hand, closed her eyes, and reached out for the cool, slippery-silver feel of Time magic.

At first, she wasn't sure she had the sense of it: the physical elements were so much easier to grasp, and she was by now intimately acquainted with Fracture, but Time she had always left to be her sister's domain. Like the whisper of an autumn wind, it glided over her skin, streaming around her without flowing into her at all—but then the taste of pomegranate blossomed on her tongue and she caught the scent of wheat on the air.

Pressure tugged on her, as though something gripped her by the shoulders and yanked, and then the world around her disappeared.

There, the Tiber River, crooking its way through the landscape. Behind Latona, the hills: the high peak of the Capitoline, the familiar crest of the Palatine, and beyond, the uneven bumps of Esquiline and Quirinal and Viminal. None of them anything like she knew them. No temples jutting up from their heights, no homes and insulae crowding their ascents. No roads at all, and only a few scattered buildings. Hardly worth the name, really, more glorified tents.

Latona realized where she was: the base of the Aventine Hill. Now, instead of a ruin of rocks, a simple hut stood, with a straw roof and mud-and-daub walls.

The man standing before her, smiling patiently as she gawped and tried to gather her bearings, was bearded, wearing a rough-woven gray tunic and something that was not quite a toga overtop of it. The draping fabric was deep green, both rougher and heavier than the clothing Latona was used to, and embellished with bronze medallions.

The man himself had a ruddy complexion, but a nose as fine and straight as anyone could ask for. Raven-dark curls spilled from his head in unruly splendor, but his beard had an auburn hue. His eyes were dark, darker than Sempronius's, but gentler, too.

She had no experience with men of his particular station. The Parthians were said to bow and scrape and touch their foreheads to the ground in the presence of their kings; the Tennic peoples had elaborate rituals for greeting royalty. But Latona was Aventan to the bone—and so was he. Surely he could expect no groveling obeisance, no prostration.

What did one say, upon being granted audience with one of the founders of the nation?

"Noble Remus, most venerable of ancients," she said, finding her voice, "I am honored."

"Welcome, beloved child of the future." His voice was rich and strong. "I have been expecting you."

The day was cool and fresh: early spring, she thought, earlier than the mid-Maius she'd been living through. She could see so far, without the familiar buildings and walls standing all around, without a single road tracking its way through the hills. Somehow she never thought of Aven as being so thickly wooded—but of course it would have been, filled with pines and cypress just as the surrounding countryside was. Wetter, too; the hollow between the Aventine and Palatine hills was little more than a swamp.

Seven hundred years, or near enough. The thought was enough to stagger her.

Still, Remus gazed on her with patience. If he had been expecting her, apparently he expected this disorientation as well.

"You are of Time," she said, surprised. "I always thought—Well, stories differ, but almost everyone agrees on—"

"Spirit, yes," Remus said. "That more than anything, as you reckon things now. We did not conceive of them quite so, in my day, nor make fine distinctions between the talents."

It fit, with what she and Alhena had been learning; Aven's magic was not static, had not always been as it was now, could perhaps change further.

She swallowed, still unsteady. "I'm not sure how this is working. I don't know enough about Time magic. Am I—" She looked around again, at the familiar-unfamiliar surroundings. Closer to the river, she could see men and women at work, hauling timber. The first Aventine docks, perhaps? "Have I been pulled back? Or did you—?"

Remus chuckled, not unkindly. "Your sister will be better able to explain it to you, someday. Great power lurks in her as well, and she has the mind to hone it. For now, let us consider this like a bridge across a river. When we meet in the middle, we are neither on one bank nor the other." His eyes seemed to glow, like the last ember of a guttering fire. "I have long known we would meet, someday, as I have met a few of my other descendants, scattered like seed across the fields of time."

"Your descendants?" Latona asked, half-choking on the word. The Vitelliae were an old family, claiming long heritage in Aven, but—

"A figure of speech," Remus said. "Neither my brother nor I will be able to carry on our family—and yet we will be more blessed than most, for this whole city is our filial line. Every soul who will be born here, or who arrives and makes it their home." He laid his hand upon her brow, a paternal blessing. "But like all parents, we have our favorites." His fingers—so rough, a working-man's hands, for all he was a king—stroked her hair. "My brother, he loves best the warriors. Generals, perhaps, but even more, those who give their last to defend Aven against terrible odds. He will die happy, thinking on their strength and valor. But I?" He stepped back, gesturing to the land around them. "I love the statesmen who will make law and justice stronger than might alone. I love the mages whom the gods favor." Two paths, two powers, so deliberately separated by modern Aventan law, yet unified here in its founder. "And I have a different vision of what will mean glory for Aven than my brother does."

When he spoke, Latona felt dizzy. So plain a man. From the look of him, he had more in common with the Tennic or Iberian tribesmen than with the venerable fathers of the present age. And yet.

It was the power, she realized, radiating off of him. Her magic recognized it like the heat of the very sun. She'd never glimpsed such strength before, such raw control of the elements—but something beyond that, too. She breathed it in, and the taste of cinnamon almost overwhelmed her: not only from the Spirit magic, but from Remus's pure sense of self, utterly at peace with his place in the world. Would Romulus feel the same, or would his energy be restless, the counterpoint to his brother's serenity? She wondered—she wondered—she wondered—

"There are so many things I should ask you," she said. "An opportunity like this—"

"Alas, my daughter," Remus interrupted, "we have not the time. Moments still pass for you, and I cannot hold this bridge for long. A limitation imposed by Grandfather Saturn, I think, to keep we mortals from overreaching and, perhaps, tripping over ourselves."

He had gestured, she realized, in the direction of the Forum, where the Temple of Saturn would someday stand.

Then, quite suddenly, he seized her head between his hands, drawing her close until they were nearly nose-to-nose. The intensity emanating from him astounded her, all that serene energy turned to sharp focus, a string plucked. "Listen and listen well, dearest of daughters. They will draw their strength from a gash between the worlds. But your power, it is all around you, in the bones and the beating heart of the city. You are of Spirit; you are Juno's, Hera's, Uni's." Three names for one goddess: Aventan, Athaecan, Truscan. "You are bid to be this city's protector, a sacred charge. And you will not fail."

A command or a prediction? Latona wasn't sure. She shook her head, tears standing in her eyes. "I will give all I have," she said, and knew it for the truth; if it took her life to protect this city, these people, then her life she would surrender. "But I don't understand how—"

"You do. You will. There is more to magic than you know, but much you can learn. The bones, the beating heart."

A pinching sensation tugged at the back of Latona's head; the Time magic, drawing on her, urging her back to the present. *'No, it's too soon, there's so much more I want—'*

Again, the Time magic tugged on her, more insistently. She was farther away from Remus then, in the manner of a dream, having moved without moving. He raised a hand in valediction. "Go with the blessings of the gods, Vitellia Latona, dearest of daughters. And good luck to you."

Alhena watched the scene as though through a thick fog, able only to see outlines, only to hear muffled speech. She was the conduit, and she felt the *snap* of reality re-asserting itself when the channel closed.

Latona crashed abruptly off of her bench. "Domina!" Merula cried, pushing Alhena aside and gathering up her mistress. "What are you doing to her?"

"Only what was necessary," Alhena said. "Only what was demanded of me."

Latona roused herself. "I'm alright," she said, unconvincingly. She popped herself on the cheek a few times. "That was odd. In more than one way." Her face scrunched up, but when she opened her eyes again, they were more focused. "Channeling an element I don't control feels... different."

"We'll have to examine it when we have leisure," Alhena commented. "Set it down in writing."

"Yes," Latona agreed. "Assuming we all survive to the Ides, that is an excellent suggestion."

Impatient, Merula tapped a foot. "What is happening? Explain?"

Latona did, filling in what Alhena had not been able to perceive, guess, or intuit. Merula's face displayed skepticism at the tale. "If he is being so powerful, reaching across centuries, I am thinking he could have been more helpful. More... direct. What useful information is he giving you?"

Latona blinked a few times, frowning. "He said I would not fail. Perhaps that will have to be help enough."

LI

As nightfall approached, a strange cohort gathered inside the Esquiline Collegium: three mages, the ladies Latona, Vibia, and Alhena; Sempronius Tarren and Gaius Vitellius, both in soldier's kit but bereft of their swords; and every many whose obedience Vatinius Obir could command.

As Obir looked at the assembly, he swelled with pride. The ladies claimed that Aven stood to tip into chaos tonight, and his collegium would fight to prevent that. He trusted his men—and the ladies, and his patron, were trusting him.

"You must strike, and strike fast," Obir told his men. "No questions. No hesitation. If you hesitate, you die, for these blasphemers will cast the evil eye upon you, steal your will, turn you into their puppets."

Ebredus, his second, nodded, unafraid. The gods only knew what strange fiends he had encountered in his homeland. Obir was not fool enough to credit *all* the stories about Tennic tribes and their magic—nor fool enough to discredit them. The tales about Numidian sorcerers and desert enchanters were typically two parts exaggeration to one part truth, and he presumed the same was true for the stories from the north. The one part of truth formed a sharp enough edge to warrant caution. Ebredus had, furthermore, been a warrior long before he joined a legion's auxiliary unit; he knew how to face down an enemy without faltering.

The same was not true of the local boys. Those who grew up within Aven's walls had no notion of real battle. Scraps in the streets, yes, and the violence that blossomed during the Dictator's reign, but not the regimented terror of being part of the rank and file. Most had witnessed the Discordian fiends in the past year, but firing an arrow at a leopard on the run was different from bearding it in its den.

"The Lady Latona will be doing all she can to shield us," Obir went on. "You all have your talismans, yes?"

A murmur of assent went around the room, and many of the men held theirs up. Red strips of fabric, woven through with Fire magic. Some wore theirs as armbands. Others had twisted them into cords and used them to hang amulets about their necks. *'No harm in that. Protection upon protection.'*

"Good. Remember, these will help, but they will not render you immune—not if these blasphemers are as powerful as we think. Keep your head about you. Pinch yourself if you start to grow dizzy. And if you feel your *animus* slipping away, remove yourself immediately. I will blame no man who makes a strategic retreat. Far better that than we have to kill you for turning your weapons on us, eh?"

They were armed with clubs and daggers; swords were forbidden within the city, and Obir would risk neither blasphemy nor legal trouble by transgressing against that prohibition. But there were many ways to kill a man.

Or, come to that—

"At least one of the Discordians is a woman," he warned his men. "Probably more. I do not want you to be moved to mercy by their sex." He shook his head. "They have declared themselves combatants, even if they are not holding swords or leading a cavalry charge. Their goal is to perpetrate great evil on this city, just as though they were aiming catapults at its walls. They will kill you, if they can. So kill them first."

Aventan men were unused to thinking of women in such ways, but many in Obir's collegium were immigrants from places where female combatants were not unusual. Most of the Aventans also nodded, however. They had accompanied Latona and Vibia to dens of horror; they had learned to see some women, at least, as fighters. Perhaps that was not the image most men had, when they thought of a warrior, but Obir could consider them no less. They put life and liberty on the line more than once, and they would do so again this night.

They had split their magical resources. Rubellia, Terentilla, and Marcus had been dispatched to the edges of the Campus Martius, to use shielding and grounding magic to keep whatever the Discordians unleashed from affecting the soldiers there, if they could. The Lady Latona suggested it, and

Obir agreed, assessing that the mages would be tempting targets, either for Discordian possession or as hostages. Guarding them would take men away from the fight. Three—for Lady Alhena refused to be parted from her sister—were easier to protect than six.

Latona stepped forward. She was dressed improperly, by the standards of her class: a knee-length tunic of unadorned fawn-brown fabric, sturdy-looking leather sandals, her hair in a long triple-plait. Yet the warrior spirit shone through her.

"You are all brave men and noble-spirited," Latona said. "Aven will owe you for your service today, and when I can, I will ensure that it honors and recompenses you. If you are ready, then let us proceed."

Aula never minded being one of the non-magical Vitelliae. Most of the time, the gods' gifts seemed far more trouble than they were worth. She'd seen her sisters struggle to control the elements that called to them—Latona, suffocating under emotions not her own; Alhena, drowning in the mists of time.

They came through it, stronger for each challenge, and she was proud of them, so proud—but she was proud of herself, too, without suffering such crucibles to test her character.

The idea that her daughter had magical talents was half a blessing, but half a terror, too. Aula would do better for Lucia than her own mother had done for Latona or Alhena, but that would still not make it easy. Lucia's life would have considerations that Aula's never had: demands upon her time and her piety, skills to master, a weight in all betrothal negotiations.

So Aula never felt like she had missed out. Her sisters had skills she did not; she had skills they did not, and far less burden.

That did not make it easier, though, to sit at home on a dark and luckless night while her sisters *and* her brother went out to face unspeakable horrors.

"We have to do something," she told their father.

"I am doing something," Aulus said. "I will tend to the rituals at the hearth, as every paterfamilias must, and that—"

"Will mean nothing if they cannot stop the threat, and you know it."

Aulus rubbed his brow, weary. "I do not know how to help against a threat I do not understand. I still can't believe I'm allowing your sisters to... and I wouldn't, if Gaius weren't with them. I don't..." He looked so much older now, in the uncertain lamplight, all his worries carved on his face, than he did when sitting confidently in judgment in his role as censor or when welcoming his clients.

'He has never done well with things he doesn't understand,' Aula realized. 'That's why he and Mother handed Latona off to Gaia Claudia in the first place, all those years ago. It's why he tried so hard to keep her contained. But it's also why he gave in, when she finally pushed back against him.'

Aula never needed to push back; Aulus let her take over her mother's role as lady of the house, content to have domestic matters arranged for him. That, he understood. Magic, he did not and never would.

Latona had several reasons for keeping her father as much in the dark as possible, lack of faith in him prime among them. Not undeserved; Aulus had failed her more than once, and she judged it safer to skirt his notice and attention than to risk telling him the truth and being penned back into a cage she had only just figured out how to unlock.

Aula knew him better. Aula knew how to manage him. And so Aula weighed the present concerns against the potential drawbacks, and she came to a decision. "I think I know how we can help," she said. "But you must listen to me first, without interrupting, without judgment. I don't understand it all, either, not the way they do. But we can make advantage of that, Father. We can help them *because* our views are not cluttered by the magic. And in helping them, we will be of service to the city."

Vibia led the procession, with her brother at her side. Whatever the Discordians planned, they had not yet unleashed its full power. Fracture magic crackled all around, but inchoate and unharnessed. She couldn't even sense any curse-charms as they moved downhill, though she was sure they were seeded all over the city, waiting to be invoked. The overbearing potential for disaster weighed on Vibia like a thick cloak, heavier the closer they drew to the Forum.

The city of Aven lay quiet, every door closed, every window shuttered. Those that had shutters, at least; in the poorer homes, a curtain drawn over the window had to suffice. In some places, carts had been abandoned, if their owners could not get them swiftly enough through the choked streets. Oxen stood in their traces, lowing petulantly; some dragged their carts behind them as they wandered in search of food. Others lay down on the bricks to sleep.

Never so still, this city, never so silent.

Silent, and yet bright. Lamps and torches glowed not in the streets, but behind every door and window. The citizens of Aven thought to burn away the horrors, like a fire purging a pestilence.

Their path wound through a deserted marketplace, stalls creaking and canopies snapping in the wind, then emerged on the Via Sacra, in front of the House of the Vestals. Lights were burning there, too, and at the other end of a small garden, the sacred flame was visible within Vesta's Temple.

As they went past, Vibia caught a glimpse of a figure dressed in white, though she was too far away to discern which of the Vestals was tending the hearth this night. Quinta Terentia, perhaps, or one of the other elder priestesses, with enough gravitas to weather any storm, mundane or magical.

Some of their cohort murmured prayers as they passed the Temple. '*Why not?*' Vibia touched her fingers to her lips, whispering her own plea. Vesta guarded the city, and right now it needed all the help it could get.

The Fracture magic around them was growing stronger, carving new channels into the world. '*That's right. Lead me to you.*'

Alhena worried as she walked. Choosing not to go with Tilla to the Campus Martius had been an agony. '*But I can be of more use here. Maybe.*'

Proserpina had allowed her to help her sister onto the pathways of the past, but the counsel they found there was too enigmatic to be useful. The future, meanwhile, flickered. Alhena wasn't sure if that was a good or bad thing, and so she fretted over it.

Optimism bid her think it good. If the future was unsettled, still in flux, then it could still be affected. They could seize the opportunity, turn the threads of the Fates to their advantage.

Pessimism reminded her that, if that were the case, so could their opponents.

Then, as they passed the Temple of Vesta, one thread of the future sharpened, a glint of metal flashing in her ethereal awareness. "Latona," she whispered, pulling on her sister's sleeve. "Latona, they're..."

"I feel it," Vibia hissed. "They've started. Gods, we have to hurry."

"Where?" Sempronius asked.

"Down by Janus." Her voice was thin, straining. "I think... I think just in front. If they've... gods, I think they opened the gates..."

Bronze gates, and hills of bones, and torn earth, and fiendish howls: all the things terrorizing Alhena's visions for the past year. *All worlds shatter*, the words emblazoned on her mind.

The military-minded men exchanged glances. "No time for subtlety and no use in stealth," Gaius said. "They'll hear us coming, if they haven't already."

Obir started to raise his whistle to his lips, but Latona held up a hand. "Wait! Let me—"

Obir could not hear the words as Latona closed her eyes and whispered, but he recognized the shape of them by now: an invocation to Juno and Venus, drawing down the shield of protection over them all. After a moment, her lashes fluttered open and her gaze roved over the Esquiline cohort, and she continued to murmur her prayer.

The casting settled over them. Obir felt its effects in the rush of blood in his limbs, the hearty sensation of strength and vigor, like a satisfying trip to the baths or a robust workout in the gymnasium. The red kerchief around his neck seemed warmer, as though it bestowed sunlight in the middle of the darkness.

Starry-eyed, Ebredus looked around with a small smile. Obir had discovered long before that Ebredus *could* see magic at work. Some god or other had laid his hand upon the warrior, and though he kept to his Tennic ways, it bestowed the ability to witness Aventan magic. *'Perhaps even to work it, if he ever tried.'*

No time to muse on that. Latona sighed, looking around at the men. Whatever she saw must have satisfied her. "Stick together as much as you can," she instructed. "I will—The magical shielding will be more effective that way."

What she was not saying, Obir suspected, was that she would struggle to keep it over all of them if they split up. Hard enough to hold a charm over so many men at once. "Strike fast," he reminded his men.

Their best bet was in ending the battle fast, before any foul magic took hold.

For battle it would be, part of an undeclared war, a shadow war. If they were successful, most of Aven might never know what transpired in the Forum this night, and so much the better. Most citizens should not *have* to know such darkness.

'*It ends here,*' Obir thought, readying his knife: no mere eating dagger, but a longer, shining blade brought from his homeland. He thought of the long terrors of so many months: of the people of his neighborhood, afraid and in distress; of the mother who wept at his door because she could not protect her children from unholy fiends; of the specter that dared to take on the face of his own brother. '*It ends tonight.*'

LII

'*What I wouldn't give for a gladius and a shield,*' Sempronius thought, as Obir's whistle cut the air and his men moved into a practiced formation. '*Better yet, a horse and a spatha, and a whole legion to trample these Discordians into dust.*'

Instead, he had a couple dozen collegium men, some with military training, but many accustomed only to city brawls. They moved with precision, though; Obir insisted on discipline, and his men learned the same whistle-signals as any legionary. As they stampeded down the paving-stones, they moved into three distinct shapes: a central cordon, surrounding the mages, and two wings.

As Vitellius said, there was no point in stealth; Mercury could have granted all their shoes winged and silent soles, but even without Obir's whistle, at least one of the Discordians would have felt Latona's magic, strong and shining. So they ran, past the long colonnade of the basilica, past tribunal benches, past the Font of Juterna and the Temple of Castor and Pollux. Two hundred paces, perhaps.

Vibia, not much given to physical exertion, was panting, but as they came within sight of the holy trees at the end of the Via Sacra, she found the breath to shout, "There!" She pointed to a group of hooded figures standing beneath the trees, in the yard in front of the Temple of Janus.

Her confirmation of their target was all the permission Obir's men needed. The wings fanned out, left and right, while the central column held tight to their defensive purpose. Sempronius wanted to yell "*Testudo*" and hear the clash of shields forming a hard shell. Some of the men had small bucklers, but most of the physical defense would come from bodies and weapons alone. The rest, the magical fortification, came from Latona.

Sempronius and Vitellius took up point positions, each in front of his sister, with Merula between them. Obir stood to Sempronius's side, whistle still in his mouth, ready to signal his men.

Sempronius only had a moment to process what they rushed in on: the Discordians, in a circle around a low-burning fire. In front of each cultist, a gruesome pile: tiny bones, dead rodents, mutilated birds. Dozens and dozens of broken things, and each break a place for Fracture magic to spawn, blended with the power of death, swelling quickly, a conduit for *lemures* and other fiends.

The cultists were not alone, however; they had non-magical protectors, too, men with clubs and knives. *'Well. We thought to guard ourselves. Small wonder they did the same.'* Obir gave a short blast, and the central cordon came to a halt, forming tight ranks. The wings proceeded, fanning around the Discordians' circle, then charging inward.

And so began the brawl.

All the violence of the past year had not prepared Vibia for the pandemonium of battle.

Not a *true* battle, perhaps, nothing like what the legions faced, but quite enough to satisfy any curiosity Vibia may have entertained about the ordeal. The night's alarming silence erupted in a chorus of battle-cries, followed by grunts of exertion, blades striking bucklers, clubs cracking limbs, infuriated curses, feet scraping against the earth, howls of pain.

The Discordians' protectors outnumbered Obir's men. Who were they? Summoned by Durmius Argus, no doubt, or by Rabirus himself. *'Perhaps after we kill them, we can trace them back to their masters.'* If the Fates were with them, those connections of patronage might provide the proof they needed to see justice thoroughly done.

First, they had to survive.

Latona was doing her job. The woman's eyes were glossy with tears, but her lips never stopped moving and her fingers stretched out toward their cohort of unlikely heroes. She would protect them, keep the Discordians from seizing control of their souls or their limbs or anything else.

Vibia's job was different. She had to hold the line—and close it. In-terrupting the ritual did not heal the gashes they had already torn in the world, and the cultists were still going, within their own protective knot, snapping the necks of mice and pigeons as fast as they could.

Each fissure wrecked the world a little more, igniting hidden curse-charms a little farther away. Vibia ground her teeth, bearing down on her magic. Larariums on the Palatine, the Carinae, the Capitoline would be fal-tering, spitting out *lemures*. Maybe further. How many charms had they planted? Over how much of the city?

Along the Via Sacra, wispy shapes drifted up from cracks and crevices. Vibia tried to ignore them, trusting in Latona's magic to keep her safe. Some of the fighters, she suspected, had wandered out of the range of the Fire-shielding, but every man wore, at least, a Fire-woven length of fabric. It would be enough. It *had* to be enough.

Some Discordians, feeling Vibia slam closed the doors they opened, turned their focus. One hooded man—a gray-haired grandfather who ought to have been dandling babes on his knee and telling them stories, not summoning up fiends to rip a city apart—struck out with Fracture magic. A bur, Vibia thought, like the one that felled Latona in November, though his was a less focused assault.

And a futile one. Latona's shields held. Vibia could not see them, but she felt the shudder as the attack hit Latona's wards and shattered, its ener-gy dissipating back into every crack and fissure of the world around them.

From behind Sempronius, Vibia saw several men she recognized among the Discordians and their protectors—but she did not find one face she expected to be at the center of the fray.

'*Corinna. Where is Corinna?*'

Merula's blood *sang*.

She had trained with gladiatrices, yes. She had fought before, spilled blood before, yes. But this—this was a *fight*! Fast and hot and thrumming in Merula's veins like the best song she had ever heard, the best food she had ever eaten. '*Is this what magic is feeling like, to them as can perform it?*'

It had to be: perfect glory, perfect purpose, knowing your role in the world and that the gods smiled upon it.

The paving-stones were slick with blood, some from the sacrifices they had interrupted, some from the cultists and their protectors, but Merula's footwork was too careful, too controlled to be thrown off by it.

The cultists were throwing magic at her, too. She could feel it in the heat of her headscarf, burning like a crown of fire, and tingling on her skin, well-shielded by the domina's magic. No more than a minor distraction, not enough to put her off her rhythm.

One of the beefier fighters approached her, a pitted knife in his hand, evidently thinking she might be easier to take down than one of the Esquiline men. *'Fool.'* Merula struck, parried, struck again. She kicked at his knee, making him stumble. Her dagger slashed into his shoulder as he tried to right himself, then she caught his arm with hers, forced it up, and jabbed her blade between his ribs. Again, again, maneuver after maneuver, until she was satisfied he would not rise.

Merula stepped back, taking a moment to assess the situation. The domina was still behind her brother and Obir's wall of men, cheeks flushed with exertion, lips moving in a constant invocation to keep their allies within the scope of her magical shielding. Beside her, Lady Vibia looked pale, clammy, and furious.

They were well-protected, and within the knot of Discordians, those at the very center, those who had not been distracted, those still performing their putrid ritual, Merula saw a man who needed killing, vulpine face showing beneath his cowl, eerily aglow in the firelight.

"Scaeva!" she screamed.

He did not raise his head or look to her, but his eyes twitched, or so Merula thought.

She growled, calculating how best to fight her way to him. "Bastard is *mine.*"

Alhena kept toward the back of their group, behind her sister and brother, with Obir's men behind her. They knew their business; while the wings spread out to attack, the central cordon was a wall against the Discordians'

defenders. A few threw themselves at the front rank, trying to get past them to Latona and Vibia, but most were engaged with the violent fighters in the wings.

Alhena's magic tingled. Something was wrong.

'Well, of course, you daft thing. Many things are wrong. You're twenty paces from the largest Discordian ritual this city has seen in centuries, men are beating and stabbing each other all around you, some of them are probably dead, and a dead king told your sister she has to save everyone. Nothing about that is right.'

Maybe the Fracture magic was affecting her, making her own gifts too unpredictable, making the future itself too mutable, its path as uncertain as a feather in the wind.

The commotion had already attracted attention. The Forum was not only a place of business and religion; the Via Sacra had houses lining it, too, and some of those doors were opening, their occupants peering out in curiosity—or, more likely, sending their door boys and housekeepers to find out for them. *'Some of these houses belong to priests and priestesses,'* Alhena thought. *'I wonder if Aemilia Fullia still thinks we're overreacting.'*

The onlookers might send reinforcements, though Alhena wasn't sure which side that might serve. Latona had to be stretched almost to her limits. Could she extend protection to many more? If lictors came, they might become infected by *furillae* and become unwitting servants of the Discordians. *'If they send to the Campus Martius, though...'* Then, if the soldiers came, they would come with their own protection—Rubellia and Marcus and *Tilla*.

Selfishly, Alhena wanted Tilla's hand to hold; in love, she was glad Tilla was far away from this danger.

Another tingle. Alhena's magic wanted her attention. *'But on what? To where?'*

She pivoted, peering into the shadows beyond her square of protection. The Temple of Saturn? Alive with energy, but not the source of concern. The Font of Juturna? No one near there, and she hoped it remained unmeddled-with. The basilica? Figures were huddled in the colonnade, but they seemed terrified onlookers, not threats. The Temple of Vesta, still aglow behind them—?

Someone was between their battle and that Temple, now. Two some-ones, both all in white. Most of the Vestals were chosen because they were mages of Light. Did they want to help?

That had to be it. The foremost figure was Quinta Terentia, hair piled high in its ceremonial ropes. One hand was held palm-up in front of her; the other bore a swinging lamp. Like Latona, she seemed to be murmur-ing to herself. Prayers, no doubt; magic, to drive away the creatures of the netherworld.

And it worked: the smoky figures rising from the crevices between paving-stones shied away from her, a mist burning off under sunlight. Quinta drew nearer, smiling serenely through her whispered invocations.

Still, Alhena's magic grew from a tingle to a buzz, and by the time she saw one future snap into place, it was too late.

The second white-clad figure caught up to Quinta, but she was no Vestal. There stood Anca Corinna, holding a bronze blade that glinted in the light of the half-moon.

Alhena screamed, as loud as she could. The men near her turned; Sempronius turned; even Latona turned, her attention diverted from her charm-casting.

They all moved at once, rushing toward the Discordian and the Vestal.

None of them were faster than Corinna's arm. In one swift motion, she slit Quinta's throat. Several people shouted. Quinta collapsed, and as her blood sprayed out on the ground of the Forum, Fracture magic flared with volcanic force.

LIII

Janiculum Hill

The walls shuddered around Neitin, and a tile slid from the roof into the pool in the center of the garden. Neitin ignored the splash, focusing on mixing the alder, angelica, and other herbs that Hanath had brought her.

The Numidian woman stayed with her again this night, though Neitin did not know if it was under orders or out of curiosity. Hanath's brow pinched in concern, and she stared past Neitin, toward the front of the house. In the atrium, Gregorius performed his own ritual, the pacing with the black beans. His wife was weeping, saying something in the Truscan tongue. "She thinks it is a ground-quake," Hanath translated. "That their god Neptune is angry. But that did not come from the ground."

"It did not," Neitin murmured, scooping the crushed herbs and powdered stones together. "That... that should be enough. I hope."

"You hope?"

"I don't know!" Matigentis, sitting on a blanket next to her, was howling again, making it hard to think. "I don't know if this will work at all. Sakarbik said... but I don't know! I've never—I've never done anything like this, I've no training, I've no talent, I just... I just have to hope. That's all."

With sullen defiance, Neitin rose and began casting the crushed mixture into a wide circle, as she had seen Sakarbik do. More wailing from the front of the house, as loud as Mati.

"What's going on out there?" Neitin asked, not taking her eyes from the circle she created.

"Better not to know," Hanath intoned. "You were not, I think, fond of the *akdraugi*..."

Neitin's fingers slipped, dropping a larger clump of the mixture than she'd intended. She stooped to try and brush it out more evenly, wondering if that would matter, if *any* of it would matter since this was such a foolish, thin hope. "There are *akdraugi*?"

"Something like them."

Neitin moved faster, finishing the circle. "Come inside." Hanath did, sitting by Matigentis and putting a hand on his back. The circle had room enough for Neitin's jailers, too, if they were inclined to trust foreign magic—but they were preoccupied, and Neitin would not waste time imploring them. *'Let their own rituals protect them, if they can. I owe them nothing.'*

She knelt, pressing her hands flat on the garden soil, and she prayed. Sakarbik had told her not to forget her gods, her people, her heart. *'Nabia, lady of the rivers, if you are here, if you know these waters at all, I beg you, hear me. I love you as I have ever loved you. I pledged my son to you. I yearn for the familiarity of my home waters, but if it is your will, I will find a way to love these, too.'*

The Tiber, they called the gray-green snake that wound its way through their hills. Neitin had seen it only briefly as she was brought to her genteel prison, but as she pressed her hands flat against the earth, she imagined it, rumbling and roiling. Whatever was happening out there, the river no longer provided a barrier, but still it rose, trying to defend itself against some unnameable menace.

'From the Tagus to the Tiber, I honor you, Nabia. Please, please, please protect me and mine.'

She held out a hand. Glancing once more toward the front of the house, Hanath passed her dagger to Neitin.

Neitin repeated the words Sakarbik had instructed her in, hoping she remembered them rightly, was not mispronouncing them. She tried to give them the same song-like cadence Sakarbik always had.

Then she looked up through the hole in the ceiling. Strange custom, in these Aventan houses, but Neitin was grateful for it now, for the half-moon shone down. ""Endovelicos of many faces, Endovelicos who blesses my sight, here!" Speaking the last words of the charm, trying to imbue them with Sakarbik's commanding force, Neitin slammed the dagger down into the earth, in the midst of the silvery moonglow.

She held her breath. So did Hanath. At first, nothing.

Then, quiet. Matigentis, Neitin realized, had stopped crying. The noise from the Aventans in the front of the house had abated. No, not stopped—but become muted, as though Neitin had pillows stuffed over her ears.

Looking up at the moon, she found its silver-white glow bore a tint now: a faint golden mist, rising from the circle she had cast, drifting through the air to protect them.

Weaker than Sakarbik's, of that Neitin was sure. If *akdraugi* hurled themselves against it, it would crumble. It was no proper dome, nor the dense wave Sakarbik had summoned on the battlefield.

But she had done *something*. Enough, perhaps, to keep the not-*akdraugi* at bay.

She did not dare to speak, barely dared to breath, lest she shatter what she had made. Matigentis stared around him, sniffling wetly, but calming. Slowly, Hanath reached out, and at first Neitin thought she wanted her dagger back, but then she took Neitin's hand and squeezed it.

The silence was eventually broken by the susurration of a bird's pale wings, as it swooped down through the hole in the ceiling and came to rest just outside the gleaming circle.

Forum

Like a wave in a tempest-tossed sea crashing upon a rocky shore, the Fracture magic ripping through the Forum hit Latona with enough force to knock her off her feet. She was assailed with pain—not her own, but brought to her through Spirit magic: Merula's shock and impotent rage; Gaius's interplay of panic and resolve; Vibia's fury and revulsion; Sempronius's flare of horror; Quinta's last terrified heartbeats.

'A Vestal. She killed a Vestal. I cannot—'

But she *could* believe it; that was the truly horrible thing. Corinna would stop at nothing to loose her horrors on the world. Now she had proved her devotion to her dread patroness.

The magical breach stretched down the Forum as though it would tear the Palatine and Capitoline Hills away from each other. The citizens living on those hills, they wouldn't see the gulf growing as Latona did, not unless they had particular magical gifts of their own, but they would feel it nonetheless, permeating their souls, hateful as any haunting *umbrae*.

Then, the physical manifestations. Dark clouds gathered above their heads, blotting out the half-moon and stars, and wild winds raced into the Forum from all directions, competing with each other to flay leaves from their branches. Harrowing noises followed, the keening of *lemures* beyond the tear in the world, eager to come through.

This was every breach she had sealed over the past year, grown hungrier and more terrible by a thousandfold. This was the maw Pinarius Scaeva had summoned in the warehouse on the Aventine, all those months ago, given full scope and force. That terror flooded Latona, along with all the borrowed fears of her friends. *'Hungry and devouring, it will leave us all cold corpses, it feeds on magic, how can I defeat a thing that feeds on what I would fight it with?'*

Despairing, Latona struggled to get to her feet. *'There has to be a way. I will not be the one who lets this city fall to everlasting strife. There must be a way—'*

The initial blast of magic had knocked everyone, Corinna included, to the ground. The protective cordons on both sides were broken, men tumbling over themselves, some crawling to get away, some trying to resume the fight even before they were back on their feet.

As Vibia righted herself, she heard Obir's whistle, attempting to restore order. But a hateful wind had kicked up, sweeping through the Forum, cold as ice and dragging a dark fog in its wake. Could Obir's men hear him? Could they find each other if they did? Already, men twenty paces away were becoming indistinct, blurred behind cloudy shapes.

But Vibia could still see Corinna, reveling in the blood she spilled.

Growling low in her throat, Vibia stalked toward the Discordian she-demon, her own bronze blade clenched in her hand. Before she reached her quarry, Corinna straightened, the blood-drunk madness in her eyes sharpening, and she held her crimson-coated knife out in a threat.

Her words, though, crooned an invitation. "Vibia Sempronia, you should be standing with us. All those jagged edges you keep trying to sand down, but oh! They do keep cutting, don't they?" She laughed and reached out with her other hand, as though to draw Vibia into an embrace. "Stop

wasting yourself! Give yourself over to Discordia, and discover true freedom!"

Vibia snorted. "You're a poor judge of character if you think that's the
way to motivate me." All her life, she had set herself against tumult and turmoil. Discordia could never offer her anything worth considering.

Corinna's smile turned nasty. "Won't have a choice much longer," she
half-sang. "She is with me, and didn't you see? Didn't you *feel*?" A wild
cackle escaped her. "Plans, plans, my brother made such plans, but I knew
they would unravel, and you! You and dearest glitter-gold and all your lovely breakable men, you were so helpful. Interrupting the ritual, yes, you did,
but you should have known! Fracture should know. You feel it, don't you?"

And Vibia did, though she hated to concede as much to her opponent:
a tautly-stretched rope, severed, snapping loose, its ends frayed. An interruption was not a cessation. An interruption had its own power, lashing
through the air. She *should* have seen that, at least, though she could never
have imagined Corinna would augment that potential with gruesome blasphemy.

Corinna still beckoned to her. "Feel it, knife's-edge, oh, *feel* it with me!
I opened the door, and it's coming through, Discordia's pet, another child
of Chaos. It comes, and it will tear this city down to its bones, and then it
will crack those bones and suck the marrow—"

"Oh, *do* shut up!" Vibia threw her own knife; she knew it would miss
Corinna, but that wasn't the point. For the blink of an eye, Corinna turned
aside, following the arc of the blade through the air, and in that instant,
Vibia pounced, hurling her full weight at the woman and bearing her to
the ground. She grabbed Corinna's wrist and squeezed hard, bones grinding beneath her fingers, until Corinna's grip loosened and she dropped the
blade.

For a moment, the two women grappled in the blood-spattered street.
Vibia seized the chain around Corinna's neck, wanting to strangle her with
it, but it snapped, and as Vibia cast it aside, she realized what it was: a
charm, perhaps the very one that had protected Corinna from magical retribution before.

Vibia grabbed Corinna's head and summoned her own magic. She, who
was always so careful, always so measured, acted on pure instinct now, let-

ting the tangled threads of Fracture guide her. *'Break her. I don't care what it takes. Break her!'*

Sempronius had to exert too much effort simply to keep his mind rooted inside his head. The instant Quinta's life rushed free of her body, Sempronius's magical senses went into riot. Water and Shadow felt death keenly at all times, but on this night, with the fabric of the worlds thin and torn, the awareness threatened to suffocate him.

Worst of all was the magical breach tearing above the Forum, pressing down on him with horrible familiarity.

Back in the Aventine warehouse, when Scaeva assaulted Latona, he tore into her essence, using the violation to call the devouring maw. Terrible as that had been, he had attacked her with magic alone, not physically. Here, the blood of a Vestal Virgin, a powerful mage, provided the gate, and Anca Corinna had chosen an exquisite moment to kick it open. The gaping wound in the world was so much worse than the one Scaeva had created, worse than anything in Iberia.

Sempronius was not a man to shrink from a challenge, but as the void called out to him, his instincts leapt for it and recoiled at the same time. A siren's song, beckoning him to doom.

He bit down on the inside of his cheek, attempting to ground himself; he touched the focale at his neck, seeking comfort in its blazing heat. *'Hold onto this. Latona's strength, Latona's care. This can protect you.'*

The terrible maw reverberating above the Forum had other ideas.

Gaius Vitellius could have lived many happy years never doing battle in the midst of raging magical forces again. The focale around his throat burned with familiar heat, and he tried to trust to his sister's magic, focusing on the immediate threat in front of him, not the howling chaos consuming the Forum and everyone in it. He fought with a lacquered rod in one hand and a knife in the other; no familiar gladius, no spatha, no shield but what Latona's magic provided.

A spear-wielding Discordian lunged at him. Not a talented warrior, but tenacious and maddened with determination: a dangerous set of traits. Vitellius knew he could do nothing to help the magical situation, and so he set himself to what was within his power. However difficult the task, he had no choice. '*Hold. You must hold. Hold them off long enough—Latona will think of something, Sempronius will think of something, someone will think of something!*'

Where were the other men? Vitellius hoped Obir's deputies had them well-engaged. The advantage of a legion was always having someone to watch your back; fighting in the open like this was more akin to gladiatorial combat, and Vitellius didn't like it.

Something was happening beyond the spearman: a flash of fabric, flapping in the air. Did someone have the female Discordian down? He couldn't spare the focus to look; all his world had narrowed to the jagged metal jabbing in his direction.

But Vitellius had learned a few tricks in Iberia.

The next time his opponent stabbed forward, Vitellius caught the spear with his rod and drove it down to the street, embedding the point in between two stones. Then he brought his dagger down hard, just below the spear-tip, hacking into the wood.

It cracked, but not enough. As his opponent tried to yank the weapon back, Vitellius stomped down on the spear, trapping it beneath his foot. The next pull snapped the shaft below the spear-tip. Vitellius kicked it behind him, away from his bewildered foe.

No time to hesitate: a jagged piece of wood was still weapon enough to do harm, but Vitellius took advantage of the man's surprise. He barreled in close, swift and silent, bringing his rod down hard on the back of the man's neck, then cutting up, until his dagger met flesh. He twisted his wrist and tore backward, feeling viscera come away with the blade.

An ugly wound, gashing open the man's belly as he staggered to the ground. A painful death.

For a moment, Vitellius wanted to let him linger in that agony. '*He helped call fiends and demons down upon this city. He is ally to the woman who killed a Vestal.*' Vitellius remembered his own soul-rending experiences with fiends pulled from behind the boundaries of the natural world. Mennenius's death. Felix's missing hand. His sister's haunted eyes. *'He ought to suffer. He deserves no better.'*

Vitellius was a better man than that, and besides, he had other foes to worry about. He ended the Discordian's suffering with a final quick strike to the heart, then looked for his next opponent.

Only then did he realize, with hollowing despair, that he had lost sight of his sister.

A noise like thunder bowled through the Forum, coming not from the clouds but from the earth itself.

Smoky wisps began to appear *everywhere*. From between the stones in the street, from cracked mortar in the temples and administrative buildings that lined the Forum, from every buried charm they had not had time to unearth. Keening *umbrae*, seeking out souls to torment; hungry *devorae*, eager to feast; vicious *furillae*, savage and inciting.

Even these were not the primary danger: the yawning chasm tearing through the sky was lord and master to these thousand other troubles. The vicious spirits would do harm enough, though, sinking their claws into the men Latona had brought to the Forum in the hope of preventing such a catastrophe.

Latona tried to re-weave the protective shielding, but she could not determine where to direct it. Everyone had scattered; the battle had devolved into utter chaos, and most of it she could not see. Thick fog swept over the Forum, an unnatural bronze-tinged sheen that obscured her vision more than a few paces in any direction. It did not move, even when whipping winds should have driven it away.

Her heart beat a panicked rhythm against her ribs, throat tightening as awareness of her acute vulnerability asserted itself. *'Corinna. Where is Corinna?'* She might slit Latona's throat just as she had Quinta's, so fast, without Latona ever seeing it coming.

Fire. Where was the nearest flame? She needed something to draw strength from, but the torches and lamps her cohort brought with them into the Forum had long since been thrown down. She did not want to draw from the Discordians' ritual fire; no telling what they might have burned in it. Many temples had lamps standing outside their doors or decorating their corners. *'So far away, though, all so far away.'* Those were little more than orange blurs beyond the mist that whirled in the Forum. Somewhere, surely somewhere, there had to be a puddle of oil flickering with flame.

All her friends were somewhere in the mist, could be falling prey to vicious shades. Her brother, reliving horrors he had only recently escaped. Her lover—

'Oh, gods, Sempronius.' She would have been worried enough for him before, but knowing what she did now turned the concern to true terror.

And if this spread, the rest of the city would fall. Her sisters, her father, her niece. The other mages would not be able to hold the line for long—kind Rubellia, merry Terentilla, sweet little Fausta, all would be lost.

'I cannot—I cannot allow it—I will not!'

But she did not have the tools to combat this massive an evil.

A shape approached her, hazy through the mist. Friend, foe, or fiend? Latona couldn't tell. Instinct had her backing up, but sense forced her to stop; there was no telling what she might back into.

She summoned what shielding she could, seizing hold of Spirit magic with the rest of her strength. Her only hope might be to use empathic projection to overwhelm an attacker.

The figure that solidified out of the mist caused her control to shudder. Pinarius Scaeva, his hood knocked back from his thin face, his eyes roving and rolling. Had Corinna's wild act knocked his last scraps of sanity loose?

But no. His attention snapped to her, and he grinned, showing uneven teeth. "I made you a promise, once," he said, voice warbling like a poorly strung lyre. "I will fulfill it now, I think." He gestured upwards. "Do you feel it? What she's done? A magnificent pupil, outstripping her teacher, and all for our lady's glory."

"All for your own foul satisfaction," Latona answered. She flexed her fingers, and a fluttering warmth responded. Nearby, a flame. She *tugged*, and while the fire itself was too far away to jump to her hand, it lent power enough to allow her to spin a shield.

"Ahhhhhh," Scaeva said, eyes widening in appreciation. "I see you've learned something since last we met."

"Many things." Holding the shield as best she could, she reached again for Spirit, scooping up the turmoil all around her. With one great shove, she thrust it at Scaeva, hoping the effect would be enough to shatter his mind for good.

He staggered back a step—but lashed out, too, Fracture magic calling to every crack in the world around them, strengthening the conduit to that churning maw. All around Latona, the spirits responded, rising up from the grooves between the paving stones and the cracks in rocks. *Devorae*, ravenous and ready to consume.

Yet they did not reach her.

Her shielding held. Growling in determination, she pushed it out further, to seal the breaches, cauterize the wounds Scaeva tore in the world.

And he pushed back. Fracture against Spirit, the two magical forces crackling as they collided. Mages sometimes dueled as part of public games, but never like this, rending the world between them. Scaeva giggled madly, as though enjoying the effort. "I told you before," he said, "how delicious it would be, to devour your radiance. I underestimated. You've grown. More of a meal, now. And if I can feel it, I assure you, so too can the child of Chaos. It will sup on every soul in the city—but it will start with you."

Abruptly, he shifted, and Latona realized almost too late that he was trading his magical assault for a physical attack. A bronze blade flashed in the air—

His arm snapped back mid-descent, caught in strong fingers and wrenched behind him. In a moment, Scaeva was on the ground, howling in agony; in another breath, he was silenced, a spray of blood arcing up from the gash in his throat. Merula, half-drenched in gore, gave him a good kick in the side to push him further away from Latona. "As I said, bastard," she declared, and spat upon his twitching body, "your death is *mine* to claim."

For the briefest of moments, Latona felt relief—but then another shuddering wind hit them, another whorl of fiends sprang up, and she redoubled her efforts on protecting Merula and anyone else she could reach.

LIV

As a new wave of *lemures* tore their way through to the world, a wrenching, ripping force yanked at Vibia's control of her magic. Shuddering, she peeled away from Corinna, retracting her assault. Her crimson mantle burned against her skin. Something wanted *through*, pressed insistently at the Fireborn barrier, trying to force a hole through it and into Vibia's psyche, a place to slither and expand.

'Not again.' She reached out, placing her palms flat upon the earth. Her fingers curled, nails scraping against stone, until each was a rigid claw. Vibia wasn't sure how much of that was her, grasping to reality with all her strength, and how much was the shade trying to seize hold, insinuating itself into her veins and nerves.

Her chest was tight. Her throat, too. And then Vibia realized that she wasn't breathing. Everything inside her had gone still, except her blood. Its rapid beat throbbed in her ears, too quick to count. *'Breathe!'* she commanded herself. *'Open your mouth and draw in air! This should not be difficult!'*

Unable to snatch control of her mind, the fiend had instead reached for her body. Her head and spine angled back, back, as though the shade were dragging her by the hair into the void between the worlds. *'If I pass out, it gets me. I will become its puppet, Janus and Fortuna preserve me. Breathe!'*

At last, her body obeyed her command. With a loud gasp, she pitched forward, gulping for air. Her head swam, her chest ached—but the magical pressure eased. She had thrown off the fiend. Could do it again, if necessary.

But while she had been distracted, Corinna had vanished into the bronze mist.

Sempronius's instincts pulled him asunder, yearning to reach out for the magical forces swirling about, frightened of losing himself to those forces. He had to find Latona and his sister—they could not have gone far. But this fog—it reminded him of the *akdraugi,* the mist that invaded men's souls.

Sempronius had touched the gates of Pluto's realm before, knew what the entryway of death felt like. Discordian magic had plunged the entire Forum into that liminal space. Above him, a gyre of clouds swirled in the night sky, silver and grey and purple and indigo. There, the maw; there, the nexus of all these horrors.

He had closed such a gash once. He could again.

"Use me."

A voice on the wind, or the shades whispering, or an echo inside his head. Perhaps it was Discordia herself, beckoning; perhaps it was madness.

"Feel this. Use this. You rejected me once before. Claim me now."

His lips formed the word "no," but his lungs did not give it breath.

"How have you liked the slow path? The long road to victory? Has it been satisfying? You know how very far you have to go. A world to win over, and with what? With words?"

A ripple of breeze tickled the back of his neck, fluttered the edges of his focale.

"Claim me. Claim me, and claim them. A legion of spirits at your command. Who could defeat you then?"

The darkest side of his ambition, which he had always denied. The tyrannical path, which he had always shunned. The reason men like him were not supposed to reach for civil or military power.

"Use me, claim me," the voice crooned, sweet as summer air. *"Claim me, and claim what is due you. Reshape the world to your liking."*

He had rejected this offer before, had denied the dark attraction. Half of him screamed to shut out that voice, to withdraw his magic, to abjure it entirely and forever if that was what it took to keep himself free of this temptation. The warmth of his focale flickered uncertainly, like a fire trying to catch on wet logs, unequal to the task of burning out the damp.

The noise of the rest of the Forum grew faint. All his world narrowed to the swirl of dark colors in the sky and the whispering voice, promising him so much.

Shadow slipped loose of his control.

The air rumbled, and Latona flinched. Not thunder, but the groaning of a world being pulled apart. *'I have to stop this. I have to—but I don't know how!'*

Latona wasn't even sure where she was. Somewhere near the Temple of Vesta? Or closer to the Rostra? She'd gotten separated from Merula again, when some club-wielding brute charged them. Noises from fights echoed all around her. The pandemonium had scattered, with combatants stumbling through the dark and the mist, but whenever they found each other, they set to bloodshed. How many had died? How many were left?

No way to tell, but the mayhem would only grow worse as the maw above split and yawned. What had Scaeva called it—a child of Chaos? How far did its influence already spread? How many nightmares were shuddering to life, in homes all over the city?

"Latona!" a high voice called, and Latona spun to face another shape stepping out of the mist. Anca Corinna, her white gown sodden with crimson, her long dark hair damp and clinging to her skin. Her face and arms were spattered and smeared, blood and dirt alike. "*There* you are!" she said with delight, as though they had gotten separated during a festival and reunited in the crowd.

Latona's hands balled into fists, but Corinna's magic whipped out, bronze thorns assaulting Latona's shields. Latona's protection held; the Fracture did not get inside her, could not yet claim her mind and soul, but its force sent tremors through her whole body, and she fell to the street, barely catching herself in time to keep her head from cracking on the paving stones.

"You've put in quite a valiant effort, glitter-gold," Corinna said, a nasty smile on that too-perfect face. "But this city, I claim for Discordia." The fluttering grace with which Corinna knelt beside her was at variance with the rough shove of her hand to Latona's chest, pushing her flat on her back.

Vibia pressed through the mist, bronze knife in her hand, to find her brother. She could not pluck out his *animus* from the fog, but she still had means. There was a place in the Forum where the Fracture magic felt excited, like a child with a new toy, and she followed its shivering thrill straight to him.

Sempronius stood near the base of the Temple of Saturn, staring at the spiraling unnatural clouds. His magic was beyond her ability to sense, but she could tell that the Discordian curse was *feeding* off of it. She didn't have to see the meal to know that teeth were snapping.

"Oh, you absolute idiot," she growled, drawing near him. "Did you think yourself impervious?"

He did not respond, but she had not expected him to, not with his eyes black as the night and bedazzled with a bronze gleam. *'Of course the great fiend would feast on Shadow. Fracture only opened the way. He must feel like home.'*

Well, she would be damned if anything was setting up camp inside of her brother. She frowned, analyzing the patterns of Fracture magic that jabbed into him, siphoning out an energy she could not see. She had no Spirit mage at her disposal now, to ease the process, as when she freed Latona. But at least she knew what to do.

"Fortuna bless us both," she sighed. Then Vibia stabbed her brother.

A small wound, in the flesh of his upper arm, not so deep as to risk nicking any major channels of blood. Enough, though, to let *her* magic in. *'Sunder!'* she commanded, focusing all her effort on the consecrated bronze blade. *'Separate! Break away from him!'*

This Discordian magic had not, at least, had long enough to burrow and snarl itself within Sempronius's soul. It would drag him under, if given time, not least because his Shadow was not fighting it in the same way Latona's Spirit had. But Vibia was not going to give it that time.

Her magic jarred against the Discordian pressures, an oppugnant *clang* rattling within her mind. She ground her teeth and would not yield, not even for so long as it would take to blink. *'Unwind, unbind, and get out of my brother.'*

A guttural moan tore out of Sempronius's throat, voicing an agony that had nothing to do with the point of her knife still embedded in his shoulder or the blood running down his arm. He twisted and sank to the ground, and Vibia moved with him, refusing to surrender.

As he yelled, the winds picked up around them, ripping at their hair and clothes, a miniature tempest swirling in the midst of the Forum. Still Vibia held fast, still she forced her magic against the Discordian invasion of her brother's animus. He was shouting, indecipherable words, in a voice seeming to resonate *through* him, not from his throat. A thousand threats, a thousand sorrows, echoing in the sepulchral tone. If the five rivers of the underworld had a voice, misery and wrath and lamentation and oblivion and abhorrence rushing together, it would sound like that.

And then, the air around them stilled, and suddenly Vibia found no counterpressure to her magical force. The Discordian influence shattered and scattered.

A moment later, Sempronius's fingers came up to touch her arm. His eyes had gone back to their usual indifferent brown, and when he spoke, his voice was his own.

"It's not that I'm not grateful," he rasped, "but would you please re-move that knife?"

The world was still howling around them, but Sempronius's mind was clear. *Too* clear, painfully clear, purged and scraped and scrubbed with lye.

"You're an idiot," Vibia said, withdrawing her blade from his arm and immediately using it to cut a strip off the sleeve of her gown. "You saw a great gaping hole tearing from reality to the realm of chaos, and what did you try to do? Rhetoricize at it?"

"No. No. I thought I... but I..." He glanced upward, then flinched away. A ragged breath, half a sob, as Vibia set to binding his wound. "I don't think I can do it, Vibia. Not like the last time. I don't dare."

The power in that maw was magnitudes beyond the first he had closed, back in the warehouse. Corinna's success made Scaeva's early attempt seem a pale, paltry thing. *'It's too potent, too dangerous, too hungry—and what a feast I gave it, opening up all my Shadow for its consumption. I cannot touch it. I should have felt that, should have known...'* But he had fallen prey to his own conceit. A force beyond reckoning, a creature of the void, and he thought he could wrangle it like a wily colt.

Latona had accused him of hubris, and she was right. So certain of the gods' plans for him, Sempronius dismissed his mortal limitations. Victory, in his mind, always meant finding the cleverest way through obstacles, a way that brought his wits and his magic and his charm and his ambitions together. There had always *been* such a way.

But this time, facing this power, that certainty led him straight into a pit, and only Vibia had pulled him out. If he fell again...

'*I would end up no better than Ekialde,*' he thought, remembering the young king, writhing and bleeding as the *besteki* ravaged him. '*I would pitch myself into the void, all because I thought I had the power...*'

What had the doomed *erregerra* told his wife, at the end? '*I am sorry I went so far away from you.*'

Sempronius did not want to go away, not from Latona, not from this world, not from his purpose. But this challenge, he could not meet. Strange, humbling thing, to encounter that constraint.

Worse, harder, to admit it out loud. "If I touch that thing again... I think you'd have to stab me in the heart to get me back." A cracking realization, terrible to admit. "I can't help."

Vibia tied off the makeshift bandage. "We're—I think we're losing, Sempronius. We haven't lost yet. But if we don't close that thing..."

He swallowed. He could not close the rift in the worlds. He did not have the power.

But someone had to.

"We have to find Latona."

"If she's—" Vibia bit the thought off; Sempronius heard the words she did not want to say: that Latona might be unconscious, or possessed by a fiend, or dead.

He knew the reality as well as she did, though. "If she's alive," he said, "she'll be trying to fix it."

And she was, without doubt. Venus bonded lovers' hearts; he would know if hers had stopped beating.

With physical force alone, Latona could have knocked the Discordian mage over, wispy thing that Corinna was. Corinna had seized control of her magic again, though, and was using it to split Latona's strength out of her. Her muscles wouldn't obey her commands to move, and the tide of terror rose within her chest.

It was too much like the advantage Corinna had gotten over her in their first encounter. The edge of oblivion was there, an easy thing to tip into, the world of shades and nightmares, and Latona knew if she fell into it again, she would not escape.

Corinna went on, calm, as though their magics were not clashing with the fury of a thousand gladiators. "It was always meant to be so. Don't blame yourself too much. This city was rotting from within long before you or I were born." Corinna shrugged prettily. "As does every city. Every place where people, flawed and selfish, gather. Society is an illusion we cast to make ourselves feel better about the yawning edge of chaos."

That laugh again, the one that made Latona want to sink her nails into the woman's throat, and then Corinna seized Latona by the hair, dragging her half-up from the ground.

"It's so much easier once you admit the inevitability. This is what we do, we brief mortals. We cannot build but we feel an impulse to tear down. We cannot gather together without scrapping and scrabbling and stabbing."

"You're wrong," Latona ground out, her throat fighting against the paralyzing force of Corinna's magic. Her own power was still there, still all around her, if only she could reach it—

"I'm not, and you know it. You've seen it yourself, the corruption and weakness. You've seen the worst of it. Strife is this city's destiny. It always has been. Nothing you can do will change that."

Corinna's words, with the splintering power of her magic, waged a war on Latona's heart. There was truth to what she spoke, no matter how Latona wanted to believe differently. Despair like a strangling vine wound its way around Latona's mind, intent on dragging her under, back to the nightmare realm, where she would have no power at all to fight against the inevitable tide of pandemonium destined to ensnare her beloved city—

And then, a shift.

The balance of magical power in the Forum changed. With Spirit's awareness, Latona sensed new signatures at work. First, her heart thudded in fear. More Discordians, here to back up Corinna?

But no. From the north, a cool thread of Air. To the east, mingling streams of Water. Behind her, approaching from the base of the Capitoline Hill, burning Fire and grounding Earth.

The mages of Aven had come.

LV

The fog began to thin, growing patchy and then clearing as new magic assaulted it. Howling in rage, Corinna released Latona and dashed away—to find her remaining comrades? Or to perpetrate some new horror?

As the bronze haze broke apart, Latona could better see who had come: first, riders, charging down the Via Sacra. One was Autronius Felix, reins wrapped around his maimed arm.

Hoofbeats to the right told Latona that the same thing was happening on the Via Nova, and there was the Lady Hanath, her swirling cloak ink-dark in the light of torches, with the Arevaci cavalry. Behind them, a line of legionaries approached, curving around the Capitoline Hill.

They were providing a guard for the mages, as Obir's men had for Latona and Vibia. Rubellia, Tilla, Marcus, faces that Latona expected—but there were more, so many more, not just mages, but other citizens. Latona saw Seppius from the Lower Esquiline, with what seemed to be half the neighborhood at his back. Others approached from the Velabrium, from the Subura, from the Palatine. Some bore torches, others buckets, others makeshift weapons, while the energy flowing from mages of all elements created a dazzling tapestry, streaming into the Forum.

'Everyone you helped,' whispered a soft voice at the back of her mind. Not her own; it resonated into her, the same feeling as when Spirit magic came unbidden, accompanied by the taste of cinnamon. 'You gave your aid freely, unreservedly. You bled for them. Did you think they would forget?'

Her vision blurred again, this time from tears springing up. She dashed them quickly away, still trying to make sense of what was happening. 'But how—how did they organize, how did they know—?'

Then she noticed the birds: dozens of them, white and grey, and *there*, in the midst, Marcia Tullia, perched on the back of her husband's horse.

She had her own protective cordon, and birds swooped to her and away again, across the Forum, directing the communal efforts with shrieks and pecks and insistent flapping, since there was no time to scribble out messages.

'*She summoned them. She must have sent out the call to every mage here, and to the legion.*'

Men and women brought buckets from the nearest fountains, which Seppius and Davina and other Water mages used to cleanse the stones of the Forum, rushing clear the poisoned earth, flooding the cracks and channels that had become gates beyond the world. Little Fausta dashed here and there, pointing out the fissures others could not see.

Rubellia and her acolytes wove a net of protection over a group of soldiers who advanced on a huddle of Discordian mages, a solid shield wall closing in around them; lining the road near them were citizens bearing torches and lamps, flames to fuel the defense.

Marcus Autronius and Terentilla marched alongside another cohort, reinforcing Obir's men in their fight against the Discordians' protectors. Marcus's deep green and Tilla's verdant spring twined around the warriors' feet, grounding their souls within their bodies, protecting them from the *furillae* that hissed and flared around them.

No swords within the city, the legionaries held to that rule: they had shields only. But a legionary's shield was a formidable construction in its own right, and as they pressed around the Discordians, those mages lost their nerve and their focus. More of the demonic spirits faltered and evaporated.

"Latona!" Vibia, rushing across the blood-streaked earth, and with her—Latona wept anew—was Sempronius, bloodied and disheveled, but alive. "Latona, the breach! We still have to seal the breach!"

Latona looked to Sempronius. "Last time—Vibia said you—"

He shook his head firmly. "No, beloved. I can't. I—" He had never looked so ashamed, not even when confessing his secrets to her. "I'm going to go help Felix and Hanath, do what I can there. I have to remove myself. The maw—it's too strong, there's too much Shadow in it. I tried, but I... I'm not strong enough to fight it." His hands grasped her shoulders. "But you are. And you have the right magic."

Her jaw trembled. There was the faith in her, the faith she'd wanted proof of, and now she didn't know if she could live up to it. "I don't know how. We've sealed breaches before, but this—"

"I know. When I tried, I touched it, I felt... I felt everything it glories in. The chaos, the contention, all the weaknesses in this city... everything it will feed on." His fingers slipped up into her hair, cupping the back of her head. "But you are stronger than it. You will find a way. I-I don't dare stay. If I fall to it again..." His face spoke the agony for him. "We'll give you as much of an opening as we can."

He kissed her then, hot and brief and desperate, and then he was gone, picking up a blade some cultist had let fall and rushing to join the fighters along the Via Nova.

The air around them shuddered again. The newly-arrived mages were creating an opportunity, yes, but if they did not seize it, the void would still win. It would demolish them all, feast upon their magic, grow stronger on their souls.

Latona grabbed Vibia's hand, pulling the other woman to stand by her side. "Just like every other time!" she shouted above the stormy winds. "Only—bigger!"

Flickers of possible futures fluttered within Alhena's awareness, so many as to nearly blind her. Some blinked out as fast as they sputtered into existence, potential snuffed before it could catch; others solidified, or consolidated from close variables into one cohesive likelihood.

Those threads, she could use to help direct the efforts of mages and non-magical citizens alike—desperate attempts to make up for her failure in not seeing the threat to Quinta Terentia in time.

Merula had been injured, a terrible gash to her thigh; Alhena sent a healer-mage in her direction. A few cultists attempted to slip into the Subura; Alhena sent a line of legionaries to the far end of the Forum to cut them off. Rubellia's strength faded; Alhena sent a Fire-forger toward the citizens bearing torches, to give her more to work with.

Then she heard a wail that cut into her soul, and she could no longer hold herself aloof from the turmoil.

Terentilla had peeled away from her cohort near the Temple of the Vestals. Tilla gathered up her sister's lifeless, blood-soaked body and was shaking her head in disbelief, too shocked even to cry.

Alhena crashed to her knees at Tilla's side. *'I'm sorry, I'm so sorry, I didn't see it in time, there were too many images, I couldn't... I'm so sorry, if I'd known, if I could've stopped it happening...'* She touched Tilla's shoulder, hoping Tilla would read comfort in the gesture, knowing no words could suffice to answer this kind of grief.

Tears stood in Tilla's eyes, and her lips moved wordlessly for a moment. Then, as if a tide of anguish hit her all at once, Tilla released a throat-ravaging scream of misery and fury.

It drew attention, and not only from mortal ears. There were yet *lemures* in the Forum, wispy shapes that darted and weaved above the paving stones, trying to evade the mages intent on purging them. Now, several of the bobbing, smoky tendrils curled in Tilla's direction. "Come on," Alhena said, firm but soothing, lifting Tilla up. "We need to move." The last thing she wanted was for some hideous shade to settle in front of them and take on Quinta's face. "Tilla. We're in danger here. We have to move."

The word "danger" seemed to have some effect, but still, Alhena struggled to peel Tilla's arms from around Quinta. Only after much effort did she get Tilla upright and moving back toward the street.

"Alhena!" Vitellius ran to them. "What's the—" The question halted mid-throat as he realized exactly what the matter had to be. "Gods. I'll get you two out of here. She's in no state to continue."

"Wait." Alhena flicked her gaze upward, where the unnatural clouds continued to swirl. Her own magic clicked into place, jagged pieces of the world suddenly forming a coherent mosaic. "The pattern's shifted."

"The—what?"

"I can feel it." Futures, winking out with each heartbeat. Options collapsing into each other, truncated. "An end. I can feel an end."

The sky above the Forum crepitated, tumultuous energy in utter riot, bucking against the restraints that Latona and Vibia attempted to place upon it.

"Latona," Vibia said, wary, "I've got the edges of it, but I can't—I can't hold it for long."

Latona drew all the energy she could from the flames that dotted the Forum and the surrounding streets, but she needed more. Those flickering lights weren't enough for what she needed to accomplish. *'I need more strength to seal a wound of this magnitude. I need—'*

Strength. Sempronius had said the maw fed on the weakness of the city, its cracks and turmoil. *'But that is not all the city is.'* She and Sempronius, they believed in Aven's potential, its strength, its myriad beauties, rough and reckless though they were. They had faith in what this city could be, if it dared, if its people chose well, chose to embrace possibility rather than fear. They loved this city, and that had power, too.

Latona glared up at the vortex of clouds and magical energy seething above the Forum. *'Right. That's about enough of you.'*

Latona reached and reached, pulling at the power of the Rostra, where words shaped the nation. She reached for the Comitia, on the other side of the platform, where the Tribal and Plebeian Assemblies voted. She reached for the Curia, not far to her left, where the Senate argued and debated. The judicial basilicas, the Temple of Saturn, the stretch of open space where Aventans gathered for law and business. *'The strength of Aven, even in its division. The heart of Aven, its greatest glories, these places where Aventans speak and shape our fates!'*

The strength of its people, too, all around her: the mages, coming together to fight this terror; the legionaries, who never expected to risk their lives within the city walls but whose shields held firm; the citizens, braving the terrors of the night, refusing to relinquish their city to horrors beyond mortal comprehension. That strength, that *love*, flooding the Forum, raw and ragged and beautiful—

That, Latona could use, and within it, find the threads that shone clarion in resonance with her own heart.

'Alhena, who is here though it petrifies her. Vibia, who has taken every wretched step of this path with me. Sempronius, oh, Sempronius, who believes in this city and its future with such fervor—'

Latona released Vibia and held out both her hands, palms up. "Jupiter Optimus Maximus," she called, full-throated, "and Blessed Lady Juno, and Mars and Minerva, and all you gods who look after this city! Divine Romulus and Remus, look here and hear me! I call your power to this place! I call on your power to *defend* this place! Give me strength and guide me! I, Vitellia Latona, entreat you! Look here, gods; look here and hear me!"

Spirit magic leapt through her, as strong as anything she had ever used Fire to bolster. It rushed into her from the Rostra, from the Comitium, from the Curia and the basilicas and the temples, from every soul fighting to reclaim their city.

The mortal world around her disappeared, plunging Latona into sudden silence. She had slipped into a crack—but not, she thought, one of Discordian making. *'Chaos is the space between. Chaos was here before the universe, and it will be here after. Discordia is its grandchild—but so is the earth and so is the sky and so are all the gods.'*

Chaos did not belong to Fracture alone; that was a fallacy they had let themselves fall into, through chains of philosophy and centuries of thaumaturgical reasoning. Chaos was primordial, neither good nor bad but simply *existing* and eternal, both grand-sire and grand-dam to all creation. It was the void above the earth and below the sky, the slippery channels between the spheres in which the planets moved, the ceaseless cycle of creation. It was every element entwined, a tangle of pure energy, the well from which every mortal mage drew when they invoked their powers. Tangible or intangible, they all originated here.

For a single heartbeat, Latona could see it *all*.

Then she snapped back into herself, dizzy with the vigor of the magic flowing through her.

She reached up with one hand, stretching it toward the black and purple clouds swirling over the Forum, the miniature tempest brewing right over her head. As close to pure chaos as this world could bear, summoned and unleashed by Corinna and her putrid rituals, her wretched fellowship, her perverted devotions.

'I have as much right to this as she has,' Latona thought. The insides of her knuckles buzzed, and she clenched her hand into a fist: yes, the magic was there, the energy, the pulsing heart of the storm, and she had a grip on it. *'And I will use it!'*

Screaming in a combination of feral agony and vindictive glory, Latona yanked her hand down, drawing as much magic as she could grab along with it.

LVI

Lightning struck the earth in the center of the Forum, a vicious pink-and-white blaze that illuminated the whole area in a blindingly brilliant flash.

Some of the mages present faltered, as did many of the non-magical citizens wreathing the Forum. The legionaries held, though; these were men of the Tenth, who had faced horrors and hauntings in Iberia. No mere flare of light was going to deter them.

Sempronius looked across the Forum, and his throat tightened. Vibia had been knocked to the ground, perhaps unconscious, but Latona stayed upright, fist still clenched. Beneath the swirling clouds, she glowed, her skin alight with the power she had drawn down from the sky. It danced up her fingers, coiled around her arms, played and leapt in her hair.

Beautiful, and terrifying. *'Gods, Latona, let go. If you hold onto that too long...'*

She had control of it for the moment, was herself the point of balance, the conduit between the earthly realm and the chaos from which all magic sprang. But if she lost control, even a sliver, it would burn through her in a heartbeat.

Instinct told him to rush to her; insight bid him hold back.

'Trust her. She won't make your mistakes.'

Latona had drawn magic into herself before, transmuting one element to another, but never had she felt so full of the gods' gifts as she did now. *'My city. I will protect my city.'* The sky above remained an unholy whorl of tempestuous weather and curse-ridden energy, a sword fit to sunder the earth in two, but Latona now had the power to seal the breach.

What came down to her as lightning, she respun and flung back up at the heavens: a golden mortar, filling the cleft torn in the world. *'My strength is the strength of Aven. My power is in this city's bones, its beating heart.'*

Slowly at first, then in a torrent, the ragged edges of the world knit back together. The maw spiraled smaller and smaller, devouring itself, until at last it snapped closed and dissipated, back into the vast realm of potential that had given it birth.

The storm winds stopped blowing; the dark clouds broke apart; stars became visible in the blue-black sky.

Latona's limbs trembled with the raw power she had absorbed. She had never channeled magic like this, never felt herself so liberated, as though any moment her soul might leap free of her body and ascend to join the stars, ever-dazzling. She stretched both arms out; her skin glowed, lines of fire crackling in her every vein.

Such a temptation, to hold onto this power, to let herself blaze with the glory of it—

A temptation that she, with a long exhale, closed her mind to.

'Release!' she told herself. *'Back to where you came from!'*

The effort stole all of Latona's strength, and she collapsed to the paving stones. Golden light bolted out of her in all directions, back to the Rostra, the Curia, the temples, the basilicas. The strength of Aven, restored; the city, made safe.

Coughing, Latona sat up—or tried, as best she was able. She found her head pillowing instead against a bony shoulder. Not the most comfortable of resting points, but Latona sighed with relief. Vibia had reached her side and gathered her up from the ground.

When she thought of what might have happened if she had not been able to release the power, if she had not returned to herself, Latona shivered. *'I would have died. I would have incinerated myself, burned up from the inside out, fried my own brain or boiled my own blood or gods know what. Gods. Maybe this is why they stopped giving mortals such power.'*

Impulsively, Latona threw her arms around her soon-to-be sister-in-law, embracing her as tightly as she would have Aula or Alhena. After only a breath's hesitation, Vibia returned the gesture, squeezing Latona. "Please stop trying to die," she said. "It does get my brother so distressed."

As the sky crept toward dawn, the Forum buzzed with activity. Mages and citizens worked together to clear the space of any remaining curse-charms. Soldiers guarded the Discordians, both the cultists and those few of their protectors who survived the fighting.

Then, there were the dead.

Vitellius had seen worse carnage, certainly. Battlefields with more blood, more bodies. But the *shock* of it—corpses being lined up along the Via Sacra, crimson pools beneath the tall columns of the Temple of Saturn—such things weren't meant to happen here, at home.

'*It's always someone's home. Segontia, Libora, Toletum... why should Aven be spared?*'

Worst of all, the lifeless form of Quinta Terentia. A horror beyond sacrilege. How would the city weather such a loss?

Her body was collected by her stunned father and still-weeping sister. Terentilla clutched at Alhena's hand like a drowning man would to a rope, and so Alhena insisted on accompanying them. "I'll be fine," Alhena said, voice small but sure. "Go find Latona. Take her home."

Vitellius found Latona still sitting on the ground, just across the Via Sacra from the Rostra, amid a cluster of concerned friends. Vibia, looking every bit as exhausted as Latona; Rubellia, making a vain attempt at tidying Latona's hair.

As he approached, Latona was making a game attempt at pushing up from the ground, saying, "There's still much to do..."

"And someone else can do it," Vibia insisted. All it took was a light poke to push Latona back on her rump. "We've quite done our part."

"She's right," Rubellia said, in a much more soothing tone than Vibia's brusqueness. "My darling, you... you just did something beyond comprehension. That magic... I cannot explain it. It shouldn't have been possible."

"There is more to magic than we know. That's what he said..." Latona frowned, as if realizing she had said something odd. "I'll... I'll explain later." She turned to Vitellius, blinking owlishly. "Gaius. Oh, thank Juno. But where's—"

"Alhena's with the Terentiae."

Rubellia nodded knowingly. "It's good of her to offer them comfort."

"What could possibly be comfort enough?" Latona asked.

None of them had any answer. Vitellius's heart ached for the guilt he knew would weigh on his sister's conscience. How terrible it was, not to be able to save everyone.

Latona swiped at her eyes. "Vibia, where's—where's your brother?"

"Resisting the urge to make a spectacle of himself by fussing over you, I expect," Vibia said. She jerked her chin toward the Via Nova. "Over there. Marshalling the apprehension of the Discordians. Do you want me to fetch him?"

Latona shook her head—then nodded—then shook it again. "No. No, I'll... I'll never find the right words, not now. My head's a muddle."

Rubellia looked past Vitellius, squinting a bit. "We're about to have more company."

"Gods." Latona rubbed at her forehead. "I'm half-tempted to faint to avoid dealing with them."

"I think," Vitellius said, leaning down to help her rise, "you're going to want to talk to this one."

Approaching was Marcia Tullia, face pale and ashy, hair blown loose by the unnatural winds. Still she moved with grace, however, and her cool voice carried a sense of calm. "Vitellia Latona. I believe I owe you an apology."

Latona leaned on Vitellius's arm, which he held stiff to help her balance. "You brought them," she said. "The mages, the legionaries, the cavalry, the *people*. It was you, wasn't it?"

Marcia nodded. "It was in progress even before that *thing* opened up." She glanced upward nervously, as though the sky were not yet to be trusted.

"A good thing, too," Vitellius said. "We could not have waited longer for reinforcements."

"But..." Latona frowned in confusion. "But if it was before... what changed your mind?"

Marcia lifted one brow. "Thank your sister."

"My—"

"Aula Prima," Marcia confirmed, "who could out-talk Mercury. She and your father paid us a most unexpected midnight call. She explained, perhaps not everything, but a great deal." Her gaze lowered; her hands busied themselves tucking her hair back into its pins. "About the Discordians, how they unsettled the city last year. About Anca Corinna and her brother and the Augians' corruption. It seemed incredible, despite... despite everything."

"They knew it would," Rubellia said. "They were counting on it."

"And we all fell into the trap. You didn't know who to trust, and I..." Marcia sighed. "Suffice it to say, I will be spending much more time in contemplation on how my own faults made me easy prey for their manipulations." She shook her head. "Still, I wish it had not come to this. I cannot be comfortable with what transpired. The killing of mages without trial... I do not like it."

"I didn't *like* it, Marcia," Latona said. "It was necessary."

"It was war," Vitellius said, voice dangerously low. For all that he respected Marcia Tullia, her words were aggravating him. "All we did was in defense of the city."

Vibia's hackles were up as much as his. "And we didn't think a civilized chat would be enough to stop them."

"I know," Marcia answered. "And with the Augian Commission corrupted, there was no justice to bring them to. But I can still regret the necessity, and worry about what happens next. It's going to be a legal mess. Even cultists have families who may sue on their behalf. Some may claim the killings were politically motivated."

Latona's hand gripped Vitellius's arm even tighter, and she swayed slightly. "Forgive me, Lady Marcia," he interrupted, "but I think none of us are adequately prepared for erudite conversation at the moment."

"No." She looked somewhat abashed. "No, of course. But, Latona, if I may, I will call on you—at your home or at that house on the Esquiline—once you've recovered." A slight, self-deprecating laugh. "Once we both have, fully. There are matters I should like to discuss with you, with a clearer mind than I did before. I cannot promise to agree with you on everything, but I want to hear you, without prejudice, and speak, without rancor."

"I would be glad for that, Marcia," Latona said. "I never wanted enmity between us."

"Nor I."

As Marcia departed, Vibia folded her arms over her chest. "That woman is too honest for her own good."

"She means well," Latona said. "And she *did* save our hides, so I'm willing to extend her a fair bit of grace. We'll need her. To achieve what we truly want... we will need her support." She looked up at Vitellius. "Can we go home?"

"Of course. Vibia was right; there's nothing here that someone else can't take care of. You've earned your rest. Do you want me to carry you?"

"Yes," Latona admitted, "but no. I... I think I cannot look weak in this moment."

Vitellius understood. "Hold my arm, then. I won't let you fall."

Rubellia kissed Latona's cheek before they parted, and Vibia pressed her hand, then went in search of her own brother. Vitellius and Latona started toward the Palatine, which had never seemed so far from the Rostra.

They passed the place where Latona had called down lightning. In a ten foot circle, the paving-stones had been transformed: black and glossy, with crackling white lines running through them, as though the lightning itself had been captured. Vitellius wondered if the stones would be repaired, replaced.

He hoped not.

It was well that they had so many witnesses, Marcus thought, because otherwise he had no idea how they would have explained what happened. Marcus himself only knew the half of it; much had been beyond his capacity to see. He felt the effects, though, and he knew just how close Aven had come to utter disaster.

Most of the Discordians—those left alive, anyway—had been surrounded by the implacable shield walls of the legionaries. Effectively, they were captives, though what was to be done with them until trial would be a matter for debate. Throwing the mages in the Tullianum, together, was unlikely to be a wise decision. No, they would need to be parceled out to the homes of men who could be trusted to keep guard over them. *'And then...'* The legal implications made Marcus's head spin.

At least the Augian Commission's involvement could now be openly investigated, even if the extent of their complicity might not yet be proved beyond all doubt. In addition to Anca Corinna and her fraternal connection, an Augian was among the captured Discordians. He sat on the ground in the midst of a circle of legionaries, sulky and silent. What methods might be used to encourage his tongue, Marcus was happier not to contemplate, but his presence alone ensured that the whole situation could not be handed over to the Commission.

Vatinius Obir had custody of Corinna herself. He had bound and gagged her, though she had fallen into a swoon at the moment that Latona called the lightning down from the sky. One of the collegium's boys was sitting on her legs, in case she should wake.

Marcus had no pity to spare for Anca Corinna, and only enough compassion to wish to see justice done fairly and publicly. Even before she murdered a Vestal, her crimes had been numerous and damaging. Whatever happened now, she was the author of her own end.

Felix rode into the Forum and dismounted unsteadily. "Damn, but that's still harder than it should be..." He shook himself, then looked to Marcus. "If I'd known you were keeping all the fun here in the city," he said, "I wouldn't have gone all the way to Iberia to find it."

"You utter ass," Marcus breathed, then embraced his brother. "Thank you for coming."

"I was glad to be able to help," Felix said, throat full of emotion. "Better than sitting on the Field of Mars, useless, waiting to hear what happened. No soldier likes missing a fight."

"I shall be glad to never see another." Marcus did not understand how his brother, and so many other men, could find it glorious. The battle of the Forum had not even been large, not as a legion would reckon it. Marcus had lived through civil strife under Dictator Ocella. When Ocella died, he hoped that he would never again watch blood run in Aventan streets. *Maybe now. Maybe now, a victory over Discordia will mean a respite from strife. Gods, give us a few years of peace, at least.*

The next night, Latona dreamed.

Aula bundled her off to bed as soon as she arrived home. The coming days would bring an endless round of calls to pay, calls to receive, dinner parties to attend. She would have to tell the story a thousand times, walking the narrow line between under-crediting her efforts and appearing too self-aggrandizing. She would, eventually, have to answer to Aventan law.

Later. All of that would come later. Latona spent most of the day unconscious. She roused herself mid-afternoon to take a little food and drink, brought to her in bed by little Lucia, but she was asleep again before dusk. And as she slept, she dreamt.

She found herself again in the swampy valley that once stood between the city's hills. This time, it was a summer's night, warm and breezy, with stars glimmering overhead. Most of the huts dotting the hills were dark and still, but a few dogs patrolled the ridge of the Capitoline, and others slept outside the paddocks of sheep and goats.

One man sat alone, outside a hut on the Aventine Hill, arms wound around his knees, head tilted up toward the stars.

Latona climbed the hill to join him. Remus looked younger now than at their first meeting: fewer lines around his eyes, his skin less weathered, his beard a little more towards red. He showed no surprise at her approach, though. *'If it is him, reaching across that bridge again, and not only a dream, some fevered fancy born of exhaustion and delirium.'*

She believed that it was Remus, in truth. The same odd sense of certainty pervaded her mind, driving away all questions.

So she sat down beside him. "We won," she said. "I think we won."

"You never win," he replied, gently. "Not completely. This is not a fight that is ever over."

It ought to have sounded wearying. Instead, a thrill ran through Latona's veins. *Purpose*, that was something worthy to hold and cherish.

"It may be that your part in the struggle is done," Remus went on, "or it maybe that the Fates will require you again. But the fight doesn't end. Liberty is fragile, and it must be rigorously defended."

"You're a king," Latona pointed out. "What care you for liberty?"

A soft chuckle—which reminded Latona, oddly, of Sempronius. "I was a king because kings were what we knew how to be, then. Athaeca and its democracy were so far away. What did shepherds in the Truscan hills know of it? No, all we knew was the example of the rulers of our region: take power and hold it, through steel and blood if you must. Defend what was yours, for someone would take it if you did not."

He sighed, looking suddenly sadder, older, wiser.

"We made mistakes. With the best of intentions, we still erred. As my powers grew stronger, though, as I trusted the gods' gifts more, I could see times and places where power would be differently envisioned." He reached out, and his fingers brushed her cheek; they were warm, as hers always were when working magic. "It will always change. And people like you can help ensure it changes for the better."

"I... I did my best," Latona said. "I will continue to do my best."

"I know you will. Because you love," Remus said, and the warmth of his regard hit her with physical force, a golden glow beneath the silvered sky. "You love with a fierce heart, and my far-distant grandmother Venus sees that, and she adores it. You love people, you love the vulnerable and the needful with protective fury, and the Lady Juno sees that, and she adores it. You love this city, though you see it with clear eyes. You love it as few since its founding have done, and I see that, and I adore it. Your vision of Aven's future is one I wish to thrive."

Lingering concerns pulled at Latona's mind. "Corinna, the leader of the Discordians, she... she was not wrong in everything she said. As much as I wanted her to be, she was not entirely wrong." Latona told him what Corinna had said, about the destiny of cities being to rise and fall. And she spoke of what she had felt, touching the raw energy beyond the void. "This city... It needs chaos, doesn't it? We seek order, but we need the wildness, too. She's right about that, but wrong about it only leading to destruction. We need chaos for good things. The new ideas, the ambitions, the inspiration..."

"Chaos is generative power," Remus agreed. "Creation itself—and destruction, too. Both inevitable. Neither un-negotiable. The trick, as your Fracture mage friend could tell you, is in holding the line. And that is not easy. The forces of Discordia have sought to tear this city asunder since its founding. They tried to set brother against brother, wanted us to rip each other apart, to commit the most heinous of sins, to bloody this whole nation with the stain of the kin-killer."

Latona shivered. "What a terrible thought."

"Indeed. So, yes, some will always be led by their most venal instincts. And some will always be led by nobler aims." A soft laugh. "Most of us are neither monsters nor paragons. We are humans. We fight, yes. We succumb to our flaws. We yearn. We love. We do great and terrible things." A shadow came over his eyes, like a cloud over the stars. "Sometimes in the same breath." Then he cast the shadow aside, turning to smile upon her. "But it matters that you have striven for better, Latona."

Latona leaned back on her hands, joining Remus in gazing up at the stars. The rest of the dream passed in meditative near-silence, only the stirring of the breeze and the chirring of tree-crickets, until Latona's consciousness faded back into the oblivion of a peaceful sleep.

LVII

Arrius Buteo paced in Rabirus's atrium. He had *not* been invited to dinner, the day after the debacle, but he turned up anyway, snorting and fuming and demanding attention, when all Rabirus wanted to do was think, in quiet solitude, and adjust his plans. "You should never have thrown your lot in with those cultists," he chided. "Foolish recklessness. I can't think what you—"

"You told me to use whatever weapons were at our disposal," Rabirus shot back. "And it was Cornicen who led me to that deranged priest in the first place." Now Scaeva was dead, the madwoman Corinna was in chains, and Durmius Argus had vanished from the city, as much an indictment as his Augian fellow caught at the scene.

"We are men of order!" Buteo insisted. "Order, and good governance! What were you thinking?"

"I was thinking that sometimes, a field is more fertile after a wildfire rolls through. I was never going to let those lunatics hold power, Buteo. I hoped they would be useful tools."

"Foolish. Foolish! You jeopardized the whole damn city!"

"You don't know that."

It had been a hellish night, true. Worse than the first two, many times worse, but the Discordians could never have sustained that level of terror. Whatever they had unleashed—and Rabirus hardly credited some of the rumors that came out of the Forum. Who did they originate with? Mages, yes, but plebeian Fire-forgers, half-trained charm-makers, and other fools. Like as not, they hallucinated a horror far beyond what the Discordians actually conjured.

"You overestimate their abilities," Rabirus said. "They were half-mad cultists. *Fully* mad, some of them. These rumors that they summoned a child of Chaos, it's ridiculous. Some storm magic, that's all, thrown in front of credulous simpletons who puffed the story up, and thus made themselves look more heroic in the bargain."

Buteo's face was stony. "You're wrong," he said, in a tone far more somber than his usual stentorian thunder. "Whatever they did, it cut deep into men's souls. It could not have been easily reined."

What had Buteo seen, in the dark and terrible night? Rabirus had not been unaffected. But soul-shuddering? No. *My friend is of an excitable nature, that's all. For all his virtues, I am steadier than he is.'*

And, to his credit, Buteo mastered himself rapidly, resuming his pacing. "You may have a point, though. We can use that idea. Make mock of the more incredible tales sweeping around the city. Point out who profits from them." He hissed. "Of course Sempronius Tarren was on the scene. I tremble to think what use he'll make of that. The speeches we're going to be subjected to..."

"It is too much," Rabirus declared. "That false-triumph he intends to throw, the laws he's doubtless to introduce. And now he'll marry that Vitellian woman, allying two of the strongest and oldest families, and pinning his own prominence alongside her newfound celebrity to boot."

"Have you heard what they're calling her?" Buteo sneered. "Just whispers so far, but if it catches on..." A disgusted noise. "'Salvatorix,' they said. A woman-savior, of all the absurdities, as though she's some demigod. *Dux femina*, more like, I've said it before and I'll say it again. Unnatural."

"Salvatorix and imperator," Rabirus said grimly. "What a fine pair."

"He won't stop at imperator, not with the groundswell supporting him and his woman. This is a man who would be king." Buteo jabbed a finger down at the ground. "We have all known it, have we not? It is what we have feared since Ocella first singled him out as a rival worthy of extermination. Like recognized like. Now the wretched man is more popular than ever, and he'll be running for consul in a few months."

Buteo continued to grouse, but Rabirus's attention meandered. Easy enough, once familiar with the cadence of Buteo's speech, to muffle awareness of the individual words. He thought instead of just how Ocella had come to power, what situations he had manipulated to get there, and how he might have been stopped. Another such Dictatorship—or worse—would be the end of Aven. *'And that must be Sempronius's goal. He can never achieve all he intends from a mere consul's chair.'*

So he had to be stopped before he reached that point.

Buteo paused for breath, so Rabirus cut in: "Perhaps you were right, friend Buteo. Perhaps we should not have invited thaumaturgical interference in our goals." Should have kept his sight clear, should have kept the matter pure. "I think it's time for us to fall back on more certain methods of removing an obstacle from our path."

It would take planning. Careful planning, with many variables to control. That had been his mistake, really, with the Discordians; too unpredictable, too complicated, and Durmius Argus hadn't kept his sister well enough in hand. Unaccounted variables.

'The next time I strike at you, Sempronius Tarren, I will not miss.'

The funeral for Quinta Terentia was held on the Ides of Maius under a brilliantly blue sky.

By popular demand, and in recognition that she had given her life while trying to protect the city, she was accorded an honor few men in all of Aven's history could claim, and which had never been bestowed upon a woman: a procession through the Forum, with a *laudatio* delivered upon the Rostra.

Quintus Terentius spoke about his daughter's devotion to Aven and to the goddess who blessed her. Hollow-eyed Terentilla stood to one side of the platform, with her mother and brothers; on the other side, Quinta's other family, her fellow Vestals, including the newly-anointed youngest, a sombre girl of seven.

Afterward, Sempronius slipped away from the sorrow. He had been unsettled since the night of the battle and his own brush with the abyss. Foul magic had gotten its hooks into him, and though his head and soul were clear now, it rattled him to know how close he had teetered to an irrecoverable edge.

His footsteps carried him to the Temple of Victoria, yet unfinished and undedicated. It would need two new murals now, the vanquishing of the Lusetani and the defeat of the Discordian menace.

The mood would pass. Another day or so, and he would resume attacking his goals with his usual vigor. There would be much to do: trials and lawmaking and anticipating Rabirus's next move, not to mention planning the Ludi Tyrenni for the end of the month. *'The games must be even more spectacular now. The city's spirits need lifting. After so many dark months, we ought to arrange as much joy as we can.'*

He would have to decide what to do with the Lady Neitin and her son, after the celebrations. Hanath had mentioned something, in the eerie dawn following the battle. Before she received Marcia Tullia's summoning bird, she had been on the Janiculum, where the Lady Neitin had done... something. "I cannot explain it, not properly," Hanath said. "It should not have been possible, not as I understood the shape of the world. You must speak to her."

So he would need to unravel that cryptic message, too. Later.

He strolled the courtyard of the temple aimlessly, thinking about pleasant things—the chariot races and theatrical pageants that might draw a city out of its fear and sorrow—until he heard footsteps approaching.

She was clad in her charcoal-gray mourning gown, with a mage's black borders upon her tunic and the mantle pinned atop her head. It ought to have made her look dull and withdrawn, but to Sempronius's eyes, Latona's beauty shone from within it like the sun behind storm clouds, golden and perfect as ever.

'Blessed Venus, forgive my transgressions. Allow me the privilege of honoring you and making this right, if I can.' A silent prayer to a deity he never had much reason to importune. *'Please, Lady of Love and Beauty, heart-warmer, passion-provoker, give me that chance. Let the intensity of my regard for her make up for the infrequency of such passions in my life. Let her heart be open to me, and I will shower your temples with gifts.'*

Strange, to see Latona without her shadow, but Merula's injury had not yet healed. The Vitelliae had all attended the funeral, of course; how had she slipped away without a guard?

"I saw you come this way," she said. "I know this isn't... Juno, it's not the right time for this conversation, but I feel we must have it."

A hollowness opened up beneath his ribs, a breathless ache. But he nodded. "Yes," he said. "If you're willing."

"Willing?" Her face cracked with a sad smile. "I am still angry with you, Sempronius. But I... I miss you. Throughout this whole ordeal, I wanted you near, even when the pain..." She winced. "We cannot go on like this. We must settle how things will be between us."

He cleared his throat, unaccustomedly awkward. "There's a nice garden on the southern side of the building. Let's—That is, would you like to take a walk?"

She nodded. "This mantle is awfully warm in the sun."

They walked to the side of the temple, where myrtles provided ample shade. Latona stood under one bower, taking in the swaying branches, the deep green leaves, the unripe blue berries. On her other side grew an oleander, eagerly blossoming into pink flowers.

Neither spoke. Then both tried, at once.

"In the Forum, you—"

"Latona, I—"

They both halted. Latona, blushing, gestured to him. "Please. You speak."

A cruel deference, though she didn't mean it that way, for Sempronius scarcely knew where to begin. This clumsiness was unbearable. Sempronius hadn't felt like a callow youth when he'd *been* one. Finding himself tongue-tied and wrong-footed now...

'Further penance for your foolishness and pride,' he chided himself.

He decided to begin where she had, perhaps, intended to. "In the Forum," he said, "I over-estimated myself. I... I was an ass, to think myself beyond the touch of hubris. To think I had..." He gestured with one flat hand, as though sighting a javelin throw. "Kept my eye on it. Guarded against it. I did try. But I was over-confident. I thought the gods would not allow me to fail, not with my work unfinished."

"The gods," Latona said, a touch wry, "are fickle."

"Yes," he acknowledged. "And your fears were valid. I should have heard them. You saw the danger I could not. " His fingers flexed; he wanted to reach for her, to touch the soft hair bobbing against her cheek, to rejoice in the warmth of her skin. "I do not have much experience with doubt, and I confess I find it uncomfortable. I don't know how to navigate it. What happened in the Forum... it was humbling."

The shadow of a smile touched her lips. "Many in this city might say you could do with some humbling."

He risked a smile in return. "And they may be right." Solemnity re-asserted itself, and he looked down, where her hands were clasped against her stomach. "I could not even rescue myself from it. If Vibia hadn't been there..."

"Vibia?"

"She saved me. Pulled me back from the edge of a cliff that would have destroyed me. I do not want to be the man that error showed me I could become. I know where that road leads." A body, writhing and wracked, bleeding on the sand. A wife, weeping and alone. All that potential, snuffed out.

He thought of the Shadow-born prophecies, the revelation that sent him to Iberia in the first place. Truth lived in them, yes, but he had erred in thinking the road to ruin or glory lay through him alone. Perhaps the gods had sent him to Iberia not to earn renown, or at least not *only* for that, but to learn a lesson from Ekialde's example.

"I still want us to shape the future of our dreaming, Latona. Our strengths, yoked together, could achieve it. And I—I appreciate that more, now. What it would really mean. It will take both of us. To shape the Aven of our dreams, to stand against whatever opposition the world may throw at us—it will take both of us."

She regarded him for what seemed an impossibly long moment. Even the birds in the garden had gone quiet, or perhaps he could not hear them over his own deafening trepidation. Then she settled her shoulders back. "Very well. I have conditions."

Sempronius's heart sped up, a flicker of hope fighting back against the hollow pit. "Conditions."

"This will not be the end of this conversation," she said. "I love you. I will protect you. I do not know that I yet forgive you." Solace and pain together, like water washing a wound, struck his heart. "So we *will* speak more of this. About what you've already done, and about what you plan to do. You're not going to treat me like other men treat their wives. You can't keep things from me. If I'm going to protect you and your secrets, then you must bring me inside. You cannot deny me the chance to prepare for whatever catastrophe might yet unfold. And I—I will vow to do the same." Her fingers went to the edge of her gown; she had pinned something just inside. The betrothal ring, he realized as she tugged it loose. "I won't try to slip things by you, the way I have my father, because there won't be a need. I will tell you my plans, my fears, my suspicions, my worries, my ambitions. I will trust you, and you must—Sempronius, you *must* trust me in return."

"I do," he promised, and it felt as weighty a pledge as any they would make on the day of their wedding. "I will. Latona, I—I want to be a partner to you. Let this be an unusual sort of marriage, because we are not usual sorts of people." He held out both his hands, palms up. "Let Jupiter, Romulus, and Remus hear these words and hold me to account: I will not keep secrets from you, nor shut you out of my decisions, nor fail again to show you the trust and honor that you deserve. May they strike me down if I fail this vow."

Latona gave one sharp nod of satisfaction. Her eyes warmed, and color came back to her cheeks. "Then I will keep your secret," she said, "though with the hopes we may rewrite its necessity. I will help you build the Aven of our hopes. And yes, Sempronius Tarren, I will still marry you." She held out the ring. "I think you should try giving this to me again."

He drew nearer, joining her in the bower of myrtle and oleander, and Latona knew she had made the right choice. Whatever his sins, and however furious his deception made her, she could not have borne a life without him in it. She needed him—but he needed her, too, and there was warmth in that.

'*Our souls are well and truly tangled, just like Alhena foresaw. And she was right. Whatever is to come, I would rather be at his side than anywhere else in this world.*'

She meant what she said: forgiveness would be a process, not a single act. But reflection had granted her some perspective. She knew what it was to hide a problem out of pride, and she knew how deep-rooted fears could drive unthinking actions. '*The world has left its wounds on him, too, even if he'd never admit it.*'

Sempronius took her left hand gently. "Vitellia Latona, brighter than sunlight and stronger than steel," he said, drawing her close, "do me the honor of wearing this ring."

"I will."

He slipped it past her knuckles, seating it firmly. "And when we wed, let it be the start of a truly extraordinary union."

She laced her fingers with his, pressing their palms together. "You tempted me with that once before. After I saved your life." She tilted her head up, noticing then the redness and weariness in his eyes. "You told me I needed a worthy husband. A partner. Someone with drive and ambition, to be my match."

"I meant every word." His fingers brushed at her hair. "And still do."

"It terrified me then. All your talk of vision and destiny. It seemed... it seemed so much bigger than me."

"I should like," he murmured, dropping a kiss above her ear, "to exact excruciating vengeance upon every person who made you feel so small."

"They weren't *all* ill-intentioned," Latona objected, thinking of her father. "But that isn't the point."

"And what is the point?" His lips drifted to the curve of her jaw, and it became rather harder to remember.

"The point is... it doesn't scare me, anymore. Not after what I've seen. What I've done."

"You were magnificent," he breathed.

A blush tinged her cheeks. "Yes, well... Now, I feel big enough for it. Whatever it is the gods want of me, whatever plans Juno intends me to live out... I am enough. I can take it on. And I want to do so with you."

He pressed his forehead to hers, holding her by the hips. "And there is much to do. We do still have Discordians to dispense justice to, Augian corruption to expose..."

"Neighborhoods to protect and revitalize."

"Land bills to pass."

"A new thaumaturgical collegium to establish."

"To say nothing of an ocean-spanning federation to build. But before we do any of that, we have a wedding to celebrate." He kissed her properly then, capturing her mouth and lifting her up onto her toes. Latona clasped him around the neck, her heart soaring with love for this impossible man and his limitless aspirations, as a gusty wind kicked up around them, rattling the myrtle leaves and swishing the oleander.

To be continued in
Book 4 of the Aven Cycle

Glossary

AB URBE CONDITA: literally, "from the founding of the city". How the Romans/Aventans measure years, in time since what we consider 753 BCE, the legendary founding of the city.

AEDILE: a mid-level magistrate responsible for public buildings, the public games, and the supply of grain to the city. Elected by the Tribal Assembly. Men generally served this office between their quaestorship and praetorship, though it was not strictly necessary to be elected as praetor.

AUGIAN COMIMISSION: the group of mages dedicated to preserving the provisions of the Lex cantatia Augiae and keeping order among Aven's magically-gifted citizens.

CAMPUS MARTIUS: The Field of Mars, a large open space used for military training and for elections.

CENATORIA: a simpler and less-burdensome garment than the toga, worn by men on informal occasions.

CENSOR: a magistrate responsible for maintaining the census and electoral rolls, supervising public morality, and some aspects of government finances. A man had to have served as consul to be elected as censor. Elected by the Centuriate Assembly.

CENTURIATE ASSEMBLY: One of three voting assemblies designated by the Roman constitution, which gathered for legislative, electoral, and judicial purposes. Originally a military organization, but later expanded and ranked by wealth rather than military status. Only the Centuriate Assembly could declare war or elect the highest-ranking Roman magistrates: praetors, consuls, and censors.

COLLEGIA: assemblies with legal purpose and some authority which could function as guilds, religious organizations, or social clubs. Most common were the crossroads colleges, which were neighborhood associations formed around shrines placed at intersections.

CONSUL: The highest and most prestigious political office in the Roman Republic. The Centuriate Assembly elected two consuls to serve together for a one-year term. Consuls held executive power. They convened and presided over the Senate, negotiated with foreign states, and served as commanders-in-chief of the legions.

CURIA: the Senate House.

CURSUS HONORUM: literally, the course of offices; the sequential order of public offices held by politicians in the Roman Republic.

DICTATOR: a magistrate entrusted by the Senate with full power and authority to act unilaterally. A temporary office intended to be held for no more than six months.

DOMINUS/DOMINA: literally, "master/mistress", but also translates as the equivalent of "Lord/Lady" when used in conjunction with a name.

DOMUS: house. In the city, generally referred to a free-standing building occupied by a single family.

EQUESTRIAN: one of the property classes of ancient Rome, ranking below the Senators but above the rest.

FIVE CLASSES: property classes including all those who held land but did not have enough wealth to qualify as Equestrians or Senators.

FORUM: a large open-air market, often surrounded by a mixture of temples and shops. The largest forum in Rome/Aven, generally referred to as *the* Forum, was the center of political, mercantile, and spiritual life.

GARUM: a popular condiment made from fermenting fish.

HEAD COUNT: the property-less class, with no land and little wealth.

IDES: in March, May, July, and October, the fifteenthday of the month; in all other months, the thirteenth day.

INSULA: apartment. Blocks of insulae could be five to seven stories, with the largest and most luxurious apartments on the bottom floor and the smallest and most miserable at the top.

KALENDS: the first day of a month.

LATIFUNDIUM: a large agricultural estate under private ownership.

LEGES TABULAE MAGICAE: a section of Aventan law governing the behavior of mages, particularly with regard to interactions with non-magical citizens.

LEX CANTATIA AUGIAE: an Aventan law preventing the ascension of magically-gifted citizens to the ranks of praetor, consul, or censor.

LICTOR: a civil servant who acted as a bodyguard to high-ranking public officials.

MACELLUM: a market, smaller and with fewer permanent structures than a forum or emporium.

MOS MAIORUM: the "proper way of things." An informal code based on precedent and custom, elevated to dogmatic status by the Optimates.

NONES: in March, May, July, and October, the seventh day of the month; in all other months, the fifth day.

OPTIMATES: one of the two most prominent political factions in Aven, dedicated to conservatism, relative isolationism, and the preservation of power among the elite.

PATRONS AND CLIENTS: the basic social unit of ancient Rome was the patronage system, by which the patron, a man of higher social status and clout, served as protector, sponsor, and benefactor of the client, who in turn provided support and assistance to his patron.

PENATES: household gods.

PONTIFICAL COLLEGE: an institution consisting of the highest-ranking priests of the state religion.

POPULARISTS: one of the two most prominent political factions in Aven, favoring expansion of civic rights and economic opportunity.

PRAETOR: a magistrate ranking just below a consul. Praetors had municipal and judicial duties, but might also serve as commanders of legions or as local governors. Their specific duties fluctuated greatly at different points in Rome's history.

PRAETORIUM: the command tent of a Roman legion, generally placed at the center of the camp.

QUAESTOR: the first rank of the *cursus honorum*, requisite for entry to the Senate, responsible for the state treasury and audits.

QUINTILIS: the month we know as July.

SENATE: the Assembly consisting of the most experienced politicians. The Senate dictated foreign and military policy and directed domestic policy, but could not actually pass laws.

SENATORS: both the highest-ranking and wealthiest social class and those men who served in the Senate.

SEXTILIS: the month we know as August.

THERMPOLIUM: a quick-service restaurant for food on the go.

TRIBAL ASSEMBLY: the largest of the three Assemblies, as it consisted of all citizens, divided into their "tribes," which largely referred to their family's region of origin. This Assembly was most often responsible for the passage of laws.

TRIBUNE: a title with several meanings. A tribune of the plebs acted as a check on the Senate and the Assemblies, able to exercise veto power over the actions of consuls and other magistrates. A military tribune commanded portions of the Roman army, subordinate to praetors and consuls; these were usually men in their early twenties, getting military experience before beginning the cursus honorum. Other mid-ranking officers were also styled tribune, generally those who were members of a commander's staff.

VILLA: a large home outside of a city. This might be a villa rustica, a country estate, or a villa maritima, a seaside home.

Author's Note and Acknowledgments

This book did not go as planned.

For one thing, it initially didn't know whether it was supposed to be one book or two books.

Then, while *Give Way to Night* was the book I had to release during a pandemic, *The Bloodstained Shade* was the book I had to write during one.

And then, a little over a year ago, DAW Books and I parted ways[1], and I found myself charting an unexpected course.

It's been an adjustment. Self-publishing was never a path I intended to travel, but I'm enjoying the opportunities for expansion that this may give me. I don't *have* to say goodbye to this world and these characters before I'm ready.

As you may have noticed in that last chapter, Sempronius and Latona still have a lot they want to accomplish. There's a lot of work to do – and a lot of enemies still to defeat. My intention is to follow them on that journey. There will be a fourth book of the Aven Cycle, eventually. There may also be other tie-in short fiction. If you'd like to hear about all of that as it develops, along with any other publishing news I will have in the future, joining my newsletter is the best way to make sure you get the major updates!

There's been a lot to learn, a lot to juggle, a lot to wrangle. Throughout all of that, I had an incredible amount of support and love thrown my way, by so many people.

Thanks, thanks, and ever thanks to:

---

1.   https://cassmorriswrites.com/2022/01/28/a-turn-in-the-road/

My parents, who have sheltered and succored me through all this drama. Thank you for only making fun of me a little when I lay down flat on the floor and flopped around, both inelegant and ineloquent in my misery.

My agent, Connor Goldsmith, who told me to write the book that would make me happy, and whose negotiating skills gave me the freedom to do so.

Cameron Montague Taylor, whose developmental edits were absolutely invaluable. Her insights and enthusiasm actually made me want to work on this book again, after I had endured several highly demoralizing months.

My delightful and brilliant co-podcasters, Marshall Ryan Maresca and Rowenna Miller. I am so privileged to work with them on Worldbuilding for Masochists, but I am even luckier to have two such good friends.

The many scholars whose work I have leaned on while creating the world of Aven. A full list of the books, podcasts, documentaries, and other assorted sources I have used are available on my website[2].

My wonderful Patreon members, whose support means more than ever. Y'all are why this book exists; your memberships helped fund its editing, cover art, and marketing. More than that, you've also kept me accountable to myself and reminded me that people care about the work I do and want to see more of it. Special recognition goes to the Consuls: Bruce and Mary Morris, Marcell Williams, and Robert Mee.

And the many, many friends and fellow authors who reached out during this process. I would try to name them all, but I'd surely leave out someone, and then I'd want to walk into the sea in embarrassment. This is why, secretly, I hate writing acknowl-

---

2. https://cassmorriswrites.com/aven-cycle/the-world-of-aven/resources-and-history/

edgements. I believe in jinxes, and I live in terror of causing un-intended offence. But for every DM, every RT, every unexpect-ed card in my mailbox, every shout-out, and every kind word, please know that you have my full-hearted gratitude.

Audaces Fortuna iuvat!

Don't miss out!

Visit the website below and you can sign up to receive emails whenever Cass Morris publishes a new book. There's no charge and no obligation.

https://books2read.com/r/B-A-AGNR-VCMCC

BOOKS 2 READ

Connecting independent readers to independent writers.

About the Author

Cass Morris works as a writer and research editor in central Virginia. Her debut series, The Aven Cycle, is Roman-flavored historical fantasy. She is also one-third of the team behind the Hugo Award Finalist podcast World-building for Masochists. She holds a Master of Letters from Mary Baldwin University and a BA in English and History from the College of William and Mary. She reads voraciously, wears corsets voluntarily, and will beat you at Mario Kart.

Read more at https://linktr.ee/cassrmorris.

Lightning Source UK Ltd.
Milton Keynes UK
UKHW010736310123
416239UK00002B/207